WICKED PLEASURES

Penny Vincenzi

WICKED PLEASURES

ORION

First published in Great Britain in 1992 by
Orion
An imprint of Orion Books Ltd
Orion House, 5 Upper St Martin's Lane, London WC2H 9EA

A CIP catalogue record for this book is available
from the British Library

ISBN 1 85797 001 2 (Csd)
ISBN 1 85797 002 0 (Tpb)

Typeset by Deltatype Ltd, Ellesmere Port
Printed in Great Britain by
Richard Clay, Bungay, Suffolk

For Paul. With love.

The heart is deceitful above all things, and desperately wicked.

The Book of Jeremiah.

Acknowledgements

I owe a great many thanks to a great many people, for their help to me with writing this book.

Primarily a large number of people working in the Square Mile and on Wall Street who not surprisingly prefer to remain anonymous, but who gave me an enormous amount of their time, and fielded my endless questions with patience and good humour.

Three books were also outstandingly valuable to me and I would like to thank their authors: Ken Auletta for the *Greed and Glory of Wall Street*, Dominic Hobson for *The Pride of Lucifer* and Bryan Burroughs and John Helyar for *Barbarians at the Gate*.

Much gratitude also to Ivan Fallon of the *Sunday Times*, who was generous enough not only to point me in several important directions but to give me several pages' worth of ideas.

For help on the New York half of the book, I could not have managed without Betty Prashker, who chauffeured me all over the Hamptons on what must have seemed to her a very long weekend. I would have been lost without Robert Metzger and Bunny Williams who allowed me to quiz them about their dazzling lives as interior designers in New York, Jane Churchill who gave me the same privilege in London, and Jose Fonseca and Dick Kreis of Models One who have forgotten more about the modelling business than I shall ever know, and were good and kind enough to share it with me.

On matters of technical expertise, legal, financial and even mechanical, I owe a great deal to Sue Stapely, Mike Harding, Pete Townend and Paul Brandon. And to Shirley Lowe, who presided over the book's christening.

There have been wonderfully crucial supplies of nuts and bolts from Lyn Curtis, Pat Taylor Chalmers, Katie Pope, Caroleen Conquest and Alison Craddock. Not forgetting some absolutely vital input from my bank manager, Peter Merry.

Wicked Pleasures could not have been written at all without Rosie Cheetham, friend and editor, who wields a brilliant, creative and most inspiring pen; my agent, dear Desmond Elliott, who encourages, guides, cheers and cajoles: and most of all, my husband Paul and my four daughters, Polly, Sophie, Emily and Claudia, who have a great deal to put up with, never complain about it, and are always there when I need them.

None of Virginia Caterham's children knew who their father was.

'They think they're my husband's of course,' she said, smiling rather defiantly at the psychiatrist. 'They have no idea there's anything remotely unusual about their background. I keep thinking I should tell them – and then losing courage. What do you think?'

Dr Stevens looked at her thoughtfully. He really had hoped she wouldn't be back. She had been doing so well. But if it had taken a relapse to get her talking, to make her reveal the reason for the drinking, then perhaps it was worth it. They had never got this far before.

'Lady Caterham – how old are your children now?'

'Well – Charlotte's thirteen. Georgina's eleven. And Max is eight.' She looked very frail, sitting there in the big chair, almost childlike herself, wearing a full skirt and a large loose grey sweater.

Her heavy dark hair fell forwards over her face; she pushed it impatiently back, her large tawny-coloured eyes – extraordinary eyes – fixed on his.

'And – are you close to them?'

He was playing for time; trying to decide how to play it.

'Yes, very. Of course Charlotte is a little awkward. Well, it's a difficult age, you know. And I'm away quite a lot, with my work. It's very important to me, my work. But – yes, I think we're close.'

He changed tack.

'Lady Caterham – '

'Can't you call me Virginia? You did before.'

'Virginia. What was it that made you start drinking again? When you'd done so well for so long. Do you know? Can you tell me?'

'Oh,' she said, 'whatever makes you? It's never just one thing, is it? There were lots of things. Too many to talk about now.'

'But Virginia, that's what I'm here for, to talk about them.'

'Oh – I don't know. I was lonely. Despairing.'

'About what?' he said, very gently.

'Dr Stevens. Please answer my question. About the children. I need to know what you think. I really do. Before we go any further.'

'Well,' he said carefully, 'well, it's very hard for me to say. There are so

I

many imponderables. Does your husband know that you – that there have been other men in your life?'

'Oh Dr Stevens, of course he does.' She smiled at him almost cheerfully. 'I would say that's almost the whole point of our marriage. That there were other men in my life.'

Chapter 1

Virginia, 1956–7

Nice girls still didn't in 1956. And Virginia Praeger was a very nice girl.

What annoyed her, and most of her contemporaries, was that nice boys did.

She remarked on this fact to her brother, Baby Praeger, as he drove them both out of New York in the crisp April dusk and towards Long Island to spend Easter with their parents in the Hamptons: it was so terribly unfair, she said suddenly, she sometimes felt her major memory of her first year at Wellesley had been of pushing eager, sweaty hands up out of her bra and down out of her panties, and being made to feel guilty about it, and then hearing girls talking about however virginal you might be on your wedding night, of course you'd want a man with some experience, one who'd know what he was doing.

'You're allowed to sow your wild oats. Why can't we sow a few?'

'Because you're female,' said Baby, easing his new and infinitely beloved Porsche Spyder into fifth gear and a speed nudging 100. 'Look out for cops, darling, will you?'

'You won't get caught,' said Virginia irritably. 'You never do.'

'I might.'

'Well anyway, that's a really logical answer. Like Daddy saying girls don't go into banking. It's just so stupid.'

'Which do you fancy more?' asked Baby. 'Banking or sex?'

'Banking,' said Virginia promptly. 'How about you?'

'Sex. We could discuss a swop,' said Baby, laughing. 'You're a fraud, Virgy, deep down, wild oats don't actually interest you. Now how about the bank? Do you really want to get into all that?'

'Well – maybe not. But I'd certainly like the option . . . Look out, Baby, there's a cop coming up.'

Baby swung over into the slow lane, the needle dropping with formidable ease. The cop pulled up alongside him, gave him a look to kill and sat alongside him for several miles before pulling off fast after a Merc that had leapt out of the twilight behind them and vanished again ahead. And Baby didn't get booked. Didn't get caught.

★

3

It was true, what Virginia said, he never did. Right from the moment they had both been toddling about together, Baby had never got into trouble. If something got broken, if they were late back for tea, if they didn't untack their ponies, if they didn't write thankyou letters, if they got bad reports, if they forgot to walk the dog or clean out the rabbit's cage, Virginia got into trouble and Baby, somehow, got off. It wasn't that he lied, or pretended he hadn't committed the crime; he was just lucky. Their father would have been out or away when he should have heard about the misdemeanour, or too busy to be bothered about it; or their mother would have been distracted, involved in one or another of her endless charitable causes; or Mrs Viney, their nurse, would have been doing something else as he scuttled in late; or the gardener would take pity on the rabbit and see to it instead of waiting for someone else to notice.

But whatever the reason, Baby never did get into trouble.

And Virginia did. In spite of being much loved, she was always in hot water. Especially with her father. And she was always permanently in Baby's shadow: whatever she did, he seemed to do better. Which was strange, because she was cleverer. She knew she was. She was quicker than he was, faster on the uptake, her grades were consistently better, her successes more frequent, her failures fewer. Year after year she got straight As, while Baby's results teetered between all right and mediocre. And yet, somehow, she always felt she'd failed. That was because of her father too; careless of, blind to, his daughter's impressive talents and achievements, he would boast of Baby's far less remarkable ones, and where there were none, would boast of that fact too. 'Boy's a lost cause,' he would say, his eyes soft with pride as he looked at his son: and 'No better at Math than I ever was,' looking to, waiting for, the laughing, flattering denial from his audience, and drawing attention to Baby's talent for appearing to be clever, purporting to work, the dangerous, social skills that some feckless fairy had bestowed upon him in his cradle, making them seem a virtue, a skill in themselves. As indeed they were, and Baby knew they were, and he invested much time and trouble honing them, perfecting them, while Virginia watched, irritable, resentful, from behind the barriers of her own dutiful dullness.

And then Baby was easier than she was, more socially accomplished: Virginia had pretty manners, everyone said, but she did not actually have Baby's charm, she didn't sit at the centre of attention at parties, she wasn't regarded as the one person who must be at a gathering to ease it into life, set a seal on it.

Of course she was popular: very popular. There was no shortage of young men trying to make their way into her bra and her panties, and her social diary was not exactly bereft of social entries. Her friends said that was because she was not only very pretty but nice; her enemies (few, but articulate) maintained it was because she was an heiress to a fortune so big that even in a college where real money was in no way a rarity it was impressive.

Frederick Praeger III was a banker. In the circles in which the Praegers moved, that meant he owned the bank. His father had owned it, and his grandfather had founded it, and it was confidently expected that in the fullness of time, Baby would take it on and be known no longer as Baby but as Frederick Praeger IV.

The seeds of the Praeger fortune had been sown in 1760 by a bright sassy young man called Jack Milton who worked as a clerk for a small bank in Savannah, Georgia. He kept hearing talk of the money to be made from financing the Golden Triangle, a chain of trade in which a ship would leave Liverpool, England, loaded with metal boxes, and tin spoons and forks, and sail to the west coast of Africa, where the goods would be exchanged for slaves. The ship would then sail on to Bermuda, where the slaves (destined for shipment to the Southern states of America) would be traded for molasses; the third leg of the triangle saw the sugar sold back into Liverpool. It was perfectly possible and indeed normal to make 150 per cent profit on each leg of the journey.

Jack Milton, who was a shrewd young man, talked to his superior at the bank about the feasibility of investing in the Golden Triangle at the American end; his superior, who was less shrewd, shook his head and said it sounded real risky to him. And there it might have ended, had Jack not found himself working late one night when the owner of the bank, one Ralph Hobson, had come back to his office, a little the worse for drink, to collect a box of cigars a client had given him. Seeing Jack at his desk, and impressed by his industry, and being in benevolent mood, he started talking to him, and Jack found himself discussing the Golden Triangle and its potential. Three months later, Hobson had invested in a small ship; nine months after that he saw his money quadrupled. He repeated the exercise, watched the bank's profits soar and, being a fair man, gave Jack shares in the bank. In the fullness of time he made Jack a partner. Milton Hobson prospered; young Mr Milton and young Mr Hobson succeeded their fathers, and their sons succeeded them. They lived on adjoining plantations in Georgia, made additional fortunes from cotton, and owned a great many slaves. Then, early in 1850, Douglas Hobson contracted cholera and died, childless; Jeremy Milton found himself sole owner of the bank, with only daughters to succeed him. His wife had died bearing their only son, and the child had followed her after a very few hours.

Jeremy was not strong himself; he had bronchial trouble, and doctors feared consumption. He looked, at thirty-five, a middle-aged man; he feared for the future of his bank.

His oldest daughter, Corinna, was a beauty, with great dark eyes and a cloud of massing dark red ringlets; moreover, being sole heiress to a considerable fortune, she was a great prize. No one could understand why she decided, therefore, not to marry any one of the handsome, charming boys who were paying her court, but a serious, albeit handsome young man with a stammer, no money and a desk at the bank, called Frederick Praeger.

They were married in 1852, Jeremy made Frederick a partner in the bank and the two young people settled down to a first year of rather stormy bliss, after which Corinna settled down as a young hostess in Savvanah society. Frederick prospered on his own account, investing hugely both for himself and on behalf of his clients in the railroads that were being built the length and breadth of the country; Jeremy watched his progress and the development of the bank and was pleased with what he saw. Frederick was showing himself worthy of his position both as son-in-law and successor.

And then as the 1850s drew to a close the talk was all of war. Of war between North and South. The South was complacent, certain not only that it could, but that it would, win, that its generals – the mighty Beauregard, and Johnston and Lee – were unbeatable, that the Yankees were a bunch of upstarts who didn't know how to fight. Most Southern citizens were unconcerned by the imminent prospect of the conflict; but Jeremy Milton had friends and associates in the North, and he knew they had superior weapons, communications and men certainly as brave, certainly as well trained as the Confederate Army. And they also had more money. Far more money.

'I don't like it,' he said to Frederick, 'I don't like it at all. Oh, we shall no doubt do well out of it. Wars are great for banks. The build-up beforehand and the reconstruction afterwards. But I am fearful for the South. Fearful for this town. Fearful for you and my daughter. I think you should send Corinna to the North if and when the war starts.'

So Corinna and her father spent the war years in Philadelphia. Frederick joined the Confederates and did not rejoin them until early 1866 – thin, a little frail from continuous onslaughts of dysentery, but safely, wonderfully alive. The family had survived. It had also survived with much of its fortune intact. From the beginning of the war, Frederick had continued to invest in the railroads. And despite the defeat, the siege, the shelling, the burning of Atlanta, the great steel arteries had survived, and were now pumping lifeblood back into the South. What was more, he

6

had for the two years immediately before the war sold huge consignments of cotton direct to Liverpool and had the money banked there, where no one could touch it. Now he reclaimed it; thousands of dollars. And then there was Atlanta to rebuild. The whole of the South to rebuild. New industries, and vigour. The Praegers had returned to Savvanah, one of the few fortunate families who were not impoverished; on the phoenix-like rebirth of the south, they grew richer still.

In 1867 Corinna became pregnant; she was a little old at thirty-two to be bearing children, the doctor said, but she was strong and in good health, all should be absolutely well. The Praegers were delighted; perhaps at last the longed-for son was to be given to them. Jeremy was as excited as they; he had dreamed of a grandchild, a successor ever since Corinna's marriage.

And indeed, the son was born: a large, lusty child, with Corinna's dark blue eyes and Frederick's blond hair; but he brought grief in his wake, not joy. Corinna, who had seemed to weather a long, hard labour with her customary courage and stoicism, took him in her arms, gazed adoringly into his small, cross face and then abruptly and without warning haemorrhaged and died before anything could be done to save her.

Jeremy, already frail, had a mild stroke a week later, and never quite recovered his full faculties. Frederick was left with the responsibility of raising the tiny baby.

He hired nurses, housekeepers, governesses, and in time the household was restored to order, but he was desperately unhappy himself; Corinna's memory lived on in the house and haunted him, and the sight of his feebly shuffling father-in-law filled him with a bleak misery, from which there seemed no escape. He lived on in this nightmare for four years, the bank his only refuge; in 1872 Jeremy died, the bank became Praegers and Frederick moved to New York.

The move was an immediate success.

Frederick had no serious business struggles; communications had opened up enormously, many of his clients had offices in New York and were delighted to find him there, and the economy was growing at a formidable rate.

The building, on Pine Street parallel to Wall Street, was beautiful, built in brownstone, with elaborate cornices on the ceilings, marble fireplaces in the larger rooms, carved shutters at the tall windows, and a great deal of fine panelling, and he furnished it charmingly, as much like a house as he was able, with lamps from Tiffany, furniture from the antique showrooms of both Atlanta and New York, Indian carpets; it was a point of pride at Praegers that there were always fresh flowers in every room, and the walls were lined not only with financial reference books but the

7

works of Charles Dickens, Mark Twain, Walter Scott, Shakespeare. Clients liked to go there, it was a small, gracious world in itself, a pleasant place to be, and to pass time as well as receive excellent business advice.

New York was a heady place; the world's first department store had been opened there by Alexander T. Stewart, followed by Lord and Taylors, Cooper-Siegel and Macys, developing slightly frenetically into what was known as Lady's Mile. The building work was formidable; Frederick watched St Patrick's Cathedral and Trinity Church go up, as well as a wealth of other fine commercial and civic constructions such as the Metropolitan Museum and Carnegie Hall. Accustomed to the gentle and genteel pace of Southern life, Frederick found the fast, acquisitive atmosphere of New York, and the potentially dangerous but heady multi-racial mix that lay beneath the city's booming fortunes, inspiring and stimulating. His formidable capacity for work, his commercial foresight and his personal, rather serious charm brought him success both business and personal; realizing early that he could not compete with the great giants of Wall Street, and that he had a genuine advantage in being able to give a more personal service than they, he specialized, taking as his clients companies in the publishing and the communications business, the flourishing cable companies along with book publishers and the growing magazine market. One of his first New York based clients was a young man called Irwin Dudley, who published romances and sold them to the young working-class women of America by the million; over dinner one night the two men conceived of a new publication for their readers, a weekly story paper, many of the works being serials, thus ensuring a steady flow of readers. When *Love Story* was launched upon a hungry female public in 1885, the first issue had to be reprinted three times; a sister paper, *Real Romance*, purporting to be true stories and incorporating an advice column for the lovelorn, sold out so quickly that emergency paper supplies had to be rushed in from mills in the South as New York could not service the huge order at such short notice. Frederick, who had seen fit to underwrite Dudleys with Praeger capital, was a director of the company, and his own fortune increased gratifyingly as a result.

But he had many many clients; Praegers flourished, and so did he, as the more ambitious hostesses of New York discovered the rarest of rare social jewels: an unattached, attractive man. He was invited everywhere; as sought after at dinner tables as on the boards of the great flourishing building and railroad companies that were among his clients, admired, revered almost, happier again than he would have believed. But any of the dozens of young women who were settled at his side at dinner, who met him at theatres, concerts, summer garden parties, with matrimony in mind were set for disappointment. Frederick had only one love in his life (apart from his son and the memory of Corinna) and that was Praegers. The bank occupied not only his intellect, but his emotions; he viewed it not so much as a company but a favourite child, the subject of his first thought in the morning and his last one at night, and very frequently even of his dreams. In vain did the New York debutantes and their mothers hint that his baby son must need a mother, that the Upper East side mansion must seem large and empty without a mistress, that he himself must find his leisure hours empty and chill; he would smile at them all in the slightly sorrowful manner he had perfected and say that no, no, they were fine, that the baby's nursemaids and governess were doing a wonderful job, that his housekeeper ran the house with energy and skill, that he was left no time by his friends to feel lonely.

His only concern was the small Frederick, increasingly naughty, even before his first birthday. Frederick was a beautiful, charming child; his nurse idolized him, and the young governess, specifically hired to teach him his letters and numbers, thought he was so wonderful that she managed to persuade herself that it must be her own fault, not Frederick's, that he found the mastery of them rather more difficult than might have been expected.

A benign conspiracy built up over the years, concealing young Frederick's just slightly limited intelligence; but by the time he was thirteen and due to go to school, facts had to be faced. Of course he could go to the Collegiate school, and indeed Mr Praeger would add lustre to the parental roll, but young Fred was clearly not going to be one of the star pupils. He sat, comfortably and cheerfully, very near the bottom of the class for five years, popular, happy, a star on the sports field to be sure, with a particular talent for athletics and tennis, and managed, with the addition of some vigorous extra coaching, to just about scrape through his final examinations. His years at Yale were spent similarly, with sex added to the range of his accomplishments; but he was at twenty-one so good-looking, so amusing, so infinitely socially desirable, that it was comfortably easy for his father to ignore his limited intellect and instal him in what came to be known as the Heir's Room at Praegers (next to his father's office), especially fitted out to young Fred's specification, with antique furniture, Indian carpets and the very latest in modern technology, including a ticker-tape machine and a telephone on which he spent much of the day talking to his friends. He spent most of his time buying and selling his own stock, taking exceedingly long lunch hours and showing a great many young ladies around the bank, greatly overstating his own role in it.

Early in 1894 Frederick I died suddenly and unexpectedly, of a heart attack, still not entirely blind to his son's shortcomings, but convinced that he had many years in which to improve young Fred's banking skills. It was his one great folly; Frederick II was in fact rather less well equipped to run Praegers than the boys who ran messages all day long between the bank and the Stock Exchange in Wall Street. This did not greatly concern him; he looked at the assets of the bank, found it inconceivable that they should be in any way vulnerable, and proceeded to fritter them away (literally at times, so great was his penchant for gambling, both on and off the floor of the Stock Exchange) to rather less than 40 per cent over the next five years. Clients abandoned Praegers; portfolios shrank; partners resigned; returns on equity were down almost to break-even point. The senior partners were heard to remark to one another over luncheon that it was as well old Mr Frederick had died, it would break his heart to see what was happening.

Mercifully for everyone concerned, a happy event occurred. Young Frederick fell in love, with a wholly delightful young person called Arabella English. Arabella, whose father was employed (in quite a lofty capacity) in Morgans, understood banking, and had heard a great deal about the tragedy of what was happening at Praegers. On receiving a proposal of marriage from Frederick II she accepted it with immense graciousness and pleasure, advised him to talk to her father the next day, and in the intervening twelve hours suggested to her father that he might, as tactfully as possible, suggest a more dedicated approach to the bank by her Frederick, if he genuinely desired to marry her. So in love was Frederick, so desperate to gain the approval of old Mr English, that he would probably have obeyed if English had told him to hang from the sixth floor by his ankles for ten minutes every morning in order to improve his business performance.

The reform was dramatic. Frederick II was in his office by ten each day, and stayed there until well after four (long hours indeed for those golden days), in growing command of the market; he lunched only with clients; he read only the financial papers (once breakfast was over); he managed to approximate as closely as was possible for a person of his abilities to a first-rate banker. When Frederick Praeger III was born in 1903, there was once again a considerable inheritance for the young princeling.

Frederick III was an interesting child; he had, along with the classic Praeger blond good looks, all the instinctive skills for making money displayed by his grandfather, combined with a formidable talent for politicking. Those around him became vividly aware of both qualities when at the age of seven he asked his nursemaid to give him a quarter to put in the school charity box. His mother, he explained, untruthfully but moist-eyed with earnestness, was too busy with her social arrangements to see to such minutiae, and the nanny, incensed (as any good nanny would be) by such a display of maternal selfishness, promptly gave him fifty cents. Frederick invested this in a packet of peppermint humbugs, bought on the way to school, the chauffeur having been persuaded to stop for a moment so that he could buy an extra apple for his lunch box. The peppermint humbugs were then sold for a penny apiece to the other children; Frederick returned at the end of the day one dollar fifty up on his initial investment. By mid-term he had made over twenty dollars. He did not need twenty dollars; he just liked the knowledge that he could earn them at will.

By the time he was twenty-five he was buying and selling the equivalent of peppermint humbugs at the bank with equal skill, and playing off the rather intense relationship he had with Nigel Hoffman – one of the senior partners who was also his godfather, his department head and a man of considerable brilliance – against the more prickly one with his father, who was already uncomfortably aware that when it came to both skill and hunch, his son and heir was considerably his superior. Young Fred would eat lunch with Hoffman one day, tell him he felt his father was holding him back, treating him like a child; the next he would confide over dinner to his father that he felt Hoffman expected too much of him. As a result Fred II became over-protective, anxious not to burden him with too much responsibility, and Hoffman gave him an ever freer rein. If he made a mistake, young Frederick could blame Hoffman, if he did well, he could point out that he deserved more responsibility than his father gave him. He couldn't lose.

By the time Fred-the-Third, as he was always called; fell in love with Betsey Bradley, who was working as a stenographer at Praegers, he was in a more powerful position than anyone at the bank, including his father, who had finally abdicated his position in everything but name, and was spending most of his waking hours on the golf course and playing backgammon at the Racquet Club.

Fred III had pulled off a particularly remarkable coup and secured Fosters Land as an account, thus greatly increasing his standing both within and without Praegers. Fosters was a vast, billion-dollar development company, whose awesomely young chief executive, Jackson 'Jicks' Foster, had been at Harvard with Fred, and had called him one morning and dropped his gift into Fred's possession as casually as if it had been a pair of cufflinks. Outside the Praeger specialty as it was, Fred still managed the business superbly, and the friendship between him and Jicks Foster was never shadowed for a day by any professional cloud. When Frederick III brought Betsey home for the first time and announced that she was the only girl in the world for him, his mother was not happy. Arabella wasn't unkind to Betsey, rather the reverse, she was charming and gracious and went out of her way to draw her out and encourage her to talk. Nevertheless, she confided to Frederick II that night that there was no way on God's earth that she was going to allow young Fred to marry Betsey, she would wreck his future, and be no kind of a wife to him at all.

Arabella spoke very firmly to young Fred about his choice of bride, saying much the same things as she had said to his father; young Fred looked at her coldly and said he loved Betsey, she was the wife he needed, and if Arabella wasn't going to accept her, then he would have to think very hard about severing connections with his parents altogether.

The rift between Fred III and his mother caused by his marriage was papered over, but never properly repaired; and its far-reaching effect on Fred was to send him out of his way to hire and promote young men from the less well-to-do and aristocratic families, partly to irritate his mother, but partly from a deep conviction that the streetwise and hungry would work harder and more cannily for him than the over-indulged upper classes. Which in turn had its effect on the personality of Praegers, giving it a rougher, tougher profile than most of its fellows on Wall Street. But perhaps the greatest irony of all, as Fred III often remarked, was that Betsey in the fullness of time proved to be just as big a snob as her mother-in-law, and spent long hours reading etiquette books and getting herself put onto charity committees as well – although never the same ones as Arabella.

The young couple settled down to a surprisingly tranquil existence; Betsey had been reared to look after her man, and look after him she did, in every possible way, running his home with an aplomb that impressed even Arabella. She was not only efficient, sharp and tough, she was warm and loving and a tender and caring mother to Baby Fred born in 1935 and Virginia in 1938. It was a source of great heartbreak to both her and Fred, who had planned for a huge family, that after the birth of Virginia, when Betsey very nearly died, the doctor insisted on a hysterectomy.

In lieu of more children Betsey demanded a new house. She liked the family home on East 80th into which they had moved, after the deaths of Fred's parents within one year. But she had always hated the overgrown cottage Fred II had built near East Hampton, and she wanted something more substantial and to her taste.

'All right, go and find yourself a mansion. Just don't bother me with it until moving-in day. I'll just sign things. All right?'

'All right,' said Betsey, and went and told the chauffeur she would be needing him that day to take her out to Long Island.

'We move in tomorrow,' she said to Fred one Thursday the following September. 'You only have to let Hudson drive you out to the Hampton's in the evening, rather than come home here. I have clothes for you at the new house. I think you'll like it.'

Fred did like it. Beaches stood proudly high on the white dunes, near a small inlet into which the ocean swung, creating two facing stretches of sand. It was a great white mansion of a place, built in the colonial style, with huge sweeping lawns at the back (studded with white peacocks, a long-time fantasy of Betsey's ever since seeing *Gone with the Wind*) dropping right down onto the white dunes. The house had three vast reception rooms, eight bedrooms, a playroom, a den; outside there was a tennis court, a pool and a pool house, a football patch for little baby Fred, a stable block, and a massive sun deck with a heated conservatory for when the breezes blew in a little too harshly from the Atlantic. Betsey had decorated the house with considerable restraint (given her natural rather excessive inclinations, to be seen in full flower in the gilded Louis Quinzerie of East 80th), and it was all shades of sea colours, pale blues and greens and every tone in between, with honey-coloured polished wooden floors, pale rugs, and a great deal of wicker and chintzy furniture. Fred and the children walked in and fell in love with it; and Fred told Betsey that night in bed as he tenderly began removing her nightdress, that if he had ever needed to be reassured that he had married the 101 per cent right person, Beaches and what she had done with it had clinched it for him.

Virginia in particular had always loved Beaches. It was a place where she and Baby and Betsey spent time on their own, in the school vacations, Fred visiting only at weekends, and she was removed from the relentless pressure of trying to please him, struggling to win his approval, to do better than Baby. She relaxed there, could be herself, enjoy quiet pleasures like walking by the sea, adding to her collection of shells, playing the piano, reading, riding sedately along the shore, without having to worry about her hands, her seat, her pony's too slow pace. Virginia had two ponies, one she loved and was happy on, called Arthur, a round, placid little grey, and another she disliked and was afraid of called Nell, a dancing, prancing chestnut, a show pony whom Fred insisted she rode whenever she was there, alongside Baby on his equally spirited bay, Calpurnia. Fred would follow them on a huge chestnut hunter, watching them, urging them on: those rides were a nightmare. Virginia would sit, tense and uncomfortable, trying to convince herself that she had Nell under control, dreading Fred's shout of 'Come along then, off we go, come on Virgy, kick on, kick on', of the petrifying fear as Nell stretched out into the gallop, the dread of falling, the greater one of being run away with. Baby would fly ahead, whipping Calpurnia, whooping with pleasure; Fred would canter along beside her, urging her to keep up, and even in her terror she could sense his irritability, his contempt. She used to arrive back at the house shaking, sweating, grey-faced with exhaustion, often physically sick (refusing just the same to allow Betsey to know how afraid she was, lest she spoke to Fred about it), thankful only that it was over for the day, perhaps even for the whole weekend. But during the week she would saddle up Arthur and set out alone, simply walking, or trotting easily and happily on the ocean edge and riding, she knew, a great deal better.

Baby, who would in the fullness of time become Fred IV, had been called Baby Fred from birth, and had become just plain Baby at Harvard, even though he was (fortunately for his reputation) six feet four inches tall and the most brilliant halfback of his generation. He was not, so far, showing quite every sign of being a worthy successor to the bank; he was clever, quick and charming, but he had a considerable aversion to hard work, only passed his exams by the time-honoured method of last-minute crash swotting, was permanently overdrawn at the bank, and spent a great deal of time not only on the sports field and the tennis court, but at parties, dances and the Delphic Club where his considerable dramatic talents found great expression in the Hasty Pudding Theatricals. He also was to be found extremely frequently in the arms (and the beds when he could accomplish it) of the very prettiest girls. He had his grandfather's golden looks, thick, blond hair, dark blue eyes, wonderful, flashing, infectious smile, and something too of Fred II's immense *joie de vivre* and somewhat irresponsible dedication to the pursuit of pleasure. Fred III, who had vivid memories of his father, and had heard much folklore about the appalling mess he had thrown Praegers into during the early part of his rule, was haunted occasionally by seeing a similar pattern evolving for Baby. But his anxiety was tempered by a pride in and love for Baby that was literally blindingly intense. Virginia, arguably cleverer, certainly harder working, more responsible, morally impeccable, would have died happy for half such indulgence from her father.

Betsey would upbraid Fred for his insensitivity, and bend almost double over-praising everything Virginia did – but it didn't help. Even her looks, which were stunning – her waterfall of thick, dark hair shot with auburn, her perfect heart-shaped face, straight little nose, sweetly curving mouth, and her extraordinary large, brown-flecked golden eyes ('Like a lioness's' as Betsey remarked gazing into them enraptured soon after the baby was born) – did not please him. 'Bad luck,' he would say, 'Baby getting the Praeger looks. Virgy takes after my mother.'

Her father's dismissal of everything she did, every accomplishment, every talent, hurt Virginia every day of her life. In theory she should have hated him and hated Baby; in fact, against all logic, she loved Fred more than anyone in the world, and tried to please him – and hero-worshipped Baby. It said a great deal about a certain insensitivity in Baby that he remained oblivious to much of her anguish.

Fred's occasional anxiety over his son was currently greatly eased; Baby had fallen in love with a most suitable girl, who was having a gratifyingly sober effect on him. Mary Rose Brookson, whose father was in real estate, had an icy beauty, spoke five languages and had graduated Phi Beta Kapa in Fine Arts and English Literature; she would have had a sobering effect on anyone. Virginia found Mary Rose at best awe-inspiring and at worst dislikeable: Mary Rose went to a great deal of trouble putting her rather ostentatiously at her ease, and asked her slightly patronizingly about her studies whenever she saw her. But Virginia could also see that she was a most restraining influence on Baby and his excesses, and should she be given the opportunity, would be the perfect consort for Baby, queen over his dinner table, make all the right contacts and connections. And no doubt provide him with several very aristocratic heirs to the dynasty.

Virginia's future too was not exactly unsettled; Fred III had drawn up a settlement on her that made dizzy reading for any prospective suitor. $1m when she was twenty-one, in stocks and bonds, a further $1m in trust until her twenty-fifth birthday and a 2½ per cent share in the bank's profits when she was thirty or when Baby inherited it, whichever came later.

When Virginia was seventeen she came out, presented by her father at the Junior Assemblies Infirmary Ball. She was among the two or three most beautiful girls there (and even Fred went so far as to tell her she looked very pretty). But Baby, who was also there, was easily the most handsome man. Blond, blue-eyed, with a knee-weakening smile and shoulders broad enough to lay a girl on, as some wag had once said, he was, not unnaturally, the focus of the mothers' attention as well as their daughters'. And although he got very drunk and spent half the evening trying to get Primrose Watler-Browne's knickers off in the cloakroom, nobody ever heard about it; Virginia, who was quietly and discreetly sick in the ladies' after her two glasses of champagne had mixed rather badly with the glass of Dutch courage in the form of a beer Baby had given her before they left the house, was severely reprimanded by her mother who heard about it from another debutante's mother.

But if nothing could shake Virginia's adoration of her brother, at least the feeling was mutual. Baby might not have been aware of her problems, but he loved her dearly in return, and one of the most important things he had been able to do for her was make her early days at college happy. When she arrived at Wellesley, he went out of his way to take care of her, to introduce her to all his friends and to see she had a really good time. Virginia was not one of the stars of her year, but she was quietly happily popular; and removed from a constant position under Fred III's heavy eye, happier and more confident than she had ever been.

Baby Praeger and Mary Rose Brookson became officially engaged at the end of August. There was a lavish party for them to celebrate, and Mary Rose stood hanging onto Baby's arm in a rather predatory way throughout the evening. People kept saying how well matched they were, and what a perfect couple they made, but Virginia found it harder and harder to agree; Baby was so warmly, easily charming, and Mary Rose was tense and almost painfully formal. She was undoubtedly beautiful, but in a slightly chilly way; she had ice-blonde hair and pale blue eyes, and her fine, fair skin showed tiny blue veins through it on her temples. She was extremely thin, and very chic; she dressed for the most part in stark, rather severe clothes, but for the party she wore a dress from Oleg Cassini in navy silk chiffon, small-waisted and long-sleeved, draped from the waist; everyone said it was gorgeous but Virginia thought it was a middle-aged dress. Betsey had a very large photograph framed for the upstairs drawing room at East 80th; every time Virginia looked at it she felt depressed.

The wedding took place in June of 1957, at St Saviour's East Hampton, and in a vast cream and peach marquee on the lawn of the Brookson house near the South Shore; Mary Rose wore cream silk with real cream roses in her hair and looked charming. Virginia, who was the only grown-up attendant, was totally eclipsed by the ten tiny flower girls, none of them older than six, dressed in cascades of cream and pink frills. Mary Rose had insisted that Virginia's dress was exactly the same, despite her plea for something simple, and in all the wedding photographs she looked, despite her determined smile, uncomfortable and overdressed.

The best man, Bink Strathmore, Baby's room-mate from Harvard, had just got engaged himself and was so deeply in love he could hardly bear to stand away from his fiancée and close to Virginia for even the duration of the photographs; and when Fred III got up to make a speech (despite the irregularity of such an event) he made a great deal of how proud he was of Baby, a perfect son, and how equally proud of Mary Rose, her charm, her beauty and in particular her brains, and if ever a female was to persuade him that she be allowed to enter the board rather than the boardroom of the bank, it would be her. 'Which is not to say that even in a hundred, a thousand years such a thing will happen,' he finished to much laughter and applause.

Later, he led Baby to the piano, his tap shoes in his spare hand, and asked Virginia to come and dance with him. She was in fact a brilliant tap dancer; it was her one accomplishment that Fred III was truly proud of, and he made her teach him to tap dance too. Virginia and Fred Praeger doing 'You're the Tops', accompanied on piano by Baby, was one of the more privileged sights of New York. Charmingly, graciously, but firmly this time Virginia refused. Fred had to do 'You're the Tops' on his own.

It was the first time she had ever got the better of him; the pleasure of that slightly eased the pain she had endured all through the long, humiliating day.

Virginia went back to college feeling depressed. She felt she had lost Baby and it was time she had someone of her own. She graduated Phi Beta Kapa, in Fine Arts, and spent the summer attending the weddings of her friends. By October she felt she could have conducted a wedding ceremony and organized a reception for five hundred in her sleep.

'So what did you think of Mary Rose's apartment?' said Charley Wallace to her at a drinks party in the Hamptons one golden autumn Sunday. Virginia had not intended to go to the party, she had promised Baby a game of tennis, but she had had a headache and pulled out of the game, and then been dragooned by Betsey into accompanying her to the party.

'Well,' she said carefully, for Charley was a close friend of Mary Rose's, 'it's a very nice apartment. Very nice.'

'Yes, but isn't she just the cleverest thing to have found Celia before anyone else?'

'Celia who?' said Virginia, slightly absently. She was wondering if she could possibly persuade herself that Charley with his dropaway chin and braying laugh was attractive (given that he was about the only unmarried or un-about-to-be-married) man in New York State and possibly the whole of the United States of America that autumn.

'Celia del Fuego,' said Charley, and then seeing Virginia's blank look said, 'don't say she didn't tell you? Most people can't stop boasting about using her.'

'Charley,' said Virginia, 'this is very intriguing. Exactly who is Celia del Fuego? Some smart new shrink or something?'

'No of course not,' said Charley, 'Mary Rose is far too together to need a shrink. Yet anyway,' he added with a just slightly sharp twitch of his mouth; Virginia promptly decided she liked him more than she had thought. 'Celia's an interior designer. Really terribly smart. She's done Bunty Hampshire's house, and Sarah Marchmont's apartment, weren't you at college with her sister, oh and she might be doing Kenneth's new salon, and they say that Mrs Bouvier, you know, Jackie's mother, has been talking to her. And her stuff's all over *House and Garden*, apparently.'

'How on earth do you know all this?' said Virginia curiously. Charley didn't seem quite the kind of person to know about fashionable designer people.

'Oh, my mother's having her penthouse done,' said Charley, 'and Celia's going to do it for her. That's how I found out she did Mary Rose's. Maybe Mary Rose doesn't want you to know. Maybe she wants you to think she did it all herself. Promise you won't tell her I told you.'

'I promise,' said Virginia absent-mindedly. She found the concept both of Mary Rose employing an interior designer and then keeping quiet about it highly tantalizing. It was very unlike her. Maybe it was because she felt as an expert on the visual arts she should be able to handle her own decor. Virginia stored the information away for future use; and resolved that on Monday morning, she would look up Celia in the classified section of *House and Garden*, and arrange to go and see her. She wasn't sure why, but she found the prospect intriguing.

She met someone else at the party at the Hamptons that day: Madeleine Dalgleish, English and a distant relative of Mary Rose, but scarcely recognizable as such, and greatly more engaging. She was scatty, more than a little shy, and slightly odd–looking, very tall, and almost gaunt with dark, deep-set eyes and a large, hook-like nose; she had been charmed and touched by the attention and genuine interest shown in her by a young woman who she was assured by her hostess was not only the greatest heiress of her generation but also inexplicably unattached.

Virginia had found her much the nicest person there and spent much of the party chatting to her, careful to avoid too much discussion on the subject of Mary Rose until Madeleine Dalgleish said, with the suggestion of a twinkle in her eye, that she was relieved to find all young American women were not as daunting as her own third cousin.

'I was always rather frightened of Mary Rose,' she said, holding out her glass to be refilled for the third time in the conversation (which was no doubt, Virginia thought, contributing to her frankness), 'even when she was quite a little girl. She was always so extremely sure of herself. Although I'm sure she'll make a wonderful wife for your brother,' she added hastily.

'I'm sure she will too,' said Virginia, and changed the subject as soon as she decently could onto which parts of New York Mrs Dalgleish had and had not seen.

'I'll tell you where I'd really like to go,' she said, 'the Stock Exchange. My father was a stockbroker and I spent a lot of my childhood in the gallery at the London Stock Exchange. I'd love to compare notes.'

'Well you must let me take you,' said Virginia. 'I spent a lot of my childhood in the one here. Why don't we go along before lunch tomorrow? I don't suppose it's very different.'

'How very kind,' said Madeleine. 'I'd love that, and you must let me buy you lunch afterwards.'

But the visit never took place; Madeleine had had to rush home to England to her young son, taken ill at Eton with appendicitis, and had missed the promised tour. She phoned Virginia, expressing genuine regret, and said when she returned, she would contact her again. Nine months later she was back, phoned the delightful Miss Praeger as promised and invited her to lunch at her hotel.

Virginia often reflected how frightening it was that her entire destiny had swung on the thread of fate that had given her a headache and sent her to that party.

Chapter 2

Virginia, 1958–59

'There are two kinds of designer,' Amanda Adamson said to Virginia, inspecting the patina on a Louis Quinze table closely as she spoke. 'The major firms, like ourselves, and Macmillan and Parish Hadley, with a great many social clients and a considerable weight of staff, and then the small individual with the right contacts and a bit of luck.'

She straightened her sliver-thin body, in its Dior chemise-line dress in herringbone tweed, and glared at Virginia, her expression making it extremely plain what she thought of the smaller individuals and their dependence on luck. 'Now if – and I do mean if – you join us, you will be a very small cog in a very large and powerful wheel. But that does not mean you will not be important. Our clients, coming as they do from the highest social spectrum, are used to everything, and I do mean everything, being The Best. From the china in which they are served their tea in this office, to the manners of the delivery drivers.'

'Yes,' said Virginia humbly. 'Of course.'

Amanda Adamson sighed. 'Most girls don't of course recognize the good from the indifferent these days. I have to say that as your mother's daughter, with your educational background, I am inclined to give you the benefit of the doubt. Perhaps you'd like to tell me why you want to pursue a career as an interior designer.'

'Well,' said Virginia simply, 'I like beautiful houses and beautiful things, and I like people, and I – well I think it would be fun,' she finished lamely.

Amanda Adamson looked at her more severely still.

'My dear girl,' she said, 'this business is not, I assure you, about fun. Decorating is big business. I run this company like a Wall Street broker house. I have a staff of twenty. I have a highly complex financial system. I never go over budget, I always deliver on time. I have furniture delivered here on memo, that is to say, on approval, worth thousands of dollars, and I have never returned anything even slightly damaged. I have clients right across the country. Only last week I arrived in Colorado with four forty-foot trailers of furniture. It may be satisfying, but it is not fun.'

'No, I'm sure it's not,' said Virginia hastily. 'I didn't mean that. But I think it must still be wonderful, to see your ideas for a house, for a room, even, turn into reality. Like a picture coming to life. With people moving around in it, and liking it.'

Amanda Adamson's face softened suddenly into humour. 'Ah,' she said. 'Yes. People. You know what drives people to me? Rather than saving thousands and thousands of dollars and getting it done themselves?'

'No,' said Virginia. 'No I don't.'

'Terror,' said Mrs Adamson. 'Terror of appearing tasteless. Our role is to advise people and give them a house that stands up to the most minute examination from their friends. Or rather the people who come to their houses.'

'Oh,' said Virginia. 'Oh, I see.'

'People are very insecure,' said Mrs Adamson. 'Very insecure. It's important to understand that.'

'I think I know about insecurity,' said Virginia, thinking of Mary Rose, so cultivated, so pretentious about taste and style, and yet driven to employ a decorator and then pass off the result as her own. 'I've seen evidence of that very close to home.'

'Oh really?' said Amanda. She smiled at Virgina suddenly. 'I think you'd do this job rather well. I have a good feeling about you. Would you like it?'

'Oh I would,' said Virginia. 'I really really would.'

She found herself employed as a shopper at Adamsons; it was something of a misnomer, she felt, as most of the time she was not shopping at all, but tidying up the showroom, making coffee for clients, taking messages, picking up merchandise. But sometimes she was sent out to shop: to visit the wholesalers and pick out samples: 'Six different blue linens, Virginia, different weights, for Mrs Macaulay's cushions, and while you're doing that, could you keep an eye open for lemon silk for the curtains.' 'Virginia, Mrs Blackhurst has changed her mind, she wants wool and silk mixture now, not slub, could you go and find the nearest to that green that she likes so much and if there's a pattern, try that as well.' 'Virginia, Mrs Waterlow wants red saucepans in her kitchen, not aluminium, could you try and track some down.' 'Virginia, Papp are sending three tables up on memo, could you just run in there and see if they have any silver frames we could use.'

This being in the days before the D. & D. building opened, and everything was more or less under one roof, the shopping was something of a challenge; many, indeed most of them, were contained more or less in the same area, around and about the Upper 50s and Third, but sometimes it was worth going down to the rag trade area and hunting there, and even to the Village; she was good at it, she often brought back something unexpected, witty, that delighted and charmed the spoilt, capricious women Adamsons spent its days making more spoilt and more capricious.

Virginia loved the new world she had found herself in; she loved its excesses, the shops like Karl Mann, who recoloured Monets to match clients' carpets, and inserted people's own pooches and/or ponies into reproductions of quite famous eighteenth-century paintings. She loved the flamboyant characters like Angelo Donghia and Joe Schmo, who had turned interior design into a branch of showbiz. She went to a party at Donghia's house on 71st Street, taken by one of the designers at Adamsons; Donghia was a great champion of the young, a mentor of many young designers, and he was charming to her. She spent a starry evening talking to actors and fashion designers and journalists in the ballroom, with its white satin banquettes, and in the great mirrored hallway.

It was all new and glamorous and exciting, and yet she felt totally at home in it, absolutely in the right place; she knew she could make something of this world, and make something of it her own.

It was a potential client, the mother of her best friend at college, Tiffy Babson, who gave her the big idea. Mrs Babson said she had bought a cottage out at Connecticut, near Old Lyme, and she wanted help with the bedrooms. 'The rest is just perfect, and I don't want to change a thing, but the bedrooms are a nightmare. Could you ask Mrs Adamson if she would consider doing them?'

Virginia asked Mrs Adamson; Mrs Adamson said that she was extremely sorry, in tones that made it clear she was nothing of the sort, but she didn't do bedrooms, as Virginia very well knew. 'I would only consider doing a bedroom,' she said, 'for somebody extremely famous. Or of course the mother or the daughter of a very important client. You can tell Mrs Babson that she won't find anyone of any note at all doing bedrooms. I'm sorry.'

Virginia relayed this to Mrs Babson, as tactfully as she could; Mrs Babson was disappointed. Virginia looked at her.

'Mrs Babson, I could – help a bit if you like. I mean we'd have to not tell Mrs Adamson, but I could certainly take a look at the cottage and make some suggestions, and maybe even get you some fabric for the drapes and so on.'

'Virginia, that'd be wonderful!' said Mrs Babson. 'Come out this weekend and take a look.'

She went and took a look. The cottage was charming, right on the shore. Virginia drew up a colour board of blues and greens and whites, with some fabric samples she had hanging around the office, and did a sketch of each bedroom, complete with lights (brass ones, hanging on chains), white wicker furniture, and rugs on painted wood floors, marbled the colours of the ocean. Mrs Babson was enchanted, and asked her to take it a stage further; Virginia said she would shop around for the furniture and the rugs, but that it was more than her job was worth to actually make any purchases. 'So it will have to be retail: expensive, I'm afraid.'

'Never mind,' said Mrs Babson. 'I'll be saving plenty on Mrs Adamson's fee. Now Virginia, that doesn't mean I expect you to do all this for nothing. You must bill me, just as if I was a regular client.'

Virginia said she wouldn't hear of it, but that if Mrs Babson was happy with the end result, she could pass her name to her friends.

Mrs Babson did so; almost immediately a Connecticut neighbour, with a New York apartment as well, both in need of restyled bedrooms, approached her; and then another. Virginia liked doing bedrooms; they were more personal, less daunting than drawing rooms. She spent a great deal of time (as indeed she had learnt from Mrs Adamson) talking to her clients, establishing how they saw their bedrooms, whether they were simply somewhere to sleep, or somewhere to sit, chat, eat breakfast maybe, read. For one client she suggested a corner that was more than a corner, more of a study extension, separated from the main part of the bedroom with wicker screens; for another, a little girl who wanted to live in a tent, a four-poster with huge draped curtains; for a third she had an artist paint a trompe l'oeil of the ocean on a tiny bedroom wall in the Hamptons. What Virginia Praeger did with a bedroom, all the ladies said, was make it speak louder for their personalities than the whole of the rest of the house put together.

And so VIP Bedrooms was born. Virginia said to Betsey that she had never thought to be pleased her middle name was Irene.

By the following autumn, Virginia felt the burgeoning of an altogether unfamiliar sensation: confidence. She had a growing list of clients, her appointment book was always full, the small study she had appropriated for herself on the garden floor of East 80th was swiftly proving inadequate as an increasing number of visitors stepped over the piles of fabric samples, paints, reference books to sit in front of her small desk and large drawing board and discuss their decor problems with her. At least one of her commissions, a small but enchanting studio apartment –

strictly speaking beyond her bedroom brief – in the Village was being considered for inclusion in *Seventeen* magazine. This was, she knew, due more to luck than anything; her client, a young designer, had a boyfriend who worked on the magazine. They were doing a supplement on single homes, and the assistant art director had been to see the apartment, loved its stark whiteness and its faithfulness to the studio style, and been impressed at the same time by the jokey trompe l'oeil on one huge wall of a door opening onto a close-up of the Statue of Liberty's head. If that came off, Virginia knew she would be made. She told Fred III and Betsey about it over dinner one night; Betsey was immensely impressed and made all kinds of unsuitable offers of bringing flowers down to the apartment herself, and maybe even have Clarry the maid clean it.

'Mother, you're sweet, but I'm afraid Janey Banks – she's my client – would see both those things as an insult. No, I'm sure if *Seventeen* do it, they'll be bringing in their own flowers and cleaners. It is exciting though, isn't it?'

'It's wonderful,' said Betsey. 'And you are just the cleverest girl. Isn't she, Fred?'

'What's that?' said Fred, who was engrossed in a report in the *Wall Street Journal* on the relative effects on the Stock Exchange of Nixon or Kennedy's arrival in the White House the following November.

'I said Virgy was just the cleverest girl, getting her work into *Seventeen* magazine.'

'Well she hasn't yet,' said Fred. 'I'll believe it when I see it. And *Seventeen* magazine, what's so great about that? A broadsheet for teenagers. Wait till she's in *House and Garden*, then I'll be impressed.'

'I'm afraid you won't,' said Virginia, getting up from the table. 'Would you excuse me, Mother, I really have a lot of work to finish.'

'Fred Praeger, you are just the pits,' said Betsey, snatching the paper from his hands as Virginia closed the door rather slowly and quietly behind her. 'How can you hurt her that way? She's doing so well, and even if she wasn't, don't you think a little encouragement would be in order?'

'I don't believe in empty encouragement,' said Fred. 'If she's going to run a business, she has to develop some guts, get a little thicker-skinned than that. Anyway, what's she doing, telling a few people what colour their walls should be? Nothing very difficult about that. That's not a career. She's just filling in time as far as I can see, until she gets married. And frankly, Betsey, I'd a lot rather she did that. She's twenty-one years old, it's time she had a husband.'

'Oh for heaven's sake,' said Betsey, 'I never heard such old-fashioned nonsense. Why should she be in a hurry to find a husband?'

'All girls should be in a hurry to find a husband,' said Fred. 'It's what they're here for.'

'You're wrecking her self-confidence. You always have.'

'Oh for God's sake,' he said, 'she's just fine.'

'She's not fine.'

'Well she seems fine to me. And when she gets a husband she'll be even more fine.'

'If you're not careful,' said Betsey, 'she'll get the wrong sort of husband. Just to put one over on you.'

Virginia was, in fact, although she would have died rather than admit it, looking out for a husband with increasing anxiety. Half her friends were married, the other half engaged; she was nowhere near either condition. She felt nervous, increasingly lacking in confidence about herself.

Her career had helped; the knowledge that she had succeeded in something, off her own bat. She no longer felt the complete no-no of a person who had left Wellesley more than a year ago. But she was surprised to find how little it really mattered. She was still uncertain of herself, or her ability to attract, to amuse – often, she thought, to feel. She looked ahead, sometimes, at her future, and saw herself growing older, unclaimed, undesired, increasingly desperate, and she was frightened. Then she would shake herself, tell herself she was only twenty-one, she was being ridiculous, she was successful in her career, she had lots of friends, her life was full. Only it was full in the way she had never really wanted, her social life already slightly lopsided and awkward – fewer dinner parties, these days, more invitations to larger gatherings, where her singleness didn't matter. Of course it was ridiculous, to be worried about such things at her age; but in 1959, in the circles in which she moved, they mattered. She didn't necessarily have to be married, but she had to have someone she could be asked around with. And to have a sexual relationship with. Virginia knew that at her age she should have had some kind of sexual experience. It was very different from being a college virgin. And it was beginning to be embarrassing.

She had boyfriends; of course she did. But they were never right. Too brash, too quiet, too sporty, too dull. This one plain, this one a dandy, this one obsessed with money, that one with his career. None of them anywhere near perfect. And Virginia was a perfectionist. She was just not prepared to settle for anything mediocre, for compromise. What she wanted, she supposed, had to admit, was someone a bit like Baby: fun, charming, witty, attractive. That would be nice. Then she shook herself. 'For heaven's sake, Virginia Praeger. Can't you do better than fall in love with your own brother?'

She had been going out for the past month or so with a banker, a solemn, rather intense young man called Jack Hartley. He was nice, in spite of his intensity, kind, interested in her, and good–looking in a dark, slightly heavy way. He took her to the theatre and to concerts, which he particularly enjoyed, and engaged her in long solemn conversations about politics and the state of the economy. It wasn't ideal, but it was better than nothing. He kissed her a little earnestly when he took her home each night, and never tried to do any more. Then he got rather drunk one night, took her out to dinner and on the way home started caressing her breasts in the cab. Virginia sighed mentally and let him get on with it, thinking it was perhaps not such a high price to pay for having a reasonably acceptable escort. She wasn't enjoying it, but it wasn't unpleasant. As the cab pulled up outside the house, she said (more to show him she wasn't shocked than for any more sexually acceptable, reason), 'Jack, do you want to come in for a nightcap?'

Jack Hartley looked at her and there was genuine surprise in his eyes. She was puzzled but ignored it.

'That would be nice,' he said, 'I'd like that very much.'

Up in her small sitting room, she handed him a bourbon, poured herself a glass of wine.

'It's been a really nice evening,' she said, 'thank you.'

'I enjoyed it too. I – well, yes, I did.'

She sat down opposite him.

Jack looked at her a little nervously.

'I – that is – would you – '

'Would I what?' said Virginia, her golden eyes dancing slightly mischievously.

'Would you come and – and sit here? Next to me.'

'Well – yes, all right.'

She knew what he was actually saying. She moved and waited. His arms went round her, the dutiful, almost automatic kissing began again. Virginia tried to respond. She wondered if there was anything she could think of that would make her feel more aroused. All she wanted was for it to be over, so she could get on with her wine, and then as soon as decently possible get rid of him and go to bed.

One of Jack's arms was moving now, making its tentative way downwards. He stroked her breast for a while, then suddenly put his hand beneath her shirt and pushed it up towards its goal again, his fingers inside her bra, feeling for the nipple. Virginia kept her eyes tightly shut, her mind on the matter in hand. It was all right. There weren't any of the darts of pleasure she had heard about, but it was all right. Then suddenly there was a darting violent pain, as the bracelet of his Rolex watch caught on the fabric of her bra, and pinched her flesh hard. She yelped, pushed him away, pulling her shirt down again.

'Sorry,' she said, 'sorry. It was – ' '– hurting' she had been going to say, but he didn't give her a chance. He stood up suddenly, smoothing his jacket, straightening his tie.

'It's quite all right,' he said, slightly harshly. 'I should have expected it.'

'Expected what?' said Virginia, too intrigued to be embarrassed any more.

'Oh – nothing,' said Jack hastily.

'Don't be silly. What should you have expected? Jack, I want to know. Come on, if you don't tell me I shall scream and my father will be down to horsewhip you.'

Jack looked genuinely terrified. 'Really, Virginia, I didn't mean anything. I'm sorry. I didn't mean to offend you.'

'You didn't offend me, Jack. But I still want to know what you meant just then.'

'Oh – oh, hell, Virginia, it's just that you have this rather strong reputation.'

'For what?'

'Oh – well, for being very – well, strict . . .'

'Strict? Whatever do you mean?'

'Well – oh, I don't know. Old-fashioned. Er – moral, you know. There's nothing wrong with that. Absolutely nothing. It's a really good thing to be. A good reputation to have. Anyway, look, it's late, I should go, I have a heavy day tomorrow. Goodnight, Virginia.'

'Goodnight, Jack. Thank you for a really nice evening.'

She was too stunned to feel anything at all.

Later, lying in bed, staring up at the ceiling, she felt alternately embarrassedly amused and humiliated. Here she was at twenty-one, rich, attractive and, in theory at any rate, a highly desirable proposition, and she was apparently a joke, a spinsterish by-word in frigidity, famous for her moral impregnability. It was a nightmare. She would never be able to confront her own social circle again. There she is, they would all be saying, all knowing nods and smiles, poor old sexless Virginia, locked into her chastity belt – funny that, when her brother's so sexy, so terribly attractive; extraordinary really, they would be saying, she should have been married by now, all her contemporaries are, poor Virginia, what a shame, no one wanting her, everyone afraid of her, how did it happen, well at least she has her career, that's something . . . on and on it went all night in her head, a dreadful litany of sexual failure. She was ready in the morning to get most publicly into bed with the first man she set eyes on. Whether she loved him, whether indeed she liked him or not.

In the event such drastic action was unnecessary. At ten o'clock her phone rang. It was Madeleine Dalgleish; she had returned to New York, and would very much like Virginia to lunch with her. Virginia walked into the Plaza, her head aching, her heart sore, miserably aware that she was doing nothing whatsoever to redeem her reputation by sitting down with a middle-aged lady from England, followed the maître d' to Mrs Dalgleish's table – and found herself gazing into the eyes of the most beautiful young man she had ever seen.

Virginia never ceased to wonder what would have happened to her life if she had met Alexander Caterham a day or two earlier, a week or two later; when she had been feeling less vulnerable, more composed. She would still have undoubtedly noticed his looks, admired his clothes, enjoyed his charm; whether she would have reacted so strongly, so emotionally, was a matter for possible conjecture. In the event, she looked at him and her heart literally turned over: she fell in love. She had always doubted the feasibility of love at first sight; she had heard it described, discussed, debated, but she had not believed in it, had never experienced anything approaching it herself. Love to her was what she saw manifested by her parents, tenderness, loyalty, a high degree (in the case of her mother) of the setting aside of self, and a clear delight in each at being in the company of the other. She could not believe that anything so central to the complexities of two people could be accomplished, even recognized, in the space of a second. But that day, in the Palm Court of the Plaza, she felt she was at least partly wrong. Certainly for the very first time in her life she experienced a strong sense of sexual desire. Standing there, slightly nervous looking at this man who had risen to greet her, she felt it, felt desire, a huge, hot bolt of pleasure lurching within her, and it was a physical shock, she was surprised by it, shaken, and (given the events of the past twelve hours) immensely relieved, almost amused by the timeliness of it, and she closed her eyes momentarily and waited for the room to steady, and then as it did, she took his outstretched hand and felt the heat and the shock again.

'Alexander Caterham,' he said, and his voice was quiet, resonant, Englishly musical. And so confused was she, so totally startled by her reaction to him that she quite literally forgot her own name and simply stood there, staring at him, trying to think of something intelligible to say.

Madeleine Dalgleish, amusedly half aware of what was happening, stood up too and said it for her: 'Miss Praeger! How very very nice to see you again. I have told so many people in England how kind you were to talk at length to a boring old woman in a roomful of charming young people that your fame has spread the length of the country. Isn't that right, Alexander?'

'Indeed it is,' said Alexander; and 'What nonsense,' said Virginia. 'It was a pleasure, you were much the most interesting person at that dreary party, and I was so disappointed when you had to cancel me next day.'

'Well,' said Madeleine Dalgleish, 'it is never too late, and Alexander and I would be delighted to be shown Wall Street and its environs whenever you have the time. Oh, how rude of me, Miss Praeger, this is Alexander Caterham. He had to come to New York on business; his mother is an old friend of mine. I invited him to lunch, and then thought perhaps the two of you would not mind meeting.'

'Of course not,' said Virginia. 'It's very nice to meet you, Mr Caterham.'

He bowed slightly, his blue eyes exploring hers: 'My pleasure entirely,' he said.

'Not Mr,' said Madeleine quickly, slightly awkwardly, smiling. 'Lord.'

'I beg your pardon?' said Virginia.

'Alexander is the Earl of Caterham. Aren't you, Alexander?'

'I fear so,' said Alexander. His eyes had still not left Virginia's.

'His mother and I came out together,' said Madeleine Dalgleish with just a touch of complacency, 'in 1920. We've been good friends ever since. Virginia dear, do sit down, and tell us what you'd like to drink.'

'I think,' said Alexander Caterham, 'we should have champagne. To celebrate. I think this is a very special day.'

'I don't know New York,' Alexander said to Virginia on the telephone next morning. 'So you will have to forgive me if this is a crass suggestion. But I would really like to look at the city from the Empire State Building with you. And then perhaps I could buy you dinner. Would that be all right? Could you bear it?'

'I think so,' said Virginia, laughing. 'The dinner sounds fine. The Empire State – well, we should maybe have a drink first. Let's meet at the St Regis. In the King Cole Room.'

'Very well. Thank you. Six thirty?'

'Six thirty.'

He was waiting for her when she got there; she looked at him, in all his languid, English grace, and she wanted him even more, even harder, than she had the day before. Her anxieties, her insecurities about her sexuality had vanished as if they had never been; for the second time in twenty-four hours she felt a harsh stabbing deep within herself, a hot throb that was half pleasure, half pain. She closed her eyes, afraid he would see the hunger in them as he grazed his lips across her hot cheek, opened them to see his blue eyes tenderly exploring hers.

'It's extremely nice to see you again.'

'Thank you. Did you – did you have a good day?'

'It was all right. I spent most of it thinking about you.'

She was shaken, startled that he should say such a thing, a great liquid wave of delight filling her, making her lighthearted, silly with pleasure.

'What a waste of a day,' she said quickly, flushing, thinking how awkward, how gauche she must sound.

'Not at all. On the contrary. I can't think of a more worthy way to spend it.'

'Oh.'

'I've ordered a bottle of champagne. I thought we'd need it.'

'How lovely.' Dear God, why couldn't she say something intelligent, memorable?

'Tell me,' he said, 'how many times have you been up the Empire State Building?'

'Honestly,' she said, 'I don't know. Probably about two dozen. Maybe more.'

'How tedious for you.'

'Well,' she said, 'the company makes a difference.'

'I'll try to be good company.'

They stood on the eighty-sixth floor looking out at the electrically spangled sky of New York, the exquisite flowery shape of the Chrysler Building, the lights drifting down the river.

'It's beautiful,' said Alexander. 'I love it.'

'I love it too,' said Virginia. 'And you should see it by day as well. It's quite different. More startling.'

'This is quite startling.' He raised his hand, stroked her cheek.

Again, the stab of pleasure. She swallowed, then smiled.

'I'm glad you like it. We're surprisingly sensitive, we New Yorkers. We need to be admired.'

'You must get a lot of admiration.'

'Well. Some.'

'Let's go and have dinner. And I can admire you.'

She had suggested the Lutèce; in the absence of knowledge of anywhere else, he had agreed. It was a measure of her father's standing in the city that she was able to get a table at twenty-four hours' notice;

30

Alexander was not to know that two weeks was more normal and could not be impressed, but he was charmed and pleased by the menu and the wine list.

'This is as good as Paris,' he said.

'And why shouldn't it be?'

'Don't be touchy.'

'We *are* touchy, we Yankees. I told you. We like to be admired.'

'I'm very admiring.'

He was easy to talk to; relaxed, interested, interesting. He talked a lot: he told her about his life in England (very feudal, he said with an almost-ashamed smile) in the great family house. He talked for a long time about the house with its parks and farmland, its lodges and its stables, its perfect eighteenth-century gardens: an exceptionally fine Palladian building, he said, designed by Robert Adam, gardens by Capability Brown, commissioned by the third Earl after he had burnt the original Elizabethan house down, smoking in bed in a drunken stupor; Hartest House, it was called: 'And so lovely it still brings tears to my eyes, when I see it again after being away.'

She looked at him, surprised at such poetry; he smiled at her.

'I'm very sentimental. Family failing.'

'Do you have any pictures of it?'

'No, nothing could do it justice. I like to carry its picture around in my head. But I could send you one, if you like.'

'I would like. And is it yours, this beautiful house?'

'Oh it is. Yes. All mine.'

'What happened to your father?'

'He died,' he said shortly. 'Two years ago. What about your father?'

She told him: how hard she tried to win her father's praise; how he was always watching Baby, how occasionally, when she had been little, he had taken her on his knee and said, 'You're pretty good – for a girl'; how afraid she was of riding with him, how he ignored her school successes, despised her new career.

He listened, politely, smiling rather amusedly; after a while, when she was describing some particularly terrible defeat at Baby's hands, he threw back his head and laughed.

'Why are you laughing?'

'Because it's so silly. Because you haven't had a hard time at all. Not really.'

'I know it wasn't hard exactly. But it mattered to me. Terribly. All things are relative, after all.'

'Of course. But you see, I had a really hard time. What you had to endure sounds like paradise to me.'

31

'All right, Lord Caterham, tell me about your hard time.'

'Oh,' he said, looking distant, 'it doesn't make very pretty hearing. I was sent away to school at seven. Got beaten a lot. Got bullied. Hardly ever saw my mother. Never got cuddled, loved, tucked up in bed at night. Except by my nanny, of course. And that was the good part.'

A wave of tenderness and sorrow swept over Virginia. She put her hand over his. 'It sounds very sad.'

'It was. A bit.' He smiled at her suddenly, a sweetly sad touching smile. Virginia felt her heart wrung.

'And nobody ever made it up to you?'

'Not really. Not yet. I'm hoping to find someone who will. One day.'

'I'm sure you will,' said Virginia.

He stayed in New York for three weeks and saw her nearly every day. She showed him the city, introduced him to her friends, invited him to dinner at the house on East 80th, when Fred III had slightly grudgingly and half-heartedly taken to Alexander and invited him to spend his last weekend at the house in East Hampton. Alexander had accepted graciously. Betsey was in a ferment of anxiety – what should they eat, who should he meet, what should they do? Baby and Mary Rose were invited, but Mary Rose had a big dinner party on the Saturday; she said graciously that they would drive out for Sunday lunch. 'So what do you think for Saturday night?' Betsey said anxiously to Virginia. 'A formal dinner? Fork supper? Or should we just have a quiet evening, the four of us? And should we put him in one of the big double guest rooms, or a single one? I don't want him to think we're just dumping him in any old room.'

'Mother, for a woman who's entertained *le tout* New York for thirty years you're behaving very strangely,' said Virginia, laughing. 'I'll tell you what would be nice, why don't we ask Madeleine Dalgleish? She's still here, and I'm sure she'd be pleased to come. And of course put him in a single room. Just don't worry about it. I can almost hear Daddy saying it: He's only a friend of Virginia's.'

She was in an intensely emotional state, feverish with excitement, dizzy with love, fretful at Alexander's lack of action. He talked and listened to her a great deal, he phoned her three times a day, he told her she was beautiful, that he loved being with her, he kissed her goodnight in an almost chaste way after seeing her home: but that was all. Virginia thought of all the boys and their fumbling fingers, their over-enthusiastic kisses, and looked back in wonder at her own icy responses; here she was, melting (literally, she sometimes felt), shaken with desire, aware of her body and its behaviour, its hungers, in a way she had never known, or dreamt of knowing, and no release, no answer to any of it. She was in despair; Alexander obviously saw her as a kind, sympathetic sister, or friend; probably he had some nobly born creature at home, waiting for him, and he was simply passing the time with her. She wondered if he realized how very much she wanted him, adored him: please God he didn't. That would be utter, total humiliation. That would be dreadful.

She withdrew from him slightly towards the end of that last week, eager to appear cool, disinterested; she could sense his puzzlement, his desire to engage her attention again, and it pleased and soothed her. But she had decided that if nothing happened over this weekend, if he didn't do or say something that indicated he regarded her in some way other than as an agreeable, albeit close, friend she would have to put him and her passion for him aside; she would die rather than appear to be chasing after him.

He arrived on Saturday morning; they had a long, boozy lunch in the garden, and then went walking on the South Shore. Alexander took her hand, raised it to his lips and kissed it; Virginia had to restrain herself by an act of sheer physical will from hurling herself into his arms.

'This is a lovely, lovely place,' he said. 'And your parents' house is beautiful. I love it.'

'It can hardly compare with Hartest, surely,' said Virginia.

'Well,' he said, 'it's different. It's like comparing you with – well, with the Queen of England.'

'Thanks,' said Virginia, laughing.

'No, it's not such a silly comparison. She's regal and important and immensely steeped in tradition. Like Hartest. You're young and lovely and unfettered and free. Like this place. I love you both.'

'Me and Queen Elizabeth?'

'No, you and this beach.'

'Shore.'

'Sorry. Shore.'

'Did you ever meet the Queen?'

'Oh yes,' he said carelessly, 'several times. I wouldn't count her among my intimate friends. But yes, I have met her. At functions. The Derby once.'

'You must,' said Virginia, her eyes dancing, 'tell my mother.'

'Alexander has met the Queen,' she announced at dinner.

Betsey had just taken a mouthful of chicken; she choked.

'Queen Elizabeth?' she said, a glass of water and a great deal of back-thumping later.

'Both of them.'

'Both?'

'Both. The current one and her mum.'

'And – and – what – well, how – ' Betsey was silenced, scarlet with awe.

'What she means is,' said Fred III mildly, 'what is she like? Does she breathe in the normal way, walk by putting one foot in front of another, chew her food, go to the bathroom, that kind of thing.'

'Don't be ridiculous, Fred,' said Betsey. 'You're making me sound like an American.'

'Funny, I thought you were one.'

'Not only Americans ask those questions,' said Alexander, smiling. 'The English are equally fascinated by her. Whenever I tell anyone I've met her I get bombarded by questions. She's very nice. Much prettier than she looks in her pictures. A bit shy. Maybe a bit bossy. But then I suppose she would be. It's her mother I really like. She's a wonderful old bird. A bit vulgar, but wonderful.'

Virginia could see Betsey shaping up to ask how a queen could possibly be vulgar and looked across the table at Madeleine. 'Mrs Dalgleish, how do you feel about a game after dinner? Shall we have a Scrabble match, England versus the United States? I warn you, I was Scrabble champion at Wellesley,' she added to Alexander.

'You never beat me and Baby, though,' said Fred.

'Baby cheats. He makes up words.'

'Nonsense,' said Fred. He scowled at her. Betsey turned quickly to Alexander.

'Do they play Scrabble in your country?' she said.

'They do,' said Alexander, 'I don't.'

'Oh,' said Betsey, confused.

'I'm quite quite hopeless at any kind of board game. Especially Scrabble. But I'd love to watch you. Really.'

'Oh no,' said Virginia. 'No of course not. Is there anything you'd rather do?'

He fixed his dark blue, intense eyes on hers. There was an odd expression in them that she couldn't read; she looked away.

'I'm sorry to be a party pooper,' he said, 'but I honestly think that I shan't be good for much. I was working until three this morning, and that walk this afternoon, and this marvellous claret has made me rather sleepy. I'm so sorry . . .'

He went upstairs to bed at ten thirty; they all assured him they were

34

tired too, and were delighted to have an early night. Fred waited until he heard the door shut and then said what a pity Baby hadn't been there, to make the evening go. Virginia, who had allowed herself to fantasize that Alexander might have been planning to get everyone into bed early, so that he could come and find her when they were all asleep, waited staring into the darkness for over an hour and a half and then cried herself to sleep.

Baby and Mary Rose arrived next day at lunchtime, late, and clearly in foul tempers. Betsey was tense, she had insisted on a formal four courses in the dining room, rather than a light lunch on the porch, and everyone pushed most of the food around their plates and returned it uneaten. Fred III was irritable because his golf game had gone badly; Madeleine Dalgleish had gone for a walk in the morning, got back late and was still flustered; Baby was morose; Mary Rose sat next to Alexander and flirted with him until Virginia thought she really might be sick; and Virginia herself was awkward, afraid to say anything in case it sounded crass or – worse – a piece of competing flirtation.

After lunch they all went and snoozed on the porch; Fred, miraculously restored, woke them all at four and said who was going to walk. 'I will,' said Alexander. 'I'd like that very much.'

'Good. Virgy baby, are you coming?'

'No,' said Virginia, closing her eyes again. She had an appalling head-ache.

They got back an hour later, beaming.

'That was great,' said Fred III happily. 'Nothing like a walk. And you know what, Virginia? Alexander here has a real passion for Busby Berkeley movies. Well, why didn't you tell me?'

'I didn't know,' said Virginia, feeling foolish. Her headache was no better.

'I told him we'd do "The Tops" for him. Go and get your tap shoes, honey. Baby, come on, to the piano.'

'Oh Dad, I can't.'

'Course you can. Come on.'

Baby got up good-naturedly and stumbled sleepily towards the house. 'Come on, Sis. Keep the old man happy.'

'No,' said Virginia. 'No, honestly. I just don't feel like it. Alexander doesn't want to see me dancing. And don't call me Sis. You know I hate it.'

'Oh, I'd love to see you dance,' said Alexander, smiling at her. 'Really. Please, Virginia. It sounds as if it would be wonderful.'

'It isn't,' she said, getting up reluctantly, seeing that giving in was easier than resisting. 'But all right.'

She got through it. She felt stupid, ridiculous even, but she got through it. Baby played carefully, following her, seeing she was nervous; Fred III was in great form. Afterwards Alexander clapped and said, 'That was wonderful. You have a real talent,' and she felt sillier still. She was just bending down to undo her tap shoes when she saw Mary Rose lean towards him and whisper something in his ear. He smiled at her. Virginia froze, locked in a dreadful misery and jealousy. Babe gave her a gentle shove. 'Go on, Blessed. Move.'

'Don't call me that,' said Virginia furiously.

'What did you call her?' asked Mary Rose, intrigued

'Blessed,' said Baby, who was still drunk from lunch. 'With two syllables, as you can hear. It was a nickname from college, wasn't it, darling?'

'Baby, please shut up,' said Virginia. 'Please.'

'How intriguing,' said Mary Rose. 'What did it mean?'

'Oh, it was short for – '

'Baby, please – '

'The Blessed Virginia.'

'Sounds all right to me,' said Alexander politely.

'No, that's not all of it. The Blessed Virginia, our Lady of Tomorrows. It was a reference to Virginia's extremely virginal state. At the time. She was famous for it. Of course nobody knows if – '

'Baby!' said Fred sharply. 'That will do. Virginia, go and find Beaumont and ask him to bring in some drinks – '

But Virginia was gone. Flying out of the room, across the hall, up the stairs, hot, ashamed, blinded with tears, her humiliation total. She ran into her room, slammed the door, locked it, threw herself on her bed. Some great wave of hurt had caught in her throat, she couldn't even cry. She just lay there, hurting, mortified, not knowing what to do. After what seemed like hours there was a knock at the door.

'Virginia. It's Baby. I'm sorry. Please let me in.'

'No,' said Virginia. 'No. Go away.'

More silence. Baby's footfalls receding. Then different ones, slower, more tentative. A gentle knock.

'Virginia. It's Alexander. Please open the door.'

'No.'

'Then I shall stay outside until nature drives you out.'

She lay for a moment, thinking. Then, half smiling blotchily, half shamefaced, she went to the door.

36

'You'd have had a long wait. I have my own bathroom.'

'Can I come in?'

'I suppose so.'

He put his arm round her, walked her to the bed. She sat down heavily and he sat down beside her.

'I don't see why you're quite so upset. It didn't seem such a bad nickname to me. Rather sweet in fact. You should have heard some of mine.'

'Oh,' she said, smiling shakily again, 'you and your childhood.'

'Yes, well you know what I think about yours.'

'It wasn't just the name. It was – well, everything. Having to dance for you. Baby winning as usual. Vile Mary Rose.'

'Vile?'

'Vile. She always puts me down. She hates me.'

'She seems all right to me. A little icy perhaps.'

'Oh well. I can see you like her.'

'Not particularly. The people I like best in your family are your mother and you.'

'Oh,' she said dully.

'You're not so – well, so sure of yourselves.'

'Oh.' There was a silence. Virginia wondered if this was the nearest she was going to get to a declaration of love. Probably.

He suddenly turned her to face him, looked into her eyes.

'Are you still a virgin?' he said.

Virginia was stunned, literally deprived of breath. She stared at him. 'Why?'

'I'd like to know.'

'Oh.'

'I'm sorry. It's a very personal question.'

'Yes.'

'Yes it's a personal question, or yes you are?'

'Both.'

'I thought you were,' he said. 'Look – there's no real connection. But will you marry me?'

37

Chapter 3

Virginia, 1960

They were to be married the following April in New York. Betsey and Fred begged and pleaded with her to have the reception on Long Island, but Virginia refused. She didn't explain why: that the wedding, however careful she was, would seem like a carbon copy of Baby's to Mary Rose. If it had been possible, she would have married quietly in a registry office, or run away to England, but Alexander said countesses had proper weddings, with their parents' blessing. He appeared not to fully appreciate the oddness of his own mother missing the ceremony.

Alexander was a wonderfully attentive and considerate fiancé: he insisted on speaking to her father, on them talking to her mother together; he went along with Betsey's insistence on an engagement party, flying back to New York after a brief trip home to see to matters there; he was charming to all the endless Praeger relatives; he took her to Van Cleef and Arpel's to choose a ring ('nothing flashy,' she said, 'nothing like Mary Rose's,' and the result was tiny rings of diamonds round tinier ones of ruby, and then still smaller ones of sapphire, specially commissioned to her rather rambling description), he went along with all Fred and Betsey's suggestions for the wedding (service at St John the Divine, luncheon for four hundred at East 80th, the conservatory extended by a marquee).

Alexander's contribution to the guest list was modest: immediate family none (he was an only child, his father dead, his mother, he explained carefully, was eccentric, rather frail and virtually a recluse); he invited an ancient maiden aunt, his widowed godfather and two dozen close friends with their husbands or wives. 'It's either that, or we charter a jumbo jet and bring the whole of England,' he explained to Virginia. 'I am planning a huge party when we get home, two actually, one in London, one at Hartest to introduce you to everybody, and we shall have to have a jamboree for everyone on the estate as well. Much better to wait.'

Virginia, mildly surprised, particularly by the non-attendance of his mother, agreed; she was too happy and too much in love to push him or question him on anything.

'Can't I come over before the wedding?' she said. 'Can't I come and see Hartest? Meet your mother? I really would be much happier.'

'I don't want that,' he said, kissing her. 'I want you to come to it as my bride, as the Countess of Caterham, mistress of the house. I want it to be perfect. For you. And for me.'

'Well,' she said, kissing him back, 'I like the sound of the mistress bit, at least. But your mother – surely, Alexander, if she won't come to the wedding, I should go and meet her. It seems so wrong that she won't set eyes on me even until after we're married. I can't believe she wouldn't feel happier that way.'

'Virginia, you must let me be the judge of my mother's behaviour,' said Alexander, and for the very first time she saw a chilliness in his eyes. 'She is a difficult and very private person. She doesn't like people. She certainly doesn't like crowds. At the moment, I have to say, she is expressing a little – hostility towards the idea of my marriage.'

'Hostility? Oh, Alexander, why?' said Virginia, a cloud of anxiety drifting across her bright happiness. 'Do you know? And don't you think she'd be less hostile if she met me, if I made the effort?'

'No I don't,' said Alexander. 'I'm sorry, darling, but I really do urge you to trust me on this one.'

She never forgot her first sight of Hartest House. Alexander had brought a great stash of photographs from England for her and she had looked at it in silence and awe: a great, perfect palace of a house settled exquisitely into the lavish, rolling Wiltshire countryside.

'Adam said what he worked for was movement in architecture,' said Alexander, 'a sense of rising and falling: Hartest for me does not just move, it flies.' A wide house, it was, perfectly proportioned, built in the Palladian style, with curving porticos, wide terraces, tall windows, the whole centred around a rotunda which formed the heart of the house, echoed in the great dome on its roof; 'and here, you see, in the rotunda, one of the most famous double flying staircases in England, people come from all over the world to see that staircase'; and the grounds were as exquisite, miles of parkland, studded with sheep and deer, a Palladian bridge set at one end of the lake – 'there are black swans on that lake as well as white' a river curving languorously through woodland ('the Hart, our own river'); 'the photographs cannot do it justice,' said Alexander, 'the stone is pale, pale grey, the colour of fine mist, and even on a dark, rainy day it seems somehow to shine.'

'I cannot imagine,' said Virginia, laughing, 'what my mother will say when she sees these. I think she'll have a coronary.'

But Betsey didn't. She looked at the pictures in silence and then at Virginia, and then she said quietly, 'It's a very big house for a little girl.'

She was very subdued for the rest of the evening. It was left to Fred to

39

admire the house (and insist on putting a price on it) and for Mary Rose to exclaim over its 'exquisite proportions', its 'magnificent grandeur' and its 'overwhelming vistas'. Baby was totally silent on the subject.

Baby was totally silent on the subject of the wedding altogether. He kissed Virginia when she told him, said he hoped she'd be very happy, and that Alexander was a lucky man, and never said another word about it, apart from discussing his role as best man (an extraordinary request, it was felt, from Alexander, who must have had a close friend of his own, but which Betsey insisted was an example of English charm and thoughtfulness, involving his new family) and initiating Alexander into such American marriage rituals as the Bridal Dinner which was held at the Racquet Club) attended by the bride, groom, ushers and attendants, and where lavish gifts were exchanged. (Virginia gave her bridegroom a gold watch on a platinum chain from Cartier; the twelve small flower girls were all given gold link bracelets, the twelve ushers Gucci belts; Alexander presented Virginia with a small Victorian locket which had belonged, he said, to his mother. Betsey was a trifle embarrassed by the modesty of the present and kept telling Fred afterwards that the English were different.) The bachelor dinner for twenty-four, also thrown at the Racquet Club, was a subdued affair; Alexander promised to do his best to enter into the spirit of the thing, he told Virginia, but was done for by midnight. 'The guy's got no balls,' Baby reported to Mary Rose in the morning; Mary Rose told him not to be disgusting.

As the months went by, Virginia felt herself in an increasingly dreamlike state. She tried to continue to work, but it was difficult; in any case she had to wind her business down. The initial intensely romantic passion she had felt for Alexander did not fade; she was obsessed by him. But beneath the passion, the romance, just occasionally she felt an odd unease, a disquiet which however hard she tried, she could find no substance in, no reason for. It was certainly not because of any fault, any lack of tenderness or lovingness on his part: quite the reverse. He loved her, adored her even, and he told her so every day, often several times a day; he was almost absurdly romantic, writing her long letters whether he was in England or New York, sending her flowers on every possible pretence of an anniversary (a month since we met, a week since we became engaged, six weeks since we bought the ring, two months since you said you loved me). He was a passionate reader, and he liked to read aloud to her, particularly poetry; Donne, he told her, came closest to his heart, to describing how he felt. He had the beautiful elegy 'On Going to Bed' (the one containing the words 'Oh, My America! My new found land') written out most exquisitely by a calligrapher, and framed for her; he commissioned a portrait of her, in the dress she had worn when he met her, and had a miniature painted as well, which he carried with him everywhere, 'in my breast pocket, next to my heart'. And yet, despite his undoubted and great love for her, despite her own intense feelings, there was this slight unease somewhere in her consciousness. Trying to analyse it one evening, after he had gone back to his hotel, she decided the nearest to it was a sense of fantasy, a lack of reality in their relationship. Then she stifled the thought, told herself not to be absurd, that the life ahead of her was indeed perfect, or as near to perfect as real life could be, and that she was crazy to be looking for flaws in it.

The other thing which disturbed her a little was his extraordinary passionate love for Hartest. He spoke of it as if it was a person, a woman, or perhaps a beloved child. His voice changed when he talked of it, became deeper, more resonant; and once, when she dared to criticize his attitude, even to tease him about it just a little, he became angry and cold.

'Hartest is all the world to me,' he said, 'I love it more than I can possibly describe. You have to accept that, learn what it means to me.'

'More than I do, I sometimes feel,' said Virginia, 'and what would you do if I didn't like it?'

'I have to tell you I think I would find it hard to go on loving you,' said Alexander, smiling rather coolly at her.

'And if you had to choose between us?'

'I'm afraid that would be intolerable,' he said. 'You take me, Virginia, you take Hartest. It is part of me, part of my heart.'

'So it would be Hartest, not me?'

'This is a ridiculous conversation,' he said, and his eyes were suddenly quite hard. 'Absurd. But of course,' he added hastily, his voice deliberately, amusedly lighter, 'that would never happen, I would never have to choose. I love you, and you are going to be there, at Hartest, it will be your home as well as mine. You will love it, Virginia, I promise you that.'

The conversation was disturbing – almost, when she dwelt on it, alarming; but she crushed the emotions. She was hardly going to give up a wedding, a marriage, a bridegroom of such near perfection, for a few puny anxieties.

Virginia's dress, made by Ann Lowe, who had made Jackie Kennedy's, was a ravishing flood of white lace, the skirt composed of descending myriads of frills, each one trimmed with tiny pink rosebuds. The skirt became a train which followed her for almost twelve feet down the aisle of the cathedral; she wore a veil that covered her face as she came down the aisle, the diamond-drop tiara that had been in the Caterham family for two hundred years, woven with real pink rosebuds, and the look of love as she put back the veil and faced Alexander brought tears to the eyes of almost every woman in the church and a few of the men as well. Even Fred cleared his throat and blew his nose loudly.

Fred's speech was surprisingly mawkish; he told several anecdotes about Virginia, extolling her talents and her charm, said she would always be his little girl to him, and that New York would be a sadder place without her. And then switched the mood and made everyone laugh by suggesting to Alexander that he might speak to the Queen of England and see about a royal warrant for the bank, and said he was thinking of buying a small tiara for Betsey and an ermine robe for himself to wear on special occasions in the future. Alexander promised to see what he could do, said he would pick out a tiara personally 'although Betsey could hardly look more regal than she does today' and then spoke so tenderly and movingly of his love for Virginia, and his immense gratitude to Fred and Betsey for giving her to him, that even Baby was mollified.

At seven, they went upstairs and changed; Virginia reappeared in a white Chanel suit, and what was known as a Jackie pillbox on her dark hair; they climbed into Fred's Rolls and were whisked off to Idlewild Airport on the long haul of a flight to London and thence Venice.

Virginia went to her marriage still a virgin; it was Alexander's wish, and her body would have had it otherwise, but her heart was touched. She was impatient and hungry (and relieved at her own hunger) but she waited. Alexander had become more ardent, since their engagement; he kissed her passionately, desperately almost, he caressed her body, her breasts, her thighs, tenderly, deliciously, gently, he told her how beautiful she was, and how desirable he found her, and she liked and enjoyed it, responding urgently to the kisses, but too shy, too afraid of appearing awkward, of offending him even, to attempt to return the caresses. But she never felt he was in the slightest danger of becoming out of control, of breaking the discipline he had set upon them both; and even one night when they had lain for hours in one another's arms on the couch in her sitting room at East 80th, and she had felt such soaring, stabbing hunger that she could hardly stand it, and had looked at him, her eyes huge and dark with sex, and said half laughing, at the situation, 'Alexander, please, there is no need for this agony,' he had set her away from him, and gazed into her eyes and said, 'Virginia, there is. For me there is. I'm just an old-fashioned guy, as they say over here. I love you

42

very, very much and I want you utterly utterly perfect on our wedding day. Please try to understand.'

They reached Venice exhausted. Virginia had not slept on the plane, or at least only very fitfully; her head throbbed, her back ached, her eyes were sore when she finally stepped out of the plane at Marco Polo airport. She was tired, fretful, hostile towards Alexander. Every time he touched her hand or tried to kiss her cheek she drew back; the magic of her wedding day, the love she had felt for him for the last six months, the desire that had been swooping through her increasingly strongly ever since she had set eyes on him, had all deserted her. She felt herself an icy, stony, exhausted shell.

And then as she stepped onto the landing stage where the water taxis waited, still silent, dull with tiredness, she saw it, the golden light of Venice, tipping onto the water, and she felt the gentle, pervading warmth of the Italian sun, touching her like a lover, and she looked out across the sea towards the tender, misty outlines of the city, and it touched her heart and she felt that in some strange way she had come home.

In the water taxi, following the white posts down the lagoon towards the city, struck with a joyous almost physical delight as it took substance before her eyes, golden and terracotta and white against the blue water, the bluer sky, disbelieving, almost fearful of its beauty, she turned to Alexander and smiled. 'You were right,' she said. 'Right to make me wait.'

He took her hand, smiled back at her. 'And this is only the foreplay,' he said.

He had booked a suite at the Danieli in the old part of the hotel.

'Chopin stayed here,' he said.

Virginia leant out of the window, gazing enchanted out at the lagoon, weak with weariness and pleasure. 'How wise of him.'

'Well,' he said, 'he lacked one advantage I have. He didn't have you. Are you happy?'

'Very happy.'

'Come here.' He opened his arms; she went into them. 'I love you so much,' he said. 'So much. Later we will explore. I want to show you everything, San Marco, the Bridge of Sighs, the Doge's Palace. All the clichés. But I expect you want to rest.'

'Oh no,' said Virginia, 'no, I don't want to rest, Alexander. I feel I could never be tired again.'

'Then – ' He looked at her, his eyes probing hers. 'Then what would you like? Now?' A smile played on his lips; he reached out and touched her face.

'Well –' and she looked down suddenly, confused, nervous, 'well, I –'
'You look nervous.'
'Alexander, yes, yes I am.'
'My darling,' he said, leaning forward and kissing her gently, 'there is nothing to be afraid of.'
'No, of course not,' she said, trying to smile. 'It's just that I – well, you wanted a virgin, Alexander. You have one. And we do tend to be a little fearful.'
'Of course,' he said. 'I understand. And I am a little nervous myself. If that makes you feel any better.'
'A little.'
There was a silence; she waited for him to make some kind of move, but he sat there, just looking at her, his eyes very tender.

There was a knock at the door. It was a waiter with champagne, and a huge dish of wild strawberries.
'Put them there,' said Alexander to him. 'By the bed.'
'Si, signore.'
He withdrew, closing the door silently. Alexander went over to the table, opened the bottle, poured two glasses. He held one out to Virginia.
'Come and lie down on the bed with me,' he said, 'and just let me tell you how much I love you.'
She drank the glass quickly: too quickly. She felt dizzy, uncertain of herself. She looked at him, and then away, her eyes shadowy with tension. Alexander put his own glass down, quickly; it was an oddly decisive movement, he seemed suddenly less patient, less gentle. He pushed her back onto the pillows, stroking her hair, his lips moving down onto her throat. He began to unbutton her blouse, to caress her breasts; Virginia, filled with sweet, hot fire, lay, her head thrown back, her arms winding first gently, then more urgently round his neck. His lips were on her nipples now, kissing them, licking them; she felt the sensation travel down through her body, increasing the heat in her loins. She moaned, moved against him; he sat up and again paused, paused for quite a while, and then began to undress her, gently, carefully, kissing her as he went, moving down, caressing her stomach, his fingers moving tenderly across it, down, towards her thighs; he removed her skirt, her stockings, her panties; she could feel her own wetness, her own heat. She was naked now, quite naked; a long, slender white body, carved out of the rich red brocade of the bed cover. Alexander looked at her, studying her, touching her, kissing her; and she opened her arms again, smiled at him, a joyous, confident, reckless smile, the smile of love. 'Come and join me,' she said.

And he hesitated once more, just for a moment, and then began to kiss her again, harder than ever, his hands exploring her, there, there in the warmth of her, and she was throbbing with sex and love, frantic for him.

'I love you so much,' he said, and he sounded gentle, almost sad suddenly, 'so very very much.' And then he pulled away from her, and began, very slowly, to remove his own clothes, and his eyes never left her face, not for a moment, and then he walked over to the window and closed the shutters so that the room was in darkness and came back to the great bed and drew her into his arms.

Chapter 4

Angie, 1963

Angie hoped she wasn't actually going to shit in her pants, but it was beginning to seem quite horribly likely.

She shifted on her chair, trying to ease her discomfort, and wondered how much longer she was going to have to wait. God, she was in agony. Maybe she wasn't cut out after all to be powerful and successful, if this was what it did to your guts. What on earth was the silly woman doing there, behind that door?

Angie looked around the tiny room she was in, trying to distract herself. She supposed it must have once been some kind of servant's room; no doubt the Countess of Caterham enjoyed keeping people waiting in it. It could hardly qualify as a room, it was more of a cupboard, nothing in it but a chair and a tiny low table, with neat piles of *Vogue*s and *House and Garden*s. She was tempted by the *Vogue*s, but knew she should be more interested in the *House and Garden*s; she had tried to concentrate on them, but her discomfort was too great. She started to count. Just as she reached fifty-five the door opened and a face that she recognized from photographs in gossip columns and magazines appeared, smiling at her.

'Miss Burbank! I'm so sorry to have kept you waiting in this horrible little room. Long long call to a very tiresome client. Please come in.' Her voice was low and very slightly husky, her accent soft and drawly, rather than the New York twang Angie had expected; she stood up, finding to her relief that her bowels had miraculously called themselves into order, and followed the Countess of Caterham into her office. On the threshold she looked around, stopped quite still by surprise and pleasure at what she saw: a room quite unlike anything she could even ever have imagined. If this was an example of Her Ladyship's work, then Angie liked it.

What had amounted to the entire basement floor of the Caterham house in Eaton Place had been converted into one great room, the supporting pillars cleverly masked by smoked-glass dividing screens in very dark greenish blue. The tiled floor was a pale pale icy version of the same colour and the walls – such of them as could be seen between endless framed antique architectural drawings, and a floor-to-ceiling set of shelves, stacked with what looked like open books with rainbow-coloured pages – were stark white.

The lights hanging low over the two smoked-glass and chrome desks were in beautifully worked wrought iron, painted white, and the chair behind what was obviously Lady Caterham's desk was not a predictable chrome and leather affair, but an exquisitely carved wooden one, with a cane back and seat.

It crowned the room, that chair; Virginia saw Angie staring at it and smiled at her. 'It's nice, my chair, isn't it? It's Charles II.'

'Really?' said Angie, carefully nonchalant. If Lady Caterham was going to try and engage her in a discussion about antique furniture, then she would know she was in the wrong place, and she wasn't going to stay and be made a fool of.

'Yes. But I really like it because it's unpredictable. Like the lights. I nearly had those stained-glass Tiffany jobs, but I thought that's what everyone would expect. Especially my being American. So I had the blacksmith at Hartest, that's where we live really, make these. Do you like them?'

'Very much,' said Angie carefully, thinking how much prettier stained-glass lights would actually look. 'What are those book things on the shelves? With the coloured pages?'

'They're fabric sample books,' said Virginia. 'You show them to clients, help them make up their minds. To be treated with great respect – the samples, not the clients – they cost a fortune. So do the wallpaper books.'

'I suppose they would,' said Angie, trying to sound knowledgeable, and surprised that anyone as patently rich as the Countess should be concerned with cost. 'That's Hartest House, isn't it? Behind you.'

She had prepared carefully for the interview. Suze had told her how important that was. She went to the big public library in Westminster and looked up the Caterhams in *Who's Who*; Alexander Caterham, she learnt, was the ninth Earl, and had inherited the title and the house, Hartest House in Wiltshire, when he was nineteen years old. He had married Virginia Praeger ('only da' it said 'of Frederick and Elizabeth Praeger of East 80th St, New York and Beaches, East Hampton, Long Island') in April 1960. They had a daughter, Lady Charlotte Welles, born in January 1962.

'Yes, it is, Hartest,' said Virginia, looking at her slightly surprisedly and then round at the original architects' drawing and plans for Hartest which hung on the wall behind her desk. 'How very clever of you to recognize it.'

'Well,' said Angie, giving her a quick, almost conspiratorial grin. 'I looked it up, you know.'

'What do you mean, you looked it up?' said Virginia, intrigued.

47

'Well I knew I was coming to see you, so I thought I should find out a bit about you.'

'I find that very engaging,' said Virginia, smiling at her; she had a nice smile, Angie thought, very warm and soft; it lit up her face, which could actually look rather sad. Angie had noticed that in several of the photographs. She also had to admit that the Countess was very beautiful. Far more beautiful than she had expected. The photographs, even if they could show her perfect heart-shaped face, her almost impossibly straight nose, her wide, curvy mouth, couldn't begin to do justice to her colouring, to the dark, auburn-tinted hair, the pale pale creamy skin, and the amazing tawny eyes. She liked Lady Caterham's clothes too: if this was class dressing, she couldn't wait to join in. Virginia was wearing a pale pink suit, in slightly bumpy tweed, with navy braid edging to the neckline and cuffs and pockets, and large gold buttons. A white flower was pinned to her jacket, rather than a brooch; she wore pearl and gilt earrings and white and navy sling-back shoes. Angie didn't know it, but she was looking at couture Chanel, in its purest form.

'Well now,' said Virginia, 'sit down, Miss Burbank. Would you like a coffee?'

'I'd love one,' said Angie, who hated coffee and would have killed for a cup of strong sweet tea, 'thank you. Black, no sugar,' she added, as Virginia paused holding the cup. God, it was going to be horrible.

'So,' said Virginia, 'let me tell you what I'm looking for. I suppose the proper name would be a secretary, and there would be some letters and things to type, but really I need more than that, or do I mean less, someone to be more of an assistant really, but in a very humble way, someone to run about and collect things, take swatches over to clients, pick up curtains when they're made, that sort of thing. Would you mind doing that, Miss Burbank?'

'No of course not,' said Angie, trying not to sound too much as if she thought it was a daft question.

'Well, you'd be surprised how many people would. Feel they're trained to be secretaries, not messengers. Um – can you drive?'

'Not quite,' said Angie carefully. 'I haven't passed my test.' Difficult to pass a driving test when you weren't old enough to have a licence.

'Well that's a pity. But maybe you could manage in taxis and things. For now.'

'Well, it might be better,' said Angie, 'I haven't got a car anyway.'

'Well that's not a problem,' said Virginia, slightly impatiently, 'you could use mine. Obviously.'

'Oh. Yes.' Christ, this job was getting more jammy by the minute.

48

'Well, now let's see. Your typing and shorthand are obviously very good. The agency was really enthusiastic about you.'

'Oh, that's nice.' Good old Suze; she'd done her proud; she hoped she could live up to it.

'Er – how old are you, Miss Burbank? Are you really twenty? You don't look it.' The tawny eyes were amusedly watchful; Angie relaxed suddenly and grinned back. 'No. No, I'm not. I'm only eighteen. Just eighteen actually. But it sounds so young, I didn't think you'd even have seen me.'

'I might. I must say I'd put you at eighteen. But anyway, it doesn't really matter.'

Angie smiled at her. 'Good.' Silly cow. She might think it mattered if she knew she still wasn't quite sixteen.

'So tell me about yourself. What have you been doing up to now?'

Oh, thought Angie, not a lot; not much I could tell you about. 'Well, I've been temping mostly,' she said.

'Really? That must be fun,' said Virginia. 'A different job every week.' She sounded slightly wistful.

'Not really,' said Angie. 'As soon as you find out how they do the filing, and how they all like their coffee, you have to leave again.'

'I suppose so. And did you learn your shorthand and typing at school?'

'No, evening classes,' said Angie carefully. She didn't want to be asked awkward questions about certificates. Anyway, the crash course she had been given by Suze and her own painstaking practising had turned her into a much more efficient secretary than all those snooty pieces like Marcie in the last place, who had been to Pitman's and could hardly bear to risk their red talons on the typewriter keys. Suze had told her that, and the first temporary job she had done had certainly confirmed it, the man had told her she was wonderful, the best girl he'd had all summer. That obviously had something to do with the fact she'd not thrown a mental when he pinched her bum behind the filing cabinets, and been careful to cross her legs particularly high on the thigh when she was having trouble with dictation, and had to ask him to slow down a bit; but the fact remained she was quick and neat, and she worked hard, and kept her filing tray empty. She couldn't understand the other girl in the office who left hers until it spilled over the top; it just made it so much more work, and she was always looking for things halfway down the pile.

'Tell me about yourself,' said Virginia, smiling at her. 'Do you live at home?'

'Well – sort of. I live with my brother.'

'And where are your parents?'

'Well, my mother died last year.'

'I'm sorry. That's sad, when you're so young. You must miss her.'

'Oh I do,' said Angie earnestly, recalling with sudden vividness standing at her mother's graveside and looking down at the coffin with a cold blank where grief should supposedly have been.

'And what about your father?'

'He left us. Years ago. We live with our gran and granddad, Johnny and me.'

'And what does your brother do? It's nice you have him, at least.' Virginia was obviously slightly thrown by this sad history, as she was meant to be.

'Yes, we're quite close. Johnny works in a shop.' Well he did. Some of the time.

'So why do you want this job?' asked Virginia suddenly. Angie was thrown slightly off balance by this change of mood.

'Well – I do prefer working for a woman.'

That was a popular one, Suze had said. And anyway it was true. 'And I do like houses. I mean I've never lived in a really nice one. But I love reading about them. And I'd like to find out how they get that way. Nice. You know? And I'm always changing my own room round, redecorating and so on.'

'It isn't just discussing colour schemes, you know,' said Virginia. 'In fact that's the easy bit. It's dealing with a lot of rather particular, very capricious people.'

Angie looked at her politely. She wasn't sure what capricious meant.

'They spend an awful lot of time – expensive time – changing their minds. They don't know what they want, or they're not sure. But they like to think they do. Or they do know what they want and it's – well, not very nice, and you have to talk them out of it. So a great deal of the job is diplomacy. You know? Flattering them, charming them, trying to work out what they're really saying.'

'Like what?'

Angie was suddenly genuinely interested. This was the kind of thing she could handle.

'Well, they say they want their room or flat or whatever to be very simple. Not fussy at all. And you look at their clothes, and they may have on one of those blouses with a huge bow, you know, and very fussy hair and lots of rings and things; and you know that what they really mean is maybe a simple colour scheme, but lots and lots of busy, pretty chintzes and things. Or a very complex colour scheme, shot silk wallpapers, two contrasting curtain fabrics, but just maybe plain upholstery fabric and some very modern-looking vases and things. You have to talk to them. And you'll get them looking at swatches – '

'What are swatches?'

'Oh, bits of fabric, samples. Like the ones in those books. And if you're lucky, they'll say, yes, that's exactly what they want, and you breathe a sigh of relief and then they'll say, but could I get it with a blue pattern on it. So it really is quite difficult and you have to be extremely patient. And they get quite rude sometimes too, and you have to be terribly nice, not answer back – could you cope with that?'

'Oh, I think so,' said Angie, thinking of the innumerable times Johnny had sworn at her, blamed her for things, and she had stood there taking it, in case he decided to hit her.

'Oh, yes, and there is one other thing,' said Virginia. 'I forgot. I need someone to do the accounts. I can hardly tell the time, I'm so innumerate. Can you do simple book-keeping, that sort of thing? And you'd have to do the invoices, work out the time we'd spent on each job, that sort of thing.'

'Oh yes,' said Angie, casually confident. 'I did book-keeping as part of my course.'

'Good. Well, look, I have to see a couple more people, and you are a bit younger than I'd – well, thought of. But I think we'd get on well. Anyway, thank you for coming, and I'll ring the agency tomorrow or the next day. Is that all right?'

'Yes of course,' said Angie, trying not to show her disappointment. She had hoped to get it settled then and there, although Suze had told her it would be very unlikely. 'Thank you for seeing me,' she added politely, holding out her hand. The Countess's handshake was interestingly firm; she had expected it to be rather limp and chilly.

Angie had spent her early years in a small terrace house in Bermondsey, just down the road from the Caledonian Market, with her mother, Stella, her grandparents, and her brother Johnny. She never knew who her father was; Stella didn't have much of an idea either.

When Angie was five, Stella got married to Eric Dobson, who owned a large draper's shop in Brixton. He seemed rather rich to Stella; the three of them moved into his house in Romford. The marriage ended when Angie screamed aloud one night, waking to find him sitting on her bed, with his pyjama trousers down; Johnny reported rather more serious abuse. They all went back to Bermondsey, where Johnny embarked on his career, nicking things from Woolworths and selling them down the market. Angie was sometimes allowed to help him with the nicking: she considered this a great honour.

When she was seven, Stella saw an advertisement for child models. She dressed Angie up in her party dress, put her unruly blonde curls into neat ringlets and took her along to the Lovely Little Ladies agency. Angie was hired and spent three very happy years being photographed in endless fluffy jumpers, holding endless kittens, or modelling clothes at fashion shows. She was known as Angel. When she was about eleven, the modelling agency work dropped off; she passed the eleven-plus, but they couldn't afford the uniform for her, so she went to Secondary Modern. Angie minded quite a lot.

When she was fourteen she got her first boyfriend. He was twenty-five, his name was Guy, he owned a strip club, and he introduced her to sex. She found she liked sex. Very much.

He also suggested she left school and started modelling again. She was too small to be a proper fashion model, so she specialized in underwear. It wasn't as nice as being Angel, but the money was good. And if the clients were allowed to come into the dressing room and supervise the fit of the bras and pantie girdles, she got tips as well. Her angelic little face, Bardot curls tumbling over her shoulders, adorned innumerable advertisements and showcards. It was around then that she changed her name from Wicks to Burbank. She got the name from one of her *Picturegoer* magazines; it was the name of a studio in Hollywood and it seemed to go with Angie. She had always hated Wicks.

When she was fifteen, she became pregnant. Guy gave her a handful of tenners and sent her off with one of his strippers to get herself sorted, as he put it. She ended up in hospital and nearly died. The doctor told her she would be lucky if she was ever able to have another baby. Shocked and weak from loss of blood, Angie couldn't see that was a great problem.

Soon after Angie came out of hospital, Stella went into it. Her smoker's cough was diagnosed as lung cancer; she died six weeks later.

And then she met Suze. Suze had a flat in the same block as Johnny and his girlfriend Dee, in Kennington. Dee's dad was rich; he lived in Spain most of the time, and paid for the flat. Johnny said he was on the run and couldn't come back to England. Angie often stayed with Johnny and Dee, especially if she was working on their stall on Saturdays. She met Suze on the stairs one wet Sunday afternoon, and they went to the pictures together; it became a weekly event. Suze seemed to her the epitome of sophistication. She worked for a secretarial agency, and she had a fur coat, and a very refined accent. She talked a lot about the life of a secretary, and how the personal ones earned a lot of money and prestige. It sounded wonderful to Angie who was beginning to find modelling pantie girdles and selling stolen goods depressing, and she said so.

'Well,' said Suze, 'no reason why you shouldn't do it, Angie. I could teach you shorthand and typing. You've got a good brain, you could do very well.'

52

'You're kidding,' said Angie.

Suze said she wasn't kidding.

Eight months later, after a baptism of fire working for a rag trade firm where she had to do a bit of modelling in between answering the phone, typing and being touched up by the owner, Suze told her she was ready for a proper job and sent her for her interview with the Countess of Caterham. 'You most probably won't get it,' she said, 'but it'll be good for you to practise your interview technique.'

Lady Caterham phoned Suze at the agency, and told her that she felt Angie was much too young and inexperienced for the job; Suze was still trying to work out how she was going to break this news to Angie without sending her into a fit of terminal depression when Lady Caterham broke into her thoughts, an amused lift to her voice, and said that even given that, Angie was so patently a worker, would clearly be the greatest fun to work with and that she had been so impressed by her taking the trouble to find out about her and Hartest before the interview that she would like to take the gamble and hire her.

No one else in her family was very pleased about Angie's new job; her brother said there was no money in office work and how did she think she was going to pay the rent out of the eight pounds a week the Countess was paying her? Pretty mean, he reckoned, when she was clearly as rich as Croesus. Mrs Wicks, her grandmother, said she supposed it was all right, but the aristocracy were a funny lot, and wouldn't a big office have been more fun? Only old Mr Wicks, struggling to get the words out between coughs, told her she was a clever girl and he was proud of her. Angie bought him a packet of best Old Holborn and told him to think of her every time he rolled a ciggy with it. The whole family had agreed there was no point taking the doctor's advice and stopping him smoking now.

Angie went to Wallis and bought what they described as a Chanel-style suit in pink tweed, which she could see was very much the kind of thing the Countess would like, and then she went to Liberty and bought two very plain wool shifts, one navy, and one beige, with a label in them that said Jane and Jane. The girl in Liberty, who was exceptionally nice, told her she had made a very wise choice and that the designer of the dresses, Jean Muir, was going to be one of the great new names in English fashion. She suggested to Angie that exactly the right shoes for the dresses would be low-heeled pumps from Russell and Bromley. 'Their end of season sale is on, you could get a bargain.'

Angie was surprised that her shoes should have low heels; to her, sophistication had always been synonymous with high, the more teetery the better. But she could see that the girl was infinitely more familiar with the look she was after than Suze, hitherto her mentor of style, and so she thanked her, told her that if she ever wanted her house done up at a bargain rate she had only to ask, and went obediently to Bond Street where she bought two pairs of the low-heeled pumps for ten pounds each, one black patent, one navy leather; she could always, she thought, wear her new white stilettos with the unbelievably pointed toes for going out dancing on Saturday nights with Suze; and finally as she was wandering up Bond Street past Fenwicks, she saw a classically plain navy coat in the window and spent her last twenty pounds on it. She didn't particularly like any of the clothes, but she could see they were all absolutely right for her new life. The whole thing after all was a bit of play-acting; she had just acquired her costumes.

After about three weeks, she stopped feeling she was play-acting, and became totally absorbed in her job. She learnt fast; she had grasped by the end of the first day Virginia's highly (and necessarily) complex filing system for the fabric and wallpaper samples, how much they all cost, and how to calculate the price of a set of drawing room curtains in both full and window length. By the end of the fourth she had also grasped which phone calls were idle inquiries and which genuine, and worth spending time and calculation on. Much of the time she was alone in the office while Virginia went out seeing people; in theory then she was catching up on her typing and filing, but in practice she was talking, endlessly talking, patiently and politely to clients, telling them that yes, Lady Caterham had been working on their colour board, or design, or room plan, that it was nearly ready, that she would be phoning them in a day or two, that she was waiting for a particular sample to come in before presenting them with her ideas, or for the architect to finalize some small detail.

Angie quickly discovered that, as Lady Caterham had said at her interview, finding the right fabric for the right sofa or whatever was only a tiny part of her job. 'You have to find out what they really want. I mean a lot of people come to decorators because they simply can't imagine the thing themselves. They want something and they don't know what. They're very insecure. And you're not sure either. So I always say, "Look, why don't we do this room, or even just the curtains, and then see how you like it? If you do, we can go further, if you don't we can rethink." We have to get their confidence, make them feel they're happy with us. Very often they say, "Oh, I didn't think it was going to look like that." They may like it and they may not, but at least you haven't frightened them. Then they're happy to go along with you, because they feel they're going in the right direction.'

'And what happens if they want something and you can see it's going to be horrible?' said Angie.

'Oh,' said Virginia, laughing, 'you say, "Oh, that sounds really nice." Then you phone next day and you say, "I thought about your suggestion, and I thought it might be even better if we did so and so." They nearly always agree. This whole thing is at least fifty per cent psychology. Some people come to a decorator rather than a shrink. And the more difficult they are, the more they seem to come to me. Maybe because I'm a woman, maybe because I'm American, I don't know. But anyway, that's what happens, and mostly I seem to make it work.'

Angie regarded her with ever-increasing respect; she had never been confronted by such a combination of creative, practical and psychological skills.

Virginia had only been running her London business for a little over a year, and she already had a large number of clients, all filed on the constantly whirling little Roladex on her desk. 'Never leave that out,' she said to Angie, 'if you leave the office unmanned during the day, put it in the safe. It's worth more to us than everything else in the office put together.'

She told Angie she wasn't sure why she had been so instantly successful. 'It's so different here, in New York you boast about your interior designer, they're starry people, the big ones, here you're more of a tradesman. Some people, in the country particularly, would die rather than admit they'd not done it all themselves. Obviously I'm not going to be working for many of them, although I did help a dear lady with her drawing room, she'd been married thirty-five years and only ever changed one cushion. But in London, well, it just took off so well.'

'I suppose,' said Angie carefully, 'it's got something to do with who you are. I mean, I don't suppose Virginia Bloggs would have been quite so successful. Even if she had been as clever as you,' she added hastily.

'Well – yes, I suppose so,' said Virginia, slightly reluctantly. 'Now look, Angie, I have to go out now and I won't be back. Mike Johns has promised to come back with the estimates for that hotel today. Chase him if he hasn't rung by four, will you? We'll lose it if we don't quote tomorrow. And when he's done it, could you slot the figure into the quotation, and be sure to get it mailed tonight. It's vital.'

'Are you sure you don't want me to take it round?' said Angie.

'No, really, because then you're out of the office. Just post it. It'll be fine. And I'll see you tomorrow. Bye, Angie. And thank you. You're doing a great job.'

The afternoon was surprisingly quiet; it was late November, and the rich ladies of London were on the whole psyching themselves up for Christmas, resigned to their houses having to pass another party season without being redone. Most of the jobs now being quoted for were small: some curtains here, some loose covers there. Angie caught up with her filing, typed some letters and invoices ('People not paying is the worst nightmare of this job,' Virginia had told her on the first day, 'invoices have to go out soonest'), dealt with some fractious clients. At four she phoned Mike Johns, who was a builder Virginia often worked with, who was quoting for a job on a small but hugely luxurious hotel in Knightsbridge they were working on. The new owner, an American, Mr M. Wetherly Stern, wanted what he called a complete restyle for his South West Three Hotel, and Virginia had presented him with plans for what she called the English Country House ('Only of course no self-respecting country house would ever look remotely like it,' she said to Angie) with a reception area and a lounge bar full of library shelves, small tables covered with magazines, low leather sofas, fireplaces with marble surrounds, and alcoves. Mike was to build the shelves and alcoves, the bars and the reception desk, which was also to resemble a large library table. Mr Stern wanted his hotel open for the early spring and was growing impatient. 'He's a funny little man,' Virginia had told Angie, 'quite nice, and obviously terribly rich, very polite, but a bit greasy. I wouldn't like to cross him.' Mike's quote was late; it looked as if Mr Stern might be crossed.

Mr Johns was out, said his secretary; he wouldn't be back all afternoon. Did she have a quote to send Lady Caterham? Angie's voice was slightly, ominously patient.

'For who was this?' Angie could almost hear her setting her nail polish aside, and sighing.

'This was for Virginia Caterham,' said Angie with an icy patience.

'Would that be trade?'

'It certainly would,' said Angie, 'and Lady Caterham has been waiting three days now.'

'Well Mr Johns is a very busy man.' The voice was growing defensive.

'He could be a lot less busy if we don't get this quote.'

'I'm afraid I don't like your tone,' said the secretary.

'I'm not smitten with yours either,' said Angie, 'but I have a job to do, and I've promised Lady Caterham and our client to get that quote in the post today. Now could you maybe shift your arse and look through your files, or maybe give Mr Johns a call. If it's not too much trouble. Or should I get Lady Caterham to call him direct? She does know where he is.'

This was a lie, and she also knew she was running a big risk, talking to the girl this way, it was probably what Virginia would call counter-productive, a favourite phrase of hers, but she was genuinely agitated; the bluff paid off.

'I'll have to call you back,' said the girl. 'Just give me a few minutes.' She clearly wanted to finish her nails, thought Angie, get them dry.

She phoned back half an hour later.

'I do have the quote, but it's very rough. And I've no time to type it myself.'

'Oh really? Well isn't it lucky that I do. Just get it over here, put it in a taxi, and I'll see to it.'

'I don't know that Mr Johns would like me using a taxi without permission.'

'I'm sure Mr Johns wouldn't mind you using his cock without permission, if it was going to get this job sorted out.'

'I find your language very offensive,' said the girl.

'Yeah, well I expect Mr Johns would find your behaviour offensive,' said Angie, 'and if I don't get that quote in half an hour, he's going to hear about it. Now go and find a taxi, and get it over here, fast, the Eaton Place address, and then you can get off early and go to the hairdresser as planned.'

'How did you – that is how dare you talk to me like that?'

'I dare. Do you want Mr Johns to hear about the hair?'

'Just give me the exact address.' The girl sounded sulky. 'You'll get it.'

The quote, in Mike's illegible handwriting, arrived three quarters of an hour later; by the time Angie had deciphered it, typed it into Virginia's estimate and made the necessary adjustments, the post had gone. She sighed. Well, she'd just have to deliver it in person. It wasn't far. Just near Harrods, off Beauchamp Place. She was getting to know the smarter areas of London rather well. Shit, it was nearly six, she'd never get a taxi. If only she could drive. Well, she could hike it. The Russell and Bromley pumps were very comfortable. She put the Roladex in the safe, locked up the office and half walked, half ran down to Sloane Square, up Sloane Street, round the back of Harrods and up Beauchamp Place, bumping endlessly into wearily irritable Christmas shoppers; by the time she reached the South West Three, she was flushed and flustered.

The glass door was wide open; a few plastic easy chairs and low splay-legged tables stood in the dingy reception area; the carpet which had once had a frenetic orange and beige print beneath years of grubbiness was worn threadbare, and the fake oils in gilt frames of beauty spots in the British Isles made the room infinitely more depressing rather than less. It was cold and the blow-heater someone had helpfully placed in the middle of the room was doing no more good than if it had been belting out hot air into the middle of Knightsbridge. A short, stout man, with dark hair and bright, currant-like dark eyes, flanked by a pair of tall girls, was standing by the blow-heater. He looked at Angie, and glowered at her.

'The hotel is closed.'

'Yes, I know. Mr Stern?'

'Sure. Yes, that's me.'

'I'm Angie Burbank. I work for Lady Caterham.'

'Oh, do you now? Well, you can tell Lady Caterham she sure as hell isn't working for me. No way, no way at all. That estimate is three days late. This is a hotel I want to open, I run a business, you know? Have you heard of business in this country?'

'Some of us have, some of us haven't,' said Angie cheerfully. 'Lady Caterham certainly has. She's been working on your plans round the clock. I have them with me. And estimates.'

'Too many clocks,' said M. Wetherly Stern. 'I wanted that estimate this afternoon latest. I'm talking to another decorator, and he'll be here in thirty minutes. I'm sorry, Miss – what did you say your name was?'

'Burbank,' said Angie. 'Angie Burbank.'

She saw one of the tall girls exchange an amused, eye-raised glance with the other over Stern's head. As always when she felt at a disadvantage, adrenalin rushed to save her.

She put her hand out, touched Stern's hand very gently.

'Please, Mr Stern,' she said, 'I know these quotes are late. It's my fault. I – I lost the original quote. Lady Caterham will probably fire me when she finds out. Please – please take a look at her plans. I know you'll like them. Really.'

Stern's eyes met hers: bright, burning dark eyes, surprisingly large, with very long eyelashes. Angie concentrated very hard, and felt tears rush to the back of her own large green ones. She had always been able to cry to order. She looked down, swallowed, then up again; Stern smiled at her suddenly, and rather slowly, and she became aware, with a swift sure rush of sexual instinct, that he was looking down at her, that there weren't many people he could look down at and that he was enjoying it. She mentally thanked the girl from Liberty once again for making her buy the low-heeled shoes – in the stilettos, their faces would have been level – and smiled at him tentatively. He said nothing. She bit her lip, looked down again, waited. More silence. She sighed. 'Very well. I don't blame you. I'll take them back.'

Stern suddenly laughed. 'Well, I like honesty. Let's take a look at them. You deserve that. That can't have been easy. You girls –' he looked up at the two brunettes – 'you girls go find some coffee somewhere, and bring it back here while I look at Lady Caterham's plans.'

'Oh, thank you,' said Angie, 'thank you very much. Could we maybe put the plans down on that table, while I go through them, explain them just a bit. I know Lady Caterham would like me to do that. I really do think you'll like them. They're very – English. I do think it's clever of you to have spotted the potential of this hotel.'

Stern still didn't look at the plans. He was still staring at her, his large dark eyes exploring her face, her tangle of blonde hair, her tiny slender body. 'You're a very little girl,' he said, 'to be doing what seems to be quite a big job. No more than a schoolgirl, are you? How old are you, exactly?'

Angie took a deep breath and, for the first time that afternoon, told the truth. 'I'm sixteen,' she said, 'well, nearly sixteen and a half.'

'Well, Miss Burbank,' said M. Wetherly Stern, 'I find myself very impressed with you. Very impressed indeed. Now let's have a look at these plans – how would you like to do that over a glass of champagne?'

'I'd like that very much,' said Angie. 'Thank you.'

'So he took me to the Hyde Park Hotel, where he's staying, and plied me with champagne, which was lovely, and looked at the plans, and asked me to have dinner with him next week,' she reported to Virginia the following morning. 'So I said I would. And he definitely likes the plans. I'm sure he'll phone any minute. He said he would, before ten. Oh, listen, that'll be him now, I bet.'

She picked up the phone.

'M. Wetherly, good morning. Yes, I'm very well. Thank you so much. Yes I enjoyed it too. Lady Caterham is here now, and she'd like to speak to you. Yes, I'll see you next Wednesday. I'm looking forward to it already.'

Virginia was amused to hear a slightly more breathy, schoolgirly note in her voice than usual.

M. Wetherly Stern told Virginia he wanted her to do the hotel; he said he was very impressed with her plans. Virginia took Angie out to lunch at an Italian restaurant in Ebury Street to celebrate and to thank her. 'But I'm worried about you. I fear he's a dirty old man. Are you sure you're not getting into rather deeper water than you can handle, Angie?'

'No, of course not,' said Angie, 'I really like him. I like older men. My first boyfriend was twenty-five and I was only fourteen. And I don't think he's a dirty old man at all, actually. I think he's sweet. He's certainly not greasy. He's got the most beautiful great dark eyes and incredible

59

eyelashes, and he's very polite and respectful, and his hair doesn't have a smidgen of grease on it, and he has a really nice smile, and he doesn't have bad breath, and he made me laugh a lot.'

'Well, you certainly seem to have studied him,' said Virginia. 'Er – Angie, can I ask you something?'

'Of course,' said Angie, knowing what was probably coming. She picked up her wine glass, and took a large swig.

'Angie, exactly how old are you? I know you told Mr Stern you were sixteen because you reckoned he had a Lolita complex, but is that the truth?'

'Well – yes. Sort of,' said Angie. 'I mean, yes it is. Oh God, is that *awful*? You're not going to fire me, are you? For lying to you?'

'Angie,' said Virginia, 'don't be ridiculous. How could I fire you? I can't imagine running the business without you now. But I wish you'd told me the truth at the interview.'

'Well you really wouldn't have hired me then,' said Angie. 'I mean eighteen was pushing it, wasn't it? Be honest?'

'Well – maybe. A bit. Anyway, here's to you, and Mr Stern. Not as a couple, I hasten to add.'

'M. Wetherly,' said Angie, 'that's what he likes to be called. And why not a couple? I think it could be fun.'

It was fun; she enjoyed the company of M. Wetherly more than she had ever enjoyed any man's. He was extremely funny; he was gentlemanly and considerate; he had a simple honesty which endeared him to her, and he was very very rich. He bought her endlessly beautiful presents, perfume, a Gucci watch, a gold bracelet, a pearl choker, silk shirts, cashmere sweaters; he took her to the theatre, and out to dinner, to places she had only ever dreamed of, but familiar to her as her own name, from her reading of the gossip columns, the Caprice, the Ritz, the Terrace Room at the Dorchester, Le Gavroche, and a wonderfully cosy, clubby place called the Guinea in Bruton Lane, off Berkeley Square. He also took her out shopping to buy evening dresses; his taste was a little different from the girl at Liberty, he liked very tight slinky black crepe dresses, scarlet lace shifts, gold and silver lamé Grecian-style numbers. Angie loved them all; the only thing she was always careful about was staying in low-heeled shoes. She discovered a designer called Jean Varon who made long high-waisted dresses with tiny bodices adorned with sequins, ostrich feathers, even smocking, in white crepe and red satin and black silk, and bought every one she could find. M. Wetherly took her dancing to Annabels which he belonged to, and plied her with champagne, and told her she was the most beautiful girl he had ever known. He was thirty-six and divorced, and Mrs Stern lived in some splendour in New Mexico; they had no children.

He had made his money from cement; had been a millionaire at twenty-three on the back of the building boom of the fifties in Europe. He had homes and mistresses in New York and Paris, he told Angie; he thought it was wrong to deceive her. He had never lived in London although he knew it well; now he was looking for a house there, to keep an eye on the hotel – the first, he hoped, of a chain. After he had taken her to dinner three times, he asked her if she would consider going to bed with him. Angie, who found him surprisingly attractive, said she certainly would; the experience was pleasant but not earth-shattering, M. Wetherly being nervous and very gentlemanly. As they lay in a companionable silence afterwards, sipping champagne, she asked him about his sexual fantasies. There was a long silence; then M. Wetherly turned towards her, circling her small firm breasts with his fingers, and said, slightly shamefacedly, that he had always rather liked the idea of schoolgirls. Angie, who had suspected as much from their first encounter, said nothing, but the next day she went to Daniel Neals and bought a gym slip, a shirt, a tie, a girdle and some dark green knickers, and after dinner that night she said she had something to show him. Up in his room, she told him to wait while she went and got ready in the bathroom; he settled excitedly on the bed, uncorking the champagne, and the expression on his face when she emerged, looking slightly shy, her long fair hair tied up in bunches, her slender legs encased in black stockings, tie slightly awry, a satchel hung on her right shoulder, was better, she told Dee, than all the presents put together.

'Oh Angela,' said M. Wetherly. 'Oh Angela, how very sweet you look.'

'Well,' said Angie, sitting down on the bed beside him, 'I've kept it all. I thought it might come in useful.'

'And it has,' said M. Wetherly fervently, 'it has.'

'But,' said Angie, who had thought about this scene quite carefully, 'I don't think all my clothes are named properly. Marked, you know, with my name. I thought perhaps you should check. And you do remind me of my headmaster so much. He was very strict you know. If we didn't have all our clothes marked, he used to get very cross with us. Sometimes he even spanked us. Why don't you start with my stockings, and work through everything?'

'Angela,' whispered M. Wetherly, as he tenderly began to unknot her tie, 'I think I love you.' The next day he bought her a staggeringly expensive diamond bracelet: 'For the sweetest seventeen I know.'

★

61

Angie didn't tell Virginia any of the details of her relationship with M. Wetherly. She thought she would be shocked. She just said he had bought her dinner two or three times, and as far as she was concerned, he was just a nice old sugar daddy who enjoyed her company.

She wasn't sure if Virginia believed her, but it saved her from having to feel guilty or worry about her. She was happy, interested, doing well at her job. For Christmas, Virginia gave her an orange fun fur coat, a bonus of £100, and a rise of £5 a week. She took Angie out to lunch at the Caprice and told her she couldn't imagine the business without her now, and that she hoped she would never leave. Angie said she never would.

It was two weeks before Christmas when she had her first proper conversation with Alexander. She had seen him innumerable times; he spent the middle of the week in London, with Virginia, travelling up on Monday evening and down on Thursday. 'He doesn't really like any of this, but he puts up with it. I'll tell you why one day,' Virginia said. He steered very clear of the office during the day, and was out a great deal; he was on the boards of several companies, and always seemed busy. But he would come down in the evening, to collect her, and as he put it 'take her home'; it was a little joke, which he seemed to enjoy more than she did. Angie wasn't quite sure if she liked him, and he seemed rather tense, fraught a lot of the time. But he was extremely good-looking; the first time she found herself looking up at him, Angie felt literally weak at the knees. She had been working one evening at about six thirty in the small outer room, sorting samples onto a colour board for a new client; she heard footsteps and didn't even look up, thinking it was the butler, who often brought down a tray of drinks for Virginia.

'My goodness,' said a voice, 'what devotion to duty!' and she had looked up and found herself gazing into a pair of eyes that were so intensely blue, so amused, so appreciative that even the memory of M. Wetherly's burning brown ones faded into nothing.

'Oh!' she said. 'Lord Caterham. I suppose,' she added, feeling even more foolish every minute.

'You suppose correctly. And you, I suppose, are Miss Burbank. I have heard so much about you, about how you have transformed my wife's working day, but I had no idea how decorative you were. It is extremely nice to meet you. How do you do?'

He held out his hand; Angie jumped and took it. It was a very firm, but rather cold hand; she felt an odd desire to take it in both hers and warm it.

'So is my wife in there? In the holy of holies?'

'Sorry? Oh, yes, yes she is. Working on something we're late with. I'm sure she'd be pleased to see you.'

'I certainly hope so,' he said, and she felt instantly foolish, cross with herself for saying anything so silly.

'I've just arrived from Hartest,' he said.

'Ah yes. The lovely house,' said Angie.

He looked pleased. 'You know about Hartest?'

'A bit. That it's eighteenth century, built by – um, Adam, and that it's considered very beautiful indeed.'

'It is not only considered so, it is very beautiful indeed,' he said, 'you must come and see it one day. You would love it.' Angie wondered how long it might be before a genuine invitation was issued: a very long time, she was sure. 'Now if you will excuse me I must go and drag my wife away from her important work, we are going to be late for a very tedious dinner if we're not careful.'

'Of course. Do go in.'

She felt silly again, as if she was playing at being hostess to him in his own house; she stood up and watched him go into the room, and as he shut the door behind him, she heard him say, 'Darling! What a funny, sweet little creature out there,' and felt sillier still. It would be nice, she thought, to feel on a slightly more equal footing with the Earl. Then she shook herself. She had a long way to go before she could expect to do that.

The week before Christmas, he came up on the Wednesday; Virginia and he were attending some charity ball. He was in his dinner jacket, pacing up and down in the drawing room as Angie came through the house to leave; she felt shy suddenly, looking at his tense back, and tried to slip past him. She was in a hurry in any case; M. Wetherly was buying her dinner before departing for New York for Christmas. He had business there, he said, sadly neglected, that he should see to after Christmas; and he had promised Sonia, his young lady in New York, to spend Christmas with her. 'Although I have to confess, Angela, I would rather be here with you.' He did not expand on this theme; Angie did not press him. She was very fond of him, but she didn't want things to get too heavy. The more Sonias and Mariannes (the name of the Paris mistress) there were, the better she liked it.

'Angie!' Alexander was bestowing his most gracious smile on her: practising for the tenants for Christmas, thought Angie irreverently. 'Are you trying to sneak past me? Let me wish you Happy Christmas. Come and share a glass of champagne with me. My wife is clearly going to be quite a while yet.'

Angie smiled at him and went into the drawing room. There was a bottle of champagne and two glasses on the black marble mantelpiece;

one was already filled. Alexander handed her the other. 'I was hoping to have a drink with my wife, but she doesn't deserve it. And you do, from everything I hear.' He poured the glass very full, smiled at her. 'Happy Christmas, my dear.'

Angie felt belittled, more than ever on a par with the tenants by the 'my dear', but took the glass, sipped it and smiled up at him. 'Thank you, Lord Caterham. And to you.'

'Oh, please call me Alexander. I hate all that, and I know you and Virginia are on best-friend terms.'

She looked at him slightly surprised. Surprised that Virginia would consider her like that, and still more so that he should know about it.

'Well,' she said, 'we do seem to get along very well.'

'I'm pleased,' he said, 'she needs a friend. She doesn't have very many.'

'Really?' said Angie. 'She – you and she – seem to be always going to parties and things.'

'Yes, yes, of course, but I don't mean a social circle. I mean a friend. There is someone in the country she is quite fond of, a neighbour, Mrs Dunbar, but apart from that she hasn't formed any very close relationships. She has found it very difficult, coming from America, having to settle down here, build a new life, more difficult than I expected.' He sounded faintly exasperated; Angie looked at him sharply and then at the bottle and realized several glasses had already been drunk.

'Well,' she said carefully, 'it can't have been easy. Leaving her family and everything behind.'

'Ah, yes,' he said, 'her family. Yes, well she certainly misses them. Especially her brother. Baby, have you heard about him? Ridiculous names, these Americans have. Baby! I ask you. He's six foot four, big as an ox.'

'Well she seems quite happy now,' said Angie, floundering slightly, not wishing to enter into any criticism of Virginia, her family or even her nation, 'and the business is a great success. I'm sure it's helped.'

She felt very foolish, all of sixteen years old, discussing the emotional stability of her employer with her employer's husband.

He looked at her and his eyes were suddenly rather sad. 'Yes,' he said, 'yes, it has helped. You're right. It's done more than I could, more than any of us, even Charlotte. Ah, Virginia, darling, how lovely you look. I've been chatting to Angie, and given her your glass, as you were so late down. Can you forgo a drink, do you think, as we're late?'

'Oh, no, I'd like a drink,' said Virginia quickly, 'you know I need Dutch courage on these occasions, Alexander. Just a tiny glass, it won't take a moment. Here, give me yours. How was the drive and how's Charlotte?'

'The drive was hell, the whole of Wiltshire, Gloucestershire and Berkshire was converging on the M4. Charlotte is fine. I told her I was coming to see you. She's looking forward to spending some time with you.'

There was an edge to his voice. So that's it, thought Angie; hardly surprising, really.

'And I with her,' said Virginia. She seemed suddenly more positive for her drink. 'Now then, Alexander, let's go.' She was looking dazzling, even Angie who was used to her beauty was surprised by her; she was wearing a white crepe dress, off one shoulder, with long drifty sleeves, and a high pearl choker at her throat; her dark hair was piled high Grecian style, and her great golden eyes were studded with fake lashes. She smiled at Angie. 'Have a lovely evening, Angie, I'll see you in the morning.'

'Thank you,' said Angie. 'Goodnight. Goodnight, Lord Caterham.'

'Alexander. I told you. Goodnight, my dear. Happy Christmas, if I don't see you again. Will you be spending it with your family?'

'Yes, I expect so.'

'How nice.'

And how impossible for you even to imagine, thought Angie, what my Christmas would be like; and how the opposite of nice it was going to be.

She did spend Christmas with the family; in an act of pure generosity, she went home to Mr and Mrs Wicks (Johnny and Dee having gone to Marbella with Dee's dad). Angie bought a Marks and Spencer lambswool sweater for Mrs Wicks, and a nice scarf for Mr Wicks, new slippers for them both, smart plaid ones for him, pink fluffy for her; she also brought two bottles of wine, one of champagne, and a bottle of port for Mrs Wicks, some crystallized fruits, a box of chocolates and a huge bag of mixed nuts all from Fortnum and Mason and a Christmas pudding, complete with its own bag of sixpences, from Harrods Food Hall. It was only when she had finished shopping that she realized she had gone automatically to those places without thinking about it, and felt almost irrationally pleased about it. Her social education, her journey towards being posh, was obviously coming along very nicely.

Mrs Wicks had cooked a capon for the three of them, which Angie kept saying was deliciously moist whenever the conversation ran out, which was fairly often. The pudding was delicious, they all wished over the sixpences and Mrs Wicks drank a great deal of the port. They both exclaimed over the champagne and told Angie she was much too generous, and who would have thought to see such a thing in their house, but neither of them liked it, so Angie finished up drinking the whole bottle over presents. Mrs Wicks asked her how Lord and Lady Caterham were spending Christmas, and said they couldn't be having a more slap-up time than the three of them, and Angie said, no, they certainly couldn't. Mrs Wicks gave her a nylon scarf, and Mr Wicks pressed a crumpled dirty fiver into her hand and told her to buy what she liked.

After Christmas, Virginia and she became very close. It was an odd relationship, but it worked. The business gave them a common base, and conversations that began in a discussion about the stupidity of one client, insisting on silk curtains in a kitchen, the appalling taste of another, covering exquisite honey-coloured parquet flooring with ankle-deep curly carpet, or the inadvisability of buying fifty yards of Sekers silk for a third, who would inevitably change her mind the minute it arrived at the office, would lead easily and naturally into long philosophical discussions and then revelations about their respective pasts. Virginia was often alone in the evenings; she stayed in town two or three nights a week, and if Alexander did not join her, if he had stayed at Hartest or was away himself on business, she would ask Angie to stay for a drink and a chat upstairs in the house. Virginia always enjoyed what she called the first drink of the day; she watched the clock, telling Angie she never allowed herself anything until after six thirty, but then right on the dot, she would pull the cork on a bottle of white wine and drink at least two of the big goblets that she kept in the office. Angie, who didn't care if she had a drink or not, would keep her company and noticed that Virginia became very relaxed very quickly as the wine went down.

'Tell me,' said Angie carefully one night, having observed the third goblet of wine fairly swiftly emptied, 'tell me, what does your husband – I mean Lord Caterham – think about you working, doing this? I'd have thought he'd have wanted you to be at Hartest, being a good wife and mother, hostessing and riding to hounds and all that sort of thing?'

'Oh well,' said Virginia with a sigh, 'he doesn't exactly like it. But he puts up with it. Like I told you.'

'Did you?' said Angie carelessly. It wouldn't do to let Virginia think she was especially interested in the subject; it was obviously very delicate.

'Yes. He has to, really.'

'Why?'

'Well, you see, after I had Charlotte I was very depressed. It was awful. I still have nightmares about it. Postnatal depression it was; Mr Dunwoody, he was my obstetrician, said it was quite natural, especially after a difficult first labour. And it was difficult. Boy, was it difficult. I thought it would go on for ever.' She hesitated, looked at Angie, smiled slightly shakily. 'I've always been frightened of childbirth. Ever since

66

reading *Gone with the Wind*. They promised me, absolutely promised me, I'd be fine, that I could have this wonderful drug called pethidine, that it was easy these days, that I wouldn't feel a thing. I believed them and I shouldn't have. I felt a great deal. Never let anyone offer you pethidine, Angie, all it does is make you feel out of touch with yourself, so the pain is worse. God, it was awful. I didn't behave very well, I have to tell you.' She smiled faintly. 'I kept thinking this was no way for an English countess to behave, yelling and screaming, but I didn't seem able to stop. Then finally she, Charlotte, was born, and they said it was a girl and I just couldn't believe it. All that had kept me going through those awful hours, was the thought that soon it would be over and I'd never have to do it again. And then the baby was a girl, and clearly I would have to do it again.'

'Why?' said Angie.

'Well, to give Alexander an heir, of course.' Virginia sounded oddly cynical, bitter almost. 'That's what I was there for. Going through all that. And then, no heir. No heir to Hartest, to the title. When they said it was a girl, I just felt utter, utter despair; I wouldn't hold her, wouldn't do anything. I remember saying to Mr Dunwoody, my husband would be so upset, he wouldn't even want to know, and he said nonsense, he would be delighted, and when Alexander came in, I said I was sorry, and he said exactly that, he said nonsense, he was delighted, he liked girls, but I knew that even if it was true, he still needed a boy. Anyway, it went on and on, for weeks and weeks, an awful, dull, aching misery, and a sort of anger; Mr Dunwoody said it would pass in a day or two, that I'd be fine, and I wasn't. I couldn't imagine ever being fine again. I was still amazingly weak after two months, and I used to cry every day, for hours and hours, at the same time every day, after lunch. I looked forward to the crying, it was a kind of catharsis. I refused to nurse Charlotte after a bit, it was such a shame, it was one thing I could do, I had loads of milk, and she was such a pretty, good baby; Nanny, that is Nanny Barkworth, Alexander's old nanny, who had always been in the house, she is such a dear, she lives at Hartest, has rooms at the top of the house, near the nurseries, started taking total care of Charlotte, giving her formula. That made me feel worse, even though I'd refused to do it myself. And then Alexander's mother didn't come. She never came to meet me after the wedding, I've never met her, can you believe that, she's obviously extremely odd, virtually a recluse, Alexander says, and that upset me and I thought that now at last that I'd had the baby she'd come, but she didn't. I decided that was because it was a girl, that it was my fault, as well.'

'It's a pretty name, Charlotte,' said Angie carefully.

'Yes, isn't it?' said Virginia. Her face was strained, white; she poured

67

herself another glass of wine. 'I chose it, insisted, they wanted to call her Alicia which is Alexander's mother's name, but I certainly wasn't having that, it was the one thing I managed to be positive about. Charlotte Elizabeth, she's called, Elizabeth after my mother, Charlotte because it was my favourite name.'

'Was your mother there?' asked Angie slightly awkwardly. She was finding this sudden insight into the neurotic behaviour of her apparently rather serene boss a little unnerving.

'Yes, she came and stayed for two months.' She laughed suddenly. 'I think in spite of everything, she had never been happier. She's a terrible terrible snob and being in an English stately home, in daily contact with an English earl, was sheer heaven for her. Even though she had a loopy daughter.'

'But it didn't help?'

'No, nothing helped. A psychiatrist came, and talked to me endlessly. He said I was in shock. Well maybe I was. They gave me drugs, they didn't help, not really. I just wandered about like a zombie, round the house and the grounds, not talking to anyone.'

'I don't understand why you were in shock,' said Angie.

'Oh, it was the ghastly birth,' said Virginia quickly. 'It was truly terrible, Angie, I can't begin to tell you.'

Angie kept her counsel. She was obviously a stronger person than Virginia. Nevertheless she didn't think she could take much more of this particular bit of the drama.

'So what brought you round? Made you better?' she asked politely.

'Well, my mother had been talking to Alexander, a lot, obviously, and together they came up with the suggestion that I should go on a trip to New York, stay with my parents, leave the baby and everything behind. And when they suggested it to me, I just felt as if a great weight had rolled off me, it was like feeling a terrible pain begin to ease. I couldn't wait to get away. Although as we drove away, I did cry, I can still remember crying, I wouldn't let Alexander come to the airport, and I cried when I said goodbye, and the minute we got to the top of the Great Drive – oh, Angie, you must come to Hartest soon, so all these names mean something to you – I just stopped, stopped crying, that is, and there was another great weight gone.'

'Don't you like Hartest?' said Angie. 'I thought you loved it.'

'Oh, I do,' said Virginia, 'I do love it. But it's – well, it's very demanding. When I first saw it, when Alexander brought me home, I couldn't believe it. I couldn't believe that anything so lovely, not just the house, but the lake, and the park, and the lodges, everything, could be my home, be mine. I cried. I remember Alexander saying that it brought

68

tears to his eyes, every time he returned to it, and it did to mine. But – well, it's a lot to live with. Or it seemed it then. I'm getting used to it now.'

'And the trip to New York cured you?'

'No, not quite. I did feel better. Gradually. Seeing old friends, easing off the pills. But there were still problems. My father, he's always been very critical of me, didn't approve of my running away, as he put it. He kept saying I looked all right and he thought I was a fraud. Lightheartedly, but meaning it, you know? That didn't exactly help. And my mother didn't really understand. And she fussed and fussed, checking up on my pills and telling me I was drinking too much.'

'Oh really?' Angie looked at her thoughtfully.

'Yes. So silly. No, it was Baby who really cracked it. He took me out to lunch at the Oyster Bar at Grand Central Station, it's just the greatest place, Angie, you'd love it, I'll never forget it, and bought me oysters, the first of the season, and said what he thought would be a great idea was if I went back to work. He said Mary Rose was working and it was all fine, and it did her good. Mind you, Mary Rose, that's Baby's wife, is a terrible pain in the – in the . . .'

'Arse?' said Angie helpfully.

'Yes, just about there. She delivered Freddy, that's their baby, in three hours flat, and she kept telling me so, in tones that implied if I'd been more careful and prepared better I'd have done the same. Well next time, she maybe won't be so lucky.'

'Let's hope,' said Angie. 'Anyway, Baby – Virginia, why on earth is he called that?'

'Oh, it's because when he was tiny, and he was called Fred, all the first-born sons are, he was called Baby Fred and then at Harvard he was the youngest player on the football team, and it kind of went on from there. It suits him,' she added vaguely.

Angie thought that if Baby was six foot four and huge with it, as Alexander had said, this was a little unlikely, but she didn't like to say so. Baby was obviously beyond criticism, at least as far as Virginia was concerned.

'Well anyway, Baby thought you should go back to work?'

'Yes. I was saying the days at Hartest were so long, and I had to go back and I didn't know that I could, I was so afraid of getting depressed again. And Baby said working would keep the days a whole lot shorter. It seemed sensible, I did miss my work, and I was lonely, terribly lonely, I found the English people I met, neighbours, old friends of Alexander's, nice but not really my sort of people. But I thought Alexander would be very against it. Anyway, I called him, and talked to him for ages, and I could tell he had great reservations, but he was terrific. He really was. I told him about how I was scared of coming back, and how much I would like to get back to my design work and he said of course if I really wanted to, then we should consider it. He said he'd been worrying about me being bored and lonely; he said he quite understood about my difficulties making friends; but he said he was worried about Charlotte. That I'd neglect her. I promised I wouldn't, and that there was Nanny, and he said he'd talk to Nanny, and she, bless her, said she thought it was a very good idea. She's my best friend here, Angie, her and you. So that was that, really. And suddenly I felt brave enough to come back. But I'm afraid he still doesn't really like it. Especially his daughter being raised by her nanny rather than her mother. Originally, we thought Charlotte and Nanny could come to London on Sunday evening with me, but she increasingly stays in the country. Well, everyone knows the country air is better for children, don't they? And Alexander certainly prefers to think of his daughter growing up in the house that he is so famously in love with. Just the same, he doesn't like it, but then he's frightened of the alternative. And so am I. God, look at the time. Angie, I'm sorry. I'd run you home, but I've had just a bit too much to drink. I'll call you a cab.'

'Don't be silly,' said Angie, 'I've enjoyed it. And I don't need a cab. I'm having a drink with M. Wetherly at the Carlton Towers. I can walk. I'll enjoy it, honestly.'

Walking quite slowly up Sloane Street, she thought how bizarre it was that someone as rich and blessed as Virginia should claim as her best friends two women as far removed from her in age and situation as it was possible for them to be.

Angie noticed a change in Virginia as the year wore on. She seemed more confident, altogether happier; Angie put it down to her increased fame and success; since the success of the hotel she had designed for M. Wetherly, offers poured in almost every day, and they were even trying to work out if they should get a third person in to help (a notion Angie was half pleased about, half resistant to) when Virginia came down rather late to the office one morning halfway through August looking pale and told Angie she was almost certainly pregnant. 'I'm over three weeks late, and I've just been sick,' she said proudly.

'Oh Virginia, that's really nice,' said Angie, slightly awkwardly. Congratulating people on prospective parenthood was slightly outside her sphere of experience. 'How do you feel? Oh, that's silly, you've just been sick. Sit down, I'll get you some water or something.'

'You're an angel, could it be herb tea? Camomile, I think. I don't feel too bad. Not really. I haven't had it confirmed yet, well I haven't had any tests, but I really don't think I need to. I went to see my gynaecologist yesterday, that's where I was, not with terrible Lady Twynam at all. I called my mother last night to tell her, and she said Mary Rose was pregnant too. Isn't that odd?'

'Yes, I suppose it is,' said Angie.

'She's just about a month ahead of me. I'm awfully glad. I've got the impression recently that Baby was just – well, rather depressed about their marriage. But my mother says he's like a dog with three tails. So that's really nice.'

'Um – how does Alexander feel?'

'Well, I only told him last night as well. He's terribly thrilled. Praying for a boy already, of course.'

'Of course. Well, I'm sure you'll manage it now.'

'Let's hope.'

'Well,' said Angie, 'let's hope you stay – well this time.'

'Yes.'

'I think you're very brave, Virginia.'

'Well, we have to provide Hartest with an heir somehow. I'm anxious, of course I am, but I think I can manage things better. I've been reading a lot about natural childbirth and I really think it will help me.'

'Well I think it's terribly exciting,' said Angie, 'and you must let me do everything I can to help. Maybe we should go ahead and take on this new person. As long as it's clearly understood she's junior to me,' she added with a grin.

'No, Angie, I've been thinking a bit about that. If – as – I'm going to have two children, I don't think I can be quite as much the career woman as I have been lately. Don't look like that, it's all right, I'm not going to pack it in and take to weaving my own nappies. And you're certainly going to be busier than ever. But I do think we should ease off a bit. Not get any bigger at least. So I've made a conscious decision that for the next year or so we'll only take on jobs – and people – we really like the look of. How does that sound?'

'Absolutely fine,' said Angie, trying to appear enthusiastic.

A few days later Alexander came up to Eaton Place. Virginia was upstairs when he arrived, having a rest after lunch. She was, despite all her protestations, feeling extremely unwell. Alexander on the other hand looked wonderful, tanned and happy, and very relaxed.

'Hallo, Angie my dear, how are you?' he said, wandering through the big office, idly leafing through the colour swatches on her desk. 'Ghastly, most of these things, aren't they? Virginia once threatened to let her skills loose on Hartest. Fortunately I managed to dissuade her – tactfully, I hope.'

'Don't you like what she does?' asked Angie, genuinely surprised.

'Not much of it, no, between you and me. Oh, I'm sure it's very clever, but I have to say that most of it is very vulgar. Well, let's say it's not for me. Anyway, where is she?'

'She's lying down for a bit. She doesn't feel terribly well.'

'No, I'm afraid pregnancy doesn't really suit her,' said Alexander with a sigh. 'Let's hope this time we have a boy, and she can relax.'

'Can't – couldn't a girl inherit Hartest?' asked Angie, half seriously.

Alexander turned to her, and she was genuinely startled by the expression on his face. It was almost fiercely intense, and beneath the smile he forced it to wear, bleak and sad; his mouth had a tight white line round it.

'Absolutely not,' he said, 'it's completely out of the question. It isn't just Hartest, it's the title. There has to be a male heir, it's imperative. I – and Virginia of course – both understand that. It is our prime role at the moment, to provide an heir.'

'But surely,' said Angie, genuinely intrigued and puzzled by his emotion, 'I can see it would be ideal – important even, but if she – you – don't have a boy, you don't. I imagine a girl – well Charlotte – could inherit the title, couldn't she? Or is there a cousin or anything?'

'There is no cousin, and I have no intention of allowing the name of Caterham to die out through being passed down a female line,' said Alexander. He was making a great effort now to sound more lighthearted; only his eyes, harsh and sad, gave him away. 'That seems to me to be taking female emancipation a little too far. No, we shall have a boy, of course we shall. My friend the Earl of Dudley has five daughters to date. I believe he is confident there is a boy on the way now. Anyway, it certainly isn't anything you should bother your extremely pretty little head about. Now I shall go and see the mother of my future son and heir to try to persuade her to come to Hartest for a few weeks until she's feeling better.'

'Oh, do,' said Angie, 'I can easily hold the fort here, there's nothing special going on. I'll be happy to cope, really.'

'I'm sure you will. And thank you.' He was his old self now, easy and charming; but Angie felt chilled, somehow, disturbed by their conversation.

Later that afternoon she wanted a telephone number urgently; a client phoned in a fury, saying the builders were insisting on re-laying a floor and it was not in the specification Virginia had sent her. Angie knew it was and she wanted to contact the architect to get him to confirm it to the client. The number was not for some reason on the Roladex, nor in any of the files; worried, thinking Virginia would be well rested, and that

Alexander had gone, she went out into the hall and quietly up the stairs to the wide landing where Virginia's bedroom stood, at the front of the house, overlooking the square. She waited before knocking, hoping to hear movement inside, or Virginia's radio on – she listened constantly to classical music on the Third Programme; instead she heard Virginia's voice: fretful, faintly fractious, but with the steely underlying note that Angie had come to know extremely well. Never being over-scrupulous in matters of personal privacy, Angie listened.

'Alexander, please listen to me. I don't think you're taking me very seriously. I want to have the baby at home. Not here, but at Hartest. I think, well I know, I shall cope better, feel less frightened.'

'What, in the house?'

'Yes, in the house.'

'Oh, darling, I don't think that's a very good idea. Supposing something went wrong.'

'I'm sure it won't. I've already talked to a gynaecologist about it.'

'Mr Dunwoody?'

'Not Mr Dunwoody. I never want to see Mr Dunwoody again.'

'But darling, he's the best.'

'Not for me he's not. No, I've found a lovely female obstetrician. She's only about five years older than me, she's terribly sympathetic, and she's going to do lots for me. She's called Lydia Paget.'

'Virginia, Mr Dunwoody is the finest obstetrician you could possibly have.'

'Alexander, he is nothing of the sort. He took me to hell and back. And I don't like him and I don't like his attitude. It's patronizing. Lydia Paget is like me; I can relate to her. Now don't look like that, Alexander, this is the twentieth century. She's not an old crone from the village with a birthing stool. She may be a woman, but she is a consultant. At Queen Charlotte's. Well, she was. Now she's in Swindon, at the hospital there, and she has a private practice herself. And the main difference between her and Mr Dunwoody is that she's had a baby. Two actually. One the old-fashioned way, one the new. And she says she certainly knows which way she preferred. She really does know what she's talking about. And she's done a lot of work on psychoprophylaxis, on handling the birthing process yourself, natural pain relief – '

'Oh Virginia, don't start giving me all that American claptrap jargon . . .'

'Alexander, it's not American claptrap, and the very least you can do, surely, is listen to me, try to understand how I feel. I'm doing this for you, if you'd care to remember, and I get the strong impression that you don't care about my feelings, my fears at all.'

'Don't be absurd.'

'I'm not being absurd. I just don't see why you won't agree to it. I'm not asking very much. I want to have the baby at Hartest, in my own surroundings, and Lydia Paget is willing to help me, to deliver the baby there, and to see I get the right sort of education.'

'Virginia, I just don't want you to have the baby there. I'm sorry. All right, you can be in the care of this woman if you like, provided I am satisfied she is properly qualified, but I don't want you giving birth at Hartest.'

'Why on earth not? You of all people should like the idea. I'm sure that until the last decade or two all the Earls of Caterham have been born there.'

'I daresay. But I'm afraid I don't like it. I know it sounds odd, but I find it very unattractive.'

'Alexander, you don't have to be there. You don't have to be in the county if you don't want to. Or even the country. Anyway, it's a big house, you won't hear me screaming or anything.'

'That's not the point. I just would rather you had the baby in hospital.'

'Alexander,' said Virginia, an odd note coming into her voice, 'either I have this baby at Hartest, or I don't have it at all.'

'Oh for Christ's sake,' said Alexander, and Angie could hear the floorboards creaking as he started pacing up and down; she fled swiftly down the stairs. She was just opening the door at the bottom of the office steps when she heard Alexander shouting, 'All right, have the bloody baby at Hartest. But don't blame me if something goes wrong and you have to have another and another and another.'

'Angie? This is Virginia. I had to call you quickly. I wanted you to be the very first to know. I've had the baby. Half an hour ago. It was marvellous. She's a little bit early, I know, about ten days. But she's fine. Six pounds. She's beautiful. Really beautiful. What? No, I don't mind a bit that it's a girl. It was so easy, I could do it six more times. Sorry? Oh, he's out riding. He doesn't even know yet. I woke up and it had started and I told Alexander to call Mrs Paget, she's been staying at the Lodge, and he said once she was here he'd go out for a while, and the baby just slithered out about an hour after that. This new way of doing it is wonderful. Absolutely no problem at all, it hardly hurt, just very hard work. I was actually smiling while she was being born. Oh, yes, and she's called Georgina. Very very long and skinny. And she doesn't look like anyone in the family at all. Now I want you to come down and see me very soon. Promise you'll come. I'll get Alexander to meet you at the station, or even drive you down. Oh, Angie, I'm so happy. Now I must phone my mother. I'll tell you the best thing too, I beat Mary Rose to it after all. Her baby's due this week, and I thought she'd have hers first, and start gloating all over again. Bye, Angie darling, see you in a few days.'

It was ten days later that Angie arrived at Hartest, on a perfect early spring day; carrying a large bunch of lilies, and a bottle of champagne, she caught a lunchtime train from Paddington to Swindon, and was standing rather uncertainly outside the station, looking for the chauffeur who she had been told would meet her, when she heard a great hooting and saw across the yard a rather old Bentley, with a radiant Alexander at the wheel. He got out and gave her a hug and then held open the other door for her; he was dressed as she had never seen him, in brown cords and a checked shirt and navy guernsey; his blond hair was untidy, and he looked a completely different person from the rather tense one who came to the house in Eaton Place, relaxed, smiling, and at least five years younger.

'You look lovely,' he said as the car pulled away, 'and it's sweet of you to come. What glorious flowers. Virginia will be pleased. And champagne too, how thoughtful. I think if you don't mind we'll put that away for a few weeks, Mrs Paget feels she shouldn't be drinking at the moment, or certainly very little, and she keeps trying to make an excuse to have some champagne. Of course she's got lots to celebrate, but still. Have you had lunch? Because Mrs Tallow has kept you something in case.'

'I have, thank you,' said Angie, 'I had a pork pie on the train.'

'Poor you, was it foul?'

'No, it was fine,' said Angie, who was still young enough, and had been deprived enough in her childhood, to like almost any food and could never see what was wrong with half the stuff that Virginia and M. Wetherly and other over-privileged people pushed away from them claiming it was disgusting.

'Good. Now I came to fetch you myself because Harold Tallow, who doubles as butler and driver for us, is terribly busy, with Virginia's parents arriving tomorrow, and besides I wanted to be the person to show you Hartest for the very first time.' He sounded excited, overwrought almost, like a small boy on the verge of a treat.

'Well, that was very kind,' said Angie, 'thank you. I didn't know Virginia's parents were coming, I could easily have come next week.'

'Angie, Virginia was dying to see you and show you the baby. She adores you, you know she does. She was all set to come and meet you, drive herself – '

'She's that well?'

'She's that well. It has been an amazingly different experience. I have to admit I was opposed to all this – I was going to say nonsense – natural stuff, home birth and so on, but I was wrong. She is up and about, happy and strong, feeding the baby herself, discussing the next time already.'

'Well that's wonderful,' said Angie. 'I'm pleased.'

Alexander didn't talk very much after that. They drove through the centre of Marlborough, which Alexander described as a classically perfect town, and which looked to Angie rather like a child's model, with its wide square set with haphazardly uniform red-brick houses and buildings, and then pulled out of it and up the hill signposted Salisbury Plain and Calne. A few miles on, the road divided into two, one fork dropping down below the great sheet of blank, almost bleak landscape that was the Plain and the other stretching straight ahead of them. Alexander took the higher road, waving vaguely in the direction of Avebury and the stone circles. 'Ever seen those, or Stonehenge?'

Angie shook her head; she was beginning to feel a little strange, almost bewitched by this silent journey through a countryside she had never imagined in England, so grand and majestic was it, and oddly nervous; after another fifteen minutes or so, Alexander turned into a lane that dropped abruptly from the road, dipping into the centre of the landscape, suddenly a softer, gentler place, oddly protected from the huge expanse of sky and grass that had been stretching as if into infinity. The lane was narrow, twisting, up and down hill; a couple of miles or so further, and he turned off again; large wrought-iron gates with stone columns stood open, and they were safer still, driving under a tunnel of trees, so dense that even without their leaves it was dim, peaceful, drenched with spring sounds and fleeting sunlight and birdsong.

'Goodness,' she said, 'it's so different,' and he turned towards her and smiled and said, 'Yes, isn't it, like some exquisite secret,' and her eyes met his, and for a brief moment something passed between them, something sweet, warm, excited, and quite indecipherable in terms of any human emotion Angie had ever known. She turned back to the road in front of her; it was lighter now, becoming broader, the trees further back, and there was a second pair of gates, bigger, grander, with a lodge on either side, a pair of perfect low, grey buildings, and the road wound past them off to the right, dipping downwards slightly. Another moment or so and Alexander stopped the car, turned off the engine. Angie looked at him, oddly nervous; he smiled at her, reached out, patted her small hands, knotted in her lap.

'It's all right,' he said, 'I'm not about to seduce you. Just to introduce you to my – ' he paused, corrected himself carefully – 'one of my greatest pleasures.'

'Pleasures?' said Angie slightly doubtfully. She wondered what on earth he was getting at; it seemed slightly creepy suddenly.

'Yes,' he said, 'pleasures.' He paused and looked at her thoughtfully. 'Pleasure is a very important factor in one's life, don't you think?'

'Well – yes,' she said, slightly warily.

'I have always made a distinction, between innocent and wicked pleasures,' he said, smiling at her, 'and Hartest for me is at once my greatest and most innocent pleasure.'

Angie wound down her window, and the air rushed in sweet, heady, earthy, with the noise of birdsong filling every corner of it; she put out her hand and it was as if she could touch the day, so rich and gold and drenched with recent rain.

'That's right,' he said, 'that's exactly what I want people to do, drink it in, feel it, be ready for the next bit.'

'And what's the next bit?' asked Angie, smiling at him, liking him as she had never liked him before, charmed by his childlike delight and pride in his possession, his land, his countryside, patently suddenly his major reason for existence.

'The next bit is the house,' he said, and he paused, staring ahead of him for a moment more, his face blank, before starting the engine again, gently, almost reluctantly, and easing the car very slowly forward. Angie was still looking to the side at the woods when the car turned quite sharply to the left; her head turned, and she saw Hartest and gasped aloud with shock and pleasure; it lay below them, about a quarter of a mile away, at the bottom of a long straight drive, with meadows rolling away from it, studded with sheep and deer, and to the right a lake, a lazy oval of blue surrounded with rushes, and in one corner a run-down wooden building with a landing stage and a boat tied to it. Beyond the lake further to the right was a wood, and winding lazily from that, a river, flowing through the parkland and under an exquisite bridge, with three arches and what looked to her like a dilapidated building on either side of it.

Angie had known what the house looked like, had seen in many photographs now the curving double flight of steps leading up to the great front door, the pillars studding the front, the rows of perfect windows, the dome looming from the centre of the roof; but the pictures had meant nothing, she could see now, nothing at all, without the colours, the tenderly pale grey of the stone, etched, carved into the blue sky, the darker colour of the roof, the white-grey of the great curving gravel drive in the front of the steps, the soft sheen of the windows reflecting the day, or the precise location in which the house lay, gentle, enfolding countryside, marked out by man as the place for it to be.

'Oh God,' said Angie, 'oh God, it's beautiful,' and she felt, almost

77

irritated, tears come into her eyes, and he saw them and smiled at her again and said, 'I'm so glad you like it so much. It makes sense for me of everything I do.'

Looking back on that remark, she realized it told her more about Alexander than anything else he ever said to her.

They drove very slowly down the Great Drive, as Robert Adam had designated it, and pulled round in front of the steps; two golden retrievers ran down to greet them, whining and slobbering ecstatically, and leaping at the car and Alexander as if they had not set eyes on him for several extremely long years. Alexander shouted at them repeatedly to get down, and as they continued to leap, got out, struggling through the flaying paws and slavering tongues, opened the door on Angie's side, and gestured for her to go up the steps. Angie looked up, awed, feeling (again to her irritation) that she couldn't possibly have any business there, and then felt instantly better as Virginia appeared, smiling, waving, shouting out, 'Angie, Angie, I'm so glad you're here.'

She ran up the steps then, and hugged Virginia, and then remembering the lilies ran down again to fetch them (noticing even in her nervousness that the bottle of champagne had been slipped under an old Barbour in the car, and feeling vaguely anxious about it).

'Here,' she said, slightly breathless as she reached Virginia again, 'for you. Congratulations. You look really well, Virginia, I thought you'd be in bed, lolling on pillows, you know?'

'I feel really well,' said Virginia, 'and I got up the very first day, didn't I, Nanny?'

A tall and very solid figure had emerged behind Virginia; five feet nine at least, Angie thought, oddly surprised, for if she had thought about them at all, she had imagined nannies tiny and round; she had iron-grey hair, set in a formidably neat roll at the back of her head, slightly sallow skin, grey, very bright eyes, an oddly pretty little nose, and a mouth that folded in on itself in repose so firmly that the lips almost vanished. She was wearing not a uniform as Angie would have expected, but a completely shapeless skirt, and a matching jumper and cardigan, all in exactly the same shade of beige. Her legs, which were surprisingly long and slim, were encased in thick beige stockings and she wore very stout brown lace-up shoes. She looked at Angie and smiled suddenly, a swift warm smile, after which her face returned to its habitual expression of almost relentless disapproval.

'Nanny, this is Angie Burbank, who works for me so wonderfully,' said Virginia, 'I've told you lots and lots about her. Angie, this is Miss

Barkworth, but you must call her Nanny, everyone does, don't they, Nanny?'

'They do, madam, and it's something at least to be thankful for,' said Nanny, slightly bafflingly it seemed to Angie, and Virginia laughed and said, 'Nanny, you have lots to be thankful for, not least two dear little girls to look after, and where is Charlotte, I want Angie to meet her too.'

'Charlotte is in the kitchen, madam, with Mrs Tallow, but of course we are shortly to go for our walk,' said Nanny, in tones that made it clear that a meeting of the United Nations would have paled into unimportance by comparison.

'Yes of course,' said Virginia, 'well, we'll go and catch her there quickly, Nanny – come on, Angie – and then we can have tea. You must be starving.'

'I'm not, actually,' said Angie, 'but I'd love a cup of tea.'

'Mrs Tallow will make you a cup of tea, she likes it really thick and strong like you do,' said Virginia, 'come on.'

She led the way through the great front doors and into the hall; it was large and tall and square and almost empty, save for a large table against one wall, on which stood a very large vase of flowers and a vast, rather shabby leather book, with 'Visitors' embossed on it in gold, curly letters. The room had a wooden floor and white and blue walls, covered with elaborate plasterwork – Angie was too confused and nervous by now to take it in in detail, but she absorbed a welter of nymphs and urns and tumbling grapes – and a very large number of doors leading off it. Virginia led the way through one at the back and Angie followed her; beyond it was a second hall, the Rotunda, she later learnt, vast and vaulted, with a great deal of light tumbling from above; looking up, she saw that she was standing under the glass dome, which was glazed in a great spider's web of sections. The room again was largely empty; there were a few chairs set about it, and a pair of matching tables at either side, and some paintings, and leading up from the back of it was a staircase, wide, curving, infinitely graceful and as far as Angie could see, completely unsupported.

'That's the famous flying staircase,' said Virginia, 'it's pretty, isn't it? Don't ask me how it stays up because I don't know, and don't ask Alexander either, because he'll tell you. Come on, down here to the kitchen and my darling Charlotte.'

A door at the back of the Rotunda led down a maze of steps and into a long corridor; this branched to the right into a longer one, with a ray of light and a door far to the end of it, and led at the left through a door into a kitchen which, Angie reflected, could easily have contained the whole of her grandparents' house. The floor was stone-flagged and the walls were also stone, with windows set in them rather high, letting in a view of the outside at foot level; in the centre of the room was a huge scrubbed pine table set with a large number of chairs, and at one end was a massive fireplace hung with tongs and bellows and other implements which looked to Angie as if they had been designed for some kind of medieval torture, and an iron grate, filled with logs.

On the opposite wall were some sinks which looked almost as old as the implements, with scrubbed wooden draining boards and wooden cupboards and plate racks set above them; and next to the sinks was an Aga, its rail hung with a series of small pairs of trousers and socks, presumably Charlotte's, airing off, and a big black cast-iron pot boiling furiously on the top.

But in spite of the size of the room and a certain potential for bleakness, it was warm and comfortable-feeling; two large shabby armchairs were set on either side of the Aga, one with a large ginger cat in it, and the air was rich with delicious smells, a heady combination of baking and roasting.

'Mrs Tallow, hallo, this is Angie Burbank who works for me, and Nanny said Charlotte was down here.'

'She was, Your Ladyship, but she's just gone with Mr and Mrs Dunbar to see the lambs. They won't be more than five minutes.'

Mrs Tallow smiled at Angie; she was round and cosy, with dark hair and bright blue eyes, dressed in a white overall, and looking much more like the conventional picture of a cook than Miss Barkworth was of a nanny. 'Pleased to meet you, miss. Would you like a cup of tea and maybe a piece of cake or something? Charlotte's been helping me, Your Ladyship, she's a wonder in the kitchen, and she's made a lovely little ginger cake, and I've just done it with butter icing.'

Angie sat in one of the big saggy chairs by the comforting warmth of the Aga, drinking a cup of very strong, very sweet tea and eating cake. Virginia, sipping a rather large glass of wine which she had extracted from the fridge – 'Left over from lunch, Angie, don't look like that' – asked Mrs Tallow what she had planned for dinner the following day when her parents arrived – 'My mother loves chicken more than anything in the world, if that might be at all possible' – and then there were footsteps along the flagged corridor and a man and a woman with a little girl between them, holding their hands, appeared in the doorway. They were both very tall; he particularly so, with a hawklike bony face, light brown floppy hair, and very pale, large, almost sunken blue eyes. He was wearing a greenish-brown tweed suit, which was very shabby, and the collar of his cream woollen shirt was frayed. He had very large hands which were, she noticed, extremely beautiful, long-fingered and slender;

his legs in the old, flapping trousers were quite incredibly long. He must have been at least, she thought, six foot six. His wife, or at least Angie presumed it was his wife, had a pleasantly plain freckled face; she was also tall, but more sturdily built and less shabby-looking, dressed in a woollen skirt and shirt with a sleeveless anorak over them, and a headscarf knotted over her fair hair. Round her neck was a string of pearls which Angie would have betted a year's salary were real.

Virginia put down her glass of wine and smiled radiantly at them. 'You are both so kind, to take Charlotte around with you so much. Angie, I want you to meet Martin and Catriona Dunbar. Catriona is my best friend in the country, she actually talks to me quite often, and doesn't even mind that I don't like hunting, and Martin is our estate manager, and keeps us all in order. Especially Alexander. This is Angie Burbank, my assistant in London. Equally invaluable.'

Catriona and Martin shook hands with Angie slightly nervously, as if contact with someone so patently not of their world might prove dangerous in some way.

'How do you do,' said Catriona. 'Welcome to Hartest. We always think what Virginia does in London is so clever, don't we, Martin?'

She seemed a very strange friend for Virginia to have, Angie thought; they could surely have nothing remotely in common.

Martin Dunbar took Angie's hand in his large bony one. His handshake was surprisingly gentle.

'How do you do?' he said and his smile was quite extraordinarily sweet, transforming his face from gaunt and hawklike to almost boyishly soft. 'It's extremely nice to meet you at last, we've heard such a lot about you.'

Angie smiled at them both rather nervously, and wished she could think of something sensible to say.

'We have to go, Virginia,' said Martin. 'I have to see Alexander, and Catriona is going shopping. Maybe I'll see you later.'

'Yes of course,' she said, 'come in for tea,' and smiled at him – carelessly, almost coolly, Angie thought. They both walked to the back door; Virginia went with them, and then returned, holding out her hands to Charlotte.

'Charlotte my angel, come and say hallo to my bestest friend, Miss Burbank. I think you may call her Angie, mayn't she, Angie?'

'Of course,' said Angie, holding out her hand, 'hallo, Charlotte, I'm very pleased to meet you,' and then she remembered Suze had told her that was one thing you never said, and she felt embarrassed again.

Charlotte however was not yet too well versed in the niceties of English etiquette and didn't seem too outraged; she smiled and took

Angie's hand and said hallo, and stood studying her face. 'You're very pretty,' she said after a moment or two.

'Well, thank you,' said Angie, 'and so are you.' And it was true. Angie didn't like children, she never had, she found them tedious and demanding, but she had to admit that Charlotte was an enchanting-looking little girl, just slightly tubby, with a mop of shining dark curls, and a cherubic face, dimpled and slightly freckled, with her mother's tawny eyes, and a round rosebud of a mouth.

'Do you work in London with Mummy?' she said, and yes, Angie said, she did, and Charlotte told her she should come and work at Hartest, it would be much nicer, and then Nanny appeared in the kitchen doorway, holding a small duffle coat and a pair of red wellington boots.

'Time for our walk, Charlotte,' she said.

Charlotte smiled at her. 'Can the new lady come too?' she asked hopefully. 'I could show her the lambs,' but Nanny's mouth folded in on itself more firmly than ever, and Virginia said no, not this time, Angie had come to see her and meet the new baby, and they were going to have boring talks about work, but they could all have tea together, if Charlotte was very good.

'Come on,' said Virginia when they had gone, 'let's go upstairs to my room, and you can meet Georgina, and then we can have a really nice chat. Do you mind the back stairs?'

Angie said not too terribly, and grinned, and they climbed two flights of dark winding stairs and went through a doorway onto a wide corridor flooded with light; Virginia walked down it a few yards and pushed open a door.

'This is my room,' she said, walking over to a crib set by the big bed, 'and this is Georgina. Look, isn't she heaven?'

Georgina, who was indistinguishable from any other small baby, being crumply, curled-up, snub-nosed and tight-fisted, was sleeping determinedly; Angie admired her as effusively as she could, and then turned to the window. Virginia's room was at the back of the house; the view was over miles of woodland, and then beyond that endless folds of fields; immediately below the window was a long terrace, with steps leading down to a formal garden, beds planted into elaborate shapes, and beyond them tall hedges surrounding what were clearly other gardens, elaborate symphonies of shrubs, and beyond them again long, deeply sloping lawns studded with masses of crocuses and early daffodils all the way to some hidden boundary – 'A ha-ha,' said Virginia, 'it's like a huge ditch, it keeps the deer and sheep out of the gardens' – to where the gardens met the park again. Some paddocks lay to the left of the house, where several horses grazed; just visible above the trees she could see more buildings, presumably stables. She made a supreme effort to say something appropriate, something sophisticated and gracious, and Angie Wicks spoke from her heart. 'You lucky bitch,' she said, and then realizing what she had said, clapped her hand over her mouth and looked at Virginia in horror. 'Sorry, Virginia,' she said, 'I don't know how that slipped out.'

Virginia laughed. 'Don't be silly. I don't mind. Of course it's much too much for anyone, and I certainly don't deserve it. I feel guilty about it all the time; here I am with everything – except maybe a boy baby –'

'Yes, but you will have,' said Angie, 'and now you say you don't mind having another, it doesn't matter, does it?'

'Not really,' said Virginia with just the slightest suspicion of a sigh. 'No, no of course it doesn't. Oh Angie, it *is* nice to see you, even if I do make you feel sick with jealousy.'

'I'm sorry,' said Angie, 'and I'm not even exactly jealous. Just knocked out by it all I suppose. You must be looking forward to seeing your mother,' she added carefully, knowing that was what women always said when they had babies, although quite unable to imagine such an emotion herself.

'I am, I am, I can't wait. If only Baby could come too, but he's still incarcerated with Mary Rose.'

'And is the other Lady Caterham coming this time? Alexander's mother?' asked Angie carefully. Virginia's face shadowed, then brightened very quickly and carefully. 'No, she's not. Well, it's her loss. I actually wrote to her and told her the baby was called Georgina and her second name was Alicia, after her, and would she please come and meet me and her two granddaughters, and she hasn't even answered. Alexander said she'd phoned, and said she couldn't make the journey. So I just give up.'

Angie reflected that she would have given up too. The more she saw of the Caterhams, the less she realized she knew about them. And the more she felt she needed to know.

Chapter 5

Virginia, 1965–6

She was drinking too much. She knew it, and she knew other people must know it, but she didn't quite know if she cared enough to want to do something about it. She never got drunk, not properly drunk, but she was tipsy every night. And most lunchtimes. Fortunately she didn't get unattractively tipsy, she stayed coherent, she didn't knock things over, she just started talking rather freely, and giggling too much, and flirting outrageously with every man in sight. Since she was in such a privileged position socially, nobody minded this too much, the men enjoyed it, and the wives looked on fairly tolerantly for the most part.

But every morning she did have an awful headache and quite often she was sick; but they weren't real hangovers, not like Baby had, when he stumbled out red-eyed and grey-faced, groaning and mixing up disgusting concoctions. A few cups of coffee and maybe a Bucks Fizz for breakfast if she was feeling really bad, and she was fine. So it wasn't as if she had any kind of problem. She could stop if she wanted to, of course she could. She just enjoyed drinking, especially champagne. And she got very belligerent indeed if anyone suggested she enjoyed it too much.

Apart from the sense of unease about her drinking, Virginia was very happy. Georgina was a good baby, and she was enjoying her. Her joy and self-satisfaction at her easy delivery under the aegis of psychoprophylaxis was greatly increased at the news that Mary Rose had gone completely to pieces when she had her second baby, screamed so loudly all the other mothers in the hospital complained and finally had to have a forceps delivery under total anaesthesia.

She had called her baby, a boy, Kendrick. Everybody thought it was a terrible name, but Mary Rose had been studying Gaelic during her pregnancy, and discovered it during the course of her reading; she would inform everybody who could be coerced into listening that it was derived from two words, Cyne, which meant royal, and ric, which meant power. Baby said he didn't quite see the connection, but never mind; he told Virginia he was very proud of his baby who looked far more like him than Freddy did. They had all come to Hartest for Georgina's christening.

★

When Georgina was just six months old, Virginia was pregnant again.

She knew it was a bit soon; but she kept saying to Angie and Alexander and her mother and anyone else who cared to listen that she felt time was running out on her, that if she didn't have a boy soon she'd be too old. It was useless everyone pointing out that she was only twenty-seven, that she had plenty of time, she became fretful and tearful and said no, no she didn't. Another girl would mean another two years passing; this time, this time she had to have a boy.

Lydia Paget tried to reassure her, to calm her, without success. 'At this rate, you'll have serious postnatal depression again, if the baby isn't a boy. You must try and relax about it.'

Alexander had gone to see Lydia with her, an almost unheard-of event. She supposed it was a measure of his concern. 'I have tried to reassure her, Mrs Paget,' he said, 'believe me. It seems to matter to my wife far more than it does to me. I have told her over and over again that I am quite content to see Hartest in the hands of my daughters, but she simply won't believe me. Or chooses not to.'

Lydia and Virginia both stared at him.

'Forgive me, Lord Caterham,' said Lydia, 'but this message most assuredly has not got through. Your wife seems to feel she's failing you. She's the first Countess of Caterham for two hundred years, I understand, not to have a boy. There's a very strong male strain running through your family.'

'Yes,' said Virginia fretfully, 'I've been terribly unlucky.' She felt irritable, uncomfortable somehow. She wished she could have a drink.

'I don't see it as unlucky,' said Alexander. 'I am just sorry that you do. It is truly of little interest to me. Well, naturally I would like a son. But I would rather you were happy and enjoying your pregnancy. It's much more important, isn't it, Mrs Paget?'

'Alexander,' said Virginia, 'I really don't think you should lie to me like this.'

'I'm not lying to you,' he said, with his most gentle smile. 'I mean it.'

'There you are, Lady Caterham,' said Lydia, smiling too. 'Now you have it from the highest authority. Try to relax about it.'

'I can't,' said Virginia. She felt terribly angry suddenly, betrayed. 'Come on, Alexander, it's time we went home.'

It was a very long pregnancy. She didn't work very much; she insisted on going to London, sitting in the office, but she was too tired most of the time, and she worked a very short day. Angie kept things ticking over, and did her best, but the business suffered. Virginia didn't care. She was increasingly uninterested in everything except herself. She was bored, irritable, difficult. She neglected the girls. She could hardly bear to speak to Alexander. She was highly critical of Angie and all her efforts. Alexander kept urging her to give up work, to stay at Hartest. It made her furious; the conversation always ended in an ugly scene. Only when she had had two or three glasses of wine was she tolerable company.

She even quarrelled with Nanny. It was unheard of, and it was over Charlotte's bedtime. Virginia had insisted on keeping her up and was lying on her own bed with her, reading her stories. Nanny had said she must go to bed, it was after seven, and Virginia had said no, that she wanted Charlotte to stay with her. There was a scene; Charlotte was finally taken away screaming.

Half an hour later Nanny came back.

'I know you're not yourself, madam,' she said, 'but that's all the more reason to leave me in full charge of the girls. I'm not as young as I was,' she added with her usual glorious lack of logic.

Virginia picked up her book. She ostentatiously opened it and turned the page, ignoring Nanny totally.

Later she phoned her on the house telephone.

'Nanny darling, please come down here. I want to say I'm sorry.'

'I'm busy just at the moment,' said Nanny firmly. 'With the children's ironing.'

'Please, Nanny.'

'I'll come down later, madam.'

'Nanny, I'll be asleep later. I've just had some hot milk. It won't take long.' She could hear the tears in her own voice; could hear Nanny relenting.

'I'll be down in a minute, madam.'

She said she was very sorry to Nanny; she said nobody understood how frightened she was, how worried. Nanny patted her hand and said she did. Then she picked up the empty cup and moved towards the door. She looked at it and stopped suddenly, turned back to Virginia.

'Excuse me for mentioning this, madam, but I don't think whisky is very good for you at the moment. Not even in hot milk.'

'Oh Nanny, really. Don't be such an old misery. Just a little drop, to get me off to sleep.'

Virginia went into labour over a month early. She was rushed to hospital. Lydia Paget only arrived for the final half hour. It was a harder birth than Georgina's, but it was still over in six hours; the baby was placed in an incubator.

She lay in bed in a state of almost awestruck happiness. She had done it.

She had had a boy. She had accomplished what she had had to do. She was the mother of a son. Her own personal miracle had been worked. She didn't have to worry any more.

Lydia Paget came to see her. 'The baby is a little distressed. But he should be all right. Thirty-four weeks isn't too desperate these days.'

The next day they wheeled her down to see him. Her son, the small Viscount Hadleigh, heir to Hartest.

She looked at him as he lay in the incubator, and felt frightened. He looked very vulnerable. He was moving relentlessly about, and his arms and legs were particularly thin, his joints oddly large. 'It's because he's premature,' said the nurse in charge of him, seeing her shocked face, 'that he's so thin. It's in the last month they gain some fat.'

He had a shock of black hair, and his eyes, oddly small even in his tiny face, looked unseeingly out at the world.

In spite of her fear, she smiled tenderly at him. 'Hallo, Baby Alexander,' she said. 'Be strong, won't you? Be strong for me.'

She felt she could do anything now. Anything. She was going to be a good wife. Be nicer and more companionable to Alexander. She was going to be a much better mother. Play with the girls. Spend more time with them. Make sure they were happy with their little brother. Make sure they didn't realize that he was a hundred, a thousand times more important than they were.

And she would give up drinking, most definitely she would give up drinking. And give up her work too. And she would take an interest in the estate and the farm. Just start being a better person, being good. She had to show her gratitude to God somehow.

Alexander, Viscount Hadleigh, died two days later. The paediatrician kept telling her there had been nothing he could do, could have done. It was not just that he was premature, that would have been nothing, he had other problems. He had a heart defect, and a slightly cleft palate; he wasn't able to suck properly, and some of his joints were malformed. Privately he told Lydia Paget that it was a clear case of foetal alcohol syndrome. The mother must have been drinking a great deal. Lydia, who had observed all the signs for herself and known there was nothing to be done, but who had hoped that somehow the little boy might survive anyway, nodded and went to see Virginia again, to see if there was anything, anything at all she could do for her.

87

Virginia was sitting in her bed, just staring out of the window. She turned to look at Lydia as she came in.

'It was my fault, wasn't it?' she said, in a dreadful dead voice. 'My fault. The baby died because I've been drinking too much. I should have stopped, I should.'

'Well – ' said Lydia helplessly, 'well maybe it didn't help.'

'Lydia, it wasn't that it didn't help. I killed him. I drank him to his death, my baby, my poor poor little tiny baby.' She started crying, sobbing, clinging onto Lydia's hands; after a while she said, 'I hate myself, Lydia. I hate myself so much. Oh Lydia, if only you knew, if only – '

'I know,' said Lydia, stroking her hair, 'I do know.'

'No, Lydia, you don't, you can't. You haven't ever done anything so awful, so wicked. Have you?'

'Well – I don't think that's very important. What I've done or not done. Did you – did you see the – the baby today?'

'Oh yes,' she said. 'Yes, I've seen him. I was holding him when he died. I felt – I owed it to him. He was so tiny. He hadn't any love in his life at all. Any physical closeness. They said I could hold him. That it wouldn't do any harm, to take him out of the incubator, not any more. So I did.' She was crying again now, tears falling freely down her face; talking feverishly, urgently. 'And I was holding him, talking to him. I really thought it might help. In spite of what they said. He felt rather cold and I held him very close to me. He felt so tiny too, almost like a little bird. I asked them to bring some more blankets for him. They were a while finding one. Do you think it might have saved him? If they'd brought one sooner? He was so cold. His feet were so cold.'

'No, I don't think it would have made any difference,' said Lydia very quietly, speaking with difficulty, 'not by then.'

'Well, I just wondered. He was so peaceful, once they took him out of the incubator. He was very restless before. I don't think he was suffering, though. Do you? You don't think I did the wrong thing, do you? Taking him out of the incubator. You don't think he might have lived if he had stayed there?'

'Oh no,' said Lydia, 'no, I'm sure he wouldn't. But I'm sure he wasn't suffering. And it must have helped him so much, to be held by you.' She had tears in her own eyes now. 'It would have soothed him. Comforted him. I'm sure you did absolutely the right thing.'

'I thought he'd just gone to sleep. Well, he did at first. His eyes just closed. Then he was very still. But he was still breathing. I kept hoping, you know, right until the end. Even after he stopped breathing. Somehow I went on hoping. I asked them. I made them make absolutely sure he was dead. The – the stethoscope looked so big on his chest. It was such a tiny chest. So tiny and thin. Too tiny, I suppose.'

'Yes,' said Lydia. 'Yes of course, he was. Too tiny altogether.'

Alexander, Viscount Hadleigh, was buried at Hartest, his grave, with its oddly pristine little headstone, looking shockingly raw and hurtful among the old, weathered ones.

'It will weather too,' Alexander had said to Virginia, 'it will fade, in time. Like our grief.'

'I don't want it to,' said Virginia.

The tiny coffin set with a crown of white roses was carried into the chapel by Alexander alone. The only other person there was Nanny; Virginia had forbidden even Betsey to come.

'This is for us to bear alone,' she said simply to her mother on the phone. 'No one can help.'

After the service Alexander carried the coffin out again, out of the chapel, towards the space under the yew tree that had been prepared for it; she saw him set it down as tenderly as if it had been a live baby. She picked a white rose from the bunch of flowers she was carrying and laid it tenderly on the coffin and kissed her fingers and laid them on the coffin too; and then she learnt what it truly meant to feel your heart break.

'Virginia, you need help,' said Alexander. They were breakfasting in the house in Eaton Place; it was a cold January day; the children had been sent on an extended visit to their grandparents in New York. Virginia couldn't cope with them, and it was felt that they were better removed from the entire situation. Nanny had gone with them, but returned after three weeks, her lips very tightly folded, saying that Mrs Praeger seemed to imagine she could look after the children herself with the help of some foolish girl, and there was certainly no place for her in such a household. She made it sound as if Beaches was a brothel. Alexander told her not to fret, that he was sure the children would be fine, and that they would soon be home now, anyway. Virginia was much better. He didn't sound at all convinced when he said it.

Virginia had gone out to the kitchen and returned with a glass of orange juice; he had asked if he could share it with her and she had said quickly no, no, she would fetch him one of his own, and gone back out of the room. Alexander tasted the orange juice; it was thick and sweet with gin.

'Oh,' she said, 'oh, no, I'll get over it. Don't rush me, Alexander, it's only just two months since the baby died. I'll be all right.'

'I didn't mean help getting over the baby,' he said, 'I meant help to stop drinking.'

'Oh,' she said, 'oh for God's sake don't start on that. Why does everyone keep talking as if I'm a drunk?'

'Because,' he said simply, 'because you *are* a drunk.'

Virginia stared at him. She knew how terrible she must look. She had turned away from her own reflection in the mirror that morning. Her face was white and puffy; her dark hair, although freshly done, was dull and lifeless. She was very thin, her golden eyes dull and dark-rimmed. But that did not mean she was a drunk. It did not.

'Don't dare to say such a thing to me,' she said. 'I am not a drunk. I may get a little drunk at night. God in heaven, I need something to dull the way I feel. But I am not a drunk. Now if you will excuse me, Alexander, I'm going upstairs.'

'Virginia,' he said, 'you are a drunk. And if you had not been a drunk all during your pregnancy, that baby would still be alive.'

'Oh,' she cried, and it was a wail of pain, 'don't, don't say such a thing. He wouldn't, he wouldn't. It's a cruel, wicked lie. I won't let you even think such a thing.'

'Virginia, it's true. If you don't believe me, ask Mrs Paget. Ask the paediatrician at the hospital. You killed that baby, and if you're not very careful, you'll kill yourself.'

'I don't know,' she said, looking at him flatly, her face icily, stonily white, 'how you can be so cruel to me.'

'I know you won't believe it,' he said, taking her hand, looking at her tenderly, 'but it's because I love you. And I want to help you.'

She began to cry suddenly, raging, dreadful tears, grabbing at her glass from time to time and drinking from it; when it was empty, she tried to get up and take it to fill again. Alexander snatched it back from her.

'No,' he said. 'No. We will start now, today. We will beat it together.'

'I can't, I can't,' she said, 'it's the only thing I have that doesn't let me down.'

She missed the raw pain in Alexander's eyes, but she saw the blaze of anger that followed, and she felt the stinging blow he delivered to her face. 'How dare you!' he said. 'How dare you, sitting there, reeking of drink, wallowing in self-pity, say everything lets you down? Does your mother let you down? Phoning every day, begging to be allowed to come and see you? Do your children let you down? Little Charlotte, sending you pictures she's painted, to make you feel better? Longing to come home to you? I daresay she feels let down, Virginia; that would be understandable. What about Nanny, caring for them all this time, never uttering a breath of criticism of you to anyone? Angie, covering up for you, working to retain the few clients you have left, has she let you down? Have I let you down? Acting out this ghastly charade, pretending to our friends, the servants, that you were ill when you were so drunk you could hardly stand up sometimes, cleaning up your vomit, trying to comfort you? How dare you say everyone lets you down? It is you who are letting us down, Virginia, and you have no excuse, no excuse at all.'

She looked at him, calm suddenly, and there was a long, endless silence. Then she said, 'Well, I think I have one or two. But not many. And I'm sorry, Alexander. I'm sorry.'

'You've said that a great deal,' he said, 'over the past few months. I should feel better if you were to try to prove it to me.'

'All right,' she said, her small, pointed chin lifting suddenly, her eyes almost amused, 'all right, I'll try.'

She did try. She told Angie what she was doing, that Alexander was staying up in London with her, to help her, that she couldn't face being at Hartest with the servants; she begged Angie to be patient with her, that it was going to be tough.

It was very tough. She stopped drinking altogether for two days, but the withdrawal was so frightening, revealing as it did how much she must have been drinking, as she sweated, developed cramps, threw up; Alexander finally, alarmed and weakened by her pleas, gave her a drink to soothe her, and agreed they should find professional help. She promised at the height of her agony to go to Alcoholics Anonymous, but later she refused, and she could see he was almost relieved, so great would the humiliation have been; and so instead he became an expert himself, reading extensively on the subject and drawing up a programme of steadily decreasing alcoholic intake for her.

It seemed to work; after three weeks she was feeling better, was sleeping better; Alexander was talking of sending for the children. Then one day he was out at a business meeting all morning; alone in the house for the first time for a long while, alone with her guilt and grief and remorse, she lost control; by lunchtime she had drunk half a bottle of gin.

'Virginia, for the love of God, what are you doing?' said Alexander wearily, looking at her as she sat slumped at the table in the small dining room. 'We've been through so much, we're getting you out of it, why drag yourself back into it again?'

'I don't know what you mean.'

'Virginia, you do know what I mean. You're drunk. Where did you get it from?'

'I'm not drunk.'

'You are.'

'Oh all right,' she said, suddenly angry, tears pouring down her face, 'yes I'm drunk. And it's lovely. It's lovely. I don't feel frightened any more. Or sick. I just feel good.'

'So where did you get it from?'

'I got it from the cellar.'

'But the cellar's locked.'

'Oh, I know. Very crafty of you, Alexander. I didn't like that. That was really what got me going. I went looking for the key. And when I couldn't find it, I got a screwdriver and took the lock off.'

'Well all right, Virginia. Let's just give up, shall we? You drink as much as you like and kill yourself, and any children you might have in the future, and I'll stop trying to help you.'

'Don't you start talking about children.'

'Why not?'

'You know why not. And it's irrelevant anyway.'

'Well it is if you're going to continue to murder them.'

She stood up suddenly, came at him with the bottle she had hidden hastily under the chair. 'You bastard,' she said, her eyes narrow slits. 'You bastard.'

He snatched the bottle from her easily, pushed her back down into a chair. 'Just stop it, Virginia,' he said, 'just stop being so melodramatic. Drink yourself to death if you want to, but leave me out of it.' He turned away and walked towards the door; she snatched her glass, splintered its rim against the table and ran after him, mad with grief and rage. She clawed at the back of his neck with the shattered glass; blood spurted everywhere, horribly.

He put his hands up to the wound, and they turned almost instantly red; he looked at them and then at her, and then said very calmly, 'I think you should call the doctor.'

It was all carefully covered up, of course; Virginia, shaking with terror, called the doctor, told him what had happened. And then he sent her away after stitching Alexander's neck and talked to Alexander for a long time and then came out to find her and said it had been a very nasty accident, Alexander falling like that, but he would be fine and all they had to do was look after him very carefully and her too, as she would need all her strength to take care of him. He said she was to go in and see Alexander, who was sitting in his chair looking rather pale but quite cheerful; he said he was fine, and she was not to feel too badly about it all. He said the doctor had said she was to go and see him in his surgery and get some advice, and Virginia, weak with remorse and misery, said of course she would, and made an appointment that very afternoon.

But she didn't go. The time for the appointment came and went, and she didn't arrive; and in the end the doctor went to Eaton Place, ostensibly to dress Alexander's wound, but actually to see Virginia and impress upon her how badly she needed help.

Virginia was not there; she had gone out early, Angie said, to see some prospective clients. She had actually given Angie a list and some telephone numbers. But she was not seeing any clients, she was driving extremely fast down the M4 and when the police stopped her she was so drunk she could hardly stand up to get out of the car.

She finally saw a psychiatrist. He sent her to hospital for detoxification. He told her it wasn't a permanent solution, that was in her hands, but it was the first step; he told her that alcoholism was a form of self-destruction, and that she must try to analyse why she was following such a course. He told Alexander afterwards that he was baffled by her case, but that the one thing that had emerged was that Virginia found the thought of being at Hartest almost unendurable. 'Presumably because of the child, and the fact that it's buried there. She wants to stay in London for a while. I would advise that very strongly.'

It was the third day, the third day without a drink. It was awful, but not as bad as she had expected. The worst thing was the fear; the fear. The nameless fear, the sense of impending doom that hung over her. And then there was another fear, even worse, not nameless at all, that of having to live without alcohol. That was terrible.

Virginia sat in her small room at the clinic and tried not to think about life without alcohol. But she couldn't. She was supposed to be reading, but she couldn't concentrate. She had a box of chocolates to eat, but she didn't want them. All she could think about was what her life was going to be like in the future, if she achieved what now at last seemed just possible. No lovely, heady buzz as the champagne hit her bloodstream; no slipping into unselfconscious confidence at parties and at the dinner table; no swift numbing of the headaches and backaches that plagued her; no instant easing of her pain as she thought, more fiercely, more agonizingly every day, of her tiny dead baby. And good food without wine; and sunbathing without wine; and chatting easily with friends over an endless lunch without wine; and not having a glass of whisky; and coping with a rude, difficult client and not rewarding herself with a martini. The whole thing looked intolerable.

And then she had hurt. She had hurt all over. Her head hurt, her eyes hurt, even her teeth ached. A drink would ease all of that. The doctor said it was temporary, that sort of pain; but it didn't feel temporary. She remembered something Scott Fitzgerald had said: that he had never managed to be sober long enough to enjoy it. She knew what he meant. It was hard to imagine enjoying this condition. And harder to visualize it becoming normal.

But whatever she was going through, she seemed to be at least managing. It wasn't so bad, she kept saying to herself fiercely, desperately trying to force her concentration on her book. It wasn't so bad.

That night it got really bad. She felt terrible. She couldn't stand it. Terror gripped her. She looked at the clock. Three. Three a.m. They had said insomnia would probably trouble her. Trouble her! This wasn't trouble, it was a screaming agony. Terror. Physical pain. She had to do something, anything. Otherwise she would run away, find an off-licence, smash a window, anything to get a drink.

What had he said, her therapist? Think of ten minutes. You can survive anything for ten minutes. Ten minutes will do it. OK, she'd do it. She fixed her eyes on her clock. Five minutes. No better. Eight. Ten. Ten minutes more of it she had survived. And it was worse. Far worse. They'd lied. Christ, what could she do?

The phone! That was it, they had said always phone. Phone her therapist. He would be on call. Night and day. He would help her through it. She lifted the phone, pressed his extension.

'Yes,' said an instantly alert voice.

'It's Virginia here. Please come. I can't stand it.'

'Virginia,' said the voice, soothing, tolerant, almost amused. 'You can stand it. You've done so well. Of course you can.'

'I can't. I need you.'

'I'll come in the morning.'

'I can't wait until then,' she said, her voice cracking with pain.

'Yes you can. Think yourself through it. Remember hitting rock bottom. Remember what it was like. You don't want to go back there. Do you, Virginia? Remember the ten minutes. You can hang on for ten minutes. Ten minutes at a time.'

'I just did.'

'Good. Well there you are. You can do another ten. And another. Make yourself some herb tea. Do you have plenty?'

'I don't want herb tea,' she cried in agony, 'I want a drink. Please, please come.'

His voice changed. 'All right. I'll come.'

He sat and talked to her for an hour, sharing a pot of herb tea. The pain eased, the panic passed. At six she was asleep. He looked at her thoughtfully. She had not been such a heavy drinker, and yet her withdrawal was so bad. Why? She was an interesting case.

94

Remember your rock bottom, they had said. It was important to recognize that. Hers had come when she had come to herself, vomiting and half clutching a bottle of whisky and scrabbling at the baby's grave. That was when she had known she had to give in and go to the clinic. Listen to Alexander, do what the doctors said. In a way it was a good thing it had been so bad, such a terrible rock bottom, so utterly, dreadfully ugly and humiliating. Stabbing Alexander in the neck, getting charged with drink-driving, they hadn't been real rock-bottom things. But lying on the grave, that was. She had to come back from there. She had to.

She was a difficult patient. She didn't really participate in the group discussions, and in her one-to-one sessions with the psychiatrist, she was reserved too. You must talk, they said, you must try to realize what first triggered off your dependence. Oh, she would say vaguely one day, it was the postnatal depression. Another it would be her low self-esteem because of her childhood, always feeling Baby was doing better than her. Then it would be her dead baby. Never consistent, never letting go.

She showed the anger, the 'reservoir of rage' that therapists all know in alcoholics, but she never revealed the real reason for that either. Once she almost did; she said, 'All right I'll tell you, I'll tell you, are you ready for it, because I'm going to tell you,' and then she didn't, she said no, she wouldn't, she couldn't, she hardly knew herself any more, and retreated once again into her shell of solitary pain.

But she didn't drink. She had stopped drinking.

She was totally resistant to going back to Hartest. She said she could manage in the clinic, she could probably cope with London, even with New York if necessary, but not Hartest. It was asking too much. Nobody understood why. They asked her, but she couldn't tell them. Or wouldn't.

After three weeks in the clinic she went home to the house in Eaton Place. She was terribly frightened, she clung to Alexander's hand, and as the car pulled up in front of the house she looked at him, stricken, and said, 'What will they all think, how am I going to face them?'

'They will all think you are brave and strong and they will be pleased to have you home,' he said, kissing her gently.

'Angie's in there, she's dying to see you, she needs your help and opinion on so many things. Lady Price Somebody or other is driving her mad. Come in, Virginia, don't be frightened. And I'll be with you.'

She tried to work, because she knew it would help, but it was very hard. She was emotionally and physically weak. She was aware of what a strain she was putting on Angie, even to insist on trying, but she couldn't help it. In fact things were very bad; they had scarcely any clients left. Perversely she didn't mind; she told Angie they could start again, that it would be fun.

It wasn't much fun though; it took weeks to get even one client. Then she found it hard to concentrate, to care even, and lost her again. Which upset her horribly, sent her into paroxysms first of weeping, then of rage.

She was sitting at her desk, next morning, staring out of the window, wondering if life was ever going to be anything remotely the same again, when Angie came in. She looked tense, oddly defiant.

'I have to talk to you,' she said.

'Yes? What about?'

'I've decided to leave.'

Virginia stared at her, trying to make sense of what she had heard. 'I don't understand,' she said.

'It isn't very difficult,' said Angie, and there was a degree of impatience and something else – scorn? – in her voice that hurt Virginia almost more than anything else. 'I'm leaving. I'm sorry, when you're so down, but I am.'

'Angie, you can't,' said Virginia, 'I need you so much at the moment.'

'Well I'm sorry,' said Angie again, 'but I really have tried very hard, Virginia, to be a support and everything. But it's been – well, never mind what it's been. The thing is, I want to move on. M. Wetherly has offered me a job in America. It's a big opportunity, and I really want to go.'

'But Angie – ' Virginia stopped suddenly. There was no future in crying, or arguing. She could see very clearly, in Angie's green, clear-sighted eyes, what she was actually saying. That she had had enough. More than enough. And hurt as she was, she did not feel she could entirely blame her.

'Well,' she said, 'of course you must go. I can't expect you to stay here looking after me for ever.'

'No,' said Angie. 'I'm afraid you can't.'

That stung badly; Virginia stared back at her, hoping the pain didn't show.

'Well,' she said again, forcing herself to sound bright, 'you'll be able to

96

meet Baby at last. I'll tell him you're coming, and that he must take care of you.'

'Oh, I don't need taking care of,' said Angie. 'I'll be fine, just fine.'

'Yes,' said Virginia, and she was aware of the edge in her voice as she spoke, 'yes, I think you probably will.'

Angie left for America a month later, flew into Kennedy at dusk on a cold, windy evening, and as she struggled wearily out of what seemed like hours in Immigration, her luggage on a trolley, thinking how foolish she had been not to wait until M. Wetherly had come back from a trip to the Bahamas before embarking on her new life, the most beautiful man she had ever seen in her life stepped forward, smiling at her, taking her trolley. He was broadly built, and very tall, and dressed in an extremely well-cut grey suit with a cream button-down-collar shirt and a red tie. His teeth were almost unnaturally white and even, his skin almost too perfectly tanned, his eyes almost unbelievably blue, and as she stood there staring at him, literally weak at the knees, he said, 'You *are* Angie, aren't you? I'm Baby Praeger. Virgy told me to be sure to meet you, and I can tell you now I've seen you, I wouldn't have missed it for the world.'

Chapter 6

Baby, 1967–8

Tidings of Joy

The Countess of Caterham, the beautiful American-born wife of Alexander, Earl of Caterham, has finally given birth to a longed-for boy, heir to the title and to Hartest, the exquisite family seat in Wiltshire. The baby, whose name has still not been confirmed, and who will be styled Viscount Hadleigh, was born in the London Clinic two weeks ago. Lord Caterham, speaking from the family's London house in Eaton Place last night, said that the baby was extremely strong and healthy, and that his wife is recovering fast and is overjoyed. 'This is a marvellous early Christmas present,' he said. The Earl said that his two daughters, the Lady Charlotte and the Lady Georgina Welles (pictured here at the annual Midsummer Garden Party at Hartest), were thrilled with their new brother, and were busy choosing names for him.

Viscount Hadleigh's christening will be held in the chapel at Hartest.

Conspicuously absent from the christenings of the two girls was the Dowager Lady Caterham, who lives as a virtual recluse in her home in the Scottish Highlands. There is much speculation as to whether she may now make the journey to England in order to meet her grandson; a source close to the family told me last night that she strongly disapproved of her son marrying an American and that she has refused to meet her daughter-in-law on those grounds. The Earl, who is still close to his mother, denies this, and says it is simply her increasingly frail health that has kept her from meeting Lady Caterham. Neighbours in the Trossachs report frequent sightings of the Countess fishing in her thigh-high waders.

'Bloody Dempster,' said Alexander, flinging the *Daily Mail* across the room. 'Why can't he leave us all alone? God knows the trouble this will cause.'

'Because he's paid not to leave us all alone,' said Virginia, who was fond of Nigel Dempster and had benefited from time to time from publicity in his column. 'Digging dirt is his job. He always says that if there's no story he can't write it. We should all keep our noses cleaner.

And if you're talking about your mother, I hope it makes her feel at least a little uncomfortable.'

'It won't,' said Alexander shortly.

Nanny came in. 'Your Ladyship, the baby is crying,' she said. 'I suppose you'll want to feed him.'

'I suppose I will, Nanny,' said Virginia. 'I'll come up.'

'You do realize that it's a quarter past nine,' said Nanny with a wealth of meaning in her voice.

'Yes I do, Nanny. Thank you.'

'I'll get him up then,' said Nanny with a heavy sigh. 'I hope we won't regret it later. As he's a boy.' She left the room, her back rigid with disapproval. Virginia winked at Alexander and stood up.

'What on earth was that about?' said Alexander.

'Babies don't get fed at a quarter past nine,' said Virginia. 'They get fed at ten. And two. And six. And ten again. The most dreadful things happen otherwise. Everybody knows that.'

'I seem to remember Charlotte and Georgina being fed more or less when they wanted it.'

'Yes they were. But as Nanny says, this baby is a boy. He has to be brought up properly right from the beginning. No newfangled demand feeding for him. He's got to go to Eton, after all.' She smiled at Alexander's slightly bemused expression and went over and kissed him. 'Don't worry, darling. He'll survive it.'

The baby was christened Maximilian Frederick Alexander six weeks later. He was a most engaging child, blond and blue-eyed like Alexander, and smiled squintily at anyone who came into his rather hazy orbit. He was a quiet and peaceful baby, needing a feed only every five hours; Nanny, who might have been expected to be pleased by this, said it was confusing and she never knew where she was, one night she had to get up at three to give him his bottle and the next night at four. When Max, as everyone called him, obliged her by sleeping right through the night from ten till seven in the morning when he was only six weeks old, she was very put out, and said she had always known that this kind of thing would lead to trouble later.

Sitting gazing out at the endless wastes of the Arctic below him, Baby, who as Godfather had attended the christening, ordered a double bourbon. He always needed something strong before he faced the combination of Mary Rose and his father. They were a formidable team.

Initially he knew Fred III had not especially liked Mary Rose; what Baby had seen then as a tantalizing coolness, Fred had interpreted (correctly, Baby reflected gloomily, gulping gratefully at the bourbon) as coldness, distance, lack of any sense of fun. But as time went by, it became borne in upon Fred that Mary Rose was a brilliantly successful company wife. Fred lost no opportunity to point this out to Baby. Not only did she entertain tirelessly for the bank, she associated herself very publicly with causes and charities which would benefit it. And if there was one thing Fred cared about more than his wife and children it was Praegers. He had grown up watching his father managing the bank less than brilliantly, had heard tales from the older members of staff how near it had come to being entirely lost, and he had a morbid fear of this happening again, and of his own son being a less than perfect guardian for Praegers. Baby knew this; and he realized as the years went by that he was not the natural instinctive banker his father was. He lacked his flair, his vision, his sense of timing. The knowledge made him nervous; and so did Fred's highly visible monitoring of his increasingly weak performance. And the further realization that Fred and Mary Rose seemed to be joined in a critical conspiracy was undermining Baby's confidence seriously. As the criticism mounted, he took refuge in other things, other pursuits, mainly that of fun. He sought out old friends from his bachelor days, spent weekends sailing with them, evenings playing poker, going to old haunts, getting drunk. And being who he was, high profile, word got around. And Fred had been very displeased and Mary Rose had been very displeased; and the two of them had formed an alliance which as far as Baby was concerned was painful.

But over the past few months he had been working very hard to redeem himself. Partly because he knew he had to if he was to take over Praegers before reaching his own retirement age, and partly for another reason altogether: a very different, happier, but equally powerful reason for becoming his own man, in command of his own destiny. He had shunned the poker games and the drinking clubs; had worked late and worked hard, had joined Mary Rose on her charity committees, had spent long hours discussing Praegers' future and the way it should go with Fred.

And it was beginning to work; winning him back Fred's respect, increasing his self-confidence, improving his own performance as a result. Nevertheless, he still frequently felt like a naughty child on probation; and after an absence, an escape from the surveillance, such as he had just enjoyed, going back oppressed him.

There was of course another, happier aspect to the situation . . .

★

That spring Fred III and Betsey suggested Virginia brought all the children to stay for the Easter vacation. Fred's love affair with Charlotte had burgeoned during her long stay with her grandparents while Virginia had been ill; he had spoilt her outrageously, and had even taken the unprecedented move of taking an afternoon out from the bank ('He certainly never did that for me,' Betsey had remarked tartly) and escorted her to the theatre or the movies; they had seen *Mame* and *Cabaret* and the all-black version of *Hello Dolly* which was the great rage on Broadway, and he had taken her to Radio City which she adored, and the Beatles' all-cartoon movie, *Yellow Submarine*. He also took her to Lord and Taylor's and Saks and Bonwits and bought her stacks of clothes, anything she fancied; Betsey said, half amused, half shocked, that Charlotte was the only child she had ever actually known who had her own Chanel bag, and she had stopped Fred III from buying Charlotte a fur coat with great difficulty.

And then he had bought her a pony, to ride on Long Island; he was called Mr P., a rather round, steady little bay, who was kept at livery at Toppings Farm, where all the Hampton children rode. Charlotte had a natural seat and a lot of courage, and she and Fred rode together in the countryside, and on the South Shore; and he had taken her sailing with him, in his boat at Sag Harbor, and even begun to instruct her in golf, and had a set of tiny clubs made for her. He thought she was altogether quite wonderful, and the whole thing made Mary Rose very cross.

And now, Betsey had said on the phone to Virginia, he had got a new pony in mind for Charlotte, since she was growing out of Mr P., and besides she was just dying to get her hands on Max.

'And you could have a holiday, Nanny darling,' said Virginia, discussing the prospective visit with Nanny. 'You look tired.'

'I don't know that I'd be able to relax,' said Nanny darkly, 'with Max over there. He might pick something up.' She still viewed America as a dangerous subcontinent, on a par with the Australian outback or the African bush.

'Nanny, Max will be fine. And his grandmother is so longing to get to know him.'

'That's another worry,' said Nanny, 'he'll be picking up American ways.'

'Well he is half American. And he's a little young to be chewing gum or saying gee whizz.'

'Well, he's your child I suppose, madam,' said Nanny, in tones that implied that Max was not really anything of the sort. 'And you must decide.'

'Yes, I think so. And I have actually decided that we shall go.'

'And will His Lordship be going?'

'Well yes, I expect so. You know he doesn't like me out of his sight.'

'Well, I'll think about it,' said Nanny.

Virginia wasn't quite sure what she was going to think about.

But His Lordship didn't go to New York. He walked into Virginia's study that evening and said he was going to visit his mother for Easter instead. 'She hasn't been well. I'm worried about her.'

'I'm sorry,' said Virginia with difficulty. 'What's been wrong?'

'Oh, just flu. But she's getting on, you know.'

'Alexander, she's sixty-two. She's a comparatively young woman.'

'Well, she would appreciate a visit. So I'm going.'

'Alexander, don't you think – well, couldn't I come with you? Heal this stupid rift? I'm ready to hold out the olive branch if she'll take it.'

'Virginia, we've had this discussion so many times. It isn't a question of a rift, and I don't think it's a good idea.'

'But Alexander, I want to get to know your mother. It's absurd.' She was near tears. 'Please.'

'Virginia, I know you do, but it isn't possible. She has this very strong antipathy towards you, and I don't think – well, I know – there's anything we can do about it. I'm sorry. You'll be all right, surely, with your family?'

'Yes. Yes of course I will. I'm – just upset about it. That's all. And I'd have thought she'd at least want to see Max, if not the girls.'

'Virginia, please. Can we leave it?'

'Yes, all right, Alexander. Let's leave it.'

They had a wonderful Easter. Virginia and the children arrived the week before, and everyone seemed miraculously happy and relaxed, even Mary Rose who came out on Thursday for the long weekend with the children; Baby, she said, was following her on Saturday, he had an important business dinner on Thursday night and wanted to catch up on paperwork in the peace of the Friday. She looked very smug as she said this.

She had looked less smug on her arrival; Charlotte was practising her swing on the front lawn with her grandfather.

'I don't know,' she said to Fred III, as he kissed her hallo, 'why you don't buy that child her own car to drive around in. I'm sure she'd like it.'

'Yes she would,' he said, deliberately ignoring the real meaning of her remark, 'and I'm sure she'd drive it very well.'

'How is her golf game?'

'Oh, it's coming along nicely.'

'You know, Freddy sometimes feels a little hurt that he doesn't get included in all this activity you share with Charlotte, Dad. Why don't you ask him along sometimes when you go the movies, or to tea at the Plaza?'

A friend of Mary Rose's had observed Charlotte and her grandfather guzzling, as she put it, cream cakes in the Palm Court one afternoon earlier in the week. Mary Rose had had indigestion herself all night at the thought of it.

Fred III looked at her. Much as he admired her, and what she had done for Baby and the bank, he still found it hard to like her personally, and she had certainly lost a lot of her early beauty; the slender, cool girl was turning into a gaunt rather chilly woman. Mary Rose was now thirty-four; elegant, still striking, but somehow a little forbidding. She was dressed that day in a rust tweed trouser suit; it accentuated her long legs, her rangy graceful stride, but it also showed off her almost painfully narrow hips, her overly tiny breasts. And her face was thin, her eyes hungry; Fred contemplated her personal relationship with Baby, and for the first time his sympathies wandered towards his son. Then he remembered the brilliant dinner Mary Rose had given for Baby's birthday, the charity ball she had co-chaired, bringing ever more useful contacts into Baby's path, and he beamed at her, as warmly as he could.

'I'm sorry, my dear. I guess I'm just an old-fashioned guy. I prefer girls. Tell you what, next week I'll take Freddy and Charlotte to the circus. How'd that be?'

Mary Rose opened her mouth to say she thought Freddy would prefer a solo outing and then shut it again. She smiled at Fred III. 'It'd be marvellous. Come on, Freddy, Kendrick, get out and say hallo to Grandpa.'

Kendrick got out first; he was a handsome little boy, with thick floppy dark gold hair and very dark blue eyes. People never stopped remarking on how exactly like Baby he was. But there was something about him that was not Baby, that was less engaging; he was quieter, slightly withdrawn, and his smile was not Baby's wide, generous grin, it was a more reluctant, polite smile. He came forward to his grandfather now, holding his mother's hand, a model child in his pale blue coat with the velvet collar, his white socks, his button shoes; Fred bent down and gave him a hug: 'How are you doing?' he said. Kendrick smiled at him politely and said nothing. Freddy followed, dressed perfectly in long trousers and polo shirt, sweater knotted on his shoulders; he was holding out his hand graciously to his grandfather. 'How do you do, Grandpa?' he said. His smile was not Baby's either, it was his mother's, taut, self-conscious, but his looks were not hers, he had the dark hair and more solid build that was a legacy from the Bradley side of the family.

Fred III shook his hand good-naturedly and then cuffed him gently round the head. 'Coming riding with Charlotte and me? We can easily hire you a pony from Toppings.'

The boy looked round at his mother, panic in his eyes.

'Er – Freddy has a slight cold,' said Mary Rose quickly, 'I think he should stay indoors today.'

'Fine,' said Fred, irritability blending with visible relief. He knew the slight cold was in fact fear of riding, and he had no patience with the child, and could hardly contain himself whenever Freddy did ride with him, insisting on walking his pony for most of the time, tense and pale with nerves, hauling at the animal's mouth whenever it quickened its pace. Charlotte on the other hand was fearless and cantered beside him on her little barrel of a pony, laughing with pleasure as the wind caught her hair.

'Charlotte honey, come over here and say hallo to your cousins, and then you and I'll go riding.'

Charlotte came running over; she was wearing jeans and a big sweater, her long dark hair was tangled and falling around her shoulders, her golden eyes, Virginia's eyes, sparkling with pleasure. Fred looked at her adoringly; the look was not lost on Mary Rose. Charlotte slipped her hand into Fred's. 'Hallo, Freddy. Hallo, Kendrick. It's nice to see you.' Her English intonation, her slightly formal phraseology, sounded charming. 'Freddy, do come riding, we're going to have such fun.'

'Er, no, I have this slightly strep throat,' said Freddy self-consciously. 'My mother thinks I really should stay inside today. I'll just go and see Grandma.'

'Freddy, take Kendrick. And mind he doesn't trip on the step.'

'Yes, Mother.'

Charlotte's and Fred III's eyes met in a moment of totally pleasurable and malicious understanding; then she looked up at Fred. 'I'll go and put on my riding things. See you later, Aunt Mary Rose.'

'She seems to be putting on a little weight,' said Mary Rose sweetly, looking after Charlotte as she ran indoors.

'Oh, she looks lovely. I don't like these scrawny children. And of course Virgy was a chubby child. But she's a wonderful kid. Plucky! And by God she's bright,' he added, punishing Mary Rose for aiding and abetting Freddy's cowardice. 'She can add up a row of figures in her head faster than I ever could. And read the credit and debit sides of a balance sheet. Extraordinary. I can see a woman president of Praegers yet. I really can.'

Mary Rose walked straight past him and into the house.

Baby drove out on the Saturday morning in his new car, a white Mustang, which he referred to as his new mistress, and which he said was making him feel young again. He enjoyed this joke; he had always enjoyed sailing close to the wind; it was a faster trip to the Hamptons, now that the new Expressway had been built, and besides he enjoyed the drive. As always as he found himself in the wide, oddly graceful streets of the Hamptons, with their endless white colonial-style buildings, picked up the leisured pace and breathed in the fresh salty air, he felt, city creature though he was, strangely at home; and as he turned into Waterlily Drive, cruising along the wide, grass-edged road, with its tall hedges, waving at various familiar faces dressed in the singular way of smart people pretending to be scruffy, he felt a warm wave of well-being engulf him, a sense of being absolutely happy and at home.

He turned in along the endless gravel drive, and up the sharp bend to where Beaches stood high above the shore, and met a torrential welcome; Charlotte hurled herself into his arms, Georgina clutched his legs, Virginia simply stood and smiled at him. She was looking great, he noticed with pleasure; well, smiling, relaxed.

'It's so lovely to see you,' she said, taking his arm as the family gradually released him, 'I miss you, you know. And you look wonder-ful.'

Baby smiled at her, and told her he felt wonderful too.

'What have you been doing, Baby? Is it some new wonder diet?'

Baby had a sudden brief vision of the new wonder diet and switched his thoughts with an effort.

'I've taken a leaf out of your book,' he said. 'I've given up alcohol. I feel terrific.'

The entire family paid lip-service to the fiction that Virginia's teetotalism was voluntary. It amused her; she was perfectly relaxed herself about her problem, but she knew it made her parents feel better about it, so she went along with it.

'Good for you. You're certainly a whole lot slimmer. No more hangovers then?'

'No more hangovers. Now that is something I miss.'

Virginia laughed. 'And Mary Rose looks better too. More relaxed. You're obviously doing her good as well.'

'Yup.' He changed the subject quickly. 'How's Alexander?'

'He's fine.'

'Pleased with his son and heir?'

'Yes. Over the moon.' She smiled at him. 'And at last I can relax. Now Hartest has an heir.'

'No more babies?'

'No more babies.'

'What about work?'

'Work's all right. Alexander doesn't like me living in London during the week any more, which makes things awkward. Well, he doesn't mind me being there too much, but he won't let me take the children. He says they have to learn that Hartest is their home.'

'Well, he could be right.'

'Oh God, Baby, how you chaps do stick together.'

Fred III was in tremendous form. He said he was busy planning his retirement party (Fred often talked about retiring, then found some reason not to), which was to be the following Christmas. He was almost sixty-five, and Baby was performing at absolutely 100 per cent capacity. The bank would be in good hands. Whenever he said that, Mary Rose looked exactly as if, Virginia thought to herself, she was about to have an orgasm. She wished there was someone she could share the thought with.

On the Monday afternoon Baby was just beginning to allow his thoughts to stray rather pleasurably towards New York City, when Virginia asked him to go for a walk with her on the shore. He went, slightly wary; he could see she was in heart-to-heart mood, and he was afraid, knowing how well she knew him, of how close his heart might come to being read.

'I meant it about missing you,' she said, taking his hand, as they walked close to the water's edge, the salty air and wind catching their hair, 'there really isn't anyone like you in England I can talk to.'

'I can't believe that,' said Baby easily.

'No really, it's true. Well, except for my friend Catriona, and she isn't quite a kindred spirit.'

'No, I can see that,' said Baby, thinking of the gangly, gushing Catriona, puzzling as a friend for Virginia at all, let alone a close one.

'And it's worse since Angie left. I miss her horribly for all her naughty ways. I was so disappointed she couldn't come to the christening. She came to stay here a couple of times, apparently. Mother really likes her. Do you get to see her ever, Baby?'

'Occasionally,' said Baby.

There was a silence.

'Is anything the matter, Baby?' said Virginia suddenly. 'You don't seem quite yourself.'

'No. No, of course not. Sorry, Virgy, I've got a lot on my mind. Business, you know. I'm back in full harness, these days, being the

Golden Boy, delivering the goods. I wouldn't go so far as to say Dad's pleased with me, but he's not as displeased as he was.'

'Well,' said Virginia, laughing, 'you certainly seem to be delivering the goods to Mary Rose. She looks a hundred times better.'

Baby felt a desire to confide in her so strong that it was like a physical hunger. 'Virgy – ' he said.

'Yes, Baby?'

'Virgy I – well – ' He stopped with an immense effort of will. He had promised himself not to tell anyone; it was a kind of pact he had made with himself. If nobody knew, then nobody could tell; and love her as he did, he was aware that even Virginia might tell someone. He couldn't think quite who, but she might. 'Oh, nothing,' he said finally, 'it isn't important. Tell me some more about life in England. How's that nice lanky guy, Martin or whatever his name is? The one married to your friend Catriona. I like him, he's a good egg.'

'As we say over there.'

'As you say over there.' He noticed that she was looking at him rather oddly.

Later that day, as he was helping Mary Rose load the luggage into the wagon, Virginia said, 'Shall we lunch one day this week, Baby?'

'Sure,' he said, 'love to. If I have a day. I'll call you from the office.' He was uncomfortably aware he sounded slightly evasive, and that Mary Rose was listening.

'Well, if not this week, next. I'm here for nearly a month. I'm planning on building up my business here again. There are a couple of people I want to see.'

'Well – I – '

'Virginia,' said Mary Rose, her voice taking up its most school-mistressy intonation, 'Baby is usually very busy at lunchtime. He has business lunches every day.'

Baby had never expected to feel grateful to Mary Rose. 'It's true, Virgy,' he said. Then he looked at her hurt face and felt remorseful. 'I promise I'll ring you, try and make a date. Anyway, what's all this about you working in New York? I thought Alexander wanted you to spend more time at Hartest.'

'Yes,' she said, 'he does.'

She wore the expression she often did these days, one he could never quite read, but which set the conversation as clearly off limits.

Virginia drove herself into New York two days later. She was working from the house on East 80th, and she had planned to stay there for twenty-four hours. Betsey, who was having a wonderful time with the children, practically pushed her out of Beaches. Fred III wasn't going back to the office for the rest of the week. He would help her with the children. He had bought Charlotte a pocket calculator as an Easter present, and he was dying to show her how it worked.

It was one of those bright, windy, blue and gold days New York is made for, the streets flooded suddenly with sunshine, the buildings lightened, less oppressive than in the winter dark; Virginia walked up Madison after a highly satisfactory meeting with a new client on Beekman Place, and a subsequent visit to the D. & D. building. Her heart lifted as it always did on such a day, at the pleasure and energy the city was charged with.

Waiting to cross the street, gazing idly into the hooting, restless cars, she suddenly realized she was gazing into a yellow cab, at an oddly familiar head. A golden head, a large broad back, that was all she could see, for its owner was totally engaged in kissing the other occupant of the cab. But as it suddenly lurched forward, he pulled away laughing and lay back against the seat, and she could see him properly, and of course it was Baby. And the other person, blonde chaos of curls fanned across his outspread arm, green eyes laughing into his, was Angie.

'Baby, I really have to see you urgently.'

'Virgy darling, not today.'

'Yes today. This evening. At the house.'

'Virginia, I can't. I'm terribly busy. I have a huge deal going through, and I'm a little behind on the paperwork.'

'I'm not surprised. You should stay in the office over lunch, rather than taking taxi rides. Or have those business lunches that Mary Rose so approves of.'

Baby's prime emotion was one of relief. At last he could talk, without having to actually break his pact with himself.

'Ah,' he said.

'Yes. Baby, are you out of your head?'

'Virginia, you don't understand. You simply don't understand.'

'Well, you could try helping me along. I don't mind how late it is.'

'OK. But I'll have to make an excuse to Mary Rose.'

'Well,' she said briskly, 'I expect you've been getting fairly adept at that.'

He arrived at East 80th at seven, and poured himself a large bourbon.

'I thought you'd given that up.'

'Oh,' he said, 'only on the good days.' He realized there had been a lot of those lately, and smiled at her, half sheepish, half happy. 'Virginia, you have to let me explain. It isn't – well, it isn't like you think.'

'Baby, I know how it is. It always is. Oh, Baby, you're such a fool. Angie of all people.'

'Well,' he said, trying to sound lighthearted, 'of all people she seemed like the best to me.'

'I'm appalled at her, Baby, frankly. After all my – our kindness to her.'

'Maybe,' he said looking at her oddly, 'it was all the kindness, as you put it, that made her more likely to do it.'

'I don't know what you mean, Baby.'

'I mean that she gets a little tired of feeling grateful. Of having to be shown kindness. Here was a chance to make a move on her own account. Because – well, because – '

'You wanted her?'

'Yeah,' he said, slightly defensive. 'Yeah, because I wanted her. I have to tell you, Virginia, I do adore her.'

'Well of course you do. She young, and she's sassy, and she's – '

'Beautiful,' he said. 'You never told me how beautiful she was.'

'I didn't think it was necessary. Yes, she's beautiful. And totally immoral. Or amoral. Well, that's hardly the point. Baby, it's so dangerous. If you had to have an affair, why not someone completely separate from us all? In a different city? You're mad. What would Mary Rose make of it? And Dad?'

'Mary Rose is benefiting from it,' he said sadly. 'For the first time in years I'm able to be nice to her. I'm so happy.'

'I believe that's what they all say.'

He looked at her and finally found the courage to ask her something he had always longed to know.

'Virginia, have you ever – well – '

'Oh Baby, don't be ridiculous.' She was flushed, plainly angry; she lit a cigarette. 'How could I risk such a thing? I'm a high-profile lady, with a dynasty to found.'

'Yes, but – haven't you ever thought about it?'

'Oh, often,' said Virginia lightly.

He poured himself another drink, and sighed. 'Oh, Virginia, if only you knew how utterly different I feel. I'm so happy. I can work properly. I really really love her, you know. That's why it's so important. It isn't just an affair, just a few times in the sack, I love her.'

'Do you think she loves you?'

'I don't know. She says she does.'

'Baby, she's a tough little nut, you know. And fearsomely ambitious. Has it not occurred to you that she might be using you?'

109

Baby had a sudden vision of Angie, sitting stark naked in the big bed in the small apartment he had rented for her in the Village, her eyes soft with tenderness, and he felt a sharp hostility towards Virginia that he could never have imagined possible.

'You simply don't understand,' he said shortly.

'Perhaps you'd better try and make me. Tell me about it,' she said.

He had thought she was gorgeous, straight away. It wasn't just the exquisite face, the green eyes, the cascade of blonde hair, the oddly reckless, slightly rakish smile, nor the small neat body, nor even the way she exuded sex, or that she found him so clearly irresistible as well; nor was it her toughness, her courage, her way of taking life on the chin and hitting back at it. She was working for a fashionable young interior designer, having left her original mentor, a Mr Stern. She and Mr Stern had parted company, at her own instigation, she told him, when Mrs Stern, with whom he had recently been reconciled, became increasingly jealous and difficult about Angie's position in his firm and his life. 'And he was never going to see me as anything more than a secretary anyway. You have to keep moving on, I think, Baby. Certainly at my stage in life.' But what was primarily irresistible about her to Baby was her sense of fun. When he suggested, after their very first lunch, that they took a walk in the park, she said she'd rather ride round Central Park in one of the carriages; only she didn't sit in the passenger seat with him, she persuaded the driver (who told her she'd lose him his licence if he got caught) to let her sit alongside him. When they first went to bed together, she refused to be smuggled into a downtown brownstone; she dared him to take her to the Plaza, and book in as Mr and Mrs Smith. She said if he did, she'd do anything – 'and I mean anything' – he liked.

Then there was the time when she insisted he waited outside Macys, while she brought him three things he would like from the store without paying for them; and the time when she wore a black wig and dark glasses and walked into a restaurant and pretended not to know him when he sat down beside her, and everyone was staring and finally she called the manager and poor Baby had ended up not feeling really quite sure himself who she was. And the night she had given him a list of things to collect before she would agree to have dinner with him, 'A kind of treasure hunt, Baby, I'm sure you played it lots of times in your over-privileged childhood'; the list had included a packet of Tampax, a blow-up lady and two tickets for *Hair*; and the occasion when she said they would have a competition 'To see which of us could think of more positions to fuck in, and the loser has to do the one the winner likes best.'

And practically every time he met her, she had some new idea, a game to play; and every time he found her more irresistible, and he loved her more.

The other thing he found irresistible was the way she thought he was wonderful. Nine years of marriage to Mary Rose had been demoralizing to Baby; nine hours into the affair with Angie had restored his self-esteem, made him feel clever, powerful, sexy, funny again. And that was heady stuff.

The affair had begun slowly; he had seen her to the small hotel Virginia had recommended, near Gramercy Park, taken her for a drink the next evening, made sure she had made contact with M. Wetherly, driven her out to Long Island to spend a spring Sunday with Fred and Betsey. He had been slightly uncomfortably aware of her sexuality, and, more beguilingly still, of her awareness of his, and they had flirted easily and almost thoughtlessly through the day (to Mary Rose's irritation but no more – although from then on she always referred to Angie as 'that little English girl', her frosty tone inserting a silent but clearly heard 'common' between 'that' and 'little'). Angie went her way, found her niche in New York, and it was autumn before he bumped into her again, quite literally, at the Thanksgiving Day Parade. He had taken Freddy, greatly against Mary Rose's wishes, who said Freddy would be able to see everything much better from the Morgans' balcony at the top of Park Avenue, but Baby said there was nothing like being on the street and he took Freddy down Broadway, and stood with him on his shoulders in Times Square, and they were craning their necks, looking up at Snow White and the Seven Dwarfs, when a voice said, 'One more step and I'll be dead'; and he had looked behind him and seen Angie, wearing jeans and a check jacket, a red scarf round her neck, her hair tied in a pony tail, laughing but half afraid of being trampled by him, and he had said, 'I'm terribly sorry,' and then recognizing her, 'It's Angie, isn't it, how are you?'

Angie said she was fine, and wasn't the parade wonderful, the best fun she'd had in New York yet, which was saying something, and Baby asked her what she was doing for the rest of the day and she said spending it with herself, and he said that was terrible, why didn't she join him and his family at the Praegers' house on East 80th Street. Angie said that would be wonderful, and she'd love to, but she should go home and change; Baby said fine and to arrive at the house any time after two. Angie turned up looking devastating in a red jersey mini dress and white boots; Mary Rose was very cool to her, but Betsey was delighted to have her at Thanksgiving dinner, and Fred III flirted with her so outrageously that Baby couldn't get so much as a wink in edgeways. Which was

111

possibly why, as he drove her home that night, he felt compelled to make it plain that he would have been flirting too, had his father allowed it, and one thing led to another and he found himself kissing her rather hard and the next day they had lunch together and that was that.

'And don't even ask me where it's going to end, because I don't have the faintest idea,' he finished, looking at Virginia with an oddly vulnerable expression. 'And you have to promise me not to tell anyone, Virgy. Scout's honour?'

'Oh for God's sake,' said Virginia, 'what do you think I'm going to do, call Cholly Knickerbocker? Of course I won't tell anyone. I just fear for you, Baby, that's all.'

'Don't,' said Baby, 'I can look after myself.'

Angie came to see him straight from a meeting called by Virginia three days later. She was in a very odd mood.

'She acts like she was still my boss, Baby. I don't like it.'

'You're being over-sensitive,' said Baby soothingly.

'I'm not. She said straight away how she'd seen me in the taxi with you, and she wished she hadn't; and then went into a lecture about you being married and everything. As if I didn't know. And then she went into this great spiel about how kind your family had all been to me. So I told her a few things.'

'What kind of things?' said Baby nervously.

'Oh – true kind of things. Like yes, you'd all been kind to me, helping a poor little girl from nowhere, showing how good you were. And like it wasn't entirely one-sided, that I'd worked my butt off for her, and covered up when she was drinking and been pretty bloody loyal. Oh and I pointed out that I was quite easy to be kind to. I said I might be a bit common, but that I didn't have cross eyes or anything, and I said please and thank you, and I wasn't exactly stupid. And then she said she hadn't meant it like that, but she was upset, that you had a difficult marriage, and I wasn't helping it. So I said I thought I was helping, that you'd said even fucking Mary Rose was easier these days.'

Baby felt slightly sick suddenly. 'Angie, I think that was going a little far. Discussing things in quite such detail.'

'I think *she* was going a little far. Anyway, she went a bit quiet, and then she just said she would like to appeal to me to give you up, that if your father knew he'd break you. And she said she hoped I didn't think you were about to leave Mary Rose for me, that Praegers didn't leave their wives. What she meant was they didn't leave them for the likes of me.'

'So what did you say?'

'I said I couldn't give you up,' she said, kissing him. 'I said all I knew was that right now we were having a great time, and I really cared about you, and you really cared about me. And then she said you'd get over it, if I moved out, and I said I didn't want you to get over it. And then I left. I quite enjoyed it all really,' she added. 'Much more than she did.'

Baby looked at her; she was wearing a black silk shirt and a gold bracelet he had given her, and some Chanel earrings, and she looked very expensive and sophisticated.

'Well,' he said, 'I expect Virginia saw some changes in you.'

'Yes, I expect she did,' said Angie happily.

That was a heady summer for Baby. It wasn't just that he was happy with Angie, or even that his marriage ironically was improved; he appeared to have recovered his place in the sun on Pine Street. This was not entirely due to a greater diligence, or even an improved skill on his part. There was a booming economy in the late sixties, albeit against an appalling background of war, violence and political unrest; the year before, as the cost of the war in Vietnam rose towards $21 billion, the stock market had touched 1,000 for the first time, and there was so much trading on the Exchange that an almost unsupportable burden was placed within its unmechanized confines. People working in the back office – the department where the paperwork and follow-through of all the business was dealt with, known in the trade as grunt work – were frequently at their desks round the clock. At one time the Exchange was closed on Wednesdays, simply to enable people to catch up; two o'clock closing became the norm for a while.

There were two reasons for this: one was that a lot of small companies were expanding, and the other was that there was a huge public interest in securities; the joe in the street was buying stock at undreamed-of levels. The smell of money was mouthwateringly in the air; it was up for grabs, and everyone was grabbing. Even some of the bulge-bracket firms, people like Merrill Lynch and D. H. Blair, had retail clients. Praegers had a great many. One leading broker, Charles Plohn, came out with so many issues he was known on the street as One a Day Charlie. As a cause – or as many argued a result – P.E. Multiples were at an all-time high. What that meant to the joe on the street was that the return on the stock he bought went roaring up as the firms prospered, and it was rated and re-rated in the extremely bullish markets. The fact that much of it was high-risk stock and its price was related to perceived value and sheer numbers rather than actual performance, and that in a more bearish market it might become less attractive and be re-rated downwardly, was not given a great deal of attention. Despite – maybe even because of – the stormy background to life, people seemed to be living totally for today; tomorrow was left to worry about itself.

Many of Baby's corporate clients were therefore making a great deal of money that summer as he advised them, with apparently consummate skill, on buying here, selling there. Clement Dudley floated a new company marketing magazines and books solely for the under twenty-fives called Upbeat; the flotation was what he described to Baby as a 101 per cent success, and the launch issue of the flagship magazine, *Pop*, a fashion and music weekly, was a sell-out. One group of local newspapers in the South trebled its investment capital; a small television network in need of finance saw an issue he advised on over-subscribed four times. Fred III, dining one night with the chairman of Gloucester Books, the hugely prestigious house specializing in superbly researched, glossily packaged art books, heard that Baby had masterminded the finance of a new and slightly more commercial venture than Gloucester had been involved with in the past, art books for schools, using stock to finance part of the deal, and savoured the somewhat unusual experience of basking in his son's reflected glory.

Typically, it was from his mother that Baby learnt of Fred's pride and pleasure. And that once again Fred was talking about retiring and leaving Praegers in a spirit of confidence and even optimism.

Baby, reporting this to Angie in bed that evening, after some extremely pleasurable sex, felt suddenly and gloriously inviolate.

In August, Angie was summoned to England. Mr Wicks was dying; he had finally been taken to hospital, haemorrhaging from both lungs, and the doctor had said it would be a miracle if he survived more than two days. He actually managed three, and he told Angie, clutching at her arm with his thin, shaking fingers, he would have waited three months to say goodbye to her. Angie sat and held Mrs Wicks's hand and watched him drift comparatively painlessly out of life, and thought of all the times he had covered up for her when her mother was cross with her, and had chuckled and told her she was a caution, and the way he had pinned up pictures of her right round the fireplace and never let Mrs Wicks take them down, and the tears blurred her vision of him so badly that she was hardly aware that his head finally lolled helplessly and suddenly to one side.

'He's gone,' said Mrs Wicks matter-of-factly, drawing her hand away from Angie's and proffering her rather grubby handkerchief. 'Here, girl, blow your nose, you look dreadful, great gob of snot hanging down, thank God he couldn't see you, fine vision to take away with him.' And then she burst into tears herself, and Angie sat holding her, breathing in the familiar smell of cigarette smoke and cheap hairspray and cheaper perfume, and wondering whatever would become of her gran now.

The funeral was actually a rather jolly affair; Angie, describing it to Baby later, made it sound a lot more fun than most of Mary Rose's supposed celebrations. All Mr Wicks's friends from the Lamb and Flag got together and organized a wake, and Angie suggested to Mrs Wicks that they should have a brass band following the hearse. Mrs Wicks had protested at the idea at first, and then suddenly caved in and said yes, it might brighten things up a bit, and it had been Mr Wicks's favourite sort of music. Johnny and Dee had sent a wreath which was elaborate even for Bermondsey (Angie explained to Baby that funerals were big events in Bermondsey, their cost usually out of all proportion to a family's income) with the letters GRANDAD twelve inches high, which stood upright on top of the coffin; Mrs Wicks had been quite overwhelmed by this and told Johnny she felt like the Queen, standing by it in the church. Johnny and Dee had also booked the best room at the Lamb and Flag and organized a slap-up lunch with beer by the barrel-load; Dee told Mrs Wicks not to worry, her dad had sent a cheque, and said as he couldn't be there himself, owing to not being too welcome with the authorities, it was the least he could do.

At least two hundred people had come to the church, and a hundred of them arrived at the Lamb and Flag; after lunch and a very nice speech from the captain of the darts team, who said he was sure old Alfred was scoring triples up there even as he spoke, the serious drinking began, and later the brass band started up again, and as they refreshed themselves between numbers Jack Hastings, who had been in the trenches with Mr Wicks ('World War One, that was,' said Angie, 'can you imagine, still alive'), took to the piano and there were some rousing choruses of 'Tipperary', and 'Show Me the Way to Go Home', and it was after eleven when the last group of mourners had finally departed, leaving Mrs Wicks flushed, tearful, and very happy. Johnny and Dee and Angie had taken her back to the little house and put her to bed, and then sat downstairs by the fire, in the spot where Mr Wicks had spent so many years, and talked quietly about what was to become of her.

'Well, we can't have her,' said Johnny, 'we haven't the room, and anyway, things aren't too settled are they, Dee?'

'Not really,' said Dee, looking at him with the resigned adoration she always did, adding (emboldened by the many glasses of Dubonnet and bitter lemon she had drunk) that she could remember it being worse, 'but we haven't got the room, it's true.'

They had both looked at Angie, who pointed out very firmly that

she couldn't possibly have her gran in New York, it was out of the
question –

'Why not?' said Baby innocently when she told him about it later. 'She
sounds like a fun old lady.'

Angie simply told him firmly that Mrs Wicks would not have
considered moving to New York, that she'd loathe it, that all her friends,
or those that were still alive, would be left behind.

'I think you should maybe try to do something for her,' said Baby,
'she's been very good to you, hasn't she? More of a mother than your
mother, you said.'

'Oh Baby,' said Angie, 'I say a lot of things. I don't know how you
remember half of them.'

'I love you,' said Baby, 'I find it quite easy to remember what you say.'

Angie leant forward and kissed him. 'Love you too. And – yes, you're
right, she was, she was very good to me. And of course I would like to do
something. But how can I? I can't spare any money.'

Baby looked at her. Her eyes were soft, her expression wistful. For
what must have been the thousandth time, he wondered quite what he
had done to have deserved her, and how he was going to keep her. There
was a silence. 'I could spare some money,' he said, 'I'd really like to think
your grandma was comfortable and you didn't have any worries about
her. If it would help, you find some nice place to settle her into, Angie,
and I'll pick up the bill. I feel a kind of debt to anyone who's looked after
you.'

'No, Baby,' said Angie, very firmly. 'I really really couldn't let you.
We're an independent lot, we Wicks, and besides, it really is not your
problem.'

'Your problems are mine,' said Baby, 'and I kind of like trying to crack
them.'

There was a silence. Angie looked at him very solemnly. Then she
smiled, her sweetest, softest little-girl smile. 'Oh Baby,' she said, 'how
can I ever ever repay what you do for me?'

'I can think of a few ways,' said Baby, his hand reaching down into the
soft moistness between her legs, 'one very simple down payment you
could make right this minute.'

What ensued was one of Angie's more imaginative pieces of lovemaking; Baby never opened a bill from the very nice private rest home in
Bournemouth where Mrs Wicks became a permanent resident, without
remembering it with a stab of almost violent pleasure.

The event in question had actually taken place on the stairs of the
Caterham house in Eaton Place; Baby had rung Virginia at Hartest the

day Angie had flown to London and begged her to let him borrow it for the weekend.

'I have to be in London anyway. Business. Just for a few days before we come and stay with you.'

With some reservations he had agreed to Mary Rose's slightly pressing suggestion the family spend a few weeks of the summer at Hartest.

'How convenient for you. Baby, no. You can't have the house. Especially if it's for you to disport yourself in with Angie.'

'Oh, Virgy, please. It's so much safer than a hotel – '

'Why?'

'Well because there's no stupid staff there who might give Mary Rose misleading messages – '

'Misleading! Really, Baby.'

'Well you know what I mean. She always has to have the hotel number and the room number, and – '

'I wonder why. No, it's out of the question. I couldn't do it to her. I do have some sense of family loyalty. And I wouldn't be able to look her in the face when you all got here. Besides there are no staff there, stupid or otherwise. It's August. You'd have to do everything yourselves. And clear up after yourselves.'

'What about family loyalty to me? And clearing up, playing house'd be fun.'

'Oh sure. I somehow don't see you cleaning the bath out, Baby, or changing the sheets. Or Angie for that matter.'

'I'll hire someone to come in and do it. Please, Virginia, it would be so great.'

'No, Baby, really. I can't let you. Besides, whatever would Alexander say if he knew? He'd go crazy.'

'Well he wouldn't know. Would he? I just have this wonderful wonderful idea of me and Angie, alone and completely safe, in our own little private universe. For just forty-eight hours. It isn't such a lot to ask.'

'Baby, I do think you should be a little more wary of Angie. I've told you before, she's such a tough, clever little thing. You seem to have built her up into something between Helen of Troy and Ella Wheeler Wilcox.'

'No, I haven't,' he said, and he was horribly aware of a tremor in his voice, 'I just love her, that's all.'

'But Baby, you know nothing can come of it. Ever. And you must know how frightened I am for you both. It's so horribly dangerous and – and stupid, what you're doing.'

'Oh, I know,' he said, his voice low and remorseful, 'but we really are trying to work something out. Really. This would be – well possibly our last proper time together. Please, Virginia. I wish you could see me, I'm on my knees here.'

'Well – ' she said, and he could hear her trying not to laugh, trying not to give in, knowing that he had, as always, managed to make her do what he wanted. 'Well, I still don't see why it should make such a difference. But if you really really want it – '

'I do.'

'Oh, all right. I'll leave the key with the agency who keep an eye on it during August. I'll tell them you're going to pick it up – when?'

'On Thursday. Virginia, I adore you.'

'Baby,' said Virginia briskly, 'you know you really should think about growing up.'

'I'd really rather not,' he said.

It was a very happy forty-eight hours. Angie, over-excited at finding herself suddenly, albeit briefly, the mistress of her previous employer's house, took it upon herself to bestow pleasure upon Baby in as many rooms and corners of it as possible. The especially memorable episode on the stairs took place on the Sunday afternoon; they had just consumed most of a bottle of champagne and a pound and a half of strawberries in the huge bed in the master bedroom; the glasses and the large, spider-like stalks of the strawberries lay on the pillows, the bottle which Baby had knocked over in a sudden excessive need to kiss Angie's stomach and thighs was dripping steadily onto the extremely valuable Indian carpet.

'We have to start clearing this place up soon,' Baby had said, looking rather apprehensively around him. 'I promised Virgy we would.'

'I'll clear it up later,' said Angie, kissing him, 'I'm terribly good at housework. And you know you like watching me while I do it. Now, Baby darling, we've done the drawing room and the dining room and the kitchen and two of the bathrooms, and lots of bedrooms: time for the stairs.'

Baby looked at her; she was flushed, and her blonde curls were in a tangle on her shoulders; her green eyes were very bright. They were both naked; he put out his hand to caress her hair, and she leant down and kissed him gently, and then sat back, smiling, her eyes on his penis, already obediently, tremulously erect.

'I'm surprised,' she said, bending to kiss that too. 'I'm surprised you can still manage that, Baby. After such a very active weekend. You really are a remarkable man. Come with me, I have a nice idea for the rest of the afternoon.'

She took his hand and slithered off the bed; he followed her obediently, watching, with what was almost an ache in his heart, her neat, muscley little buttocks, her slender, graceful legs. They reached the top of the stairs, and she turned, smiling at him.

'Halfway, I think,' she said, 'like the Duke of York. You know about the Duke of York, don't you, Baby?'

Baby said he didn't.

'Well when he was up, he was up. Like you,' she added, sinking to her knees, taking his penis in her mouth, caressing it gently, rhythmically, with her tongue; he could feel the pulling, the working of it, and closed his eyes, groaning aloud. One of the things Angie had taught him was not to mind making a noise when they were having sex; Mary Rose conducted the whole thing in a kind of almost church-like silence.

She rose suddenly, stood right up, pulled his head down to her and kissed him very hard; he could taste himself, salty, earthy, in her mouth.

'And when he was down he was down,' she added, after a while, 'and when he was only halfway up, he was neither up nor down. Let's rewrite the script, Baby.'

She led him downstairs, to where the stairs curved in the half landing, pushed him down, kissing him again, her hands on his stomach, his thighs, his balls. He groaned again, reached out desperately for her; she pushed his hands away, behind him, made him lean back. He felt his penis aching, yearning for her; to be in her, in her warmth, her tightness, her wetness, her soft, tumescent hunger. Slowly, with infinite gentleness, she turned her back to him, presenting him with her arse, moving over him, onto him; then more slowly still, urged him, soothed him, welcomed him in. He felt the familiar, melting softness, the flow of her own pleasure; felt her moving, tenderly, quietly at first, then as always in a gathering greed. He cried out, sat up sharply, put his arms around her waist, clutching her to him, feeling his penis reaching further and further into her, exploring her, seeking her out, loving her, having her, part of her, making her part of himself, and then soon, so often it was too soon, in a great surge, a rush, a waterfall of release, he felt his orgasm, and her own, as it always seemed to do, falling onto his, in sweet, soft, thrusting spasms; and afterwards, they lay there for a long time, she above him, her head turned backwards towards him, her hair splayed across his chest, holding his hand, and he listened to her saying over and over again, 'Baby, that was so good, just so good,' and thought that never, even in a life that had known a great deal of pleasure, had he known any so intense and so joyous as that.

Twelve hours later, she left; to return to New York. She had not, after all, done anything about tidying up the house. She had offered, but she had been sad, and seemed tired; Baby told her to forget it, that he would get an army of cleaners in in the morning. He fed her raspberry ice cream in the kitchen, washed down with the rest of the champagne, and they sat in the drawing room with the shutters closed, and watched a very bad play on television. Halfway through it Mary Rose phoned; Baby took the call in Alexander's study, where he felt he might at the same time manage to sound comparatively level and normal, and spare Angie the pain of hearing him tell Mary Rose he was looking forward to seeing her at the airport three days later. He found the prospect so dreadful that the slight headache the champagne had given him deepened into thick, almost sickening pain.

They slept together, in a different, clean bedroom, that night, and did not make love; Baby awoke holding Angie so tightly she was struggling, half frightened, to be free. He found with some embarrassment that he had tears flowing down his cheeks; when she left, they flowed again. He realized then that he had not, whatever he might have thought, experienced love before.

He spent most of the two weeks at Hartest trying to talk to Virginia about Angie; he became increasingly aware that she was not over-receptive to his soul baring. Mary Rose had been working on a book on eighteenth-century paintings and had taken herself off a great deal to galleries and houses all over the country; he had expressed his earnest intention to keep all the children happy and amused, but in fact he neglected them hopelessly, so that the burden fell on Virginia and Nanny. The children were all difficult in their different ways; Kendrick and Georgina both possessed an awe-inspiring capacity to throw temper tantrums over something as minuscule as the relative brownness or otherwise of their boiled eggs at breakfast; Charlotte spent most of the time showing off on her new pony, deliberately making Freddy look a wimp, and making everyone fear for her limbs, and Freddy suffered an endless series of what his mother called sick headaches, and what the other children called making a fuss. Only Max was no trouble, sitting placidly in his playpen hour after hour, but even he developed a tummy bug towards the end of August; Nanny, as Charlotte remarked, was getting what she called very bristy.

Alexander kept well clear of everybody, and was out on the farm most of the time; they were short of hands, he said, and it was harvest time. He came home exhausted every evening, very short-tempered, and fell asleep over the dinner table.

'I'm very fond of your brother,' Baby heard him say to Virginia, in the library late one night, when he came back down the stairs in search of a last brandy and soda, 'but please don't ask them all to stay here together again. I don't think I could stand it.'

'They're my family, Alexander,' said Virginia. 'And I love them. And this is my home as well as yours and right now they need me. Quite apart from that, I need them.'

'Well I need you too,' he said, 'and I think my claim is a little stronger.'

Baby slipped back up the stairs, not wishing to be embarrassed any further and not quite sure why he found this exchange so oddly sinister.

Chapter 7

Baby, 1969–70

Just after that Christmas, Mary Rose had announced that she would like to have a summer house of their own. After a month of intensive searching, during the course of which she had examined with typical and laudatory thoroughness no fewer than thirty-seven houses, she announced she had found exactly the right one, on Nantucket. It had all the advantages of Long Island, she said, without being Long Island, the same white beaches, peace and quiet, a leisurely pace of life and charming mainly nineteenth-century houses, reminiscent of those in the Hamptons. The house she wished to purchase was at Siasconset, and was, she said, an overgrown cottage.

'Sconset, as they call it, is delightful, Baby, originally an artists' colony. The beach is beautiful, I know you'll like it. I said we would take a trip there next weekend, stay over on the Saturday. We can show it to the children. It will be so good for them to be there, so away from the pressure of city life. Most of the people travel around by bike, it's extremely peaceful and safe, and there's even a children's drama festival in August. I feel absolutely confident that it's the house for us, and we're very lucky to have the opportunity to buy it. I have actually negotiated a very good price. Houses on Nantucket very seldom come up, especially at Sconset. I have told the agent your visiting it is largely a formality.'

'Well in that case,' said Baby, unusually irritable after a particularly bad day with Fred, 'is there any point my visiting it at all? Why don't you just go ahead and buy the damn thing? You've obviously made up your mind about it.'

'Oh, Baby, don't be ridiculous,' said Mary Rose, 'this is a family house, and it must be a family decision.'

'Of course,' said Baby.

In fact he did very much like not only Nantucket, but the house. It was called Shells, and seemed just a little more than an overgrown cottage, having six bedrooms, a huge kitchen, a dining room, a living room and a den, but it was charming, low and white, built in stone and cedar tiles, like so many of the houses on Long Island, and it had a big garden with a play house and a swing hanging from a tall cedar tree, and a large porch, big enough for a family dining table, with a rose-covered trellis, overlooking the shore.

They spent the whole of August there, together with the children's nurse and a steady stream of visitors. There were rather more of their New York friends there than Baby had anticipated, which he actually liked; it made for more action and more fun. Fred and Betsey came and were particularly delighted with it; there was a golf course just along the Milestone Road, and a children's course at J. J. Clamps's just along from there which, Fred pointed out with some malice to Mary Rose, would suit Charlotte and him just fine. Towards the end of August, Virginia and Alexander and the children came; Baby was surprised to see Alexander, having heard his views the previous summer on holidays with Virginia's family, but Virginia explained rather vaguely that Alexander wanted them to be all together. There was something faintly unsatisfactory about her explanation; Baby wondered if and when he might hear a more likely one.

While the Caterhams were there, Fred and Betsey came back for a long weekend; the resultant family tensions were considerable. Charlotte ran to her grandfather's side the moment he arrived and never left it. They were like sweethearts, Betsey said slightly plaintively, and it was true; they sailed, walked and played golf and tennis together, sat next to each other at meals, shared little jokes and generally shut the rest of the world out.

On the Monday evening, before Fred and Betsey left for New York, the four older children were allowed to stay up for dinner; afterwards, inevitably, Fred told Baby to play while he and Charlotte did 'You're the Tops'.

'I don't think so,' said Baby. He was quite drunk; he was quite drunk every night. Fred looked at him sharply.

'I'll play,' said Virginia quickly. 'Baby's tired.'

The performance was charming; but Betsey and Virginia were the only enthusiastic applauders. Baby was half asleep, Alexander was looking embarrassed, Freddy was slumped in a chair playing solitaire, Kendrick and Georgina had sloped off to the kitchen in search of extra ice cream, and Mary Rose was trying to conceal her distaste for the proceedings, clapping limply while smiling icily at the performers.

'Very good,' she said when they had finished. 'But I'm surprised you haven't learnt a new number by now, Charlotte. Don't you go to your dancing classes any more?'

'Oh yes,' said Charlotte, 'but I don't have a partner to practise any new numbers with. Well, not a decent one.'

Fred III smiled at her, and pulled her onto his knee.

123

'That's my girl,' he said. 'A good partner's everything. That's what Ginger used to say.'

There was a silence; it was broken by the sound of Baby snoring. Fred looked at him with distaste.

'Baby,' said Mary Rose, in a voice that was quiet, yet piercing enough to splinter glass, 'Baby, could we all have some more to drink, please.'

Baby woke up and shambled out to the kitchen; Betsey looked distressed.

'I think he's probably had enough to drink already,' she said.

'Oh, he's all right,' said Fred, ever contrary. 'He drinks a lot, but he knows when to stop.'

He looked briefly at Virginia; there was an uneasy silence.

'I think,' she said, feeling the tears stinging behind her eyes, 'I think if you'll excuse me, I might go up to bed. I'm terribly tired. Max had me up at half past five this morning, singing nursery songs.'

'Of course, dear,' said Betsey, 'you do look tired. Freddy, will you come over here and show me what you're doing?'

'I can't make it come out,' said Freddy, showing her the solitaire. There were five solitary marbles impossibly far apart.

'Hey, that's not very clever,' said Fred. 'Charlotte can do that in a trice, can't you, honey? Show Freddy how you do it.'

Charlotte took the solitaire board from Freddy, smiling at him rather complacently as she put the marbles back in position.

'It isn't very difficult,' she said, 'look.'

Sixty seconds later she had reduced the board to one solitary marble, positioned dead centre. Fred III was smiling triumphantly. 'Isn't that just something? She showed me that this morning. Charlotte honey, would you share your secret with me?'

'Only if you promise to play golf with me in the morning.'

'I will. I promise.'

Mary Rose looked as if she might be sick.

Sometimes, Virginia thought as she went out of the room, sometimes she could actually sympathize with her.

Alexander did not behave well either. He was plainly and painfully bored. He didn't like sailing, he didn't like Baby and Mary Rose's friends – rich, clannish, painstakingly Old Money, the wives as earnestly cultured, as painfully devoted to their roles as Mary Rose, the men an uncomfortable blend of ferocious ambition and locker-room camaraderie; they all moved through the days together, in a close-knit, rather self-conscious group, arranging the next day's sailing and tennis and drinking before they parted each night as if in terror of a day's solitude.

He spent much of the time mooching around or swimming on his own or with Georgina, patently very much his favourite, and refusing to take any of the other children with him, saying it was too much of a responsibility, and that in his opinion there should be one adult to each child in the sea.

Virginia announced that she had to go to New York. 'And then on to Long Island,' she said to Alexander over supper. 'There's a problem on that cottage at Sag Harbor. I'll be gone the rest of the week. Is that all right?'

'Not really,' he said, looking at her oddly, 'but I suppose it will have to be.'

'Yes, Alexander, it will.'

Left without Virginia, Baby felt oddly lonely. He suddenly realized how much he was missing Angie. And he was worried about her on her own in New York. She had been to England to visit Mrs Wicks, and she and Suze had been on holiday in France, which he had paid for, glad to be able to rid himself of some of the guilt he felt at enjoying the time with his family; now she was back in the city.

'I'll have to get back to work by then, Baby. It'll only be a week before you get back, and then we can have the most wonderful, noisy, exhausting reunion. Don't worry about me, I'll be fine.'

'I can't help worrying about you, Angie. You seem very vulnerable to me. I don't quite know why.'

'I don't know why either,' said Angie.

Friday was a perfect morning, mistily golden, the sun forcing its way determinedly through onto the just-blue sea. It was clearly going to be very hot. Baby woke up early, found himself feeling more optimistic and calm than he had done for almost the whole of the past month, and decided to go for a swim. The children were all up and in the kitchen, being fed by the harassed nurse; Freddy and Charlotte demanded to be allowed to go with him.

'Sure,' said Baby good-naturedly. 'I'd be glad of the company.'

Freddy was good at swimming; it was the one thing he could beat Charlotte at. The surf was quite big, and there was a strong undertow to the waves.

'Be careful,' Baby warned them, 'don't go out of your depth.'

Charlotte rather uncharacteristically did what she was told, but Freddy swam out, bobbing over the breakers, diving under them, riding in on them, laughing with pleasure. Baby's heart contracted with love as he looked at him; whatever he had to endure at Fred's hands, at Mary Rose's, it was worth it, to see the children happy, to know Freddy's future was safe.

Later, they sat on the deck, wrapped in huge towels, drinking hot chocolate. Alexander had appeared, smiling. He seemed better humoured than he had done for weeks.

'Virginia just phoned. She'll be out here first thing tomorrow.'

'She all right?'

'Yes of course she's all right. Why shouldn't she be?'

'Oh – I – just wondered,' said Baby. 'She was looking a little pale.'

'She's fine,' said Alexander shortly. Then he appeared to pull himself together again. 'I'm going for a bike ride. Anyone want to come with me?'

'I would,' said Baby, 'but I'm bushed with that swim. You kids want to go?'

'I will,' said Charlotte. 'OK, Daddy?'

'Of course. Go and get dressed.'

Baby looked after him curiously as they set off, Alexander in front, laughing over his shoulder at Charlotte, wobbling wildly on her bike. He really was odd, so buttoned up and tense most of the time, so difficult to talk to. Maybe it was being English.

Baby sighed and settled himself on the deck, throwing off the towel, stretching out his long legs in the warm sun. Only three more days of this, then back to New York. And Angie. Life, he thought, as he relaxed into a sleepy, warm, half-suspended state, was still pretty good.

Later he swam again. Then he went to the tennis club, played three sets of tennis, and chatted to his friends over a couple of sodas rather than beer: aware as he did so that he was trying to get himself into prime condition for Monday and Angie. The thought of Angie, so near in time now, made him frantic for her; in an attempt to soothe his hungry senses, he stopped worrying about his health, drank the best part of a bottle of Californian Chardonnay with a very late lunch, and lay down in the hammock in the back yard, confused and conflicting images of Angie's small neat body bobbing in the waves as Freddy's had done that morning. He put a sunhat over his shorts, in case anyone might notice the enormous erections these visions were responsible for, and drifted off to sleep.

He was awoken by the phone ringing. It was Fred.

'Get back into New York will you, Baby, right away. I do mean right away.'

The dreadful, ghastly terror that it was something to do with the bank, some dreadful, crass thing that he had done: the sensation of dropping into a great white vacuum of panic. And then an almost worse horror at Fred's next words, in his most icy, contemptuous tones.

'You're a cheat, Baby. A cheat as well as a fool. Does Mary Rose have any idea what kind of a skunk she's married to? After all she's done for you.' And then the dreadful, fiercer panic as he realized it was Angie Fred was talking about, him and Angie, that he knew, that someone had told him. And then, as he was hastily throwing some things into a bag, trying to think of some reason he could give Mary Rose for needing to get back to New York at three on a Friday afternoon, Virginia on the phone, her voice thick with tears and pain, to say it was she who had told Fred, she he must blame.

'But I had to, Baby, I simply had to, you've got to understand, I'll explain when I see you. I'll meet you at Grand Central. Oh, Baby, I'm so sorry, so terribly terribly sorry.'

And then the long journey into the city, fretting and fuming on the ferry, feeling so physically sick on the train that he spent half the journey in the rest room, sitting on the toilet, his head in his hands, arriving at Grand Central finally as New York fell into dusk, still almost unbearably hot and humid; Virginia was there at the station, ashen, her lips oddly as white as the rest of her face. She was in Fred's car with Hudson at the wheel, and Baby sat away from her in the back seat, his hostility and his nausea growing, listening while she told him what had happened; someone on Cholly Knickerbocker's column had called Betsey just before lunch and asked for Fred III. 'And of course Mother said he wasn't there, he was in the office, and this guy said he would try again there, but he'd been out just earlier, and he was very anxious to get hold of him. And Mother said why, and he said well, he didn't know if she had heard any of the stories that you were running around town with an English girl half your age, who used to work for me. And Mother said obviously, of course not, that it was total nonsense, and where on earth had this story come from, and the man said from a good friend of Fred Praeger Senior, and could Mother have Dad call him right away after he got in from the office so he could check it out. And well, Baby, that was what panicked me, both of us, that Dad was going to find out, either from a friend or this journalist. And he so obviously had the story 100 per cent right, all the details, it wasn't some kind of stab in the dark, and we felt, Mother and I, that somehow we had to get to him before anyone else. To try and make him understand.'

'Well,' said Baby bitterly, 'you seem to have done a good job there. Virginia, for Christ's sake, why didn't you call me?'

'I did. I did call you. You were at the tennis club. Freddy said no one knew exactly when you'd be back. And then – well, I agreed with Mother

I should talk to Dad before the press got onto him, and I called his office and found out where he was having lunch, and went to meet him at the restaurant. Baby, don't look at me like that, time was running out, I just had to get to him.'

'Didn't you think of calling Angie?'

'Oh yes,' said Virginia, looking at him with the first glimmer of defensiveness, 'of course I did. She wasn't there. In the apartment.'

'Well of course she wasn't. She was at work.'

'No, Baby, she wasn't at work. They said she had called in sick two days ago.'

'Well –' Baby's face had gone, impossibly, even whiter. 'Well, I expect she's with a friend.'

'I expect she is.'

'So you just told him?'

'Yes.'

'All about it?'

'Well – some of it. Most of it. Yes. Yes, I did. I'm terribly, terribly sorry.'

'And you didn't even think to call Cholly Knickerbocker first?'

'Baby, there didn't seem a lot of point. You know what these people are like, the more you say, the deeper you get in. I thought Dad would probably be able to fix it, anyway.'

'Virginia, there are some things no one can fix. Not even Dad.'

'No. Well, maybe not.'

Fred tore into him. He told him he was spoilt, and self-indulgent as well as a fool; that he had no self-control, no dignity, that he was lucky that the story had not come out before; that he deserved none of the considerable advantages Fate had seen fit to send his way.

'I should disinherit you for this,' he said simply. 'Just throw you out. You don't deserve that wife of yours, your family, certainly you don't deserve Praegers.'

'Oh for Christ's sake,' said Baby, stung suddenly beyond endurance. 'You're being extremely naive. Do you really think I'm the only married man in New York City having an affair?'

'I'm not interested in all the others,' said Fred. 'You're my son, and I don't like scandal. You seem to me to be getting increasingly like your grandfather and it scares the hell out of me, Baby. It really does. I don't want to leave Praegers in the hands of an incompetent libertine. And if you must have an affair, you could at least choose some woman from your own class, someone who might employ a little discretion. Not some cheap girl who used to work for your own sister.'

'Please don't describe Angie as cheap,' said Baby. He was angry now, a flush rising in his waxily pale face.

'Of course she's cheap,' said Fred. 'And where is she anyway? I'd like to see her. I have a few words to say to her as well.'

'Look,' said Baby, 'I know you think you run this family. That we all do what you say – '

'Baby, I don't just think it. It's a fact,' said Fred briefly.

'Well, maybe. But the rest of the universe just may not be quite so impressed.' He felt sick as he said this: he had never stood up to his father in quite this way before. 'What makes you think Angie is going to do what you say?'

'She'll do what I say,' said Fred simply.

'I don't think she will. This isn't what you think. A quick fling. I love Angie. And she loves me.'

'Oh really? Well, we shall see. Where is she, anyway?'

'She's – out of town.'

'Well,' said Fred, 'I think we'd better get her back in, don't you?'

Angie arrived, very composed, after a three-day break 'with a girlfriend' in Florida. She was carefully dressed for the occasion in a very short but strangely modest-looking grey flannel dress with a white collar, her hair tied back with a black velvet ribbon; she sat with her hands in her lap, listening carefully to what Fred had to say, without even glancing in Baby's direction.

Fred's proposition was simple: she was not to have anything to do with Baby in the future, in any way whatsoever. She was not to talk to the press; she was not to talk to anybody. Those of her friends who knew about her relationship with Baby were simply to be told that Baby had terminated it.

'It would be better,' said Fred, 'if you left New York altogether; went back to England. What would you feel about that?'

'I'd hate it,' said Angie simply. 'I like it here. I like my job. I have – friends here. I don't like England any more.'

'Well, we shall see about that. I would be prepared to make it worth your while, if you were to go back there.'

Baby felt an outrage so violent it was a physical force, thrusting itself in the depths of his stomach. 'Dad!' he said. 'Don't talk to Angie like that. Don't.'

Fred looked at him. 'Why not?' he said quite mildly.

'Because she's not used to it. You. It's a fearful insult. Angie and I are – were – very deeply involved. You can't just – buy her off. I won't let you and she won't let you.'

Angie shot him an odd look. Then she turned to Fred again.

'So – what happens if I don't do what you say? If Baby and I were to decide to stay together.'

'Oh,' said Fred with great finality, 'oh, that's completely out of the question.'

'It is?'

'Completely.'

'Baby,' said Angie, 'what do you have to say about this?'

'Well,' said Baby, 'well I – '

'Good God,' said Angie, 'you're going along with it, aren't you? Doing what Daddy says. Like a good little boy. Poor Baby. Poor little defenceless Baby.'

'Angie,' said Baby, 'you don't understand.'

'Oh,' she said, 'I think I do.'

'No,' said Fred, 'not entirely. The thing is, Miss Burbank, if Baby's marriage ends, if this – relationship continues, then Baby loses his position at the bank.'

Angie stared at him, an incredulous expression in her green eyes. Then she half smiled at him.

'I don't believe it,' she said, 'you'd actually disinherit him, because he's been screwing around a bit! Mr Praeger, you really do need to come into the twentieth century, you know. It's archaic. It's absurd. Baby, you're not going to accept this, are you? I mean it doesn't even matter about me, but you really have to learn to stand up for yourself a bit.'

'Angie,' said Baby, and he spoke very quietly, and he didn't look at her, 'Angie, I have to accept it. I'm married to Mary Rose, and I have my future and, far more importantly, my son's future to consider. I can't put that at risk. I really can't.'

'So that's what the deal is, is it?' said Angie. 'You stay with Mary Rose and stop sleeping with me, and you keep the bank for yourself and Freddy. And if you don't? If you stand up for yourself, start behaving like a grown-up?'

'Then he doesn't keep the bank,' said Fred smoothly. 'I should change its share structure, pass the majority over to the partners.'

'You'd really do that?' Angie stared at him.

'Oh yes. Yes, I'd do it tomorrow. This family is very important to me. And Mary Rose has been magnificent, she is prepared to stand by Baby.'

'You mean she isn't prepared to go through a divorce? Well Baby, you really have sold out, haven't you? I suppose it's understandable really. You're what – nearly thirty-five now, aren't you? A bit late to start again, I suppose, to be poor, struggling, rejected. Without your beautiful houses and your fancy clothes, and people at every turn running round after you, doing your bidding. I suppose nothing could really compensate for that; certainly not me, it seems.'

She looked briefly at Baby, then coolly back at Fred.

'So what's in this deal for me?'

'Well,' said Fred, 'if you go back to England, I will settle – let's say, a hundred thousand dollars on you. So you can set up your own company. Buy yourself a house. Whatever you like. I don't really care. Naturally, it will come in stage payments; I wouldn't like to see you changing your mind the minute the cheque hit your bank account. If you decide to stay in New York, on the other hand, the – let's say, the backing – would be cut by half – fifty thousand. It really is up to you.'

'Oh Dad, don't,' said Baby wearily. 'You really can't buy people like this. Angie won't accept this kind of blackmail. She isn't one of your financial institutions. It's immoral, what you're proposing.'

'Do be quiet, Baby,' said Angie, quite politely, 'I think I have a right to decide here. I don't think your role in all this is particularly moral. As I see it, and in spite of all the things you've ever said to me, this whole thing has nothing to do with love. It's all about money.'

The pain Baby experienced was very bad. Very bad indeed. Apart from missing Angie almost beyond endurance, having to submit to Mary Rose's contemptuous forgiveness, and the knowledge that he had, as Angie had pointed out, sold out to his father entirely: apart from all that was the dreadful hurt that Angie had taken Fred's money, had been prepared to be bought off herself, coolly, cheerfully even, with not a backward glance at him, at their relationship. He knew it was illogical that he should feel this way, but what he had seen that morning, in those cool green eyes, heard in that clear amused little voice, opened his eyes to another Angie altogether, one he felt he had never known. And all the comfort, all the warmth, all the self-esteem their relationship had brought him was gone, taken from him, not easily and cleanly, but in a slow and horribly painful death.

For days, fearfully, the family opened the papers, scanned the gossip columns; nothing appeared, nothing at all.

'Do you think,' Virginia said wearily that morning to Baby in his office, 'do you think Dad did fix them? Stopped them running it?'

'No,' said Baby, and the expression in his eyes as he looked at her was nearer to dislike than anything she had ever seen from him. 'No I don't. I don't think he could have done. I begin to think it was all a terrible mistake. A hoax. Which you could have stopped, Virginia, if you'd been a little more careful, taken a little more time.'

'I'm sorry,' said Virginia, for the hundredth time, 'I keep telling you, I thought I was acting for the best. I'm so sorry, Baby, Mother was sure it was authentic. She had no doubt that the man was a reporter, that he spoke with a very thick Brooklyn accent. He said . . .'

'Oh sure,' said Baby bitterly, 'all newspaper men have Brooklyn accents, don't they? I mean that really clinches it.'

'Baby, I – '

'And on the strength of that one phone call, Virginia, you decided to rush in, where not an angel had so much as tiptoed, and talk to Dad about it. Without checking first. It was an insane thing to do. Insane. I just cannot understand you. OK, it had to end some time, but not so painfully, not so publicly.'

'I'm so sorry, so terribly terribly sorry,' said Virginia. She felt as if she was in some kind of nightmare: that any moment she would wake up. 'I just didn't think – well, all right it was rash. Ill-judged. I was wrong. I'm sorry.'

'I must say,' he said, 'I would not have believed it of you.'

Virginia looked at him for a long time, her eyes heavy and sad. Then: 'Baby,' she said, 'Baby, I did have your good at heart. I really did. I thought I could help.'

'Well,' he said, 'you didn't. You'd better get along and sort our your own affairs. I hope you make a better job of them.' He turned away from her.

It was months before he spoke to her again.

Chapter 8

Virginia, 1973

It had been Baby who had brought them together again; Virginia lacked the emotional chutzpah to force it through. She was awoken early one morning in London by his voice on the phone, loud and cheerful, forcing through her sleepiness. 'Darling, it's me. Baby. Look, I don't know about you, but I can't stand this any longer. Can we make up buddies?'

Making up buddies was an expression from their childhood; on the rare occasions when they quarrelled, usually as a result of Baby getting away with something that he should not have done, Virginia getting blamed, that was how it would end, with Baby coming to her, a silly expression on his face, waving a white handkerchief, and chanting, 'Truce! Pax! Make up buddies.' Virginia had always said then, 'I don't want to be buddies with you,' and he would protest and argue and win her round; that morning on the phone, struggling to sit up, laughing and crying at the same time she said, 'Oh Baby, yes, yes please.'

'Thank Christ,' he said and she realized he was drunk, that his words were slurring, that it was two in the morning in New York. 'That's great, Virgy. I guess I've been a little – stiff lately. Come and see me next time you're here, OK?'

'OK, Baby. And I guess you deserved to be – stiff. Where are you?'

'Oh, at home.' This was accompanied by much muffled laughter and spluttering.

'At home? Baby, you can't be.'

'Oh, but I am. Not my home, of course. Somewhere much nicer. A very lovely home indeed. With very lovely people. I have to go now, Virgy. See you soon. Take care.'

'You take care, Baby.'

That had been over a year ago, and since, they had been if anything closer than ever; the only unspoken rule between them being that they should never refer to Angie or her place in their past. It upset Baby and angered Virginia; it was best left.

'Well now,' he said. 'what can I do for you?'

'Baby, I've rung for advice. Well not for me. It's Alexander. He's got – financial problems. He wondered if he could come and talk to you.'

'Well – yes. Yes of course he could.' For Alexander to be prepared to discuss his financial problems with Baby was the equivalent of Baby discussing his sexual peccadillos with Alexander: a totally unlikely scenario.

'You don't sound very – enthusiastic.'

'Well, it's a difficult time. But Virgy, I'd love to help if I can. Really. Why don't you come and meet me for lunch – let's see, on Monday. I have a meeting with the bank's analysts I'm just desperate to cancel. Four Seasons at twelve thirty?'

'Thank you, Baby. That'd be wonderful.'

Baby was looking wonderful, she thought; well and happy. She hadn't seen him since Christmas. She stood up, smiling, as he approached the table; he gave her a hug, rather than kissing the air beside her head as their fellow lunchers were all doing to one another, and grinned back.

'You look great. I love that dress. And the hat's a peach.'

Virginia looked down at herself, smiling; she was wearing a beige silk dress with a slightly droopy hem, from Valentino, and a matching cloche hat. She had changed her look altogether, she seemed older, more sophisticated; her eyes were darkly smudged, and her lips were darkly, shinily plum-coloured. She could tell it was all not quite to Baby's taste – the all-American college girl look (epitomized, somewhat ironically, by Angie) – but he would like the stir she was causing. Baby liked attention. She was not only looking extremely glamorous, she was a big name in smart New York society these days, to the people who lunched at the Four Seasons, an important designer. Several people came over to their table to greet her, to establish their claim on her; she had revamped the enchanting Oxford Hotel in the Upper Eighties, made it look like a very smart, but very elegant private house, restrained but extremely luxurious, a blend of New York glamour and European chic, and it had received a great deal of publicity, been featured in *New York* magazine and *House and Garden*; now the owner, an oil-rich Texan of breathtaking vulgarity who nevertheless knew style when he saw it, had asked her to do three more hotels for him, in Los Angeles, Palm Beach and San Francisco.

'Well,' said Baby, 'so what's new? Tell me what the problem is with Alexander.'

The problem with Alexander was Hartest. Dry rot, Virginia said. Right through the building. 'It's going to cost at least six million pounds.'

'Well that's certainly some help he needs,' said Baby. 'I don't know. Things are bad here, you know. The recession is still hitting the stock market. A lot of people have lost a lot of money.'

'I don't suppose Dad has lost a lot of money.'

'No he hasn't. One jump ahead as always. Pulled some money out of the market, bought a lot of forestry land. For paper,' he added, seeing Virginia's puzzled face. 'It's the big new thing. And with our base in the publishing industry – well. Oh, and a few more thousand head of cattle.'

'Well, but what about the bank?'

'The bank's fine,' said Baby with a slight sigh.

Virginia looked at him. 'And Dad?'

'Dad's fine, and getting younger every day, he says. Seeing the recession out, he says. Then he'll go.'

'Baby! Do you think he will?'

'No, I don't.'

He smiled at her, forced his tone to stay light. 'Let's order, shall we? That lobster they're eating looks awfully good.'

'Yes, let's. But what do you think, Baby? Would you let Alexander have that sort of money?'

'No,' said Baby instantly and automatically. Then he pulled himself up. 'Look,' he said, 'I'll talk to Dad first. See what he says. He might just – well, no he won't. Let me handle it, I was going to say. But at least I can spare Alexander the agony of having to spell out every hideous detail.'

'Thank you, Baby.'

He called her that night and said it hadn't done a great deal of good. Fred III had been slightly contemptuous of Alexander's problems.

'You know what he's like, he doesn't understand anyone else's lifestyle,' said Baby, careful not to offend her. 'He doesn't understand how hard Alexander works. But he says that of course he must come and talk to him, he'll see what he can come up with.'

'Doesn't sound too hopeful.'

'No, I'm afraid not. But you never know with Dad. As long as Alexander doesn't expect a blank cheque.'

'Of course not,' said Virginia. But she rather thought Alexander did.

Alexander phoned Fred III who told him to come over as soon as he could and to bring Charlotte with him; Alexander said he thought it would be better if Charlotte stayed at home, but he would certainly be happy to bring all the family to Long Island in August. Fred III said he was thinking of going to the Bahamas; would they all join him and Betsey there? When Virginia heard that Alexander had said he would love to go to the Bahamas she realized just how serious his problems must be.

Baby offered to go with her to meet Alexander at Kennedy, to brief him on the ride back into the city and Fred's office; Fred had insisted he come straight to Pine Street.

'I'm busy the rest of the day,' he said to Virginia, 'and then out of town tomorrow and Friday. If he wants to have my attention, he'll just have to grab it while he can.'

Virginia sighed. Fred was obviously savouring the situation.

Virginia sat appalled while Alexander talked to Fred III. She occasionally exchanged a nervous glance with Baby. Fred said he wanted Baby there, in case he could contribute to the discussion; Baby knew the real reason was a deeper humiliation for Alexander. And the humiliation was considerable. He had made some silly investments on the stock market and lost hundreds of thousands; he had lost hundreds of thousands more on an abortive stud farm project. None of that would have mattered particularly, the estate and his personal fortune could stand it, Hartest was the real problem.

'And how much would that cost?' said Fred.

'The initial estimates are between five and six million. Pounds.'

'Jesus,' said Fred.

'Yes,' said Alexander, 'and I don't think he's going to help. I've asked him,' he added, trying to lift the mood of the meeting.

'Well,' said Fred, 'how are you going to raise it? What advice can I give you?'

Virginia watched Alexander carefully. She knew what he was hoping for, and she knew that Fred knew too; and he might get it and he might not, but a long and elaborate game of cat and mouse would have to be played anyway.

'Well, I don't know quite,' Alexander said.

'You must have a very large fortune tied up in those pictures.'

'Yes. About ten million.'

'Well then. Sell a few.'

'Fred, I can't. A Van Gogh. A Monet. I couldn't part with them. They're part of the house.'

'They'll look pretty silly with the rain falling in on them. Sell one; raise collateral on the rest.'

'Well – yes.'

'What about Virginia's money? She has a great deal. Can't she help?' He spoke as if Virginia wasn't there.

'I wouldn't dream of using Virginia's money,' said Alexander quickly. 'Besides, it's hardly on that sort of scale.'

'Isn't it? I seem to remember settling a fair amount on her.'

136

'Yes but Dad, a lot has gone,' said Virginia quickly, 'a lot of the investments I'd made went in the recession.'

'Well,' he said, looking at her coldly, 'you shouldn't have changed them without consulting me.'

'I – well, I know.'

He looked at her sharply. 'Who advised you? Some half-brained ex-Etonian with a daddy in the City?'

'No.'

'Well?'

'A – stockbroker in England, yes. But not half-brained . . .'

'I'd like to know his name. So I can be sure never to do business with him. What about your investments here? You have your shares in the ranch still, don't you? And in Dudleys?'

'Yes of course. But Father, they don't amount to six million pounds. That's nearly – well, pushing ten million dollars.'

'I can handle that kind of conversion, thank you. It seems to me that you could surely help.'

'Yes. I could certainly help.'

'And what's your opinion on all this anyway? You seem a little surprised by it, in my observation. A wife should make it her business to know her husband's problems. Your mother has always known about every tiny detail of my life.'

This was so outrageously untrue that Virginia was unable to let it pass.

'Dad! She hardly knows the name of all your companies.'

'She would if any of them were going wrong,' said Fred briefly. 'I'm surprised at you, Virginia.'

'Yes, well, she's very busy with her own work,' said Alexander, 'and the children of course, and the house. I didn't want to worry her.'

'She doesn't seem too involved with the children,' said Fred, 'she's always away from them. Anyway, this isn't getting us very far. I'd have thought it was perfectly obvious what you should do. Open Hartest to the public. Set up a fun fair, that sort of thing. Hire some guides. Start a motor museum. Run a lottery. Turn it over to the nation, give it to the Queen. Then you get state grants, don't you? That's what to do.'

Alexander winced. Virginia felt a stab of sympathy for him. Fred III was clearly enjoying himself greatly. She didn't say anything, her father was already clearly ranged against her, and it would have made things worse, but she went over to Alexander's chair and stood behind it. She felt it lent him at least some moral support; he looked up briefly and smiled at her, a weak, wan smile.

'Did you want to say something, Virginia?' said Fred.

'No. Thank you.'

137

'You could give up that bloody silly business of yours and help. If you turned Hartest over to the National Trustees or whatever they're called. Show people round yourself.'

'Well – yes. Yes, I could,' she said, anxious to keep him in a positive mood.

'I would never ask Virginia to give up her work,' said Alexander firmly, 'it's terribly important to her.'

'Well you're a fool,' said Fred briskly. 'But that's between you and her.'

'And besides, I don't think it would make very much difference. To the bottom line.' He smiled briefly. 'Er – '

'Yes?'

'I was actually wondering about a loan. On a strictly business basis, of course.'

'Oh good heavens no,' said Fred. 'I couldn't possibly advise the bank to lend that sort of money. Not just to mend the roof of some building.' He spoke as if Hartest was a small garden shed. 'Unless of course you were to open the house to the public. Then I should feel a little more secure about it.'

'Oh well,' Alexander sighed. 'Well obviously I shall think about what you've said.'

'Yes, do. And if you want a buyer for that Monet, I do know a very interested party.' He smiled at Alexander, his bright blue eyes oddly sinister in his handsome old face. 'In fact I'd give you a better price than most. You can get some estimates if you like. Just to check.'

'No,' said Alexander briefly, 'no really, it isn't for sale.'

That night, Mary Rose insisted on having Virginia and Alexander to dinner. It was an uncomfortable occasion; Virginia was depressed, Alexander exhausted, Baby irritable. He had tried very hard to dissuade Mary Rose from issuing the invitation, but she insisted.

'It would be discourteous,' she said, 'and you know how I feel about discourtesy. Baby, do stop picking at those nuts, you're getting appallingly overweight.'

Inevitably they discussed Fred's offer.

'I think,' said Alexander, 'if I had to open Hartest to the public I would die.'

'Why? Why would it be so bad?' said Virginia, determinedly positive. 'It would still be beautiful. Look at Blenheim. Beaulieu. Castle Howard. They aren't spoilt.'

'Oh Virginia, I'm quite shocked to hear you talk like that,' said Mary

Rose. She made it sound as if Virginia had suggested turning Hartest into a brothel. 'Once these places are turned over to the public they lose their soul.'

'Mary Rose, with respect I think I have more idea what I'm talking about than you do. I do actually live in England, you know.'

'Some of the time,' said Mary Rose with her frostiest smile. 'And my book on the art heritage of the eighteenth century took me inside a great many English houses. It seemed to me that the ones still in private hands had preserved a mystique, a personal quality, a sense of care that was quite gone from places like Blenheim. Of course it was an extremely subtle thing – '

'Yes, well subtlety doesn't pay bills,' said Baby. He was very drunk.

'Paying bills isn't everything,' said Alexander.

'I thought,' said Baby, 'that's why you were here.'

'Well at least the house would be safe,' said Virginia quickly. 'If you – we did open it to the public. I would have thought that was what mattered.'

'You don't understand, do you?' said Alexander, and she shrank slightly from the great darkness behind his eyes. 'You just don't understand. It's just a place to you, just a building and some land.'

'And what is it to you?' said Virginia. She felt suddenly violently angry. 'I can see it's very beautiful, that it's a marvellous thing to own, to pass to your children. I can see that's important to you. But what would change if you charged a few people to go round it every now and again? I'd have thought you'd have liked that, showing it off.'

'Sometimes,' he said, 'I think you're jealous of Hartest. Of how I feel about it. It's the only explanation I can find for your attitude.'

Virginia stared at him. She was flushed.

'Mary Rose,' said Baby hastily, 'coffee, do you think? In the drawing room? It's getting very late.'

Alexander left for England the next day. Virginia stayed to tie up some problems on her latest project, then left two days before Easter. She said she had promised Alexander and the children to spend it with them.

When she got to Heathrow, Harold Tallow was waiting for her at the airport.

'Tallow! I was expecting my husband. And possibly even the children.'

'Charlotte and Max are in the car, madam, with Nanny. I have a letter for you from Lord Caterham.'

'A letter! Good gracious, how formal. Just wait a moment, Tallow, and let me read it.'

She read it in silence. Tallow watching her saw a red flush sweep up her face from her neck; and then a few moments later, she turned very pale. Then she smiled at him, a quick, bright smile.

'Right. Let's go and find the children. I hope they've been good.'

'Very good, My Lady.'

They approached the car; Max burst out of it and hurled himself at her.

'Mummy, Mummy, you look beautiful, what have you brought me?'

He always said that, and it always made her laugh.

'A stetson, Max, that's what I brought you, a real ten-gallon hat like they wear in Texas. Charlotte, my darling, you've grown so much taller! And thinner! I told you you would. Oh, you look so pretty. But I think the jeans I got you in Bloomies will be too short. And too loose. Never mind, it's a nice problem. Give me a kiss. Nanny, hallo, how are you?'

'Very well thank you, madam,' said Nanny. 'It has been rather cold of course, but Max has been very good.'

'Good,' said Virginia, slightly uncertain, as always when confronted by Nanny's non sequiturs, which one to respond to. 'Oh, I'm looking forward to getting home. We've been circling round Heathrow for over an hour, trying to land. I hope you knew that and haven't been waiting all this extra time.'

'We checked, My Lady,' said Tallow. 'They told us you were delayed.'

Charlotte looked at her mother critically. 'You're terribly thin, Mummy. And you look tired.'

'Burning the candle at both ends, I daresay,' said Nanny sternly. 'Like His Lordship.'

'Well a bit, maybe,' said Virginia. 'But anyway, I'm home now. And Lord Caterham is away, I understand.'

'Yes, madam.' Nanny's face was expressionless. 'He went to see his mother yesterday.'

'And took Georgina with him?'

'Yes indeed, madam.'

'Isn't that amazing, Mummy? All these years and Granny never sets eyes on any of us, and then suddenly out of the blue, she phoned and asked to meet Georgina. And – ' Charlotte paused for maximum effect – 'and Max and I are going next week. Did you know that?'

'No,' said Virginia. 'No, I didn't.' She leant against the window suddenly; Nanny looked at her sharply.

'Are you all right, madam? Is it that lagging you're feeling?'

'Jet lag, Nanny. Yes, I think it is. I'll be all right. Charlotte, when did this happen? This invitation to stay with your grandmother?'

'Daddy phoned this morning. He said she liked Georgina so much she wanted to look at me and Max. I can't wait. She lives in a castle, you know, a real one, with turrets.'

'How exciting! Well, I shall be waiting with bated breath to hear about it all. I shall have you here for a few days, though, shall I?'

'Well – yes. Sort of. I've been invited to stay with Joanna Lavenham for the weekend. Is that all right? Daddy said it would be. But Max will be here.'

'That's fine,' said Virginia automatically. Her head was beginning to ache.

Easter without the children was bleak. The house seemed large and very silent. Virginia wandered about trying to work, and determinedly staying cheerful. It was only a few days, she told herself. After all, she often left them. It was probably unreasonable to expect them to be sitting waiting for her all the time.

On Monday, Georgina phoned.

'Mummy! It's wonderful here. Granny is really nice, not like we all thought at all. She's quite young-looking really, and guess what, she has a pony for each of us. We did the Easter egg hunt in Granny's woods yesterday with her dogs helping. They're lurchers, not very nice to look at, but very clever. One of the bitches is in whelp and Granny says I can have one of the puppies. Tomorrow we're going fishing. Hang on, Max wants to talk to you.' (Much giggling in the background.) 'Mummy, sorry, he doesn't, Granny's cook has just called him, he's going to help her make the supper. Oh, it's brilliant here. I wish we'd come before. See you next week. Bye, Mummy.'

'Mummy? It's Charlotte. Yes, it's just the best fun. Granny is really really nice. I've got a lovely room, overlooking the loch, and I've got a four-poster bed. Look, would you mind if we stayed another week? The thing is Granny has organized a bit of what she calls a jolly at the weekend, asked lots of people over, lots of people my age, it's going to be brilliant. You don't mind, do you? Daddy sends his love. No, he's out now, fishing. He's terribly good at fishing.'

'Virginia? How are you? Not too lonely? Good. Yes, they seem to love it. They're getting on very well indeed with Mother. She says she should have invited them years ago. What? No, I really don't think she's quite ready for you. But give her time. Look, I completely forgot to tell you and I'm terribly sorry, a Miss Ward phoned, the day you were getting back. She wanted you to ring her. She said it wasn't urgent, but she wanted to discuss her rugs. Would that be right? I really do apologize for not telling you. But she's probably phoned you herself by now. She hasn't? Oh well, you'd better ring her. I'm so sorry. Yes I'm all right. Worried of course. Desperately worried. It's so sad your father won't help. What's that? Virginia, I'm afraid I don't see that as help. I'm sorry. No, I know you can't influence him. You keep telling me that. I'm afraid I feel very alone in all this. Look, I have to go. Goodbye, Virginia. See you soon.'

She had never heard him so cold, so distant.

Susannah Ward was very cool when Virginia phoned her.

'I'm sorry, Virginia, but I simply couldn't wait. I thought I made it plain to whoever it was I spoke to that it was urgent.'

Arrogant bitch, thought Virginia. She clearly hadn't, Alexander was always painstakingly careful about messages. 'So I've gone ahead and chosen the rugs myself, and now I've had a chance to think carefully about them, I can see they don't quite tone with the wall colour you proposed. So I'm deepening that a little, and I'm taking a further look at the fabric for the blinds as well. It's a pity, but there it is. I did tell you at the beginning I was in a great hurry to get this done.'

'I'm very sorry,' said Virginia more humbly than the situation probably allowed.

She put the phone down and went for a long walk. It wasn't a great deal of fun; Alexander had even taken the dogs with him.

Later she ate lunch and then tea alone. It was at times like this that she most longed for a drink. She drove into the village and bought some chocolates and some French cigarettes. When she was low, she needed such things.

She decided to talk to Catriona Dunbar. Catriona had been urging her for months, on and off, to come onto her Riding for the Disabled Ball committee; Alexander had been urging her to do it, she had told him she didn't have the time. 'You would have time if you were around here a bit more.' Suddenly even that seemed a more attractive prospect. At least it would mean she could go over and see Catriona, have lunch maybe.

Catriona's voice was guarded, cautious. 'Oh, Virginia. Hallo.'

'Hi, Catriona. How are you?'

'Frightfully well, Virginia, thank you.'

'Er – Catriona, I'm ringing about the Riding for the Disabled.'

'Oh – yes?'

She sounded very cool. Had she been that difficult about it, Virginia wondered. 'Well, Catriona, if it's not too late, I really would quite like – '

'Virginia, I'm frightfully sorry, but it is too late. We don't have unlimited time, you know. The Ball is in September, and Jennifer Compton Smith has joined us now.'

'Oh. Oh, I see. Well, if there's any small thing I can do.'

'Yes, well thank you, Virginia. Jolly nice. Look, I have to go, Martin and I are going to a point-to-point.'

'I couldn't – ' 'come with you?' she had been going to say, suddenly and slightly foolishly hungry for company; then she hauled herself up. She wasn't that bad and Catriona was clearly feeling the opposite of friendly. She hadn't realized there had been a time limit on the wretched committee, and anyway, she was sure she'd told Catriona she'd give her an answer when she got back at Easter. God, these women and their minutiae-filled lives.

'Sorry, Virginia. Must dash.'

'Bye, Catriona.'

She put the phone down rather slowly. Silly bitch. What a fuss about absolutely nothing at all. Jennifer Compton Smith was welcome to it all. Thank God she had a career to occupy her. She decided to go to London for the day and do some shopping, and go and see a couple of people. She and Alexander had met a woman called Anne Lygon at a cocktail party just before she'd gone to New York, a property developer who'd asked her to come to see her about doing a show flat in a new development in the City. It was a very nice high-profile job and she'd been excited about it. She'd done some preliminary sketches in an entirely new mould for her, the currently buzzy high-tech style, all perspex and stainless steel mesh and black and white, which Anne had liked, and asked her to develop; she decided to ring her.

'Anne? This is Virginia Caterham. Look, I'm in London today and I have some more ideas; I'd love to come and see you about them. Would that be convenient?'

Anne Lygon sounded polite but guarded. 'Well, Virginia, I'm very busy today.'

'That's OK, I didn't expect you to drop everything for me.' She struggled to keep her voice light and amused, to staunch the creeping sensation of chill in her stomach. 'I could come tomorrow or even Friday.'

Anne sounded embarrassed. 'Look, Virginia, I'm sorry, but I really don't think this is going to work out. I'm sorry. I really do have to proceed very fast now, and I was hoping to have got further down the line with you. Another time, maybe.'

'Yes,' said Virginia, not even trying any more to keep her voice from bleakness. 'Yes of course. Goodbye, Anne.'

'Goodbye, Virginia.' Anne Lygon sounded relieved.

She went to London and spent a great deal of money on a new mink coat.

143

If Alexander was short of six million, three thousand wasn't going to make much difference.

Charlotte had telephoned from her grandmother's, and left a message asking her mother to ring back. Virginia had never rung the number before, it was an eerie feeling. She hoped Alexander's mother wouldn't answer the phone. That would be awful. She would just have to ring off. Virginia realized suddenly she was shaking slightly. She put the phone down quickly, mid-dial, and lit a cigarette. That was better. She redialled. A male Scottish voice answered the phone.

'Kinloch Castle.'

'Good morning. May I speak to Lady Charlotte Welles, please?'

'May I ask who is calling?'

'It's Lady Caterham. Her mother.'

'One moment, Lady Caterham.'

She waited, tapping her fingers on the table, looking round the room, newly aware of it, studying the ornate carvings on the cornices, the perfect lines of the fireplace; occasionally, just very occasionally, she could see why Alexander loved the house so much. She must try to help him more with it, with everything. She hadn't been much use to him lately.

'Lady Caterham?'

'Yes?' She hadn't expected this, not to speak to Charlotte.

'Lady Caterham, I am so sorry, but the children have gone.'

'Gone.' The word seemed oddly threatening. She realized she was panicking, quite illogically. 'What do you mean gone?'

'Well, Lady Caterham, they have gone away for two or three days. Lord Caterham and the Dowager Lady Caterham have taken them on a trip to some of the islands. They should be back by Saturday.'

'Oh,' said Virginia. 'Oh, I see. Well – well I expect my daughter just wanted to tell me that.'

'Yes, My Lady, I expect so.' The voice was soothing, oddly patronizing. She felt irritated.

'Well, when they return, please tell them I called.'

'Yes, Lady Caterham. Of course.'

She put the phone down, chilled. They all seemed rather lost to her suddenly. Then she shook herself. That was ridiculous. They would all be home in another five days or so. She would just make herself a very strong coffee. She lit one of the French cigarettes and went down the hall to the kitchen door.

There was only one thing for it, really. She had hung on for the rest of the

144

day, she had smoked, drunk coffee, eaten a whole box of chocolates, but in the end it seemed just the only, blindingly obvious thing to do. Have a drink. Just one. Only one. To ease the pain and the loneliness and the hurt.

What a nightmare week. Everything, everything gone wrong. The children away, apparently under the spell of their grandmother; a client upset, the job with Anne Lygon cancelled, even her friendship with Catriona on the rocks. It was horrible. Horrible. And always there, underneath it all, the nagging awful fear about Hartest and the money, and Alexander's dreadful, alienating misery. And there was no one, nothing to turn to. Except – except a drink. The one friend she had always had. It had suddenly become the only thing she could think about. Comforting, consoling, soothing; anaesthetizing pain, stilling anxiety. So accessible, so undemanding.

Red wine, that's what she wanted. Uniced champagne wouldn't be cold enough, and she wouldn't be able to have just one glass of champagne, it would be a waste. She could cork the red wine up, keep it maybe until dinner tomorrow. She picked out a bottle of claret, tucked it under her arm, and went quietly upstairs again. There were plenty of corkscrews in Alexander's study, she could get one from there.

His study was cold, creepily tidy and impersonal. It was as if no one had ever used it. She took a corkscrew off the tray, went along the corridor to her room, and locked the door behind her.

She no longer cared about the children going off without her, or whether she was losing all her clients. She felt excited, exalted even. She felt as if she was going to meet some long-lost lover. Well, perhaps not lover. Friend. Her heart was beating very hard. She sat down on the bed, drew the cork, poured a very small amount of the wine into the tumbler from her bathroom. She sat and looked at it for a moment, thinking, waiting. Then she raised the glass and took a small, contemplative sip.

When they came home, the children and Alexander, swooping down the Great Drive in the Daimler, she was out on the steps waiting for them, her eyes full of tears of pleasure. She was almost drunk.

When she saw Charlotte and Georgina off to school – Georgina off bravely to board for the first term – giving in to Alexander's suggestion that he should drive them there and leave her to do some work, she said goodbye to them and went upstairs and got drunk.

And when Max had gone back to school too, to his little pre-prep school in Marlborough and had hugged her goodbye at the gate and said, 'Soon I shall be away at boarding school too, I can't wait,' she drove up to

London, to the house in Eaton Place, and stayed there for twenty-four hours, twelve hours drinking and twelve hours trying to sober up. And then another twelve, and then another.

In the end Alexander came to find her; he looked at her, sadly loving, and said, 'Come along, darling. Let me take you home.'

And then there was treatment, therapy, a short spell in the clinic, and home – safe, she thought – but then Alexander had to go away for a few days, to talk to people about the house, and it was so quiet, so lonely, so frighteningly lonely she got drunk again.

And while she was drunk, hopelessly drunk, Baby phoned; Alexander had suggested he did, just to cheer her up, had said he knew she missed him and that she was alone; and she was weeping with happiness, babbling down the phone, and she didn't realize how quiet he was at the other end, and how he said goodbye rather suddenly.

Alexander was still worried, still distracted about Hartest, about money; he said that after all, maybe, he would have to open it to the public. He said nothing would ever persuade him it was the right thing to do, but it was beginning to seem the only thing to do. Virginia offered to sell all her shares but he said it simply wasn't worth it. 'It wouldn't even sort out the walls.'

Virginia got very drunk indeed that night. She carried on drinking all the next day, and the next. In a very short time, she was in the clinic again.

She was sitting in her room reading a week later, the worst over (again), when Alexander walked in, looking remarkably cheerful.

'You look better, darling.'

'I feel better. I'm so sorry, Alexander. So terribly terribly sorry.'

'I know.'

'This time I won't, I really really won't go back.'

'I believe you. We'll lick it. Together.'

'You're very good to me, Alexander.'

'Well, I love you. It's easy.'

'I can't believe that.'

'It is.'

'You look better too.'

'Yes, well, I've had some very good news.'

'What's that?'

'Your father phoned me this morning. He's reconsidered. He's made a loan available to me.'

'Alexander, that is just fantastic. I'm so pleased.'

'Well, it should be a boost for you too. Help you through. No more worry about being on the streets.'

'No. Oh, it's marvellous. Simply marvellous.' She looked at him thoughtfully, almost awestruck. 'It's really an extraordinary volte-face. I wonder whatever made him change his mind.'

Alexander turned and walked over to the window. 'God knows,' he said.

Chapter 9

Charlotte, 1974

Asking her mother That Question, as she always thought of it, was the hardest thing Charlotte ever did. It was much more difficult than the other difficult questions like when she might get a bosom, and what was a tampon for and what exactly was a lesbian, and the awful irony of it was that unlike the other questions, she had to keep asking it, or variations on it, over the years, without ever getting an entirely satisfactory answer.

That Question had first been put into her head (as indeed had the one about lesbians) by another girl at her school. Charlotte had been eleven when it was put there, and in her last year at Southland Place, the boarding prep school where both she and Georgina had been sent at eight.

Charlotte and Georgina had been sitting side by side on the bench on the rounders field when the subject was first raised; Georgina's skinny arms hugging her endlessly long legs, her small pointed chin resting on her knees, Charlotte's considerably less slender form, glowingly damp from having just scored seven rounders, her dark curls plastered to her plumply pretty little face.

'Shove over, fatty,' said Rowena Parker not unkindly to Charlotte; 'I'm zonked.'

Georgina turned to glare at Rowena. 'Don't call my sister fatty.'

'Why not? She is a fatty. She's as fat as you're thin. Are you two adopted or something?'

'What on earth do you mean?' said Charlotte, looking at her more in interest than outrage. 'Of course we're not adopted.'

'Well, I never saw two sisters look more different,' said Rowena. 'I mean honestly, you're short and – well certainly not thin, and dark, and she's tall and skinny and sort of mouse-coloured.'

'Don't be so rude,' said Charlotte. 'Anyway, you don't look much like your sister either.'

'No, but at least she's not a foot taller than me and two years younger. I think it's quite peculiar.'

'Well I think *you're* quite peculiar,' said Charlotte. 'Come on, Georgina, let's go and find some tea.'

'Don't eat all the cake,' said Rowena. 'I know you, Charlotte Welles.'

'Stupid cow,' said Charlotte when they were out of Rowena's hearing.

'Well she is a stupid cow,' said Georgina, 'but it's true, Charlotte, isn't it? We do look very different. I've often thought about it myself.'

'You're joking!' said Charlotte, turning to stare at her.

'No I'm not. In fact Max said something about it last holidays. He said he was so glad he didn't look like either of us, because we were both so ugly, and I hit him, and then he said it was true and what was more, we were both so ugly in different ways. And we are.'

'Ugly?'

'Well, I'm ugly. You're not. But we do look very different.'

'Georgie, you're not ugly.'

'Well, I'm plain.'

'I don't think you're plain,' said Charlotte staunchly. She was very fond of Georgina; her voice nevertheless lacked any great conviction. Georgina at nine was at best what the French call *jolie laide*, with a long narrow little face, sharply painful cheekbones, a large mouth and a high forehead; she was extremely tall and angular with legs that looked too fragile to support her, and a set of ribs so prominent they even showed through a T-shirt. Her nickname at school was B (short for Biafra); whenever she got the wishbone or it was her birthday she wished to put on some weight. Charlotte wished precisely the reverse; she was prettily, peachily round, with a tumble of dark curls and dimples, and although she was beginning to grow taller and to slim down a little, she did look, beside the faun-like Georgina, like an engagingly cuddly little puppy. Which was not what she wanted and grossly unfair, as she wailed at least twice a day, since she was painstakingly careful about what she ate, while Georgina could and did consume four Shredded Wheats for breakfast and then some toast and honey, always had seconds of everything including treacle pudding and brought back twice as much tuck after the holidays as Charlotte, none of which ever seemed to touch her skeletal frame.

'Well anyway, we don't look like sisters. Have you really never thought about it?'

'No,' said Charlotte, 'I haven't. And I'm sure we'd know if we weren't, you know what Mummy's like for being open with us, as she puts it.'

Nevertheless, the thought began from that moment to haunt her.

She summoned the courage to ask Virginia about it next holidays; she had to wait until they were alone, which wasn't very often, but one afternoon they were sitting in the old wooden dinghy on the lake, pretending to catch fish, just the two of them. Georgina had gone to play with a friend, and Max was riding with Alexander. It had been a good summer, the endless restoration, reroofing and underpinning of Hartest finally complete.

149

It took a lot of courage, the asking; three times she opened her mouth, felt a rush of fear and then shut it again, but finally she got out the word 'Mummy?' in a questioning voice, so that Virginia was bound to say 'Yes, what?' as she always did, and then she knew she had to go on.

'Well, could I ask you something? Something awkward?'

'Charlotte! Not more about lesbians,' said Virginia, laughing. 'Darling, of course you can, and it can't be awkward, not between you and me. I'm your mother.'

'Are you?' She felt quite sick when she got that out, sick and breathless; but she met Virginia's eyes very steadily.

Virginia stared back without flinching, but she flushed; then she smiled slightly awkwardly.

'Darling, of course I am. What an extraordinary thing to say. Is that the question?'

'Yes. Well, sort of. Sorry. I – well I just had to ask. Some of the girls at school think we're – adopted.'

There, she had got it out. Said the word. She sat forward in the boat, staring at her mother's face.

'Charlotte! What an astonishing question. What on earth, what on earth could make anyone think that?'

She began to look cross now, her golden eyes snapping. 'Who's been putting that sort of nonsense into your head?'

'Oh, some stupid girl called Rowena. But – '

'Yes?'

'Well, you can see why she should think that, can't you?'

'Not really,' said Virginia icily. 'I can't.'

'Mummy, don't get upset. It doesn't matter that much.'

'I am not upset and it does matter. Perhaps you could tell me why she thinks it.'

'Well, it's just that we do look awfully different,' said Charlotte. 'All of us, but specially me and Georgie.'

'Don't call her that,' said Virginia automatically. She hated Georgina's name being shortened.

'Sorry. But she's about six feet tall and a beanpole and I'm six feet wide and sort of shortish, and I'm dark and she's mousey. And then Max is blond and good-looking and sort of normal-shaped.'

'Like Daddy.'

'Well, yes. Like Daddy.'

'And you're dark and pretty. With maybe just a tiny bit of a weight problem. Like I used to have.'

'Well – yes.'

'And Georgina is exceptionally tall and thin, at the moment, but I understand Granny Caterham is very tall.'

'Yes – she is.'

'And you and Georgina both have my eyes. Which are a very unusual colour. Haven't you thought of that?'

'No, I s'pose not,' said Charlotte. She wished she hadn't said anything, her mother was clearly very upset.

'Darling,' said Virginia, making a great effort to smile, to appear relaxed, 'I do promise you you're not adopted. I gave birth to all of you, personally, and if you don't believe me, I can introduce you to my nice obstetrician who was there at the time. Well, for Georgina and Max, she was. For you I had a dreadful old trout called Mr Dunwoody, who I'm sure would vouch for me as well. All right? Do you believe me now?'

'Yes,' said Charlotte, and she did. And she felt much better about it. For a while.

It was Max who raised That Question again. It was the Easter holidays after his seventh birthday, and he was being sent off to Hawtreys to board, as part of his inevitable progress towards Eton. Max caused his tutors, as he did his parents, considerable anguish; although he was not brilliant or even clever he was certainly not stupid, but he was what his pre-prep headmaster had billed 'creatively lazy'. Max (rather like his Uncle Baby) set fun at a high premium; he was immensely charming and good-natured, popular, and highly inventive, and he found school work tedious and pointless. Had he devoted even a quarter of the energy he put into avoiding it into his homework, Charlotte told him prissily from time to time, he could have been top of the class in every subject.

'No I couldn't.'

'Of course you could.'

'Well I don't want to be a swot like you.'

Charlotte was always being accused of being a swot; to an extent it was true. She was awesomely clever, and she did actually rather enjoy studying; as a result she did so extraordinarily well that the girls in her class would refer to being 'first except for Charlotte Welles'. She wasn't just good at the sciences or arts subjects, she excelled at everything; in the end-of-year exams she had achieved the almost unheard-of distinction of full marks in Latin, Maths and French. Maths was her overall favourite, she worked at it for recreation as well as study, working out complex equations and problems in the evenings at school while the other girls wrote to boys, or sewed or watched television.

'I plan to run a business,' she said when anyone asked her what she was

151

going to do when she grew up. 'Possibly a bank. Like my grandfather. Or I might be a lawyer.'

A boy at school called Fanshawe, Max reported, had also said they must be adopted, 'Because we all look weird in different ways.' Max had responded by hitting Fanshawe, who had started to blub and said he had heard his mother talking about it. Max said he quite liked the idea, it might mean he had a really interesting father, like a gypsy or a burglar, instead of a boring earl; Georgina looked upset and worried and said she was so frightened of anyone else being her parents it made her feel sick. Charlotte told them both to shut up and that it was all nonsense, that Virginia had told her so; but she still couldn't quite shake the thought out of her head. It was no good talking to Virginia; she had got so cross the last time (strangely cross, Charlotte thought, reflecting upon it again, almost – what? scared?). And it certainly wasn't the sort of question she could ask Alexander. There must be some other way.

Virginia was in London for a few days; Charlotte waited until everybody was busy one morning then went into her mother's study, and opened the bottom drawer of Virginia's desk very slowly and carefully, as if its contents might sting her – like Pandora and her box, she thought, irritated with herself at her fear. Her hands were clammy and shaking slightly; and she closed her eyes briefly before taking out her own file, the one labelled Charlotte, and opening it. Her birth certificate was right on the top.

'So you see, it's true. Mummy wasn't lying. You can tell Fanshawe, Max, and hit him again if you like. We're all in order, parents definitely Mummy and Daddy, everything's fine.'
    'Was it your idea to look at the birth certificates?' said Georgina. 'You really are clever, Charlotte. You'll have to be a detective when you grow up.'
    'Oh no, I'm going to run a business,' said Charlotte. 'A huge powerful business. I should like that.'
    'You should get rid of that stupid Freddy,' said Georgina, 'and run Grandfather's bank.'
    'Yes, it'd be easy,' said Max, 'he's such a wimp. You could push him in the lake and he'd drown, or get him up a tree and he'd never get down again, and he'd starve to death.'
    Charlotte looked at him thoughtfully. 'I think there are rather better ways than that,' she said.

Chapter 10

Baby, 1978

It was Fred III's birthday. His seventy-fifth birthday. And it was being marked by his retirement. There had been a farewell dinner two days earlier with his colleagues, friends, compatriots and admirers on Wall Street. And now tonight, a huge party for family and friends at the house on Long Island.

And then he and Betsey were going away on a long vacation, to Bermuda, so that, as he put it, he wouldn't be messing things up for Baby his first few days alone at the bank.

Baby could hardly believe it was finally happening. Just when he had given up all hope, Fred had walked into Baby's office one morning and simply said that he wanted to spend more time on the golf course and would retire in three months' time, on his birthday. Just like that. And then walked out again, and Baby had heard no more about it for three days when he had announced it to Pete Hoffman (son of Nigel, long since retired) and the other senior partners at the end of a meeting, as calmly as if he had been telling them their half-yearly bonuses were up or he was taking another day off over Thanksgiving.

Baby hadn't even dared tell Mary Rose until then; that night he went home with a vast bunch of red roses in one hand and a bottle of very best Bollinger in the other.

'I did it,' he said, simply. 'Correction. We did it.' She didn't even need to ask him what he meant.

Every day since then he had been terrified, terrified his father would change his mind, terrified that he would do something stupid, terrified there would be another stock market crisis that would make Fred feel he had to after all stay on and just 'see it out', his favourite expression. But the days had turned into weeks, and nothing had happened to change Fred's mind; and in the last month he had given a series of luncheons for the major clients, the senior partners and Baby, telling them of his decision. The partners had been apparently pleased and highly supportive, pledged their help to Baby, and privately told one another behind extremely closed doors that it was about time too. Pete Hoffman had been particularly delighted; strange, Baby thought at first, until he realized that Pete's son Gabriel was about to leave Harvard and take his first faltering steps into Wall Street. Fred III had taken against Gabe; he said he was too much impressed with himself by half. As Fred never changed his mind about anyone, this clearly did not bode too well for Gabe's future with Praegers; with Baby in charge, there could be a better outlook for him. Baby thought Pete could sweat on that one for a bit. He wasn't too sure about Gabe himself. He could hardly believe it was happening at last. That the bank was to be his. To run, to shape, to work on. Now that it was so near a reality, the prospect excited him more than he would have believed.

And now, here it was, the Saturday before the Monday, and he was moving out of the Heirs Room, which would stay empty for a few years until Freddy settled in, and into the dark, massive office with its great mountains of bookshelves, its ancient desk that Frederick I had brought up from Atlanta with him, its ticker-tape machine, silent now, in the corner, its beautiful lamps, switched on night and day – and its memories. They were almost tangible, those memories, Baby thought; he had watched his father standing very still in the doorway for the last time yesterday, reliving so much: his early days, the crash, the accession, the day when Jicks Foster's call came through – 'Fred? Fred Praeger? Fred, I need a bank,' the arrival of Miss Betsey Bradley in the steno pool, the war, the depression, the frenetic growth of the city, and behind and beyond them all, a backdrop to those memories, the vast, almost fearsome ebb and flow of money into the city, the huge power it yielded, and its attendant hopes and fears, defeats and victories, that any good banker can stand in the street and smell and sense with a physical force. Baby's only real anxiety now was the degree to which he could personally experience that force.

'Baby, you look wonderful!' said Virginia. 'About five years younger.' She had gone into the great yellow and white marquee in search of her children; the space was so big that it took her a few moments to see them all, hanging around the stage, fiddling with the microphone, studying the place cards on the top table. It was a mass of flowers, the marquee, all yellow and white also: great ropes of freesias twisted into moss and twined around the poles, huge urns set with yellow and white roses right around the perimeter of the room, and at either side of the stage, arrangements of smaller yellow and white flowers, all spelling out seventy-five on the tables.

Baby was standing watching the children, taking in the scene, with an odd expression: smiling, but oddly tense . . . It was true that he looked wonderful; dressed in his dinner jacket, his face bronzed and his hair bleached from the summer on Nantucket Island, his eyes very blue and clear, he looked as he had used to again, handsome, relaxed, happy. 'You look like Prince Charming,' she said.

Baby smiled at her. 'Not so much Prince,' he said, 'King. At last.'

'At last. I'm so happy for you, Baby.'

'You look pretty good yourself,' said Baby. 'Incredible that you're the mother of those two grown-up young ladies over there.'

Charlotte was sitting on the edge of the stage, swinging her slightly plump legs, clearly aware that she looked sexily ripe in her cream chantilly lace dress from Chloë, with its ruffled, tantalizingly low bodice, and full, just-short-of-long skirt. Her dark hair was brushed wildly full, her tawny eyes were outlined with kohl, and she wore very shiny pale pink lipstick on her sensuous little bee-sting mouth. She was a very pretty girl, Baby thought; and her looks belied her; anyone seeing her for the first time would assume she was a sweetly dumb little thing. It was an oddly dangerous combination, he thought, the baby face and the sharp mind.

He knew that really he should regard her with the same suspicion that Mary Rose did, knowing that she was the Crown Princess, the best-beloved grandchild, but she was such a disarmingly nice child, so unspoilt, so nicely mannered that he found it impossible to do anything but like her.

Freddy, on the other hand, viewed her rather differently, Baby knew. He couldn't stand her. Right through their childhood he had hated her, for outshining him, for being cleverer, and braver, than he was, for bossing him about whenever she had the opportunity – and for being a great deal closer to their grandfather. Baby (who found his eldest son difficult to get along with, with his distant, rather jumpy manner, his shyness which manifested itself as coldness, his lack of any sense of fun) had tried to reassure him on this; to make him realize that he was the heir to Praegers, that no one could take it away from him, that his grandfather was a traditionalist and an accessionist, and nothing on earth would persuade him that Freddy should not have Praegers as his own in the fullness of time, that the constitution of the bank was such that the 30 per cent of the shares that would pass to Freddy on Fred III's death were as safely and assuredly his as the 50 per cent that would become his own. But Freddy was still uneasy. He was afraid and suspicious of Charlotte, afraid and suspicious of her power over his grandfather, and nothing his father could say would assuage the fears.

It was taking Freddy a long time to grow up physically, Baby thought; maybe that was a lot of his problem. He was nineteen now and he still looked like a boy rather than a man, and he had none of the exuberance, the air of self-confidence that both Fred III and Baby possessed in such exceptionally generous quantities. Kendrick was more of a classic Praeger, bigger, bolder, more instantly charming, but Baby found him harder to understand. He was very artistic, and he dressed rather flamboyantly whenever he was allowed, which wasn't often; he was due shortly to go away to the Lawrenceville School, which he was privately dreading, being very unsporty, but which he professed to be looking forward to greatly. He was only modestly clever, and he worked very hard for his just-above-average grades, but he had one outstanding talent and that was for drawing. When he grew up, he said, he was going to be an architect, and he spent a lot of time, whenever he was there, making painstaking sketches of Hartest, which he loved. He had so far displayed no interest in girls whatsoever; the terrifying thought occasionally entered Baby's mind that Kendrick might be gay. He crushed it ruthlessly, but it wouldn't quite go away.

'Hi, Daddy. You look really handsome. Oh, Charlotte, that is one great dress.'

'Thank you, Melissa. You don't look too bad yourself.'

Charlotte jumped off the platform and gave her little cousin a kiss. Melissa (born a neat nine months after Angie's departure from Baby's life) was dressed up in a myriad of frills, a large pink velvet bow holding back her golden curls. She was at eight an enchanting child, sweet-natured, friendly, easy-going, and everyone loved her: 'The only one of the batch who seems to be Baby's,' Virginia had remarked to Alexander once; he looked at her and laughed and said he thought Melissa was prettier than Baby, but even he – who found any children, apart from his own, tedious – liked and played with his little niece.

'When will the people start coming?' Melissa asked Baby as her brothers joined them.

'Oh, in about quarter of an hour, I should think. Now, Kendrick and Freddy, I want you two to be really watchful this evening, for anyone who might be looking a little lost; make sure everyone is talking to someone, make introductions. And don't head the rush to the buffet, any of you. Children last.'

'Father, none of us would rush to the buffet.' Freddy sounded faintly pained. 'You know that.'

'I would,' said Melissa. 'Really fast. I'm starving now.'

'Then you'd better go to the kitchen and fix yourself a sandwich, because you've got a long wait. And don't go bothering Mrs Berridge, she has enough to do. Just sort it out for yourself, OK? And don't go missing, and don't get peanut butter on that dress or Mummy will have a fit. And so will I,' he added hastily. 'Maybe I should go with you.'

'I'll go with her,' said Charlotte, taking Melissa's hand, 'and watch out for the dress.'

'Now for that I would be grateful,' said Baby. 'How do I repay you?'

'I'll think of something,' said Charlotte, smiling at him.

The three hundred and fifty people gathered into the marquee were all what Fred III called family. What this meant was that he and they went back a long way. In several cases, there were three generations of a family there, and in a great many two; several of them actually childhood friends of Fred's (although no childhood friends of Betsey's), rich, powerful, moneyed people, who saw the progression of father and son and then grandson through their companies, or at least their fields of work, and their pursuit of the same lifestyles, as being as inevitable as the progression from night to day, or winter to spring. You were born into this particular world and you stayed there, you married into it, you raised your children in it and you strayed from it at your peril.

Clement Dudley was there, looking disdainful and distinguished, with his still more disdainful and distinguished wife Anunciata, and so of course was Jicks Foster with Mrs Foster IV, who was only a little older than her stepson Jeremy. He was there too, in high spirits, with his fashion model wife, Isabella; their marriage had taken place two years earlier on Staghorn Cay, the Bahamian island Jicks owned, in front of a thousand close family and friends.

There had been rumours since then that all was not well in the paradise Jeremy and Isabella inhabited in a Park Avenue duplex; she had continued to pursue her career and spent rather less time with Jeremy than she did with her hairdressers and exercise gurus, and Jeremy's name was constantly in the gossip columns, usually at rather unsavoury clubs. But now things seemed better; Isabella was very publicly pregnant, and had already given her just slightly uninformed views on motherhood to countless journalists, and Jeremy had taken to staying at home at night and in his office during the day. American Suburban, Jeremy's personal slice of the Foster property empire, was flourishing, despite the rocky market of the past two years; in one of his infrequent but brilliant pieces of lateral thinking, Jeremy had launched an innovation in property development, the Cut Out House. The Cut Out House was well constructed, but totally unfinished inside; it did not even have window frames. It was extremely cheap and for a young couple, desperate for a home of their own, a godsend; they could buy it, and do all the final work themselves, installing doors, windows, plastering, painting, fitting the electrics, building the kitchen – all at a fraction of the professional cost. Investors in American Suburban were almost alone that year in the property world, seeing their stock increase in value.

Baby had personally seen through the financing of the Cut Out House, and Fred III had been delighted with the result; Baby was not sure how Fred would feel if he knew quite how much of the personal proceeds Jeremy had taken from the company were stashed away behind a brass plate in Nassau, safe from taxation, but he certainly saw no need to tell him.

The Fosters and the Dudleys sat with the family at the top table: Fred III and Betsey in the centre, with Virginia and Alexander on Fred's right and Baby and Mary Rose to Betsey's left. They must have looked a bit like the Last Supper, thought Baby irreverently, looking down into the main section of the marquee, with its mass of murmuring, candle-lit people, sharply aware of the oddly stylized picture they all made. It always irritated Baby to be told how similar he and Alexander looked, but he had had to admit this evening, catching sight of the two of them in the large mirror over the fireplace in the drawing room, that they could have been brothers, tall, blond, blue-eyed, the sharp differences in their personal styles cancelled out by their dinner jackets. Their wives on the other hand were looking more than usually different, Virginia in a slither of white crepe, with the Caterham tiara in her swept-up dark hair, Mary Rose in her ice-blue full-skirted satin, her blonde hair sleekly bobbed, her only jewellery the diamond pendant Baby had given her on their wedding day.

The children were behaving beautifully, although plainly a trifle subdued and bored by now: Charlotte, placed next to Freddy, was working hard at a conversation, but Georgina and Kendrick sat eating in silence; only Max and Melissa, their plates piled dangerously high, sat talking, relentlessly animated, Max pausing in his conversation every so often to offer Melissa some particularly delicious morsel from his own plate, or to beckon a waiter over to refill her glass with Coca-Cola.

'That boy,' said Betsey to Fred, after watching him fondly for a while, 'has the makings of a real lady's man. I never saw anyone of his age flirt so professionally.'

The meal was finished: the glasses had been brought round, filled with champagne for the toasts; Baby stood up, banging on the table with the heavy silver salt cellar.

'My lords, ladies and gentlemen,' he said, 'this is a very auspicious occasion. We in this family are very happy to be here this evening, and happy that you could share it with us. Most of you have known my father for many many years – and those of you who are not old enough to have known him for many years will certainly have grown up hearing about him, aware of him. He is, without doubt, a remarkable man: a remarkable family man, and a remarkable businessman. I could stand here for a very long time enumerating his talents and his achievements, but I won't. In the first place because you would grow weary, but more importantly, and in the second, because he would hate it. My father doesn't like adulation, and he doesn't like fuss. What he does like is fun. Fun is what he has given all of us, and fun is what he wants you to have tonight. So – no more eulogies, except to say, "Dad – You're the Tops." ' Much laughter. Baby looked at his father, raised his glass. 'Could I ask you all to raise your glasses to my father on this, his seventy-fifth birthday?'

The room and the glasses rose: 'Fred' went up the cry, 'Happy birthday, Fred.'

Fred stood up. 'Thank you. Thank you all. I would like to say a few words, a very few you will be surprised to hear. Bur first, I want you all to sit down again and enjoy what will certainly be the high spot of the evening. Charlotte, darling, are you ready?'

Baby looked sharply over at Virginia, who had been half poised to stand up, to step forward, her tap shoes already placed on her feet, after a tactical visit to the ladies' room. She was sitting back in her chair, looking half relieved, half hurt. He knew exactly what was going on in her head: she had not really wanted to do the dance, and without the comfort of champagne, the thought of facing so large an audience was fearful for her. But it would have been right, on the other hand, for her to do it; it was her rightful role, partner to her father, she had shared that particular piece of adulation with him all her life, it was her own personalized place in the sun, and to be so publicly removed from it was humiliating.

Baby looked at Charlotte, standing up, smiling into the applause, slightly confused, moving down towards her grandfather, taking his outstretched hand, saw him kiss it; Baby moved to the white grand piano that stood on the corner of the stage, and began to play, confused himself, hardly hearing Charlotte's clear, surprisingly sexy, throaty singing voice joined to Fred's in the words.

The applause was tumultuous. There were cries of encore, and it was only Charlotte's repeated head-shaking, her flight into the welcoming arms of Jeremy Foster who was applauding with excessive zeal on the edge of the floor, that declared the cabaret unequivocally over.

Fred stood there, just a little breathless, his hands up, asking for silence. 'Great, partner,' he said, 'absolutely great. I'll say those few words now, but best get your glasses filled first. They may take just a little while.'

'And while that is going on,' said Betsey, standing up, beaming into the room, 'we have something else for you. Happy birthday, Fred.'

The lights in the marquee dimmed; there was a light from the doorway as two waiters wheeled the cake in: an amazing piece of work, a sculpture of the bank, four feet high, in perfect detail, the doors, the steps, the pillars, and, leaning out of the middle window above the door, a man with silver hair, smiling out onto the world, holding a balloon with '75' on it. There were several people on the sidewalk outside the bank, also holding balloons, and the entire edifice was outlined with candles and fizzing sparklers. The band played 'Happy Birthday'; everyone joined in; Fred stood, smiling just slightly bashfully. Then he went over and kissed Betsey's hand.

'Come help me blow the candles out,' he said. 'I never could do anything properly without you beside me.'

A great wave of 'aahs' swept through the room; everyone smiled; the children all joined in blowing out the candles.

And then they were motioned back to their seats, Fred walked back to the microphone and people sat expectantly, as he stood there, looking out, smiling benevolently. Virginia, recovered now, sat back studying him. He looked, in his tuxedo, no more than sixty-five. His silver hair was still thick and wiry, his tanned face still firm; he was slim, fit-looking. He and his immense vitality had cheated the years; he was an astonishingly attractive man.

He was relaxed, enjoying himself; he was never happier than when he had a captive audience. Betsey, who had played that particular role with great charm and skill all her life, sat as attentive as anyone. There was a long, expectant pause.

'Well,' said Fred, 'thank you all for coming. Thank you for the presents. It could take until next birthday to open them all. You've all been very generous.'

He has stopped smiling now, was looking round the room almost soberly.

'I have much to be grateful for,' he said. 'It's been a wonderful seventy-five years, forty-five of which I have shared with my lovely wife Betsey. I ask you to give her a toast. Betsey Bradley Praeger: the best wife a man could have.'

'That's true,' said Betsey, smiling through her tears; everyone laughed, it broke the tension.

'I have loved it all,' Fred went on. 'My family: my beautiful grandchildren; my children have been lucky too. Alexander, Mary Rose: you would adorn any family. Thank you for becoming part of us. The bank of course is family to me: as much a part of me as my flesh and blood. I've seen it grow – even shrink occasionally' (much laughter) 'develop, change, increase in strength and stature. To be part of that process is a great privilege. It is also a great joy.

'A company is like a family; it has many facets, many elements. And you must respond to those elements, give each branch of the family what it needs.

'And just as you never quite leave your family, it remains with you, always, a source of strength as well as a commitment; you can never quite leave your company, let it go . . .'

Baby's heart lurched suddenly, his mouth went dry. He saw Mary Rose's eyes close in a momentary, involuntary agony. Dear God, he thought, he's going to change his mind.

There was a long silence. The assembled company was spellbound; not a pair of eyes left Fred's face. Even little Melissa was listening as if her life depended on it.

'Of course the family grows up; gains independence; your attitude to it changes. But you still keep a watchful eye. You must be there when you are needed.'

Another pause. 'You can never say "My job is done. My children no longer need me." They always need you. They need your attention, your concern, your love. And sometimes you can see what they need before they know it themselves. So it is, my friends, with the bank.'

Another endless silence. Baby felt the sweat break out on his forehead. His nails were grinding into his hands.

'I am seventy-five years old now. Time to hand the bank over. Which I do today. With great joy.'

Relief, sweet, cool, flooded into Baby's body, like a physical presence.

'My son, Baby Praeger, or as I suppose he should now be called, Fred Praeger the Fourth, is to take over the bank. He will be chairman; it will be his to do as he sees fit with. To develop, to change, to take care of. He has served a long apprenticeship; too long, he would tell you – possibly has.' (more laughter) 'He will do a great job. I have every confidence in him. I ask you to raise your glasses to – Fred the Fourth.'

'Fred the Fourth!' The glasses went up again. Baby smiled, then suddenly dashed his hand across his eyes. Mary Rose, unusually gentle, covered his other hand with hers. She smiled with extreme warmth at her father-in-law, and half rose. He gestured to her to sit down again.

'Just a few more words. A very few, I promise. To continue with my analogy about the family: I see new needs, new challenges, to the bank. We are in the middle of great social upheavals; new classes, new races are achieving power. And there are fundamental changes to be made everywhere. The world is not what it was. To ignore those changes, those challenges, is dangerous.'

'For heaven's sake,' muttered Mary Rose to Baby, 'what is he talking about?'

'This bank, this family of mine, has always been very much a personal affair. I am the third Frederick Praeger to run it. Baby will be the fourth. Freddy, his son, stands in line, heir apparent. That is as it should be. Freddy, stand up, take a bow.'

Freddy stood up, boyishly awkward, and bowed, nervously, uncertain. Everyone applauded.

'However,' said Fred, 'however . . .'

'Dear God,' said Baby. His knuckles were white.

'There are new contributions that can be made, from a new source. The fastest rising, strongest source to hit mankind since man rose onto two feet. A powerful, clear-sighted, courageous source. I refer to – woman. Now this may surprise many of you. I have not been known for my championship of women's cause. Indeed I have, to my shame, obstructed it. But it is a mark of strength and of courage to admit a mistake, and I am admitting mine. I have come to respect, to admire, to value women.'

'And about time too,' said Betsey, providing yet again a hugely welcome break in the tension.

'Indeed. And without you, my darling, I would not have made this leap. However, there are practical considerations to my change of heart. I want the bank to be equipped to receive this bounty. I want it receptive to every kind of change. I want it to contain women, therefore, in high places. Consequently, I have drawn up a new constitution for the bank.'

The silence in the room was tangible, thick; nobody stirred.

'I have made provision, as I can, within the share structure, for a change in its constitution. I have arranged – ' he waited, his gaze resting upon her, tender, benign – 'for my eldest granddaughter, Charlotte, to inherit the bank equally, together with her cousin, Freddy. I would ask you all to stand, and to drink to Charlotte. And the new future that she represents.'

Everyone rose once again, slightly awkwardly, a little uncomfortable, raising their glasses, saying 'To Charlotte' oddly half-heartedly.

Baby looked at Freddy, white-faced and still, staring blankly in front of him, and then at Charlotte, receiving congratulations, flushed, half smiling, plainly (but charmingly) overwhelmed by it all, and hated her so much that he could in that moment have quite easily killed her.

Chapter 11

Charlotte, 1978–80

Charlotte always said afterwards that that had been the moment when she had grown up – swiftly, unequivocally, irreversibly. She changed, publicly, dramatically, from a pretty, charming child into a young woman, one already branded successful, immensely rich – and potentially powerful. It was the last that seemed at once most exciting and most scary. She sat there, the picture of modesty, looking down at her hands, and felt a surge of almost physical excitement, of triumph at the thought of what she had been given. And then that sensation passed, and she was suddenly and immensely aware of, concerned for, Freddy. She was quite proud of that afterwards; she felt she must be a nicer person than she had always thought. Time seemed to have frozen; nobody at the table moved or spoke. She looked at him sitting there, next to her, rather pale, staring fiercely ahead of him, clenching and unclenching his fists, and she felt sick and just didn't know what to do; and then she saw Baby coming towards them, his blue eyes concerned, gentle, as he looked at Freddy, putting his hand on his shoulder, saying something in his ear; Charlotte jumped up and said, 'Have my seat, Uncle Baby,' and he smiled at her very nicely and said, 'Thank you, Charlotte. Congratulations,' and she thought how extraordinarily generous a person he was, not to hate her, not to be tempted to strangle her, or at least kick her hard under the table (and the unbidden thought also came into her head at that moment, surprising her, that he was perhaps too nice, too easy to manipulate for his own good and the position he was in), and she started to move off the platform, towards the room and the smiling, indulgent crowd of people, all wanting to congratulate her.

'Charlotte,' said a voice suddenly, 'or should I say, Lady Charlotte. May I have the pleasure of this dance?'

Charlotte looked up and found herself confronted by an extremely handsome young man. He was tall, and very heavily built; he had curly dark hair and brown eyes and the alarmingly perfect teeth possessed by so many rich Americans, and he was undeniably and powerfully sexy.

'We haven't met since you were twelve,' he said, holding out his hand to pull her up from her chair. 'I'm Gabriel Hoffman. Known as Gabe. My father is a partner at Praegers. It looks like we shall be working together in due course.'

'Really?' said Charlotte coolly. For some reason she didn't like him in spite of the good looks and the sexiness. 'Have you already started working there yourself?'

'Not quite,' said Gabe. 'But that's what I shall be. A partner like my dad. So like I say, we shall be working together.'

'I hadn't realized partnerships were hereditary,' said Charlotte coolly. 'So maybe we won't. I'm sorry, but I have to go have a word with Freddy.'

She walked past him and over to Freddy who was standing in one of the doorways, looking as if the end of the world had come and staring at her intently over his glass of champagne. His eyes, she noticed, and wondered why she had never done so before, were exactly like his mother's, very pale and very cold: and at that moment fearsomely filled with dislike.

'Come on, Fred the Fifth,' she said, taking the champagne out of his hand and setting it down on a nearby table. 'Dance with me. And let's be friends. We're going to be in this thing together, after all.'

Freddy looked at her for a moment or two without speaking; then he said, 'I'm sorry, Charlotte, I don't like dancing. And I think it is a little naive of you to imagine we could be friends. Business partners, yes, it seems, but friends, no.' And he turned away from her and walked out of the marquee.

Charlotte stared after him. A knot of panic that was almost physical had formed in her chest; she felt cold and very alone suddenly. She realized very vividly in that moment the full extent of his hatred for her, and realized too how naive, how crass she had been to think she could simply chat him up, charm him into accepting her, regard her as anything but a bitter, deadly threat, a claimant to his birthright, the thing he had been brought up to believe from babyhood was his and his alone. Charlotte was not easily frightened, but she was frightened now, looking down the years ahead at the feud that she would inherit along with the bank, a feud that nothing could save her from; and then following swiftly on the fear came a rush of sheer reckless courage with which she always greeted danger, and she smiled at the retreating back and turned back to find Gabe Hoffman. But he was gone, and she saw him dancing with a very pretty girl, laughing down at her; he glanced over and saw her watching them, and his expression was distant, unfriendly. Charlotte stared back at him, and realized with sickening clarity that she had made a serious tactical error. She needed Gabe; she needed all the allies she could get. She had already lost not one but two of her skirmishes in what was clearly going to be a very long war. And playing silly flirtatious sexual games was clearly no way to win any of them.

Charlotte had discovered the power of her own sexuality the previous summer; and having discovered it, she had enjoyed exercising it. She had spent a week with her friend Joanna Lavenham and her parents in their house near Salcombe in Devon. Joanna's brother Toby had been there, and Toby had not only found Charlotte very exciting, he had seen that she found him very exciting too.

Toby was nineteen and at Oxford; he had successfully seduced half his year, and he quite fancied his chances with the sexy, brainy Lady Charlotte Welles. He engineered a sailing afternoon with her, alone in his dinghy, moored the boat in a cove, suggested they swim in and had then proceeded to kiss Charlotte with an unhurried confidence that left her confused, hungry and flattered.

After half an hour or so, one of his hands found its way into her bikini top; she pushed it away rather half-heartedly once or twice and then closed her eyes and surrendered herself to the increased pleasure; shortly after that the hand was moving confidently and insistently down to her bikini bottoms and her pubic hair. That was even nicer; but just as she was drowning in the pleasure of it and the added pleasure that the gorgeous Toby Lavenham found her so plainly desirable, he pulled away from her and started pulling off his trunks.

'Oh no,' said Charlotte firmly, sitting up herself and readjusting her top. 'No, Toby. Sorry.'

'Darling, I'm not going to do anything,' said Toby, 'honestly. I just want to be really close to you. That's all.'

Charlotte lay back on the sand and looked at him thoughtfully. He was very tall and well built; he had brown floppy hair and very sexy grey eyes. His body was slim, but not skinny, with a lot of dark hair on it; and the object hitherto concealed by his swimming trunks was dauntingly large and rather awesome. Charlotte tried to imagine herself accommodating it and couldn't; well, that was all right, she thought, she wasn't going to have to.

'Frankly,' she said, smiling at him very coolly, 'I really don't think I believe you. Please put your trunks back on, Toby, I really think this has all got a bit out of hand.'

Toby looked at her for a while; then he smiled, a mildly mocking smile. 'It's all right,' he said, 'I don't fuck schoolgirls. Come on, let's go home.'

He didn't speak to her unless he had to ask her to pass something at the table for the rest of the week; then on the last night they were all invited to a party, Charlotte got very drunk and asked him to dance with her, and Toby took her outside after a few minutes and kissed her for so long and so expertly that she hardly knew what she was doing, she wanted him so much; her body seemed to be no longer hers, no longer under control, she could feel it reaching for him, a sense of odd emptiness, a quivering, almost painful heat somewhere in its depth.

'You're an amazingly sexy girl,' he said to her finally, drawing back, breathing rather heavily, 'and I would like to screw you right into the ground.'

'Well,' said Charlotte, speaking with some difficulty, 'why don't you?'

'Would you like that?' said Toby, grinning down at her.

'I think so. Yes, yes I would.'

He took her hand, and started walking with her towards the summer house at the bottom of the lawn; Charlotte felt a mixture of fear and a great excitement, a disbelief that she could have come thus far. She was beginning to wonder, somewhat anxiously, what if anything she should do or say about contraception, when she heard Mrs Lavenham's voice calling from the french windows.

'Toby! Charlotte! Are you there? Time to go home.'

'Fuck,' said Toby. 'Fuck. Or rather, no fuck. Sorry, Charlotte. Another time maybe.'

Ever since then, her body seemed to have taken on a completely new and disturbing life of its own; it was restless, curious, and extremely wilful. She thought of sex a great deal, after that, what it might be like, what its range of pleasures might be; she was fascinated by it, she wanted it; and more than anything, she liked making boys want it. She was still a virgin; but she was impatient not to be.

And now, in one evening, one hour, one moment almost, she had discovered the necessity of growing up. And in consequence the matter of when and indeed whether she should go to bed with someone had become of very paltry importance.

It was difficult after that to go back to school, to obey rules, to wear a uniform, to be a child. She felt quite different about herself. Everything she did was directed towards this great and totally absorbing end. She could think of very little else. She pretended to; she pretended she was pleased, but no more than that, that she was also scared, of all the implications, the necessary manifestations of her birthright, leaving her family, going to live in America, having her entire life pattern prescribed for her, but she actually felt nothing of the kind, she was desperately

166

excited, frantically impatient. And also, she discovered, oddly confident. Not even the thought of Freddy's hostility worried her seriously. She had no doubts that she could handle that, as well as she would the work, the new world she was to find herself in; she sat from her viewpoint as Deputy Head Girl in an English public school with no real knowledge of what she was confronted with, and did not doubt for one moment that she would be successful at it.

She enjoyed her two A-level years. The work she found easy; exploring subjects in depth was an intense pleasure. She read far more and more widely than any of her contemporaries; nevertheless the actual examinations she found stressful, she became exhausted, tearful, unable to sleep. No one could understand it, they kept telling her she was bound to do well, she was so clever, and even if she didn't, it wouldn't matter. This simply made Charlotte even more fretful. The eyes of the entire world, or at least that part of it she cared about, would be on her results; she needed, for her own self-esteem, to be seen to perform not well but brilliantly, to show that she had not been given her great prize for nothing, just because her grandfather favoured her, petted her, but because she deserved it, and could justify the gift in every day of her life.

She lay awake half the night before the results came, staring into the darkness, sweating and afraid; she was actually sick twice. Towards dawn she fell finally asleep, and surfaced what seemed like a moment later, to hear Max's voice light with excitement.

'Georgie, look, they're here.'

'Max, don't call me Georgie. You know how cross it makes Mummy. What's here?'

'Everything makes Mummy cross. Charlotte's results.'

'Je-sus!'

'Georgie, don't swear. That's the one thing that makes Daddy cross. Shall I take them up or will you?'

'Bags I do!'

So much for getting up early and meeting the postman at the top of the drive; Charlotte flung out of bed, feeling angry and sick again, and opened her bedroom door. Her heart was thumping so hard she could feel it in her throat, a great lump. She swallowed, took a deep breath and ran down the stairs.

'Give those to me!' she said, snatching them from Max's hand. 'And go away, both of you, go away.'

Max and Georgina retreated, into the library; Charlotte ripped clumsily at the envelope, closed her eyes briefly, then opened them, forced them down. There was a silence, then a great, almost primitive cry of triumph echoed up into the dome of the Rotunda.

'Grandpa? Grandpa, it's Charlotte. How are you? Good. Listen, I got my results. Four As. Isn't that great? Aren't you proud of me? Yes, so I go up to Cambridge next term. Yes, she's thrilled, and so is Daddy. Anyway, I'll see you next week, won't I, on Nantucket. I feel I can really look forward to it now. How are the others? Give my love to Grandma. Bye, Grandpa.'

She went for a walk on her own, into the woods, savouring the happiness, the relief, the certainty of pleasure that lay ahead. Cambridge! Freedom, adulthood, endless endless fun; and at the end of that, her heritage, at Praegers: it was almost too much, she thought, she was too blest. She didn't deserve it. Something had to go wrong.

It certainly didn't go wrong on Nantucket. She went determined to accomplish the one thing that still seemed to her outstanding: the loss of her virginity; and she accomplished it in the bottom of a sailing boat a mile out to sea one afternoon, with the enthusiastic cooperation of her sailing instructor. She had heard so often that the first time was painful and disappointing; for Charlotte it was neither. She lay there, afterwards, her body almost surprised with pleasure, and laughed for joy; the sailing instructor, whose name was Beau Fraser and who wasn't really a sailing instructor but a law student at Pittsburgh, looked down at her and smiled and asked her if it really had been the first time, he would never have believed it, and most people didn't come once the first time, never mind twice. He was just about to try to accomplish what he called (rather wittily, Charlotte thought) a third coming, when the wind suddenly got up, and he had to see to the boat; sitting on the tiny foredeck, struggling to put on her bikini, she slipped and fell into the water. Beau Fraser hauled her back in, but the bikini was lost; she arrived back at the landing stage of the sailing club with nothing on but her life jacket. Fortunately the only person around was Baby, who cast his eyes over her slightly eccentric dress and without saying a word gave her a huge grin, removed his linen jacket and put it round her.

'Sir Walter Raleigh lives on, you see,' he said, 'better come inside quickly and borrow something, your grandfather's coming along to pick you up and give you tea.'

Charlotte had always been very fond of Baby; from then on, she would have died for him.

She would also from then on, or certainly until she left Nantucket, have died for Beau Fraser; every day they went sailing and every day he made love to her. She could not have enough of him; it was as if she had been starved all her life and now at last she was able to eat. She couldn't think of anything else, in those weeks; she woke up, her body already excited, anticipating the pleasures that lay ahead of it; she spent the mornings trying to concentrate on golf with Fred or tennis with Baby, or trying to crack Freddy's icy reserve, chattering determinedly to him through breakfast, while all she could think of was Beau Fraser's infinitely skilled mouth and hands, working on her body, the growth and heat of her hunger for him, and the infinitely variable, infinitely reliable pleasure as he entered her, moved within her, and her body welcomed him, and rose and fell and shook with passion. She lived in terror of their afternoons being disturbed, interrupted in some way; she would sit at lunch, uncharacteristically silent, ignoring the family discussions and plans about picnics, riding, barbecues.

The last week they were there Alexander and Virginia arrived. They were clearly not very happy and seemed to be determined to annoy one another as much as possible. Alexander as usual spent a lot of time on his own, went to bed early and refused to join in all the family games; the only person he would do anything with at all was Georgina, whom he took cycling and swimming a great deal, so that she was removed from the family group as well. He called her Georgie a lot in front of Virginia, which always annoyed her, and which he never did at home; he also refused to take seriously Baby's report that Max had been necking, as Baby put it, with Melissa in the summer house, and his demand that Alexander should chastise Max.

'For God's sake, Baby, they're children. What do you think can happen?'

Baby said that wasn't the point, and Alexander said he couldn't see any other and walked out of the room; the subject was not raised again. Charlotte had a sneaking sympathy with Baby's point of view; she felt her father was being insensitive. Which was extremely unlike him.

After four days, Virginia left again; she had a client to see in New York, who had asked to do his beach house on Florida Key West; she had done his apartment at the Sherry Netherland, in what she described as French provincial style.

'I cannot imagine how anything French provincial could sit in that brash heap of a hotel,' said Alexander lightly. 'Georgie, don't eat so fast, anyone would think you hadn't been fed for a year.'

'Imagination was never your strong point,' said Virginia. 'And don't call her Georgie.'

She was in particularly tetchy mood; even Max had to admit it was better without her.

Alexander took the children back to England alone; Virginia had gone to Key West. She had called Nantucket to say she would be anything up to two weeks.

'It won't matter, will it?' she said to Charlotte. 'Max and Georgina will be at school, and you'll be off to university. I won't be missed.'

'You will,' said Charlotte, 'but we're used to it.' She put the phone down without even saying goodbye.

Left on her own, with a month to kill before she went up to Cambridge, Charlotte was bored and lonely. She did some reading, and she rode a lot, but she missed Beau unbearably, and she missed her brother and sister as well. Alexander was busy with the estate, distracted; she sought other friends, but found them unsatisfactory. She was just thinking of going back to the States to see her mother and do some groundwork on the bank when Toby Lavenham rang.

'Charlotte! Hi, how was your summer?'

'Oh it was fine. How was yours?'

'Excellent.'

She saw him almost every holidays, but they had never resumed their relationship; the opportunity had not presented itself at first and then he had had a relationship at Oxford which Joanna had said was serious. 'But he still does hold a bit of a torch for you, Charlotte. I wouldn't be surprised if he comes back to you after all. Don't despair!'

Charlotte didn't say she was extremely far from despair; Joanna adored her brother.

He sounded pompous and stiff after Beau; she could hardly bear to talk to him.

'Charlotte, I'm down this weekend, with my parents. Could I come over and see you?'

'Of course. Any time.' She sounded bored, uninterested.

'Well – I wondered if you'd like to have dinner on Saturday? In Marlborough somewhere? Would that amuse you?'

'Oh – yes. Yes, that'd be really nice.' Come on, Charlotte, she thought, make an effort. He can't help not being Beau.

'OK. I'll call for you about six thirty. Then we can have a drive and a drink first.'

'Fine. Bye, Toby.'

Oh well, it would be better than dinner with Nanny.

Somewhat perversely, Charlotte went to considerable trouble to look nice for Toby. She wanted to show him that she was now a grown, fully mature woman. Not a schoolgirl.

She wore a black jersey dress that clung to her body, buttoned right through from neck to hem; she left several of the top buttons undone, and most of the bottom ones, so that when she sat down a great deal of leg was revealed. Charlotte's legs could not compete with Georgina's but they were shapely nonetheless. She had lost quite a lot of weight, she thought happily; her summer with Beau had done more for her than show her the delights of sex. She had had a lot of difficulty eating dinner at night, after her rapturous afternoons, and she had been so strung up at lunchtime anticipating them, she hadn't been able to eat then either. It would probably all go back on now, she thought ruefully.

She put on a lot of eye make-up, brushed her dark hair rather wildly back from her face, sprayed herself liberally with Rive Gauche, and went down to meet Toby feeling rather pleased with herself. He came towards her smiling, his hands stretched out to take hers. She found herself surprisingly pleased to see him; she had forgotten how good-looking he was, and leant forward and kissed him lightly on the lips.

'Charlotte! You look gorgeous. I love the hair. Is that how they wear it in Massachusetts?'

'It's how I wore it in Massachusetts.'

'Well I wish I'd been there. Was it fun?'

'Great fun.' An image of Beau, stark naked, kneeling above her in the sailing boat, swam suddenly in front of Charlotte's eyes; she smiled rather weakly at Toby.

'Good. Well, shall we go? Or is your father about? I'd like to say hallo to him.'

'No, he's out on the estate somewhere,' said Charlotte hastily. Alexander didn't like Toby.

'Right. Look, like my new wheels?'

The new wheels were an Aston Martin convertible, dark green with whitewall tyres. Charlotte whistled admiringly.

'It's gorgeous, Toby. Is that the fruits of your new job in the City?'

'Well – Father thought I should have a decent car. It's important, you know. To give a good impression.'

'I'm sure.' She smiled at him. Pompous idiot, she thought.

Toby drove her very fast into Marlborough; they stopped halfway at a pub and had a drink. Or several drinks. By the time they reached the restaurant, Charlotte's head was spinning agreeably.

Toby had ordered a bottle of champagne; it was waiting in an ice bucket by their table.

'Toby!' said Charlotte. 'What largesse.'

'Yes, well, it seemed a rather special evening to me. We've never managed to go out on our own together. And I – well, I was wondering if – '

He looked at her rather seriously; she laughed awkwardly and looked about her. 'I love this place, don't you? Oh look, there's Sarah and Dominic. Let's go and say hallo.'

They didn't just say hallo to Sarah and Dominic, Charlotte suggested they joined them. 'It'd be much more fun. Come on, just get the waiter to bring over two more chairs, and maybe another bottle of bubbly, Toby.'

'Fine,' said Toby. He was looking a trifle tight-lipped.

They were all four friends from childhood; Sarah was a plain, rather horsey girl, and Dominic was a hearty, rugger-bugger type who was struggling through his degree course in agriculture at Cirencester with some difficulty. He had always admired Charlotte; she was quite drunk by now and flirting outrageously with both men.

'Come on, Sarah, now you sit in the corner, and Dom, you go there on the inside. Then Toby can order the waiter about more easily. Oh Dominic, it's heaven to see you, you look sort of weather-beaten and sexy – a sort of upper-crust Mellors. Is that what agricultural college does for you? Toby darling, maybe you should have done agriculture instead of going into the City. You wouldn't be quite so pale and interesting-looking. Now what shall we all have to eat? They've got lobster. Oh, you should have seen the lobsters we had on Nantucket. Huge, with those enormous phallic claws. I used to have the most odd dreams afterwards. Now what have you two been doing all summer while I've been disporting myself with lobsters? Oh, I'm so glad we all found each other. I've been so bored, with everyone away, this is just the best fun in the world.'

By the end of dinner, Toby was in a serious sulk, Sarah was giggling and trying to behave as outrageously and sexily as Charlotte, and Dominic was nodding off over his port. Charlotte decided she wanted to go dancing. Toby could take her to Tramp.

Out in the car, Toby looked at her in silence. Then he started it and moved off at great speed down the main street.

'Toby, this isn't right. This isn't towards London. Turn around.'

'No, Charlotte. I'm not turning round. You're in no fit state to go to Tramp. I'm taking you home.'

'Toby! Are you implying I'm drunk?'

'No. I'm telling you you're drunk.'

'I am not.' She reached out and stroked the back of his neck. 'How masterful you are, Toby. How wonderfully masterful. Wasn't that a fun evening? Don't you think?'

'No,' said Toby. 'No, I don't.'

'Oh. Well that's a shame.' She looked at him in silence for a moment, then said, 'You're really very good-looking, Toby. Very good-looking.'

'Thank you.'

'Do stop the car a minute will you?'

He gave her a startled look and pulled over to the side of the road. Charlotte leant towards him and kissed him hard on the mouth.

'Gorgeous,' she said briefly. 'Gorgeous. Goodness, sex is fun.'

Toby started the car again and drove it very hard out of town; then he swung left and took a turn that said Savernake Forest. Charlotte lay back, a smug expression on her face, half asleep.

She came to herself with a jolt when she felt the car stop. Toby had parked at the end of a rutted lane. He was looking at her with an odd expression.

'Goodness,' said Charlotte, sober suddenly, 'what happened? Did we break down or something, Toby?'

'No,' he said. 'No we didn't break down. But I might in a minute. Come on, Charlotte, let's get out.'

'No. Oh all right. Just for a bit.'

She got out. Toby dragged a rug out of the boot and draped it on the grass verge. He sat down on it. 'Come on,' he said, 'come on, Charlotte. We have a lot of unfinished business to pursue. Don't we?'

'Well, I – '

'Oh, Charlotte, don't go all coy on me. You know I've always fancied you.'

'Toby! You've been having a wild old time, from what I've heard.'

'Yes, I have. But I never quite got over you, Charlotte. I've never forgotten that night at the party. Have you?'

'No,' said Charlotte. It seemed easier. What party? What was he talking about? Her head was spinning.

'Come down and join me,' said Toby patting the rug again. 'Come and be comfy.'

Charlotte looked at him doubtfully. Then she sat down. Toby pushed her onto her back and began to kiss her. He had always kissed well; she remembered now. Not as well as Beau, but it was all right. She returned the kiss.

Toby's hands began to move into her dress. She felt them caressing the mounds of her breasts; then confidently, deliberately on her nipples.

Charlotte, briefly torn between enjoying the sensations he was evoking and a sense of disloyalty to Beau, relaxed suddenly. Beau was thousands of miles away. A little heavy petting wouldn't hurt. Toby's hands were under her dress now, exploring upwards, stroking her bare brown legs, working his way up her thighs. He reached her pants; she felt his fingers rather awkwardly, tentatively in her pubic hair. She squirmed, aroused in spite of herself, and Toby felt the signal.

He sat up suddenly, away from her, unzipping his fly, dragging down his trousers; Charlotte carefully averted her eyes.

He leant towards her again, started pulling at her pants; she smiled at him, and tugged them off herself. The combination of the drink and the sudden sharp reminder of sexual pleasure was too much for her. She lay back, her face, her eyes, her wild hair an irresistible invitation. She felt excited now, everything blotted out, except the hot, beating urgency of her own desire; Toby started kissing her again, and then as she thrust her body upwards, against him, entered her quite suddenly, hard and relentless. Charlotte closed her eyes again and abandoned herself to pleasure.

Only there was none. Toby thrust into her four or five times, kissing her frantically; she had scarcely begun to soften to him, to feel any kind of pleasure when he moaned, came and collapsed onto her. Charlotte lay in the moonlight, looking up at the sky, with a sense of total betrayal. Where was it, the joy she had learnt to experience, the mounting leaping heat, the tumbling explosion, the sweet peace? All she felt was a dreadful aching emptiness that was almost pain. She lay and she didn't move and she felt quite sober, and deeply ashamed suddenly.

'That was great,' said Toby, moving off her, turning onto his back. 'Really great. Are you all right?'

'Er – yes,' said Charlotte slightly uncertainly.

'Sorry I didn't put a johnny on. Got a bit carried away. But you should be all right, shouldn't you? Dates OK?'

'Er – yes,' said Charlotte again. 'I think so.' Outrage was beginning to replace the emptiness. There was no way she was going to tell Toby she was on the pill; let him worry for a while.

'So was that OK for you? I thought it was terrific.'

Charlotte turned to look at him. She thought she had never hated anyone so much as she did Toby at that moment, lying there with a self-satisfied expression on his face, his trousers still around his knees. 'Actually no,' she said coldly. She sat up, looking around for her pants.

'What? Oh sorry, darling. Look, don't worry, it's often not too hot the first time. You'll get better at it.'

Charlotte looked at him in silence for quite a while, deliberately bestowing a lingering gaze on his small limp penis. Then she smiled, a tight, cold little smile.

'Toby,' she said, 'I think you have a little to learn. A lot even, it seems. That was not the first time, you will obviously be surprised to learn; I am equally surprised that you should have thought it was. Moreover, I don't think I have to get better at it, I have very often managed to enjoy it enormously. On the other hand, I think you need to get quite a bit better at it. Your technique, if indeed what I have just endured can be dignified with such a term, leaves a great deal to be desired. Now perhaps we could go home. I'm very tired.'

She stood up, pulling on her pants, and then walked towards the car; as she reached it, Toby grabbed her by her shoulders and turned her roughly round.

'You bitch,' he said, 'you slut. You filthy little self-satisfied slut. Well, blood will out. It's obviously all true.'

Charlotte stared at him. 'I don't have the first idea what you mean,' she said.

'Oh really? Well you would say that, wouldn't you?'

'Toby,' she said, 'please explain. And please let go of me. You're hurting me.'

'Oh, get in the car,' he said suddenly, obviously regretting his words. 'Just get in and let's go.'

'Toby,' said Charlotte, 'I want to know what you meant by that. What's obviously all true?'

'Nothing,' said Toby. 'Get in the car.'

Charlotte got in in silence. He started the car, backed up the track, and started driving fast along the main road. Charlotte looked at his face, set and white in the moonlight, and felt a great shudder of unease. She didn't say any more until Toby pulled up in front of Hartest. Then she turned to him.

'Toby,' she said, 'if you don't tell me what you meant, I shall run up those steps and wake up the whole house and say you just raped me.'

'You wouldn't dare. They wouldn't believe you.'

'I would certainly dare, and they would believe me. I'm a very good actress, I have mud on my legs and leaves and twigs in my hair and certain irrefutable evidence in my body. My father would find it extremely difficult not to believe me. Now then, just tell me what the hell you were talking about.'

'Oh, Charlotte, don't make me. Please. I shouldn't have said anything. I'm sorry.'

'It's a little late for that. Toby, would you just begin, please?'

175

'No.'

'Right.' She opened the door, stepped out and opened her mouth to scream. Toby, moving with impressive speed, dragged her back in and put his hand over her mouth.

'Shut up. Just shut up. I'll tell you.'

'All right, I'll shut up. Get talking.'

'You – you won't like it,' he said.

'I don't mind.'

'And it's only gossip. Stupid Wiltshire gossip.'

'Fine. I like gossip. Just begin, will you.'

'Yes, all right, Charlotte. I'm only amazed none of it has reached you before.'

'None of what?'

'This. The gossip.'

'Well it hasn't. You're in the privileged position of being Lead Gossip. Go on, Toby.'

'Well – all right. Don't blame me, that's all.'

'Oh, I wouldn't dream of it.'

There was a long silence. Toby looked frantically out of the window. Charlotte moved to open her door again. He grabbed her hand suddenly and held it, surprisingly gently.

'I just hate this,' he said, 'hate having to hurt you. I've always liked you so much. I might not have shown it this evening, but I have. But – well, Charlotte, the gossip is that – well, you and your sister are not actually your father's. And that your mother has had a lot of affairs.'

There was a long silence. A very long silence. Charlotte sat quite still, her face set, staring at him. She did not take her hand away. Then she said, 'When did you hear this?'

'Oh,' he said, 'I've heard it a few times. Honestly. I've never said anything to anyone. Said I didn't believe it, actually.'

'Who have you heard it from?'

'Oh – a couple of girls. You know how girls gossip.'

'No, actually,' said Charlotte.

'Well they do. And I once heard my mother and a friend of hers talking, by the tennis court. Georgina was playing with someone, you weren't there. My mother said how unlike the two of you were, and her friend said well, surely my mother had heard the gossip, that neither of you were your – were Lord Caterham's children – Charlotte, don't look like that, you and Georgina are amazingly different looking. That at least is true. And neither of you looks in the least like Max. Now he *does* look like your father.'

'Yes he does,' said Charlotte absently. 'Exactly.' She was talking oddly, as if in shock. 'Well, you see, Toby, I look just like Grandma Praeger. Everyone says so. And Georgina, well she is like – well, all sorts of people. Granny Caterham is very tall. And she has Mummy's eyes. We both do. Lioness's eyes, Grandpa Praeger says. So it obviously is nonsense. Just gossipy nonsense. Goodnight, Toby. Thank you for dinner.'

She got out of the car and walked very slowly up the steps and round to the small door at the side of the south front which the family often used, and went in without turning round.

Charlotte went downstairs to the kitchen and stood looking around her for a moment or two. She felt as if she had never seen it before; she felt as if she had never been in the house before, and that she did not know where she was.

Then she went over to a cupboard, got out a mug, and made herself some warm milk. She sat down at the table, staring at the Aga and thinking about what she had just heard, trying to process the information, trying to analyse her feelings.

Confusion, that was to be expected. Panic, also. But her major emotion was something that contributed to the panic, something that frightened her. It was a kind of calm, dull acceptance that what she had just heard made sense. A lot more sense than that they had all been adopted.

She hated the acceptance, hated recognizing it. But she did. And she wasn't sure why. Most people, confronted by what she had just confronted, would have been outraged, indignant, denying it. Why wasn't she? Her parents always seemed happy enough. Of course her mother was away a lot, but when she came back, her father was always so happy to see her, he was joyful, singing about the house before going to meet her. They never quarrelled, or hardly ever. He never for a single moment said anything remotely disloyal about Virginia; he went out of his way to defend her absences, to explain to them all why it was so important to her to work, to have a life of her own. And to make sure they believed that she loved them. And her mother also never ever spoke harshly about Alexander. She hardly ever argued with him, even. She was a little distant, of course, a little cool, but that was the sort of person she was. She wasn't like him, openly loving, physically demonstrative. But she did quite clearly love him.

They often went off for long long walks together, around the estate, hand in hand, talking, endlessly talking. They were famous, those walks. Max particularly always wanted to go with them, and often he did, but sometimes they would discourage him, laughing, saying they wanted to be alone.

Of course her mother had had problems. There had been the drink, and revivals of the drink; but she had beaten that, and her father had been so wonderfully supportive over it. Surely, if a man's wife was so compulsively unfaithful to him that two of her children were not his, or even one of them, that man would not stay loyally by her while she went on alcoholic benders for days at a time, got picked up by the police, was committed to clinics; surely he would take that as a reasonable excuse to end the marriage.

And she had been so terribly depressed after the first little boy was born, Charlotte could still just remember that, the endless crying, and the collapse on the grave, and then being sent away to America; and she could remember how tender, how patient her father's voice had been, never exasperated, never giving in, as her mother cried at the table, and in the car and all over the house. Surely he couldn't have managed that, if there had been any doubt, any doubt at all, about the baby's parentage.

And then there was Max. If ever a child looked like his father, Max did. The blond hair, the blue eyes, the long slim body. Obviously Max was his. So, clearly even if she and Georgina were some other man's children, the marriage had been mended, sufficiently, to conceive Max. To begin again. And would that have been a possibility, if your wife had been so blatantly unfaithful to you?

And that was another thing. Alexander was so loving, so terribly terribly loving towards them, to her and Georgina. If he had a favourite, it wasn't Max, it was Georgina. Surely he wouldn't be able to do that, if he knew they weren't his? Or suspected it.

Of course that was another thing. She hadn't thought of that. She was assuming Alexander must have known, if it was true. But maybe he didn't. But then, he wasn't stupid. And if your wife was away a great deal and kept on getting pregnant and having children who didn't look remotely like you, like anyone in the family, you'd have to be pretty stupid not to suspect something.

And then, for heaven's sake, thought Charlotte, her mother was a sophisticated woman; surely if she had been having affairs all over the place, she wouldn't have got pregnant. She would have been terribly careful, this wasn't the nineteenth century. Erring wives just didn't come home with bastard babies. A bastard baby, she thought: is that what I was? Am?

No, clearly it couldn't be true. It didn't make sense. It was a vile, filthy lie and one that her father had managed to rise above, because he was a gentleman and a loving husband and father, and to refute it, to force it into the open, to publicly deny it, would have been to perpetuate it, to give it credence in some strange way.

But then why had it started in the first place? And why then, why, why, did she still feel as if it did make some sort of sense?

Charlotte shook her head, put her cup in the sink and went slowly up the small staircase that led out of the kitchen. It came out finally on the first-floor back landing, and then there was another flight up to the second floor where the nurseries were and where Nanny slept. As the children had grown older they had been given bigger, grander rooms on the first floor, but the nurseries had remained, 'ready for my grandchildren' Alexander had said, smiling, more than once. Charlotte looked up towards the second floor now, thinking in a kind of wonder that she could never again view her childhood peacefully, happily, and sighed; she took her shoes off and went up. She smiled as she passed Nanny's door; thunderous snores were coming out. She went into the day nursery, light with the brilliant moon, went over to the window, pushing absently at the rocking horse as she passed it. She stood looking down at the parkland; the moon was reflected in the lake, the swans slept on it, their heads tucked within their feathers, and the tall reeds at the side looked darkly mysterious, part of their own shadows. She could see every detail of the Palladian bridge and the wide stream flowing beneath it; a deer and her fawn, awake in the moonlight, moved slowly across the park, towards the water. How beautiful it was, she thought, diverted from her unhappiness, not just the house, but all of it, the land, the whole small country that was Hartest, their heritage, that their father loved so much, that he invested all his energy and money and strength in. She leant her head against the window, drinking in the beauty, and tried to sort her whirling thoughts.

Charlotte made her way wearily down the front stairs and along the landing towards her own room. She felt desperately tired and rather sick.

On the wall, outside her mother's room, was a painting that had been done of her and Georgina and Max eight years earlier by the celebrated portrait painter Leopold Manners: she and Georgina dressed in cream lace dresses, Max in a blue velvet page-boy suit with a lace collar. It was a very flattering portrait; Leopold Manners had not made his name and his fortune by telling the truth about his subjects, and she looked a great deal slimmer than she had actually been, and Georgina (who had then been at her plainest and scrawniest) a great deal softer and prettier. Only Max stood there as he had truly been, a ravishing small boy, with a mop of ash-blond curls and huge blue eyes. But oh, God, thought Charlotte, switching the picture light on to study it more carefully, oh, God, they all looked so different. Nobody, nobody, had they not known, would have thought them brother and sisters.

'For God's sake, Mummy,' she said aloud as she finally got into bed and lay wide awake, staring at the ceiling, 'for God's sake, if you had to commit adultery, couldn't you have been a bit more careful to choose lovers who looked at least a bit like Daddy?'

Chapter 12

Charlotte, 1980

'You're disgusting,' said Georgina. 'Disgusting. I don't want to hear any more. I just want to go back to school again and forget about it.'

'Georgie – '

'Don't call me that. You know how angry it makes Mummy.'

'Georgina, Mummy's not here. *Plus ça change.*'

'What's that meant to mean?'

'Nothing,' said Charlotte wearily. 'Just that she's not here, to be angry. She's away. As usual. That's all I meant.' She put her hand up to her reddened face where Georgina had struck it. 'That hurt, you know.'

'Good. That's what I intended. I wish I hadn't come home.'

Georgina picked up a sugar lump and started dipping it into her tea. She was always doing that, eating sugar. Charlotte watched her, resentment added to her misery and guilt. It wasn't fair. If she ate sugar lumps she'd be a size sixteen instead of just squeezing into a twelve.

'Charlotte,' said Georgina, 'are you somehow implying that because Mummy's always away, your foul story must be true?'

'No I'm not. I don't think.' Charlotte spoke slowly. 'Although it's what you might call circumstantial evidence.'

'Oh for God's sake. Don't start talking your legal jargon.'

'Sorry. Georgina, I can see why you're so upset. But can't you also see why I had to talk to you?'

'No. No I can't. I really, genuinely can't.' She embarked on another sugar lump.

'Look,' said Charlotte patiently. 'You would have found out. Honestly. I mean you would have heard the rumour. Just like I did. And it would have been horrible for you. As it was for me. I'm sorry, Georgina, I just had to talk to you. I felt I was going mad.'

'Well I still don't see why you should think it has to be true.'

'I'm not sure myself,' said Charlotte, 'but I just do.'

'What about Max? He's clearly a Caterham. You've only got to look at him and Daddy together. They're terribly alike.'

'Yes,' said Charlotte, 'I agree. I don't think there's any doubt about Max's parentage.'

'It's much worse than the adoption idea,' said Georgina with a sigh.

'And that's another thing,' said Charlotte, remembering. 'Mummy was so funny about that, so cross. I didn't think much about it at the time, but lots of children think they're adopted, and their mothers don't fly off the handle. That was obviously why. Raw nerves.'

Georgina looked at her, weary suddenly, her aggressiveness dispersed. 'Is it really going to do any good, digging over all this dirt?'

'I don't know if it'll do any good, exactly. But don't you feel that really, really we ought to know? It seems pretty crucial to me. I want to, if you don't. If I'm not Charlotte Welles, then who am I? And did Daddy know? And if he did, why did he put up with it? I just have to know, Georgina. I really do.'

'I hate it,' said Georgina. 'I simply hate it. And now what are you going to do,' she said, angry again suddenly, 'go to Daddy and say, "Hey, we just heard you're not our real father. We'd like to hear more about it, please." Or "Mummy, we understand you've been having affairs, and conceiving babies all over the place, would you be kind enough to let us know who our fathers are?" '

'Well, don't you want to know?'

'I know who my father is,' said Georgina, her face closing again, 'it's Daddy. I know it is. I couldn't be anybody else's. I know I couldn't.'

'Yes,' said Alexander, 'yes, I'm afraid it's true.' He smiled at Charlotte, a shaky, careful smile. 'I'm more sorry than I can ever tell you that you had to find out this way. I had always hoped, prayed, that the gossip would never reach you. I suppose it was stupid. Naive. But then I could see no alternative.'

'You could have told us the truth,' said Charlotte. She was flushed, angry. 'It would have spared me, and still more spared Georgina a lot of pain. It was a horrible thing to happen, Daddy. Horrible.'

'Darling, I can see that. I'm appalled by it. By what you've been through. And I have to say I do wish –' He looked at her very seriously – 'I wish you'd come to me before you'd spoken to Georgina. Together we might have been able to make it easier for her. She's very young still. And we've always been so close. It must have been a terrible shock.'

'Yes it was. Terrible. Well, maybe I shouldn't have talked to her. But I had to talk to someone. And she is the person most intimately concerned.'

'Well,' said Alexander, 'I think I am fairly intimately concerned myself. If I might say so. But I can see, darling, you did have to talk to someone. And that you'd have wanted to discuss it with her. Of course I can.'

'Why didn't you tell us?' said Charlotte, a note of exasperation in her voice. 'Why?'

'Darling, how could I? How could I? At what point? How would I have known? When you left school? Sixteen? When you reached puberty? When you learnt the facts of life? Impossible. I just kept putting it off. And praying. As I said.'

'You could have done something,' said Charlotte stubbornly. 'You could have told us we were adopted, at least.'

'I wouldn't have wanted to do that,' he said. 'I wouldn't have wanted to lie to you.'

'Oh thanks,' said Charlotte. Her voice was bitter. 'That was really nice of you.'

Alexander was sitting at his desk. He leant forward and took one of her hands.

'Darling, don't be angry.'

She turned on him, her face white and tense. 'Daddy, of course I'm angry. What do you expect? I've just discovered I – Georgie and I – are the victims of a monumental piece of – of fraud. That we're not who we thought we were. That we're illegitimate. And you have never taken any steps to protect us from the knowledge. And then you tell me not to be angry.'

'Charlotte,' he said, and there was great pain in his voice, 'Charlotte, you might spare a thought for me. In all this. How do you think it has been for me? Living with this all these years. It hasn't been easy. I love you both very very much, and I would hate you to think otherwise, but dear God, it hasn't been easy.'

He sounded angry now; she looked at him, startled.

'No,' she said, 'no I don't suppose it has. I'm sorry. I haven't thought about you enough. What – what did actually happen? I mean how did it happen?'

'Oh,' he said, 'I don't really want to have to go into all the details. It would be painful for both of us. But your mother has always been – well, independent. You know how much time she spends away from me. From us. And she is – well, very attractive. Very sexually attractive. I found it hard to hold her. From the beginning, I'm afraid. But I loved her and I went on forgiving her. In so many ways she was a wonderful wife, you see.'

'Oh wonderful!' said Charlotte. 'Superb. Daddy, you should have divorced her.'

'I couldn't,' said Alexander simply. 'I really couldn't. I didn't want to lose her, I didn't want a scandal, and you see – ' he looked at her almost shamefaced – 'I would have looked terribly terribly foolish. To have admitted that she had lovers so very early in our marriage. That may sound very silly to you, but I was brought up in a very different way. Appearances were important to me. To my family. To – Hartest.'

'Oh.' She looked at him and her heart softened, started to ache for him. He looked so infinitely sad and humiliated suddenly; she put her hand out, tenderly, onto his.

'Poor Daddy.'

'Well. I expect I was foolish. Weak. But there it is. What we – I – decided to do seemed simplest. At the time.'

'And at least you had Max.'

'What? Oh, yes, of course, I had Max. He was my son.'

'Daddy – '

'Yes, Charlotte.'

'Daddy, I hate to ask you this but I simply have to. Who – who was my father? And Georgina's? What was he like? Where is he? Please tell me. I need to know.'

'I don't know,' he said. 'I really do not know.'

'That's absurd. You must know.'

'No, no I don't. I didn't want ever to know. I told your mother that it was the only way I could stand it, never knowing, who she had been – who – well, it was the only way I could go on. And go on loving her. I did, you know. I still do. Very much.' He suddenly put his head in his hands; a sob broke in his voice. Charlotte put her arms round him.

'Daddy. Daddy, don't. I'm so sorry, so terribly, terribly sorry. Don't cry, please don't cry.'

He put his arms round her then and clung to her, as if she was the parent and he the child. 'I'm sorry, Charlotte,' he said, 'so terribly sorry. Tell Georgina how sorry I am. Please tell her.'

There were still ten days before she had to go up to Cambridge. She couldn't imagine how she was going to get through them. She fixed her mind on getting there, on starting a new life; somehow, she felt, it would matter less there, she would be safe, a different person, she could escape from it all. She and Alexander hardly spoke, read at mealtimes, avoided one another after dinner. She knew she should go back to Georgina, report on the conversation with her father, but somehow she kept putting it off. She couldn't face another scene and she felt she had handled the last one completely wrongly.

Georgina phoned from school a couple of times, sounding almost cheerful. She said she wasn't thinking about it, and she was quite sure it was all evil gossip. Charlotte, sounding noncommittal, said she was glad Georgina was feeling better.

What she longed for, and yet dreaded, was her mother's return. She wanted to talk to her, and yet she was afraid to, wanted her reassurance and was terrified of not getting it. Virginia was due back just before she went up. 'I'll be able to drive you up, darling,' she had said gaily on the phone, last time Charlotte had spoken to her, before her dinner with Toby. 'We can have a lovely day together.'

'Yes, sure,' Charlotte had said, aware she was sounding cool, still upset that her mother hadn't come back with them to see Georgina and more importantly Max back to school. God in heaven, how was she ever going to be civil to her now, if that had upset her? And yet – yet, she wanted to see her so much, wanted to talk to her, wanted – yes, wanted to fight with her if necessary. It would be healing, comforting. Just to unscramble not just the story, but her own emotions.

She wondered if her father had told Virginia that she knew. No, clearly not, or she would have come straight home. Or would she? No, that wasn't fair; her mother was nothing if not morally brave. On the other hand if Alexander hadn't told her, why not? It was something of a crisis. He must have done. He must. And her mother must have decided to stay away. Working out what to say, shrinking from facing her. It made Charlotte's misery worse.

Alexander said he was going to meet Virginia at Heathrow. 'I'd like to talk to her. Try and explain how you feel. Try and persuade her to come home with me.'

'If she's got any imagination at all,' said Charlotte bitterly, 'any proper maternal feelings, she won't need it explained.'

'Darling, you must try not to be so angry with her. She would no doubt feel she had – had her reasons.'

'No doubt.'

He phoned from Heathrow. Virginia's plane had been delayed, she was exhausted, he was taking her to Eaton Place. 'But she will be down first thing in the morning. She's dying to see you.'

'Of course she is.'

A little later, pacing the house, she suddenly felt she couldn't stand it any longer. She phoned the house in Eaton Place. Virginia answered the phone. Charlotte was so pleased to hear her voice she stopped being angry.

'Mummy? It's Charlotte.'

'Charlotte! I thought you'd gone up to Cambridge.'

'No,' said Charlotte coldly. 'You know I haven't. Well, you did. You said you'd take me.'

'Yes, but – oh, I must have been confused. Are you all right, darling?'

'Yes, I suppose so,' said Charlotte. 'More all right than Georgina, anyway.'

'Charlotte, I'm so sorry you had to find out. Like this.'

'Yes, well,' said Charlotte, her voice coolly polite, 'it might have been nicer if you'd trusted us enough to try and explain.'

'You sound very hostile.'

'I don't feel hostile exactly. Well I do, but more than that I feel confused. Mummy, I do want to talk to you. About it. About everything. I just have to. Are you really coming home tomorrow?'

'Yes. Yes of course I am. I'm very glad you do want to talk. I think I might find it easier to explain than Daddy. Some of it anyway. Why – how it all happened.'

'I wish you were here now,' said Charlotte. She sounded wistful suddenly.

'Well, darling, I would have been. If I'd known you were there.'

'Well now you do. And I do feel terribly lonely.'

'I'm sure you do. Charlotte, what about Max?'

'What about him?'

'Well, he has to be told; I wondered if you'd spoken to Daddy about that.'

'No. No, not really. But anyway, it's different for him, isn't it? I mean, yes of course he has to be told about us. But it's not the same. Not really.'

'Well of course it is.' Virginia sounded puzzled. 'Of course it is.'

'Mummy, it isn't. How can it be?'

'Charlotte, what are you saying?'

'Well – as Max is really Daddy's. There just isn't so much to cope with. For him. That's what I'm saying.'

There was a long silence. Then Virginia said, 'Charlotte, I think I'll come down tonight after all. I've got my Golf here. I'll drive myself down. I'll be there by ten.'

'Oh Mummy, thank you. That sounds wonderful.'

She wasn't there by ten as she had promised. She wasn't there by eleven. Just after twelve the police arrived. There had been a crash on the M4 just after the Marlowe turn-off. Virginia's car had been in the wreckage. She had died very soon after getting to hospital.

Chapter 13

Baby, 1980

Baby stood in the chapel at Hartest, looking at Virginia's coffin, his eyes heavy with tears he dared not start to shed, and remembered her. She was a very particular person, the one he remembered; not the ravishing and successful Countess of Caterham, nor the beautiful young girl who had walked down the aisle towards him and Alexander in her white rose-strewn dress; not the tear-stained remorseful woman who had betrayed him and Angie to his father, nor the mother of the brilliant and dazzling child who was robbing his son of his birthright; she was not the fragile, vulnerable woman who had become an alcoholic, God only knew for what reason, nor the heartbroken one who had buried an infant son. And she was not even the graceful, laughing figure partnering her father in their ritual dance, nor the protesting Blessed, the virginal toast of Harvard. She was a little girl, a plump, slightly anxious little girl, with tangled dark curls and a resigned expression in her tawny eyes, who always got caught and was always in hot water, while he, Baby, having committed the same crimes, got away safe, unpunished, scot free.

And now she lay there, dead, still, lost to him, to her children, to her husband, to everyone who loved her and he remembered her in her vulnerable, often sad beauty; and once again, she had been the unlucky one and he, Baby, had got away, and was standing here, quite safe, still unpunished, and still scot free.

The remorse, the guilt, was almost worse than the pain.

It was a stricken little household that he found himself in. The two younger children were more visibly upset than Charlotte; Max was struggling and failing to be brave and Georgina wasn't even struggling, and cried most of the time. Alexander was moving about like an automaton, frozen-faced, silent, making arrangements; Nanny appeared to be furiously angry and went about all day frowning and slamming doors, her lips folded in upon themselves even more tightly than usual. Baby did his best to provide comfort, support and even a little cheer; he cuddled the girls, encouraged Max to cry as well, thinking it would be good for him, and tried to talk to Alexander, who rebuffed him firmly and just politely.

Charlotte, he found, was suffering from guilt as much as grief; she kept saying it had been her fault Virginia had died.

'Darling child, how can it be?' said Baby. 'She was driving probably too fast, she was a lousy driver, and she crashed her car. That's not your fault.'

'No, but I said I wanted to see her badly. I said I wished she was here. She was tired, I knew she was, she'd only just flown in. I should have waited.'

'Charlotte, you can't blame yourself for that. You only told her you wanted her. I expect she was pleased.'

'No, but I shouldn't have, I shouldn't have. Not when she was so tired. And it was raining. Oh God, why, why didn't I leave her alone?'

'Well, you didn't, I'm afraid.' Baby sighed, hugged her closer. 'We all have to live with what we have done. And nobody, nobody on earth would blame you for what you did. But I can understand your blaming yourself.'

'Does that mean you blame me?'

'Of course not. I just said I didn't. Listen, poppet, you just have to hang onto the thought that she would have been glad you wanted to see her. OK?'

'Yes but – '

She didn't say any more. He got the feeling that she wasn't telling him everything, but he didn't press her.

Fred and Betsey and Mary Rose and the children arrived after four days for the funeral; it was a relief to see them, it took the pressure off him. His children were subdued, upset; they had been extremely fond of Virginia. Even Freddy managed to overcome his hostility to Charlotte, told her how sorry he was, how much he would miss his aunt. Charlotte was too numb with misery to notice.

Betsey was shattered, shrunken in her grief, but Fred was angry, as Nanny had been, angry with the other drivers, angry with Alexander for not being with her, angry with Virginia herself. 'If she'd been where she should have been, with her family, instead of rushing around the United States worrying about that damnfool business, it would never have happened. Ridiculous, the whole thing, ridiculous bloody waste.'

Baby sat nodding. There was never any point arguing with Fred; and besides he did feel there was something in what he said. Virginia had neglected her family, there was no denying it; she clearly felt she had her reasons, and Baby did not think they were entirely personal ambition, rather the reverse, Virginia had always seemed to him one of the least ambitious people he had ever met, but they had to be slightly spurious set against the demands of her family. Anyway, it was too late now; but if it did Fred good to rail against her, then Baby thought they should let him be.

Alexander came down to breakfast the day before the funeral and said his mother was coming down and he was meeting her at Heathrow in two hours' time. Having dropped what was clearly a very large bombshell he disappeared again.

'I don't want her here,' said Georgina, staring at the doorway after him. 'She never even saw Mummy when she was alive, why suddenly arrive on the doorstep when she's dead? I'm going to find it very hard to be nice to her.'

'Oh don't be silly,' said Charlotte wearily. 'Of course you must be nice to her. She's always been very nice to all of us. She's obviously feeling remorseful. I think it's quite brave of her to come.'

'I don't want her to come either,' said Max.

'Er – put me in the picture here,' said Baby, putting down his coffee cup. 'This is the grandmother who would never come and meet Virginia, yes?'

'Yes, that's right,' said Charlotte. 'We never knew why. Mummy never knew. When we met Granny Caterham, she just never mentioned Mummy at all.'

'I asked her why she never came,' said Max suddenly. 'She told me it was the journey. She said she hated trains and gets car sick.'

'Well, but that doesn't explain why she would never have Mummy up there,' said Charlotte.

'Daddy said she would,' said Georgina, 'Granny would have liked her to go, but Mummy got in such a strop because Granny wouldn't come to the christenings or anything, she refused.'

'I didn't know that,' said Charlotte wonderingly.

'I'm finding this all very confusing,' said Baby wearily.

Charlotte turned to him. 'The thing is, Granny Caterham always refused to come and meet Mummy. Or to see us when we were born. And we weren't allowed to ask why. I mean we weren't even allowed to ask Daddy. It was out of bounds. Even after we'd been up there and met her. But there was obviously some big row behind it.'

'And – what is she like?' asked Baby.

'Oh, she's fun,' said Charlotte. 'Really she is. We liked her. It was difficult, because we couldn't tell Mummy that. She gave us one or two lovely holidays up there. We see her about once a year.'

'And your mother never ever met her?'

'Never ever.'

★

The Dowager Countess arrived at lunchtime. Expecting some kind of madwoman, Baby was rather charmed by her. She was very like Alexander, tall, erect, with a remarkably deep voice; she was dressed in sturdy tweeds, her grey hair pulled back neatly into a bun, her brilliant blue eyes fixed on her son throughout the meal. There was an odd expression in those eyes, Baby thought, trying to analyse it, not quite concern, and certainly not tenderness or affection, rather a detached interest as if she was studying some unusual species of animal she was not quite familiar with.

She didn't talk a great deal, but when she did it was to the children, whom she was clearly fond of; after lunch she suggested they all went for a walk with her. Alexander excused himself and followed them out of the room.'

'Well,' said Betsey, struggling with a natural, grandmotherly jealousy. 'I really didn't like her at all.'

'You could have fooled me,' said Fred, 'you practically curtseyed to her when you were introduced.'

'I did not. I thought she was a very odd, cold woman.'

'Just like her son if you ask me,' said Fred.

'We didn't,' said Betsey.

The day of the funeral was in an odd way easier than Baby had feared. The adrenalin required to get them all through it, the forced bonhomie of the luncheon afterwards, the plentiful supply of drink, all helped. Baby sat next to Catriona Dunbar at lunch; he had met her before and found her nice, although extremely unattractive and so unlike Virginia in every way as to make the friendship totally inexplicable.

'You must be feeling quite dreadful,' she said in her slightly braying voice, passing him the hollandaise sauce. 'I'm so frightfully sorry.'

'Thank you,' said Baby. 'You'll miss her too.'

'Yes, I will. Very much. Of course I didn't see her very often, but whenever I did it was such a pleasure.'

'But I thought –'

'Yes?' She smiled at him, too widely; some salmon had become stuck in between her rather horsey front teeth, she looked oddly fearsome.

'Oh, nothing. I thought you and she were great friends.'

'Oh how nice. That she should think that, tell you that!' said Catriona. 'But no, not really. Martin is here quite a lot of course, being estate manager, and is a great friend of Alexander's, and Virginia was kind enough to invite us here quite often for meals, largely so that Alexander and Martin could talk. But no, we weren't especially close. I was always

190

rather in awe of her, to be frank with you.' She smiled at him again; the salmon had been joined on her teeth by a shred of watercress; Baby averted his eyes. She had dropped a splodge of hollandaise sauce onto her navy suit, and was scraping at it rather ineffectively with her knife, spreading it further. He wasn't surprised she had been in awe of Virginia. 'She was so glamorous, so sophisticated, and the clothes she had! And that wonderful job of hers, I never quite understood what she did, but it was obviously frightfully clever and interesting . . .'

'I didn't understand it either,' said Baby. He was puzzled. Virginia had always made rather a meal of her friendship with Catriona, said she was the only person in Wiltshire she could really talk to, and how she loved having her over to Hartest. Maybe she hadn't been able to admit to not having a friend at all and had more or less invented the relationship. Poor Virgy. What a sad life she had had, one way or another.

He looked across at Martin Dunbar; he was very pale, drinking a great deal and not eating much. He had been one of the pallbearers, together with Baby and Alexander and Freddy, and had looked very shaken indeed in the chapel. But then he always looked ill, he was so gaunt and drawn; Baby had met him several times, and the first occasion he had really expected him to keel over and die any moment. In fact Alexander told him Martin enjoyed the best of health. 'It's a certain type of English look that, the dead on the feet style. Awful lot of them at Winchester, for some reason.'

'Did Martin go to Winchester then?' said Baby.

'What's that? Oh no. No, he's a Harrovian.'

Sometimes Baby felt the entire English race talked in non sequiturs like Nanny.

He found Nanny looked very fierce in the library after lunch, most unusually holding a glass of sherry. He put his arm round her.

'Worst's over,' he said.

'Worst's only just begun,' said Nanny briefly.

Betsey came in quietly. She had been crying again.

'Hallo, Nanny,' she said.

'Good afternoon, madam.'

'I was wondering if I should stay on for a few days, to help look after the children,' said Betsey.

Nanny looked at her, her expression dark and disapproving. 'I don't think that would be at all a good idea,' she said, 'they're very upset. Very upset indeed.'

The implication was that Betsey had neither grasped this fact, nor was remotely capable of doing anything about it; Betsey looked at her coldly.

'I am aware of that, Nanny,' she said, grief lending her courage. 'I would ask you to remember I am the children's grandmother. I think I can help them just a little.'

'I don't need reminding,' said Nanny, unmoved, 'and no one could have loved Her Ladyship more than I did.'

She clearly felt this closed the subject and moved away and out of the room; for the first time since the news of Virginia's death had reached Betsey, as she sat leafing through the Neiman Marcus catalogue picking out Christmas presents ('How could I ever have thought that mattered, how could I?' she had said over and over again, as sublimely illogical in her grief as Nanny herself), she smiled; a small, wan, but unmistakable smile.

'The old witch isn't all bad, is she?' she said to Baby. 'Virginia always said she was such a good friend to her, I never believed it before.'

'She's nearly all good, actually,' said Baby, smiling at her gently. 'Just has a funny manner. She's English, don't forget. Are you all right, Mother?'

'No, not really,' said Betsey, 'how about you?'

'The same.'

They were all due to leave the next afternoon. Baby, guiltily relieved to be getting away from the claustrophobic atmosphere, was sitting in the library after breakfast reading, when the Dowager Countess of Caterham came in. He smiled at her rather distantly.

'Good morning.'

'Good morning, Mr Praeger. We haven't spoken very much. I'm sorry.'

'Force of circumstance,' said Baby politely.

'Yes indeed.' There was a pause. The bright blue eyes looked at him rather intently. 'You were very fond of your sister, I believe.'

'Yes,' said Baby slightly shortly. 'Most people are. Fond of their sisters, I mean.'

'Not at all,' said Lady Caterham. 'I loathed mine.'

'Ah well.'

'I would have liked to have met her, you know. Your sister.'

'Really?'

'You sound rather unconvinced.'

'Well, Lady Caterham, forgive me, but Virginia was very hurt by your – reluctance to meet her. Very.'

'My reluctance? Mr Praeger, I don't quite understand. There was no reluctance on my part.' Lady Caterham was looking at him with a chilly near-distaste.

Baby stared at her. 'But . . .'

She sounded impatient. 'Mr Praeger, if somebody tells you they don't want to meet you, you don't push it. As you might possibly say. Even if – especially if, I would say – that person has married your son.'

'Lady Caterham, I do assure you Virginia would not have said that. She longed to meet you. To have you here. I don't understand.'

'Well, Mr Praeger, she may have told you that.' The deep voice was growing impatient. 'But I do assure you, the message came over very loud and clear. I was not welcome at Hartest, and never would be. I have to say I found the items in various gossip columns, implying that I had refused to come, very hurtful. Your sister had a lot of friends in the press, I understand.'

'You could have sued,' said Baby mildly, 'if what they were saying really wasn't true.'

'Mr Praeger, I am not a rich American. I have better things to do with my money than throw it into the coffers of a national newspaper. I can tell you that any effort I could have made to correct anything your sister's friends wrote would only have rebounded on me badly.'

'Not if it wasn't true,' said Baby again.

'Some things are very hard to prove. Anyway, let's not get sidetracked into that one. I preferred to retain some dignity over it.'

'But – I still don't see how the confusion arose,' said Baby. 'The idea that she didn't want to see you. Did she write to you or something? Who told you?'

'No, we never had any contact,' said Lady Caterham. She was looking increasingly distant. 'Never. She never even thanked me for giving her the Caterham tiara. Of course it was hers by right, but even so, I would have liked – well. Never mind. It's too late now. I'm only glad to have been allowed to meet my grandchildren, albeit a little late. I'm sorry, Mr Praeger, to talk like this about your sister at such a time, but you are clearly under some considerable misapprehensions.'

'Yes, clearly I am. And I have to admit to being totally baffled – '

'I also, Mr Praeger.' She smiled at him suddenly. 'I can't imagine how I could have struck such terror into someone. Do I look like a monster?'

'No, you don't,' said Baby politely. 'But – who did tell you? If it wasn't Virginia.'

She sighed. 'My son of course. Alexander. Who else? And very upset and saddened he was by it too.'

He went to find Alexander. He had to. He had always been so sorry for Virginia, in her rejection by Lady Caterham. She had minded so much. What on earth was Alexander playing at? Fucking up the relationship,

193

pretending it came from Lady Caterham, telling Virginia lies. Alexander was sitting in his study, working at some papers. He still looked dreadful. Baby felt a pang of remorse, tempted to withdraw, and then went in and shut the door.

'Alexander . . .'

'Yes, Baby?'

'I have to talk to you. It's about Virginia and – and your mother.'

'Oh yes?' The blue eyes were very cold suddenly.

'Alexander, why on earth did you tell her those lies?'

'What lies? To whom?'

'To Virginia. About your mother refusing to come and see her?'

'I didn't.'

'Oh, Alexander, come on. Virginia was always talking about it. It was a source of terrible sadness to her. Now your mother says she would have welcomed Virginia.'

'It's true.'

Baby stared at him. 'What's true?'

'She would have welcomed her. Virginia was obsessively jealous of her. She refused to meet her.'

'I don't believe you. I just don't believe you.'

Alexander shrugged. 'Look – I'm sorry. But it's true. Baby – I know you loved Virginia very much. So did I. Very very much. Always. I would have done anything for her. I did. But she had – a darker side. She was an alcoholic. As you know. But that wasn't all. There are many things she couldn't handle. And like all alcoholics, she – well she lied. A great deal. I didn't mind. I knew it all and I loved her anyway. But I had to face these things. And I think you should too. She was – not entirely balanced, Baby. I've never admitted it to anyone before. But I think you have to know. I'm sorry.' He looked up at Baby, and there were tears in his eyes.

'But – ' said Baby. 'But you see I – '

'Baby,' said Alexander, 'Baby, I am finding it very hard to get through this. All of it. I'd rather we left it for now. If you don't mind. I did my best for her, you know. My very best.'

'Yes,' said Baby slowly. 'Yes, I really think you did. I'm sorry, Alexander. Very sorry.'

He left the study and went for a walk in the woods, wretchedly shocked and unhappy, and realized that in some strange way he had lost Virginia not once now but twice.

He went straight to the office when he got back to New York, desperate for work, for something to think about other than Virginia. Amongst all

the other letters on his desk was one with an English postmark. It was
from Angie.

Chapter 14

Angie, 1980

Angie often thought how terrible it was that her first reaction to the news of Virginia's death had been pleasure. She hadn't actually thought she was quite that bad a person. She had felt other more suitable emotions very soon afterwards, sorrow, a sense of very real gratitude, and regret that she had never tried to heal the rift between them. But initially there had been a stab of intense delight, and it had come, that stab, because it gave her a valid reason for getting in touch with Baby.

She had not thought she had actually loved Baby. She had always imagined that she was simply using him: his money, his patent adoration of her, his ability to give her fun. She liked him, she liked him enormously, and she found him immensely attractive – although his capacity actually to deliver the sexual goods was a little disappointing. She really did like those blond, aristocratic, WASP looks best; she had sampled sexy intellectuals, randily intense Jews, bits of rough, blacks, Arabs, and they all had this that or the other going for them. (Especially the Arabs at the moment; the last one she'd gone out with had worn a money belt beneath all his clothes which he'd removed with some reluctance; there was five million pounds in it, he'd told her. She hadn't believed him and had sat there, stark naked, making him count it in front of her, noticing with some interest that his erection remained rampantly rigid throughout; he obviously found the money as exciting as she did.) But at the end of the day Angie liked breeding; and Baby had had plenty of that. And she had also liked the way he treated her, the respect he gave her, the way he had talked to her, told her things, asked what she would like to do, and not just in bed, but where she wished to eat, walk, stay. Pretending he was the greatest stud since Casanova had been a small price to pay for that, for being treated like a lady. He had been a bit of a soft touch, a slight sucker, which she didn't actually approve of; the way he had just come up with the money for Mrs Wicks (never cancelled, in spite of everything), paid for her holidays, believed all the lies she had told him. But actually she hadn't told him that many. She'd liked him too much. And when it had been over, and she had watched his father wiping the extremely expensive floor with him, she had expected only to feel scorn, distaste, perhaps a little nostalgia; and she had felt real pain, genuine grief and loneliness, and she had been glad she had agreed to go to England, not merely because her fee was higher, but because it meant there was no danger of running into him, no frequent stories to read about him in the financial press (and occasionally the gossip columns), she could just begin again, start life on her own, and try to pretend she had never known him.

She had done well; she had arrived back in England with the first cheque from Fred III and a very good idea. It wasn't entirely original, but it was good. She combed the then rapidly gentrifying streets of the less fashionable parts of London – Battersea, Clapham, Peckham – for ungentrified houses. If they were bang next door to gentrified ones, so much the better. And she would post letters through the doors, saying she was looking for just such a house and could offer them what was very slightly below the market price. She could do that because she was going to be buying them direct and would thus save them agents' fees. For every hundred letters she delivered, she would get roughly ten replies; from each of the ten, she would find two houses. This was 1970; the property market had gone mad. She reckoned to buy a small three-bedroomed terrace house for £10,000, tart it up – and she did it nicely, Virginia had given her standards, no bubble glass in the windows or phoney Georgian doors for her – put in a bathroom and a fitted kitchen, set a couple of tubs by the front door and sell it for £15,000 three months later. And she did it over and over again, dozens of times. When the property slump came briefly in 1972, she simply held her fire; it didn't last long. In four years she had doubled Fred's capital; before she was thirty she was a millionaire.

She was never tempted to move into a higher price bracket; the profits might be larger, but so, she said, were the risks. And there weren't so many houses. She did get involved briefly in the flat market, buying three- and four-storey houses and converting them, but it was more complex, the conversions were often a nightmare. She could work in the small houses, the chi-chi cottages, with builders she knew personally. The whole thing could be easily controlled. And she liked it, she liked watching dingy little houses, and even rows of dingy little houses, growing pretty and graceful under her skilful eye.

She had bought herself a rather beautiful house in St John's Wood, in 1975, a small, early Victorian villa, covered in wisteria, with the original shutters, cornices and fireplaces, and an exquisitely planted courtyard at the back, filled with small trees, including a fig, vines and shrubs and several charming stone statues. The house stood quite high above the street and had a large, light basement; Angie converted that into a flat for Mrs Wicks.

She had never been happy, seeing her in the rest home; Angie had the deep conviction of her class that you should look after your own. She went and fetched Mrs Wicks one Saturday afternoon, told them at the home that she would like to leave the standing order running, as a token of her appreciation – well, she thought Baby wouldn't miss it, and the home had done well by Mrs Wicks – and drove her back to London.

'You can do exactly what you like here, Gran,' she said, 'have a different man in every night, keep cats or budgies or tropical fish, give French lessons, just please yourself. You can keep your pension, no need to give me any rent of course, and if you need a bit of extra, just ask. I've got plenty. Only thing you're not to do is interfere in my life, OK?'

'OK,' said Mrs Wicks cheerfully. 'I'll do for you, darling, keep you nice and spick and span. I'd like that. This is very good of you, Angie.'

'You were good to me,' said Angie.

Mrs Wicks was very happy in St John's Wood once she had settled down. She and Angie went on some shopping sprees, and she bought herself a lot of silk blouses and what she called smart trousers, and the one thing she had always wanted, a fur coat. It was a mink and Angie told her she'd got it very cheaply; it actually cost over a thousand pounds. It had to be extremely warm for her to go out without it. She had her hair dyed red and styled every week at the salon in St John's Wood High Street and her nails done as well. She still smoked forty a day, but she used a cigarette holder, 'Like my friend Marje Proops,' she told Angie. She had advanced on Mrs Proops, who had then lived in St John's Wood and often shopped in the High Street, one Saturday afternoon and told her she admired her more than any woman in the world, and that included the Queen and Barbara Castle; Marje had been charmed and they had a cup of tea and a pastry together in Gloriette and from then on Mrs Wicks modelled herself on Marje, and even got glasses like hers and changed the wedding ring she had worn for forty-nine years for a wide band exactly like her heroine's. She was sixty-seven years old, but she looked younger every year; she had always been very slim, but poverty had aged her. Released from worry about the rent and Mr Wicks she looked quite girlish at times.

She was bored for a while, once she had got used to her new life, and the hairdresser and the shopping; but then one morning, as she walked rather slowly down the road, enjoying the sunshine and wondering what she might do for the eight hours or so before Angie came home, she saw the woman who lived next door to them, standing at her gate.

'Good morning!' she said. 'Lovely day!'

'Won't last,' said Mrs Wicks. 'Rain coming in from the west.'

She always said that, whatever the forecast, whatever the weather. It impressed people.

'Oh really.' The woman was very smart-looking, dressed in a white suit. 'Look, I hope you don't mind my approaching you, but I gather you work for the young woman next door. I wondered if you were fully occupied.'

'Not quite,' said Mrs Wicks truthfully.

'Well you see,' said the woman, 'my char has left me, just like that, these people have no concept of loyalty – '

'No,' said Mrs Wicks.

'And I do have to have someone, naturally, it's a big house – '

'Naturally,' said Mrs Wicks. She got out her cigarettes and her holder. 'Smoke?'

'No thank you. So I – well I wondered if you might have a little time to spare.'

Mrs Wicks looked at her thoughtfully. 'Well, I might. What are you paying?'

'Four shillings.'

'Oh I couldn't do it for that.'

'Really? Well I'm afraid that's my top rate. What a shame.'

'Yes,' said Mrs Wicks.

'What does Mrs – Miss – ?'

'Burbank. Miss. Well, I live in, you see. So it's different. But it's the equivalent of five bob. We worked it out.'

'Oh. Oh, I see. Er, would you be able to iron?'

'Probably. If you paid me.'

'And come in each day for a couple of hours?'

'Yes, I expect so.'

'Well – maybe I could do five shillings.'

'Well, please yourself,' said Mrs Wicks.

'Right. Yes, let's agree on that. When could you start?'

Mrs Wicks was feeling very bored. 'Now,' she said.

Angie was slightly irritated. 'We're supposed to be going up in the world, Gran. You can't go charring for neighbours.'

Mrs Wicks was indignant. 'Course I can. I like housework, and she's paying me five bob an hour. That's well over the rate. She wanted to know what you did for a living.'

'What did you tell her?'

'I said you were a doctor.'

'Gran! What on earth for?'

'I knew it would impress her. Stuck-up cow.'

Mrs Hill had huge delusions of grandeur, and treated Mrs Wicks with a gracious condescension at first; she also followed her round the house watching her, telling her she had left smears on the taps – 'It's so difficult to clean real gold plate' – and not replaced the ornaments in exactly the right places – 'A great many hours have gone into arranging those, Mrs Wicks, my husband is quite an artist.' Mrs Wicks dealt with the condescension by the simple expedient of wearing her mink coat to work, handing it to Mrs Hill and telling her to hang it up carefully.

Mrs Hill looked at it and said what a very nice coat it was, and a wonderfully good imitation.

'That's no imitation,' said Mrs Wicks, 'that's the real thing.'

'Oh Mrs Wicks, I don't think so. I do know mink when I see it.'

'Fraid you don't,' said Mrs Wicks cheerfully, 'it come from Maxwell Croft, and if you don't believe me I can show you the bill.'

Mrs Hill went a little pale and said that would not be necessary.

After three more session of being followed around as she worked, Mrs Wicks handed Mrs Hill a duster from her overall pocket, and told her she would be leaving. 'You've obviously got the time to do it yourself, you're wasting your money paying me.'

Mrs Hill said she was sorry, and left her alone; she told several friends about her wonderful new char and two of them approached her. In no time she was working full time, always arriving in her mink coat and the diamond watch Angie had given her for Christmas, both of which she handed over to her employers as she arrived. 'I don't want to get them messed up,' she would say.

Very often in the afternoons she would go to bingo in Maida Vale, where she was inordinately lucky; it was rare for her not to win something each week; and once a week she went to a ballroom dancing class in Paddington, where she met several gentlemen friends; one of them took her out to tea every Sunday, to the restaurant in Regent's Park and then on to the cinema. His name was Clifford Parks and he told her she was the most ladylike person he had ever met. Angie liked him, and often gave him a drink when he brought Mrs Wicks back; he had assured her quietly that he had every respect for her grandmother and she was not to worry. Angie said she wouldn't worry.

In the evenings if Angie was home on her own, they ate TV suppers in Mrs Wicks's kitchen diner, which was much cosier she said than Angie's dining room; if Angie gave a dinner party Mrs Wicks would put on a black dress and wait on the guests, which she did with surprising skill. And about once a week Angie would take Mrs Wicks out to a posh restaurant and teach her about good food; at the end of the first year the mink coat had been hung up in the cloakrooms of the Ritz, Claridges, Grosvenor House, the Caprice, Rules, Wheelers, the Meridiana, San Frediano and the Gavroche.

Through all her fun and success, Angie never forgot about Baby; never ceased to compare him (albeit not always favourably) with other lovers, other friends, never ceased to wonder what would have happened if they had not been parted, or indeed if they were to meet again. The prospect tantalized, fascinated her; as time went by it became almost an obsession.

And now Virginia's death had made it attainable; and she could not pass the opportunity by.

Dear Baby (she wrote)
I was so sorry to hear of Virginia's death. She was so extremely good to me, and I was always sad that we never renewed our friendship. You must be extremely unhappy, and I wanted to let you know I was thinking of you. Please pass on my sympathies to other members of the family if that would seem appropriate.

I shall be in New York next month [this was quite untrue] and I wondered if you would like a drink for old times' sake. It would be good to see you again.
Yours,
Angie

'I'm going to New York,' said Angie to Mrs Wicks over their TV supper.

'When?' said Mrs Wicks, spooning up the sauce of her spaghetti bolognese with great relish. 'What for?'

'On business,' said Angie, meeting her piercing gaze steadily.

'I didn't know you had business in New York.'

'Well I do.'

'What kind?'

'The same kind. Houses.'

'Oh yes? You're not going to see that man are you?'

'What man?' said Angie innocently. 'Look out, Gran, you've got bolognese on your sleeve. I don't buy you real cashmere jumpers to trail in tomato sauce, you know. Cost a lot of money, that jumper.'

'Don't try and change the subject,' said Mrs Wicks.

'Well,' said Baby, 'you haven't changed a bit.'

'Liar!' said Angie. 'I'm a middle-aged woman. I'm thirty-two.'

'Dear God. I wish I was thirty-two again.'

'How old are you, Baby?'

'Forty-five.'

'Well, you look pretty good yourself. And you have changed.'

'I should think so,' said Baby, laughing, 'I'm not middle-aged, I'm almost old.'

'Oh nonsense,' said Angie, 'you look terrific. And when I said you'd changed, I meant for the better.'

'Oh really?'

'Yes. You look – well, more in command. Sleeker. Smoother. It's nice,' she said, smiling at him. 'Suits you.'

'Thank you. Well, I am in command. I have the bank now. I'm chairman.'

'I know. I read about it. I'm pleased, Baby. Congratulations. Is that good?'

'It's wonderful,' he said simply. 'I'm loving it. But it was a long wait. And there are still – let's say – problems.'

'Really? What?'

'Oh – Dad pulled a bit of a rug from under my feet. Our feet. He's cut Charlotte into the bank. She'll get half of it, one day. Freddy has to share it with her.'

'Good God,' said Angie.

'Yes. Neat work.'

'What's she like now?'

'What? Oh, sweet. A nice child. I don't see her giving me any problems of any kind. She's very eager to fit in, do what I say . . .'

'Good. Pretty?'

'Yes, very pretty. In a babyish sort of way.'

'What about the others?'

'Well, Georgina has turned into a bit of a beauty. Very unusual-looking, immensely tall. And Max is a great charmer of course. Precocious. Now I don't trust him. I caught him in the summer house with Melissa this summer and – '

'Baby! He's only what?'

'Thirteen.'

'And Melissa's your new daughter?'

'Yes. Well, quite new.'

'Born after – well, since we were together.'

'Yes.'

There was a silence. Angie looked at him. It had been true what she had said, he did look more self-confident, more in control. But he had also aged, there was silver in the blond hair, his tanned face was lined, and his extremely well-cut suit did not entirely conceal his considerably increased girth. He was not fat exactly, but he was very heavy. Angie remembered

202

with a sudden sharp pang the beauty of Baby's body – muscley, firm, brown – and felt sad.

'Well now,' he said, 'what about you? Have you prospered? I hope so.'

That was nice of him, she thought: considering that any prospering had been done on the back of the pay-off his father had given her and that she had accepted so readily.

'Yes,' she said, 'I have.'

'In what field?'

'Property.'

'Indeed. A tycoon, Miss Burbank.'

'Well – not quite a tycoon. But doing OK.'

'Good. I'm pleased to hear it.' There was a silence. Then he said, quite suddenly, 'I've missed you, Angie. I've missed you so much.'

She looked at him, and his blue eyes at least were just the same, dancing at her, full of sweet sadness, and the time changed suddenly, turned back, and she was eighteen again, hungry, impatient, looked for nothing but fun; and she said, 'Oh, Baby, I've missed you too.'

There was a long silence and she knew exactly what he was doing: thinking, weighing up; the dangers, the delights, the pleasures, the pains, and she knew if she was anything at all of a nice person she would make it easy for him, jump up, say she had to leave, that it had been nice seeing him, that next time she was in New York they must do it again. She would be concerned for him, for his marriage, for his children, for his struggles to do the right thing, for his new position in life – and it couldn't be easy running that bank, it was a huge, a pressing responsibility. If she really loved him, she thought, she would go, now, at once, and leave him in peace.

But it was too late, he had got there before her, he was speaking now, saying the words, the deadly, dangerous words: 'I wonder if you have time for dinner one evening – ' and she was quite quite powerless to do anything about it, to resist, and moreover was totally unwilling even to try, and she smiled at him and said, with something oddly like a break in her voice, and cursed it, that break, for betraying her, for revealing the emotion, 'Yes, Baby,' she said, 'yes I think so. That would be lovely.'

Chapter 15

Georgina, 1981

Georgina was just beginning her orgasm when her Housemother came in; just rising on the great tumbling rapids of pleasure, opening herself to them, folding herself around Jamie Hunt, her long long legs wrapped round him, her body arched, her head thrown back, biting her lip to try to contain the cries of pleasure that would surface, would emerge, however much she told herself they must not.

And then the light snapped on, she opened her eyes; and instead of seeing Jamie's face, contorted itself with pleasure, she looked over his naked, plunging back and buttocks, and saw her Housemother standing there, an expression of total disdain on her face, and as her body retreated, slipped away from delight, she felt no fear or shame, only a sense of outrage that she had been cheated, and at the same time, one of intense amusement, and the sound that finally escaped her was not an orgasmic cry, but a throaty, joyous giggle.

She was expelled immediately; Alexander was sent for, and she was dispatched with him the same day. The school was very nice, very fair; but as they said to him, she had been warned twice about her behaviour, it was not the first time a boy had been found in her bedroom, although this was the first time she had been caught in flagrante, and her attitude did not encourage them to give her any more chances. She did not appear remorseful, or even apologetic; she had simply said that the House-mother should have knocked, that any reasonable person would have knocked, before entering someone's bedroom.

She was silent in the car as they drove rather too fast towards Wiltshire; she sat looking out of the window apparently perfectly relaxed, although tearing occasionally at her badly bitten nails. As they came into view of the house, at the top of the Great Drive, Alexander stopped the car, looked at her and said, 'This is very upsetting for me, Georgina, very upsetting indeed. I can't quite understand your attitude. Your behaviour – just. Your attitude not at all.'

'I can't see a lot of difference,' said Georgina. 'I can't see what we were doing was wrong. So I don't see why I should be dreadfully sorry about it. But I am sorry if I've upset you.' She felt very odd; she was not

normally aggressive, in fact she was rather the reverse, gentle, conciliatory, almost excessively compliant at times; but ever since Charlotte had
told her about her mother and still more so since Virginia had died, she
had felt disoriented, lost, detached from her real self. And she looked at
her father now, so hurt, so baffled, so angry, and she simply did not know
how he could not understand.

'Oh for God's sake,' said Alexander, 'how can you possibly say you
don't know you were doing something wrong? It is explicitly forbidden
in the school rules, you'd been warned before, and besides, Georgina, I
expect you to have more self-respect that to go hurling yourself into bed
with the first boy who asks you. I really do.'

'He wasn't the first,' said Georgina.

'Georgina! Oh God.' He put his head on his arms on the steering wheel.

'Well I'm sorry, Daddy,' she said, knowing she still sounded cold and
wishing she could do something about it. 'I guess it's my bad blood
coming out.'

Alexander lifted his head and stared at her. 'I'm afraid I don't know
what you mean.'

'Don't you? Don't you really?'

'No. I really don't.'

'Oh Daddy. I mean obviously I take after my mother. Sleeping with
everyone. Don't forget I have no idea who my –'

Alexander raised his hand and struck her hard across the face. 'Don't
ever, ever let me hear you saying that about your mother again.'

'Why not? It's true isn't it?'

'It is not true. And I will not have you saying it.'

'Oh.' She was silent for a while, holding her face, staring at him,
wondering at the same time how he could be so loyal and how she could
be behaving like this, hurting him, the person she loved best in the world.
'Well,' she said finally, 'I'm very impressed you can be so loyal to her.
Very. I won't say it again. But I'm afraid I can't help thinking it.'

There was a long silence; Alexander sat looking down at the house, his
face very old suddenly, an expression of utter despair on it. Then he
turned to her and took her in his arms.

'Georgina, I'm sorry. I'm so sorry I hit you, I cannot imagine – oh God,
what can I say – do you want to talk about it all –'

'Daddy, please please don't . . .' She hugged him back and stayed
there very still for a while, then sat back and looked at him, and her
bravado was suddenly gone, she looked smaller and vulnerable and very
near to tears. 'I deserved to be slapped, I'm sure. And no, I don't want to
talk about it, I hate it all so much. Please. I'm trying to handle it and it's
very difficult. But I don't want to talk about it. With you of all people. I

feel so sorry for you, and I'm terribly sorry to have been expelled, sorry I've disgraced you. But please don't make me talk about Mummy and please even more don't try and make me think well of her. OK? Now can we go home, please? I'm awfully tired.'

'Yes of course.' He started the car again. As he drove down the Great Drive she looked at him cautiously. The overriding expression on his face was interesting. It was one of relief.

They ate supper alone in the kitchen. It was surprisingly relaxed.

'I can't imagine where you can go to school next,' Alexander said quite cheerfully. 'It's not easy, after an expulsion.'

'I don't want to go to any school.'

'Well of course you must go to school. You're only halfway through your A-level course.'

'I know. But I told you I didn't want to do them. Not these, anyway. I want to go to a sixth-form college and do architecture. I can go to the one in Swindon, can't I? They'd be pleased to have me, I'd have thought.'

'I have no idea. They might not welcome you either. I don't imagine they will fall gratefully upon you, simply because of who you are.'

'Oh, Daddy. Don't be silly. That wasn't what I meant. And anyway –'

'Yes?'

'Oh, nothing. I meant because my O levels were quite good and right for the course, and because I know so exactly what I want to do.'

'Well perhaps. We shall have to write to them. In any case I would imagine you'd have to go back and start again, do two full years there. It's May now, you'll never catch up.'

'Well I wouldn't mind that. Anything to get away from Ancient Civilization and Latin.'

'Yes, well I can't imagine why you took those particular options in the first place.'

'Just to be awkward, I expect,' said Georgina, with a slightly weak grin.

The sixth-form college at Swindon couldn't take her, but Cirencester said they would give her a place: on the condition that she agreed to repeat her first year. Georgina was suddenly much happier. She still felt lost, but life seemed to be making a little more sense. She went round Hartest singing, helped Mrs Fallon with the cooking, helped on the farm with the haymaking, and generally was a great deal more agreeable than she had been for some time. Charlotte arrived home early in June, flushed with triumph at getting a First in her First Part Tripos, and left almost immediately again with a party of friends travelling round Europe; she agreed to meet everyone on Nantucket in August.

Then towards the end of June Georgina began to feel unwell. It started with a general lassitude, and then she became nauseated; within a week she was being sick at least three or four times every day. Nothing seemed to help. She couldn't keep anything down, and she grew alarmingly thin very fast.

Old Dr Summerfield had a look at her, diagnosed delayed shock, and told her to rest, take plenty of glucose and eat small, regular meals. The small regular meals went the same way as the large irregular ones. Another week went by.

It was Nanny who realized what the matter was. Nanny who sat her down in her room and looked at her steadily and asked her when she had had her last period. Georgina tried to remember, realized exactly what Nanny was actually saying, and felt shaky and breathless suddenly and as if she was falling very fast into a long dark hole.

'Oh dear,' she said, 'oh my God.'

'We'd better go and see someone,' was all Nanny said.

They went together to Swindon (telling Alexander they were seeing a specialist Dr Summerfield had suggested, relying on his busyness and general distractedness to prevent him from ringing Dr Summerfield himself to discuss who the specialist was and what he specialized in), visiting Virginia's own gynaecologist, Lydia Paget, who had listened to Nanny's slightly coded telephone message and agreed to see Georgina immediately.

The journey was a nightmare; they had to stop the car three times for Georgina to be sick, and when they got to the hospital she had to bolt into the loo twice while she waited to go in. It was a shaky, white, hollow-eyed creature who finally sank into the chair in Mrs Paget's consulting room. 'I may have to run,' she said, with a ghost of a smile, 'I warn you.'

Lydia Paget smiled at her encouragingly 'Of course. There's a loo through there.' She gestured at a door behind her desk. Georgina sat and tried to think what to say.

'Well now,' said Lydia, 'you don't look very well. Are you always so thin?'

'Yes,' said Georgina. 'Always.'

'Well there's nothing wrong with being thin. It's healthier than being fat. So what do you think the trouble is?'

She smiled encouragingly at Georgina. Georgina relaxed suddenly and smiled back. She looked remarkably cheerful.

'Well I suppose I'm pregnant,' she said, 'I don't know why I didn't think of it before. I was really stupid.'

'Well – maybe. When was your last period?'

'April twenty-fifth.'

'Right. And it's now June twenty-ninth. That is quite a long time. How is your cycle normally?'

'Oh,' said Georgina matter-of-factly, 'four weeks dead regular. Always.'

'Well – it certainly sounds like circumstantial evidence. And when did the sickness start?'

'About three weeks ago. Only a week before that I just felt terribly tired.'

'And it didn't occur to you before that you might be pregnant?'

'No. I know it sounds dumb. But I'd had lots of upsets, you know.'

'Of course,' said Lydia quietly. 'You must miss your mother so much. I'm sorry.'

'Oh, well thank you,' said Georgina, briskly brief. She saw Lydia look at her sharply and she rushed the conversation on, anxious to get away from the quagmire of her feelings about her mother. 'But actually I didn't mean that. I'd been expelled from school –'

'For?'

'For getting caught in bed with a boy.'

'Ah. Well that does sound a bit dumb. Not to have thought that you might be pregnant, I mean.'

'I know. It was Nanny who made the suggestion. Well, asked me when I last had a period.'

'Well good for Nanny. It's the same one, I suppose. Wonderful old lady.'

'Yes,' said Georgina, 'yes, she's here with me now.' The thought of Nanny sitting outside waiting for her, fiercely anxious, made her eyes fill with tears as the thought of her mother had not done. She looked down at her lap.

'Well now,' said Lydia Paget carefully, standing up, smiling at her gently, 'let's have a look at you. We may all be wrong.'

They weren't all wrong. She pronounced Georgina about seven or eight weeks pregnant. 'Of course we'll do a test to make absolutely sure. But your breasts are swollen as well, and there are various other changes in your body. I don't really think there's any doubt. Now then, do you want to discuss practicalities with me?'

'I'm not sure,' said Georgina, 'I mean what kind of practicalities?'

'Well,' said Lydia, 'I'm very happy to help. With any arrangements and so on. I imagine you'll want to think about everything a bit. But if you want a termination, we don't have very long. And of course you'll have to tell your father. Or does he know?'

'No, of course not,' said Georgina.

'Well – what about the father? Of your baby I mean. Do you want to tell him?'

'I can't,' said Georgina.

'Fine. Any particular reason why not?'

'I don't actually know who it is.'

Lydia Paget was trained to be emotionless. Never had her disciplines been more strained.

'I see. Well, in that case, I think I would urge you very strongly to consider a termination. But of course it's up to you. And I'm here any time, any time at all, if you want to talk to me. I expect you must feel very alone. I'm sorry.'

'Well – just a bit,' said Georgina. She realized she was suddenly feeling rather cheerful. 'But I think I'll be all right. I've got Nanny of course. But thank you anyway.'

'That's quite all right. Now if you go and see my nurse she will sort out the test for you. I'll phone you later today.'

'Thank you. Thank you very much, Mrs Paget. You've been terribly kind.' She smiled radiantly at her. 'I really do feel much better now. In every way.' She hesitated and heard herself saying, almost to her own surprise, 'Oh, and I think I probably should tell you, I'm certain I won't want to have a termination.'

Lydia was looking down at the note she was writing for her nurse; she stopped for a second, and looked up at Georgina plainly startled. Then she carried on.

'Fine. It's up to you, of course. But do think about it all, won't you? All the implications. Very carefully. And come and see me again in a few days. Whatever you decide, you need help to sort you out physically. You can't go on like this.'

'No. No, I can't. In fact –' she stood up suddenly – 'excuse me, I need that loo of yours now.'

She didn't say anything to Nanny until they were back at Hartest, beyond nodding and saying 'Looks like yes' as she came out into the waiting room.

Once home she said, 'Can I come and see you? In your room?'

'Of course you can. I'll put my kettle on.'

'Lovely. Very weak tea, I just might be able to keep that down.'

★

'Well now,' she said, sinking into Nanny's rocking chair, her hands clasped happily over her stomach, 'I am pregnant.' She felt filled with joy; she smiled at Nanny, enjoying the sensation of happiness.

'Well,' said Nanny, 'there's no going back now.'

'No,' said Georgina. 'No, and I wouldn't want to. Thank you for sorting me out, Nanny. I don't know what I'd have done without you. Given birth at Grandma's on Christmas Day, I should think.'

'That's all right,' said Nanny, 'you never were very sensible.'

'I know. But isn't it lovely?'

'No,' said Nanny, 'I don't think I'd say that.'

'Oh but it is. I'm just so pleased, I can't tell you.'

'Georgina,' said Nanny, and the shock pushed her into an absolutely standard reaction for once, 'you are talking nonsense. Of course you can't be pleased. How can you possibly be pleased? You must be more sensible. What are you going to do?'

'Have it, of course,' said Georgina, 'I can't tell you how good it makes me feel, Nanny. Even though I do feel so awful. I'm just terribly terribly happy.'

'Georgina, you can't have that baby,' said Nanny, 'you can't. It will break your father's heart.'

'Yes well,' said Georgina, 'I just have the feeling it will help to heal mine.'

She looked at Nanny. 'Look, I don't want to talk about it too much, I hate talking about it, any of it, but it might help you understand. How I feel. It's about – about Mummy. You see, we – that is Daddy – oh dear, this is going to be horrible for you – '

Nanny looked at her and there were suddenly no secrets between her and Georgina whatsoever.

'Georgina,' she said simply, 'I know.'

Georgina felt as if someone had told her the world was rotating the other way round. She said nothing at all, just stared at Nanny for a long time. 'How do you know?' she said finally.

'I know a lot of things,' said Nanny.

'Well – but – ' Georgina spread her hands out in a gesture of disbelief. Of all the people in the world she might have suspected of knowing, Nanny, with her strong disapproval, her immense moral sense, her devotion to Virginia, was the last. 'But Nanny, you were so fond of Mummy. You wouldn't ever hear a word against her.'

'Of course not,' said Nanny. She had picked up her knitting and started doing it very fast. She didn't look at Georgina. 'I was your mother's friend. She was very lonely.'

'But Nanny, you used to look after Daddy, you surely loved him.'

'Oh yes,' said Nanny. 'Yes, I loved him. I loved them both.'

'But Nanny – ' A new thought struck her, a blinding shot of relief. 'If you know, you can explain perhaps. We don't know, Charlotte and me, how, why – Daddy won't talk about it – '

'Of course not,' said Nanny, almost primly. 'Why should he?'

'Well because we're – ' 'his children' she had been about to say, and then stopped.

'It's a grown up-matter,' said Nanny, 'not for children.'

'Oh Nanny, we're not children. And we need to know.'

'No you don't,' said Nanny. 'You want to know. You've forgotten what I always told you, Georgina, there's a big difference between want and need.'

'Well I think we do.'

'Well I can't tell you,' said Nanny, 'I promised your mother I'd never tell anyone.'

'But we know, Nanny.'

'Only as much as you need. How did you find out anyway? And when? You should have told me before.'

'Oh – Charlotte heard some gossip. From Toby Lavenham. She asked Daddy, and he said it was true. It was just before Mummy died.'

'I never liked that boy,' said Nanny. 'Too well mannered. And your father didn't say any more than that it was true?'

'No.'

'Quite right.'

'Oh Nanny!'

Nanny looked at her and her face was softer suddenly. 'It can't have been easy for you,' she said, 'and I'm sorry. I often said to Her Ladyship that she should tell you herself. She said she would when you were older.'

'Well, she didn't,' said Georgina slightly bitterly, 'and as soon as we found out she went and died.'

She started to cry again and moved across to put her head in Nanny's lap; Nanny put down her knitting and stroked her hair.

'Poor little girl,' she said, very gently.

.

After a while Georgina looked up at her. 'I can't believe that you know. That you knew all the time. Oh God. And you won't tell me any more? Any more at all?'

'No,' said Nanny simply. 'It's not for me to tell you.'

'Well – all right. We can leave that for now. But Nanny, the thing is, what I was going to say, I was feeling so lost and alone and I suddenly feel I know who I am again. Having this baby. Can you understand that?'

'No I can't,' said Nanny, stern again. 'I certainly can't understand how you can contemplate having a baby. Without a husband. At your age.'

'I don't quite see what my age has to do with it,' said Georgina. 'But anyway, I can and I will have it. I'd have thought you'd like the idea, Nanny, of having a baby to look after again.'

'Well I would like a baby,' said Nanny, 'if it had a father. Who is the father, Georgina? Someone at that school? I never did like the uniform.'

'Er – yes,' said Georgina carefully, aware even in her euphoria that Nanny would not be able to cope with the news that the father of her baby could be any one of three boys, 'yes. Someone at school.'

'So he'd marry you, would he? I don't know if we've got time to organize a wedding.'

'No, Nanny, he wouldn't marry me. Definitely not.'

'Well he should,' said Nanny, 'and I shall tell him so myself.'

'No, Nanny, you can't. I'm not going to tell you who it is.'

'Well your father will want to know.'

'Yes,' said Georgina with a sigh, 'I know he will. Look, Nanny, I will tell him, I'll have to, I know. But not for a day or two. Is that all right?'

'I suppose so,' said Nanny, 'as you're not eating.'

The logic of this was too difficult even for Georgina to follow. She stood up and gave Nanny a kiss.

'Thank you,' she said.

Lydia Paget phoned the following day. The test had been positive. 'As I thought. Now, Georgina, I am relying on you to contact me when you feel ready.'

'Thank you,' said Georgina.

'And could I just say – and you can tell me it is none of my business – that any girl as young as you, even as financially fortunate as you – should not enter into motherhood lightly. It really might be better – to consider a termination.'

'It *is* none of your business,' said Georgina cheerfully, 'and I don't mind a bit. But honestly, Mrs Paget, I wouldn't dream of having a termination. I really want this baby very badly.'

'I'm sure,' said Lydia, 'and I can understand that. But do you think it wants you? In your present situation? Think about that one, Georgina. Please.'

'I'll think about it,' said Georgina, 'but I won't change my mind.'

She was very brave about telling her father. She told him everything. That she didn't know who the father was, that she could only narrow it down to three; and that she couldn't possibly therefore – how could she –

tell any of them. And that she was going to have the baby and that there was nothing he could do to persuade her otherwise.

Alexander listened in silence. He didn't shout, he didn't rant or roar. He just listened carefully and attentively, looking at her all the time in a cold, detached way. She had never seen him like that, never known him anything but warm and loving and good-humoured, or normally naturally angry, as he had been when she had been first expelled. It was very frightening.

When finally she had finished, had said, 'And Mrs Paget can help me where to have it and so on,' he said, 'Georgina, there's very little I can do about all this. You can stay here, of course, and your child as well. I am not going to cast you out like the father in some Victorian melodrama. But don't expect me to forgive you. Or to love it. I'm afraid you are no daughter of mine.'

And 'No,' she had said, illogically wounded by his reaction, 'no I'm not. Maybe that's why it has happened.'

'No of course you are not,' he said, 'you are not my daughter. Not my own flesh and blood. But I have always loved you so much, been so proud of you, you have been, God forgive me for admitting it, my favourite. There are other things apart from genes and chromosomes that form us all. To me, you were my daughter. My beloved daughter. I stress that you were. This has made me feel otherwise.'

And he turned and walked out of the room.

She had a termination in the end. She thought and thought until she could think no more, on a rack of guilt and grief, and then, shaking with violent misery, she phoned Lydia Paget and asked her to arrange an immediate operation. 'And don't, don't tell me I'm doing the right thing,' she said. 'or I shall go quite quite mad.'

'I won't,' said Lydia, 'I promise. And I won't allow anyone else to tell you so either.'

It was painless, easy, swift. Georgina would have preferred that it could have been otherwise. She felt she owed it to her baby, that she loved so much, to suffer something for it, in killing it. It seemed an ultimate betrayal to throw it out of her warm, nurturing body, carelessly, painlessly, without so much as a breath of discomfort. She lay bleeding in the narrow bed in the clinic after she had woken up, willing her body to suffer. It wouldn't.

'I want it to hurt,' she said, clinging to Nanny's hand later, when she came to visit, tears streaming down her face. 'Can you understand that? I want it to hurt. I can't stand it not hurting.'

'It's hurting all right,' said Nanny, pushing back Georgina's hair. 'It just isn't hurting the way you want it to.'

Georgina stared at her. 'Yes,' she said, 'yes of course. You're right. How wise you are, Nanny. What would I do without you? What would any of us do?'

It did hurt, after all, in the end. She got an infection, developed a high fever, and lay for days with a temperature of 105, rambling, calling for her mother, for Alexander, for Nanny.

'She did it for you, you know,' said Nanny. 'You will remember that, won't you, Alexander?'

'Yes,' he said, 'yes, I'll remember it. I promise.'

Slowly, she grew better. After a week she was sitting up in bed, drinking the sweet weak tea she was addicted to, pale, but recovering.

'That's better,' said Nanny, coming in to collect her cup and a plate of bread and butter which Georgina had requested. 'You're on the mend.'

'Yes. I'm so glad I was ill. It's made me feel better. Less guilty. You know.' She smiled suddenly. 'I sound like you, Nanny, don't I?'

'I don't know what you mean,' said Nanny. 'Your father's looking very peaky.'

'Yes, I know. He came to see me earlier. We had a talk. He said he hoped I would forgive him.'

'And what did you say?'

'I said there was nothing to forgive. It's very sad, and I still feel wrenched in pieces, but I could see in the end I had to – to do that for him. He's done so much for us all our lives, just loving us. I'd never realized before.'

'I had,' said Nanny.

'Yes, well of course you had. You're old and wise.'

She smiled, and sighed in the same instant. 'I'm not doing very well, am I, Nanny? But it isn't easy. Any of it. You know.'

'Yes,' said Nanny, 'yes, I know.'

'I'm so jealous of Max,' said Georgina, suddenly starting to cry again, looking like a stricken child, 'so terribly terribly jealous.'

'You mustn't be,' said Nanny, taking her in her arms, stroking her hair, patting her shoulder. 'There's nothing really to be jealous of. Nothing special about boys,' she added darkly.

'Well of course there is,' said Georgina, looking at her puzzledly, brushing away her tears, 'something to be jealous of, I mean. Surely you must be able to see that.'

'Why?' said Nanny. 'I don't see.'

'But you must,' said Georgina. 'It's different for him. Quite quite different.'

'No, Georgina, I don't,' said Nanny, and her faded blue eyes were genuinely puzzled. 'No, I don't see at all, I'm afraid. Why is it different for Max?'

Chapter 16

Charlotte, 1981–2

'I'm beginning to think Daddy must be mad,' said Charlotte. 'Or maybe that we're all mad.'

'Maybe she drove him mad,' said Georgina, 'with her behaviour.'

'What on earth do we do now?'

'I don't know. I just don't know.'

They were sitting in the library at Hartest, watching the August rain falling determinedly down. 'Thank God for Nantucket,' said Georgina moodily. 'It's been doing this for weeks.'

It was the day before they were all leaving for America and Charlotte had only just returned from her travels; Georgina had had to wait for an agonizing six weeks to talk to her. The one time she longed, ached for her sister's presence and counsel had been when she had been wrestling with her conscience over her pregnancy: and that had been the one week in the whole summer when Charlotte had not called.

Charlotte was filled with remorse, savagely sorry for her beleaguered sister. 'Oh, Georgie, if only I'd been here. I wish I'd known.'

'Well, I was all right. I had Nanny, she was so wonderful. She's such a mass of contradictions, you'd have thought she'd be shocked, and she was just a rock. The most disapproving thing she said about the whole thing was that she never liked the school uniform.' She grinned at Charlotte. 'Yes, I did it for Daddy. I suddenly saw how much he had done, loving us, caring for us, never letting us down, never letting Mummy down, never giving us the slightest idea for an instant that we weren't his. And I thought what having the baby would do to him, and I thought, well, I just couldn't. However much I wanted to. I mean I can always have other babies – '

'Georgina – ' said Charlotte, 'I'm not going to read you a lecture. Of course I'm not – '

'You'd better not,' said Georgina, slightly grimly. 'You'd bloody better not.'

'I'm not. I just said I wasn't. But I do think you'd better get yourself sorted.'

'If you mean the pill, I have. Lydia Paget put me on it.'

'Good. But not just that, you can't really go round sleeping with every man with an erection you come across.'

'Why not?' said Georgina. 'It's fun.'

'Yes, well it may be fun. But you won't do yourself any good, apart from getting a foul reputation and probably VD into the bargain. OK? Find someone you at least like, and stay with him.'

'Yes, miss,' said Georgina. She scowled at Charlotte and then grinned.

'Sorry, Georgie. Lecture over. I suppose,' said Charlotte, carefully casual, 'I suppose, if we'd still had Mummy, none of it would have happened.'

'Possibly not. But God knows what dreadful genes she's passed on to us. It seems to me – well, never mind.'

'That you might be following in her footsteps? Is that what you're afraid of?' She had been hoping to lead Georgina into this thought.

'A bit.'

'Well, don't be. That way lies madness. We're obviously a mass of rogue genes, all of us. We can't let them be an excuse or a justification for anything we might be doing. We're ourselves. That's all we know. We have to make do with that. Now look, what are we going to do about Max?'

'Tell him, I suppose. We have to.'

'Well, yes. But when? He's still awfully little.'

'Charlotte, he's not little. He's fourteen going on twenty-four. And awfully worldly. I dread to think what he and that little sexpot Melissa are going to get up to all day long on Nantucket.'

'Well, yes. In some ways. In others he's a baby.' Charlotte sighed; she found her attitude towards Max ambivalent. On the one hand she disapproved of him dreadfully, on the other she doted on him. 'But – oh, I don't know. I mean does he really have to know yet? Tell me again what Nanny said. How it came out.'

'Well I was just saying how I was jealous of Max, I was very upset anyway, and she said, why, and I said because it was different for him, and she said it wasn't any different for Max at all. And then realized she'd told me something I didn't actually know, and got in a frightful fluster and said she couldn't say any more, that she'd promised Mummy never to tell. Poor Daddy. Poor poor Daddy.'

'Yes.'

Charlotte was silent, and then she said, 'Well, let's not tell him yet. Little bugger'd probably only use it as an excuse to do even less work than he's doing already. And there's no gossip about him. At least our mother had realized the wisdom of choosing blond blue-eyed lovers by then.'

'Oh don't,' said Georgina. Her face suddenly looked very tender and vulnerable. 'Don't. I hate it all so much.'

'I know. I'm sorry. So anyway, we can afford to wait a bit. I really don't think I can face talking to Daddy about it.'

'No. No nor can I. I feel he's more and more in a world of his own. So – we leave it for now? Telling Max?'

'Yes. I think so. But I'll tell you one thing. I'm getting increasingly desperate to know more about my – my father. I really am. And I'm going to find out. It may take years, but I'm going to find out. I don't know how I'm even going to begin. But I am.'

It was a year later that she found out about the christening robe. Right through her second glorious year at Cambridge – deputy editor of *Granta*, frequent speaker at the Union, shining star of the Dramatic Society, she promised herself that come the summer, she would not go travelling or even spend the entire three months on Nantucket with Beau Fraser, as he begged her in every letter to do, but devote herself to unravelling her history.

Home in late June, with the house more or less to herself (Georgina departing for Cirencester at eight and generally arriving home again well after midnight, Max still at school, and her father as always at this time of year fully occupied outdoors on the estate), she had long uninterrupted days to pursue her task.

She began with Virginia's personal papers. Her father had never emptied her desk; it was still in the perfect order that Virginia had maintained in every department of her life.

It was a huge mahogany pedestal desk, in the window of Virginia's study, overlooking the park and the woods; the first day she had sat at it, Charlotte had been filled with an overwhelming sense of Virginia's presence as she opened neatly stacked drawers, studied bulging address books filled out with sloping American writing, went through files kept in perfect chronological order, and gazed out frequently and almost unseeingly at the view that must have filled her mother's head.

The top few drawers, the top row of files, were entirely devoted to her work; letters to and from clients and suppliers, photocopies of drawings, estimates, invoices, tax returns, all in impeccable order.

Diaries yielded nothing. Business appointments, family occasions, parties, holidays. Not a hint of any impropriety, a name that was less than extremely familiar to her, a meeting that could possibly have been interpreted as anything but totally respectable.

Personal letters, from her parents, from Baby, from Angie Burbank – she thought she had stumbled on something when she found a scribbled note from Angie saying 'I'm so thrilled for you, he sounds wonderful', but she was forced, slightly regretfully, to match even that up with Max's birth.

Then personal documents: the marriage certificate, all their birth certificates (including one for the tiny Alexander, filed heartbreakingly with his death certificate). Photographs, of all of them, just odd, fleetingly precious ones, Alexander before the marriage, smiling at her against a background of New York on the Circle Line ferry; herself, stark naked, splashing happily in her bath, and another one, lying smiling in her Viyella nightie on Virginia's lap; Georgina, tall and sulkily lanky, even at four, holding Nanny's hand on the steps of the North Front, in her very first school uniform; Max in his christening robe, held in Baby's arms; Baby at graduation, in his robe and mortar, laughing, his arms held out to the camera and Virginia; Fred III and Virginia, dancing in the drawing room at Beaches, laughing, obviously rehearsing for some early performance, years before.

'Oh dear,' said Charlotte, her eyes blurring with tears for the umpteenth time in a week, 'oh Mummy, I do miss you.'

Only one drawer left to go, and not a promising one. The drawer held files, and the files held invoices; personal ones for clothes, jewellery, furniture, children's toys, Christmas presents. She sat there, sifting through them, visualizing what some of them recalled: the wonderful dolls' house they had been given one Christmas, painstakingly made for them by a craftsman carpenter in Yorkshire, ball gowns her mother had worn, the new grand piano she had bought when Charlotte had been ten and showing particular promise at her music, her and Georgina's confirmation dresses, Max's clothes for Eton, almost the last entry.

She had reached the last file now, the first in fact, for she was working backwards: the bills for all their baby stuff, dresses and coats from the White House, full layettes from Harrods, cribs, prams. Her own christening robe, now there was a pretty letter-heading, not a bill, just a compliments note – and here Charlotte stopped, just for a moment ice-still, wondering, more than wondering, alert suddenly. Why a christening robe? Why did she have to have a new one? There was the family one, made from Alexander's great-grandmother's wedding dress, as they had all been told, so many, oh so many times. There was the picture of Max wearing it in Virginia's drawer, and the picture of Georgina, resplendent in it, held by a smiling Virginia, stood on the grandest of fireplaces in the drawing room. It was an important part of the family folklore, that robe, they had all heard a lot about it; why, why then, hadn't she worn it? Probably, she told herself, shaking her head at her own foolishness thinking it might be significant, probably, because she had been the first baby. Maybe Betsey had wanted to give her a robe; maybe the robe had been temporarily lost or was being mended, or being cleaned. Maybe. Maybe.

★

The heading on the slip of paper was 'Maura Mahon' in a rounded, pseudo-Gaelic-style script; the address was Trinity Street, Dublin, with a Dublin phone number. 'As ordered,' it said. 'One white lawn christening robe. Self-embroidered.'

Impossible, thought Charlotte, quite quite impossible, that Maura Mahon was still operating; but it was worth trying, worth telephoning. It was too late now; after seven. It would have to wait until the morning.

Reluctantly, oddly disturbed, she stood up, looking down at the handwritten note. Why had her mother bought it, or maybe had it made; and was it, could it be, a clue?

She wandered down to the kitchen to make herself a cup of tea and to ask Mrs Fallon about supper; Nanny was there, pottering about, filling the biscuit tin she kept in her room.

'Cup of tea, Nanny?'

'Well, I suppose so,' said Nanny, 'as it's June.'

Charlotte debated unravelling this one herself and decided she couldn't.

'Nanny, can you remember my christening?' she said, carefully casual. 'I was just looking at my christening mug. Was I good, or did I cry?'

'You cried a bit,' said Nanny.

'And did I look beautiful in my robe? In the family heirloom? That was Great-Great-Grandma's wedding dress?'

'Well, you would have done,' said Nanny, 'but you didn't wear it.'

'Why not?'

'Your mother didn't want you to.'

'How odd.'

'Yes, well. She said it didn't suit you. Very silly really, when you were such a pretty baby. But she insisted. Your father gave in to her, as she was so depressed. But he was upset. Well, disappointed. You know how much family traditions mean to him. Of course old Lady Caterham would have minded, only she wasn't there.'

'No,' said Charlotte. 'Of course not. So – what did I wear?'

'Well, you must have seen photographs,' said Nanny briskly, 'it was quite nice really, I suppose. But too short. Not at all suitable.' She spoke as if Charlotte had been baptized a leggy sixteen-year-old in a mini skirt.

'Ah,' said Charlotte. 'So where did it come from?'

'Oh, your mother got it. She had it before you were born. I don't know where it came from. She knew I didn't like it.'

Charlotte felt her mother's courage and willpower in the face of such opposition required some kind of acknowledgement.

'Well,' she said, 'I suppose she had a right to choose what I wore.'

'That's a point of view,' said Nanny, making it clear that to her mind it was no such thing. 'I suppose.'

'Have you still got it? The robe? I'd love to see it.'

'I think so,' said Nanny. 'It'll be in the trunk. In the night nursery. I'll have a look later.'

'Don't bother, I'll have a rummage myself.'

Nanny looked at her suspiciously. 'What's brought this interest in your christening on?'

'Oh – nothing really,' said Charlotte. 'I just want to see what I wore for my first public appearance.'

The christening robe was right at the bottom of the trunk, a simple little dress in white lawn, exquisitely smocked, with tiny covered buttons and self-embroidered collar and cuffs. It was carefully folded into tissue paper, tied loosely with a pink ribbon, and a piece of yellowing paper, in Virginia's handwriting, tucked into the folds. 'Charlotte,' it said. 'March 14th 1962.'

Just that. Not terribly significant.

But the family robe was not wrapped, nor did it have a piece of paper with the dates of Georgina's and Max's christenings. It seemed just a little interesting.

In the morning she phoned the number in Dublin. It was unobtainable. Discontinued, they said at Directory Enquiries; no, they couldn't say when the discontinuation had taken place. No, they had no new number or address for any Maura Mahon. Either as a person or a company. Charlotte sighed. This wasn't easy.

Finally she sat down and wrote a letter to Maura Mahon. She said that she had worn a christening robe, with her label in it, twenty years earlier, that her mother, who had ordered the robe, had died, that the work was so exquisite she would like possibly to commission something similar for a friend's baby; and that even if Miss Mahon was no longer in business, it would be a great pleasure to hear from her.

She addressed it to the house in Trinity Street, marked it 'please forward' and posted it, feeling fairly certain that she would never get a reply.

She was wrong. But before it came, other events rather overtook it in importance.

She was sitting on the swing seat just after breakfast three weeks later on the deck of the house on Nantucket, chatting idly to Melissa about the comparative merits of Bruce Springsteen and Bob Marley and wishing she didn't find Beau Fraser quite so overwhelmingly sexy when she heard the phone ringing.

'I'll go,' she called out to Mary Rose, who was lying in a hammock in the yard. 'It's probably Daddy anyway, he said he'd call today.'

It wasn't Alexander. It was St Vincent's Hospital, New York. Baby had had a coronary and was on the critical list.

Charlotte flew up to New York with Mary Rose and Freddy and Kendrick. The news that greeted them when they reached St Vincent's was not good. Baby was critical: it had been a major attack. On the other hand, Dr Robertson assured them, his vital signs were good: he was no worse. The next twelve hours would be crucial. Mary Rose stayed at the hospital for the duration of the twelve hours and then for another six; at the end of them Baby opened his wide blue eyes, winked at the pretty nurse who was adjusting his ECG contacts, and closed them again.

Dr Robertson was summoned and said cautiously that it was an encouraging sign; twelve hours further on, he pronounced Baby as being out of danger. At which point Mary Rose, released suddenly from strain, had hysterics and then demanded to know what had been puzzling her ever since she first heard the news: why Baby had been taken to St Vincent's Hospital, down in Greenwich Village, and not to the New York Hospital, near their home.

Geoff Robertson, unable to find a satisfactory explanation, was driven to telling her that Baby had been taken ill in the bed of a young lady who owned an apartment in the Village, and that it had been she who had called the ambulance.

'Poor old Uncle Baby,' said Max when he heard this piece of news. 'What rotten luck.'

Charlotte, trying not to sound too prissy, said that having a major coronary was rather more than rotten luck, and Max retorted that it hadn't been the coronary itself he was talking about, but the place Baby had chosen to have it.

'I bet Aunt Mary Rose is giving him a hard time. It's enough to give him a second heart attack.'

'I wonder who the girl was,' said Georgina.

'Some hooker, I expect,' said Max.

'The really bad news for poor Uncle Baby,' said Charlotte, 'is that Grandpa has moved back into the bank.'

Chapter 17

Baby, 1982

Baby had not been in bed with a hooker, as Max had so confidently supposed, he had been in bed with Angie. And if anyone had asked him if the heart attack had been worth it, he would have told them yes.

He looked back on the ten years without Angie in amazement: that he could ever have considered himself happy, content even. What he felt for her was not just lust, affection, excitement, not even just an intense pleasure in her company. What he felt for Angie, and he knew it with a certainty that in itself made him happy, was love.

She had changed greatly in the ten years; sophistication had replaced glamour, shrewdness guile, sensuality the raw sexiness of her youth. She was successful and rich; he found that oddly pleasing. He had always been haunted by the thought that perhaps she might have been using him, however slightly, for his money, been bewitched, to however small a degree, by his power. Now she was rich and powerful herself, she had no need to be with him for the things he could give her, do for her, she clearly wanted him for himself and it made him happier than he could ever remember. The rush of emotion that he had felt when he saw her rather ugly, tidy handwriting on the envelope had been literally shocking; he had had to sit down, have a cup of strong coffee, before he could even bring himself to open it. And then he had sat there reading it, noticing his hands shaking, touched that she should have taken the trouble to write, excited that she was coming to New York and pleased that she clearly wanted to forget the past and be friends.

And then the moment he had set eyes on her, sitting there, so beautiful, so warm, had talked to her, touched her, smelt her, he knew that whatever happened, whatever the cost, he had to have her back.

It hadn't been very difficult. She had made it plain she wanted that too. They had had dinner two nights later, and gone straight back to her room at the Pierre. 'Isn't it funny,' said Angie, handing him a glass of champagne from her fridge, 'that I should be entertaining you in style now, Baby, rather than the other way round? It feels lovely.'

'It feels pretty good to me too,' said Baby. 'What a waste of ten years.'

'What a waste indeed.'

223

There was a silence; they were both slightly awkward, tense, as they had not been in the restaurant. She went over to the window.

'We ought to have some fun. For old times' sake. How about a ride in one of the horse cabs? They're around.'

'Only if you promise to sit in the carriage with me. I don't want you up there with the driver.'

'Baby, I promise to sit with you. Come on.'

They went down, ran across to the waiting line of the carriages. 'The longest ride you do,' said Angie to the driver, clambering in.

The carriage set off towards the park; Baby sat there, half terrified he would suddenly see someone he knew, half overwhelmed by pleasure. Angie looked at him and grinned.

'I know what you're thinking. Don't. Whoever do you think would recognize you in one of these things? Give me your hand.'

Baby gave her his hand; she kissed it tenderly and drew it beneath the rug the driver had tucked around them.

'Now,' she said, 'a little reunion, I think.'

He felt, with a stab that was almost fear, her thighs, smooth, warm, silky soft; she was wearing stockings, not tights, and she pulled his hand very very slowly, gently upwards, into the heat of her, pausing every now and again, and then suddenly, it was there, his hand, where it wanted to be, placed on her bush. Baby froze, stilled with desire and delight; she had no panties on, she was naked beneath her black jersey dress. Angie, having guided his hand to its destination, moved her own, under the blanket, seeking out his fly; he felt her moving towards it, stroking his own thighs with infinite gentleness, and then slowly, slowly undoing the fly, reaching, tenderly tentative, inside for his penis. He felt her fingers on it, moving, feathering up and down, lingering on the tip; he moaned, and she giggled and leant over and covered his mouth with her own. As her tongue sought out his, her hard, thrusting, greedy tongue, Baby felt as if he had been given food after a long long period of hunger, had come into shelter from burning sunlight; he lay back, and began to explore her with his hand, feeling into the soft moistness, remembering vividly, joyfully, her infinitely greedy tumultuous depths; she moaned herself then, and turned her back to him, suddenly, carelessly, lifting herself onto him; Baby felt her, wet hot, felt his penis suddenly inside her, felt her closing round him, pushing, pulling at him. He put his hands around her waist, pushed his fingers down over her stomach, into her bush, seeking out her clitoris, finding it, hot, hard; she was panting, moaning herself now, clenching and unclenching her vagina, and he felt in a great torrential primeval urge his orgasm rising, rising in him, into her, and as he came, as his pleasure exploded, broke,

224

she thrust harder, harder against him, drawing it into her own; and then it was over, and they lay there beneath the blanket, staring up at the stars, eased of hunger, oddly at peace, as the carriage proceeded in a more respectable and orderly way around Central Park.

After that it was simply a matter of logistics. There was no way he was going to let her leave his life again.

'I love you,' he said as they lay in bed in her hotel, after a second, more leisurely piece of lovemaking. 'I was mad to let you go.'

'Yes you were,' said Angie. She reached across him for her champagne. 'I read somewhere that if you dip a cock in champagne, it tastes absolutely delicious.'

'The cock or the champagne?'

'Not sure. Let's try.'

'My cock wouldn't fit into that champagne glass,' said Baby.

'Bighead.'

'No, just the cock.'

'I bet it will.'

'OK.'

It didn't, to his considerable complacency; so she poured the champagne over it, and then wriggled down and started lapping it off. Baby smiled at her golden head, stroked it, felt his penis rising again.

'Baby Praeger, you certainly haven't lost any of your potency in these ten years,' said Angie.

'Oh but I have,' he said, his eyes momentarily heavy. 'It's only you working your magic.'

'Really?' She was clearly charmed by this thought. 'You mean you sometimes can't? With. . . ?'

'I sometimes can't. With anyone.'

'Baby! Does that mean other ladies? Apart from Mary Rose.'

'I'm afraid it does,' he said, his eyes heavy with love as he looked at her, 'but I have to tell you that I have never been to bed with anyone, in this whole long ten years, without thinking of you.'

Angie sat up suddenly and looked at him. Her eyes were oddly bright; she brushed at them impatiently.

'Shit,' she said, her voice slightly shaky. 'Shit, Baby, you mustn't say things like that.'

He asked her about her own life; she told him there had been a couple of relationships, neither of them long-lasting, a couple of briefer ones. 'I really haven't been very into sex,' she said, suddenly efficient. 'I've been too busy being a tycoon.'

'And I'm really proud of you. I think you're wonderful. Do you live alone?'

'Yes, in a house in St John's Wood. It's really pretty, I can't wait to show it to you.'

'A whole house to yourself?'

'Well, most of it. I have my grandmother in the basement.'

'You do? Well that's wonderful.'

'I felt I owed her one. As they say. And she's fun, even if she is seventy-something. Oh my goodness, Baby, that reminds me, I haven't got around to cancelling that standing order to the rest home in Bournemouth. I'm so sorry. It's only been two or three months, I'll do it right away.'

'All right, darling, no rush. Talking of rushing, I really do have to go.'

'Where are you supposed to be?' she said, stroking his shoulder with her finger.

'Oh, at one of my schmoozing sessions. I have a whole host of new activities, Angie, you'd be amazed. I've gone into showbiz banking. My father hates it.'

'But your father doesn't have any say any more?'

'He has a great deal of say,' said Baby, laughing, 'but that's where it ends. Thank God.'

'Tell me about your showbiz activities.'

'Another time. How long are you here for? I didn't dare ask you before.'

'Oh,' said Angie, 'another week. Maybe two. I have some clients looking for property over here.'

Baby was very impressed.

Praegers, it was generally agreed, had changed more than a little since Baby Praeger's ascension to power. There were those who thought the changes were for the better, and those who thought quite the reverse; but nobody could deny their existence. Baby had gone in for glitz: had sponsored causes and charities, donated generously to the arts, established high-profile sporting events. The Praeger Vets Baseball Team took on all comers (almost invariably losing to them) in a blaze of media attention, and attendance at Baby's annual Celebrity Golf Game in Palm Springs was mandatory for anyone who was anyone (or indeed wanted to be).

Fred III hated the whole thing and said so; he was suspicious of it, he said, and particularly of Baby's own high-profile role.

Baby, warmly confident in his own abilities and the clement climate of Wall Street altogether at the time, told him he didn't understand, that it was the age of the personality, that Fred should take a look at Bruce Wasserstein, Peter Cohen, Dennis Levine. 'You hear those names and you think smart and you think dynamic, the clients rush in.' Fred retorted that it was dangerous, that the guys pulled in the clients all right, and then left with them; what was right was the system at Goldmans where you had to be ten years just to get to be a partner.

'Times have changed, Dad,' said Baby.

Baby was actually just a little concerned about the partner situation at Praegers. The senior guys were just fine: Pete Hoffman, Chris Hill, Mike Stevens, and the other seven, all rocks: experienced, strong, able, backing him to the hilt. But he was uncomfortably aware he had put in some just slightly less rock-like, less able people as junior partners over the past year: notably Chuck Drew, charming, golden friend of Jeremy Foster, brought in from the considerably lower echelons of Chase and placed on the board more to please Jeremy than to promote the greater good of Praegers, and Henry Keers, sharp, funny, ambitious, and showing promise but no more in the fast-developing M & A (Mergers and Acquisitions) department. Henry was a prime mover at the MidWeek Meeting, and he had an eye for his own superstar status; he was exactly the kind of man Fred worried about. What was really dangerous about these promotions, Baby knew, was that it weakened his defence amongst the board against men he didn't want in. Pete Hoffman was rooting for his own son, Gabe, now a senior vice president, brilliant, hard-working and ferociously ambitious. But Baby didn't worry overmuch about any of it; life was too much fun.

The development of the relationship with Angie proved complex. Her business was in London, and that was where she had to be. She was not playing at it, she explained to him, it was worth a lot of money, and she had to take care of it. He could see that.

After the first fortnight, while she looked (unsuccessfully for the most part, she said) for properties for her client, she went back to London. Baby missed her almost beyond endurance. It was as painful, if not more so, than the parting ten years earlier. Then he had been resolute, putting her out of his mind, determinedly ignoring the pain; now newly in love he could hardly stand it.

He made a trip to London, a forty-eight-hour stop-over; he booked in at the Savoy, and there they stayed for the entire time, never leaving the room, and hardly the bed. Once or twice he told the switchboard to say he was out, just to create the impression, to his office and to Mary Rose, should she phone more than once or twice, that he was indeed engaged on business and not confined to his suite. But the only expeditions he really made were into Angie's apparently insatiable small person; and one brief one in her company to Harrods, to buy presents for the children. When he left she cried, and said she would come to New York when she could, but not for at least a month, she was very busy with several transactions, and there was no one else to handle them.

'Can't you get an assistant?' said Baby gloomily, downing a treble brandy in the VIP departure lounge at Heathrow, and no, she said, no she certainly couldn't, she would find herself ripped off totally, and would he consider leaving Praegers in the hands of Pete Hoffman and Chris Hill for more than a few days? Baby said he certainly would, and frequently did, when he went on business trips or vacations; and in any case he hardly thought the comparison was valid. Angie had a one-woman property business, not a billion-pound investment bank.

'I daresay,' said Angie, looking at him with a dangerous light in her green eyes, 'I and my company are worth proportionately more than you and your company.'

'Maybe,' said Baby hastily. He realized he had absolutely no idea how to deal with professional and powerful women.

The compromise they reached would have seemed highly unsatisfactory if it hadn't made him so happy. Once a month at least Angie flew to New York; once a month at least he went to London (or occasionally to Paris or Zurich, to allay Mary Rose's suspicion). They were greatly aided in this by Concorde, which cut four hours off the flying time; Angie particularly enjoyed the phenomenon of leaving Heathrow at eight and arriving at JFK at exactly the same time or even a little earlier. One day just for the hell of it she flew over for lunch with Baby and back again; she had some news she wanted to share with him (a purchase of an entire row of very pretty Georgian cottages in Camberwell she had beaten two of the big boys to, by the simple process of getting the residents on her side and offering to pay their removal expenses) and lunching at the Lutèce seemed, she said, a particularly good way of celebrating. She wouldn't even go to bed with him that day, she said it made the journey seem more extravagant if its purpose was simply lunch; Baby's frustration was very largely alleviated by the charm of her gesture. After a while, when Angie was in New York she lived in her old apartment in the Village, which Baby had always found himself emotionally unable to sell; an agent had leased it out for him, on short-term lets, and he reclaimed it easily. It was an exceptionally nice apartment, with big light lofty rooms, just off Vincent Square, and Angie after an initial protest agreed that it was more sensible than running up huge hotel bills. In any case, as Baby pointed out, they were a lot less likely to be recognized by anyone in the Village than in the environs of the Pierre Hotel.

As a cover for early morning visits to Angie, Baby took up running. He bought track suits and trainers, got up early every day, and set off at an extremely brisk pace in the direction of Central Park. Once out of sight of the apartment he would saunter on for a while, picking up a coffee at one of the early morning delis, and if the day was nice enough, actually go into the park and sit on a bench and admire the landscape and any passing female joggers or dog walkers. This routine only varied when Angie was in town, when he hailed a cab, drove down to the Village, removed the track suit and climbed into her bed. Mary Rose, who always left the apartment by seven thirty to go to her exercise class, consequently never saw him return (to remove a clean, unsweaty track suit and to climb, quite unnecessarily, in the bathtub), but she approved very much of his new regime, having urged him for years to take some exercise. It added considerably to Baby's pleasure, as he lay entwined in Angie's arms, to contemplate the rather different nature of the exercise he was actually taking from what Mary Rose complacently imagined.

He was charmed and delighted by the new Angie; he had never forgotten the pleasure of her, of her beauty, her just slightly sharp charm, her sense of fun, her innate sexiness, and those qualities, rich as ever, had been heightened, sharpened by absence, by not having her. But there was something else now, something totally unexpected and every bit as important, as valuable, and that was that she was in some strange way an equal, a business partner, someone with whom he could talk problems through. She had always listened, made observations, talked sense; but now she could look at a situation from every angle, proffer suggestions, examine arguments. The hours they spent talking money, tactics, successes, dangers, came to mean as much to Baby as the hours that preceded them making love; and in some strange way he found them as exciting. Talking a deal through with Angie, describing its conception, its progress, its traumas, its conclusion, was an oddly intense pleasure.

What he did not discuss with her – until it was far far too late – was what he came to think of as the Chuck Drew affair.

It was Pete Hoffman who first alerted him to Chuck Drew's activities; he seemed to be getting overly involved in the M & A side, Pete said, and talking too much about the deals as well. He was also very buddy-buddy with Henry Keers. 'He moves in a circle of extremely high-profile people, Baby. I think you should have a word with him about discretion. It only takes one slip to get hoisted with insider dealing.'

Baby smiled politely and ignored the advice. He also managed to ignore the fact that Chuck appeared to be living beyond his means, and within a fairly short space of time had bought himself a Maserati, commissioned the building of a house in Florida and was having his New York apartment done out by Robert Metzger. Even Jeremy Foster remarked on it over a dinner with Baby, much of which was spent bemoaning the parlous state of his marriage, and Isabella's threat of instituting divorce proceedings if he didn't start, as she put it, behaving like an adult. Baby told him he should take Isabella's advice. Jeremy said he was really, genuinely trying, that he loved Isabella more than anything in the world, and after sinking several more glasses of bourbon, returned to the subject of Chuck Drew.

'Metzger doesn't come cheap, I mean he charges a hundred grand just to walk in the door. And nor do Maseratis. I'm pleased for him, don't get me wrong. But you must be paying him a fortune.'

Still only mildly concerned, Baby called the salaries division next day.

Praegers were not paying Chuck Drew a fortune; what he was getting was clearly not enough to finance Maseratis and mansions in Florida. Pete Hoffman's words about insider trading suddenly resounded in Baby's head.

He had a showdown with Chuck; asked him where he was getting his money from. Chuck told him, fairly pleasantly, to mind his own business, and Baby said he felt it was very much his business, that he needed to be assured that there was nothing untoward going on under Praegers' aegis, and that if Chuck wouldn't tell him he intended to find out anyway. He asked Chuck for details of all his financial affairs, and if he had any accounts in Zurich or the Bahamas. Chuck swore he hadn't; he remained calm, almost complacent in the face of Baby's agitation. Baby was baffled by his reaction and tried to reassure himself that if Chuck had genuinely been up to something, he would have been a lot more worried. A check on his credit rating and bank accounts appeared to reveal in any case that he was telling the truth. But Baby didn't believe him. He told Chuck if he wouldn't tell him the truth, he might be forced to call in the Securities and Exchange Commission. Chuck looked at him with the same complacent calm and said nothing.

Two days later Jeremy Foster called him; could they meet, to talk about Chuck?

Jeremy was shocked, shocked to death, he said; Chuck had admitted to him that he had been involved in insider trading, had made a fortune on several recent Praeger deals, purchasing the shares in the name of two aunts, one in Iowa, one in Wisconsin, neither of whose names most conveniently was Drew, and paying the resultant profits into their accounts. Baby, equally shocked, said he would have to report Chuck to the SEC, that Praegers' reputation was at stake.

Jeremy looked at him. 'Do you really mean that?'

'Jeremy, of course I really mean it.'

'I don't want that, Baby.' Jeremy's eyes were hard, suddenly, and blank. 'Our association, that is Fosters and Praegers, go back a long way,' he said. 'It would be very sad if anything damaged our good relations.'

'Jeremy,' said Baby, 'what on earth are you saying?'

'You know what I'm saying,' said Jeremy, and his eyes were blanker still. 'I want Chuck kept on. As a partner. I promise you nothing untoward will ever happen again. Just wipe the slate on this one, will you, Baby, please.'

Baby looked at him. He thought of the Foster account, the billions of dollars that were involved, year on year; the way the sheer weight of their business gave Praegers a status beyond its size; he remembered his father's words about how there was nothing, nothing you would not do for a client, an important client; and he waited for quite a long time, and then he said, 'Very well, Jeremy. But I want Chuck's assurance that nothing of the sort will ever happen again. OK?'

'OK,' said Jeremy. His relief was visible; his relaxation almost tangible. 'Thank you. Thank you very much, Baby.' He smiled, his most winning smile; he had changed again, into the old Jeremy, no longer stern, no longer hostile. 'Can I buy you lunch?'

'No thank you,' said Baby, slightly distantly.

It was Isabella that explained it all to him, many months later. She didn't know what she was explaining, but Baby found her crying, very drunk, in one of the bathrooms at a party they were all at.

'Hey,' he said, 'it's not so bad is it? I thought you and Jeremy were all right again.'

'Oh,' she said, 'oh, Baby, I don't know. I keep forgiving him, and then I learn some other awful thing. The latest is some black tart, and I do mean tart, he's seeing all the time.'

'Poor Isabella. Can't you poison her tea or something?'

'Baby! If only it was *her* tea. The tart is male. I can't stand it. It is total humiliation. I thought it was all over, that – that particular little behaviour pattern. Ever since he had that thing with Chuck, I – '

She stared at him, her tears abruptly stopped, her eyes wide with terror. 'Oh God, Baby, oh shit, I never said that, I forgot Chuck worked for you, please please forget it, forget I said . . .'

'Of course I will,' said Baby, patting her hand absent-mindedly. 'Of course I will. Don't worry, Isabella, I'm a great keeper of secrets. Here, take my hanky, and let me get you a drink.'

He went out to the bar to find her a drink. His mind was whirling, and he felt rather sick.

He had been feeling particularly good the day of the heart attack. He and Angie had had a very good few days: Mary Rose and the children safely in Nantucket, most of New York away. He had been sleeping at home, in case Mary Rose phoned, and getting up as early as three or four, putting on his running clothes and going down to the Village and Angie; Nancy the maid, who was a sound sleeper, only knew when he came home again, and had several times told Mary Rose that Mr Praeger was out running, and had more than once added that in the dreadful heat of a New York August, she thought it was a little unwise.

Baby often reflected later that if he had in fact done a little genuine running, he might not have had the coronary at all.

Chapter 18

Charlotte, 1983

Wild Rose Cottage, Watery Lane, Tellow, Nr Skibbereen, West Cork

Dear Lady Charlotte,
Thank you for your letter. It was so very nice to hear from you, and to have your very kind comments on the robe you wore for your christening. You must forgive me for not replying sooner; your letter took a little while to reach me [three months, thought Charlotte, very Irish] as it not only had to be forwarded from Dublin, by the extremely tardy landlord who now occupies what was once my workshop, but spent a goodly while in the village post office in Tellow, where all my letters were being held for the duration of my visit to my sister in America.

I would have been so pleased to make one for you, but alas, have to refuse; my eyesight is extremely poor now and I have had to give up my work. It is a great sadness, but what will be will be. Perhaps your friend would like to have your own robe for her baby? To pass along a christening robe is a lovely thing to do.

If you were ever to be passing this way, please do me the kindness of calling in, and be sure to bring a photograph of yourself at your christening with you. It would give me the greatest pleasure. With best wishes for a very happy Christmas,

Yours sincerely,
Maura Mahon.

Charlotte booked a flight to Cork on 6 January and then booked a car as well. The car-hire company at Cork was a small one; they told her they would be sure to save her a fine car.

She had intended to go alone, but two days before she left, Georgina came to her room where she was desperately trying to catch up on some reading, and said that Max was drunk.

'At least I think he's drunk. He's behaving very strangely anyway.'
'Does it matter?'

'Well yes it does, a bit, Daddy wants to see him immediately, to sort out this skiing trip at half term, and he's absolutely plastered in his room. Daddy'll go mad.'

'Oh all right, I'll go and try to sort him out. God, he's a nightmare,' said Charlotte with a sigh.

'Yes, he is. Look, you go and see him, and I'll tell Daddy I can't find him, and he must have gone for a walk. Stick his head under the cold tap or something.'

Max wasn't drunk, he was stoned. He had a large supply of cannabis in his room, Charlotte discovered, stacked under his mattress in several small silver parcels, and he had been smoking it fairly restrainedly, he told her, all over Christmas. Today, bored and depressed at the prospect of going back to school in a few days, he had decided to take a little more than usual.

'I'm sorry,' he said, giggling helplessly as Charlotte scolded him, piling all the parcels into the pocket of her jacket, 'I'm really sorry. It's no use you doing that, I can easily get some more.'

'Oh Max, how can you be so stupid? Where are you getting it from anyway? School?'

'Course not. A friend. A good friend. Meeting him tomorrow actually.'

'Where? Who is this friend?'

'In Swindon. Can't tell you who. Good friend though. You'd like him. Charlotte, come and join me, come on, you need to relax a bit. I've got a joint right here, we can share it.'

'Max, for Christ's sake, don't you realize what you're doing? You're mad. Daddy'll flog you personally.'

'Course he won't. He won't find out. Charlotte, stop fussing. Come and sit down here with me. Come on. Now just pass me that box, would you, and we can – '

'Max, I'm going downstairs to tell Daddy you're ill. He's looking for you. And I'm going to lock you in your room. And tomorrow I'm going to try and knock some sense into that stupid, empty head of yours. What on earth do you think is going to become of you at this rate? You're already in trouble for running a casino at school, of all places. You'll get expelled if you're not careful. And then Daddy says he won't even try to sort anything else out, it'll be the comp for you.'

'Well that's fine by me,' said Max, smiling slightly groggily at her, 'I've always fancied co-education. So much more healthy. And then I could go to the sixth-form college like Georgie, and do something meaningful like cookery or woodwork.'

'I don't know what makes you think they'd have you,' said Charlotte.

'You're being really silly,' said Max, rolling onto his back and smiling radiantly up at the ceiling, 'really really silly. I can't begin to tell you how silly you're being.'

'You can try in the morning,' said Charlotte, picking up the box of cigarette papers and the cigarette rolling machine Max had on his desk, 'meanwhile I'm taking this lot out to the stable yard to burn it.'

'Enjoy!' said Max. 'It's good stuff.'

In the morning he was totally uncontrite, but slightly nervous that Charlotte might tell Alexander.

'I won't,' said Charlotte, 'if you promise never to do it again.'

'Oh, I don't want to do that,' said Max, looking quite shocked.

'Why?' said Charlotte. 'Because you're hooked, I suppose.'

'Oh Charlotte darling, you're so naive. You don't get hooked on hash. It's no more addictive than – than cornflakes.'

'You can tell that to the marines,' said Charlotte briskly. 'And Daddy.'

'Oh Charlotte, you wouldn't tell him would you?'

'I will if you don't promise.'

'Oh shit,' said Max. 'Oh Charlotte, you wouldn't.'

'Oh Max, I would.'

'All right,' said Max with a sigh. 'All right, Charlotte. You win.'

'You are never, ever to do it again. And if I find you are, I shall go to the police. And I'm not daft, Max, I shall check. All the time. And I do hope you're not stupid enough even to take it to school.'

'No. Well, not much of it. Occasionally I have a bit. A very weedy weed. But no – all right. Don't look at me like that. I'll stop. I'll enjoy stopping, actually, just to show you how easy it is. So you can see it's not addictive. All right?'

'All right,' said Charlotte slowly. 'But I'm going away tomorrow for a few days. I certainly don't trust you not to if I'm not here. So I'm going to take you with me. Just to keep an eye on you.'

'Where are we going? Goody goody. I like little trips.'

'Ireland.'

'Ireland? What on earth for?'

Charlotte looked at him and felt her mind go into overdrive, the long-postponed decision made almost for her. 'I'll tell you when we get there. Now sort some stuff out. I've already booked you onto the flight.'

'Is Georgie coming?'

'No. She's got exams as soon as she gets back, and she says she can't go away.'

'Does she know why you're going?'

'Oh yes,' said Charlotte.

It was raining when they landed at Cork, a soft, grey, misty rain. Charlotte sniffed the air; it was oddly sweet and silky.

'I'm going to like it here,' she said.

She had booked them into the Hillskellyn Farmhouse Hotel; they reached there rather late, as Max had insisted on visiting Blarney on the way, and making the eighty-six-foot ascent up to the castle battlements in order to kiss the stone. Hillskellyn was a small Georgian house, halfway between Cork itself and Bandon, and not remotely like the rather rickety tumbledown place she had imagined. They ate dinner (smoked salmon, grouse and syllabub, served with a series of delicious wines) in a dining room of such perfect proportions it would have sat well in Hartest. After dinner, they say by an immense fire in the drawing room and drank Gaelic coffee; Charlotte looked at Max, as he sprawled in the chair opposite her, and thought how grown up he looked suddenly, and what an agreeable companion he was, and sighed.

'What on earth was that for?' said Max. 'I feel like jumping for joy, not sighing.'

'Oh – nothing.'

'OK. It was for nothing. Now then, are you finally going to tell me what you're doing here?'

'Yes I am. But you're going to need your glass refilled first. Hold onto your seat, Max, you're in for a bit of a bumpy ride.'

'Blimey,' said Max, when the very long conversation had finally finished. 'Cor blimey.'

'That's a very elegant response, Max.'

'Well, I know.' He was very pale suddenly, and clearly and determinedly making a great effort to be lighthearted, to be seen to take the news in his stride. 'Clearly I'm not quite the elegant person I thought I was.'

'Oh, I don't think any of it should alter your personal style in any way,' said Charlotte, responding to his mood with care.

'Well – I don't know. I mean dear old Dad might have been a bank clerk. Or a dustman. I'm not a viscount at all. Not a genuine one. I'm a fake. What a turn-up for the books.'

'Well, I know,' said Charlotte slowly. 'But you're still called the Viscount Hadleigh. You're still going to inherit and everything. You look like an earl. You look just like Daddy. That's what had us fooled for so long. I don't think anything's going to change for you.'

'I suppose,' said Max rather slowly, 'I suppose that's why I'm so thick.'

'Max, really! That's a ridiculously snobbish thing to say. There are a great many thick earls in the stately homes of England.'

'Yes, but not at Hartest. Dad – Alexander is very clever. And Mummy was clever too. And gifted. Creative. I'm not any of those things.' He kicked the hearth moodily. 'I had begun to wonder. Now I know. Good God. Good God. I wish you hadn't told me.'

'Oh Max, don't be silly. I had to tell you. I waited as long as I could.'

'Why did you have to tell me? I was perfectly happy before.'

'Well, you can be perfectly happy again.'

'Maybe.' He looked morose, more dejected than Charlotte could ever remember.

'Max, I'm sorry, but I really did think you had to know. We both did. I mean sooner or later you'd have heard the gossip about Georgina and me. And wondered. It would have been a horrible shock.'

'Well, it is a horrible shock anyway.' He grinned at her rather shakily. 'I don't know how you can take it all so calmly.'

'Max, I didn't. At the time. It was awful. But it was over two years ago. I've got used to the idea now. And Georgina was very very upset. You know she's always been Daddy's favourite. They just adored each other. Well, they still do. She's all right now.'

'And he won't – talk about it? You've no real idea why it all happened? What made Mummy do it?'

'No. He won't talk about it. I mean apart from just saying, as I told you, that yes, it was true, and she had always had a life of her own. It's obviously horribly painful for him. And he does think, incidentally, that we all imagine you're his own child. Of course there may be some perfectly simple explanation, like maybe he couldn't have children, that's what Georgie and I both thought at first, but then that doesn't make sense, there wouldn't have had to be all that secrecy, he would have told us, and they could just have adopted or something.'

'God,' said Max, 'poor old sod. Poor old bugger. What a dance she must have led him. How horrible for him.'

'Yes. Yes it must have been. And he's always been so marvellous. And so loyal to her. I mean with the drinking and everything. He never, ever implied for a minute that she was anything other than perfect. I suppose that's love.'

'Yes, I suppose so. You don't –'

'I don't what?'

'You don't think that I might actually be Dad's? I mean I really do look like him.'

'Well,' said Charlotte, 'honestly Max, no I don't.'

'Well,' he said, standing up suddenly, looking very tall and grown up,

237

'the bastard son is going to bed. He's very tired. See you at breakfast, Charlotte. Don't wake me up too early.'

Charlotte watched him go out of the room, walking rather more heavily than usual, his head drooping in a very un–Max-like way. She sighed. She hadn't expected him to be quite so upset. Silly of her. Stupid. It must have been the most awful shock. He was such an arrogant little bugger under all the golden charm. And sixteen was a delicate age. Specially for boys.

Max was more cheerful in the morning. He appeared at breakfast slightly pale, but otherwise entirely himself. 'I have decided I actually rather like the idea. I could be anyone, after all. Which is rather exciting. Maybe I have a hitherto undiscovered talent for sculpture or ballet dancing.'

'I have to say I doubt it,' said Charlotte, 'but time will tell.'

'It will. But I don't think I want to take your route and try to find my own dear dad. I might not like him. I think I prefer being the son of the Earl of Caterham, and it's certainly much simpler.'

'Well,' said Charlotte, 'that's up to you. Are you going to say anything to Daddy?'

'Oh no,' said Max, 'I don't see any point in that. Upsetting him and everything. It can't be very nice for him. But I'm very excited about your search for identity. When can we leave to find the mysterious Miss Mahon?'

'Straight away after breakfast,' said Charlotte, relieved but slightly surprised by his swift recovery. 'Look, Max, kippers on the menu. Or do you want bacon and eggs?'

'Both,' said Max.

The drive to Tellow was enchanting; they hit the glorious, heart–catching coast at Kinsale and turned west towards Clonakilty; the day was wild, with great sheets of storm clouds fighting off the sun, the sea black and grey and every shade of green, with great white bursts of water rolling up and foaming against the cliffs. The road followed the curves and curls of the coast westward, wilder and wilder now, past Ballinaspittle and the glorious Old Head of Kinsale; the tiny inland lakes were oddly calm and still, set against the wilderness of the sea.

'Oh, I love it here,' said Charlotte, parking the car suddenly on the edge of the road, and gazing enraptured and moody out at the sea. 'I feel as if I've come home.'

'Maybe you have,' said Max.

They reached Skibbereen at midday and swung inland on the road to Tellow.

Watery Lane was a tiny turning, no more than a track, at the bottom of the village; it wound, steeply and true to its name, back up the hill, a stream running fast down either side of it. There was a grey stone cottage set back and tucked into a small hill of its own about half a mile along it.

'That must be it,' said Charlotte. 'My God, the rain is getting worse. Get ready to run, Max.'

She parked in front of the small wooden lych gate (grown rather predictably over with wild roses), and then in spite of the driving rain and her own warning to Max, walked rather slowly up to the front door. She suddenly felt oddly frightened, and in awe at what she was undertaking.

The bell was a pull; its jangle had died away altogether before they heard a latch being clicked up. It was a stable door; the top swung gently back, to reveal Maura Mahon's gently smiling face scarcely reaching over the bottom half. It was a sweet, rosy face, with fiercely bright green eyes, and surrounded with tight carefully arranged curls; it took Charlotte a little while to realize that its owner was not standing but sitting, and that her seat was a wheelchair. Miss Mahon was very thin, and her little stick-like legs, twisted with arthritis, looked most painfully useless. But her smile was radiant, and her eyes snapped with pleasure at the sight of her visitors. Charlotte fought to find her voice, which seemed to be eluding her.

'Miss Mahon?'

'Yes, this is she.'

'I'm Charlotte Welles, Miss Mahon. This is my brother Max. May we come in for a little while?'

'For more than a little while, I hope. How brave of you to come on such a dreadful day.'

They sat by the fire and looked around them fascinated; the room was a shrine to what was presumably the Mahon family. Where there was a space on the wall, a surface on a table, there was a photograph, a miniature, a sampler: sepia Victorian photographs sat side by side with lurid school snaps, wedding photographs with christening ones, single portraits with huge family gatherings. A firescreen exquisitely worked with a picture of the cottage was signed off (in silken thread) 'Amy Mahon, aged 8, 1862'. Another showed a silver dove, with the words 'Desmond and Maureen, Silver Wedding. 1850–1875. Whom God hath joined together'. And over the stone fireplace, hung very much in pride of place, was a picture of the Queen when she had been Princess Elizabeth, smiling and shaking a young woman's hand.

'I wonder who that can be,' said Charlotte.

'It's me,' said Maura Mahon.

'When did you meet the Queen?' said Max.

'Oh, when I was very much younger, as you can see, and working in Dublin. We presented her with a linen dress for the infant prince when he was born, I have the letter still, you see, there it is, on the wall. And when she came to Dublin on a visit, she came to the workshop as part of her tour.'

'How exciting,' said Charlotte. 'So you worked in Dublin for very many years?'

'Oh, very many. From let me see, 1949 to 1979. It was a wonderful time.'

'And did you – did you make many christening robes? To order, I mean?'

'Oh, not so very many. We mostly made the little dresses and coats, supplied the White House and just occasionally Harrods. And I took personal orders from just a few special customers. Such as your mother would have been.'

'So – so do you actually –' Charlotte was having trouble with her voice, it kept rising unnaturally. 'Do you remember my mother?'

'Oh Lady Charlotte, now that would be a small miracle. Not so very small either. You were born when?'

'In 1962.'

'Well now, that is twenty-one years ago. I have a fine memory, but not that fine.'

'Oh.' Charlotte's voice sounded bleak.

Maura Mahon smiled at her. 'There is no need for such dejection. I have a note of all the work I did privately. In a big ledger. A little later, when we have had our tea, you can fetch it for me, it's upstairs, and I don't venture there very often these days. Now tell me exactly what you are doing in County Cork, and where you are going. And I hope you have brought your robe with you, so that I can see it. I hope it doesn't sound too terribly big-headed, but I do love to meet up with my own work.'

It was an hour before Charlotte managed to extricate herself from the conversation and go upstairs to Maura Mahon's tiny bedroom.

'Well, it's no longer my bedroom of course, and I miss it, but there we are. The ledger is under the bed and I fear it may be a little dusty, but you won't mind that too much, I don't suppose.'

'Of course not,' said Charlotte.

The book under Maura Mahon's high brass bed was huge, thick, leather-covered, and indeed a little dusty; she wiped it with her sleeve and, looking at it in a kind of awe, fearful for what it might not contain, went slowly downstairs.

'Here it is,' she said. 'How far back does it go?'

'Oh, to 1949. It has a few stories to tell, that book. Look, here we are, a wedding dress for the bride of Lord Kilkirk, and see, a christening robe for his baby son, and then, and this is a wonderful thing for me, another wedding dress for that baby's bride. I feel I am a part of so many histories, and it makes me very proud. Now then, my dear, 1962, where are we, yes, let's see. Ah now, a fair lot of table linen; some hand–embroidered sheets; people don't often want those these days; and – yes, here we are. A christening robe. And another. My goodness, would you believe such a thing, I did three that year. There must have been some write–up in one of the magazines. That always had a great effect. Which month were you born, Lady Charlotte?'

'In January.'

'Well then, it would have been ordered in the year before, now let's see, there was one in August, and one in September, and then another in November. Yes, there must have been some publicity. They were always so very kind to me, the papers. Now then, my dear, which of these was for your mother? I don't see her name.'

'No,' said Charlotte, and her voice sounded bleak and flat, 'no, neither do I. You didn't sell the robes through any shops, did you? So it wouldn't be shown in your book?'

'Not if the label was hand–worked. Which yours is. Well now, maybe someone ordered it for her. As a gift. Have a look at the names.' She looked at Charlotte, her fiercely bright green eyes sharply interested. 'You didn't say it was so important to you, that I should remember your mother.'

'Oh,' said Charlotte quickly, 'I just thought it would be nice if you had. As she's died. It's lovely to find unexpected contacts, that's all. And now I'm intrigued. If she didn't order it who did?'

In the end, she wrote down the names of all three people who had ordered christening robes: a Mrs Harley Robertson, with an address in the Boltons, a Lord Uxbridge from Leicestershire and an S. M. Joseph, who had an address in the Whitechapel Road.

'Some old Jewish rag trade rip-off merchant that one, I expect,' said Max, as they looked at them over dinner in the Hillskellyn Farmhouse that night, where they had returned like homing pigeons. 'Probably copied hundreds of the things and sold them off his stall. Not even worth bothering about, I wouldn't think.'

Charlotte wrote to all three, saying (at Max's suggestion) that she was writing a book on royal dressmakers, and would they be kind enough to get in touch with her. Mrs Harley Robertson phoned immediately, offering to show Charlotte the robe, made for her son; Lord Uxbridge wrote and said his wife had ordered theirs, but had passed away, though Charlotte was welcome to come and look at it if she liked.

'So it was neither of them,' said Charlotte sadly.

And from Mr S. M. Joseph there was no word.

'Old bugger's probably snuffed it,' said Max, 'or retired to the Bahamas.'

Just as she had given up hope, she got a phone call. She had come home for the weekend, and was working in the library; a lady for her, Harold Fallon said, on the telephone, a foreign lady. He couldn't quite catch the name. Charlotte picked up the phone.

'Hallo?'

'Lady Charlotte Welles?'

'Yes.'

'Lady Charlotte, good morning. I work for the Whitechapel Hospice.'

'Yes?' said Charlotte warily.

'You sent us a letter.'

'I did? I'm afraid I don't remember.'

'It was addressed to a Mr Joseph. But we don't have any Mr Joseph here. No Mr anything.' The voice sounded amused.

'Oh,' said Charlotte. 'Oh, I see.'

'We are all nuns, Lady Charlotte. Our order sends us here to work together. From convents everywhere.'

'Oh, I see,' said Charlotte again.

'I think perhaps the person you wanted was Sister Mary Joseph. She lived and worked here for nearly fifteen years.'

Charlotte's heart thumped painfully: slowly at first, then with gathering speed.

'Sister Mary Joseph. Yes. Yes maybe. How stupid of me.'

'Not at all.' The voice was warmly amused. 'How could you have known?'

'Well,' said Charlotte, rather helplessly. 'But – er, do you know where she is now?'

'I do. I hope I do. She went back to her convent in Ireland.'

'In Ireland!' Charlotte closed her eyes briefly, trying to unscramble all these messages, to make sense of a nun ordering a christening robe for her mother, a nun in Ireland, no, not Ireland, not at the time. A nun working at a hospice. What could that possibly have to do with her? And her mother's lover?

'Yes. But she wasn't very well. That is why she was sent home. The

242

last time I heard from her, the news wasn't good. We have all been praying for her.'

'Oh, I see.'

'Anyway, would you like to write to her?'

'Oh, yes please, Mrs – er Miss – er –'

'Sister. Sister Mary Julia.'

'Oh, how stupid of me. I'm so sorry. Sister. Yes, I would like to write to her.'

'Do you have a piece of paper and a pen?'

'Yes. Yes I do.'

'Very well then. The Convent of our Lady of Sorrows, Ballydegogue, Near Bantry, West Cork. Do send her our love if you see her, and I hope you find her well.'

'S. M. Joseph wasn't a rip-off rag trade merchant,' said Charlotte to Max triumphantly when he arrived home two weeks later for half term, 'she was a nun, a lovely lovely Irish nun, and she's written me the most wonderful letter. She remembers Mummy and she says she would like to meet me. Isn't that lovely? I'm going at the weekend, do you want to come with me?'

'Yes, thank you, I think that would be jolly nice,' said Max.

Charlotte was too excited to notice that he was looking rather pale.

Chapter 19

Charlotte, 1983

Charlotte sat looking at Alexander, her eyes wide with horror.

'Oh, Daddy, why? What's he done? Oh God, I'm so sorry. So very sorry. He didn't say a word just now.'

'Oh, he got caught handing out marijuana. To just about the entire school. And then some boy who's obviously got it in for him went to Dr Anderson and told him he'd been running his casino again. So that was that. Expelled. On the spot. I had to go straight in to Anderson when I got there. Max was in his study, with his bags packed. There was nothing I could do. Or wanted to, indeed. Expelled from Eton, Charlotte. My son. I don't think I can stand it. I don't think I can stand any of it.'

He looked up at her, and there were tears in his blue eyes; his face was suddenly very drawn and grey. 'I miss her,' he said, 'I miss her so much, you know. Still.'

'Oh Daddy,' said Charlotte, her own eyes filling with hot, stinging tears, 'Daddy, I know. I'm so sorry. About her. About Max. Everything.' She put her arms round his shoulders.

'I was so proud of him,' said Alexander, wiping his eyes, reaching out for the glass of whisky that was on his desk. 'So proud. My son and heir. A chip off the old block.' He laughed suddenly, a harsh, ugly laugh. 'Some old block. Stupid bloody idiot. Oh, Charlotte darling, I'm sorry. I've no business to be burdening you with all my grief and guilt. And disappointment.'

'Don't be silly, Daddy. I love it that you talk to me. It's the only way I feel I can help.'

'Sweetheart, you do far more than talk to me. Just your being here is a tremendous comfort. You remind me so much of your mother. I have to tell you, and I know I shouldn't, I dread your departure to New York. Absolutely dread it.' He sighed. 'Anyway, you're going to be around for the next few weeks, aren't you? Because I'm going to need you badly.'

'Oh yes,' said Charlotte, mentally abandoning, with enormous regret, her trip to Cork to visit Sister Mary Joseph. 'Oh yes, Daddy, of course I am.'

*

'It's no use scolding me,' said Max. 'I wasn't being stupid. I got caught on purpose. Because I wanted to.'

'But Max, why?' said Charlotte, anger mingling with fear at the change in him. 'For God's sake why?'

'Oh, why do you think?' he said, and his expression was oddly angry and withdrawn. 'Because I don't know who I am any more, that's why. Because we have a mother who was a whore. Because the person I grew up hero-worshipping is a weak fool.'

'Max,' said Charlotte, 'that's not true. Daddy is nothing of the sort. Of course you're upset, but – well, you can't blame Daddy.'

'Well I do,' said Max, 'in a way. If he'd been a bit less bloody weak with our mother, none of us would be in this fucking situation.' He grinned at her suddenly. 'Fucking being the relevant word. Anyway I can't bring myself to have anything to do with him. At the moment. Maybe I'll get over it in time.'

'Well,' said Charlotte briskly, 'in that case, perhaps you should think about giving up all your rights to the title and the house and everything.'

'Oh no,' said Max, looking at her rather oddly, 'I'm certainly not going to do that. As far as everyone out there is concerned, I'm the next Earl of Caterham. There's a lot coming my way. I have no intention of giving any of it up. That's about the only thing I feel sure about at the moment.'

'Oh Max, I'm so sorry,' said Charlotte, putting her hand on his arm. Max shook it off.

'Charlotte, I don't think you are. You broke the news that my father was some person totally unknown to me as if you were telling me that it was going to rain. I don't understand why you had to do it, Charlotte, honestly I don't. I was perfectly happy before. Now I feel – I feel – oh fuck it, what's the point of having this conversation? The harm's been done. I'm going out.'

Charlotte and Alexander were just finishing a kitchen supper that evening when Max came in, slamming the door, and went over to the fridge.

'Why isn't there any beer?'

'There isn't any beer because you've drunk it all,' said Alexander coldly.

'Well, Tallow should get some more in.'

'Tallow is not in this house to run around after you, Max. He buys a fixed amount of alcohol every month, perfectly adequate for our needs. If you want any more, you can buy it with your allowance.'

'Well,' said Max, 'it's a good thing our mother isn't around any more, isn't it? She'd have had to be spending the entire Praeger fortune on extra alcohol.'

'Maximilian, please take that back,' said Alexander. His face was white, his mouth pulled down painfully at the corners. 'I will not have your mother spoken of in that way.'

Charlotte held her breath, fearing Max would refuse; but he didn't. He looked as if he was going to cry. 'Sorry,' he muttered. There was a long silence.

'Anyway, Max, I have phoned the comprehensive in Marlborough and they are prepared to take you immediately after half term,' said Alexander finally. He looked at Max almost disdainfully. 'You've got your O levels to do, and you can't afford to miss any time. I don't imagine your performance will be over-impressive, in any case.'

'I'm not going to a comprehensive. If you want me to pass my exams, you'll have to get me a tutor.'

'I can assure you there is no possible chance of your having a tutor. I have thrown enough money after you. You're going to the comprehensive and you're going to work very hard there.'

'No,' said Max, 'no I'm not.'

'Max, you are.'

'If you try and make me go there,' said Max, 'I shall tell everybody that I'm not your son. That my mother was some kind of a whore, and that you appear to be some kind of a pervert, condoning her behaviour. All right?'

'Dear God,' said Alexander. He brushed his hand across his eyes. 'Well, it is true, you are not my son. Not my blood son. I have no idea whose son you are. I have loved you and brought you up and been proud of you, but you are not my son. I wish you were. And I hope you can come to terms with it in time. But I will not have you talking about your mother. I will not. Do you understand?'

'I don't understand you,' said Max, 'I don't understand you at all. And I don't want to talk about it any more. To anybody. But I am not going to the comprehensive.'

'Very well,' said Alexander, 'I'll get you a tutor. But only for two terms. After that you're on your own.'

'I feel on my own anyway,' said Max.

It was Nanny who put things near to right. She found Max sitting moodily in the kitchen one day, eating his way through the biscuit tin, and said, 'Making your teeth rot won't help.'

'Nothing'll help me, Nanny,' said Max. 'I'm utterly miserable.'

'That's just silly,' said Nanny, 'you've brought it on yourself. Getting expelled from school like that. Don't you go telling me you're miserable now. It's your father who ought to be miserable.'

'You know about it all, don't you, Nanny?' said Max suddenly. 'About my mother and everything.'

'No,' said Nanny briefly.

'Charlotte told me you did.'

'Charlotte always did talk too much,' said Nanny.

'I hate it all,' said Max sulkily, 'I wish – '

'If wishes were horses,' said Nanny, 'beggars might ride.' She brought this out as if it was some very important and original thought of her own.

'I never understood that,' said Max. 'What does it mean?'

'It means you can't have everything you want, and quite right too,' said Nanny firmly.

'Oh.'

'Your mother didn't have everything she wanted,' said Nanny suddenly, 'and I don't want you thinking she did. And you've had a great deal that you want. So you can stop feeling so sorry for yourself. It'll make you peevish. I can't stand peevishness.'

'Is that all you're going to say?'

'Yes,' said Nanny. 'There's nothing else I can say. Except that you're behaving very badly. He loved her,' she added, as an afterthought. 'Very much.'

'I can't think why. It's sick, if you ask me.'

'No one's asking you, Maximilian. No one's asking you anything. You don't know enough to be asked. What you need is some fresh air,' she added. 'You're beginning to look pasty. You'll get spots next.'

Charlotte, who had been standing quietly in the doorway for much of this conversation, holding her breath, laughed aloud as Max pushed back his chair and almost ran over to the utility room and the dusty old mirror it contained.

'You've obviously managed to put things in proportion for him, Nanny,' she said.

'Charlotte, there's a letter for you. From Ireland.'

'Oh God.' Charlotte took the envelope from Georgina and made a face. 'I do hope Sister Mary Joseph isn't going to put me off. I daren't go any later, my finals are only weeks away. Let me – oh God. Oh Georgie, I can't bear it.'

'What? Charlotte, surely you can take a few days off. Surely.'

'No. No I can't. But that's not it. Georgie, she's died. Sister Mary Joseph has died. This is from the Reverend Mother at the convent. I didn't realize she was so ill. Both her letters were so brave, so hopeful. Now it's too late. My last link with Mummy, and she's gone. Oh Georgie, it's so sad.'

247

Charlotte put her head in her arms on the breakfast table and burst into tears. It was so unlike her that Georgina was alarmed. Charlotte was so indefatigable, so brave; she never gave in, never cried. She put her arms round her.

'Charlotte, darling, don't cry. Please. I know it's sad, but you didn't know Sister Mary Joseph. And maybe someone else there could help. Please don't cry. Please.'

'Oh, I'm sorry. But it isn't just her dying. I really did feel she was a link with Mummy. And I've so hated seeing Daddy sort of crumble away, these past months, over Max. And Max is being so vile to that poor tutor of his. Everything's horrible. And I'm going to fail my finals, and then I've got to go to New York and leave you all. I just feel desperate.'

'Well you're not going to fail your finals and you certainly don't have to go to New York,' said Georgina. 'You can stay here. You can give the bank up and do your law, you always said you wanted to be a lawyer, before Grandpa Fred gave you half the bank.'

Charlotte looked at her, clearly startled and even shocked at the very suggestion, her tears drying on her face.

'Of course I have to go to New York,' she said, 'that really is nonsense. Freddy's starting this autumn as well, and that vile, self-satisfied Gabe Hoffman is there already. No, obviously I have to be there. Stake my claim very firmly. I feel better already, just at the thought of it. Give me that letter, Georgie, I'll write back to Reverend Mother and see if she'll see me instead.'

Reverend Mother wrote by return of post and said that she would be delighted to see Lady Charlotte. She said perhaps Lady Charlotte would like to come over as planned and attend the burial mass for Sister Mary Joseph, which was to be held on the Saturday, as she understood that there was a connection with her mother. It was always so nice, she said, for as many friends and relatives to be at a funeral as possible. Of course the sisters would all be there, but anyone from the outside world was a wonderful support for them. Then they could talk afterwards. Charlotte took a deep breath and wrote back to say that yes, she would be delighted to come.

She had thought Roaring Water Bay beautiful; Bantry Bay made her cry out loud with delight. She stood on the cliffs on the Sheeps Head, looking out to sea, and then up at the great backdrop of the Caha Mountains, and felt almost awed at its beauty. 'If I have any connection with you,' she said to the scenery conversationally, 'then I shall be proud indeed.'

★

The convent was inland, about five miles, in a small lush valley, a large Georgian house with a huge walled vegetable garden, and some magnificent greenhouses, all in a state of feverish fertility, kept by the nuns. It was a small order, just twenty sisters; they ran a tiny primary school for the neighbouring villages, nursed the sick, and financed themselves to a large degree by their garden produce. They had a vine in one of the greenhouses, already covered in tiny green grapes: 'We make wine from that every year, many many hundreds of bottles,' said Reverend Mother, as she took Charlotte on a tour of the grounds, 'it is a great favourite, not just locally, we get orders from Kerry and Limerick as well, and even occasionally from Dublin. You must take a few bottles home with you. Now if you would like to come with me, you can pay Sister Mary Joseph a little visit, she is in the chapel, and we shall be saying our mass for her in the morning.'

Charlotte had been prepared for this ordeal and had known she must not flinch from it; nevertheless she was trembling and had to clench her teeth to stop them chattering as Reverend Mother opened the door to the chapel set just slightly apart from the house, and distanced from it by a small covered walkway. Reverend Mother looked at her set face and smiled, took her arm gently.

'You have no need to be afraid,' she said, 'it is nothing, death. Sister Mary Joseph was in a great deal of pain for many months. She is at peace now. She looks beautiful. You'll see.'

Charlotte saw. She saw a small, still shell, a white peaceful face, dressed in the white robes of her order, her wimple carefully arranged, her rope belt loosely tied, lying in her coffin. Her hands were arranged to hold a single white lily together with her rosary; she seemed to Charlotte to be neither alive, nor dead, but in some remote place in between. Her face, which Charlotte looked at curiously as her courage grew, was wide-browed, squarish; the mouth, in the set smile of death, was full-lipped, the nose small and straight. Reverend Mother stood looking into the coffin tenderly, as if at some sleeping child; without thinking, without knowing why she did it even, for she was not a Catholic, had never been to a Catholic church even, Charlotte made the sign of the cross.

Outside again, she smiled and said, 'Thank you. Thank you for taking me.'

'That is perfectly all right. I knew it would be nice for you. Once you had found the courage.'

'Well,' said Charlotte, 'I think you found it for me.'

'If I did, I count it as my own good fortune. Now will you come and take some tea with me, or are you in a great hurry?'

'I would love to have some tea. Please.'

They sat in Reverend Mother's study, a quiet, painfully tidy room, all shades of beige and white, with a statue of the Virgin in one corner, and a large tropical fish tank in another, an exotic colourful bubbling country, all of its own.

'I like to look at the fish,' she said. 'They make me feel calm.'

'I can't imagine you not being calm,' said Charlotte, smiling at her.

'Well now, you might not see me not being calm, and that makes me sound very Irish, I know. But you would see me feeling it. I am a most tumultuous person. It is my worst fault. Sister Mary Joseph had great peace. I had to work very hard not envying her, not resenting it. It was so very sad you were unable to meet her. You would have liked her so much. Is the situation at home better now?'

'Oh yes,' said Charlotte, 'yes, I think so. It's very difficult for my father, coping with all of us, without my mother.'

'Tell me about your mother. And how she knew Sister Mary Joseph.'

'Well I didn't know she did. But – well, it's a long and complicated story. And of course I found out too late. You see, my mother had a christening robe made for me. By a lady called Maura Mahon, who lives about – let me see, fifteen miles away. Near Skibbereen.'

'I think I know the name. But go on.'

'Well, my mother died, and I was going through her things, and I found the robe. And I was interested, because you see there is a family robe, an heirloom I suppose you could call it almost, and my sister and my brother wore it, but I didn't. So I was just – curious. And I thought any link with my mother would be nice to explore. So I came to see Miss Mahon. And found, by a rather circuitous route, that it was Sister Mary Joseph who had ordered the robe. And she said, when I wrote to her, that she remembered my mother. And you know the rest.'

There was a silence. Charlotte thought how crazy Reverend Mother must think her, haring around Ireland after some woman who had ordered a christening robe twenty-one years earlier. She sighed. 'I'm sorry, there is more, but it's very complicated. I don't think – '

'My dear child, I would not dream of expecting you to tell me anything at all. It is entirely your own business, what you are doing. I am simply delighted to have met you. Now then, I wonder how much I can help you. Sister Mary Joseph was a very private person, not a great talker. She certainly never mentioned having a christening robe made.' Her lips twitched slightly. 'But then of course she wasn't here at the convent then, she was at the hospice in London. Well, maybe her brother will be able to talk to you.'

'Her brother?' Charlotte looked at her in wonderment; for some reason she had expected Sister Mary Joseph to be all alone in the world.

'Yes. Her brother, David St Mullin. He will be here tomorrow.'

The burial mass was very moving. The sisters filed into the chapel as a small choir sang 'Pie Jesu'. Sister Mary Joseph's coffin, closed now, and covered with pure white flowers, lilies, roses, freesias, stood on a plinth near the altar. The service, which Charlotte had expected to find tedious and incomprehensible, was lyrically beautiful; she sat and gazed at the beautiful stained-glass window above the altar, and watched and listened as the priest dispatched Sister Mary Joseph to join the angels; as they knelt in final silent prayer, one of the sisters sang 'I Know that My Redeemer Liveth', and Charlotte found herself suddenly and sharply back in her grief for her mother; at the end her face was wet with tears.

So engrossed was she in the service that she forgot about the importance to her of the man seated just behind the nuns, a slightly short, stocky figure with grey hair, wearing a rather shabby black coat, and carrying a very battered-looking black homburg.

Afterwards she followed, far behind the rest, as Sister Mary Joseph was borne out to the small graveyard behind the chapel; David St Mullin had left the chapel, his head bowed, and she had still not seen his face. She stood a little apart as the coffin was lowered into the ground, feeling a sudden chill at her heart; David St Mullin threw the first clods of earth onto it, and then stepped back. She saw his face then for the first time, heavy with sadness: square-jawed and wide-browed, like his sister's, and she liked what she saw. It was a kind face, and the mouth was gentle, and humorous; she felt she could approach its owner without too much trepidation.

Reverend Mother led David St Mullin over to her, as the procession of sisters and the priest filed back to the convent; she was smiling, although her face too was tear-stained.

'Thank you for coming, Lady Charlotte,' she said, 'it was so nice to have you with us. I wish Sister Mary Joseph could have known you. Mr St Mullin, this is Lady Charlotte Welles. Lady Charlotte has just discovered that her late mother, Lady Caterham, knew your sister when they were both young.'

Charlotte took the hand that David St Mullin was holding out to her. 'How do you do, Mr St Mullin. I do hope you will forgive me being at your sister's funeral, stranger that I am to your family, but yes, my mother did know her. Your sister wrote and told me so.'

'Indeed?' he said, courteously interested.

'I wonder, Mr St Mullin, do you remember my mother? . . . Virginia Caterham?'

There was a silence. Charlotte felt herself growing ice cold and sweaty at the same time. Was he trying to remember? Trying to duck the question? Calling up an alibi?

Finally he said, 'No. No I really don't. I'm so sorry. Should I?' He sounded absolutely genuine; regretful, charming, eager to help.

She sighed. 'Well – I thought you would. Or rather I suppose I hoped you would. Does – does the name Maura Mahon mean anything to you?'

'I don't think so. Who is Maura Mahon?'

'She's an old lady. Who made my christening robe.'

There was another silence. Then he said, 'Lady Charlotte, I'm sorry, but you are talking in riddles, I think. Why should your christening robe have anything to do with me?'

'Oh,' said Charlotte, feeling suddenly, heavily hopeless. 'I'm sorry. I just met Miss Mahon, you see. And she was asked to make my christening robe by your sister, Sister Mary Joseph. And – well, I thought you might know of some connection. Because I don't. My mother is dead, you see. It's not important really – just a small mystery.' She smiled at him, determinedly casual.

David St Mullin was silent. Charlotte was just going to start saying thank you, don't worry, it doesn't matter, all the silly, conventional, untrue things, edging towards the end of the conversation, when he said, 'Well, it certainly wasn't for me. My wife made our children's christening robe. She's a very fine needlewoman. She would have been most affronted at the suggestion anyone else did.' His voice sounded amused. Charlotte's heart felt as if it had turned to some icy, heavy substance.

'Oh,' she said, and getting any words out at all seemed almost impossible. 'Oh, I see. Well obviously I am mistaken. I'm so sorry. As I said, it's not important.' She tried to smile.

'Well, no,' he said, 'there is one possible explanation. It might perhaps have been my younger brother.'

'Oh!' said Charlotte. 'Your brother! I never thought of that. I didn't know you had one.' Her voice died away. God in heaven, he must think she was crazy.

His voice was amused. 'How could you have done? Anyway, he's been in America for a year. He couldn't get over. He'd seen Felicia a month or so ago. Reverend Mother wrote and told him not to worry to come. She said the sisters and I would all see her safely on her way. He's very busy and not – terribly well off.

'Anyway, that might be an explanation, don't you think? Although why he should have ordered a christening robe for your mother, I cannot imagine.'

'No,' said Charlotte, almost humbly.

'Perhaps he was going to be a godfather or something. Although then you would have known him, wouldn't you?'

'Yes,' said Charlotte.

'A mystery. Well, now, have I solved your problem for you, do you think?'

'I think probably yes,' said Charlotte. 'I'm sorry, you must think I'm quite mad.' She was recovering herself now, regaining confidence. 'But it's one of those infuriating loose ends that just won't be tied up. Er – what does your brother do?'

'You seem very interested in him!'

'I'm sorry. I don't mean to be rude.'

'It's all right. Charlie's a barrister. His chambers are off Fleet Street. I'll give you the number. But as I say, he's away till September. There's no great rush though, I imagine?'

'No,' said Charlotte. 'No, not at all. And thank you very much. You've been terribly kind.'

It was many hours later, as she lay staring into the darkness, still trying to persuade herself that it was highly unlikely that the impoverished Mr St Mullin could actually be anything to do with her, that she properly realized that his name was Charles.

'Dear God,' she said aloud, 'does that mean something or is it just a very strong coincidence?'

God, clearly feeling he had done enough for her for the time being, declined to answer.

'Dear Mr St Mullin,' she wrote. It was the fourth time she had begun her letter. 'Please forgive me for writing to you like this, but . . .' For the fourth time she scrumpled the piece of paper, threw it into her waste paper basket. But what? But I think you are probably my father. But I think you had an affair with my mother. But I really have to meet you. But what do you look like. But . . .

'Oh shit,' she said. 'Shit shit shit.' It was no good; a letter wasn't going to work. A phone call was easier.

She picked up the phone, dialled the number; she already knew it by heart.

'May I speak to Mr St Mullin, please?'

'Who's calling?' The voice was bored, distant.

'My name is Welles. Lady Charlotte Welles. Er – Virginia Caterham's daughter.'

'One moment please.'

There was a long silence; now what, wondered Charlotte, now what was she to say – 'Oh hallo, I wondered if we could meet, and talk about

253

my mother . . . Oh, hallo, my name may not mean anything but . . . Good morning, Mr St Mullin, a voice from your past.' Now what was it she had thought, worked out, oh yes – 'Mr St Mullin, I wonder if you remember meeting my mother, many years ago.'

She licked her dry lips, took a deep breath as she heard clicking, meaning she was being put through. This was it. Mustn't flunk it now. A voice spoke: a deep, very beautiful voice, more resonant, more mannered than that of his brother.

'Charlotte? Virginia's daughter? How wonderful. I've spent a lot of time thinking about you and her down the years. Would you like to meet and have lunch? I'd love to have a look at you.'

'Oh yes please,' she said, 'I can't think of anything I'd like more.'

Chapter 20

Virginia, 1960–1

'Oh yes please,' she said, 'I can't think of anything I'd like more.'

It had been worth enduring what had so far been a terrible evening, to hear Virginia Caterham say that.

Charles had not wanted to go to the cocktail party. He was studying terribly hard, he was tired, he was going away for the weekend, and the last thing on earth he had in mind for himself was standing and shouting for upwards of two hours with a glass of warm gin and tonic in his hand.

But the cocktail party was being given by his pupil master, who had expressed a very strong hope that he would be there, and he could see he had absolutely no option.

And so at half past five he changed into a clean, slightly less shabby shirt in the cloakroom of Lionel Craig's chambers, reknotted his tie (and then wished he had not done so, as it fell into a just different position and looked even more creased and worn out than it had before), rubbed his shoes one at a time on the back of his trouser legs, brushed his rather unruly dark hair (wondering how he was going to find the requisite three shillings to get it cut as Lionel Craig had rather strongly hinted it should be) and walked down Chancery Lane and into the Strand to wait rather hopelessly for a number eleven bus. Lionel Craig had departed half an hour earlier in his Rolls; it had naturally not entered his head to offer his impoverished young pupil a lift.

The traffic was appalling; it was almost a quarter to seven before the bus lumbered into Sloane Square. Charles leapt off it and ran frantically up Sloane Street, tore up the steps of the mansion block and pressed Lionel Craig's bell. A maid in a black dress let him in, with the observation that the party was nearly over and, smoothing his wind-blown hair, gulping his breath into some semblance of normality, he walked casually into the drawing room. Barbara Craig was standing by the door; she was a large, imposing woman with a shelf of a bosom (encased that evening in red lace), impeccably pleated iron-grey waves, and a sternly pleasant face.

'Ah, Mr St Mullin,' she said. 'What a pity you're so late, all the canapés have gone.' She rather liked Charles, he was so handsome with his wild dark hair and dark blue eyes, and she felt sorry for him because he was so patently poor and so thin.

'I'm sorry, Mrs Craig,' he said, 'no buses.' He was still slightly out of breath.

'I know how bad they are,' she said sympathetically, patting his hand, 'my daily is very often late. Now then let's get you a drink. Jarvis, bring the tray over here please, now what would you like, all the usual, and there's some Bucks Fizz, that's lovely, I always think, and of course it makes the champagne go so much further.'

Charles took this to be a sign that she would like him to have the Bucks Fizz, and took a glass; it was gloriously welcome. 'Now then, come along and I'll introduce you to some nice people . . .'

Charles moved stealthily away after sixty seconds or so and made for the table in the corner where a few of the less popular canapés still remained. He was just downing a third mini ham sandwich and wondering if he could consume the entire bowl of stuffed olives without being observed when a slightly amused voice behind him said, 'You seem to be starving. Don't they have lunch where you come from?'

'They do,' said Charles, turning round slightly shamefaced, trying to swallow the six olives he had already put in his mouth, 'but that was six hours ago and –' and promptly choked. Before he did so, before he found himself gasping and fighting for breath, spluttering into his handker-chief, desperate not to spray the room with what was left of the mouthful of olive and ham, he took in the fact that the owner of the voice was tall and beautiful with creamy skin, a cloud of dark hair just touched with auburn and extraordinary eyes, golden in colour and flecked with brown. And she was wearing a plain white dress which set off her beauty to perfection, and a very fine pearl and diamond choker. After that he lost the capacity to absorb anything; he was dimly aware for the next thirty seconds that someone was thumping his back, and presumed it was the owner of the voice; as his breath came back, his lungs refilled and the world returned to normal, she swam into focus again, half concerned, half amused, holding out a glass of water.

'Here, try this. Are you all right?'

'Yes, thank you. I'm fine. How kind of you.'

'Not really. I think it was my fault.'

'Not at all. Serves me right for pigging out.'

'Well you do look half starved.'

'Oh I'm not really,' said Charles. 'It's just a device to win sympathy for myself at cocktail parties.' He held out his hand. 'Charles St Mullin.'

She took it. 'Virginia Caterham.' She was American; the accent was quite gentle, but distinct.

'You're not from these parts then?'

'No, I'm from New York.'

'And your husband also?'

'No, he's very English, very much from these parts. Name of Alexander Caterham.'

'Not the Earl of Caterham? Owner of Hartest House?'

'The very one. You're extremely well informed.'

'Well, you see, I am employed, if that it could be termed, by our host. Your husband once retained him.'

'He did? How exciting!'

'Not really, I'm afraid. It was to do with some land law and a rapacious neighbour. Rapacious in the land law sense, that is to say.'

'Oh yes, I remember Alexander telling me. We had a neighbour who objected to our hunting across his land. Apparently. It was before my term as chatelaine at Hartest. He – and Lionel – won, of course. The poor man moved away.' She sounded amused; Charles smiled at her.

'Of course. Do you enjoy being chatelaine of Hartest?'

'Oh yes, naturally I do.' She spoke quickly, smiled brilliantly. 'It's a beautiful house. And estate. A wonderful place to live.'

'Did you know it before your marriage?'

'No, I was raised in New York, as they say. Never even been to England.'

'It must have been something of a culture shock.'

'Well it was, but I am something of a survivor. I have learnt to speak English. If you know what I mean.'

'Of course I do,' said Charles.

'And what about you, Mr St Mullin?'

'Please call me Charles. Oh, I'm Irish. A broth of a boy. We too have a rather nice house. Not as fine as Hartest, but extremely pretty. In West Cork.'

'I've never been to Ireland,' she said, 'I understand it's very beautiful. What does "we" mean? Are you married?'

'Oh my goodness no,' said Charles. 'Can't afford such luxuries.'

'Really? I thought barristers were very rich people. Lionel seems to be.'

'Barristers are. I am a pupil barrister. An apprentice. Last year I earned twenty pounds, fourteen shillings and sixpence.'

'Well, I can see not many wives could be kept on that. So who is this "we" you speak of?'

'My family. My father. He is a gentleman farmer, and runs the house and the estate. Rather like your husband, I imagine. And occasionally he throws a few shillings at me, and says, "Here, cur, take this for yourself," and I eat for a few weeks longer.'

'What a sad story. And will you inherit this house, this beautiful house, in the fullness of time?'

'Sadly not. I have an elder brother. But actually, much as I love Ireland, I prefer London. I plan to settle here. At the moment of course I am forced to live on a bench on the Embankment. But in time I may graduate to something a little better.'

'I hope so.' She smiled at him, and there was an odd quality to that smile, it was warm and amused and very friendly, but there was a sadness behind it that Charles found intriguing.

'You must come and meet my husband. He's over there, rather unusually being the centre of attention. He's actually rather shy. He'd like you.' She took him by the hand, a warm, surprisingly firm grasp, and led him across the room; a tall, outstandingly good-looking man with blond hair and blue eyes stood telling what was obviously a very funny story to a circle of people all laughing extremely loudly.

The joke finished, Virginia smiled indulgently at her husband and ushered Charles forwards.

'Alexander, darling. This is Charles St Mullin. He works for Lionel. I thought you should meet him. He remembers the case, over the right of way, you remember, and the hunting.'

'Oh yes of course.' Alexander Caterham took Charles's hand, shook it hard. 'How do you do. How clever of you to remember it.'

'Well, I'm interested in land law,' said Charles. 'It fascinates me. My father has land in Ireland, and we have had a couple of disputes with our neighbours. Paricularly intriguing as the neighbour is the Mother Church.'

'Indeed? What a very formidable adversary she must be.'

'She is. But we won,' said Charles with a modest pride.

'Then you must have very fine lawyers. Are you really interested in land law?'

'Yes I am. In fact I'm working on a thesis on the subject, eighteenth-century land law.'

'The land laws for Hartest are classically complex. If it would amuse you, I could let you loose in the library there for a while. You could come down one Saturday.'

Charles said it would amuse him very much and that he would be delighted to accept. As he caught Virginia Caterham's golden eyes, her warm, oddly sad smile, he thought that it would be amusing to spend a day in her house as well.

'I'll phone you then, shall I?' he said, and 'Oh yes, please do,' she said, 'I can't think of anything I'd like more.'

★

'So, Charles. Has the morning been useful?' Alexander gestured to a place at the table; they were eating in the small dining room at the front of the house. Charles looked out of the window; the stretch of parkland, studded with sheep and deer, unrolled gently away from the house; the winding languor of the River Hart shone in the mist-strewn autumn sunshine.

'Useful and very pleasant. What a beautiful place this is. How fortunate you are, Lord Caterham.'

'I know it. Very fortunate. I count this as the greatest possible blessing, to live here. To own Hartest. To have it to pass on to my children. It is part of my very self. If that does not sound too pompous.'

'Alexander, yes it does,' said Virginia, 'do stop. You really are a bore about Hartest at times. Not everyone can quite see its immense charm, you know. Sometimes I get quite jealous,' she said to Charles. 'He loves this house far more than he loves me. It is his mistress. He is always leaving me for it.'

'Oh nonsense, Virginia,' said Alexander lightly; but Charles heard a more serious note in his voice. 'There is no comparison between how I feel for you and how I feel for Hartest. I much prefer Hartest.'

He smiled at her, brilliantly; but she did not smile back. Her eyes were hard and dark, and the fingers she was holding round her glass were tightly clenched.

'I know it,' she said, 'I just said that. Perhaps you could stop talking this nonsense, Alexander, and give me some more wine. My glass is empty, as you might have noticed, had you not had your mind so very firmly on your house. And so is Charles's.'

'I'm sorry. How stupid of me.' He got up and refilled their glasses; Charles noticed that Virginia's emptied very fast, three more times. She had recovered herself and was laughing again by the end of the first course; but Alexander was awkward suddenly too, just slightly ill at ease, they both talked too much and too intently. All was clearly not quite well in the Garden of Eden.

After lunch Virginia said she was going to walk her dog.

'If you've had enough of land law for a while, come with me.'

They walked down to the lake; there was a path round it, carved out of the long reeds; she walked ahead, and the dog, not the classic labrador he had expected, but an exquisitely elegant afghan hound with long, silken beige hair loped beside her. She was wearing a trenchcoat and wellington boots over her slacks; she looked very English, very at home in the country and the mud.

'What an enchanted life you lead,' said Charles carefully, curious for some clue as to her unhappiness.

'Indeed,' she said, her slightly throaty voice calm and almost complacent. 'Enchanted.'

'Do you miss the States?'

'A lot. Sometimes. Not so much the States, but my family. My brother most of all.'

'What does he do?'

'Works in a bank.'

'Ah. And your father?'

'Owns the bank.'

'Ah.'

'I'm quite a family person,' she said suddenly. 'I like to have my own people around me. Alexander doesn't have any family. Only a mother who refuses to meet me.'

'Oh dear. Why?'

'Because I'm an American. Sullying the family name. I think. I have tried very hard, written to her several times, even sent her flowers when she gave me the Caterham tiara to wear on my wedding day, but all to no avail.'

'Silly old lady. Well, never mind, no doubt soon you will have your own dynasty, and then you can make the rules. And you won't be lonely.'

'Yes,' she said. 'Yes, no doubt. Quite soon.'

He sensed a tension and changed the subject.

'What bank does your father own?'

'It's called Praegers. It's an investment bank. It doesn't have an office over here, so you won't have heard of it.'

'No. No, I haven't. He must be a very powerful man, your father.'

'Yes, he is. Too powerful for his own good.' She turned and smiled at him suddenly, and said, 'We're giving a ball at Christmas. Why don't you come?'

'I'd love to,' he said. 'Thank you.'

Looking back on that moment, remembering her standing there in the reeds, her dark hair wild with the damp air, her pale face at once thoughtful and pleased at his reply, he knew that was the moment it really began.

The ball was held on the Saturday before Christmas; Hartest was in festive mood. There was a most thoughtfully provided full moon, flooding the parkland silver, the trees lining the Great Drive were all studded with fairy lights and in the centre of the Rotunda stood a vast Christmas tree, twenty feet tall, dressed in turquoise and silver. There was a dinner for two hundred chosen guests before dinner and three hundred more arrived at ten; Virginia and Alexander stood on the front steps receiving them. Charles, who was in the second contingent, thought he had never seen a woman look more classically resplendent as she did, standing there in a black velvet dress with a great sweeping train, and with a drop pearl tiara in her hair. She wore no other jewellery apart from a pearl bracelet; her face, pale and beautiful in the moonlight, with its great tawny eyes, looked exotic, strange, almost unreal.

Alexander in white tie and tails, handsome, charming, laughing, stood by her, showing them both off, his two loves, his wife and his house; Charles was struck by his patent childlike pleasure.

He shook Charles by the hand, said, 'Charles! How nice. How is the thesis?' and then turned to the people behind him; Virginia took his hand in both hers and said, 'It was lovely of you to come. I do hope you can find a friend. If not, come and find me.'

He had been asked to bring a partner, but hadn't wanted to; he was too intrigued by the whole event to be hampered by some half-known girl. He wanted to be free, to explore, both the party and his hostess's motives in asking him; he was happy to be alone, he said, when he wrote to accept, he had no particular partner to bring and if that would not foul up numbers too much, then he preferred not to. It was a very grand occasion; there were two discotheques, a live band and a jazz band, there was dancing in the ballroom and in the Rotunda and a cabaret at midnight, supplied by a young man who sang charmingly, and then suddenly switched to brilliant impersonations by request; Charles, intrigued, asked him to do the Queen Mother, and there she stood, quite unmistakable, plump, gracious, smiling, waving, asking banal questions, dressed in a dinner jacket, and looking more herself than in her Hartnell gowns.

At the end, Father Christmas suddenly appeared with a sackful of presents; one for everyone. The men got silk handkerchiefs, the women slim, gilt-edged leather-bound diaries. 'And what a status symbol they will be,' Charles heard one girl murmur to another. 'People will be very sure to let everyone know where they got them, won't they?'

As Father Christmas disappeared, the jazz band started; the younger guests began to dance. Charles, who had been quite happy until then, felt suddenly a little bereft; he found himself a glass of champagne and went in search (rather hopelessly) of Virginia.

In the event he found her quite easily, sitting on the stairs with a crowd of people; she saw him and stood up, holding out her hand.

'Charles! How nice. Have you come to ask me to dance? I was hoping you would.'

'Yes, I have,' he said, and she led him onto the floor.

She was a superb dancer; she made him feel helpless and hopeless.

'You're wonderful,' he said, standing still, watching her, laughing, 'you should be on the stage.'

'Well, I did think of it. But my mother said it was common. I dance with my dad. I taught him to dance, actually. We do a number together. Song and dance.'

'I'd love to see you.'

'You wouldn't. It's really flash and showy. It would never happen here. It's very New York.' The music changed, grew slow; she relaxed against him suddenly, he could feel the length of her body, warm, friendly. She put her arms round his neck, looked into his eyes, and smiled.

'You have such a nice face, Charles St Mullin. Not exactly handsome – '

'Thank you.'

'Don't be uppity. I was going to say, but very very sexy. There's something about that Irish colouring, the blue eyes and the dark hair, that – oh, I like it very much.'

She was quite drunk; she had had a lot of champagne.

'Yours is quite sexy too,' he said suddenly, risking it, risking a rebuttal.

'Thank you. Thank you very much. Do you think the rest of me is sexy?'

'Oh no,' he said gravely. 'Dead dull.'

She laughed, and dropped her head onto his shoulder. 'I hope you don't think I'm very forward.'

'Well I do, rather,' he said. He had meant it as a joke, but he realized, appalled, that she had taken it seriously; she drew back as if he had hit her, looked at him and then turned and fled along the corridor, disappearing into one of the rooms.

Charles followed her, trying all the doors; most of them were locked, and the ones that weren't seemed to be cupboards; but right at the end was a small sitting room; he thought at first she wasn't there, but then he saw her, hunched into a chair, by the window, looking out onto the parkland. She heard him come in. 'Please go away,' she said, without even turning round.

'Virginia, you're crazy. Of course I was joking. Of course I didn't mean it. It's – well, it's – '

'It's what?' she said.

'It's just that the biggest division the Atlantic makes between your country and mine is in our senses of humour. Your lot isn't very good at the flippant remark. You take them too seriously. I should have known. I'm sorry. Of course I don't think you're forward, I think you're beautiful and very sexy. And charming. Please don't be upset.'

262

She turned to him then, and he could see, in the moonlight, that she had been crying; great tears still rolled down her face. He was puzzled.

'Virginia, don't cry. Please. I meant nothing. Really. You have no reason to be upset.'

'Oh, but I do,' she said, and there was a great shuddering sigh, right through her body. 'I have every reason. But none of them to do with you. I'm sorry. I'm a fool.'

'You're not,' he said, and went and knelt by the chair, taking her hand. 'You're not a fool. Foolish, perhaps, but not a fool.' He reached out and touched her face, brushing the tears away with his fingers; suddenly she took his hand, and kissed the fingertips. 'Salty,' she said. 'It's always surprising, isn't it, that tears are salty.'

'Yes,' he said, 'yes, I suppose it is,' and then he leant forward and kissed her very gently, on her wet cheeks, and said, 'I'm so sorry, so very sorry I upset you.'

'Do you think,' she said idly, looking down, fiddling with her dress, her lovely head drooping suddenly, 'do you think we could have lunch one day? In London? I would so like that.'

'I would like it too,' he said, 'I'll ring you, straight after Christmas, if I may.'

He left soon after that; and all the way back to London, driving his battered, noisy Mini, he wondered why women with everything, and moreover with everything to lose, newly married to one of the wealthiest, most famously charming men in England, should be instigating an affair with a penniless barrister.

They had lunch twice before he took her to bed, in his small flat in Fulham; two lunches, exquisitely arousing affairs, where she sat and looked at him, and listened to him, and talked most politely, of legal matters and his career and his childhood and her own, and the shared interest they discovered in Impressionist paintings, and the comparable delights of Ireland and England and America, and all the while gazing into his eyes with an expression in her own that told of an acute physical hunger.

Charles knew what she wanted, and he wanted it too; it would have been a man of some madness, he said to himself, who would not. But he was terribly afraid. He was afraid of appearing foolish and presumptuous (even while his every instinct told him he was neither); of rebuttal (although the same instincts told him that was unlikely too); of having to take her in all her exquisite, expensive beauty to his shabby flat, with the creaky bed and the worn, darned sheets, presented to him by his mother when he moved to London; of the wrath that might be visited upon him, and the retribution extracted from him by the Earl of Caterham, should he come to hear of the turn events had taken; and most of all, perhaps, of not performing in bed as well as the Countess must surely be expecting. Charles had been to bed with a few girls, and indeed considered himself a modestly good performer, but the girls had either been young and naive, or prostitutes; none of them with remotely the kind of experience that a married woman, who before she had been a married woman had been an American heiress of clearly considerable sophistication, would be bringing to his bed. And yet, and yet, clearly he was what the Countess wanted; and she was equally clearly what he wanted; and so it was, at the end of the second lunch, as she sat, gently massaging his palm with her thumb, snaking one of her long legs around his under the table, her tawny eyes molten with tenderness, that he said, 'Would you – would you care to progress this thing a little further?'

And yes, she said, yes, she would care very much for that, to progress it as far and as fast as he saw fit; and he said that he had a flat in Fulham, which she was very welcome to visit should she so wish, perhaps one day next week, he really had to be getting back to chambers now, and she had laughed and said she found it a little hurtful that he so clearly preferred Lionel Craig to her, but that next week would do very nicely.

And a week later, the day carefully chosen to fit in with Lionel Craig's weekly round of golf, he opened the door of his flat in Parsons Green and showed her in, and she looked round, smiling with pleasure and said, 'Let's go straight into the bedroom, shall we, we don't want to waste any more time.'

She was determined, efficient, almost detached, undressing straight away, without bashfulness or self-consciousness even. He lay on the bed and watched her: predictably perfect she was, with her long slender body, her surprisingly full breasts, with large, dark nipples, her endlessly good American legs, and then she lay down and said, 'Now I shall watch you, if I may.' He had felt foolish then, and turned his back, tearing his clothes off quickly, tumbling into the bed beside her; but she had turned to him with an expression of such tenderness, such pleasure that he felt a surge of confidence and happiness, and took her in his arms and smiled and said, 'I am not the most experienced man in the world, Your Ladyship. But I am proud to be of service to you.'

'I am not very experienced either,' she said, and began to kiss him; tenderly, searchingly at first, then more greedily. Charles felt his mood change, lift, into absolute certainty of what he was doing; he turned her on her back, looked down into her tawny eyes, and then bent and began to kiss her breasts, slowly, thoughtfully. She lay, her head thrown back, her eyes closed, thrusting her body slowly, gently against him; she did not caress him, did not touch him even, simply followed where he led, carefully, almost dutifully.

But she was eager, desperate for him by the time he entered her, wet, tender, yielding; he sank into her, joyfully, thankfully almost, feeling her tight, taut pleasure, following it with his own. And then it changed for both of them, grew urgent, frantic, fast; he forgot everything, forgot caring for her, forgot pleasing her even, simply tumbled into the quagmire of his own pleasure, thrusting, pushing, drowning in her hot deep places; and then as suddenly it was over, and he came, in a great shuddering, rushing moment, and he cried out and then lay on her, very still, immediately ashamed, shocked, that he had not cared for her.

'I'm sorry,' he said, 'so sorry. I should have waited. But you were so lovely.'

'It was all right,' she said, 'it was fine. It was lovely. Next time, it will be perfect. But this time was good. Don't be upset, don't worry, I'm all right, just lie, be still, don't leave me, don't, don't leave me.'

He lay, quite still, wating while she quietened; then he drew away from her gently and looked at her.

'Are you really all right?'

'Yes I'm really all right.'

'I should have – well, I should have asked you before about – ' His voice trailed off in confusion.

'Contraception?' she said, smiling. 'Don't be silly. I'm a good American girl, I'm on the pill.'

'That's very avant-garde of you,' said Charles. 'Hardly anyone here takes it.'

'I know. We're an avant-garde nation. It makes such good sense.'

'Yes, I suppose so.' He was silent. Then he smiled at her and traced the outline of her breasts with his finger. 'You are quite amazing, you know. Amazingly beautiful. Amazingly nice. I can't think what you're doing here with me.'

'Having some amazingly nice sex,' she said simply.

He often tried, after that, to question her about her marriage. He was puzzled by her unfaithfulness. She didn't seem like a cheat. She didn't even seem particularly voracious. She was modestly sensual, and after the first time she always climaxed, sometimes more than once, but she was certainly not inventive in bed, she showed none of the outrageous hungers that he might have supposed her to possess, such as would lead her from her marriage bed and into an adulterous one. She simply liked, she said, being with him, knowing him in the biblical sense, and that was as far as it went. She refused to discuss her marriage, or Alexander, refused to reveal whether she was unhappy, refused to discuss her past.

When he broached the subject of what might happen if Alexander found out, she said, 'He won't. I promise you he won't.'

'But what does he think you're doing, up here in London, week after week?'

'Shopping. Seeing my friends. Whatever any woman does in London for the day. He's very busy, Charles, on the estate. He leaves me to my own devices a lot. He won't wonder. Honestly. You mustn't worry about it.'

After a while, in the way of all lovers, they became greedier. Lunchtimes, and the inevitably swift, disturbing partings they brought, were not long enough. They spent the occasional evening together, and once Charles took the day off and they stayed in bed all day, picnicking at lunchtime on cheese and grapes and champagne, listening to music, talking. He did not learn much of her marriage, but he learnt about her; her sadness at not pleasing her father more, her love for Baby, her pleasure in eventually finding work she loved, her friends – 'You'd love Tiffy, she is just the best fun in the world.' And he talked too, of his own childhood, lyrically happy, growing up on the magically beautiful west coast of Ireland, with his brother and his sister, his beloved sister Felicia, now a nun, he told her, at the convent in Cork; he had been allowed to stay at home until he was thirteen, and even then only going to school in Dublin, not being sent to England, to Eton like his brother. 'I was my mother's favourite, she would die for me.' Doing all the country things, playing with the local children, riding, fishing, climbing trees, 'Although I fell one day, thirty feet, and broke my arm, the doctor said I was lucky not to break my head, I've never liked heights since,' reading Law at Trinity College Dublin, 'A place of such charm, you never quite get over leaving it,' and then the long slow haul upwards into practice. 'You can't do it, you know, without a private income, and mine is very very small.'

'How lucky you are,' said Virginia, 'to have had such an uncomplicated life.'

'Well – yes. I suppose so. Is yours so very complicated?'

'Very,' she said, 'but I am learning to live with it.'

Towards the spring, she became obsessed with the idea of spending some real time with him. 'It's all right, I'm not going to become embarrassing and want to run away with you. But it would be nice, so nice, to have whole days and whole nights, without worrying, without watching clocks. Wouldn't it?'

'It would, but how would that be possible? Don't be silly.'

'I'm going to visit my mother at Easter. I could come home two days early. Or fly out there two days late.'

'Virginia, my darling Virginia, it sounds horribly risky.'

'Not really. Alexander is going to visit his old bat of a mother. He wouldn't know. What do you think? You must like the idea, you simply must.'

'Of course I do, but I'm scared. For you, but also for me. Just suppose Alexander found out. Just suppose.'

'He won't. He won't. He isn't – possessive. Honestly. Oh, Charles, let's try. Please.'

'All right. I'll try to think of something. But I'm not spending two days in Fulham. OK?'

'OK.'

In the end he thought of a cottage on the edge of his father's estate.

'No one ever goes there. It's right down by the sea. About two miles from the house. We could stay there.'

'It sounds wonderful.'

'It isn't. It's cold and damp, and there's no electricity. The water has to be pumped from a well. The fire has to be lit and the lamps are oil. The bed is lumpy and I'm sure there are mice.'

Virginia kissed him. 'I think you're trying to put me off.'

'I am.'

'Well you're failing. Dismally. We'll go there. And fuck and fuck for two whole days. And then I'll fly to New York and go to church on Easter Day with my mother and do penance for my sins.'

'It's all right for you,' said Charles. 'I'm a Catholic, I'm being condemned to eternal hellfire for all this.'

'I'll be worth it. I promise.'

He smiled at her. 'I think you will. Well, don't forget my Easter egg. Otherwise I'm not coming.'

'I won't.'

They met at Cork airport and drove down in an old car Charles had hired. 'God help me if anyone I know sees me. My mother will kill me.'

'What, for being here with a married woman?'

'No, for not going to see her first.'

'Ah.'

The cottage was tiny and stone built; it was evening when they got there and freezing cold. Charles had bought logs and coal, and food and wine.

'And what have you brought?'

'Just myself.'

'Bloody aristocracy,' he said, kissing her. 'Incapable of looking after itself. Make yourself useful and go and pump some water.'

She came in looking shamefaced. 'I can't make it work.'

'You're useless. Here, you carry on making this soup. I'll do it.'

She looked pleased. 'Cooking I'm good at.'

She was. She added cream and wine to the carrot soup, served it up with bread warmed on the wood stove, and champagne.

'It's a bit warm, I'm afraid. But it's vintage.'

'So you did bring something.'

'Yes. And some gorgeous cheeses, and some glacé fruits and some nuts and some wild strawberries and some fresh figs. All in my overnight bag.'

'An overnight hamper. How unusual. Where on earth did you get fresh figs at this time of year?'

'Fortnums.'

'Of course. How silly of me to ask.'

After they had eaten he said, 'Well, we'd better get down to business.'

She looked at him, startled. 'What do you mean?'

'Airing the bed. Don't panic.'

'Sorry. How do we do that?'

'Hot-water bottles.'

'You haven't brought them too?'

'I have.'

'You're wonderful, Charles.'

'I know.'

The bed was freezing, even with the hot-water bottles, and lumpy as Charles had promised: Virginia climbed into it, shivering violently.

'I've never been in a cold bed before.'

'Spoilt bitch.'

'I know I am. I can't help it.'

'I'll make you warm. Come here, nestle up.'

She pulled herself into his arms, holding him tightly to her. Her body did feel unnaturally cold.

'Are you all right, darling?'

'Yes of course. Let's just lie like this for a while. I'll be fine.'

'I don't think,' said Charles, his hands moving tenderly, exploringly over her, 'I can just lie. I'm sorry.'

'Well, try. Every time you move a blast of cold air comes in and hits me.'

'Serves you right. This was your idea.'

'It was a wonderful one. Wasn't it?'

'I think so. I wonder if you could just – '

'Yes?'

'Let me have my wicked way now, quickly. Then I'll lie quietly. I promise.'

'Oh all right.'

Afterwards, they lay in front of the fire, naked, on a thick blanket. The little room was warm now; dark, except for the firelight. Charles fetched a bottle of wine; they drank it, talking idly, smiling.

'Oh, here,' she said suddenly, 'I have your Easter egg.'

'Not from Fortnums too, I hope? Too predictable.'

'No. It's from Fabergé.'

She dug into her bag and produced it, an exquisite, golden, ruby-encrusted egg, wrapped up in a roll of cotton wool in her toilet bag.

'It's to say thank you. For you'll never know how much.'

'Virginia,' said Charles in awe, 'you can't give me this. It must be worth a fortune.'

'What you've given me is worth a fortune,' she said, smiling, 'to me. I want you to have it. My father gave it to me when I was twenty-one.'

'Well,' he said, turning it over and over in his hand, in awe. 'I will have it then. If that's what you want. But I don't know how to thank you.'

'Don't. You don't need to. And if ever you're starving, you can sell it. I promise not to mind.'

'I would much much rather starve,' he said solemnly, and meant it.

In the morning they woke early, driven out of bed by the cold, and the dead fire. Charles sent her out to the pump again, said he would not let her in until she managed to work it.

She came in triumphant with half a kettle full; he made coffee and they ate rolls and honey and some of Virginia's figs.

'Now we're going out. Enough of this intimacy.'

'Charles! I thought we were in hiding.'

'We'll be quite safe where I'm taking you.'

He drove her down the valley to the sea; they walked on a beach so wide and long it was like a country of its own. Behind them were the mountains, the small valleys, the jaggedly primeval cliffs, before them the sea, wild, cold, relentlessly beautiful.

'Oh my God, it's glorious. I love it. I want to live here.'

'I know a little place you can have. At a modest rent.'

'You're on.'

They got back to the cottage hungry, for food and each other. They made love with a gentle, sweet familiarity; afterwards Virginia turned her head from him, and he realized she was crying.

'What is it? Darling, what is it?'

'Nothing. Release. Happiness. I don't know. I just feel utterly utterly at peace. And it makes me cry. Does that sound silly?'

'Very.'

'You're too frank, Mr St Mullin.'

'I know.'

They ate in front of the fire, and then slept again, in one another's arms; woke up starving. Charles cooked dinner, chicken in wine; it was delicious.

'You're wonderful,' said Virginia.

'I know.'

'Come to bed. Let me say thank you.'

'On one condition.'

'What's that?'

'You wash up first.'

'You're so romantic.'

'I know.'

'This script is getting predictable.'

'Sorry. Come here, My Lady, let me screw you. It seems suddenly terribly important.'

'I thought you'd never ask.'

She was particularly abandoned that night; in a way he had not known her be before. She clung to him crying out, over and over again, in great seemingly endless cascades of orgasm, and when finally she was finished, spent, she lay back, smiling at him almost triumphantly, and said, 'That was very special. Very very special.'

'I thought so too. Am I allowed to go to sleep now?'

'Yes you are. But thank you.'

'For what?'

'Everything. But specially that, then. Specially.'

For years after he remembered her saying that, wondering what she had meant, really meant.

In the morning they were depressed, their holiday mood vanished. They had to leave at lunchtime and go back to Cork.

Virginia was particularly sad, withdrawn, an odd look in her golden eyes.

'Don't be sad,' he said. 'We have some lovely memories.'

'I know. Lovely ones.'

'I love you, Virginia. Very much.'

It was the first time he had said it, the first time he had allowed himself to even think it. There was no future in any of it, he knew, and certainly not in loving her. But it had crept up on him, a gentle, tender warmth, a shock of sweet pleasure, and he wanted her to know.

She sat and looked at him, very serious, concerned, her eyes heavy; he could tell at once that she did not feel the same. It hurt; but he preferred to know. 'Charles. Look – I – '

'It's all right, Virginia. I understand. You don't love me. I shouldn't have said that. I don't know why I did. Of course we can't have any more than this. Ever. It's fine by me. Honestly. Well,' he added, an oddly hurt, crumpled smile working its way into his face, 'well of course it's not. Of course I should like to take you off into the sunset and make you mine. For ever more. But it can't be. I'd be crazy even to think it.'

'Crazy, but very lovely. Charles, I'm sorry. Sometimes I think I should never have started this. It was selfish and wrong of me. I – '

'Virginia.'

'Yes?'

'Virginia, why did you? Why did you start it?'

There was a long silence. Then she said, 'I can't tell you. I just can't. Not all of it. But one reason was I wanted you. I thought you were the most engaging, sexy man I had ever seen. And I knew I could trust you.'

'Trust me.' He felt a stab of hurt, of anger. 'Ah. Well, that was convenient. Nice for you.'

'What do you mean?'

'Well, obviously you need a lover you can trust, don't you? In your position. Your important, high-profile position. Someone who won't blab all over London. Someone who won't jeopardize your standing, make you look cheap, put your marriage at risk. Yes, I can see it was very important you should trust me.'

'Don't, Charles. Please.'

'Why not? Has it never occurred to you I feel slightly used, Virginia? A nice handy, rampant cock stuck on a nice dutiful, trustworthy body. Just what you wanted. Well, maybe I wanted something too. Some love, some future even. But I'm not going to get it, am I? I just have to carry on, doing my bit, fucking away, making you satisfied and then going quietly back to work, not asking for anything, not saying anything. Well, I might just get tired of it soon. After this little honeymoon of yours is over. You might have to find some other poor sucker to do your bidding, fulfil your fantasies.'

'Charles, please!' She was crying now, tears pouring down her face.

'And don't start crying. This whole bloody thing started with you crying. Very useful things, tears. Do you cry for Alexander when he doesn't exactly come up to scratch?'

271

'No,' she said quietly. 'Alexander never makes me cry.'

Later he was remorseful. He went out to her, where she was sitting in his car, silent, white-faced, and got in beside her, taking her hand.

'I'm sorry, darling. Terribly sorry.'

'It's all right.'

'No it isn't all right. It's all wrong. I shouldn't have done it, spoilt your little idyll.'

'Why do you keep calling it mine? Haven't you liked it at all?'

'Yes of course I have. But it was very much your idea. And it was a wonderful one.'

'Well, I hope so. Anyway, I'm sorry too. It must be awful for you. I can see that. Maybe we should end it. For your sake.'

'No,' he said, 'don't let's end it. It's my problem if I can't handle it. If I've been messy enough to fall in love with you, I certainly don't want to lose you before I have to.'

He did lose her though. He had to, two months later.

She came to meet him one day in London, pale and tired-looking. She smiled at him wearily as she came in the door, and then sat down heavily on his couch; she was obviously not feeling well.

He hadn't seen her for a fortnight; he had been busy, she had been involved with planning the Hartest midsummer fête.

'Darling, what is it? You look terrible.'

'I feel terrible,' she said. 'I'm pregnant.'

'What? But you can't be.'

'Oh but I am,' she said, and despite her weariness, her pallor, there was triumph and happiness in her eyes.

'By – whom?'

'By Alexander, of course.'

He did a swift calculation, an instant recall of everything she had said on the subject.

'Now look. I thought you were on the pill.'

'Well – I was. But my doctor said it was disagreeing with me. So I came off it. And – well, I'm pregnant.'

'And just exactly how do you know it isn't mine? My baby?'

He felt a rush of pleasure and pride as he said those words; almost as if she had told him it was his, congratulated him on it herself.

'Oh Charles, of course it isn't yours.'

'How do you know?'

'The timing, for a start. I'm – well, just over a month pregnant. We haven't – well, seen each other much since Easter. That was two months ago. And I was still on the pill then.'

'How very tidy.'

'What?'

'That you should have become pregnant by your extremely potent husband the moment you came off the pill.'

'Yes, well, it does that.'

'Does what?'

'Increases your fertility.'

'I see. Well, congratulations, Lady Caterham. How very excited you must feel.'

'I do, quite.'

'I'm sure.'

'Charles, please don't.'

'I'm sorry if I'm upsetting you. So what does this mean for us?'

'Well – I suppose, and it's terribly sad, but it's over.'

'Really?'

'Yes. It has to be.'

'I suppose so. You can't come here, great with child, and beg for a fuck, can you?'

'Charles, please.'

'I'm sorry, Virginia, but I can't be genteel and self-effacing over this. I'm too upset. I told you before I felt used. I feel it more now. My time is past. I have no more use in your life.'

'Well, you can see it like that if you want to.'

'I could tell a few tales, you know, about you and your pregnancy. About what I thought of it. About it. Its history.'

'I know. But I hoped you wouldn't.'

'You knew I wouldn't, didn't you?'

'I – suppose so, yes.'

'Virginia, can you look me in the eye and tell me that you know for an absolute certainty that baby is not mine?'

She turned to him, her golden eyes clear and determined.

'Yes, Charles, I can.'

He never really believed her. But because he loved her, he pretended he did.

The christening robe had been his idea. Because he was so sure the baby was his, he wanted to lay a claim to it. Not destructively, not aggressively. But a claim nonetheless.

He talked to his sister, Felicia. He told her everything. She was a nun, at once the pride and sorrow of her family, torn as they were between a wish

273

to see her married with a love and a family of her own, still belonging to them, and an intense delight that she had fulfilled the great Catholic dream of a Vocation. She had done her novitiate at the convent at Ballydegogue, and was now working at a hospice in the East End of London; a tall, gentle, beautiful girl with a wisdom and a delicious humour the whole family relied upon.

She sat in the flat at Fulham, the flat that had rung with Virginia's hungry, frantic cries, the flat he could hardly bear to stay in now, and listened carefully to everything Charles had to say.

'So you think the child is yours?'

'Yes, I do. I really do.'

'Why?'

'I can't tell you. I don't know. I just feel it. There is something strange, wrong, with that marriage. She would never talk about it, but there is. And there is the timing. We had those two days in Ireland, together – '

'Really, Charles. That was naughty. Whatever would Mother have done, had she found you?'

'I don't know, Felicia. But she didn't. Anyway, those two endless, wonderful days, so much lovemaking, she seemed so intent somehow – oh, I'm sorry, Felicia, I shouldn't be talking to you like this.'

'Why not?'

'Well – it doesn't seem right.'

'Because I'm a nun? Charles, I'm always telling you, we are not removed from the world, and from worldly knowledge, simply because we are distant from it. We can look on it more calmly, more carefully even, and not judge, but we know it is there. So please don't be troubled. What you are saying, as I understand it, is that she seemed to you to be intent on having as much intercourse with you as she possibly could. At that particular time. So that she might have been thought to be trying to conceive?'

'Well – yes, I suppose so.' He felt faintly shocked, embarrassed even, that she should grasp so swiftly what he was trying to say.

'But Charles, why should she do such a thing? She is married, and very suitably so. She may not like her husband very much, however charming and agreeable he may be, and that would certainly be a reason for her to be having an affair with you, but it would hardly be grounds for her to be conceiving a child, your child, deliberately. Would it now?'

'No. I know that. And I have been over and over it in my mind, and I can't make any sense of it. But I do know – or I think I know – that that baby is at least possibly, probably even, mine. I mean, her story about coming off the pill and getting promptly pregnant by her husband seems altogether too neat.'

'But – have you been seeing her since Easter?'

'No, I haven't.'

'Well then.'

'But Felicia, it's only June. I don't know a great deal about pregnancy and the female body, but she was in New York until nearly the end of April. If she was pregnant, by her husband, it would only be a month or so. A bit soon to be feeling sick, or to be sure, even.'

'Women have a great affinity with their bodies, Charles. She would know, before any tests or doctors could confirm it. But in any case, there is clearly nothing to be gained and a great deal to be lost by your continuing with your claim on this baby.'

'Oh I know.' He looked at her suddenly and she saw a great sadness in his eyes. 'I wasn't dreaming that I should. It just seems such a sorry, unsatisfactory state of affairs, that's all. And I miss her. I miss her so much.'

'You really loved her, didn't you?'

'I really really loved her. She is beautiful and tender and sad, and I know,' he added with a certain defiance in his voice, 'I know I have been committing a mortal sin, but I am not sorry. I should be, but I am not.'

'Well, that is debatable,' said Felicia briskly. 'God has different ways of making us repent. It could be said that yours is in your own unhappiness, and uncertainty. It is certainly not for me to reproach you in any way. I am simply unhappy that you are unhappy. And I have no doubt that Lady Caterham is unhappy too. She does not sound to me a person to enter into adulterous liaisons lightly. There is clearly more to her story than perhaps we shall ever know. Your only way now, Charles, is acceptance, I am afraid.'

'I know. And the hope that one day I shall know what it all meant, what it was about.'

'Yes, but even that may be denied to you. It would be unfortunate to place too much faith in that, Charles. She is lost to you now, your Virginia, and you have to accept that. Otherwise you will be far more unhappy for far longer.'

'I suppose. But anyway, I do want to give her a present. Desperately I do. A farewell present, a relevant present. Not jewellery, nothing silly and obvious. Something to do with the baby. My baby. A shawl perhaps, I don't know, what do babies like, what could she possibly take and keep from me?'

'The baby,' said Felicia. 'I can see that. Well now, let me think about it for a day or so. I'll come back to you. In the meantime, would you consider taking your poor poverty-stricken sister out to lunch? I have a great longing for a glass of Guinness, and if you would take me where I can obtain one, I shall be able to turn my mind to your problem with greater attention.'

'Of course I will,' said Charles, kissing her. 'It will be a great pleasure. Are nuns allowed to go to the pub?'

'Nuns are allowed to go anywhere,' said Felicia. 'As long as their consciences are at peace. I do not find mine greatly disturbed at the prospect of spending an hour in the Dog and Duck in your company.'

'A christening robe,' said Charles. 'What do you think about that? Isn't that what all babies have to have? I could send one to Virginia. One I had had made, perhaps. That wouldn't be an aggressive gesture, would it?'

'A little, perhaps,' said Felicia, smiling at him. 'It's a very personal thing, a christening robe, there is probably a family heirloom that the baby would wear, like all his or her ancestors. We all wore the same one, after all. But it might be a very acceptable and charming gift for your countess, nonetheless. After all, it could be worn not as a christening robe, simply as a dress. Now I do happen to know someone who might well be able to make one for you. If she could, you could rest assured it would be exquisite. If you would like me to, I will speak to her, and perhaps order one for you. Then you can send it to the baby yourself.'

'Thank you,' said Charles. 'I would like that very much.'

Dear Charles,
What a lovely, lovely extravagant present. How kind of you, and how kind of you to remember me.

I shall indeed dress the baby in your robe for his christening (I am quite determined, you see, that he shall be a boy).

If I may, I shall send you a photograph of the occasion, so that you may see your gift in use.

Thank you.
With my love,
Virginia Caterham

And that was the last he ever heard from her.

Chapter 21

Baby, 1983

Confidence is a powerful ally. It trails success in its wake. It lends authority, assists in decision-making, bestows mental and physical stamina and clarity of thought. The confident are charismatic, effective, persuasive; they can hardly help but win.

It was fairly apparent to everyone at Praegers in that summer of 1983 that Baby Praeger had lost all confidence.

He knew himself he was floundering; he watched himself, appalled, as he blundered from meeting to meeting, desperately trying to impress, to be positive, creative, thoughtful, and succeeding only in looking foolish, constantly outmanoeuvred, taking up an endlessly defensive position against his father. Fred III had not lost any confidence, he had acquired a large new issue of it; and, returned to his natural habitat, the tall brownstone in Pine Street, after a period away from it which he cheerfully described to everyone as a living hell, was having the time of his life.

He had, in fact, after six months, and initially under cover of Baby's illness, managed to retrench himself in his old position, as chairman; the senior partners, in a mixture of emotions, watched helplessly as he moved from department to department, making them his own once more, midwifing on the biggest mergers, countermanding advice on investments, insisting on various underwritings whether the traders agreed or not, backing his own stock hunches, speculating on the rise and fall of interest rates, and assisting personally on the progress of at least two very large-scale leveraged buy-outs.

The junior partners in particular were outraged; promoted by Baby, accustomed to a degree of autonomy, they found themselves reduced to glorified clerks, and held anguished meetings with the senior partners, to complain and to question. The senior partners, who had seen it all before (and had watched, moreover, with a mixture of despair and admiration the sharpening up, the injection of vision, the hugely increased feeling of urgency in the bank since Fred III had returned to it), told them they were wasting their time, but they should see him themselves, should they so wish.

Baby had come back to the bank just before Christmas; relieved to be back, impatient to be working again – and not unnaturally fearful. He was right to be so; he had spent almost twenty years trying to carve out his own role at Praegers, and twenty seconds of cardiac arrest seemed to have robbed him of it almost entirely. Within days Baby was totally demoralized. His father was, as the board remarked privately, out to cut off his balls.

Even his relationship with Angie was less stable than it had been. All through the long period they had been kept apart by his illness, he had clung to her, the thought of her, like a lifeline. They were totally estranged, he couldn't speak to her, couldn't even write to her. While he and Mary Rose were staying at Beaches during his recuperation, she mailed all his letters every day, and he could hardly ask Beaumont to post something for him when Mary Rose wasn't looking. And she was looking very carefully.

And then when he finally got back to New York, and Mary Rose had returned to her work as a commissioning editor at Doubleday, he was able to call Angie, and she was gratifyingly pleased to hear from him; she told him she'd be over on the next Concorde. But: 'It's no good,' said Baby gloomily, 'I'm still under lock and key. She calls me several times a day and if I'm not here, she wants to know from the maid exactly where I went and when.'

'Tell the maid a lie.'

'Darling, I can't. Well I can, but you have no idea the amount of cross-questioning I'm subjected to. Mary Rose comes home for lunch every day, and early in the evening; I really think we'll have to wait until I'm back at work.'

Angie sounded sharp. 'Baby, I've been waiting for you all this time. I'm beginning to think you don't want to see me.'

'Oh Angie, if only you knew. I want to see you more than anything, anything in the world. Be patient, please. And then we can have the reunion of a lifetime.'

'It had better be,' said Angie.

In fact, the reunion was less than satisfactory. They met in the apartment in the Village; Angie was looking thinner, almost gaunt ('I've been missing you,' she said), and was more than slightly irritable, which was unlike her. She did have a temper, but it normally was reserved for major matters, and day by day she was very level. It made Baby nervous. His anxiety and his not unnatural fear of becoming physically overexerted resulted in a poor performance in bed; Angie was very sweet and patient with him, but neither of them could pretend the earth had moved, or even that a breeze had passed across it; Baby was saddened, further discomfited.

'Christ almighty,' he said, turning away from her finally, angry to feel tears at the back of his eyes. 'What is my life coming to, that I can't even fuck you properly?'

Angie's small hand stroked his shoulder, reached for his hand. 'Baby, don't. Don't put yourself down. You've been very ill. I thought I'd lost you that day. You're having a tough time at work. Let's both be patient.' She clambered over him, smiled into his eyes. 'I've waited a very long time for you. I can hang on a bit longer.'

Baby sighed and folded her into his arms. 'I love you so much,' he said, 'I wish we had some kind of future together.'

'Well, I don't think we do,' said Angie lightly. 'Less than ever now. I mean your dad is back in the driving seat, isn't he? So he certainly isn't going to take kindly to news of me.'

'He's only there very temporarily,' said Baby, trying to believe it himself, 'but no, you're right, it would be a disaster if he heard anything about you – about us – at the moment.' He sighed heavily. 'Angie, you're terribly thin. Have you been eating properly?'

'Oh yes,' she said. 'Of course I have. I've been worried about you, Baby. And missing you. I told you. Now look, let's not waste any more time talking about what we can't have and enjoy what we can. Just relax, Baby, and try to be happy. Let me see what a little therapy can do . . .'

She wriggled down in the bed, started tonguing him. Baby looked down at her golden head, and tried obediently to relax. It wasn't a total success, but it was better than the first time.

Maybe everything would be all right.

He didn't see her nearly so often these days. He wasn't able to make his trips to London and Paris. He got tired easily. Mary Rose was watchful. He suggested (at his doctor's genuine instigation) that he should start running again, and Mary Rose said it would be a wonderful idea and she would come with him. Baby had always hated running, but never as much as now, as he panted round Central Park with Mary Rose just behind him, shouting encouraging remarks, thinking of what he had been doing at this time a year ago.

Chapter 22

Max, 1983

Five hundred guests [confided Jennifer to her diary and her readers in *Harpers & Queen* magazine] attended the brilliant dance for Lady Charlotte Welles given by her father the Earl of Caterham, and held at Hartest House, the exquisite eighteenth-century Caterham family seat. The dance retrospectively celebrated Lady Charlotte's twenty-first birthday and was the first big party to have been held at Hartest since the tragic death of the Countess of Caterham three years ago. Lord Caterham, who has been increasingly reclusive recently, was looking relaxed and handsome, receiving the guests on the South Front of Hartest with his eldest daughter. Lady Charlotte, who left Cambridge earlier this summer and is confidently predicted to achieve a double First in Economics and Politics, is to take up residence in New York in the autumn, where she is to join Praegers, the merchant bank founded by her great-great-grandfather in 1872.

Lady Charlotte, who was looking very beautiful in a white tiered lace dress from Yves Saint Laurent, danced the night away with friends from both sides of the Atlantic. Her sister, Lady Georgina Welles, who is studying architecture at Bristol University, was also looking quite lovely in her red Emanuel crinoline, and their brother, the Viscount Hadleigh, was turning all heads in a genuine Victorian tailcoat. Other members of the family present included Mr and Mrs Praeger Senior, Mr 'Baby' and Mrs Mary Rose Praeger and their children Mr Frederick Praeger and Mr Kendrick Praeger and Miss Melissa Praeger, a delightfully pretty and well-mannered young girl who told me she hopes to train as a dancer when she is a little older at New York's Juillard school. All in all it was a wonderful evening and I met many friends, both old and new.

It had indeed been a wonderful evening; everybody said so. Alexander had appeared genuinely to enjoy himself, and had even danced several times, twice with Mary Rose, albeit with a slightly distant expression; Baby, who had been subdued but cheerful, had danced every dance, mostly with friends of Charlotte and Georgina; Georgina's new boyfriend, a fellow architect called Simon Cunningham, told her he had never known what love meant until he had seen her standing on the steps of Hartest in her red dress; Melissa was invited to go upstairs with at least five boys and refused all of them; and even Freddy appeared to be enjoying himself and became very slightly tipsy on the excellent Bollinger which Fred III had insisted on supplying in excessive quantities for the occasion.

'I want my favourite grandchild to be launched on her adult life in style,' he wrote to Alexander when he accepted his invitation to the ball, 'and it can be one of my presents to her. I know you farmers are having a hard time of it.'

And Max, who had behaved perfectly and never left the dance floor for long enough (in his own words) to smoke a joint, get drunk, or get anyone's knickers anywhere near down, had hated every minute of it. He hated everything these days; he was bored, lonely and frustrated and he couldn't see what was to become of him. He had scraped through his O levels and got five C grades; he had no interest in taking his academic career any further, and very little interest in doing anything at all.

Having two brilliant sisters who knew exactly where they were going made it worse, of course: Georgina had gone through a bad patch briefly when she had been expelled from her school, but she was doing extremely well now with her architecture, and of course Charlotte, bloody Charlotte, was doing wonderfully as always, with her fantastic future laid out before her, and all she had to do was simply step into it and reap the rewards.

Max was very fond of Georgina, but he found Charlotte hard to love. She was so bossy, so sure of herself, so permanently in the right. He wondered if she had ever been to bed with anyone. Presumably she had, she was twenty-one years old, but it was almost impossible to imagine. Max cheered himself up briefly, as he watched Charlotte dancing (she even seemed to do that better than anyone else), picturing her having sex with someone: telling them exactly what to do, how to do it, how long to take over it, when to finish, and what to say when it was all over. And God help the guy if he didn't quite deliver to her brief. He knew that some people thought she was very sexy, but Max couldn't see it. Too confident, too self-contained. Georgina, now she was gorgeous. She radiated sexiness, although in a very off-beat way. She was a bit skinny for his personal taste, but she had that kind of frail look about her, and a sort of – what? A restless quality that was very attractive. If she wasn't his sister he could really fancy her. Max sighed, remembering, as he did possibly a dozen times a day, always freshly painfully, that she was not his sister. Or not entirely.

He was still finding it almost impossible to come to terms with the news about his parenthood. The shock he had experienced when Charlotte had told him, in her brisk, matter-of-fact manner, as if she was giving him some kind of medicine that he needed, had been horrible. For weeks he had not slept properly. He would wake up two or three times a night, feeling afraid, lost, in some sort of swirling nightmare. It was as if all the security, all the love he had been surrounded by through his childhood had been taken away from him, and he was totally alone in the world.

He thought of the mother he had known and loved so much, whose favourite he had been, and it was as if she had never existed. She died for Max not that night of the car crash on the M4 but in the lounge of the hotel in Ireland, while Charlotte told him that Alexander was not his father. He had cut her out of his life from that moment, determinedly not thinking about her, struggling to wipe out even the smallest memory of her. He had taken her photograph from the frame by his bed, and torn it up; he had ripped snapshots of her out of his photograph albums; he had thrown away all the letters she had sent him, and that he had kept since he was eight years old; and he had sold, in an act that had hurt him horribly, the gold watch she had given him for his twelfth birthday, and the gold cufflinks she had given him when he had gone to Eton. He had taken them to a dealer in Swindon and accepted the absurdly low price the man offered without a moment's argument and then persuaded Tallow to put the money on a horse for him. The horse had obligingly lost and he had seen that as a fitting end to his mother's gifts to him.

And then he was estranged from his father; they communicated as little as possible, barely polite strangers. Max found it hard to explain to himself, let alone anyone else, the hostility he felt towards Alexander. He knew he should be feeling, as the girls did, sympathy, tenderness, loyalty. Instead he felt contempt and a strong sense that Alexander was to blame. If your wife was sleeping around, you put a stop to it; you didn't endure it, bring up her illegitimate children, continue to protest that you loved her. It was all so bizarre, so ugly: the mystery of it haunted Max.

He would have liked to talk to the others about it, but he couldn't; something stopped him. He didn't want them to know how badly it hurt, how unbearable he found it. He preferred to present his careless, tough front, and try to believe in that himself. He had spoken the truth when he had said he had got expelled from Eton on purpose; he had done it partly because it seemed suddenly and unbearably claustrophobic and partly to hurt Alexander. He wanted to reject everything to do with him.

Except, as he had said to Charlotte, his inheritance. For some perverse reason, Max was very determined to make sure he stayed the heir to Hartest. He didn't feel about it the way his father did, always drooling over it, and Georgina too, but he did like it: it had style, and Max liked style. And he liked privilege too, and status; and even more he liked money. There was no way he was going to lose all that, just because he was, strictly speaking, illegitimate. It was that word that hurt Max most. Illegitimate. Every time it entered his head, it was like a physical pain.

It was hurting even during Charlotte's birthday ball. He had set it aside determinedly and went and asked Melissa to dance with him. She was clasped rather tightly in the arms of a handsome boy, but she promptly disentangled herself the moment she heard Max's voice. Melissa's adoration of Max was a joke in the family, but Max found it oddly comforting.

The dance finally wound up at four; the family regrouped for brunch at noon next day and sat discussing it over croissants, scrambled eggs and a great many cups of strong coffee.

'What a charming man your neighbour Mr Dunbar is,' said Mary Rose to Alexander. 'I was telling him about my book on eighteenth-century watercolours and he seemed extremely interested.'

'I didn't think old Martin knew about anything except horses,' said Max, 'he certainly married one. The only thing missing last night was the nosebag.'

'Don't be rude, Max,' said Alexander. 'Catriona is a very nice woman and she was extremely kind to me – to all of us – when your mother died.'

Max scowled at him. Georgina leapt into the silence, rather uncharacteristically: 'Martin is amazingly knowledgeable about all sorts of funny things,' she said, 'I often talk to him about houses and things, he really likes them. He loves Hartest.'

'Well you'd think he might have found somewhere a bit nicer to live himself,' said Charlotte, 'that house of theirs is a horror. Inside as well as out.'

'Yes, well not everyone is born with a silver stately home in their mouth,' said Max, who had actually often remarked on the ugliness of the small 1920s farmhouse the Dunbars lived in, but would have argued that black was white and then that it was black again if Charlotte had made a statement to the contrary.

'I like it,' said Georgina staunchly, 'it's homely and cosy. And I like them both very much. Especially Martin. He's so gentle.'

'Charlotte,' said Melissa, who was growing bored with the conversation, 'Charlotte, who was that perfectly dreamy black boy you were dancing with such a lot? I tried and tried to get to meet him, but he was always dancing.'

'Oh, that's Hamish,' said Charlotte. 'Hamish Mabele.'

'He didn't look like a Hamish,' said Melissa.

'Well he is. His father is a king somewhere in middle Africa, and he was at Cambridge and he became very keen on Scottish dancing, joined the Muckleflugga which is a club and when his first son was born he gave him a Scottish name. I think there's even a Mabele tartan.'

'Golly,' said Melissa, 'I'd like to see him in a kilt. Or better still without a kilt.'

'Melissa, do be quiet,' said Mary Rose.

'A prince!' said Betsey. 'Well that was one I missed.'

Betsey had had a particularly good time; she had met, as she told them completely unabashed, three baronets, a countess and a duchess. 'And she, the Duchess that is, told me she had had dinner with Princess Diana last week, and that girl is just darling apparently, so shy and natural.'

'And is Prince Charles darling too?' inquired Fred mildly, winking at Charlotte.

'Well I'm sure he is,' said Betsey.

'He's very nice indeed,' said Simon Cunningham, who was eager to impress anyone to do with Georgina, 'my father is an artist and had a painting in this year's Academy, and I met Prince Charles at the Private View. He's charming, very gentle and courteous. You'd like him, I know. Maybe next year you should come, I'm sure we could arrange a ticket for you.'

'Oh God,' said Fred, 'you've done it now, Simon. She'll be putting in calls to you twice a day for the next twelve months, reminding you.'

Betsey looked hurt; Max, who was very fond of his grandmother, went over to her and put his arms round her shoulders.

'I think Prince Charles would be really lucky to meet you,' he said.

'Me too,' said Baby, who had been very quiet right through the meal. 'Look, I'm sorry to break up the party, but I have to leave you for a while. I have a meeting in London this afternoon.'

'You do?' said Fred. 'Who with?'

His voice was mildly hectoring; Max noticed that Baby stiffened suddenly, shot him a look of great distaste.

'A guy from Hambros,' he said. 'Things are very interesting over here at the moment. Something he refers to as Big Bang is on the horizon.'

'What's Big Bang?' said Max. 'Sounds like fun.'

Baby laughed. 'Fraid not. It's what's going to happen in 1986, when the fixed commission system on the Stock Exchange here ends. It's just been announced by Cecil Parkinson in the House of Commons, apparently. The old-fashioned brokers will lose their monopoly to buy and sell shares and it'll be a free-for-all. More like what we have at home. Very exciting. I want to hear more about it.'

'Oh really?' said Fred. 'You must tell me more about your plans.'
Again the hectoring voice.

'I don't have any plans,' said Baby. He looked very sombre suddenly.
'Unfortunately. Anyway, I'm off. Charlotte darling, could I borrow
your car to drive to the station? I may be quite late back.'

'Of course you can,' said Charlotte. 'Just remember it's only a Mini
now, Uncle Baby, not one of your Mustangs or Porsches.'

Bossy cow, thought Max.

'Max, telephone.' Georgina's voice pierced his sleep; he had sat down by
the fire in the library after lunch and drifted off. I must be getting old, he
thought.

'I'm asleep. Who is it?'

'Some man.'

'I'm still asleep.'

'Don't be so lazy.'

'Georgina, take his number, there's an angel. I'll call him back.'

'Oh, all right.'

'It was some photographer guy,' said Georgina, sitting down on the
footstool by his chair. 'Apparently one of the press photographers at the
dance told him to ring you.'

'Oh for God's sake. I don't want to buy any of his rotten pictures.'

'I don't think he wants you to. He wants to talk to you. Do, Max, he
sounded really nice. Here's the number.'

'I'll call him,' said Melissa brightly, 'I love photographers. They're so
sexy.'

'Melissa, you think milkmen are sexy, and solicitors, and window
cleaners and accountants and art historians and insurance salesmen,' said
Charlotte, laughing. She was sitting on one of the windowseats, reading.
'Go on, Max, ring the guy up. I'm curious.'

'OK, I will. Later. I have some serious revision to do.'

'Good God,' said Georgina, 'what on earth about?'

'The female anatomy. I'm going riding with Sarah Elliott.'

'You're disgusting,' said Georgina.

'Yes, I know.'

He phoned the number while everyone was having tea; he went back into
the dining room doing an exaggerated, campish walk, trying not to look
as excited as he felt.

'Hey, guess what? He was a fashion photographer. He wants to take some pictures of me. He says I have – wait for it, everyone – a great look. What do you think about that?'

'I think it makes me feel sick,' said Georgina. 'You're not going, I hope.'

'Of course I am. Why not?'

'Oh Max, really,' said Charlotte. 'He's probably some social-climbing gay who fancies you.'

Max, who had actually only been half serious about going to see the photographer, promptly decided nothing would stop him.

'You're such a snob, Charlotte,' he said.

'And you're not, I suppose,' said Charlotte. 'Max, you're not serious about this, are you? Whatever do you think Daddy would say?'

'I couldn't care less about what he'd say,' said Max.

He never called Alexander anything these days unless he had to.

The photographer, whose name was Joe Jones, was out when Max turned up at his Covent Garden studio next day. A girl dressed entirely in black with white spiky hair and long green fingernails looked up coolly from reading *The Face* when he walked in.

'Yes?'

'I've come to see Mr Jones,' said Max.

'What for?'

'To have some pictures done.'

'Are you a model?'

'Not yet.' Max gave her his most dazzling smile; she met it blankly.

'Who's your agent?'

'I haven't got one.'

'I should get one if I were you.'

She went back to her magazine.

Max was not used to this kind of treatment.

'Look,' he said, 'I don't have a great deal of time.'

She shrugged.

'I can't conjure him out of the blue for you.'

'But didn't he say I was coming?'

'No. Not that I remember.' The magazine had re-engaged her interest. Max began to feel irritated.

'There must be somewhere you can contact him.'

'No, there isn't. He's on location.'

'What's that?'

The girl looked up again. Her blank brown eyes flicked briefly and contemptuously over Max. 'It's out,' she said, 'out working.'

'I think,' said Max, 'you should take my name. And tell him I came.'

And if he wants to see me he can contact me. I really don't have the time to hang around here all afternoon.'

She shrugged. 'Fine.'

'Well shall I give you my name?'

'If you like.'

'It's Max Hadleigh,' said Max. 'Viscount Hadleigh actually,' he added, thinking to impress. It was a very big mistake.

'Oh really?' she said, and for a moment there was some emotion behind her eyes and her lips twitched. 'My goodness. Do I curtsey?'

'I must say,' said Max, 'I think you're one of the rudest people I've ever met.'

'I can live with that,' she said. 'Cheers. I'll tell him you came.'

Max was just slamming the door behind him when a cheerful-looking young man, dressed in jeans and with a shock of untidy black hair, pushed past him. He was laden with bags and a large silver umbrella. Max scowled at him and walked away; thirty seconds later he heard a shout: 'Hey! If you're Max, come back.'

Max turned; it was the cheerful-looking man.

'Are you Joe Jones?'

'Yup. Sorry I was out.'

'That's OK. Your secretary wasn't exactly helpful.'

'Who, Sula? Oh, she's OK. Looks after me all right. Look, stay there, and I'll do some shots now in the street. Then I'll do a few in the studio.'

'Well, I don't know if I've got time now,' said Max. He was still feeling sulky.

Joe Jones looked at him and grinned. 'If you're going to model,' he said, 'you're going to have to do an awful lot of hanging around. You'd best start getting used to it. Stay there, I'll get my camera.'

They went out into the designer-styled streets and patios of Covent Garden. Joe told Max to lean against a pillar in one of the arcades, and shot off a roll of film there; he did another one of him standing in the middle of some stalls; yet another with the buskers as a background, and then a final roll in front of the Opera House. Some Japanese tourists formed a small crowd, following them round, giggling, pointing, smiling at Max.

'Ignore them,' said Joe.

'They don't bother me,' said Max, and it was true. He was enjoying himself more than he could remember for a long time, moving easily and naturally from one frame to the next, gazing into the camera as if it was some very pretty girl. 'We should do a shot with them. They're half my size. It'd look great.'

Joe told him he was a cocky little bugger and did the shot.

'Great,' he said. 'Now then, let's go into the studio. Did you bring anything else to wear?'

'No, I didn't. Sorry.'

'That's OK. You look all right. And they're only tests. But if they turn out all right, could you work tomorrow? I have a job to do for the *Evening Standard* and the guy I'd booked has gone sick. I really need someone.'

Max thought fast. Tomorrow he was supposed to be going for an interview at the sixth-form college in Swindon. But he had no intention of going there. There was no point even turning up.

'Sure,' he said.

Joe rang him at nine that night.

'They're great. You look terrific. Be at the studio by eight, OK?'

'I don't think I can,' said Max.

'Why the fuck not? You said you could work.'

'Well, I'm in the country. I don't think I can get up to London by eight.'

'Haven't you got a car?'

'Well – yes.'

'Well get your arse into it and drive it here. OK?'

'Yes, OK.'

Max put the phone down. He would take Georgina's car. She had gone off for two days with Simon. OK, so he hadn't passed his test. He wouldn't get caught. And if he did, his father would bail him out. Or rather, he thought, with the now familiar slightly nauseated feeling, the man who was supposed to be his father. It'd be a good laugh. And he'd earn – what was it Joe had said – a hundred pounds? He could use a hundred pounds. Money for old rope. Or rather new dope, Max thought, smiling at his own wit. Much more rewarding than talking to some moron about what A levels he could do.

No one in the family saw the pictures in the *Standard*, being very much ensconced in the country that week, but one of Nanny's nieces who lived in Bromley had recognized Max and sent the paper to Nanny with a note saying how excited they all must be.

Nanny looked at the three pictures of Max, wearing white tie and tails, helping various pretty girls out of punts. The article was about dresses to wear at balls which, the writer said, were making a comeback for the very young. She didn't think Alexander would be in the least excited, except in a manner rather different from the one her niece had meant. She put the pictures in her pocket and went to find Max, who was ostensibly studying in the library and was actually reading *The Sun*.

'I've got some pictures of you,' she said briefly.

'Oh Nanny, have you? Let me guess. When I was four or when I was five?'

'When you were sixteen.'

Max looked at her face. 'Oh.'

'Yes, oh.'

'Well, let me see them. Do I look nice?'

'You look all right. I suppose that was the day you took Georgina's car?'

'Well – sort of, yes. How did you know?'

'I'm only seventy-two,' said Nanny.

'Ah,' said Max. 'Yes, I see.'

'You're a fool, Maximilian. You missed your interview, didn't you? What are you going to do if you don't get into college? Go into that the deal, I suppose?'

'The dole, Nanny. No, I'll do more of this,' said Max, gazing enraptured at himself. 'I look older, don't I?'

He did; he gazed moodily out of the page, his blond hair slicked back from his elegant, rather bony young face. He looked very tall and slightly more heavily built than he actually was. 'Joe said it would put half a stone on me.'

'Who's Joe?'

'The photographer.'

'I see. Well it's no job for someone like you, Maximilian.'

'But Nanny,' said Max, looking at her oddly, 'I don't think we can be sure about that. Can we? It might be exactly the job for someone like me. Um – you won't show them to Dad, will you?'

'I will,' said Nanny, 'if you don't rearrange that interview. You're lucky no one else spotted you. Including the police on the motorway,' she added grimly.

'I suppose so. All right, Nanny. From this moment forward, I'll slave night and day. Would you like to be my agent? You can have twenty per cent of everything I earn.'

'It wouldn't be enough,' said Nanny. For once her meaning was rather clear. 'Anyway, how much money did you get for those pictures?'

'A hundred pounds,' said Max.

'That's much too much,' said Nanny, 'I hope you're going to invest it properly, Maximilian, not waste it.'

'No, I'm not going to waste it,' said Max. 'I'm going to buy an air ticket to New York with it.'

The day after the pictures had appeared in the *Standard*, Dick Kreis had called from Models One in London.

'Come and see me. I'm starting a men's agency here. I think we might be interested in you.'

'Sure,' said Max. 'I'll be in town tomorrow.'

'Good. Do you have any shots, other than those in the *Standard*?'

'No, I'm afraid I don't. But Joe Jones has a few. Some tests he did.'

He was learning the jargon already.

Dick Kreis was a thoughtful, intelligent man; Max liked him.

'I think we can talk business. Are you readily available for work?'

'Oh yes.'

'Have you left school?'

'Er – yes.'

'Not going back to do any more exams? Or to university?'

'Nope.'

'Would your parents be happy about you modelling?'

'My mother's dead.'

'I'm sorry. And your father?'

'No, he thinks it's a great idea.'

'I'd like to talk to him, really. As you're so young.'

'Well, he's away at the moment. On a business trip.'

'OK. Ask him to call me when he gets back, OK?'

'Yes, I will.'

'Now then. We'll take twenty per cent of your earnings. If you're desperate for cash until you get going, we'll take five per cent and you can repay us later. Advertising rates are four hundred to five hundred pounds a day. Editorial by arrangement. If it's *Vogue* or *Harpers & Queen* it's something ridiculous. Maybe forty pounds a day. You're working for the honour of it. The others around twenty pounds an hour. It's pathetic, but it gets your face known.' It didn't sound too pathetic to Max. 'Now you'll need a good basic wardrobe. A dark suit. Black shoes, black socks, dinner jacket, some white and blue shirts, an assortment of ties. Can you manage that?'

'Yes.'

'You'll need to get some cards done.'

'Cards?'

'Yes. With several pictures on them. We'll get that done, dock it off your money. It'll also say your name and your measurements. Anything you can do that might be interesting? Do you ride or anything?'

'Yes, I can ride.'

'Well?' Dick had been assured by countless limp-wristed young men that they could ride; a swift encounter with anything more spirited than a seaside donkey had them whimpering back to him.

'I hunt a bit,' said Max.

'Fine. Anything else? Unusual, that is?'

'I can tap dance.'

'Oh really? Who taught you that?'

'My mother.'

'She sounds like a fun lady.'

'She was OK,' said Max briefly.

'Right. You'll have to do the rounds with your book.'

'What book?'

'The book with your pictures in. We get prints made of any particularly good shots, tearouts from the magazines, that sort of thing. And you'll have to get some test shots done straight away. I'll send you over to Rich Fuller later this morning. He does a lot of our tests. Got any other clothes with you?'

'No. Sorry.'

'Well, maybe you'd better do your tests another day. How's your physique?'

'Pretty weedy,' said Max.

'Well, never mind. You're young. And because of that you'll get mostly fashion work for now anyway. It's not big money, but it'll teach you. The odd commercial, probably. And maybe some shows.'

'Shows?'

'Fashion shows.'

'Oh,' said Max, 'I don't think I'd like that.'

'I'd advise you to do it,' said Dick lightly, 'if you're going to do well in this game, I'd advise you to do everything you can. Learn. It would probably be abroad, rather than here. Milan. Paris.'

'Oh, well that'd be OK,' said Max hastily.

'Got a passport?'

'Of course.' Max was surprised.

'Well, lots of boys your age don't have. Look, I'll fix now for you to see Rich one day next week.'

Rich Fuller had taken one look at Max and recognized that this was more than a few fashion shots, a couple of commercials; this was a whole new trend. What Max had, what Rich saw, gazing at him out of the developing tray in his darkroom on a few sheets of contact prints, was something exciting, something rare, an original quality, one that had not been around before. He was good-looking, he was photogenic, he was graceful and he wore clothes well, but so did dozens, maybe hundreds of boys. What was important was the quality he projected, an extraordinary combination of class and – Rich groped in his head for the right word –

riffraff. Sexy riffraff. Max was a high-born slut. He stood there, arrogant, well bred – and patently available. For sale, and quite cheaply for sale, to anyone who engaged his sexual interest. Just take the trouble to intrigue me, arouse me, said those rather contemptuous, just slightly blank large eyes, that full, frankly sulky mouth, and I'm your man. It was a look that was not so much about sex as about discovering sex: raw, hungry, curious. It would sell anything, that look: clothes, products, moods; but most of it would sell Max. To the very highest bidders.

Rich picked up the phone and called Dick Kreis. 'This boy is going to be huge,' he said.

Max was packing to go to New York when Dick Kreis rang.

'These shots are quite good,' he said, 'I can have you working soon, I think. Can you start right away? Going to see people and so on?'

'Well,' said Max, 'I'm going to the States for a couple of weeks at the beginning of September. But after that I'm free.'

'Good. Well, you won't get much work now anyway. It's very dead in August. But you may as well start doing the rounds. No other plans? Not going to college or anything?'

'No,' said Max. 'Nothing.'

'Fine. What are you going to be doing in the States?'

'Oh,' said Max, 'nothing much. Just staying with my grandmother.'

'Grandma, can I ask you some questions about Mummy?' Max sat looking very soberly, very respectfully, at Betsey; they were on their own in her small upstairs sitting room at East 80th Street, after Fred III had left for the bank.

'Darling, of course you can. There's nothing I like better than talking about her. It brings her back somehow.' Betsey forced a bright little smile. 'What sort of things?'

'Oh, you know. First of all I'd like to know what she was like as a little girl.'

'Oh well, now that's easy. She was just the most darling little girl. So beautiful. But always in trouble.'

'Oh,' said Max, 'so I get it from her. Being so naughty.'

'Well maybe you do, dear. But it wasn't so much that she was naughty, just that she always got caught. And your Uncle Baby just never did somehow. And she was very brave, she used to stand up to your grandfather. I probably shouldn't say this, but he was a little hard on her. And she tried so much to be good, too, she worked so hard, and of course was very very good at her dancing, and in fact she wanted to go on the stage, just as Melissa does, only of course she was a very different

292

personality from Melissa, less – confident. Now did I ever tell you about the time she ran away and – ' Her voice poured on, warm, affectionate, alive; Max listened, patiently bored. He had not the slightest interest in his mother as a child. Almost half an hour had gone by and they had reached her presentation as a debutante when he was able, with grace, to interrupt.

'She sounds as if she was really fun. I wish I'd known her then. And the other thing I'm interested in is her work. Because, you know, I did wonder about doing something a bit similar myself.'

'Did you, dear?' Betsey was surprised; Max had never seemed in the least artistic. 'Well, she didn't start that, you know, until a while after she left college.'

'Oh really? And do you know who trained her, who she worked with, that sort of thing?'

'Well it's a long time ago, Max, of course. I don't remember all the names. She didn't go to college, she started as an apprentice to a Mrs – what was her name? Adamson, that's right. Oh, she was a nice woman, and from one of the very best families, that was how she got so much work of course, people knew they could trust her. And she knew Virginia was also from the same type of background, it's very important, you know. So that was how it began. I remember the very first job that Mrs Adamson let her do, it was an apartment on Sutton Place and she had to do the nursery, and she did such a beautiful job . . .'

'Yes, I'm sure she did,' said Max. He was beginning to wonder how much more of this he could take. 'Er – did she work from this house ever? Might she have had an address book, or something like that, that I could find some names in?'

'No, darling. She kept all her books and files in England with her. I do know that. And more recently, she worked from hotels. She said she needed to feel really independent.' Betsey's voice sounded strained; she had obviously found this hurtful. 'It was sad, because I always found her work so interesting, and I loved to hear about it, make little suggestions. You know.' Max tried to look sympathetic. He could see exactly why Virginia had wanted to work from her hotel room.

God, this was boring. But he did have to find out. He had to know what his mother had been doing in the spring of 1966. Who she had been seeing. She had been in New York – or at least in America, on an extended business trip. Max did know that. He had been through the diaries. As his sister had before him.

'So – who were her friends in New York? I somehow feel – ' he hesitated carefully – 'I sort of feel I would know her better if I knew her friends. I'm trying to bring her to life for myself. If you see what I

293

mean. Men, as well as women,' he added, as casually as he could manage it.

Betsey thought for a bit. Then she said, 'Well, there is someone who probably could help you. With learning about her work, as well. His name was – oh now, what was it, my goodness my memory is getting so bad. Just give me a moment, Max darling, would you – '

Max sat in an agony of frustration. He wanted to jump up and down and scream and he didn't even move in case he disturbed his grandmother's meandering train of thought. Here he was, maybe moments away from knowing who his father was, and the old bat couldn't remember his name. He fixed his concentration on the pattern of the carpet and waited.

Betsey suddenly leant forward and patted his hand, beaming at him triumphantly. 'Dusty. That's it. Dusty Winchester.' Even in his frenzy, Max found himself hoping to God he didn't have to have a father called Dusty. 'He used to say he was her rival, he's in the same business, you see, but it was only a little joke, he was in it in a much bigger way than her, but he helped her endlessly. They were very fond of each other. They used to skate together at the Rockefeller Center. And go to Radio City a lot. They both loved that kind of thing. He was a little strange, but very nice.'

It didn't sound right to Max. He wasn't sure why even, but it just didn't. He hoped not. He certainly didn't want to be the son of someone a little strange who liked ice skating. But clearly the guy had to be seen. And at least he could give him some more clues.

He put off phoning Dusty Winchester straight away. It was too scary. He was surprised how scared he was. He seemed to be getting deeper and deeper into his own nightmares. He would do it tomorrow. But he had had to get away from Betsey. She was going to drive him crazy. He had something else important to do anyway. And it would distract him, cheer him up. He wanted to visit a New York model agency. It had been Dick Kreis's idea.

'Go to Zoli,' he had said, 'it's the hottest agency in New York at the moment. They probably won't use you, but you never know. It's all experience.'

Max was confident that they would use him. Modelling was just the biggest joy ride he had ever known.

Zoli were polite, but noncommittal. They told Max his look was a little young for New York: 'You'd do better on the West Coast. Leave your card, we'll call you. But probably not yet.'

Max was taken aback; he was used to a warmer reception. Although the few London editors and art directors he had visited before he left for New York had also tended to tell him he was a little young, they had been polite to him, and he had had a couple of bookings from *The Face* and *Blitz*, and had a provisional put on him for a commercial for a motor bike. *Vogue* had told him to come back in three months when they were doing a feature on the new young look in Men in Vogue; *You* magazine had promised him a job in one of their Christmas issues. He had grown confident very fast; now here were these arrogant Yanks telling him he hadn't got what it took.

'Sorry,' he said, 'I have to be back in London in a fortnight. You won't get me.'

'We'll live,' said the girl who had looked at his book.

It wasn't easy to get through to Dusty Winchester. The first time he got a secretary, who made him feel he was unbelievably privileged even to be on Mr Winchester's telephone line; she took his number and said she would certainly tell Mr Winchester he had called, but he was terribly busy, and he already had three calls waiting and was late for an appointment. Maybe he could call back at five?

Max called back at five, and got a male voice. 'Dusty Winchester,' it said, in a slightly reverent tone.

'Mr Winchester, my name is Max – '

'Oh no, this is not he,' said the voice, sounding shocked. 'This is one of Mr Winchester's assistants. May I take a message?'

'Well I was told to call him at five,' said Max, 'and – '

'He's in a meeting,' said the voice. 'Could you call back at six?'

'Yes, all right,' said Max tiredly.

At six he got a different male voice.

'Mr Winchester?'

'No, I'm sorry. This is one of Mr Winchester's assistants. May I ask who's calling?'

'My name is Max Hadleigh. My mother – '

'I'm terribly sorry but Mr Winchester is in a meeting right now. I can't possibly disturb him. You could call back tomorrow.'

'At what time?'

'Well, he gets in around nine. You could call then.'

'Yes but,' said Max, trying to keep calm, 'I was told to call at five and at six. I never seem to be able to catch him. Could you ask him to call me?'

'Well I could *ask* him,' said the voice, making it very plain that it was an extremely foolish idea, 'but you'd be better calling him. He's *very* busy.'

'Yes, but I do need to speak to him quite urgently,' said Max. He was beginning to feel desperate.

'Well I told you,' said the voice, sounding more disdainful than ever, 'you can call at nine.'

'Will he definitely be there?'

'Well obviously I can't say *definitely*. He should be. I can't do any more than that.'

'Thanks a lot,' said Max, slamming the phone down.

He went reluctantly to dinner with his cousins and Baby and Mary Rose; it was hard to imagine what he could have wanted to do less. In the event, it was fun. Baby was pathetically pleased to see him, and poured a great deal of very nice wine into him, Melissa was adoring, Kendrick was languidly funny, and Freddy was out. Max, who understood, rather better than Charlotte appeared to, Freddy's hostility towards all of them these days, was sympathetic to his absence. He felt he would have done just the same. Mary Rose was tired and asked to be excused soon after dinner; the four of them played Liar Dice for a while, which Max won, and then made reckless by the wine, he told them about his problems getting through to Dusty Winchester.

'Whatever do you want to talk to that old tart about?' said Baby.

'Oh – Grandmama said he was a great friend of Mummy's and he might be able to help me. I'm thinking of going into that field,' said Max.

'Really? You must be mad. Anyway, pull rank,' said Baby. 'He'll be on the line before you can say viscount.'

Max didn't like the old tart idea too much, indeed it haunted his dreams that night, but at nine o'clock sharp he took Baby's advice.

'Good morning,' he said to the first reverent voice. 'This is the Viscount Hadleigh calling. I'd like to speak to Mr Winchester urgently, please.'

Dusty Winchester was on the phone in seconds.

'Max! It's so good to meet you. Your mother talked about you so much. She was so proud of you. Come on in and sit down.'

Dusty Winchester came across his black and white Japanoiserie-styled office, holding out his hand to Max. He was tall, with dark, close-cropped hair and piercingly blue eyes. He was dressed entirely in white, white linen suit, white silk shirt, white leather shoes; only his tie, brilliant peacock blue, patterned abstractly in white, broke the monotony. Even his watch, diamond-studded by Cartier, had a white strap. Max smiled at him, charmed, while recognizing with an instinct finely honed in the bedrooms and studios of Eton that Dusty Winchester clearly did not have the right sexual inclinations to be father to anyone.

'How do you do, Mr Winchester. It's very good of you to see me, sir.'

Nothing sophisticated New Yorkers liked better than old-fashioned English manners.

'Not at all, Max, not at all. Would you like coffee? Coke? I am having rosehip tea, would you like to try that? It's very nice.'

'Oh I'll try that,' said Max. 'I like funny teas and things. My father has a whole armoury of them at home at Hartest.'

'Oh, that house!' said Dusty. 'Such a lovely, lovely thing. Your mother was always promising to ask me over, and then cancelling me at the last minute. There was one ball I was actually going to attend, but then Suky, that's my wife, wasn't well at the last minute, so we couldn't go.'

Max's confidence about Dusty Winchester's inclinations was only slightly shaken by the revelation about Suky; he made a note to ask Melissa if such things were common in New York. Melissa was a powerhouse of knowledge about social mores, far in advance of her years. He returned to the subject of Hartest.

'Yes,' he said, 'it is very beautiful. You really should come and see it. I know my father would be delighted to show it to you. He loves it more than anything in the world, you know. Far more than any of us.'

He expected the usual protestations, but they didn't come.

'Yes,' said Dusty, and his voice was serious, even slightly sad, 'yes, I know, that's so.'

Max looked at him, startled; the angular face smiled quickly, carefully.

'Oh, I'm sorry, Max. Talking about your mother does make me sad. Terribly sad. I miss her. I miss her so much.'

'Tell me about her,' said Max. 'I mean, tell me what she was like as a friend. You see –' he had his speech word-perfect now, it did seem to go down awfully well – 'I was so young when she died, still a little boy, and I'm trying to bring her alive as she might have been if I'd grown up, been a little older.'

'Well, that's very charming. Very charming.' Dusty Winchester smiled and picked up the large black mirror that served as tea tray in his office. 'Max, why don't we go and sit on the balcony? It's a lovely day, and the view of the park is just gorgeous.'

There were black canvas chairs on the balcony; he motioned Max towards one and climbed himself into a black hammock, strung between two chrome poles. He swung there gently, sipping his tea and gazing out over Central Park. Then he looked at Max.

'I really loved your mother,' he said quietly. 'Very very much. We were so close. She was such fun, Max, so brilliant and so warm.'

'Yes, I know,' said Max, 'I do remember that.' In fact, Dusty's remarks puzzled him; the mother he remembered had been cool, almost distant. Warmth had been Alexander's domain.

'And she was such a good friend. So thoughtful. We were so close, she and I. So very close. I have to tell you,' he added, smiling conspiratorially at Max, 'that Suky was a little jealous of your mother. I had to be careful, after my marriage, not to be quite so overt in my friendship with her. Which was difficult. I came to rely on her greatly. There was nothing we didn't talk about. Absolutely nothing.'

Max sat looking at him politely. This was a lot more interesting than Betsey's reminiscences.

'Your mother was a lovely lady. Beautiful. And such fun. Oh we had such fun together. We both adored going to Radio City, and we used to sneak off there sometimes together. And we went to dance classes, tap dance classes together, that was tremendous. She was very much better than I was, of course, she had such a talent for it, I often said to her that if she hadn't married your father, become the Countess, she could have earned her living as a dancer.'

'But then,' said Max, smiling, leaning back, crossing his long legs, aware of Dusty's eyes, lingering, however briefly, on his crotch, 'then she wouldn't have had me. Or the others. And been the Countess. She liked being a countess, you know. Everyone said so.'

'Indeed she did. And it became her. She was very aristocratic. Everyone said she was more English than the English in the end.'

'Really? Where did they say that?'

'Oh, everywhere,' said Dusty vaguely. 'And yes, she did like it. But – well, it wasn't entirely easy for her.'

'Really?' said Max. The guy was obviously more loony than he'd thought. 'In what way? It seemed pretty nice to me. Having Hartest, and the title, and everything.'

'Yes of course,' said Dusty. He seemed to consciously pull himself together again, 'But I always felt there was such a lot of sadness in her. She would never talk about herself very much. She was very – brave.'

He looked up irritably as the secretary, a surprisingly large, flashy creature with an immense bosom, came out to the balcony. 'Yes, Irene dear, what is it?'

'Dusty, Mrs Gershman is here. I don't think we should keep her waiting.'

'Can't Noel see her?'

'She won't see him. She says only you will do.'

'Oh. Oh well.' He sighed. 'Max, forgive me. I'm very busy as you can see. If you want to talk some more, we could have dinner next week some time. How would that be?'

'I won't be here,' said Max, 'I have to go back to England. But maybe later in the year.'

'That would be very nice.'

'Er – Mr Winchester?'

'Yes, Max.'

'Is there anyone else you think might be able to talk to me about her? Bring her alive?'

'Why not talk to Michael Halston? He was a good friend, too, and he knows just about everybody anybody ever knew. He was the gossip writer on the New York *Mail*, you know. He isn't there any longer, he's gone out to live in the depths of Maine, but he'd love to talk to you, I'm sure.'

'Do you have a number for him?'

'Yes I do. Let me see now, here we are, Freeport 71234. Call him. And be sure to tell him Dusty says hallo.'

'OK, so what's this really all about?' Michael Halston looked at Max, a sharp amusement in his dark brown eyes.

'I told you,' said Max.

'Yes, I know what you told me, and it's the biggest load of hogwash I ever heard. You're playing for much higher stakes than trying to establish who your mother's friends were, and how they passed the time between breakfast and dinner. What do you want to know, Max, and why? If you tell me, I'll try and help you. If not, you can get right back on the train to New York City. I'm a busy man, and I don't like people trying to make a monkey out of me.'

'Well I –' Max looked at him thoughtfully. He quite liked Halston. He was tough, and he was shrewd, but he was straightforward. He wondered if he could trust him enough to tell him the whole story. Probably not. The man was a journalist. He might splash it all over the New York *Mail* or his new novel. He sighed.

'It's very difficult,' he said. 'I don't know what to do.'

Halston smiled. 'When you sighed then, and looked kind of baffled, you reminded me absolutely of your mother.'

Max started to smile back, and then to his absolute horror, felt his eyes fill with tears. Suddenly, sharply, he remembered his mother: and sitting there, in front of this stranger, he couldn't crush the memories any more the way he had been doing, they rushed in on him, like a physical force, he remembered her vividly, and he remembered her clearly all of a sudden, and truthfully; she ceased in that moment, for that moment, to be a hostile monster and became herself again, the way she had really looked and sounded, the way she had smiled at him when he was telling her something, stopped whatever she was doing and given him her full attention. The way she indicated the chair next to her at the table when Alexander was out and said, 'Be my dinner date tonight, Max,' and poured him a glass of watered-down wine even when he was quite little, and asked him if it was a good one. The way she always laughed at his stupid, puerile jokes, and the way she was never shocked at his bad reports, but would smile at him gently behind Alexander's back while he droned on and on about wasting his opportunities and his talents; the way she brought him clothes from London and New York and would always always know what he'd really like and what would suit him; the way she enjoyed the music he enjoyed, and never complained it was a dreadful noise, the way most mothers did.

They way she liked to tie his stock before he went hunting, and would pat his bottom and kiss him and say 'Don't ride too dangerously, Max' as he ran out to the stables; the way she sided with him, most unfairly, against the girls when they were all fighting, because she said he was outnumbered.

And the way he had been so proud of her, longing for her to come to school to pick him up because she was so much more beautiful, so much better dressed than all the other mothers; the way she drove her car, just a bit too fast, when they were alone together, the music playing terribly loud: 'I don't do this with anyone else, Max,' she would say, 'this is our fun, our secret.'

And he wondered if she had been driving too fast, playing the music terribly loudly the night she had died, and he remembered that the very last thing he had said to her was 'I might' when she had told him on the phone to be sure to let her know the very first exeat she could come and see him, because he had been so upset that she wouldn't come home to take him back to school.

And he remembered the dreadful, awful sound of the first clods of earth dropping on the coffin, from his father's hand, and the sensation he had experienced of being physically torn and twisted somewhere in the depths of his body, as he had watched it going into the ground, and he looked at Michael Halston and the great tears filled his eyes and spilled over, splashing down into the glass of beer he held in his hand.

'Hey,' said Michael Halston, 'hey, what did I say?'

'Nothing,' said Max. His lips were quivering and his voice sounded strangled and odd; he felt utterly humiliated. 'I'm sorry.'

'Max,' said Michael Halston. 'Don't apologize. I understand. I think. You've lost your mother. And you were right, you weren't very old. You must miss her like hell. And I brought her back for you rather painfully. I like it that you're sad. That you're crying. I like it much better than all that schmaltzy claptrap you were feeding me before.'

Max smiled at him rather shakily. 'Thank you. Yes, you're right. You did bring her back.' He got a handkerchief out of his pocket and blew his nose. 'That's better.'

'Finish your beer. Have another. Why don't we walk round the garden? I have some new neighbours, arrived just today.'

He led Max towards a wide stream that ran through the middle of his large lush garden; sitting on it, resplendently stupid, were a large Canadian goose and her five goslings.

'Aren't they great? I hope they stay. I had some ducklings earlier, but they left me.'

'Yes, they're very nice.' Max looked at him doubtfully. Halston was the epitome of smart town mouse doing some country visiting, with his close-cropped grey hair, his beige linen suit, his Piaget bracelet watch. 'I – wouldn't have thought you'd be interested in birds.'

'Max, after a life spent studying people's foolishness, greed and adultery in the fleshpots of the world's fleshiest city, I find birds ineffably charming.'

'It's a nice house,' said Max, looking back at the low white clapboard building, with its high, dormered roofs and great windows, open on four sides to the lush Maine countryside, 'I really like it.'

'Thank you. I do too. My ex-wife likes it so much she's considering coming back to live with me. I'm considering letting her. Come on, let's go and have some more beer, and you can tell me what's bothering you. Or not, as the case might be.

'Well you see,' said Max, feeling his way carefully, 'I think – well I know – that my parents' marriage wasn't quite – quite what it seemed.'

'You mean they weren't happy.'

'Well – yes.'

'Well, your mother certainly wasn't. She was a very tortured woman. Poor Virginia.'

'Tortured!' said Max bitterly. 'I don't know why everyone's so sorry for her. It's my father who was tortured. Not her.'

'What makes you think that?'

'Well – I happen to know she was – well, having affairs.' He suddenly looked up at Halston, horror in his eyes. 'I'm sorry. Did she – were you –'

'No we weren't and no she didn't. Although I have to tell you it was not for want of trying on my part. And maybe she had relationships and maybe she didn't, but she was not a promiscuous lady, Max. She was too serious for that, too fastidious. I never heard anybody speaking carelessly, disparagingly of her, ever, and I knew her a long time. Her reputation was immaculate.'

'But I –' Max sat staring at him. Halston seemed perfectly serious, to be telling the truth; he was not covering up for his mother in any way.

'But you what?'

301

'Oh – nothing. It's just that in England there's been a lot of gossip.'

'What sort of gossip?'

'Well that she had been sleeping around. Worse.'

'Really? In what way worse?'

'Oh – it doesn't matter.'

'Well,' said Michael Halston, 'there never was any here. Gossip, that is. Certainly not of a serious nature. And I can't believe that if your mother had been a seriously promiscuous woman, she would have confined her behaviour to England. Where she was far more likely to become notorious, where the talk would have mattered very much more.'

'Oh, I don't know,' said Max. He sounded sulky. 'I just don't know anything any more.'

'I don't suppose you've been able to confront your father with this? In any way?'

'Yes,' said Max. 'Yes I have as a matter of fact.'

He suddenly wanted Halston to understand that this was not mere gossip he had been listening to: that he was not simply idly curious, but that it mattered, that it hurt. That there was some reason for his inquiries. 'My father said that it was true. That she had had lovers. But he wouldn't tell me any more. And I have to know why. And I have to know who they were.'

'Why? You're only buying yourself a lot of grief. She's dead, Max. Let her be the woman you loved, you remembered.'

'But I don't know who I'm remembering!' said Max in a sudden agony of frustration. 'I don't know who that woman was. What she was really like.'

'Virginia was one of my dearest friends. I miss her sadly. She was a life-enhancer. Things were brighter, better when she was there. In spite of the sadness underneath.'

'Yes, well, she didn't do all that much life-enhancing for us,' said Max, 'she was always away.'

'Always?'

'Well a lot.'

'She needed to be away, Max. Not from you, but from the pressures at home. I only saw her in England twice, with your father, once at a party in London, once at a ball in the country. She was quite different. Tense, withdrawn. Rather brittle. She never asked me to the house. I think she felt she wanted to keep us, her New World friends as she called us, separate from her life there.'

'My father is a really good man,' said Max staunchly, realizing with a slight shock that he was thinking, albeit briefly, of Alexander as being truly his father, the friend in this enemy territory. 'He really is.'

'I'm sure. I liked him. He was charming and most courteous to me. Whatever was wrong with the marriage wasn't his fault. I'm not saying that. It was – well, the nearest you can get, I suppose, is chemistry. The wrong formula.'

'People say,' said Max carefully, 'that I look exactly like him.'

Halston looked at him thoughtfully. There was no trace of emotion in his dark brown eyes, other than a gentle interest.

'Yes,' he said, 'yes, I think you do. Exactly. It's all right, Max, I'm not about to start dissecting your parentage.'

Later, as they ate lunch, Michael said, 'I can give you a few names of people your mother saw quite a bit of here. Mostly in New York. And she had some good friends down in Florida Key West. There was one man in particular she was close to – ' he looked at Max carefully – 'called Tommy Soames-Maxwell.'

'Thank you,' said Max. 'You've been terribly kind.'

'My pleasure.' He looked at Max rather oddly. 'I'd go a bit easy if I were you,' he said, 'with these investigations of yours. They can't really help you very much. And they might even hurt.'

Chapter 23

Angie, 1983

Angie didn't quite know when it had happened, but she did want to get married. She couldn't work out why exactly; but she did. And she wanted to marry Baby. Maybe it was children she wanted.

It really irritated her, that she loved Baby so much. She would actually have given quite a lot to feel differently towards him. He had so many disadvantages. He was much older than she would have wished; she actually (and particularly as she had got a little older herself – she was thirty-five now), preferred younger men. He wasn't really all that hot in bed. He never had been – and she had never been able to understand why she didn't mind that more. And of course he wasn't nearly so much fun these days; he seemed so down and depressed a lot of the time. And it really got up her nose how frightened of his father he was. She really couldn't see why he couldn't stand up to the old bugger a bit more. After all, he had got the bank. Technically. All right, Fred III had moved back in after Baby's illness, and was making mincemeat of Baby now, but he wouldn't be able to do that to nearly such an extent if Baby would only stand up to him. Angie had come across a lot of bullies in her life, and there wasn't one of them who hadn't run away squeaking when she'd stood up to them. If they were married, she could help him more: make him the old Baby again.

All these thoughts drifted through her head as she sat in a traffic jam, on her way to her office in Hanover Square. It was a very tenderly beautiful October day, golden and slightly misty. It made her feel tranquil and happy; Angie was surprisingly susceptible to the weather. Baby would be here in another week; she hadn't seen him since the time of Charlotte's dance, when he had paid a flying visit to London under cover of some meeting with a banker. Highly unsatisfactory that had been too: he had been so shit scared of Mary Rose or Fred finding out he had hardly been able to get it up at all. She had been angry, frustrated, outraged almost that they were of so much importance to him, even when he was with her, in her bed, and they had had a terrible row, and she had told him she wanted to end it; but then as she watched from the bed as he got up, and very slowly and heavily began to get dressed, his face etched with misery, she couldn't bear it, and jumped up and took him in her arms and started

304

kissing him and telling him she hadn't meant it, that she never ever wanted it to end, and he had looked at her with absolute tenderness and gratitude and then started to smile, that great joyful all-encompassing smile of his, and looked totally and utterly different and twenty years younger. That was the kind of occasion when she realized she loved him.

But what, in the name of heaven, was to become of them? He would never leave Mary Rose, he would never leave the bank – God, that would be awful, thought Angie with a shudder, the millions and millions he was worth, or rather that bank was worth. There was absolutely no doubt in her mind that she would find it much harder to love Baby without his wealth. The fact that she had money of her own was neither here nor there. Wealth meant power; it made even weak men like Baby strong and sexy. And power turned Angie on.

She had been at a party the night before and met a merchant banker. His name was Christopher Holden and he was tall and dark, very smooth, very Etonian, and he had turned her on too. He was telling her about some deals he was doing: 'The real fascination about them is pulling numbers out of the air, playing games with them, and knowing when to cash in the chips.' He told her he wouldn't even look at a deal that was worth less than a billion. Angie had felt a stab of sexual hunger at those words; she accepted his invitation to dinner (cancelling another date at twenty minutes' notice) and sat entranced in the panelled dining room of the Connaught, as he talked for three hours about the way he passed his days, the coded contacts, the secrecy, the high-level meetings, the twelfth-hour consultations, the creeping share prices, the tactics, the tension, the gambling, the heady exaltation when everything came together at the right time at the right price. He made it sound much more exciting than when Baby talked about it.

'I have a friend who's an investment banker,' she said, 'in New York.'

'Oh really? Who's he with?'

'Praegers.'

'Ah. Interesting one. Outside the bulge bracket, it's one of the most desirable little houses there are. Fascinating combination of being small with a couple of really triple-A clients. I mean, them having Fosters Land is ridiculous really. And old man Praeger still controls it. Fantastic. Eighty or something and running the show.'

'Well, he does and he doesn't,' said Angie, defensive on Baby's behalf. 'Control it. I mean, his son is in charge now. He has been for years.'

'Yes, of course, I'd forgotten that. But Fred the Third came back when Baby Praeger had his heart attack, didn't he? Poor old Baby. Not quite the same calibre as Dad, I believe. But what I mean is, the shares are all in the hands of the family, aren't they? Except for a tiny handful with the partners.'

'Yes, they are,' said Angie. 'It's unbelievable really.'

He looked at her, amused. 'What does your friend do at Praegers?'

'He's a trader,' said Angie.

'Ah. That really is fun. Lucky fellow. I wish I was ten years younger. Those boys are going to make a fortune over here now. Are Praegers going to open a London office?'

'I don't think so,' said Angie, surprised. 'Why should they?'

'I bet you they're thinking about it. In three years' time one hell of a big balloon is going up. Everyone's going to want to be here.'

'Why?'

'Big Bang,' said Holden. 'Heard of that?'

Angie laughed. 'Well – '

'Just as exciting,' said Holden, grinning at her. 'The Stock Exchange as we know it will cease to exist. Free-for-all instead, buying and selling shares. It's going to be very interesting indeed. And the banks will want to be in on it, and in order to accomplish that, they'll be buying the stockbroking firms.'

'Oh, I see,' said Angie. She looked at Holden thoughtfully. 'Well, I must ask my friend.'

'Well, he'll need to tell them to get their skates on. It's all going to happen very fast. There won't be many firms left to buy in a month or two. Look, this has been a really nice evening. Would you like a glass of champagne in Annabels to round it off?'

Angie said she would; after several glasses of champagne, and a very arousing half hour on the dance floor, Holden offered to drive her home. He had a black Porsche which he drove extremely fast; Angie invited him in for a brandy. He said he had to get back to his wife, but that he would certainly be in touch.

The human brain works in a very complex manner. Looking back on her actions over the following few weeks, Angie could see they all dovetailed very neatly into one another, but at the time they seemed rather haphazard and disconnected. She started reading the financial pages in the papers very carefully; she talked to some public relations firms with a speciality in financial and business matters, with a view to appointing one of them; she instructed a City stockbroker, Edwards and Dawson, to open a share portfolio worth £10,000 for her, and to keep her closely informed as to which shares they were buying and selling and when and why; she booked several flights to New York, at four-weekly intervals, telling Baby she had a new client who was looking for property there; and she left her contraceptive pills to gather dust upon the bathroom shelf.

Chapter 24

Charlotte, 1983–4

Charlotte had always been a star. She had been top of every class in every school she had ever attended; she had always scored straight As in exams; she had gained a double first at Cambridge. She had won enough rosettes to cover an entire wall in the tack room; she had a golf handicap of seventeen, she had been tennis champion of her school, house captain, deputy head girl, a leading light in the Union, a major contributor to *Granta*. She had been, moreover, she knew, a tower of strength in the family, had taken over in many small ways from her mother in duties on the estate; she was popular, she made people laugh, she was pretty, she was admired. Moreover she had been her grandfather's favourite for the whole of her life, and much talked about in her role as heiress elect. She had confidently expected to arrive at Praegers in this capacity, follow a short induction programme, and then settle into some junior but important job, using her brain and the considerable administrative skills she also knew she possessed to their full capacity. Instead she found herself appointed a junior associate, seconded to a senior vice president, doing grunt work. And grunt work meant very very menial. It meant sitting at her boss's desk, listening to his conversation, in a respectful silence; it meant taking minutes of meetings; it meant setting out the meeting room with paper and pencils and calculators; it meant Xeroxing; it meant proof reading; it meant stapling pages together; it meant making coffee; it meant putting a presentation book together at three in the morning; it meant never getting in after seven thirty in the morning, and often staying until after eleven at night; it meant having a bleeper with her wherever she went, even at weekends, in case she was needed for some extra urgent bit of grunt work. Occasionally it meant doing something just a little bit interesting like analysing the rate a stock had been trading over a twenty-year period, or doing financial models for a company, or phoning around individual shareholders to enlist their support in a bid. But mostly it was boring. And exhausting. And if that wasn't bad enough, Fred III, in more than usually Machiavellian mode, had decided the vice president she worked for was Gabe Hoffman.

'I know you two have met a few times,' he said, when he took Charlotte down to Hoffman's office.

'Yes, we have,' said Gabe, holding out his hand to Charlotte. 'Most memorably on Fred's birthday. Welcome.' He smiled at her, revealing his perfect teeth; but his eyes did not smile and they did not say welcome either.

'Thank you,' said Charlotte, returning the handshake briefly. 'I'm certainly looking forward to working with you.'

'Lesson number one,' said Gabe, smiling the same cold smile. 'Not with. For.'

From that moment it was war.

Gabe was outstandingly unpleasant to her. If he had been a woman, she would have described him as a bitch. He was critical, demanding, discourteous. While she would not have expected him to stand up when she came into the room, or hold the door open for her, she was not prepared for the way he interrupted her when she was talking to shout at someone else across the room, ordered her to put the phone down mid-conversation because he wanted something done, hauled her in early or at weekends, and then kept her waiting sometimes for over an hour before he appeared himself. He would exclude her from any conversation, any discussion even, unless it was necessary for him to explain something to her; ignored any comments, crushed any suggestions she made with an abruptness that in the very early days at least brought tears to her eyes.

To make it worse, he was doing very well at Praegers. His star was indisputably rising. Fred III thought he was wonderful. His father was due to retire in five years' time and it was generally assumed that when that happened, Gabe would be made a junior partner.

What made it almost worse than anything was that every other female in the bank was dying of love for Gabe. Much as she loathed him, Charlotte had to admit that he was extremely sexy. He was thirty-two years old now, and patently carnal. She remembered him as being tall, but he was very big now, heavily built, with huge shoulders, and yet lean and surprisingly graceful when he moved. The combination of that with his size was extremely sensual. It was said that he could dance extremely well, and his game of tennis was exceptional. He had a year-round tan, and sailed almost all year from the family house in Sag Harbor. His brown hair, which was cropped very short, somehow still managed to look unruly, and his eyes, which were exceptionally dark and ringed by lashes which would have looked girly on anyone else, could, when turned on most members of the female race, inspire an almost slavish desire to please. They did not inspire that in Charlotte.

Charlotte would have given anything to displease Gabe Hoffman: only she didn't dare.

And then there was Freddy. Freddy was not rude to her as Gabe was, he was icily polite in public, and in private he ignored her totally. Charlotte found this initially almost amusing; as her morale crumbled, she began to find it horribly hurtful. He and Gabe often lunched together, and had endless early morning meetings; Charlotte had a shrewd suspicion that Gabe did not actually like him very much, but he went along with him, in a typically pragmatic Gabe way. Freddy would after all one day be his boss. And they were united over one important matter: a determination to put her down, to disabuse her of any notion she might have of her own importance, to impress upon her that her life at Praegers was never going to be anything else but tough.

She was very lonely. She hadn't yet made any friends in New York; she had not yet found any kindred spirits at Praegers, and as she was working virtually round the clock she was hardly able to form any relationships outside it. The young men at Praegers were wary of her, daunted by her relationship with the family, her ultimate destiny in the bank and her attitude, which they all agreed was typically British and high-handed. And there weren't any other women, so far as she could see, except secretaries, and she had nothing in common with them.

She was staying, very reluctantly, with Fred and Betsey; she felt in her bones it was politically unwise, but she really did not feel brave enough to move into an apartment of her own yet, and she had no time to look anyway.

After six weeks she returned home for a few days, taking advantage of the Thanksgiving holiday period, excusing herself from Betsey's invitation to join them at Beaches with the explanation that Alexander was lonely and depressed. She put up a brave front to him, and to Max, saying it was fascinating and fun, that the work was a breeze, that she was learning loads, that she had never felt more sure that she was doing the right thing, but on the day before she went back she had lunch with Charles St Mullin at Simpsons in the Strand and surprised and shocked herself by bursting into angry tears.

'I hate it. I hate everything to do with it. It's boring, my boss is a pig, I don't have any friends, and everyone treats me as if I was some kind of a puffed-up princess.'

'Well,' said Charles, surprisingly calm, passing her his handkerchief and then her glass of wine, 'you can hardly blame them. You may not be puffed up but you are a princess. It's not your fault, but you are. And even this boss of yours, this Gabe, he must find it a little hard to take. That however hard he works and well he does, he can never hope to be more than a partner with a very minority shareholding in a business you're going to own and run.'

'Co-run,' said Charlotte, correcting him automatically.

'Well all right, co-run. In any event, you can hardly blame him for lording it over you now, while he has the opportunity.'

'I suppose not.' Charlotte gave him a watery smile. 'I hadn't thought of it like that. So what do I do? Don't tell me to start telling him I think he's wonderful. I'd be sick all over his Quotron.'

'What's a Quotron?' said Charles. 'No, of course not. But I think you should altogether give a little. I still don't know you very well yet, Charlotte, unfortunately, but I can see that you are a formidable package. I think you should act a little helpless, if you could bring yourself to do that. Not just with this Gabe person, but everyone. Ask for a little help. Don't mind looking silly now and again.'

'Oh God, I can't stand looking silly,' said Charlotte fretfully. 'Do I really have to?'

'Well, it's only my opinion,' said Charles, 'and I'm only a humble barrister. But I think you should try it.'

They had become very close, very quickly. As she had said to Max, whom she had sought out, breathless and excited after the first meeting (knowing it was unwise, but wanting, needing to talk to someone), 'I know he's my father, Max, I just know it. I looked at him sitting there in the restaurant and there he was.'

'But how did he actually tell you?' said Max. 'I can't believe he sat down and said, "Hey, young lady, yes, I am most definitely your dad, let me tell you all about this affair I had with your mother." ' He looked sulky and wary; Charlotte sighed.

'No, of course he didn't. We danced around one another for a long time first. It came out in bits, as we talked, in between sort of – well, checking up on one another. About halfway through lunch, he suddenly said, "It can't have been easy, tracking me down. Via that robe." And I said no, it hadn't been, but it had been very exciting and I'd been determined to do it. And I said it had been wonderful to see Ireland, that bit of Ireland, and I had never in all my life thought anywhere so beautiful. Then he said suddenly, "Tell me more about your family. How is your Uncle Baby?" Then he said, and looked terribly terribly sad, that he had been so upset when Mummy died, he had read about it in the papers, and he thought of writing to us all then, but wondered what he could possibly say. And then I said, I don't know why but I suddenly felt brave enough, probably because I'd had quite a few glasses of wine by then, and it just all came out in a rush, I said, "Look, this is an awful question, and terrible cheek, but did you and Mummy have an affair?'' And he said, looking really quite angry, "Yes it is, terrible cheek," and he really didn't think he could possibly discuss such a thing with me, and why should I have thought that anyway? Which I took to mean a sort of go-ahead. In an obtuse way. And I said, well, because I had discovered we had this very irregular family background. But that perhaps he was right and I shouldn't discuss it with him. And then he said, looking very solemn and also rather embarrassed, yes, he had had an affair with Mummy. He said it very quietly and rather sadly. And then he asked me if I could possibly tell him what sort of irregular family background I'd meant. And I said, well, you know, that we'd found we all had different fathers. All three of us. And that Daddy knew.'

'Charlotte. You can't go blabbing that all over London.'

'I wasn't blabbing it all over London. Max, I told you, I know this man is my father. And he's honest and honourable and I just knew it was all right. To talk to him.'

'How very fortunate for you,' said Max.

'So then he said, yes, they had been lovers, for quite a long time, and he'd loved her very much. And that he'd always suspected I was his child, even though she denied it, and ended the affair as soon as she'd found out she was pregnant. He said he'd seen pictures of me from time to time, in the papers and so on, and felt even more sure.'

'Do you look like him?'

'Yes and no. He has dark curly hair, and blue eyes and a lot of freckles. He's not exactly skinny, that's the thing that's most like me. But it's more than that, there's something about him, that makes me feel – well I don't know, at home. Can you understand that, what I mean?'

'Not really,' said Max. 'Did he have any idea why she might have had this affair? And conceived you deliberately? When she was only recently married?'

'No. He didn't. He said he had never been able to understand it. He said she was obviously a very nice person, that she was utterly loyal to Daddy –'

'Oh, extremely loyal!' said Max. 'Funny kind of loyalty, sleeping around all over the place.'

'Not all over the place. Just with him.'

'Oh yes, sure, and with Georgina's father and my father.'

'Well, I think the one thing we really do know is that we don't know anything much yet. We have a long way to go. A lot of discoveries to make.'

'Yes, well you're all right, aren't you? You've found your father, and surprise surprise he's charming and clever and civilized and nice. Everything works out for you, doesn't it, Charlotte? Everything.'

'Max,' said Charlotte quietly, 'Max, I'm terribly sorry you're so upset. That you mind so much.'

'I could never understand,' he said, 'why you didn't mind more. You obviously have a lot of our mother in you.'

Charlotte turned and walked out of the room.

She saw Charles St Mullin several times after that and before she left for the States; they lunched twice a week. They never talked about Virginia again, they talked about each other, what they did, what they enjoyed, each of them feeling they could not have enough.

Charles was charming, civilized and amusing; he was only modestly successful as a barrister, and he lived with his wife Grace in a house in Fulham with their three children, two girls and a boy, and had some difficulty paying their school fees. Grace was a music teacher, she gave piano and flute lessons and the youngest child was very talented and had won a music scholarship to St Paul's Girls' School. 'Thank God.'

He had a great love for his old home and for Ireland: 'I should like to go there with you,' he said slightly regretfully, 'but I think it cannot be.'

'I don't suppose Grace knows about – ' said Charlotte and no, he said hastily, no of course not, she must never know. They never returned to the subject again.

Charlotte was utterly delighted by him; he was warm and affectionate and very appreciative of her. She spent hours telling him about her hopes and fears, her ambitions, the tortuous convolutions of the family relationships, about her worries about Georgina and her greater ones for Max. 'God knows what will happen to him when I'm not here to keep an eye on things.'

'How I would like to meet them all,' said Charles. 'But I am afraid it is not to be.'

'I'm afraid not too,' said Charlotte. 'Not for a long time anyway.'

'Talking of time,' he said, jumping up, 'I must go. I'm late back already.'

'It's been lovely – again,' said Charlotte. 'Probably I won't see you again before I go. Promise you'll write?'

'I promise.' He gave her a kiss.

She watched him go out of the restaurant. He was a little overweight, and his slightly shabby suit didn't flatter him. He looked tired although he was so determinedly smiling and cheerful; his life obviously contained a lot of worry. It would be nice to be able to spoil him a bit, she thought. That was what fathers were for.

She took his advice about Praegers very seriously. She got back and tried very very hard to crack the hostility; she knew it was no use trying to get friendly with Gabe, but she went out for drinks with the others after work, more or less forcing herself on them. It was very hard; she knew they didn't want her to go, but couldn't refuse. She laughed at all their jokes, asked their advice, told endless stories against herself. It didn't seem to work. Two weeks before Christmas, she went out to get a sandwich at lunchtime, and rushed back to a report she had to finish, hardly noticing that the large outer office was empty. An hour later she did notice; it was still empty. They all came back at four; they had gone for a Christmas lunch and had either forgotten her, or chosen not to tell her. Charlotte wasn't sure which explanation she found more hurtful.

Two days later she was walking along the corridor towards the end of the day when she bumped into Gabe. 'Oh, there you are,' he said, dumping a corrected set of minutes into her hands. 'Look, get these Xeroxed, will you, and distributed. The boys and I are going out for a small celebration. See you later.'

Charlotte took the minutes and wandered back in the direction of the Xerox machine. She looked down at them, to see which of the dozens she had done that week they were, and found them blurred; it took her a few seconds to discover the reason: that she was crying. She fled in the direction of the office she shared with Gabe, and finding it mercifully empty, sat down with her head on her arms and started to cry, quite quietly, but very hard. She would probably have gone on for some time, had she not felt a hand on her shoulder, and heard a voice that combined an odd softness with what she now recognized as a thick Brooklyn accent, saying, 'Is this a private party or can anyone join in?'

Charlotte turned round sharply and looked up into a face that was so genuinely interested, so sympathetic, so concerned, that (those being such unfamiliar qualities to her these days) she cried harder than ever. 'I'm sorry,' she said, hiccuping mildly into an already sodden Kleenex, 'really sorry. I'm not doing the cause of the professional woman a lot of good here, am I?'

'The professional woman can take care of herself,' said the owner of the face, passing her a handkerchief. 'I never liked her too much anyway. Here, blow your nose on this, it's spare and dry.'

'Oh no, I couldn't. Really,' said Charlotte.

'I promise you, I always have a spare handkerchief for ladies in distress. My raincoats I lose, my handkerchiefs I keep. It's a different way round from most people.' He smiled at her. 'Now what is the matter?'

'Oh – nothing. I'm being a baby,' she said, blowing her nose and looking at him. He had an extraordinarily nice face; not good-looking but oddly sexy, with its concerned brown eyes and slightly lopsided smile.

'I like babies. Boss been unkind to you?'

'Very.'

'Nasty people, bosses. I have been known to be quite unkind on occasions myself. What do you do here?'

'Oh,' said Charlotte, with a sigh, 'not a lot. And I don't like what I do.'

'I should leave in that case,' he said. 'There's nothing worse than doing work you don't like. I'm quite serious. You're English, aren't you?'

'Yes, I am.'

'So what misfortune brings you to this godforsaken city?'

'Oh – the opportunity,' said Charlotte. 'Of working here.'

'I should hurry home. Whereabouts in England do you live?'

'In Wiltshire,' she said and at the thought of it, the rolling hills, Hartest, the kitchen fire, Nanny and Mrs Tallow, she started crying again.

'I never went to Wiltshire,' he said thoughtfully. 'I only know London and Scotland.'

'My grandmother lives in Scotland,' said Charlotte.

'She does?' he said. 'I wonder if I ever met her. Is she anywhere near Edinburgh?'

He gave Edinburgh at least five syllables; Charlotte had to laugh.

'I don't think so.'

'So who is this sadistic boss of yours? I wonder do you know Baby Praeger, by any chance? I'm looking for him.'

'Wrong floor,' said Charlotte. 'I'll take you down. Yes, I know him. He's my –'

She stopped herself. She didn't want this sympathetic stranger thinking she was pulling rank. 'My boss's boss.'

'Now listen,' he said, 'I really mean you should leave here if you're unhappy. It's crazy spending your days somewhere you don't like. It's the most important thing in the world, I always think, your work. Or rather being happy in it.'

Charlotte stood up and said, 'I can't really leave. Honestly I can't. I wish I could, though. Thank you for being so kind. And for the handkerchief. Follow me.'

They were halfway down the corridor when they met Fred, lost in a cloud of cigar smoke, his arm round Freddy's shoulders.

'Michael!' he said. 'Looking for me?'

'No, I'm looking for Baby. We have a little bit of business to finish. I got lost and this very kind and rather sad young lady is showing me to Baby's office. You should take better care of your staff, Fred. I found her weeping into her company minutes.'

'Indeed?' said Fred slightly ominously. 'Well, people who work here have to learn to be a little resilient. And I really don't have time to watch over every tiny emotional crisis. All right, Charlotte, I'll show Mr Browning to Baby's office.'

Charlotte smiled rather weakly at her new friend and made her way back to her own office. So that was the legendary Michael Browning. It had been a very big coup for Praegers, getting some of his business. He was worth at least three billion dollars, she had heard, most of it from his BuyNow Supermarkets; he had not been in the least how she had imagined, from all the awestruck descriptions she had heard of him. Gabe had had to do a report for him only two weeks after she had arrived, and had gone into paroxysms of nerves and hyper efficiency. Charlotte would never have dreamt the instigator of such neurotic activity could be a person with spare handkerchiefs to dry the eyes of weeping females and spare time to listen to their troubles. She could have fallen in love with Michael Browning, no trouble at all, given even half an opportunity. Which of course she wouldn't be.

She had just settled back at her desk, sorting through the minutes Gabe had given her, when her phone rang. It was Fred.

'Get down here, will you?' he said. His voice was expressionless.

Charlotte brushed her hair, sprayed herself with Dorissimo, dabbed some make-up onto her still blotchy face and set off down the corridor again. If she was to have the pleasure of renewing Michael Browning's acquaintance, she wanted to look as good as possible.

She wasn't: Fred was alone.

'How dare you,' he said, 'go whining and whinging to a client? An important client. How dare you?'

He was terribly angry; Charlotte, who had never seen anything but adoration in his eyes, suddenly discovered a new Fred Praeger, and why everyone was so frightened of him. She met his eyes steadily. 'I didn't know he was a client and I didn't go whining to him. He – he found me. Crying.'

'Crying! In the office!' Fred looked at her contemptuously. 'For the love of God, Charlotte, how old are you and what do you think you're doing here? This is not some fancy house party, this is a business. Involved daily in the transaction of several billions of dollars. Kindly try to remember that and adopt a professional approach to it.'

'But – '

'Charlotte, you're in a grotesquely privileged position here.'

'I am not! That's not true. Gabe Hoffman treats me like – like dirt.'

'And has it not entered your pretty, pampered little head to think why? Because one day, unless my patience fails me, and Baby's patience fails

315

him, you will be in a position to treat Gabe Hoffman like dirt. And he knows it. You may find that a pleasing prospect. I do assure you, Charlotte, he does not. What he's doing is extracting revenge. Before rather than after the event. Try to remember that. And behave yourself in future, otherwise it isn't going to happen. Ever.'

She went home for Christmas, exhausted, discouraged, sore at heart. She managed to persuade everyone that she was having a wonderful time, except for Nanny, who found her sitting in the library on Boxing Day, staring blankly out of the window.

'It's not quite right for you at the bank, is it?' she said.

'Not quite,' said Charlotte. She was too tired to argue with Nanny. 'How did you know?'

'You've put on weight,' said Nanny severely. 'You always did eat too many sweets when something upset you.'

She got back to New York on 2 January and went back to work on the third; she sat on the downtown express train and felt more miserable than she could ever remember, apart from when her mother had died. She walked rather slowly up out of the Wall Street subway and up William Street towards Pine Street. It was only seven o'clock and it was still dark. The narrow streets seemed as heavy as her heart. She remembered how she had felt as she had walked that way the very first morning, how excited she had been, and she wondered, just for a moment, if it was worth it. Then she physically gritted her teeth. 'This won't do, Charlotte Welles,' she said aloud. 'Pull yourself together.'

She had scarcely walked into the door, asked for her key, when Baby suddenly appeared at the bottom of the staircase. He was white, and he was breathing very heavily.

'Baby!' By common consent they had dropped the Uncle. 'Happy New –'

Baby ignored her. He didn't even see her. He walked straight past her and out of the door. Charlotte had never seen such rage and such determination on his good-natured face.

Baby had come into the bank that morning early, walked into Fred's office and told him he was asking Mary Rose for a divorce.

'Apparently he has a – a mistress,' Betsey told Charlotte later, hardly able to look her in the eye, 'and she's pregnant.'

'Pregnant!' said Charlotte. She was silent for a moment and then the English schoolgirl spoke. 'Golly.' She was torn between shock that anyone of Baby's generation could be so foolish and so irresponsible and a certain sneaking pleasure that the uncle she loved so much was at least still having some fun out of life.

'Yes, dear. I'm sorry, you must find this so upsetting. Apparently this girl lives in London. She's English.'

'English!' said Charlotte. 'It surely can't still be Angie? Angie Burbank?'

'Yes, dear, it is. Why, have you heard of her?'

'Well, she used to work for Mummy.'

'Yes, that's right. Well, it's been going on for many years. There was some scandal many years ago. Fred – got rid of her. Or so he thought.'

'How on earth did he do that?' said Charlotte, amused.

'Oh, I don't know. There's very little your grandfather can't do if he puts his mind to it, you know.'

'I know,' said Charlotte. 'Goodness, Angie Burbank.'

'You don't remember her, do you?'

'No, not really. So what's going to happen?'

'Well, Baby has told your grandfather that he's leaving Mary Rose. And of course your grandfather told him he was to do no such thing – '

'Uncle Baby is nearly fifty – ' said Charlotte.

'Not to your grandfather,' said Betsey briskly.

'So then what?'

'Well, your grandfather said he would disinherit Baby, if he left Mary Rose, but of course he officially and formally made Baby chairman when he retired. As Baby pointed out. Oh, I do believe there was a terrible row. Anyway, Baby has gone over to London tonight, to see this woman, and your grandfather is locked in with the lawyers seeing what can be done.'

'Well it's ridiculous,' said Charlotte. 'I mean, I just don't see what Grandfather can do about any of it. What it's got to do with him at all, really.'

'Oh dear,' said Betsey, 'I'm afraid you still don't know him very well, Charlotte.'

Chapter 25

Angie, 1984

Well, the easy bit was certainly over, Angie reflected, swinging down Harley Street in the pale January sunshine, after a very satisfactory consultation with her gynaecologist. Yes, everything was fine, Miss Burbank was roughly ten weeks pregnant, no, there was no need to worry about anything, and no, mid-thirties was not in the least old to be having a first baby, provided she took reasonable care of herself and didn't work too many eighteen-hour days. They would run all the tests, just to make sure, but he was convinced she had nothing to worry about. The gynaecologist was too fashionable and expensive to inquire about the baby's father; Miss Burbank was clearly not about to be taking up residence in a home for single mothers, and was clearly going to be able to pay his bill, and beyond that he had no interest in her circumstances.

'So,' he had said, smiling at her over his large desk, 'a late summer baby. Let's hope it's not too hot.'

Angie looked down on her entirely concave stomach, encased in a sliver-slim black silk skirt, and tried to imagine what it was actually going to be like, to see it, feel it burgeoning with this child. It was still so much a fantasy, she still couldn't quite believe in it. But it was definitely going to happen. She was going to have a baby. And she felt wonderful, strong and happy and not even sick, and Baby would feel wonderful too, when he stopped wetting himself and worrying about his father and Mary Rose and the bank. That was a bit of a worry, but she knew she could handle it; she was only after all at the end of Stage One of her plan. Which so far was proceeding more quickly, if not more smoothly, than she had hoped. She had expected to spend a little more time becoming pregnant; but it had only required one trip to New York. She had of course timed that trip extremely carefully. It coincided exactly with the middle of her cycle.

Baby hadn't looked quite as she'd imagined he would when she'd first told him; he had come over to London for forty-eight hours just before Christmas and they'd been having dinner at the Gavroche and she'd said Baby, I have some news, and put her hand on his and he'd said, looking very excited, was she going to be able to spend more time in New York and she'd said no, rather the reverse, she was actually going to have to settle down a bit and take things a bit more quietly and he'd looked at her rather oddly and said why, and she'd said, 'Well, Baby, because I'm going to have a baby. No, that's wrong. We're going to have a baby.' And he'd gone quite white, and just stared at her and she'd said, 'You don't look very pleased,' and he had sort of shaken himself and said, forcing a smile, 'Well of course I'm pleased,' and she'd said, 'Well, aren't you going to give me a kiss or something?' and he'd said, even more oddly, 'Angie, I don't understand. How did it happen?'

And 'Baby really!' she had said, 'I'm amazed you don't remember. Just about seven weeks ago, that lovely week we had in New York,' and he'd said, 'Of course I remember, but surely you're on the pill?' And she'd said yes, of course she was on the pill, but her doctor had changed the brand, because she'd been getting a lot of headaches, and put her on a lower dosage one, and that did put up the risk of a pregnancy. 'But of course I never thought it would happen. Never. But it has. And I'm so happy about it. So terribly happy. Aren't you? Baby, you're not upset are you, or cross or anything? Because I couldn't bear not to have your baby. I really couldn't.'

And Baby had said, no of course not, he was terribly happy too, and he managed to smile at her again, and ordered some champagne, but he still looked very shaken and strained, and suggested they left the restaurant soon after that. And they had lain in the big bed in his suite at the Savoy, and he had been very quiet, and made love to her rather awkwardly and silently and then gone to sleep. Angie had begun to feel just a little nervous at that point; she had expected tenderness, excitement even, long discussions about what they were going to do, and what the baby might be and what its name might be, not this odd, quiet nothingness. She had woken up in the middle of the night and he had not been in the bed, and she had sat up and looked across the room and he had been sitting in a big chair by the window, staring out across the river.

'Baby?' she said, panic rising slightly uncomfortably in her throat. 'Baby, what is it?'

'Oh,' he said, 'nothing, I have indigestion, that's all. Ate too much. You don't have to worry about me. Go back to sleep.'

'Don't be silly,' said Angie, getting out of the bed and going over to him, putting her arms round his neck, 'of course I have to worry about you. I love you. That's why I'm here. That's why I'm pregnant.'

'Do you?' he said, and his face was very sad, and something else, almost frightened. 'Do you really?'

And in a rare moment of truthfulness, she had looked into his eyes and said, 'Yes, Baby, I do, I really love you.'

'Oh God,' he said, 'that makes it almost worse.'

The panic rose again. 'Why?' she said.

'Well because I love you so much. So terribly much. I can't imagine life without you. You're the one thing that's kept me sane this last year. And now, you're going to have a baby. My baby. And how am I going to go on living apart from you now? How am I going to bear it?'

'Well,' she said, sliding onto his knee, kissing his neck, his cheek, his hair, 'well, Baby, you could start living with me.'

'Oh Angie,' he said, 'how can I? How can you even think such a thing? Life is terrible at the bank, worse than ever. My father's totally taken over control again. I'm fighting for survival. Only the other day he – ' He was silent for a moment, she felt fear run through his body at the memory. 'Only the other day he said he really felt that maybe the share structure should be broken up, changed, that the senior partners should have much more of a controlling interest.'

'Shit,' said Angie, 'do you think he meant it?'

'I don't know. Possibly not. But it was just one more body blow, to humiliate me.'

'I thought,' she said carefully, the panic rising again rather nastily, 'that he had actually appointed you chairman or whatever. That he couldn't do that any more.'

'Yes, I'm chairman. In theory it's mine,' he sighed. 'Although we all know it isn't. And I do hold now a thirty per cent share. He has fifty per cent still and the partners the remaining twenty per cent. I don't get that fifty per cent until he dies.'

'And Charlotte and Freddy?'

'At the moment their holding is notional. Well, they have a few shares. When I truly inherit, they take over my thirty per cent. Between them. It's very complex.'

'Baby, he'll never turn over that bank,' said Angie firmly, 'he loves it more than anything in the world. You've always said so, and I saw a bit of it for myself, over the years. But you'll get it in the end. I know you will.'

'Well, maybe,' said Baby. 'But in the meantime it's one hell of a struggle. And Dad uses every bit of ammunition he has to get me down. And he would sure as hell use this. He'd never let me leave Mary Rose. Never.'

Angie turned his head towards her. She started to kiss him, very slowly and tenderly. Baby's arms went round her, tighter; she moved her hands slowly down his body, slipped her fingers between his buttocks; she felt him tense, felt his penis rising beneath her. 'I love you,' she whispered. 'I love you so much.'

She slipped off his lap, knelt in front of him. She pushed his legs apart, took his penis in her mouth, working on it gently, greedily, pulling at it, caressing it, drawing at his desire. Baby groaned. His hands were in her hair, his head thrown back. 'I love you,' he said, and it was almost a cry of despair.

Later they lay quietly in bed; it was four in the morning, and the traffic was beginning to thunder along the Embankment. Angie's head was pillowed on Baby's shoulder; she turned her head and looked up at him. She could just see his face; it was less sad now, more thoughtful. She waited for a moment, thinking; then, because the thought had to be voiced some time, could not wait for ever, she said, carefully, casually serious, 'Baby, have you ever thought of moving Praegers to London?'

He had laughed at first, as she had known he would; she had agreed it was a crazy idea, and left it, had not even menioned it again. They had slept for a while, then got up late, gone shopping. Angie bought him a cashmere coat, grey, with a black velvet collar: 'That's what they wear in London,' she said, 'in banking circles.'

'How would you know?' said Baby.

'Oh, I know a lot of bankers,' she said casually.

Baby bought her a ring, a great rock of a diamond, to wear on her wedding finger.

'That's for the baby,' he said, 'our baby. We can at least pretend we're married.'

They were back in the suite at the Savoy; Baby was to leave in two hours. Angie smiled at him, kissed him. 'Maybe it won't always be pretend.'

Baby looked at her very steadily. 'Angie, it will, I'm afraid. It has to be. I'm sorry.'

At which point she had moved into Stage Two. She hadn't wanted to, she had hoped she wouldn't have to, but she had been perfectly prepared to. She pulled away from him, walked over to the window and looked out, rehearsing the next few lines; she concentrated hard, her eyes filled with the obedient tears.

'Baby, I don't know if I can bear this,' she said, turning towards him again.

'Oh, darling, don't,' he said, moving towards her. 'Don't cry. Don't talk like that. I'll be with you more, I promise. I'll take great care of you. I'll get over much more often. Or maybe you could move to New York.' He moved to put his arms round her; Angie pulled away.

'Don't. I can't live in New York. You know I can't. My work is here.'

'You don't need to work. I'll look after you.'

Angie lifted her head. Her green eyes were very stormy. 'I'm sorry, Baby, but I can't live like that. I can't be that exposed. I'm an independent woman. I need my work. In lots of ways. If you're not prepared to make any kind of commitment to me, then I have to make my own plans.'

Baby looked at her and there was real fear in his eyes.

'Angie, what kind of commitment can I make?'

'You can leave Mary Rose.'

'I can't leave Mary Rose.'

'For fuck's sake, Baby, why not? You say you love me. You've been saying it for fifteen years. I've been very loyal, very patient. Now I'm going to have our baby. And all you can say is you can't leave Mary Rose. Well, I'm sorry, but I can't handle that. I really can't.'

'What do you mean?' His face was grey with fear and pain.

'I mean we really have come to the end of the road. Our road. And a fine old junction it's turned out to be. I'm going to turn round and find a new one. On my own.'

'And the baby?'

'Well, clearly I will have to decide about the baby.' Her eyes were snapping with contempt. 'I had thought of it as our baby. It's obviously simply mine. Don't worry, Baby, I'll look after it. One way or another.'

'Angie, please. Please, I can't bear it.'

'*You* can't bear it! What about me? Hearing you, year after year, say I can't be with you, I can't stay with you, I have to hurry back, my father might find out, my wife might find out. For God's sake, Baby, you're almost fifty. When are you going to grow up?'

She had been a bit frightened at saying that. It was very corny, and it was very cruel. It just might be counterproductive. She waited, staring at him; she saw his face turn completely white, watched him walk over to her, raise his hand, felt it hit her hard, right across her face. She flinched, but didn't move, didn't even look away. Then he suddenly came at her in a great rush of remorse and love and tenderness and concern, holding her, stroking her hair, shaking, weeping himself. 'Angie darling, I'm so sorry, so terribly, terribly sorry. Please, please forgive me. I love you so much, so very very much. I'm a bully and a coward and I don't deserve you. Christ, how could I have done that? Please forgive me, Angie, please.'

Angie said nothing, just stood there, drained, weak, genuinely shocked herself. Then she heard him say, as if from a great distance, very slowly, his voice strangely deep, 'Angie, I would like you to marry me. Will you, please? Marry me?'

He was coming over tonight, for a long weekend. She had decided he should not stay at the Savoy, but at her house in St John's Wood. As their relationship was now to be formalized, they should start being together openly. In preparation for this, she had had a very long talk with her grandmother. Mrs Wicks had initially been rather opposed to the idea of her marrying Baby, and still more opposed to the idea of her having his child, but being a romantic at heart, she was now rather charmed by the whole thing and had spent the past twenty-four hours giving the house what she called a Total, which meant cleaning it from top to bottom, touching up the paintwork here and there, and filling every room with flowers. She had offered to wait at table while Angie and Baby had dinner that night. Angie had said she didn't think that was the best idea, maybe another evening, but she would like her to join them for a drink before dinner. Mrs Wicks had had her roots touched up, and a manicure in preparation for this event; when Angie came in she was waiting for her in her kitchen.

'Kettle's just boiled. There was a phone call. From his secretary in America. The plane left late, so he won't be at Heathrow till five. Probably not here until eight. I said that would be fine.'

'Oh good,' said Angie, wondering briefly what other response there might conceivably have been to the secretary's message.

'What did the doctor say?' said Mrs Wicks severely. 'Told you to rest up, I expect.'

'No, not really. He said I should be sensible.'

'He doesn't know you very well.'

'No he doesn't. Cheers, Gran.' She lifted her mug to Mrs Wicks.

'Cheers,' said Mrs Wicks. 'I really am looking forward to meeting this friend of yours, Angie. I was telling my own gentleman friend about him, and he said he had heard of your friend's bank.'

'Really?' said Angie, surprised.

'Yes. Well, you see, Clifford is very interested in the financial world. He often has a flutter on the Stock Exchange, and he reads all the financial papers.'

'Oh does he?' said Angie. 'Well, perhaps they could meet some time. That'd be fun.'

She didn't tell Mrs Wicks that she very much hoped her friend Clifford Parks would be reading quite a lot more about Praegers in the next few weeks.

Baby arrived looking tired but cheerful, with a large bouquet of slightly tacky flowers obviously bought from some stall outside the airport. Angie took his coat, led him into the drawing room.

'Drink?'

'Please. This is a lovely house, darling.'

'Isn't it? All my own work. Champagne? Thought so. How was the flight? Oh, now Baby, this is my grandmother, Mrs Wicks. Mainstay of my whole life, and the most glamorous woman in the whole street. Gran, this is Frederick Praeger the Fourth. Otherwise known as Baby.'

'Pleased to meet you,' said Mrs Wicks, holding out a well-manicured hand. She was indeed looking very glamorous; she had a new hairstyle which Henri in the High Street had been urging on her for months, a French pleat culminating in a pile-up of curls on the top of her head. She had worked out a new make-up as well, with a stronger glossier lipstick, and she was wearing a bright blue silk dress with very wide shoulders (as worn by Alexis in *Dynasty*), and extremely high heels.

'I'm very pleased to meet you,' said Baby, smiling and bowing slightly over her hand. 'But I certainly can't believe you're Angie's grandmother. Her mother maybe.'

'Well of course I was very young when her mother was born,' said Mrs Wicks, smiling at him and fluttering her eyelashes rather hard. She had been practising this lately in front of the mirror and using it on Clifford, who had certainly found it very affecting.

'I've heard a great deal about you,' he said, 'and I'm very pleased you're well now. It must have been very tedious being in that rest home all those years.'

'Gran, champagne?' said Angie hastily. 'Perhaps you'd like to pour.'

'Now that's a gentleman's job,' said Mrs Wicks briskly. 'Remember your manners, Angela. Whatever would Mr Praeger think if I took over?'

'I'd think it was rather nice,' said Baby, sinking down onto the sofa, his eyes closing. 'I'm very tired. It's one in the morning New York time already.'

Angie sighed to herself. She clearly wasn't going to get any joy out of Baby tonight.

In the morning he was more cheerful.

'All hell's broken loose,' he told her, drinking the Bucks Fizz she had brought him in bed at eleven o'clock. 'Dad's threatened to disinherit me, Mary Rose says she'll never give me a divorce, and the partners are all winding up for a battle royal. Talk about vultures.'

'And such a succulent little morsel,' said Angie, nibbling gently at his ear. 'It's going to be exciting isn't it, Baby?'

'I'd put another word to it, I think,' said Baby. He sighed but he still looked cheerful, more positive than Angie had seen him for years.

'He can't really disinherit you, can he?'

'Not strictly speaking. But he's making me feel he can.'

'And Mary Rose?'

'Oh, frightful. Verging from martyred to humouring me, like some small boy who's wet his pants.'

Angie kissed him. 'I can't wait to get into your pants.'

'Let me finish this champagne. It's much too good to hurry.'

'Oh God,' said Angie. 'Husbandly mode already.'

'Yes, and it's wonderful. I'm loving it. How's Junior?'

'Junior is just fine. He had a full service yesterday.'

'Good. And how's Mrs Praeger elect?'

'Oh, I like that! Say it again!'

'Mrs Praeger elect.'

'She's fine too. Not really even very sick. Happy. Happy you're here.'

'I'm happy I'm here. It's much nicer here than in New York. I'm living at the Sherry Netherland and it's hell. I might try the Plaza next week.'

'Now look,' said Angie, taking the glass from him and setting it down, 'we only have a few days. We don't want to waste them discussing the rival merits of New York hotels.'

'I guess not,' said Baby. He looked younger, more self-confident as he pulled her in beside him.

Later they went for a walk on Primrose Hill, then drove into London, saw *Superman II* (Angie had a passion for Christopher Reeve which Baby said verged on the insulting), had an early dinner and went back to bed. Even that had definitely improved, Angie noticed.

'This isn't bad for Junior is it?' he said anxiously, as her noisy orgasm faded and she quietened beneath him.

'No. Well, Mr Fisher did say to be a little careful. To avoid times when I would have had my period. This is absolutely not one of them.'

'Are you sure? I'd hate to lose him now.'

'I'm sure.'

'Good. Christ, I love you.' He turned to look at her. 'I still can't believe I've done it. It's so wonderful, not to be hiding.'

'I told you.'

'I know. Now look, what are we going to do? Now that I'm at least struggling to make an honest woman of you, would you consider moving to New York?'

'Of course I'd certainly consider it.' Angie waited, hauling her courage up. This was it. There wasn't going to be a better moment. And if she failed, well, it wasn't the end of the world. It would just be more comfortable, easier for her, if she could get him to agree.

'Baby – I really do think you might consider moving to London. With Praegers, of course.'

★

325

She didn't mention it all next day. He had said Praegers certainly might be opening a London office, that he was personally quite keen on the idea, although Fred was less sure, but that in any case he wouldn't be in it. Angie asked him whyever not, and he had said slightly shortly that his place was in New York, running the bank. Angie, knowing that he did nothing of the sort in New York, left the matter for the time being. It obviously wasn't going to be at all easy; Baby seemed uncharacteristically irritated by her interest in the whole thing.

In the morning they lay in bed until late, chatting over the papers, then went into London for lunch at the Ritz.

'Nowhere nicer than the Ritz on Sunday,' said Angie. 'And all that exercise has made me hungry.'

'I'm not surprised,' said Baby, 'I still think you should be a bit more restrained.'

'With you in the bed?' said Angie, kissing him. 'Impossible.'

They had just ordered lunch when Baby suddenly stiffened.

'What's the matter?' said Angie.

'Oh – nothing. It's perfectly all right. I keep forgetting I don't have to worry about it any more. About people seeing us.'

'What people have you seen?'

'My nephew. Max. Look over there, with that extremely beautiful girl.'

'Where? Oh, my goodness,' said Angie, 'he's fairly extremely beautiful himself.'

Max was sitting at one of the small corner tables, holding the hand of a small dark girl with exquisite features. As people do, he suddenly became aware of being watched; he turned his head, saw Baby and grinned, said something to the girl and got up and walked over to their table.

'Uncle Baby. What a nice surprise. How are you?'

'I'm extremely well, thank you, Max. Can I introduce a friend? Angela Burbank. Angie, my nephew, Max Hadleigh.' There was a silence. Max looked down at Angie, and Angie looked up at Max. He was wearing a pair of black cord trousers and a white shirt, a black sweater knotted casually round his shoulders; he pushed his blond hair back from his blue eyes, and smiled at her, a languid, careless smile. He was patently very aware both of the way he looked and of what her reaction would be. Angie's eyes took him in, all the arrogant young self-conscious sexuality of him, and she reacted deep within her body, in a hot, liquid sweetness that surprised and pleased her with its violence; then she pulled herself

326

together. This was no way for a nearly married woman to feel. She smiled quickly and took his outstretched hand.

'Max! How nice to meet you.'

'How do you do,' said Max, and while the well-brought-up boy shook her hand, the man's eyes moving shamelessly and appreciatively over first her face, then her body.

'How long are you here for, Uncle Baby?' he said, breaking the slightly awkward silence.

'Oh – only a few days.'

'Business I suppose?' said Max. There was an insolence in the polite voice that made Angie want to slap him.

'Yes,' said Baby shortly. 'Er – how's your father?'

'Alexander's fine,' said Max. 'Thank you.'

'And Georgina?'

'She's great.'

'Charlotte's enjoying herself, I think,' said Baby.

'Well, I don't know about that,' said Max. 'She says this guy Gabe is giving her a pretty hard time.'

'I'm sorry about that,' said Baby, genuinely concerned.

'Don't worry about it,' said Max cheerfully, 'somebody should. My sister Charlotte,' he said to Angie, 'is a straight cross between Matron and Head Girl. Very bossy indeed. Oh, hi Claudia. This is Claudia Grossman. Claudia, this is my uncle, Baby Praeger, and a friend of his, Angie Burbank. Claudia's a model. Like me,' he added with a touch of childlike pride.

'Hallo, Claudia,' said Angie. 'Nice to meet you. Models, huh?'

'Yes, I'm off to Florida tomorrow on a job,' said Max. 'To Key West to be precise.'

'Oh, I forgot,' said Claudia, carefully ignoring Baby and Angie, 'the agency asked me to tell you. You're not going to Key West after all. You're staying in Miami.'

Max scowled.

'Shit. That's all I need.'

He looked very upset; disproportionately, Angie thought.

'Miami's OK,' she said, 'they have some great restaurants. And shops. And the Everglades are fun.'

'I think it's a dump,' said Max. 'I've been there before.'

'Well, the Keys are nicer. That's for sure. But it isn't far. There's an airport at Key West, even. You could fly down in half an hour. Take a day off. I'm sure the agency won't mind.'

'I expect they would,' said Max. 'But thanks for the information anyway.' He smiled at her, then at Baby. 'Well, it's really nice to – '

'Come on,' Max,' said Claudia. She looked more bored than ever. 'Our food is getting cold.'

'Cheers, Max,' said Baby. 'Give my regards to your dad.'

'What a charming girl,' said Angie, looking after them, and then slightly sharply at Baby.

'Yup. Pretty though.'

'So is your nephew. Funny kind of career for a lord.'

'I guess so. Alexander certainly hates it. You never met Max then?'

'No, he was just a twinkle in Virginia's eye when I left England. My goodness, aren't we getting old?'

'Some of us older than others. Could Junior handle a little more champagne?'

'Could you just stay there a moment,' said the radiologist. 'I'd just like to get Mr Fisher in to have a look at this.'

'Have a look at what?' said Angie. She was lying in the X-ray department of the Princess Grace, with her stomach covered in oil, having her first ultrasound done. 'There isn't a problem, is there?'

'Absolutely not,' said the radiologist. She was a fresh-faced girl with rosy cheeks, and looked as if she had been captain of games at her school. 'I promise there isn't. Just a bit of a funny position, and I can't quite see everything. No, your baby's moving around and the right size and everything. Don't worry. Hang on a minute, I'll see if I can find Mr Fisher.'

Angie lay, her heart beating rather fast. If there was something wrong with this baby, if she was going to lose it, if it had died, she really didn't think she could bear it. Everything was going so well; too well maybe. She stared at the tiny screen, blank now, wondering what on earth it had revealed, what could have made it so necessary for Mr Fisher to have a look at it. Surely at this stage you couldn't detect abnormality, could you? Might it be that? She had an idea that spina bifida showed up on the ultrasound. God, a deformed baby. She had been so afraid she was too old. Well, she wouldn't, she couldn't go ahead with that. She suddenly and rather surprisingly wished Baby was here, out in the waiting room with the other fathers. She had never thought of him as a source of strength, rather the reverse, but now that it was his baby that was under threat she wanted him very badly. But he was three thousand miles away.

She stared at the ceiling, the walls, she counted the tiles, the lights, the robes hanging behind the door. Why was Mr Fisher being so long? Was the radiologist telling him some dreadful thing she'd found, and they were debating how to tell her? Was he furiously looking some problem, some condition up in a book, something so rare that even he wasn't able

328

to put a name to it? Was he having a quick drink, to get the courage to confront her? Five more minutes of this and she'd scream. She would count to sixty, five times, and then she'd scream very loudly.

She had just got to sixty for the third time when the door opened and the radiologist and Mr Fisher came in. They smiled at her.

'Feeling all right, Miss Burbank?' said Mr Fisher.

'Well I was,' said Angie crossly, 'until I was left lying here, worried to death.'

Mr Fisher patted her hand. 'Nothing to worry about, I promise you. Now let's have another look, Sarah. Ah yes. Yes, that's very interesting. Quite right. Clever girl.'

'Oh for God's sake,' said Angie. 'What is it?'

Mr Fisher came to the side of the bed again and took her hand, giving her his smoothest, most self-congratulatory smile. 'Feeling strong, Miss Burbank? You're going to need to be. You're having twins.'

'Baby? This is Angie. Yes I know you're in a meeting. I don't give a shit. Listen, I have something really important to tell you. Really important. Baby, be quiet and listen. I'm – that is we're – having twins. Yes, I said twins. Of course I'm sure. I just saw them for myself on the ultrasound screen. What? No I don't know what sex they are. What does it matter? The thing is, Baby, I really do feel I need you. More than ever. Can you come over soon? I don't know why, but I'm scared. All right, call me back. But don't be too long.'

It hadn't been entirely untrue. She was, if not scared, very thoughtful. Having one baby had seemed like fun; having two looked extremely daunting. Being pregnant with two was going to be awful (she was so small and she would have to get so big); and as for giving birth to two – God! Angie, who was physically quite brave, shrank from the thought. And then equipping a nursery for two, hiring a nanny – or would it be nannies – for two, getting around with two. Difficult. She paced the house. She didn't know what she was going to do. But she needed Baby and she needed him in London, and not in some bloody hostile city across the Atlantic.

Baby sat looking at her rather helplessly.

'Angie, darling, I can perfectly understand how you feel. And I have to say I am feeling fairly – well, nervous, myself.'

'Oh great!' said Angie testily. Baby ignored this.

'But I have to be in New York. I can't be in London. I really can't. I will make a home for you there, we'll be together all the time, I'm not

329

reneging on any agreement, but I can't leave New York. And Praegers. I can't.'

'I'm not asking you to leave Praegers. I'm asking you to bring Praegers to London. Like every other sensible American bank.'

'Angie, I don't know how you got this idea into your head, but I do assure you every other sensible American bank is not coming to London.'

'Did you discuss it even?'

'I told you, we already talked about it. A lot more, as it happens. My father still feels that it's not a good idea. He says everyone thinks they're going to get a ninety per cent share of the market, and that even that isn't going to be very much.'

'Oh, your father. What do you think?'

'I agree with him.'

'Well my goodness gracious me!'

'Oh for God's sake. And Angie, even if Praegers did come to London, I certainly wouldn't be coming with it. It would be run by one of the senior partners. I've told you. Angie, I don't tell you how to run your company. Please don't try and tell me how to run mine.' He smiled at her slightly nervously. 'Now look, darling, I have lots of details of apartments and duplexes and even triplexes here. You run through them, and I'll go and see them all and report back.'

'Baby, I don't want to go to New York. I don't want to have this – these – babies in New York. Mr Fisher is here. My hospital is here. I'm scared, Baby, and I want to feel safe.' She willed the tears up; Baby looked at her helplessly.

'Angie, I'm sorry. Terribly sorry. But I – '

'Oh fuck off,' said Angie, turning away from him. 'Just fuck off back to New York, Baby. I'm getting very very tired of this conversation. It seems to be going on for ever.'

'It does to me as well,' said Baby.

Angie stared at him. He didn't often stand up to her. She wasn't sure that she liked it very much.

She was reading the business section of the *Sunday Times* in bed two weeks later; it was just as well she was in bed, she told Baby, or she would have fallen over.

'Praegers joins American invasion' read the headline, quite modest, but very clear on page three.

The family-owned investment bank, Praeger and Partners, is to open a branch in London later this year. This makes it one in a very long line of American banks moving into the city in preparation for Big Bang in

October 1986. Praegers, who list Fosters Land and Dudley Communications among their clients, is small (only 27 partners, 10 of them senior) but extremely blue chip, its control handed over a few years ago by Frederick Praeger III to his son 'Baby' Praeger. It is known that Praegers are looking for a stockbroking firm to incorporate with their operation; Mr Praeger Senior said yesterday that no bank, large or small, could afford to be left behind in the battle for a share of the London market that lay ahead.

'Fucking hell!' shouted Angie to the paper. 'Fucking fucking hell.'

She reached for the telephone, dialled the number of the Sherry Netherland. 'Give me Mr Praeger in Suite Three,' she snapped to the polite voice (extremely polite, given that it was four in the morning) which answered the phone.

Baby's voice, slurred with sleep, answered. 'Yes? Baby Praeger speaking.'

'Baby, what the hell do you mean by not telling me you were coming to London?' Angie found to her irritation she was crying; bloody, bloody hormones, she thought.

'Angie, what is this? I'm not coming to London. Not for another week. Are you OK? Are the babies OK?'

'The babies are fine. Their mother isn't. Baby, why do I have to read an article in the *Sunday Times* to learn Praegers are coming to London? Why?'

'Angie, I really don't know what you're talking about.'

'Well get a hold of the London *Sunday Times* and find out.' Angie slammed down the phone.

Three hours later Baby phoned back. He sounded subdued and cautious.

'I'm sorry, darling. You really have to believe me, I didn't know. I had no idea. I'm as angry as you are. Once again, I've been made to look a fool. I'm going over to see my father now. I'm very very sorry. I'll get back to you when I've talked to him. But I have to tell you, Angie, it isn't going to alter my situation. I certainly won't be coming. Dad has arranged for Pete Hoffman to run the London office.'

Angie arrived at the building in Pine Street five days later. She was looking extremely chic, in a white Chanel suit; her blonde hair was slicked back in a large black bow. She was pale, and slightly dark-eyed, but there was an expression on her face that Baby at least would have quailed from.

'I want to see Mr Praeger,' she said.

'I'm terribly sorry, but Mr Praeger is out of town,' said the girl, smiling at her rather coldly from behind the large curved and carved reception desk.

'Yes, I know that. I don't mean Mr Baby Praeger. I mean Mr Frederick Praeger the Third.'

'Well, I'll try for you. Do you have an appointment?'

'No,' said Angie briefly.

'Well in that case – '

'Please ask Mr Praeger if he'll see me. My name is Burbank. Miss Burbank. You can tell him I have a debt to settle.'

'Oh. Well.' The girl looked flustered. 'Well if you just take a seat, I'll ring up to his office.'

Angie sat down, and picked up the *Wall Street Journal*. She liked the *Journal*; it looked so nice. She remembered Virginia using it once to paper the walls of some financial man's study.

'Miss Burbank?'

'Yes?'

'Mr Praeger says you're to go up. Third floor. His secretary will meet you at the elevator.'

The elevator was very old, with elaborate gilded gate-style doors; Angie was glad when it arrived to much groaning and rattling. A very pretty girl in a pink suit was waiting for her.

'Miss Burbank? Hi, I'm Candy Nichols, Mr Praeger's secretary. He says will you wait just a moment, he'll be right along. Can I get you a coffee?'

'Yes please. Black,' said Angie.

'Fine. You're like me, you like your coffee strong and your men weak, huh?' Candy gave her a ravishing smile.

'I like my men strong,' said Angie. 'That's why I'm here.'

'Oh, I see,' said Candy, who clearly didn't.

Fred III kept her waiting for ten minutes. Angie didn't mind. She knew what she was doing, and she knew he had made a huge concession seeing her at all with no appointment. She smiled at him as he came into the room, and stood up, holding out her hand. Her first thought was that he had hardly aged at all in the fifteen years since she had last seen him. He was, she knew, over eighty, but he was still a powerful, forceful man, tall and erect, and, with his thick silver hair and brilliant blue eyes, still attractive. In a strange way, she thought he looked younger than Baby.

'Mr Praeger,' she said, 'how nice to see you again.'

'What do you want?' he said. 'I don't have very long.'

'Two things,' she said. 'I wanted to give you this.' She held out an envelope. 'It's a bankers' draft for one hundred thousand dollars. You said I should return it if I – got together with Baby again. I'm a good businesswoman. I don't renege on a deal.'

'You should give me more than that,' he said. He scowled at her, but there was a flash of amusement in his eyes at the same time. 'That money is worth a lot more now.'

'I know, but inflation was not written into the agreement. I have witnesses to that. Sorry.'

'Well,' he said. 'Thank you. I hope you're not expecting that I shall tear it up. I intend to pay it into my personal account immediately.'

'I'd hate you to tear it up,' said Angie. 'I'd be insulted.'

'Good. Well, you're looking well. Pregnancy suits you.'

'Yes it does. Which is just as well. The only thing is, I'm not having just one baby. I'm having two. Had you heard that?'

'I had not. I am not in the habit of discussing my son's personal affairs.' Again, in spite of the hostility, there was amusement in his eyes. Angie smiled at him, and drained her cup of coffee.

'Yes, well I'm having twins. At the end of July.'

'How nice for you.'

'Well I hope so. It's a bit of a daunting prospect.'

'Well,' said Fred III, 'you made your bed, Miss Burbank. Now you have to lie on it.'

'I don't know what you mean.'

'Of course you do. Girls like you don't get pregnant unless they want to. Nor do their lovers risk getting them pregnant.'

'I'm sorry?'

'Angie.' Fred leant forward, patted her lightly on the cheek. 'May I call you that? I'm a very old, very worldly man. I don't deceive easy. Of course you trapped Baby into this. I know that. It's a measure of what a simpleton he is that he doesn't. What did you tell him? That your diaphragm had a hole in it? That you forgot to take your pill?'

'Mr Praeger – '

'And then what did you tell him? That you hadn't realized until it was too late to do anything about it? That you were a Catholic or a paid–up member of the Pro Life group?'

'Baby and I have been very much in love for years,' said Angie coldly. 'I find your assertions very insulting.'

'I find your expecting all of us to believe that the whole thing was an accident equally insulting. However, let us not spend too much time debating that. You've done it finally, gotten Baby away from his wife and family. Very good. What's the second thing you want?'

'I want Baby to come to London,' said Angie briskly.

'Oh really? Well that's very interesting. Is there any other little demand I can meet for you at the same time? Perhaps you'd like my house in New York as a pied-à-terre? A small clothing allowance? My blessing on your liaison? I'm finding this conversation very interesting.'

'Look,' said Angie, leaning forward. 'It's a very sound idea.'

'Oh really? For whom?'

'For you,' she said.

Fred leant back and looked at her. He pulled a cigar out of his pocket and clipped off the end. Then he pulled a box of matches out of the other pocket and started lighting the cigar, puffing very hard in her direction. It took a long time, and he said nothing at all. Angie waved the clouds of smoke away from her, coughing.

'Oh, I'm so sorry,' said Fred, heavily polite. 'I didn't think. Forgive me. Shall I put it out?'

'No,' said Angie. 'I know how much you all rely on your cigars. Didn't I hear somewhere that Lehman Brothers' annual cigar bill is thirty thousand dollars?'

'Sounds modest to me,' said Fred. 'Well now, tell me a little more about this arrangement you have in mind. What it will do for me.'

'It'll get Baby out of New York.'

'And why should I want that?'

'He's an embarrassment to you,' said Angie briefly. 'I know he is. He isn't really terribly clever. I love him, you may not believe that, but I do – but I can see he isn't terribly clever. And he's certainly no banker. Incidentally, why did you suddenly change your mind about the London office?'

'Nothing to do with you. But I didn't suddenly change my mind. I always intended to do it. I just don't like putting my cards on the table until I'm ready.'

'Well that didn't do a lot for Baby's morale either,' said Angie. 'Or his standing, I imagine.'

'You're very arrogant,' said Fred, looking at her. 'How did you come to all these conclusions?'

'I listen to Baby. Telling me things. I can see it. But – he does better when you're not there. You destroy his confidence. Make him make more mistakes than he would.'

'Oh really?'

'Yes. Really. So either you should retire again. Or you should give him a second chance in London.'

'How altruistic you are. And no doubt you'd prefer the former option?'

'No. The second. I want him in London. I don't really like New York.'

'Baby does,' said Fred, looking at her carefully.

'I know, but he'd like London too. He'd love it. And you could carry on here for years, having fun, get back in your old office, have everyone say what a miracle you are, and he'd be in London, out of your hair, and everyone would be happy.'

'Including you?'

'Well obviously.'

Fred stared at her for a while. Then he said, 'No. Out of the question.'

'Why?'

'I want Baby here. I'm still trying to do something with him. Make a banker of him.'

'It's not working. He's miserable. Demoralized. What's more, he's diminished in authority here. And that must be bad for the bank's image. The clients can't respect him. He'll do much better in London. Given a fresh start. He did much better without you before. When you were retired. Before he had his heart attack. You're not allowing him any stature. Why can't you see that?'

'I'll allow him what I choose, when I choose,' said Fred III, but he sounded thoughtful suddenly, and his eyes were distant.

A month later there was an announcement in the trade press. Baby Praeger was to head up the new Praeger operation in London, where Praegers had made a successful bid for the stockbrokers Rutherford and Whyte. Fred Praeger III would remain in control of the New York office until such time as he saw fit to retire once more. Mr Praeger told a journalist from the *Wall Street Journal* that he had no intention of retiring again until he received notification from a much higher authority than anything Wall Street could offer.

Chapter 26

Max, 1984

Max got out of the plane in Miami feeling irritable and restless.

This trip was in theory going to be great fun; three girls and Max (always a happy proportion, and he knew one of the girls, Dodo Browne, extremely well already), a photographer called Titus Lloyd, who was famously able to drag sex into a photograph of anything, even a boiled egg, the hairdresser and make-up artist, a deceptively sweet-looking gay boy called Jimbo, with a tongue that could very efficiently savage anyone who crossed or upset him in the least little way; and then there was the client, a shirt manufacturer from the East End called Terry, and the account exec from the agency, a slightly plain, very clever girl called Jennifer Collins.

'If you have to lay anyone, Max,' the agency had said to him slightly plaintively (for last time there had been just the suggestion of a complaint from the client about Max Leigh's extremely active behaviour after hours), 'do include Jennifer, there's a good lad. She's just the teensiest bit sex-starved and sensitive.'

Max, who was sitting next to Dodo, looked at Jennifer, reading *Time* magazine, sighed mentally at her rather earnest clever face intent on an analysis of President Reagan's fiscal policy, then reflected rather more pleasurably upon her undeniably long legs wrapped comfortably around one another, and thought he could throw a bit her way. Particularly if she would agree to his nipping down to Key West for a day.

Therein lay the source of his irritability and frustration; he needed, desperately, to get to Key West. Michael Halston had given him the name of a bar frequented by a group of his mother's friends; and the news that Miami was the last stop had been a serious blow. It had been too neat to be true, really, getting a free trip down there; he was absolutely skint (despite his large earnings, which were disappearing horribly fast into the bottomless pit dug by a growing addiction not only to clothes and clubs and expensive girls and fast cars but to the occasional sampling of cocaine as well) and there was no way he was going to be able to find the time or the money to go again for months.

They were staying at the old end of Miami, near Coconut Grove; they arrived there at five in the afternoon, were told they had the evening to themselves, although they could eat dinner in the hotel should they so wish, and warned that shooting was to start at six in the morning. 'I don't want any baggy eyes looking at my lens, thank you,' said Titus Lloyd, 'and that goes for you as well, Max. OK?'

'OK,' said Max.

He ate dinner that night with Titus and Jennifer, and went to bed early.

They were shooting around the pastel-painted, fake deco shops of Coconut Grove that first day, and using the hotel as a base; the girls were twittering about trying on and rejecting the shirts, slagging them off to one another and oo-ing over them whenever Terry Gates hove into view.

He was hovering rather a lot, continually wandering into the girls' dressing room and then saying sorry, sorry, his mistake; in the end Dodo complained to Jennifer, and Jennifer suggested to Terry that perhaps he might sit down with Titus and look at the layouts; Terry said he had looked at the layouts until they were coming out of his arse and he wanted to see the shirts on the girls. Jennifer shot a despairingly conspiratorial look at Max, who promptly went over to Terry and said, 'Got a fag?'

'Sure,' said Terry.

'Let's have it outside, shall we? Can't stand this farting around any longer.'

Outside, he said, 'Look, mate, stay out of the girls' dressing room, will you? They like to make believe they're virgins, you know; they get edgy if someone's spoiling their act. And edgy girls don't do a thing for shirts.'

'OK,' said Terry. 'Can you put in a word for me with the blonde? I gather you know her.'

'Sure,' said Max. 'No problem.'

He sidled up to Dodo a bit later, as she stood waiting to go into a shot; Jimbo was tutting over her hair. 'You really should get this cut, darling, it's in terrible condition.'

'No way,' said Dodo. 'Not here anyway.'

'Look,' said Max, 'watch yourself tonight, Dodo. Tel Boy is after you.'

'I'll have his balls for garters if he tries anything,' said Dodo equably. 'Nasty little squirt. Thanks for the warning. Oh, hi Terry. These shirts are just fab. Did you design them yourself?'

'Some of them,' said Terry modestly, whose only input into the design was to decide how many of each size to make up. 'That one you're wearing was one of mine.'

'It's brilliant. Could I buy it after the shoot?'

'You can have it, darling. For the price of a smile.'

'Oh, I couldn't possibly,' said Dodo. 'You must let me give you something for it.'

'You can give me something for it if you like,' said Terry, moving round and putting his hand on her neat little bottom, only just encased in cut-off jeans.

Dodo looked at him and moved away.

'Suddenly I've gone off the shirt,' she murmured.

'I've warned him off,' said Max. 'As best I could. He's like a filthy little mongrel with a set of pedigree bitches on heat.'

'Thanks, Max,' said Jennifer. She looked harassed. 'These things are hard work, aren't they? Now Jimbo's thrown a wobbly because none of the girls will let him trim their hair, and he's told them they've all got zits. They're sulking, and Titus is going mad because the sun's already too high for the shadows. Or something. And I thought it was going to be fun.'

'It can be,' said Max easily. 'If you just lie back and enjoy it. Look, I have to go and stand moodily in a background now; I'll buy you a drink later.'

It was already hot, and it was only nine; a small crowd had gathered, mostly elderly Miami folk with leathery, weather-beaten faces. Dodo was astride a very large motorbike that Titus had commandeered from somewhere, and the other two girls were standing on either side of her. Max was standing just out of focus, he knew, so he could afford to squint into the sun. He felt bored and irritable again, and the sight of Dodo's buttocks thrust towards him was giving him an erection which he knew would be showing, so tight were his jeans. He would have to lay her tonight, he hadn't had any sex for days and he was randy as hell.

And oh, shit, how on earth was he going to get down to Key West; they were only here for four days, and each one packed with shoots. And he was the only guy; in theory he couldn't be spared.

'Max, do pull yourself together,' yelled Titus, suddenly. 'I know you think you're out of focus, but you're not. Give me a pout. That's better. Jimbo, Cary's hair is too wild. Can't you calm it down a bit?'

'It's too wild because it's too long,' said Jimbo. 'It needs trimming.'

'Then fucking trim it,' said Titus. 'You're the hairdresser, for Christ's sake.'

'He's not cutting my hair,' said Cary, clutching it to her frantically. 'Leonard would have a fit.'

'Cary,' said Titus, 'as far as I can see, Leonard has very little to contribute to this shoot. And you are being paid a great deal of money to stand here in the Florida sunshine and thrust your tits out of a few shirts. If

I say your hair needs trimming, it needs trimming. Otherwise you can fuck off home. At your own expense.'

'Oh all right, all right,' said Cary. Jimbo advanced on her with his scissors, smirking.

'Who's a naughty girl then?'

'Bitch,' said Cary.

'Come and have a drink,' said Max to Jennifer. 'Titus is busy gathering props, and the girls are trying to console each other about their ruined hair.'

'But he's only taken off about half an inch.'

'I know. They wouldn't even have noticed if it had been done in their sleep. But they get very worked up about their hair. They feel about it rather like an artist does about his brushes.'

'Oh, I see. Well, they do all have very nice hair,' said Jennifer carefully.

'I'd rather have yours. Less fucked about,' said Max. He meant it. Jennifer had a neat, swinging shiny bob; it was the sort of hair he liked.

'Thank you. Yes, I'd love a drink. Orange juice and Perrier.'

'Fine. I'll have the same. Funny how it feels like cocktail time on these shoots at – what is it? – ten in the morning. It's the emotional energy we all spend.'

'You don't seem much like the average male model,' said Jennifer, looking at him.

'I don't? How's that then?'

'Too posh,' she said. 'You're Viscount Hadleigh really, aren't you?'

'Yup. 'Fraid so.'

'So what on earth are you doing, doing this?'

'I like it. It likes me. Why shouldn't I be?'

'Well, I'd have thought you'd be at Oxford, or some agricultural college or something.'

'Darling, I'm as thick as shit,' said Max, smiling at her radiantly. 'One O level to my name. Never get into a college, I wouldn't. Besides this is fun. I may not do it for ever, but it sure beats working. As the man said.'

'Oh well. I just wondered. Nothing to do with me really. Thank you anyway. You've helped an awful lot already.'

'I have? How?'

'Oh, having dinner with me last night. I was feeling really nervous and shy. Everyone else knew each other and I could see Titus felt stuck with me. So it was really nice that you joined us. And then warning off Terry this morning, and now calming me down. I'm really glad you came.'

Max smiled at her, his most guileless, beautiful smile. 'All part of the service. Honestly.'

339

Titus came over. 'We're going to move along to the beach for the next shot. We'll need transport. And somewhere for the girls to change. Do we have that Campervan, or not, Jennifer, that I asked you to organize?'

'Well, we did,' said Jennifer, looking helplessly into the car park. 'It was here last night. But it seems to have vanished.'

'Oh Jesus H. Christ,' said Titus. 'Darling, are you in charge of this shoot or are you some kind of kindergarten teacher along for the ride? Look, ask in reception, will you, and get something organized. We really need it.'

'I'll come with you,' said Max.

The girl in reception was regretful but unhelpful. Another client had taken the van; it was hotel property, Miss Collins hadn't made it clear she needed it every day. She could have it tomorrow, but not today.

'Could you try Hertz maybe?' said Jennifer. She looked distracted.

'No hope,' said the girl. 'I just rang them for this other client. They don't have anything. Sorry.' She returned to the brochure she was studying. Jennifer looked as if she might cry.

Max stepped forward. He put his hand on the girl's.

'Look,' he said, 'there are other car-hire firms. I can see you're terribly busy. But would you let me use your directory and see what I can do?' He smiled; the girl looked at him.

'I'll do it for you,' she said and picked up the phone without moving her eyes from his face. Half an hour later an Avis Campervan pulled into the forecourt of the hotel.

'You've been marvellous,' said Jennifer. 'I don't know how to thank you.'

They were eating lunch at a table on their own; Dodo occasionally shot them a resentful glance.

'I have a suggestion,' said Max. Jennifer looked up startled, nervous. He grinned at her. 'It's all right. Nothing like that. I need to get down to Key West. Just for a day. Could you help me fix that?'

He flew down to Key West in a tiny plane early on the third day. The girls were all outraged; Dodo threatened to go on strike.

'Listen, Babe, I've worked for this.'

'Oh yeah? In her bed? Virginal cow.'

'No,' said Max quietly. 'On the set, with you lot of animals.'

He got out of the plane and took a taxi into town; he was enchanted by it, its narrow streets, the trolley car with the ringing bell that served as a tourist transport system, the white board houses with the wide verandahs, hung over with palms, the technicolour painted shops and

340

restaurants, the swinging signs that said 'Dentist' or 'Attorney at Law', the lack of cars, the smiling, lazy crowds.

'It looks like a film set,' he said to the cab driver.

'Better than that. It's a little country. Called the conch republic. Casts a spell on you. You can't hurry here.'

'OK,' said Max. 'I'll get out and walk. Where's the Parrot House? And will it be open yet?'

'Parrot House is always open. Cept between four a.m. and breakfast. It's two blocks down, on the left. Now don't miss sunset in the Square.'

'I'll try not to, but why?'

'Everyone goes there to watch. If it's a good one they clap.'

'I'll be there,' said Max.

He found the Parrot House easily; it was a restaurant, with a rainbow-coloured (or rather parrot-coloured, he supposed) frontage, a deep dark interior and a wide courtyard at the side, with tables set amongst the palm trees. A large and splendid parrot swung in a ring outside the door.

Max sat down and ordered a beer; a very pretty boy brought it to him.

'Thanks. Is the manager here?'

'Not yet, sir. Too early. Give him an hour or two. Who shall I say?'

'Say a friend of Michael Halston's.'

Shit, thought Max, this is going to take more than all day.

A fat, smiling man with a great deal of curly grey hair eventually appeared in the courtyard. He walked over to Max, holding out his hand.

'Hi. Johnny Williams. I understand you know Michael?'

'Yes, I do. He suggested I see you.'

'Any friend of Michael's is a friend of mine. How can I help you?'

'I think once you might have known my mother.'

'Young man, I've known a great many mothers. Created a few as well.' He laughed, his great belly heaving. Max felt sick.

'Well, my mother's name was Virginia Caterham. She used to come here a lot, apparently. Had a circle of friends.'

'Virginia! Virginia. What does she look like?'

'Well, reddish brown hair. Very tall. Um – very beautiful. American.'

'Most of my customers are American.'

'Yes of course.' Max felt foolish.

'When would this have been? Here, let me get you another drink, and we can talk.'

'Thank you. It would have first been oh, about eighteen years ago. And I think she came back occasionally from time to time. But I believe her friends still come here. Quite often. It's a base of theirs.'

'Tell me some more about your mother. Where is she now, that you can't ask her yourself about these friends?'

341

'She's dead,' said Max quickly.

'Oh. I'm sorry. When did she die?'

'About four years ago. She was killed in a car crash. In England.'

'Why was she in England – I'm sorry, what is your name?'

'Max. Max Leigh. She lived in England. She was married to an Englishman.'

'Called?'

'Lord Caterham.'

He had been saving that. Americans still loved lords. Johnny's eyes lit up. 'Lord Caterham? Lady Caterham. Ah, now I begin to hear some bells. She never came here with him, did she?'

'No. No I don't think she did.'

'What did she do, your mother?'

'She was an interior designer.'

'Ah! Virgy! Virgy Caterham. Of course I remember her. She was a real lady. A very lovely lady. She hasn't been here for – oh, ten years. Ted Franklyn's crowd, that's who she was with. Oh, she was amazing. Beautiful. Beautiful! She used to dance, didn't she? Tap dance. She taught Ted to dance. And sing. Oh, they were good times. We used to go off on Ted's boat, oh, for days sometimes. Out to the reef, down to the Bahamas. Life was one big party. They were great days. I miss them, I really do.'

'So – where could I find Ted Franklyn?' asked Max, his heart thudding very hard in his chest.

'I'm afraid the same place as your mom. He died. Oh, about three years ago. Too much of everything.'

'Oh. Oh, I see. And was he her greatest friend?'

'Yes, he was. Although she did have a kind of a penchant for Tommy. Tommy Soames-Maxwell. They were very fond of one another. He was a great guy. Wonderful fisherman. I have a picture of him somewhere. Wait, I'll go find it.'

He disappeared. Max sat thinking, imagining, seeing his mother with these people, these idle, self-indulgent, hedonistic people. It was so unlike her. And yet – was it? Who was to say what she was like, who she had been? And who she had been with, and to bed with and drunk with and danced with. Ted Franklyn. Tommy Soames-Maxwell. The names alone told a story. Soames-Maxwell – what a name. What a – Oh God. The implication of it suddenly hit Max hard. Charlotte and her Charles St Mullin. And now him and Tommy Soames-Maxwell. It could, it almost had to, make sense, add up. He looked up suddenly; the courtyard seemed to have blurred, the indistinct figure of Johnny looming out of the shadows. He was coming towards him, smiling, a photograph in his

342

hand. Max took it, shaking slightly. And old, smudgy torn photograph, inscribed 'To Johnny. Remembering fun. Tommy.' Max sat and looked at Tommy Soames-Maxwell. Tommy Soames-Maxwell stood and looked back at him. Tall, smiling, blond, with a look in his eyes that invited danger. Hanging onto a huge rod, with a massive fish strung up beside him. Max felt sick, excited, almost awed.

'And where could I find Mr Soames-Maxwell? Does he live here?'

'No. Tommy lives in Vegas. He's a gambling freak these days. He used to do battle with fish, now it's the wheel. Sad, really.'

'Yes,' said Max, 'very sad. Do you have an address for him?'

343

Chapter 27

Charlotte, 1984

Charlotte knew exactly when she had fallen in love with Gabe Hoffman. One minute she had been thinking how much she loathed him, how much she couldn't wait to be rid of him, away from his office, and the long, miserable boring days with him; and the next she had been staring at him, fiercely and almost painfully aware of the extraordinary dark brown of his eyes, the wild unruliness of his hair, the oddly rakish way he smiled, the thick dark hair on his arms, right down to his wrists (she normally loathed hairy men), the urgent impatient way he moved around, the size of him, oh God, the size of him. Charlotte imagined, very briefly, lying underneath Gabe Hoffman and felt faint; allowed her mind to linger, more briefly still, on the particular part of his anatomy that might be most intimately engaged with hers, and felt first hot and then chilled with horror at herself. What was she doing, thinking, reacting to him like this, in precisely the way the entire female population of Praegers did? At – she glanced up at the array of clocks on his wall, showing the time in New York, Tokyo and London – at half past ten in the morning, for God's sake, stone cold sober. Then she forced her mind back onto what he had just said to her, what she was supposed to be replying – and she realized what had made the difference, what had done this to her, what had turned all the emotions she had in a great tumbling heap inside her head. Or rather her body. Oh well all right, her head and her body.

'You've got it,' he had said. 'That's it. You've fucking got it. You're a fucking genius.' And he had picked up the telephone and stabbed out a number, staring at her at the same time with an expression of profound and almost awed admiration. Charlotte stared back at him, still only half understanding, but understanding also that this was what she had been waiting for, looking for ever since she had been handed this bank, her legacy, at her grandfather's birthday party, all those years ago, ever since she had been working, day after day on the seemingly endless boredom of her apprenticeship. The real world, the heady world of deals, of buying and selling and grabbing and protecting: a sense of tension, excitement, urgency; the smell of money in the air, an almost tangible feeling of greed. And she was part of it now, as Gabe was, she was no

344

longer a trailing, reluctant accessory, she was in there, part of it, adding to it. And as if almost in celebration, she had toppled over into love with him. Just like that.

It hadn't even seemed to her that she had said anything particularly clever. Gabe had been wrestling for days over a hostile bid, unable to establish quite why the target company – a paper manufacturer that was only modestly successful – should be so attractive: Charlotte had looked up casually from her desk and made the observation that one of the company's original parts – small stationery goods and office equipment – had to be of almost inestimable value in terms of customer good will – 'greater than its whole, in a way,' she said. And Gabe had stared at her, very white and still, his hand frozen on the keyboard of his Quotron. 'Shit,' he said, 'of course. Of course. Crown jewel sell-out situation.' And then he made his pronouncement. And then she fell in love with him.

Gabe explained to her about crown jewel sell-outs. 'You sell off the one bit of a company that's most valuable. Quickly. So it isn't really very desirable any more. We do that, and the others'll drop their bid. It's the customers they want. Watch.'

The crown jewels were sold; the bid was duly dropped. Everyone was very excited. Gabe was very fair and told Fred III it had been her idea about the retail outlets. Fred told her he hoped she wouldn't start to think she was the best thing in banking since the invention of the dollar bill. Charlotte assured him she wouldn't. He was smiling at her as he spoke; Freddy was in the room, and she saw his face suddenly, coldly furious. It almost frightened her.

Charlotte had watched in a state of acute excitement as Blackworth sold off its stationery division, and Wrightson dropped their bid. She was invited to the celebratory lunch. She thought how dull it would be without the deal and that afternoon she found herself beginning all over again, on a new bid, for another company, a new set of stockholders, a new buyers' list. She wondered how she could ever have thought Praegers was boring. Her own work had scarcely changed, but she was suddenly completely enraptured by the process. Gabe was, along with the rest of Wall Street, deal-obsessed. The stream of negotiations, of bids and counter-bids, of rumours and counter-rumours, of leaks and denials, was like a physical presence in the office. Gabe sat at his computer, hour after hour, like some large restless bird of prey, watching it with his brilliant dark eyes, ready to swoop into its permanently shifting network of information, opportunity, challenge. For the first time, she was aware of the bank as a vital, living force. Its ability to convert money into power and thus to manipulate people seemed to her almost mystical. It held her in thrall. She knew it was a huge factor in her new, helpless passion for Gabe; but that seemed to her irrelevant. The two things, the two excitements were two halves of a whole. She was constantly if uncomfortably happy.

Gabe had shown absolutely no signs of reciprocating her feelings. Apart from saying 'well done' when a particularly difficult deal had been finally accomplished, he treated her exactly as he treated the other people who worked for him – carelessly, arrogantly, thoughtlessly. Charlotte didn't care; if anything it intensified the way she felt. She was uncomfortably aware she was feeling rather like a schoolgirl with a crush on a prefect, but she didn't really care about that either. She didn't care about anything, except getting to the office in the morning, and being with Gabe. Physical proximity to him was all she asked. Occasionally his hand would brush against hers, and once he put his arm round her shoulders, to move her out of the way; Charlotte could not believe he wouldn't recognize the scorching hunger in her reaction. Her only anxiety was that he might, in some dreadful way, realize what she felt. It was hard to imagine that such feeling, such highly charged sexual intensity, could go unremarked. She tried to make sure that her behaviour was, if possible, cooler than ever, and told herself he was too arrogant, too insensitive to see beyond the end of his desk.

As far as she knew, he had no regular girlfriend; he never mentioned one, and the office gossip was simply of an endless stream of long-legged cool beauties seen waiting for him, with commendable patience, in the reception area of the bank. Charlotte being neither long-legged, nor even, strictly speaking, beautiful, found this slightly disturbing; but so long as none of them moved into his Upper West Side apartment for longer than a night at a time, she felt she could stand it.

She was still living with Fred and Betsey, but she had made a friend at last, a real friend, someone to talk to, and to laugh with, to spend at least some of her very limited spare time with, and that had given her confidence: a girl called Chrissie Forsyte who was a trader on the foreign exchange floor. Charlotte had noticed her first in the queue at the staff restaurant in the basement, handing over her polystyrene box of salad to be weighed at the check-out with a confident '324'.

'That's 331, Chrissie,' said the girl behind the till, 'you did good.'

'Excuse me,' said Charlotte, intrigued, from behind her, 'but what did that mean?'

Chrissie turned and smiled at her. 'I was betting on the weight. Want to share a table?'

'Yes, that'd be nice. Thank you,' said Charlotte. Her difficult situation at Praegers meant she didn't often find someone to eat with; people were still either suspicious of her, or nervous. Most days she carried her own box of salad back up to her office, rather than sit conspicuously alone in the restaurant.

'I don't normally sit down here,' said Chrissie, 'I eat at my desk. But it is *really* quiet today, and I guess I can take a fifteen-minute break.' Her voice was light and pretty, her accent Southern and musical, straight out of *Gone with the Wind*. She smiled at Charlotte. She was tall and very thin, pale, with long brown hair and thick, wire-framed glasses. Most of the traders wore glasses.

'Do you always bet on the weight of your lunch?' asked Charlotte.

'Traders bet on everything,' said Chrissie. 'The floors the elevator will stop at – not that that amounts to much here – the number of wrong buses that come by before the right one arrives, the number of messages waiting when you get back from lunch. Or even the bathroom.' She laughed. 'We're wildly superstitious too. There are lots of stories about people who won't make a single trade until three people have said good morning to them, or who've bought or sold on the toss of a coin. My boss always makes his first trade of the day on multiples of the change he got from his cab fare. We're all a little crazy.' She smiled at Charlotte again. 'You spent any real time on the trading floor?'

Charlotte shook her head. 'Only whizzing through on my first day.'

'Yes, I remember. Come and spend some time there one day. It's really fun. I still love it and this is my sixth year. Only problem is my eyesight. When I started on this I had forty-forty vision. Now I have two new prescriptions a year.'

Charlotte had been up several times since then, and sat enthralled at Chrissie's side in her small empire, measuring roughly three metres by three metres, watching her as she stared for long hours at the screen on which her destiny was fixed, talking into one of her three telephones, another tucked beneath her chin, a half-drunk can of Coke and a half-eaten sandwich on her desk.

'All you have to be in this game,' she said to Charlotte, 'is quick, efficient, bossy and aggressive. For some reason I don't find that too terribly difficult.' She grinned. 'It's a war between yourself and the market. The trading floor is the cutting edge. It's the centre of the universe, I tell you.'

And Charlotte had looked around her at the bedlam of shouting voices and ringing, endlessly ringing phones, of white faces and shirt-sleeved arms waving in the air, of foul language and puerile behaviour, and contrasted it with the investment banking floor, where all was sobriety

347

and suits, Bostonian voices and Bulgari watches, and the three-hour lunch was as crucial as the morning's work that preceded it, and her own department, where ambitious young men like Gabe Hoffman spent their days almost frantically matching one man's need to another's greed, and building their own reputations and futures in the process, and marvelled that something as basically simple as the manipulation of money could manifest itself in so many and diverse ways.

She could see now why Fred had put her to work with Gabe; it was like attending a masterclass every day. She watched him as he sniffed out possible deals, pulling them apparently from the air, persuading colleagues, clients, to go along with him, back his judgement; she listened as he coaxed and urged a deal along, counselling caution one day, steadying nerves the next, arguing with the lawyers, playing with the press; she stared at him transfixed as he talked confidently of buyers where there were none, of money that was not raised, of imminent completions that were not remotely in sight. And always, every time, it seemed, he pulled it off. One of his biggest coups, which had won them their biggest client since the BuyNow TV sales business, had been advising Myonura, the Japanese electronics company, to buy into a TV network. It had been a bold and brilliant move, and much talked of in Wall Street. He was regarded as a star, in spite of his youth, his inexperience, Fred's suspicion of such animals. And some of the stardust rubbed off on Charlotte, she was seen as part of his team: admired, envied, often resented, sometimes disliked, but always noticed.

And Freddy Praeger, of course, was not in their team.

Chapter 28

Max, 1984

The girl pushed her knee between Max's legs hard. She was standing behind him, and her arms were round his neck, her hands pressed, palm downwards, on his naked chest. Gradually she slithered them downwards, towards his crotch. Max tensed; he could feel his erection forming, growing. The sweat pants he was wearing were mercifully loose, but not entirely all-concealing. The girl felt his tension and giggled, reaching down inside the waistband of the pants. 'What have you *got* in there?' she whispered. 'That is quite something, little Lord Max.'

'OK, Opal, that's great. Really fucking great. Hold it right there.'

'My pleasure, darling. My great pleasure!'

'Now don't smile. That's better. That's great.' Flynn Finnian, current darling of New York's fashion photographers, started firing his Hasselblad.

'Max, relax, baby. She isn't going to eat you. No, for Christ's sake I said don't smile. Oh shit, or laugh. Opal, stop laughing. Look, you two, you can go and fuck yourselves stupid in the dressing room in five minutes, but right now can you spare a thought for a poor starving photographer and pose! Pose! Did you ever hear of posing? It's the new thing in modelling. That's better. Pose pose pose! Gorgeous, Opal. God, I could almost fuck you myself when you look like that. Max, that's good. That's great. Now turn a bit. Yeah, that's right. Look at her. Look at her mouth. No, that's no good. Try the other way round. Opal, what happens if you put one hand behind him. Right into the pants, yes, that's right. Yeah, that's great. Fantastic. Good. Good. Max, get a grip. Think wanky, OK? Fine. Great. Fantastic. OK, that's it. Take a break. I'll see you guys in half an hour.'

Max walked into the dressing room, frantic for a cigarette. He was shaking. He was lighting the cigarette when Opal appeared in the doorway behind him. She smiled at him in the mirror, walked lazily forward and slipped her hand back into his pants; he could feel her long nails scratching him slightly as she sought out his anus, and lazily forward, towards his balls. He looked at her, all six foot of her; she was a black African, her hair cropped close, an incredible beauty, with a neck at least nine inches long. She was wearing nothing but a pair of extremely small red briefs and a four-strand pearl choker. The long red boots, which had been her only other clothing for the shot, had been kicked off. She was a year older than he was, funny, raunchy, bi-sexual. Her agency had put it about that she was a princess from some remote African kingdom, but actually she was third-generation Bronx.

'Snort?' she said. 'I have some in my bag.'

Max shook his head. 'Can't when I'm working.'

'Why not?'

'I just can't handle it. Makes me hyper.'

'Poor little baby. I can make you hyper anyway, Max. You don't need coke if you're with me. Here, turn around.'

Max turned round. Opal pushed his pants down, slowly, her eyes fixed on his rampant cock. 'My,' she said, in her thick, gravelly voice, 'that is a *nice* one. Really nice. A good well-bred English cock. I like that.' She squatted down on the floor in front of him, her head on one side, contemplating it; then she looked up at him and grinned.

'I'd really love to,' she said, as if he had invited her to tea, 'but Serena's about to arrive, and you know how I feel about her. And how jealous she is. Can we take a rain check?'

The outer door of the studio opened and Flynn Finnian's voice called out, mockingly camp, 'All finished, you two? Your fashion editor's here.'

Opal stood up swiftly, blocking Max from view. 'Oh hi, Serena darling, how are you? Do you have the furs? I can't wait to try them on.'

Max hauled his pants up frantically, his erection collapsing with merciful speed; Serena Sandeman, famously brilliant (and even more famously lesbian) freelance fashion editor, appeared in the doorway, her arms filled with furs, her ice-cool blue eyes flicking over Opal.

'You've put on weight,' was all she said, 'you need to drop at least four pounds.'

'Serena, I can't,' wailed Opal, 'I only eat once every two days now. I am starving almost to death.'

'I have a new man,' said Serena, lighting a cigarette, 'he gives you a shot every other day. You don't want to eat at all, and it makes you feel great too.'

'Not hyper?' said Flynn. 'The last one of those guys I went to, I was right out of it. I got done for drunk driving.'

'Not really,' said Serena. She gave Opal a card. 'Call him,' she said briefly. 'I can't use you for swimwear with that weight on you.'

Max looked at Opal's rangy frame, the collar and hip bones jutting out of the coal-black skin, the hollow cheeks, the concave buttocks beneath the scarlet panties, and wondered where four pounds could go from. Her fingernails perhaps.

Serena saw him looking at Opal and smiled an icy smile, her pale eyes fixed on his. Keep off, that smile said.

'You must be Max Leigh.'

'Yes I am.'

'I wanted someone dark,' she said to Flynn. 'How come we got him?'

'He looks great with Opal,' said Flynn, 'better than a dark guy. And he's a new face.'

'English huh?' said Serena.

Max nodded.

'He's a lord,' said Opal. 'An earl.'

'Really?' said Serena, icier still.

'Well only a viscount so far,' said Max modestly.

He was only in New York for a week. After this session he was going on to Las Vegas, to find Tommy Soames-Maxwell. He wasn't quite sure why he had taken almost six months to do so; partly cowardice, he supposed, partly lack of time and funds. But in the end he had had to do it. He couldn't turn his back on his roots any longer. He didn't think he was going to like the roots, but a combination of deadly curiosity and a desire to lay the ghost drove him to make the necessary arrangements.

He arrived in Vegas at midday. He couldn't believe anywhere could be so awful. It was like some grotesque fantasy town, sprung up in the middle of the desert he had been gazing at awestruck from the plane: ugly, graceless, charmless, full of appallingly massive hotels, with their thousands of rooms, endless flashing hoardings and the interminable wedding chapels. And the noise; the unique Las Vegas noise, the whine of electronic slot machines and clattering jackpots, that began in the airport and followed him everywhere, down every street, into every building. The heat was intense: 105 degrees. Dry, hard heat; but it was actually better than the awful humidity of New York.

Max took a cab downtown, as advised by Opal, who had been to Vegas on a trip, and booked into a small hotel on Las Vegas Boulevard. It was the area he wanted to be: and Opal had said it was cheap and comparatively secure.

He lay down on the bed in his room, exhausted and scared; he half wished now he had taken Opal up on her offer to come with him. But then he would have had to explain so much and lie so much; better make out on his own. Thinking he should go and explore this legendary place, he fell asleep, and woke with a start to find it was after five. He was hungry; he set out and walked along the boulevard towards Fremont Street, picking up a burger and a Coke on the way. The whole place was almost surreal: if this was his father's natural habitat, he didn't think they would have much to say to one another. Then suddenly he remembered his gambling days at Eton, and the excitement he had felt even then, watching the wheel spin, praying his number would come up, an excitement so great it had been worth risking expulsion for, and decided he had no right to be so judgmental.

He had planned to walk, but it was too hot; he took a cab to Caesar's Palace, which he felt he must see, whether Soames-Maxwell was there or not, and found himself conveyed on the 'people mover', a moving walkway into the strange fantasy world of the ultimate Vegas, the miniature Roman City, Cleopatra's Barge, the Appian Way: all of it windowless, doorless, nightmarishly impossible to find a way out of. He was totally bemused by it, drunk both with the wine that literally flowed in a fountain in the lobby, to be caught in a plastic cup, with the fearsome noise, the literally dazzling vulgarity of it. That took almost two hours, and then feeling increasingly like a lost child, in some strange, half-hostile country, he moved on to the Flamingo Hilton, and the ultra exotic Barbary Coast, with its huge thirty-foot stained-glass mural (where he strayed into the equally exotic stained-glass McDonalds for a second hamburger); until finally it was late enough to start looking for Soames-Maxwell. He took another cab downtown and started at the Golden Nugget; it seemed incredible to him that anyone could have heard of anyone in there, extending as it did an entire block; but he liked it more than Caesar's Palace, it made at least a nod in the direction of taste, with its white and green awnings, and he went to the cashier's cage, where a flashy blonde said yes, sure, she knew Mr Soames-Maxwell, he came in all the time.

'You're in luck, he just came in.'

Max's heart gave a heavy, jerking thud.

'Thanks,' he said. 'Where do I find him?'

'He's at the big table over there,' she said, and led him over to the centre table; a very large back with a mop of greying blond hair confronted them. The girl tapped it.

'Tommy?'

'Hang on, Donna, hang on, wheel's just going now. Shit, shit, come on baby, come on, come on . . .'

His voice tailed away; he turned round, looked at Donna and smiled. Max, expecting some violent rush of emotion, studied him, feeling oddly detached.

He was tall, taller than Max, and very broad; he was about two stone overweight, with a paunch tightly buttoned into his thick denim shirt. His hair was thick and just slightly too long; his face, heavily lined and very tanned, was good-natured, his eyes startlingly blue, the teeth showing in the just-too-wide smile very white and even. He had a moustache; he wore a heavy gold chain round his neck, and a Rolex bracelet watch on his wrist. He looked what he was, a man who had had too much of everything, all his life: too much money, sex, luck and love, and now all of them had run out on him, and he was desperately running after them all, trying to get them back.

'Donna darling. What can I do for you? You're looking gorgeous, gorgeous. You wouldn't get an old man a beer, would you?'

'Sorry, Tommy, I'm just going on the table now. Tommy, this guy's been looking for you. He's – what are you, Max?'

'A journalist,' said Max briefly. He held out his hand. 'How do you do, sir. Max Leigh. I work with Michael Halston.'

The handshake was firm; very firm and heavy. Max resisted the temptation to rub his own hand when it was released.

'Mike Halston eh? How is he? What's he doing? I would really like to buy you a beer, Max, but I don't just at this very moment have any cash.'

'I'll get you a beer,' said Max. 'Can we sit down somewhere and talk?'

'Sure.'

Soames-Maxwell led him through to a bar; it was very dark, very noisy. They sat down in a corner, Max called the waitress.

'Is a beer what you'd really like? Or can I get you something else?'

'I could sink a bourbon or two,' said Maxwell.

'Fine. Could we have a large bourbon, please. No, make it two.'

'Put a pack of Marlborough on that as well, would you, honey?' said Soames-Maxwell. He flashed Max his dazzling, press-button smile. 'You don't mind do you?'

'Of course not,' said Max.

'Now then. What can I do for you? How is old Mike?'

'He's fine. Very well. Retired, actually, living out of town.'

'So how come you're working for him?'

'Well, he's a writing a book. I'm doing some of the research.'

'Uh-huh.' The drinks had arrived. Soames-Maxwell raised his glass and drank gratefully. The glass was empty. 'Er – could we have another of those?' said Max to the hostess.

'Hey,' said Soames-Maxwell, grinning at him, lighting a cigarette with a gold Dunhill lighter, 'I like your style.'

'That's OK,' said Max.

'So what's this book you're working on?'

'It's called *The Last of the Playboys*,' said Max simply. 'It's about all the great playboys of the – well the thirties on. Aly Khan, Douglas Fairbanks, the Prince of Wales, Rainier, you know. And – '

'And you wanted to include me? Well that's nice. I don't know if I'm quite in that league, but I'd be delighted. To reminisce for you. That's what you want, isn't it? What are you paying?'

Max hadn't thought of that; he was taken aback.

'Er – well, I'm not absolutely sure. It's negotiable. I mean several people didn't want payment. They just liked the idea of being in the book.'

'They didn't? Then they're fools. Well, you can tell Mike Halston from me I'm not going to talk to anyone and increase his royalties for any less than – what shall we say – give me a price. And I want it up front.'

Max thought fast. The most, the very most he could raise in cash, on his American Express card, was £500. Which was about – what? $700. He took a deep breath. 'Could we say five hundred dollars?'

Tommy Soames-Maxwell burst into laughter.

'You could say it, my dear Max, but you wouldn't get me saying anything back. I want at least five grand. OK?'

Max took a deep breath. He had a strong hunch about two things. One, that $500 was actually quite a lot for Soames-Maxwell at the moment, and two, that he was a man of immense vanity who would want to be included in the book.

'Sorry,' he said, 'can't do that. I'll just have to tell Michael Halston you didn't want to be in the book.'

'Oh, will you? I see.' Soames-Maxwell looked at him thoughtfully. 'Well – how about we say five hundred down, and maybe some more negotiable.'

'Well – maybe,' said Max. 'But I don't think so. I certainly can't promise.'

'Do I get the five hundred right away?'

'Sure.'

'OK, I'll take a promissory note in the form of bourbon, and we'll settle up in the morning.'

'Fine,' said Max. 'I understand you were a terrific fisherman. Maybe we could start there.'

'Funny place to start, Max. Pretty clean wholesome sport, fishing.'

'I know. But didn't you fish with Hemingway?'

'I did.'

'So that scene must have been all quite interesting.'

'Yes it was. OK, I get you. You want the sporting me. The sporting ladies' man?'

'Well – yes.'

'I was a very fine fisherman,' said Soames-Maxwell, and he lay back in his chair, his brilliant blue eyes soft with reminiscence. 'Nothing I couldn't catch, if I put my mind to it. We fished just about everywhere, off Cuba, off the Keys, off the Bahamas. I had a beautiful boat, a hundred-footer, and I tell you, Max, if you haven't laid some beautiful women on the deck of a yacht after a day catching beautiful fish, then you haven't lived.'

'I haven't lived,' said Max, smiling at him. He was beginning to warm to Tommy. He brought the conversation round to Key West.

'You should go down to Key West and meet Johnny Williams,' Tommy said.

'I already did,' said Max. 'He told me I might find you here.'

'OK. Well, talk to Johnny some more. We used to sit in the Parrot House for days on end, sometimes, just drinking and talking.'

'And – dancing, I heard?' said Max carefully. 'Wasn't there some woman who could tap dance and taught you all?'

'Yes, there was. Virgy. Virgy Caterham. Dear God, she was a beautiful woman. I loved Virgy. I really did.'

'And was she – was she one of the beautiful women you laid on the deck of your yacht?' asked Max. He felt rather sick suddenly, and his hand was shaking. He put down his glass and forced himself to smile at Soames-Maxwell.

'She was. Boy, she was. Beautiful. So beautiful. But she wasn't, I don't want you to think, a one-night stand, some kind of a tart. She was a lady, a real lady. But she was one of our little group. Down there. She used to leave her stuffy old English husband and come down for a week here and there. He was an earl and he had some house he preferred to her. And yes, she could certainly dance. She could dance, I swear it, better than Ginger. Did she have class! She died, I heard. Ted saw it in the papers. I cried when he told me, I really cried.'

His glass was empty again; Max called the waitress.

'Two more bourbons, please.'

'Yeah, she'd come on the boat, for days sometimes, we'd sail right down to the furthest tip of the Bahamas. What days. Six or eight of us, Errol Flynn used to join us a lot, it was Errol who taught me to like coke, God damn him. And there would be Ted and one of those film stars he could always get hold of. Rita, Ava, they all came. Rita was a great girl. Boy, did she have staying power! And yes, Papa Hemingway joined us occasionally. Heavenly days they were, fishing, swimming, and then at night, the parties. I tell you, Max, they don't make parties like those any more. The games of strip poker we played – '

'Excuse me,' said Max. 'I just have to go to the men's room.'

He almost ran to the lavatory, and threw up. He sat on the toilet seat for a long time, tears rolling down his face. So that was what his mother had been like. A tart. Stripping off at parties, dancing in bars, abandoning her family for days on end, to go sailing with a load of expensive trash. And all the time coming over all cool and ladylike and pretending she was doing up people's houses.

He finally forced himself to go back.

'Sorry,' he said. 'Must have eaten something. Would you mind if we carried on with this in the morning?'

'Sure. Are you all right? You look all in. Here, I'll see you back to your hotel.'

'I'm fine,' said Max, managing to take in, even in his misery, that Soames-Maxwell was at least capable of concern and kindness. 'Really. But if we could carry on in the morning, with some more tangible stuff, dates and things.'

'Sure thing. Goodnight, Max.'

'Goodnight, sir.'

'Call me Tommy. Everyone does.'

Chapter 29

Virginia, 1966

'Call me Tommy. Everyone does.'

He looked down at her, this beautiful woman, smiling up at him from the harbour, tall, slender, dark-haired, indisputably classy, dressed in white slacks and a navy and white striped sweater.

'All right – Tommy.'

'I told Virginia she could come out with us for the day.' Ted Franklyn had his arm round the woman's shoulders, the other round his own current girlfriend and Hollywood's latest rave discovery, Kristen de Wynter. 'She's lonely. Came down here with Mike Halston, and he's gone off on a story somewhere.'

'Sure,' said Tommy. 'I'd love it.' He meant it. He didn't like Kristen, she was stupid and she irritated him, and Ted acted like she was Einstein and the Queen of Sheba rolled into one. It would be nice to have what promised to be congenial company for the day.

'Thank you, that's really kind.' Her accent had a strong tang of English. 'Shall I get my swimsuit?'

'If you like. We tend to swim in the raw,' said Tommy, grinning at her.

'My goodness. Perhaps I'd better not come.'

'Of course you had. Go get it, if it'll make you feel better. Are you staying at the Pier House?'

'Yes I am. Can I bring some champagne or something?'

'You certainly can.'

She was back in ten minutes, carrying a big white bag; she was smiling, happy, like a child.

'This is such a treat,' she said, 'I love boats.'

'It's a treat for me too,' said Tommy.

They made for the reef. 'Would you like to snorkel?'

'Oh yes, please.'

'Ted? Kristen?'

'No thanks. We'll watch you and save our strength.'

'Best wear a T-shirt,' he told her, 'you'll burn your back in this sun.'

'Well I would,' she said, 'but I don't have one.' She grinned at him. 'A T-shirt sounds a little overdressed, after your earlier remarks.'

'Well, just swimming's different. Here, I'll lend you a T.'

He gave her one and a snorkel and a visor; she slithered into the water. 'Follow me,' he said, 'I know a very pretty bit.'

He had snorkelled on this reef maybe a hundred times; he never got used to it, the colours, the sweet peace of the world beneath the water, the friendly dazzle-coloured fish.

'What's stinging?' she said, suddenly pulling her mouthpiece out. 'It feels like a thousand stinging nettles are at me.'

'Minute jellyfish. They're harmless. You must have really sensitive skin. I can't feel a thing.'

'Oh I do,' she said laughing. 'I'm like the princess in the fairy story. I feel everything. This is gorgeous. In spite of the jellyfish.'

They lay on the deck afterwards in the sun. She took her top off following, after a moment's hesitation, Kristen's lead; her breasts were startlingly white, the nipples dark and very large. Tommy kept his trunks on.

'You're a fraud,' she said, 'I was led to expect nudism.'

'I don't want to burn my cock,' he said, 'it's very sensitive.'

'Like my skin.'

'Seems like they're made for one another. Drink?'

'Do you have any lemonade? Oh, here, I brought some champagne,' she said diving into her white bag. 'And some fruit.'

'That's nice. Won't you have champagne?'

'No,' she said, 'I don't drink.'

'Never?'

'Never.'

'Well, we all do. May we drink your champagne, just the same?'

'Of course. That's why I brought it.'

He called the steward; he had employed him for years, a little monkey of a man from Tangier. He lived on the boat, all year round, whether it was in use or not, acted as cleaner, cook, valet, butler. His name was simply J, he said, and the yacht, and Tommy, were all the family he had. Tommy had always suspected he was on the run from the police, but he had never asked any questions. J was too precious to risk losing.

'So, tell us all about yourself,' said Ted Franklyn. 'How did you come to be here with Michael?'

'Oh, he's an old friend. I was in New York and he said his house down here needed doing over, I'm an interior decorator and I've seen all I need to of it, made my notes and done my plans, and I'm waiting to go back with him.'

'Which is when?'

'Day after tomorrow.'

'Ah. And where does your English accent come from? It's very pretty.'

'A long sojourn there, I guess. With my husband.'

'Ah, you have a husband then?'

'I do.'

'Name please.'

'Alexander. Alexander Caterham.'

'And does he not mind you coming away with a lot of dissolute types on boats?'

'He's in England.'

'Ah.'

'But no, we're not divorced,' she said, smiling. 'We lead – well, very complicated lives.'

'Would you like to be divorced?'

'No,' she said coolly, 'not in the least.'

'Well that's excellent. Now then, Virginia Caterham, what would you like for lunch. J! What do we have for lunch?'

'A fish mousse.'

'Did I catch the mousse?'

'No, sir.'

'Good. Ted, Kristen, you OK?'

'Sure,' said Ted. 'I think we might go below for an hour before lunch. It's terribly hot out here.'

'Fine. Virginia, are you OK?'

'I'm OK.'

'Good. Now I'm afraid the boat may rock for a while,' he said to her as Ted and Kristen disappeared. 'They have terribly energetic sex.'

'I see.'

He looked at her for a while, amused.

'You're very English, aren't you? Terribly cool and composed.'

'Not always,' she said.

After lunch, they slept for a while, under umbrellas; they awoke at four, hot and uncomfortable. 'Let's swim,' said Tommy. 'But we need to move off the reef. I'll use the engine.'

Twenty minutes later they stopped again. He came out of the cabin, grinning. 'Time to swim.' He peeled off his slacks. 'Just to prove I meant it.'

'All right,' she said, 'I believe you. Do I have to follow suit?'

'Not if you don't want to.'

'I may as well.'

She stood up too, and pulled off her own slacks and the T-shirt he had lent her. She looked at him, her eyes very cool and distant. Her pubic hair

359

was very neat, very dark, and she was so thin her stomach was almost concave.

'You don't eat enough,' he said, and then watched her as she turned and dived neatly into the water. Her buttocks by contrast were rounded and high; starkly white, oddly arousing.

'That was nice,' she said afterwards. 'I really enjoyed that. Could I have some more lemonade?'

'Why don't you drink?'

'I don't like it.'

'I see.'

'Tell me about you,' she said suddenly, sitting up, towelling her hair. There were drops of water spangled on her eyelashes, on her brown skin, on the rich darkness of her nipples. She was slightly sunburnt; she looked suddenly freed from her rather formal self and oddly wanton.

'Not a lot to tell.'

'What do you do?'

'Spend my money.'

'Which comes from?'

'Stocks and bonds.'

'I see. And how do you spend it?'

'Enjoying myself. Fishing. Gambling. Sailing. Giving parties.'

'Do you have a house?'

'Yes I do. In California, near Santa Barbara. And another in Monaco. And a little place in Aspen.'

'I used to ski in Aspen. When I was a child.'

'You did? I wish I'd known you then.'

'I wasn't very pretty. I was tubby and I always had skinned knees.'

'It sounds fine.'

'And do you have a wife?'

'Not at the moment. I have had several. Of course.'

'Of course.'

'The most recent is still, strictly speaking, my wife. But she has decided to marry a young man from Texas. He can provide her with even more than my alimony. So I think shortly I shall be free again.'

'Is that good news?'

'Neither good nor bad. Just part of the pattern.'

'Do you have children?'

'No. Do you?'

'Yes, two,' she said, and her eyes shadowed. 'Two girls.'

'And is that the final tally?'

'No, it can't be.'

'Why not?'

'I have to have a son. For the dynasty, you know.'

'What dynasty?'

'Her husband's a lord,' said Ted, waking slowly to the conversation. 'She has to provide an heir.'

'A lord. So you're a lady?'

'Yes I am. A countess, to be precise.'

'And do you like being a countess?'

'Yes,' she said. 'I'm afraid I do.'

'Do you have to get back tonight?' he said as the sun started to sink and the water turned dark turquoise. 'I mean we can call Michael, tell him you're safe. I thought we could sail on for a while, have dinner, maybe drop anchor for the night. Get back some time tomorrow. It'll be kind of easy that way. But we don't have to if you're concerned.'

She turned and looked at him, her strange, cool, almost preoccupied look.

'I'm not concerned,' she said, 'and certainly no one will be concerned about me. As long as we can tell Michael.'

'Fine.'

It was cooler; she went below, took a shower, came back up dressed in her slacks and a cream silk shirt.

'You look gorgeous.'

'Thank you.'

'You intrigue me,' he said, 'everything about you intrigues me.' His eyes moved over her body, very slowly, resting on her breasts, her crotch, moving back to her face.

'Why?'

'I don't know. You seem – well, oddly rootless. In spite of the husband, the children, the dynasty.'

'I'm not. But I am a free spirit. Or try to be.'

'That must be difficult.'

'It is. But I work at it.'

After dinner, on deck, under the stars, Ted and Kristen smoked pot.

Virginia declined, laughing. 'It just never works for me.'

'I'm going to have a little cocaine,' said Tommy. 'Just a little. Would you care to join me?'

She looked startled, almost frightened. 'No. No thank you.'

'Don't you have any vices?' he asked, laying out the two lines of powder, carefully rolling a five-dollar bill, looking at her thoughtfully before he took it.

361

'Oh yes,' she said, 'one or two.'

'I like you very much,' he said. 'You're fun.'

'Thank you.'

'Do you mind if I smoke a cigar?'

'Not at all. My father smokes cigars. I like them.'

'Who is your father? Would I know him?'

'I don't know. Fred Praeger.'

'Fred the Third?'

'The very one.'

'So your brother is Baby Praeger?'

'Yes he is.'

'Baby – how is he?'

'He's fine,' she said, smiling.

'You're very fond of him, aren't you?'

'Yes I am.'

'And you're not very fond of your husband.'

'Oh but I am,' she said quickly. 'Very fond.'

'Well then, what in God's name are you doing here? With me?'

'If I told you,' she said lightly, 'you'd never believe it.'

'Can I fuck you?'

The question was so direct, so unexpected, it startled her. She looked at him, her eyes very wide.

'Well – I – '

'Come on, Virginia. If I'd been talking sexy to you for an hour, telling you how lovely you were, gazing into your eyes, kissing you, you'd be ready for it wouldn't you?'

'Possibly, but you haven't.'

'OK,' he said, slightly wearily. 'Let's get this show on the road. Virginia, you are one gorgeous lady. I get a hard-on just looking at you. Just thinking about you. I want to introduce my sensitive cock to your sensitive skin. Er – Princess. You have the most erotic arse I ever saw. No, I mean it. And a little later on, nothing would give me greater pleasure than to be allowed to look at it again. For some time. Right. How am I doing?'

'Not very well,' she said, laughing. 'Tell me, where do you come from? Where did all this money that is too much for you to count come from?'

'My dad. And he got it from shipping. Good friend of Mr Onassis.'

'Is he?'

'He was. He's dead. Which is why I have the money.'

'And are you American born and bred? Good WASP stock?'

'American born and bred, yes. WASP stock, no. My dad started in the engine rooms. He made enough to send me to Yale, though.'

'And don't you ever feel a need to do anything other than fish and sail and gamble and throw parties?'

'No. No, I don't.'

'And your mother?'

'She was a whore,' he said briefly. 'Can I kiss you now?'

'Yes you can.'

She was nice to kiss: warm, friendly. He stopped kissing her mouth after a bit and moved down to her breasts. The nipples were huge, hard and erect. He pulled back and smiled at her, then knelt down in front of her chair. 'Take your clothes off.'

She took the pants off, sat astride; he started kissing her, tonguing her. She was wet, salty, but oddly tense. He looked up at her.

'Relax.'

'I can't.'

'Why not?'

'I don't know. I think I'm frightened.'

'Of what?'

'You, I suppose. Did you really go to bed with three girls, like Ted said?'

'Oh, frequently. And I've been in bed with one girl and two other men. And all kinds of other variations.'

'Why?'

'Because it's fun. Don't you ever do things like that?'

'No, never. I've led a rather sheltered life in that department.'

'So the Earl is a missionary man?'

'You could say that.'

'Virginia. Let me show you some fun.'

His tongue probed further; she moaned, squirmed.

'That's better. Much better.' He put his hands under her buttocks, moulding them, exploring them. 'Beautiful,' he said, 'beautiful beautiful arse. Where did you get such an arse?'

She smiled suddenly, took his head in her hands, kissed his mouth, hard, violently, then pushed his head back into her crotch, moaning, crying out.

'There,' he said, 'there, that's lovely. You taste gorgeous.'

He eased her backwards then, moved up, kissing her stomach, slowly, hard, making it burn; then returned to her breasts again, licking them, working on them violently with his tongue. She suddenly cried out, slithered down onto the floor, her legs spreadeagled, pulled him down onto her.

'Please,' she said, 'please. Quickly.'

'Oh no,' he said, and smiled into her eyes. 'We have a long way to go yet.'

He made her wait for a long time; he was surprised by the desperation, the urgency in her, but he still made her wait. He worked on her patiently: he talked dirty to her, he turned her over and over, kissing every corner and fragment of her; he brought her almost to orgasm twice with his tongue and then pulled back; he stood her up, holding her and then pushing her down onto his cock, and then as she cried out, began to throb, to flower, pulled away, again, and lay beside her just looking at her, laughing gently at her greed; and then finally he turned her, thrust into her, hard, feeling her frantically wet, softening, unfolding to him, and allowed her to come, at last; he felt her rising, tumbling, pulsating, and it went on and on, surprising even him, until he felt lost himself, in the tumult of her. And then she shrieked, loudly, fiercely, and arched her body violently under him, and held it there, in some great wild spasm that seemed nearer pain than pleasure; and then slowly, she came down, quietened, stilled; and when he finally released himself and then opened his eyes and looked into her golden ones, they were moist, and her cheeks were wet with tears, but she was smiling, radiant, oddly triumphant.

Next day they put Ted and Kristen ashore, with a note for Michael Halston, and went off again. She stayed with him for three days and then flew back to New York alone; he did not see her for almost two years. But he read in the papers, some time a little less than ten months later, that she had had a baby, a son; his name, the Viscount Hadleigh, was Maximilian.

She came back to him, many times; she seemed to need him. He knew she didn't even like him particularly, that she disapproved of his wanton, hedonistic lifestyle; but he also knew that in some strange way he was important to her.

He taxed her with it once, the baby, with his name; the baby born such a neat nine months after their first meeting, and she had laughed and told him not to be so arrogant, why should she, the Countess of Caterham, conceive a child out of wedlock when she had a husband who loved her and was waiting for an heir, his heir, to be born.

And when he asked her what it was, what he gave her that she craved so much, that drew her back to him so relentlessly, against all her inclinations, all the odds, she gave him her level, cool look and said simply, 'Fun. I'm very short on fun.'

Chapter 30

Georgina, 1984

Georgina had, from the beginning, been quite determinedly opposed to the idea of seeking out her real father. She half admired Charlotte for having the courage and the willpower to do so, but she knew she lacked both. She was also very frightened at the thought of what – or who – she might find. Charlotte had been lucky: Charles St Mullin, as far as Georgina could make out, was charming, civilized, intelligent, all the things you might wish your father to be. And indeed that a father of Charlotte might be expected to be. Georgina found it very difficult at times to cope with being Charlotte's sister. She was so clever, and so admirable, and so altogether competent, she never seemed to do anything foolish or ill-advised, her personal life was as smoothly and perfectly under control as everything else: nothing ever fazed her, got her down for long. She would never fall helplessly in love with the wrong person, and certainly she would never get pregnant, thought Georgina, with a sudden throb in her heart.

Georgina wondered where Charlotte's assertiveness and positiveness came from: from Charles St Mullin, perhaps. Or maybe from Fred III. Those genes had to be rolling around in some of them at least. Well, they certainly hadn't come her way. Georgina would have given anything to be assertive and positive. The only place she seemed remotely able to be that, she thought with a sigh, was in bed. Otherwise, anyone could push her around. She sometimes felt she hadn't quite become herself yet; she felt she was waiting for something to happen, to make her turn into a complete person. Max of course was much more positive too. Although not in the admirable way Charlotte was. Georgina thought it was probably a very good thing Max seemed so firmly opposed to seeking out whoever had sired him. Given his character as a clue, all kinds of problems might be unleashed. Georgina was very fond of Max, in fact she was more at ease with him than she was with Charlotte, but he didn't seem to be turning out quite as anyone might have hoped.

Especially Alexander. Poor Alexander. Georgina still adored him; she still found it almost impossible, in the bottom of her heart, to think of anyone else as her father. Partly because she was his favourite, and because they got on so well, but partly because it was easier that way, safer. He was such a good person, so kind and straightforward. No daughter could wish for anyone better. There was no way she was going to risk hurting herself or him by setting out on some wild-goose chase herself.

She had been looking forward to the summer. It was nearly August, and Kendrick and Melissa were coming to stay at Hartest. It had been Charlotte's idea, clever, thoughtful, kind: Mary Rose had been too upset to contemplate going to Nantucket on her own, and wanted to get away with a friend (Georgina couldn't imagine what a friend of Mary Rose's might be like), and it had seemed to suit everybody.

Kendrick loved England and Hartest, and Melissa could spend several weeks in the company of her beloved Max (who was flattered and charmed by the adoration despite his protestations of boredom at it). And then Georgina was very fond of Kendrick. He was taking a course in Fine Arts at New York University, which gave them a lot to talk about, and although he was slightly shy, once relaxed, once embarked on a topic that intrigued and interested him, he actually had a great deal to say and he said it well, forcefully, amusingly even. He had an oddball, slightly black sense of humour; Woody Allen was his hero, and (he said) his inspiration, and he had seen every one of his films at least half a dozen times.

He had straight, floppy, streaky-blond hair which he wore quite long (to Baby's disgust), and the family blue eyes: soft, large, gentle eyes, with oddly beetling brows. He was tall, taller than Freddy, taller than Max; and he was more graceful than they were, there was an oddly languid quality to Kendrick, he walked and moved rather slowly, and despite his shyness, he was a superb dancer, and if he could be dragged onto the dance floor, he would, against his own inclinations, become the focus of attention, people would watch him, stop dancing themselves. Consequently, he tended to remain rather determinedly off it. He dressed well, in a very individual way; his other passion, Woody Allen apart, was Scott Fitzgerald and his era, and he spent many hours and much of his allowance in thrift shops, buying up everything he could find that was from the 20s; he would not have dreamt of wearing a modern dinner jacket, or tails, and he had a huge collection of hats: panamas, slouch felts, boaters, which he wore at every possible opportunity. He liked linen suits, silk shirts, greatcoats, and his most prized possession was a genuine 1920s one-piece black bathing suit with a white belt, which he insisted on wearing on the beach on Nantucket Island, to everyone's embarrassment. 'For such a shy person,' Melissa had once said tartly, 'you're one huge show-off.' To Georgia, for whom style was immensely important, Kendrick's clothes were a matter for great admiration.

Charlotte had also written in her letter to Georgina suggesting the visit, that as it was Alexander's fiftieth birthday early in September, they could maybe make something special of it and have the whole family there. 'I'll come over for it, and bring Freddy, and we can ask Uncle Baby. He'll be in London.'

'What about Angie?' said Georgina when she spoke to Charlotte. 'Do we have her as well? And what about Grandpa and Grandma?'

'Mercifully, they'll be in the Bahamas. I checked. Otherwise it could have been dodgy. And Angie, well, she's got to come some time. So I thought probably yes. She'll have had her babies by then, won't she? And she is actually living with Uncle Baby. So we can't not ask her. Of course she might not come. But I bet she will. And as it's a big party, it might be less awkward for everyone. It will break the ice, very painlessly.'

Kendrick had been at Hartest only twenty-four hours before Georgina found herself, slightly to her surprise, telling him about the abortion. She had been feeling particularly weepy, and not particularly well, and trying to disguise both facts; they went for a walk and when they got back he sat down on the front steps beside her, put his arm round her, and asked her what the matter was. Somehow it was a great relief to talk about it.

'That's sad,' was all he said.

Georgina looked at him and thought how immensely good-looking he was with his blond hair and blue eyes. If he wasn't her cousin and she hadn't known him since they were both in nappies, she thought she could quite fancy him.

Georgina was in the kitchen with Kendrick when the phone rang. Mrs Tallow answered it, handed it to him.

'It's for you. Your father.'

'Oh,' said Kendrick. He had gone rather white. 'Hallo? Yes, hallo, Dad. Oh. Oh, well that's wonderful.' He was clearly trying very hard to sound enthusiastic. 'Congratulations. No, that's great. Yes, I am, but I'm not sure if – well, I shall have to ask Georgina. Of course. Yes, fine. Congratulations again.'

He put the phone down, and looked at Georgina rather awkwardly. 'That was Dad. He rang to say that – that Angie has had her babies. Both boys. I just didn't know what to say.'

'Well, you didn't do badly,' said Georgina carefully.

'He wants me to go up to London and see them,' said Kendrick. 'Meet Angie. Take Melissa. He seemed to think I ought to. I really don't want to. What do you think?'

'What does she think about what?' said Melissa, coming into the kitchen. She had been riding with Max, and was flushed and over-excited. Max was behind her, his arm round her shoulders.

'Oh – nothing,' said Kendrick.

'Kendrick, don't start going grown-up on me. What?'

'That was Dad. Angie's had the twins. Both boys.'

'Oh really! That's exciting. What are they called?'

'I haven't the first idea,' said Kendrick irritably.

'Well, you should have asked. They are your half-brothers.'

'Yes, I suppose so. Anyway he wants us to go up to London and see Angie and the babies. I hedged a bit.'

'Oh Kendrick, why? I'm dying to see Angie. And the babies.'

'Melissa, why?'

'Oh – curiosity. And she is going to be our stepmother after all. I want to see how wicked she is.'

'Very wicked, I'd say,' said Max. 'But probably the fairest of you all.'

Georgina stared at him. 'Have you met her?'

'Yup. Months and months ago.'

'You might have said.'

'Couldn't see the point.'

'Oh Max. Well, what was she like?'

'I told you. Very wicked clearly, and very pretty. Very sexy.'

'Excuse me,' said Kendrick. He walked rather quickly out of the room.

'Max, you're so insensitive,' said Georgina. 'Just think how he must feel about Angie. His father's left his mother for her, it's horribly upsetting for him.'

'And for me,' said Melissa.

'Nothing would upset you,' said Max, patting her small backside. 'Skin as thick as leather, you've got.'

'I have not. Anyway, I want to meet her. See the babies. What do you think?'

'I think we should all go together,' said Max. 'It'll be a lot easier for you that way.'

Georgina stared at him. It was very unlike Max to have the slightest consideration for anyone's else's feelings.

She took an immediate dislike to Angie, who was sitting in bed in the clinic, surrounded with flowers, in vases and baskets and arrangements, and looking more as if she was going to a cocktail party than having just given birth. Her hair had clearly been professionally done within the last few hours, and her face was carefully made up. She was wearing a 30s-style white satin nightdress, which revealed a great deal of very large, very suntanned breast, and at the side of her bed, rather than the cots and

369

the babies, was an ice bucket with a bottle of champagne in it. She smiled at them all as they came in, but didn't say anything. Baby, who was sitting on the bed, stood up and pumped Kendrick and Max by the hand and then hugged Melissa and Georgina.

'It's great to see you. What a day for the family.' If he had any idea how ironic his words were, Georgina thought, he certainly wasn't showing it. 'Two new brothers for you, Melissa. And you, Kendrick. Now before you meet the boys – ' he made them sound like baseball players, ready sprung from the womb – 'I want you all to meet Angie. Max you've met, haven't you, darling?'

'Oh, I have,' said Angie. 'Hallo, Max. Nice to see you again.'

'Congratulations, Aunt Angela,' said Max gravely, bending over her to kiss her, handing her the large bouquet of flowers they had all clubbed together and bought. Georgina couldn't see his face, but there was something in his voice that was unfamiliar: something grown-up and infinitely more worldly.

'And this is Kendrick,' Baby was saying, smiling proudly and indulgently, 'and this is Melissa. And Angie, this is Georgina, Virginia's second daughter. I don't know if you ever met her.'

'Yes, I did.' Angie smiled at Georgina. Her voice was very attractive, slightly throaty, her accent absolutely bland and unplaceable. 'Hallo, Georgina. But she wouldn't remember me. She was around eighteen months old, I think. Anyway, it's really nice to see you again. Oh, these flowers are just beautiful. How very kind of you all.'

They were actually, compared with the splendour of some of the offerings, rather modest; Georgina felt she was being patronized, and smiled back, rather uncertainly. Angie turned her brilliant smile on Kendrick. 'And this is the big brother. Hi, Kendrick. And Melissa. It's very nice to meet you, Melissa. I didn't expect you to be so grown-up.'

She could hardly have said anything better to Melissa, who beamed at her ecstatically. 'Well,' she said, 'I am fourteen, you know. What do we call you? Aunt Angela or what?'

'Oh please!' said Angie, laughing. 'I have absolutely no wish to be an aunt to such a grown-up collection of people. No, you must call me Angie. Mustn't they, darling?'

She put out her hand to Baby, who took it and kissed it. Kendrick looked down at his feet and flushed. Melissa sparkled at them.

'Can we see the babies then? I can't wait. When were they born?'

'Yesterday morning, at five o'clock,' said Angie, pushing a bell by her bed. 'Ten minutes between them. Early little birds, weren't they, Baby? Your father was hoping to stay in bed and leave me here, doing all the work, Melissa, but I wouldn't let him. He was there, right through to the end, holding my hand. Didn't faint or scream or anything. Very brave, weren't you, darling?'

Poor Kendrick, thought Georgina. He looked as if he might be sick or pass out himself. She was standing by him; she took his hand and squeezed it. He looked at her and smiled gratefully.

'Oh now look, here they are,' said Angie, as the door opened, 'thank you so much, Nurse.' She took one baby in each arm, and cradled them, sinking back into her pillows. 'You'll have to forgive me, I must just check their name tags, I can't tell them apart myself yet. Oh, yes, this is Sam, already renamed Spike by his father, and this is Hugh. Aren't they fine-looking chaps?'

Georgina looked at the two awesomely identical little creatures, swaddled up in blankets, their primeval features crushed into concentrated sleep, and felt a sudden and terrible sweep of sadness.

'Can I hold one?' Melissa was saying. 'Oh, please, do let me.'

'Probably best not, just for now. They'll wake up and start screaming, and then this nice party will have to come to an end,' said Angie. She looked down at the babies slightly warily, as if she expected them to break, or take off. Georgina, pulling herself together, forcing herself to smile at her, thought that Angie wouldn't mind the babies crying, someone else could see to that; what she would mind was having the charming tableau in which she starred destroyed.

'They suit you,' said Max, slightly uncannily echoing Georgina's thoughts, smiling at Angie with that same new, worldly smile. 'Very nice accessories, Angie. Great picture.'

Angie's eyes as she smiled back at him were interestingly thoughtful. 'Thank you, Max. Done any nice jobs lately?'

'Yeah,' he said, 'yeah, I was just in New York.'

'Oh really? Well that must have been very interesting. Baby, could you take this child a moment, I'm really uncomfortable.'

'Yes, darling, of course. Are you getting tired? Would you like everyone to go?'

'No of course not. Don't be silly.' But as she settled back on her pillows and took the baby, she winced slightly; she was clearly genuinely uncomfortable. Well, thought Georgina, it was hardly surprising, giving birth to over eleven pounds' worth of babies was quite an undertaking.

The babies woke simultaneously and began crying. A nurse put her head round the door. 'You're going to have to feed these babies,' she said, 'they're starving.'

'Right,' said Angie with a resigned sigh, 'does anyone mind?' She started easing one brown breast out of her nightdress; Kendrick, clearly terrified, looked out of the window very fixedly. Georgina noticed that

Max on the other hand stood looking rather amusedly and interestedly as Angie took the first baby and, oddly tender suddenly, offered a large dark nipple into its small rooting mouth. 'There you go, Spikey,' she said, 'that'll do for now. I can't do a duet yet. Nurse, take Hugh, would you, and keep him quiet.'

'I think we should go,' said Max suddenly. 'You've got a lot to do here, Aunt Angela. We're not helping. Come on, you guys.'

'Don't call me that, Max,' said Angie, looking at him. She was smiling, but her eyes were sharp. 'I really don't like it.'

'Sorry. Can't seem able to help it.'

'I think Max is right,' said Baby, 'it might be an idea if you all went. Very thoughtful of you, Max. Give me a kiss, Melissa. Bye, Kendrick.'

'Oh, by the way,' said Max, looking over his shoulder as they left the room, 'we're having a party for Alexander, next month. Fiftieth birthday. Charlotte's coming over, and Freddy of course. You will both come, won't you?'

Kendrick and Melissa stayed behind for a moment talking to Baby; Georgina and Max went down the corridor. 'Max!' said Georgina, looking over her shoulder. 'Max, that was naughty. We haven't even checked with Kendrick and the others that they want Angie.'

'Why on earth shouldn't they?' said Max, his blue eyes very wide, very innocent. 'She's family now. We have to have Angie, whether we like it or not.'

'And you do, don't you?' said Georgina, looking at him sharply.

'Yes, I do quite,' said Max.

Apart from a slight unease about the presence of Angie, and Mrs Wicks (who was now family in Baby's view and had been invited at his request), Georgina was looking forward to the party. A lot of the planning had fallen on her, and she had spent hours with Mrs Tallow and Nanny, sorting out food, and with Fallon, sorting out wine; Alexander was touchingly pleased by the whole idea. They had wondered about making it a surprise, but it had seemed impossible; and in fact Georgina was glad he knew, looking forward to it had seemed to cheer him up, and he was even making suggestions, asking if it could be black tie – 'It's ages since we had a smart dinner party here' – and taking a great interest in the guest list.

'It's so nice of Freddy to come, really charming. And I thought it might be nice if we invited the Dunbars. I would like that very much. Would you mind?'

'Well of course I wouldn't mind, Daddy, I love them both, specially funny old Martin, but they're not family, are they? Well, not strictly family.'

372

'No, they're not, but Mummy was so terribly fond of them both. It would be a nice sort of link with her, I feel. And Catriona was so good to me when Mummy died. I couldn't have managed without her. I just feel they would make the evening complete somehow.'

'Well, it's your evening,' said Georgina, kissing him, 'and you must complete it however you like. And they're certainly more family than Angie's gran.'

'Yes,' said Alexander, who had taken the news that Mrs Wicks was to be present with great equanimity. 'Yes, indeed. I am looking forward to seeing Angie again. I always rather liked her, you know.'

'No,' said Georgina, surprised. 'No, I didn't know.'

The day of the party was perfect: 'Very mists and mellow fruitfulness,' said Melissa.

'What on earth are you talking about?' said Max.

'Oh, you wouldn't recognize it,' she said loftily. 'You're so illiterate, Max. It's Keats. "Ode to Autumn". Isn't it, Uncle Alexander?'

'Quite right,' said Alexander, smiling at her across the breakfast table. He was in a perfect mood. Georgina had gone riding with him earlier and they had cantered through the parkland and up the hill to the top of the Great Drive. Hartest sat below them, looking more than usually as if it had been carved out of the landscape itself, the grey stone merging into the drifting mist, the windows reflecting the hazy light of the clearing sun. 'It's so lovely isn't it?' she said. 'I never stop thinking how lucky we are.'

Alexander smiled at her, put out his hand to touch hers.

'Good,' he said, 'that's exactly how I want you to feel. All of you.'

They sent him off after lunch, to do things on the estate; Georgina phoned Martin Dunbar and asked him to keep Alexander busy. 'He'll just get in the way,' she said, 'offering to help and everything. Do you mind, Martin?'

'Of course not,' he said. 'You know I'd do anything for you, Georgina.'

Georgina was surprised; he was not usually so effusive. Perhaps he'd had rather too much wine with his lunch.

Kendrick had decorated the front hall with great swathes of greenery from the woods, and Melissa had spent the afternoon fixing fifty candles into fifty saucers, and setting them all around the Rotunda and up the stairs. Baby and Angie arrived at five o'clock, and Baby and Kendrick moved the piano from the morning room into the Rotunda. Baby had promised to play after dinner, and people could dance if they liked. 'But not "You're the Tops",' said Georgina. 'It will simply upset Daddy.'

Charlotte, who had arrived the day before with Freddy, and had plainly been expecting to take over everything, had simply told Georgina after the first hour that she had done a terrific job, and asked, quite humbly, what she should do. Georgina was so thrown by this she couldn't think of anything, and Charlotte and a distant Freddy were reduced to helping Mrs Tallow in the kitchen.

Charlotte seemed altogether not quite herself, slightly subdued, rather jumpy, and considerably thinner. Every time the phone rang, she looked very edgy, and at one point she disappeared in her car and went off for an hour or so, returning looking rather more relaxed. She said she had been for a long walk to get over her jet lag; Georgina was surprised, Charlotte's constitution was of such strength that she had never been troubled by jet lag before. She was clearly wary of Freddy, and there was something of a frost between them; they avoided one another whenever possible, and Charlotte was inclined to shoot sharp little glances at him before she spoke; if Georgina hadn't known her sister better, she would have thought she was afraid of Freddy.

Tallow had lit log fires in all the downstairs rooms; by dusk, the house was filled with a sweet-smelling warmth. Alexander, who had been sitting in the library with two of the dogs, stood up abruptly at seven o'clock and said, 'I'm going up to get ready. Otherwise I shall fall asleeep and be a pooper at my own party.'

He put his arm round Georgina's shoulders and gave her a hug. 'I know you've done most of the work,' he said quietly, 'and thank you. Give your old father a kiss.'

Georgina gave him a kiss. She watched him as he walked out of the library, in his shabby old cardigan, and his socks pulled up over his jeans, and thought how much she loved him, and she felt very aware suddenly of the sense of family in the house, of closeness and happiness. It didn't always work, in fact it very often didn't, but when it did, it was unbeatable, the most tangible sense of security, of strength. Nothing could threaten them, nothing could harm them. It was a feeling of pure and very gentle joy.

Charlotte stood up.

'Quiet please,' she said. Everyone was quiet. Charlotte had that effect on people.

'Now,' she said, 'I certainly don't intend to make a speech.'

'Oh, what a shame,' called out Max, grinning at her over his glass.

Everyone looked relaxed and happy, Georgina thought. It had been a magically successful evening. Even Martin, usually so shy, was sitting next to Angie and talking more animatedly to her than Georgina had ever seen him.

When he was not talking to Angie, he was listening to Mrs Wicks, who was on the other side of him and who clearly saw it as her social duty to put him at his ease. Mrs Wicks was also having a wonderful time, drinking glass after glass of Dubonnet and bitter lemon, which went down much better with rich food, she said, than wine. She had arrived in a hired Rolls with a uniformed chauffeur, wearing a bejewelled crinoline that would not have disgraced the Queen Mother, and bearing a huge bunch of red and silver balloons saying 'Happy 50th Birthday'. She had insisted on tying these to the rail of the flying staircase; it was a tribute to Alexander's great courtesy that he thanked her most graciously and agreed that they did indeed brighten the room up a bit.

Georgina stopped looking at everyone and turned her attention back to Charlotte, who, she was aware, was looking at her rather pointedly.

'I just wanted to say two things: first thank you to everyone who's helped to make this party such a success, and especially Georgina who's done most of the organizing. Georgina, everyone!'

'Georgina,' said everyone, and raised their glasses to her. The tribute was totally unexpected; she looked at them in the candlelight and it blurred with her tears. 'Thank you,' she said rather weakly.

'And the only other thing I am going to say,' Charlotte's crisp voice broke through her emotion, 'is would you raise your glasses to Alexander on this perfectly lovely occasion and say, yet again, happy birthday.'

Everyone stood then, smiling, and toasted Alexander, saying his name first disparately, then in unison; he sat smiling, looking with a charming and patent delight into the faces of his family, flattered, youthened by the candlelight.

'Doesn't he look wonderful, I could quite fancy him,' whispered Melissa hoarsely to Max. Her remark caught a silence as they all sat down again, and everyone laughed.

'Thank you, Melissa,' said Alexander, 'may I say the compliment is absolutely reciprocated. Thank you all. Thank you for coming. It has been the most wonderful evening.'

'It's only just begun,' said Georgina, who had slipped over to the light switch and dimmed the chandelier. 'Mrs Tallow, we're ready.'

Mrs Tallow and Nanny came into the room together, bearing, on a silver tray, a vast cake or rather two, in the shape of a five and a one, each loaded with candles; they all sang 'Happy Birthday', and then: 'Come on, Daddy, blow,' said Charlotte, and he stood again, laughing, and bent and blew hard at the cake and all the candles went out, and everyone clapped. Then Baby stood up, holding up his hands.

'I would like to say a few words now. About our great admiration for you, Alexander, for the role you have played as master of Hartest and head of your family, the charm and grace you have brought to it, and the courage too, in recent years. I know that all your children particularly, and mine too, feel a great affection and warmth for you. I don't think it will cast too much of a shadow to say that I am sure that somewhere, somehow, Virginia is with us this evening. If only in our thoughts and our memories.'

There was a slightly tense silence; then Baby raised his glass again, and said, 'Alexander. Our Love.'

'And now, Daddy,' said Georgina, when the clapping had died away, 'Kendrick and I have a very special present for you. You may have noticed there was nothing from us.'

'I didn't,' said Alexander. 'So ungracious an observation could not have crossed my mind.'

'Well anyway. Nanny, Mrs Tallow, could you hold the door open for us please? And Tallow, could you maybe help us carry the present in?' She and Kendrick went out of the room. There was a long silence. Nobody spoke. Then slowly, carefully, they came in again, bearing their gift. Alexander, expecting he knew not what, saw as if in a dream, materializing out of the soft darkness, his house coming towards him, magically smaller, but exquisitely and perfectly beautiful, the grey stone, the great windows, the curving steps, the Palladian pillars, the huge front door; he held out his arms to it, as if to a friend or a lover, his face solemn, intense with delight.

'Oh my dears,' he said, 'my dears. How very very wonderful.' And then he was silent and his blue eyes filled with tears, sparkling in the candlelight. There was a great stillness in the room; nobody moved as he stood, gazing at it, his eyes moving over it, drinking it in.

'We made it,' said Georgina, finally, 'Kendrick and I, we knew you'd like it more than anything. It comes to you with our best love.' And she leant forward and kissed Alexander's cheek, and then with Kendrick set the model carefully on the floor.

Alexander sat down, brushing the tears from his eyes. 'You did know, my darling, you did indeed,' he said. 'Thank you. Thank you, Kendrick. How hard you must have worked. Oh, I don't deserve so beautiful a present.'

'Yes you do,' said Charlotte, bringing the room briskly back from its slightly strained emotionalism, 'that's what birthdays are for, for getting what you deserve. Now you're not allowed to sit and play with it, because we want you to open all your other presents in the Rotunda. Not that they can compete with that, but they certainly deserve looking at.'

They all stood up; Alexander led the party out of the dining room, his arms round Georgina's and Kendrick's shoulders. Angie and Baby followed, holding hands, and then the rest of the table.

'Let's dance,' said Kendrick, and held out his hand to Georgina. 'I wanted to tell you how beautiful you look. That dress is sensational.'

'Oh Kendrick, you are silly. With competition like Angie and Melissa, I look like one of the ugly sisters.' She glanced anxiously at her reflection in the tall window; she was wearing a long, slithery, white crepe dress, cut on the bias: 'Very Ginger Rogers,' Melissa had said when she first saw it.

'Georgina, I can only presume you're fishing for compliments. I never heard such nonsense. You are twice as pretty as either of them. They're like – like flashy little orchids, and you are a very cool, aristocratic lily.'

'Well, thank you,' said Georgina, smiling just a trifle too quickly, 'you look pretty good yourself, Kendrick, if I might say so. That is a tremendous outfit.'

'Thank you,' said Kendrick modestly. He was not wearing a dinner jacket like all the other men, but white tie and tails, the tailcoat vintage 30s, his shoes patent Fred-Astaire-style lace-ups; he had arrived complete with cloak and top hat. 'I got it in the Village last winter.'

'Why do you think you like clothes so much?'

'I like all visually pleasing things. Houses. Paintings. Clothes. You,' he added, smiling into her eyes. 'Georgina, please relax. I don't know what's happened to you lately. Don't you like me any more?'

'Oh Kendrick,' she said, her eyes filling with easy tears, 'I do like you, of course I do.'

'And now you're crying again. God, you're a nightmare. What's the matter now?'

'I'm not sure. I feel odd. Very emotional. I expect it's the occasion.'

'Well, that's allowed. You can be emotional. As long as it's friendly emotion. Friendly to me, that is. My God, look at Angie, she certainly is coming on strong at that extremely tall neighbour of yours. She surely can't fancy him?'

'Angie could fancy anyone, I should think,' said Georgina, slightly sombre, 'but actually I can see it. Martin is so mysterious-looking, so sort of tortured and – well, romantic I suppose. He looks as if he has some deep dark secret that he'll never reveal to anyone.'

'Well if anyone can get it out of him, Angie will,' said Kendrick. 'Now do be careful, Georgina, you looked quite normal and cheerful for a minute then.'

She was dancing with Alexander when Angie, walking just a little unsteadily, came towards them, holding out both her hands.

'This has been a lovely party,' she said. 'Thank you for asking me. I feel part of the family already.'

'You are part of the family,' said Alexander. He was clearly very taken with her. Georgina found it irritating, a piece of grit in the honeyed mixture of her evening.

'No I'm not,' said Angie, 'not nearly. Not Mrs Praeger yet, not by a long shot.'

'Maybe not. But I've always thought of you as family,' said Alexander. 'Virginia counted you as one of her very closest friends. I haven't forgotten your kindness to her. So – welcome back.' Georgina stared at him. He was not usually so forthcoming; in recent years he had been almost pathologically shy. Maybe because Angie was part of so much the distant past he found her reassuring. 'May I perhaps have the pleasure of this dance?' he said. 'Georgina darling, do you mind?'

'Of course not,' said Georgina, feeling more embarrassed than ever. She looked around wildly for something else to concentrate on and caught sight of Mrs Wicks, who was jiving very energetically with Kendrick, her jewel-encrusted skirts flying. 'Your grandmother is having a wonderful time, Angie,' she said.

'Yes she is,' said Angie, smiling at her sweetly. 'It was so kind of you all to invite her.'

Alexander took her into his arms and started moving very slowly to the music; Georgina watched them, slightly awkwardly, as Angie pressed her body against his, rested her head on his chest. She was clearly very drunk.

When she saw Angie pull her father's head down towards her, whisper something in his ear, Georgina turned away.

She moved over to one of the windows, and stood looking out at the park.

'There's a car coming down the Great Drive,' she said suddenly. 'I wonder who on earth it can be, calling at one in the morning.'

'Oh, could be anyone,' said Baby, going to join her.

'Let me see.' Max looked out at the approaching lights; he was very pale.

'Are you expecting someone, Max?' asked Angie. She was looking at him very curiously.

'No. No, I don't think so.'

The car pulled up at the bottom of the steps; a very large white Daimler. A man got out, looked up at the house. 'Oh Christ,' said Max.

'What is it?' said Alexander. 'What on earth is the matter, Max? Here, let me go out.'

He opened the door, looked down the steps at the car. Georgina and Kendrick followed him.

The man was very tall and heavily built, wearing a greatcoat over denims, and cowboy boots; he gazed up at Alexander for a moment, then grinned and walked slowly up towards him. As he reached the top of the steps, he held out his hand.

'Lord Caterham?'

'Yes. How can I help you? Do come in.'

'Thanks.' He moved into the house; Georgina stood aside, staring at him; she felt extremely frightened and she wasn't sure why. She felt for Kendrick's hand; he gripped hers, held it tightly, aware of her fear while not understanding it. The man had an American accent; as he stepped into the house, they could see that he was tanned, that his eyes were startlingly blue, his wide and careful smile showing oddly perfect white teeth; and that he was overweight, that the blond hair was greying, that the boots were scuffed and down at heel.

'Hi,' he said, 'I see you have a party going. I'm sorry to disturb you. Soames-Maxwell is the name, Tommy Soames-Maxwell.'

'Yes?' said Alexander again, politely puzzled.

'Is Max here? Oh, hi Max, there you are. Nice to see you again. I promised you I'd look you up and I have.'

'You know Max then?' said Alexander.

'Oh sure, I know Max. Intimately, you could almost say. Chip off the old block, Max is. As you would say over here. Aren't you, Max?'

Max was silent. His face was greenish, sweating slightly.

'I'm afraid I don't understand,' said Alexander. He sounded slightly less polite.

'Oh, I'm sorry.' Soames-Maxwell smiled at him again. 'Of course not. Let me put you into the picture a little. I – knew your wife, Lord Caterham. Extremely well. I was so sorry to read that she had died.'

'Thank you,' said Alexander. Georgina noticed that he was clenching his fists, that the bones of his jaw were taut.

'Did she ever mention me?'

'No,' said Alexander firmly, 'no, I don't believe she ever did.'

'Well, I'll put you in the picture a little some time. It's Max I've really come to see.'

He looked over at Max and smiled again.

379

'He's a very fine young man, isn't he, Lord Caterham? A son to be proud of, wouldn't you say?'

Chapter 31

Georgina, 1984

Georgina had not realized quite how miserable it all made her until she sat in the library with Charlotte and Baby next day, listening to Charlotte's clear, precise voice as she told him who Tommy Soames-Maxwell was. Charlotte had insisted on talking to Baby about their parentage; she said they needed grown-up help. Thinking of Max's defiant, almost angry face the night before, of Alexander's, grey with shock, and his retreat into his own, withdrawn world that morning, and of Tommy Soames-Maxwell's horribly relaxed, over-confident entry into their lives, Georgina had agreed. She hated the thought of telling anyone, even Baby, but Charlotte was right: they couldn't manage on their own. 'That man is dangerous,' Charlotte had said, 'he could resort to blackmail, anything. I may have to talk to Charles as well.'

Baby was clearly as upset as they had been. He downed three large bourbons very quickly and then sat staring at Charlotte when she had finished with an expression of dreadful sadness on his face.

'I just don't get it,' he said, over and over again, 'I just don't get it.'

'Nor do we,' said Georgina quietly. She heard her voice wobble.

'And your father won't talk about it?'

'Not beyond that very first day. He just acts like nothing had happened, like we didn't know.'

Baby was silent, and then he sighed very heavily. 'Well,' he said, 'I don't know what to think, but I do know that your mother was a very special person and in no way some kind of scheming adulteress. There has to be an explanation, we just have to find it.'

'Yes, well, maybe,' said Charlotte. She sounded faintly impatient. 'Meanwhile, Uncle Baby, will you talk to this Soames-Maxwell for us? We're frightened of what he might do.'

'Well –' He looked wary. Then he said, 'Yes, darling, of course I will. I don't know how much good it will do, but I'll try. One thing's for sure. There's no great rush; he's not going to go away. Not now he's found us.'

Georgina felt tears beginning to well into her eyes again; she brushed them impatiently away. Baby looked at her and opened his arms; she crawled into them as if she had been ten, rather than twenty.

'Don't worry, darling,' he said, and his voice was gentle and almost cheerful, 'don't worry. We'll sort it out. It'll be fine. Don't worry.'

Georgina wished she could believe him.

'This feels all wrong,' said Georgina. She was lying in her rather large bed, Kendrick's head on her naked breasts. 'I heard your dad saying to mine last night that we were like brother and sister.'

'It feels great to me,' said Kendrick. 'If this is incest, let's go with it.'

'Well, I suppose we are only cousins. I think that's just about legal.'

'I'm sure it is. You've got family relationships on the brain.'

'So would you have.' She sighed.

'I guess so.'

She had told him. He had found her late that afternoon, sitting, fretful and tear-stained, on the back terrace; Max had whisked Tommy up to the Eaton Place house very early that morning, Charlotte was riding with Alexander, who was consumed with a terrible restlessness, and Angie and Baby had gone. The house was empty.

'Georgina,' he had said, his voice tenderly amused, 'you're crying again! Whatever is it?' and she had stood up and said, 'Oh Kendrick, you don't know, you just don't know,' and he had held out his arms to her, and she had taken his hand and walked him round the lake, and told him, and very soon after that they had fallen, relievedly, frantically, half awed, half amused, into bed. The sudden flare of sexual desire between her and Kendrick (born of her heightened emotional state, his kindness and concern for her, the extraordinary situation they were all thrown into), the discovery that they were actually more than just loving friends, the intensely urgent, desperate need to consummate their relationship, and then the delicious discovery that sexually they were quite extraordinarily compatible, greedy, uninhibited, sensual, imaginative – all these things had driven, briefly, her misery and anxiety from her mind.

Now it was almost dark; they had heard Charlotte and Alexander come back, had lain, holding their breath, as Charlotte called her, knocked at the door, tried the handle, gone away again. Later Georgina had hauled on her clothes, gone to find Charlotte, said she had a bad headache and was trying to sleep it off, and Charlotte had said yes of course, she would stay with Alexander, and then guiltily, greedy for more of Kendrick and the delights he had brought her, Georgina had gone back into her room and her bed.

'We should go down,' he said finally with a sigh, looking at his watch. 'I promised Melissa we'd play Monopoly after supper. And Freddy's here, and we're all going back tomorrow. It's our last evening, we ought to make a nice occasion of it.'

'Oh God,' said Georgina, 'I don't want you to go. What am I going to do without you?'

'You'll be all right,' said Kendrick, kissing her shoulder gently. 'You'll be very all right. You're going back to college. I'll see you at Christmas.'

'Christmas is ages away.'

'No it isn't. And I'll say I want to come and spend it in England with Dad and you can see they're all asked down here, can't you? I'm sure everyone will like that idea. Angie certainly seemed to be getting the hots for your dad last night.'

'Angie has the hots for everybody, I'm sure,' said Georgina.

'Fraid so,' said Kendrick gloomily. 'I don't really rate Dad's chances with her for too long, do you?'

'Oh, I don't know,' said Georgina. 'It's been going on for long enough, apparently.'

'Well, I hope so. He certainly deserves a bit of happiness. I really can't blame him for leaving Mother. She treats him with rather less affection than the cats. I just wish he'd chosen someone a bit – warmer than Angie. Although she is extremely sexy.'

Georgina looked at him. 'Do I have to be jealous?' she said with a smile.

'Absolutely not. I like tall girls,' he said. 'Your dad, whoever he was, must have been pretty tall.'

'George – I think his name must have been George,' she said absently.

'You do? Why?'

'Well, there was Charles and Charlotte, Tommy Soames-Maxwell and Max. It seems to follow. But it's not exactly a lot to go on.'

'You could be right, there.' He tightened his arms around her.

'You won't ever tell anyone about that, Kendrick, will you? Not your mother, not Freddy, not anyone? And you will make sure Melissa doesn't get wind of it, won't you? Just think how she'd love to tell. I just couldn't bear it to get around. Poor Daddy, he'll never, ever be able to stand it.'

'Of course I won't. I swear I won't.'

'And your dad won't, will he?'

'I'm sure he won't,' said Kendrick soothingly. His head was beginning to spin; he felt he had strayed into some latter-day Restoration comedy. 'It's not the sort of thing he'd do. He's not a gossip. And he was so terribly fond of your mother. I just can't understand – '

'Don't talk about it, please,' said Georgina. 'I just don't even want to think about it. It's horrible. Suppose my father's vile, like that Tommy creature?'

'He couldn't be,' said Kendrick, kissing her breasts tenderly. 'Your father has to be very very nice. I just know it.'

★

383

Next day they all left. Charlotte, to Georgina's great surprise, had agreed to extending her stay slightly, spending a couple of days in London, talking to Baby about the London opening, waiting to see what came of Soames-Maxwell's reappearance. 'And I can see Charles too, that will be nice. And ask his advice if necessary. I wish you could meet him, Georgie, you'd love him.'

'Well, maybe I will one day,' said Georgina doubtfully.

'I hope so. I really do.'

Georgina drove her cousins to Heathrow at lunchtime; it was a strange experience, pretending she felt no more for Kendrick than family-style affection, under Melissa's watchful eyes. They managed a swift farewell while Freddy and Melissa rather frantically searched for a present for their mother; but that was all. When her cousins had finally gone through the boarding gates she sat down and cried in the ladies', to the concern of the kind Indian lady in charge, who gave her a packet of Kleenex and some chocolate biscuits. And then, feeling surprisingly cheerful, she drove back to Hartest.

Alexander was waiting for her on the steps. He smiled, put his arm round her.

'You look tired, darling. Come along in.'

'I'm fine. Have you had supper?'

'No. Not yet. I waited for you.' He hesitated. 'Max phoned.'

'He did? What did he say?'

'Oh, just that he was all right. That he was sorry about – about the other night. That he and – Soames-Maxwell were staying in London. He asked if he could bring him down for the weekend. I said no.'

'Good. Although I suppose we should try to like him,' said Georgina carefully.

'I really don't see why,' said Alexander, looking very cold suddenly. 'Why should we try to like him?'

'Well – because of who he – who he is.'

'Georgina, I really don't know what you're talking about. Mr Soames-Maxwell is simply a rather unsavoury friend of Max's. Who we are under absolutely no obligation to like whatsoever.'

'Yes,' said Georgina. 'Yes of course. You're right.'

She walked through the house feeling slightly alarmed. He was obviously more vulnerable than they had all realized.

They ate supper in the kitchen, and then Alexander said he was going to read.

'I'm very tired,' he said.

'I'm going up to see Nanny,' said Georgina. 'She's more and more alone now.'

Alexander frowned.

'I think she likes it that way,' he said, 'I shouldn't disturb her. In fact I really would rather you didn't.' For the first time, he seemed agitated.

'All right,' said Georgina, anxious not to upset him, 'I'll come and read with you. We'll both go to bed early.'

She sat in the library with him, but she couldn't read. She felt excited, in disarray. Apart from concern about Alexander, distress over Max, her relationship with Kendrick was disturbing her, making her restlessly happy. For the first time in her life the sex she so enjoyed had a purpose to it, beyond sheer physical pleasure and self-indulgence; it had invaded her sweetly, tenderly, it was an emotion in itself, a raw, joyful, powerful emotion, it was altering her perspective on life, giving her courage, and hope. She sat looking at Alexander, wondering for the thousandth time just what it had been about the marriage that had made her mother behave as she had; but for the very first time she was thinking without misery, without rancour. Somewhere, somehow there had to be an explanation; it seemed to her tonight, in her new happiness, that the explanation might be, if not happy, at least bearable.

She looked across at Alexander; he was asleep over his book. He looked very old suddenly; her heart wrenched. She went over to him and kissed him.

'Come on, Daddy. Up to bed.'

He woke immediately as he had a trick of doing, and smiled at her, immediately alert.

'Yes, of course. Goodnight, darling.'

'Goodnight, Daddy.'

It was still early; when she was sure he was asleep again, she went to Nanny's room. She was sitting by her fire, looking into it, a book in her lap.

'What are you reading, Nanny?'

'*Pride and Prejudice*. Such a stupid book. I've read it twice. Can't see why anyone bothers with it.'

'Perhaps,' said Georgina, greatly daring, confronting Nanny's lack of logic, 'perhaps you should read something else.'

'Oh no,' said Nanny. 'I have to finish it. There's such a lot of dreadful news in the papers.'

'Yes there is. You're right. Books are safer. Er – Nanny – '

'If you're going to ask me about that man,' said Nanny, 'don't. I didn't like the look of him.'

'Well, none of us did, Nanny. I just thought – '

'If he's anything to do with Max, he shouldn't be here,' said Nanny. 'Max never did have any respect.'

'Well – it's certainly very hard on Daddy.'

'Yes,' said Nanny. 'Of course you could say it was his fault.'

'What was?' asked Georgina. Her heart was thudding rather hard.

'Well – the way he brought Max up. Spoilt him.'

'Nanny, it's not his fault. Really it isn't.'

'That's what your mother used to say,' said Nanny, her face softening. ' "Nanny," she used to say, "it's not his fault." '

'Nanny, please tell me what you know. Please. I'm desperate to sort it out.'

'I really don't know very much, Georgina,' said Nanny. 'I never did.'

'You knew about us.'

'Yes, I did. But not a lot more.'

'Not why it happened?'

'Georgina, I promised your mother I would never tell you. She said it wasn't right that you should know.'

'But Nanny, we need to know. We really do.'

'No you don't,' said Nanny, 'you want to know. That's different. I always tried to tell you that, Georgina, the difference between want and need. You never could see it. I need a new bike, I need a new sledge. You didn't need either. You wanted them. You don't need to know, Georgina. It won't help. It's too late.'

'But Nanny – '

'I can't tell you,' she said, setting her old face into particularly stubborn lines. 'I promised, and it wouldn't be right. But I will say one thing, and it's important. You shouldn't feel too bad about him. About Lord Caterham. Is that any help to you?'

'No, not really,' said Georgina with a sigh.

Chapter 32

Charlotte, 1985

Fred III called all the partners into his office late one March afternoon (and included Charlotte: she had been at once touched and intrigued by that) and told them that Jicks Foster had died, quite suddenly, of a heart attack. He was upset, as upset as Charlotte could ever remember seeing him. There were tears in his bright blue eyes as he talked to them; he and Jicks went back a long way, he said, as they all knew, buddies from Harvard. His account had been the making of the present-day Praegers; it was a sad day on many counts. And a sad day for Fosters Land, thought Charlotte, from what she knew of Jeremy, the son and heir; and the disloyal thought came to her that there was a parallel with Fred III and Baby, the tough, hard-working, exemplary father and the beloved, indulged, playboy son. Not that Baby was indulged any more, she reflected, or even beloved; quite the reverse, Fred had nailed him personally to the cross and planted the crown of thorns of his own dissatisfaction on his head. But for too long he had given him too much, believed in him too deeply; and Jicks Foster had done the same with Jeremy. Only Jeremy had escaped the crucifixion; and now he had inherited the kingdom and was to rule over it alone.

She was working her way through some files three evenings later when there was a tap at her office door. She was working on various financial models, different ways of presenting its liquidity, for a company for which they were currently looking for a buyer; briefed by Gabe to make it look as good as possible: 'Which won't be easy.'

'Charlotte? Hi.' It was Jeremy Foster.

'Oh. Hallo, Jeremy.' Ever since the fracas over Michael Browning she had been very wary of doing more than nod to important clients in the office.

'I just dropped by to talk to your grandfather. Charlotte, are you busy? Can I buy you a drink?'

'Well – well, I don't know. I have to – '

'Oh Charlotte, please. Isabella is out of town tonight, and I'm feeling thoroughly blue. And besides, I want to talk to you about something.'

'Jeremy, I don't think I should. My grandfather is very strict about my – my – '

'Your what?'

'Well, my fraternizing with the clients.'

Jeremy went into peals of laughter. 'You're kidding me.'

'I am not kidding you. Honestly.'

'Well in that case, I shall buy you a very expensive dinner somewhere and have le tout New York talking about it. Just to annoy him. And I shall tell him I am placing American Suburban entirely in your hands.'

'Don't be ridiculous. I'd be fired.'

'He can't fire you, honey, you're family. Look, come and have a drink. Cheer an old man up.'

'Oh – oh all right. That'd be nice.'

They went to the Oak Bar; Jeremy ordered a bottle of champagne.

'Gorgeous!' said Charlotte. 'I really feel I need that. Maybe not all of it,' she added carefully.

'You're not going to get all of it. Not even half.' He smiled at her again. 'So how's banking, Charlotte? How's the president elect?'

'Oh,' said Charlotte. 'Sometimes I see that as purest fantasy, Jeremy. I just can't believe any of it. It seems so remote, as I sit there at that horrible little tin desk, binding pages together. But banking, yes, it's great, I love it. Just love it. There can't be many jobs that give you the most instant gratification.'

'Sounds very sexy!' said Jeremy.

'It is sexy,' she said, earnestly serious. 'When you've brought something off, done a deal, there is a tremendous high, a feeling of winning, of overcoming the odds; you really feel you could fly.'

'I see. Maybe I'm in the wrong business. And that uppity young man you work with. Gabe Hoffman. Do you love him too?'

'Certainly not. I can't stand him,' said Charlotte, who was currently having to invest more time and energy than usual into persuading herself that was true. 'Oh God, Jeremy, that's the champagne talking already. Don't repeat that, will you? Not to Grandpa, or to Pete.'

'Charlotte, of course I won't repeat it.' Jeremy looked genuinely hurt. 'Don't you get homesick for England?'

'Yes I do,' she said with a sigh. 'I miss my family. Specially now Baby's working in London. He was my security blanket. He's a terrible loss.'

'He certainly is. One of my best friends. He's such fun, dear old Baby. I think I shall be spending a little more time in London than I used to. Which brings me to what I wanted to talk to you about. Did you know he was ill?'

Charlotte stared at him.

'No. No of course not. What sort of ill?'

'I'm not sure. He says it's nothing. Some kind of muscle problem, he said. You know how he laughs things off. He wouldn't have said anything if I hadn't seen him fumbling in his wallet the other night. He absolutely couldn't get some money out. In the end he asked me for some. And tried to change ths subject. But I pressed him, and he said well, yes, he did seem to have some kind of problem but he was sure it wasn't too serious. He's promised me to see a specialist anyway. I just wondered if you knew.'

Charlotte frowned into her glass.

'No, I had no idea,' she said. 'I mean I hardly ever see him now. But I'm having supper with him tomorrow, before he leaves. I'll try and talk to him. And I'll have a word with Freddy.' She sighed.

Jeremy looked at her sharply. 'Don't you like Freddy?'

'Oh – yes, of course. I don't know how much he likes me, though.'

'Well, I suppose he would hardly be human if he could actually think of you fondly. I think he's a terrible guy,' he added with a grin.

'Why?' said Charlotte curiously.

'Oh, he has that awful constipated manner, just like his mother. I can't tell him good morning without feeling I've seriously goofed. And between you and me, I don't think he's very bright. Well, he may be bright, but he is most definitely not a great banker. I asked him to give me his opinion on a little window manufacturing company down in Detroit that I was kind of interested in, and he sent me a twelve-page document saying it was nothing out of the ordinary. Then your friend Gabe just happened to point out that they were one of the very first companies to use recycled aluminium for the frames, and that that would be a great PR thing, so I bought them. Only don't mention it to Freddy, will you?'

'Golly, I wouldn't. It would be more than my life was worth,' said Charlotte. 'I'm glad you told me, though.'

Jeremy laughed and leant forward suddenly and kissed her on the cheek.

'What a lovely, well-brought-up English girl you are. Talking boarding school slang. Don't change too much, Charlotte, don't turn into a Wall Street whizz kid, will you?'

'I don't think there's much chance of that,' said Charlotte. She was confused, disproportionately warmed and touched by the kiss, the admiration. She had been holding her feelings in check for so long she felt they must have become stunted, warped things, unused to any kind of life; she stood up quickly and smiled down at him, carefully casual. 'Jeremy, I have to go. I have a zillion things to do before tomorrow, and Gabe and I are flying down to Miami at five a.m. for a breakfast meeting. Will you excuse me?'

'Only if you promise to do this again some time. Soon. Very soon.'

'Jeremy! Whatever would Isabella say?'

'She would tell you you were welcome to me,' he said.

She had been about to laugh when she saw an entirely unfamiliar expression at the back of his eyes. It was sadness.

'There definitely is something wrong,' Charlotte said to Jeremy the day after she'd dined with Baby, 'but he isn't going to tell me what it is. I suppose he thinks I'll tell someone. Freddy was very frosty about it, basically told me to mind my own business, but he certainly doesn't know anything either.'

'Well, like I said, Baby's promised me that he'll see a specialist,' said Jeremy. 'We must just keep an eye on him, make sure he really does. And keep in touch with one another. I have to go away for a few weeks; when I get back, I'll call you, and we can have – dinner do you think? Just so that we could discuss exactly how we could monitor Baby's progress.'

'Jeremy, I really don't think dinner's necessary for that,' said Charlotte, laughing. 'But call me anyway.'

Jeremy called her. She had no news from Baby, did she?

'No, none.'

'Well, we should have dinner anyway.'

'Jeremy, why?'

'Why not? You'll get a good dinner, you look as if you need feeding up, I shall have a really nice evening, and Elaine and her clients will benefit considerably by having something to gossip about.'

'Jeremy, you know perfectly well it's gossip I'm worried about. I'm certainly not going to Elaine's with you.'

'Oh, all right, darling. We'll go somewhere very quiet. If that's your only worry. We can take a suite at the Pierre for the evening, if you like.'

'Don't be ridiculous,' said Charlotte, laughing.

'I'm not being ridiculous. What about your place? We could get a delivery.'

'I haven't got a place. I'm still living with Grandma and Grandpa.'

'Well, I can see that wouldn't be absolutely ideal. I'll think of somewhere, and I'll call you later. OK?'

'OK,' said Charlotte, giving in suddenly. Being wanted, being desired, was virtually irresistible after the endless months of humiliation at the hands of Gabe Hoffman.

'You won't regret it,' said Jeremy. 'I promise.'

Those words were to haunt her in the months ahead.

★

He rang her again at five. 'I'll send a car for you at eight. Pine Street or 80th?'

'Will you be in this car when it comes?'

'I might.'

'Well, you'd better come to Pine Street. I hope we're not going anywhere smart, because I won't have a chance to change.'

'We're going somewhere very smart. But you won't need to dress up.'

'Is this some kind of a riddle?'

'Think of it as a game. I like games.'

'All right,' said Charlotte, smiling slightly foolishly into the phone.

Gabe came into the office at seven, tired and bad-tempered from a long session with Fred, and asked her to start work on the minutes of a meeting they'd attended that afternoon; his watch was off, and his hair was extremely tousled. Charlotte looked at him, and her heart turned over. Shit. If only she could hate him in the good healthy way she used to.

'Gabe, I really can't. I'm sorry. That is – ' She hesitated. She was aware she wasn't being at all professional.

'Yes, what? I suppose you have some social engagement.' He made it sound as if she was planning to indulge in some particularly unpleasant perversion.

'I do as a matter of fact. But – is it very important that I'm here?'

'Yeah, it's very important,' said Gabe. 'I'd be most grateful if you could possibly spare the time. Lady Charlotte.' His eyes were hostile, darker than usual.

Charlotte sighed. 'OK,' she said. 'I'll cancel my evening. Perhaps you could allow me to just make a phone call.'

He turned and walked out of the office again: didn't even thank her.

She called Jeremy's office; he'd gone. She could hardly call the house. Well, she'd have to go down and explain when he got to the bank. It was probably Fate stepping in, to prevent the evening with Jeremy, and she should be grateful.

She started working through her notes on the meeting. Gabe had come back and was hitting his keyboard as if he would like to kill it. She was upset, angry; and nervous about Jeremy's arrival. It was hard to concentrate. She sat without lifting her head, her stomach churning increasingly, drinking endless cups of coffee, aware that Gabe was watching her, aware of her discomfort. At eight o'clock exactly her phone rang.

'There's a car for you, Charlotte.' It was Dick, the night porter.

'Oh, thank you, Dick. I'll be down. Excuse me please,' she said to

Gabe, her voice sarcastic, 'I just have to go and send a very disappointed friend on his way.'

'I thought you'd called him.'

'I did. I missed him.'

'Fine. Don't be long.'

She ran down the stairs. An extremely long stretch limo stood in the street. There was a shadowy figure in the back. She went over to it and knocked on the window, and then jumped as it slid down; there was an old woman sitting in the back, wearing rags, with a scarf over her head.

'Oh, I'm so sorry,' she said. 'I thought – '

'Don't be sorry,' said Jeremy's voice in a theatrical hiss from the depths of the rags. 'Just get in and we'll go and hide some place else. I have a false beard you could put on . . . now where did I put it . . .'

'Oh Jeremy,' said Charlotte, laughing. 'Jeremy, you are ridiculous.'

'I am not,' he said, sounding hurt, 'I went to a lot of trouble to get into this gear. I thought you'd be impressed. Come on, darling, jump in.'

The driver was standing behind her, his face impassive.

'Jeremy, I can't. I'm sorry. I really can't.'

'Why not?'

'Well – because I have to work. Gabe wants me to do something for a meeting in the morning.'

'Oh for fuck's sake. Tell him you can't. Tell him you have a prior engagement.'

'Junior associates aren't allowed to have prior engagements.'

'Hell, Charlotte, you're going to own that bank one day.'

'That's all the more reason why I can't.'

'Well, I'll wait,' said Jeremy easily, after a pause. He smiled, his eyes dancing up at her. 'I'll just sit here till you come down. I have plenty of work to do. Champagne on board. It's fine.'

'Jeremy, I might be hours. It might be midnight.'

'That's fine. I like eating late.'

'But – '

'Charlotte, go and get on with your very important work. I'll wait. I'm not going to go away. You can't get rid of me as easily as that.' He smiled at her, his engaging, boyish smile. Charlotte contrasted it with Gabe's fierce brooding face, and smiled back, wishing she found Jeremy's more moving and Gabe's less.

When she got back to her office, Gabe wasn't there; the draft of the minutes she had given him was thrown onto her desk, a post-it note stuck to the sheet saying 'This needs entirely reworking'. Almost every sheet was scribbled over in his large, black scrawl. Charlotte stared at it in disbelief. She knew she had done a good job; she knew the minutes were basically absolutely fine. And they were only minutes. Bastard. He knew she wanted to get through quickly, he was doing this entirely to hurt her. A white-hot temper ripped through her suddenly; she longed to leave him a short, extremely pithy note and walk out again. She even began to draft one; then she threw her pen down, and picked up the notes again. There was no way out of this one, but through it. Gabe's victories were her defeats; for that reason alone she had to keep winning. And winning right now was getting the fucking report right. And not showing him she cared. One day, one day . . . Charlotte wrenched her mind from the pleasurable thoughts of one day, and forced herself to concentrate.

Ten minutes later Gabe came back in. He was carrying a brown paper deli bag; he put it down on his desk, looked at her and said, 'I thought you might like a coffee. And a bagel.'

'No thanks,' said Charlotte briefly. 'I'm too busy to eat.'

She heard, enraged, her voice tremble slightly. Gabe shrugged and took the lid off a coffee, unwrapped a bagel.

'Please yourself,' he said through a mouthful.

'I find it rather difficult to do that around here,' she said.

There was a silence: then he suddenly laughed. Charlotte looked up startled. It was a rare event.

'Did I say something funny?'

'No. Yes. A bit.'

'I'm glad I manage to amuse you,' she said.

There was another silence. Gabe sat down and continued to look at her as if she was a new and interesting object set down in his presence.

'What you need is a good fuck,' he said, almost conversationally.

Charlotte stared at him. For the first time in her life, she realized the true meaning of literally not being able to believe her ears. 'What did you say?' she said at last.

'I said you needed a good fuck. Calm you down a bit. You're one huge jangling nerve.' There was something almost approaching a smile on his face, challenging, aggressive. Charlotte sat, utterly still, wanting to feel rage, outrage, but aware only within the deepest heart of herself of a violent, snaking lash of sexual excitement.

'And I suppose,' she said icily, 'that you feel you should deliver it in person.'

The moment she'd spoken, she could have bitten her tongue out. She should have been dignified, hurt, shocked, anything really, other than coming back to him with some crude wisecrack, a wisecrack moreover that laid her open to further insults. What a fool she must appear to him now: crass, gauche and, worse than those, arrogant, self-opinionated.

She braced herself for mockery, sneering, aware of a flush rising up her neck.

Gabe looked back at her for a moment or two, in silence; then he said briefly, 'No, I hadn't thought it through that far,' and went back to his work.

It was one thirty before she finally finished, and Gabe told her to go home; he was still working furiously, his watch pulled off as it always was when he was intent on something, consuming endless cans of diet Coke, and glaring at his terminal. He was working on a series of financial models for a paper company; the price of the stock was roaring up. Charlotte looked at him and thought with a touch of something near sadness that he had no idea that he had said anything particularly outrageous, anything that might have caused her to feel hurt, humiliated. Had she pointed it out, it would have intrigued him, she supposed, on an intellectual level puzzled him even, but it would have been totally inexplicable. A waste of time and energy. He was totally arrogant, chauvinist, insensitive; she felt a sense of strong sudden relief now that she had not made a scene, not reacted badly, come on all tender and girly, given him that kind of satisfaction. For the hundredth, possibly the thousandth time she reflected on the revenge she would extract from him one day, picked up her things and walked out of the office without a word.

She went into the ladies' room, looked at herself and sighed. She was pale, and her eyes were dark with tiredness, her mascara smudged. Her hair was a mess; her skirt was creased. Well, at least it should put Jeremy off.

'You look gorgeous,' he said. 'I like tired girls. Their resistance is lower.'

'My resistance is very high,' said Charlotte firmly. She sank into the seat beside him. He had shed his rags and was wearing a pair of Levis and a beige cashmere sweater. There was a bottle of champagne in an ice bucket on the floor of the limo.

'What the hell have you been doing in there?' he said, opening the bottle, pouring her a glass. He was good-naturedly interested, not in the least reproachful at the delay.

'Oh – working on figures, and lists of contacts. Gabe's still in there.'

'Do you often spend the night together?'

'Yes. Very often. Unfortunately.' The car moved off; she sipped her champagne, feeling she was watching someone else in a bad movie.

'You really don't like him, do you?'

'I loathe him,' said Charlotte, Gabe's words suddenly reiterating

394

themselves in her head. 'He's arrogant, crude, and totally insensitive.'
She heard her voice tremble slightly again, and sighed.

Jeremy looked at her thoughtfully. 'He's upset you, hasn't he?'

'No! Well – maybe. Let's not talk about him, Jeremy, please.'

'OK. We'll talk about everything else but. Tell me, Charlotte, how is
the Chinese wall in that bank of yours?'

'Very strong,' said Charlotte firmly. 'Why?'

The Chinese wall – the invisible security structure to protect clients
from the hazards of information leaking out from the banking floor to the
dealers – had been one of the first things she had learnt about on Day One
at Praegers.

'Oh – there's such a lot of insider dealing going on. Someone was
telling me the other day that in a lot of banks they're not too much like a
wall. More of a net curtain, I was told.'

'Jeremy, I'm sure you're wrong, and anyway, I don't want to talk
Praegers.'

'No, I know. I'm sorry if I upset you. I didn't mean to.'

'Anyway, where are we going?'

'Oh – nice little dining room I know.'

'Jeremy! It's not a hotel?'

'It is not a hotel.'

The car was moving into Manhattan; the streets looked twice as wide
in the deserted pre-dawn emptiness. Just past the Rockefeller Center they
turned right, wound their way down a few blocks, and pulled to a halt.
Charlotte looked up at the huge building towering above her.

'Where on earth are we? Your office?'

'Not exactly.'

'Jeremy, either it is or it isn't your office.'

'Well, it kind of is. Come along, darling, let's go in.'

The driver was holding open the door, his face if anything blanker than
before. Charlotte got out and allowed Jeremy to take her arm, shepherd
her into the building. 'I wish you'd explain,' she said slightly irritably.

'I will in a minute. Come on, into the elevator.'

Had she been anyone else, had Jeremy been anyone else, Charlotte
thought, she would have refused, been afraid of being raped or attacked.
But she felt (and told herself she was right to feel it) that she was protected
by her position and his. She stepped into the elevator, watched him press
the button for the seventy-third floor. The elevator roared up; she had
never got used to New York buildings, she felt sick and her ears popped.
Jeremy stood the other side of the elevator, smiling at her.

It stopped, they stepped out into a long wide corridor. Jeremy took
out a key and unlocked the door to the left of the elevator. 'Come on in.'

'But Jeremy, where are we? Is this some kind of a night club?'

'It is not,' he said, sounding mildly indignant. 'It's my – workroom.'

The door opened into a small lobby; he pushed it open without switching on the light. Charlotte gasped aloud. She seemed to be standing in the middle of the night sky. She was in a large room, two walls of which were windows; presumably they were on the extreme outside edge of the building, and it had some complex, geometric structure. The view was breathtaking; she could see the graceful lace-like shape of the Chrysler, the great pointing needle of the Empire State and a hundred others, the lights shining starrily at her against the dark sky. The room had a marble floor and marble walls, and was almost entirely unfurnished apart from a couple of large couches in the window. She realized there were some very dim lights set in the walls; Jeremy turned a switch by the door and they brightened slowly. There was a discreet cough; Charlotte turned and saw a waiter in full white-tied splendour standing in the doorway.

'Shall I serve the champagne, sir?'

'Yes, Dawson, do. Thank you.'

Dawson withdrew; Charlotte looked at Jeremy, her eyes wide and sparkling.

'Jeremy, whatever is going on?'

'Dinner. In a minute. First a drink. Thank you, Dawson.'

'But where are we?'

'I told you. In my workroom. This is where I work. Where I think, and have ideas. There's what you might call a studio through there. And when it gets very late, I don't go home. Hence the kitchen. Oh, and there is also a bed.'

'I just thought there might be,' said Charlotte tartly.

Jeremy looked hurt. 'You just thought wrong. It's a single bed.'

'Yes, I know the New Yorker's idea of a single bed,' said Charlotte. 'It would contain a whole English family. Let me see this studio.'

Jeremy handed her a glass of champagne, and took her hand.

'It's here,' he said, leading her through the lobby again. The studio was parallel to the first room, and almost as big; it did indeed have a huge artist's desk in it, completely empty of pencils, paints or paper. There were two plan chests, a table with a computer terminal on it, and some architectural drawings hung round the wall. It did not look as if it was very frequently used.

'Very nice,' said Charlotte. 'I can see you burn the midnight oil here a lot.'

'Come and eat,' said Jeremy, 'you must be starving.'

★

Dawson served dinner with extreme formality at a table which he produced from the kitchen and set up in the wall-windowed room. It was a superb meal – 'Very light,' said Jeremy, 'as it's a little late' – asparagus, salmon in filo pastry, and summer pudding. 'I know it's only spring, but I like to look forward.'

Charlotte wasn't really hungry, but Jeremy was so pleased with the meal he had orchestrated, so eager to give her pleasure it seemed churlish not to eat. She drank as little as she could, aware of the dangers of getting even mildly muddle-headed, but the champagne in the car and the second helping on arrival had shot into her bloodstream dangerously fast. By the time she had finished her summer pudding, she was pleasantly confused about exactly where she was, precisely why she was there, and certainly about how she was going to get home.

If Jeremy had set out to disarm her, she thought, he was going the right way about it. He had made no attempt to seduce her, had not even tried to flatter her; he had simply talked, charmingly and amusingly, about himself, and had led her, equally charmingly, to talk about her own life; Charlotte, who had thought she was too tired to speak at all, heard herself talking easily and happily about her childhood, her schooldays, Hartest, her family, her relationship with her grandfather, and then less happily about her hopes and fears for herself at the bank. 'It's so horribly complex. It sounds so wonderful, doesn't it, just to inherit this huge golden egg, and it is, I suppose, but it's a nightmare as well. So many people resenting me, jealous of me; I still have to take a deep breath before I walk into the restaurant at lunchtime, even though at last I have some friends. But they're outnumbered by the enemies.'

'You poor kid,' said Jeremy, looking at her, sympathy liquid in his light brown eyes. 'Did you ever think it would be so bad?'

'Stupidly, no. I suppose I realized Freddy would be upset, but I didn't bargain on the remaining ninety-nine per cent of the bank.'

'I don't really see it, I must say,' he said, reaching to refill her glass. Dawson had disappeared into some discreet back room. 'I mean, Praegers have always inherited the bank. It's been passed on for – what – four, five generations. Nobody resented Baby or even Freddy.'

'Yes, but I'm not a Praeger. I'm a stuck-up English debutante with a very dubious claim to my position, apart from being my grandfather's favourite. Poised to throw my weight about, cash in on a lot of unearned benefits, all that sort of thing.'

'Whose words are those? Gabe's?'

'Yes. And everybody else's. Gabe is the only person who speaks them, that's all.'

397

'He clearly is a very charming young man,' said Jeremy lightly. 'Does your grandfather know about all this?'

'No,' said Charlotte, looking at him with alarm in her eyes, 'and he is not to, either. He already practically killed me for what he called whingeing to a client.'

'Tell me about that.'

She told him; in her exhausted over-emotional state, remembering that day, her hurt at being excluded so brutally from the Christmas lunch, her eyes suddenly filled with tears. Jeremy looked at her and his expression was very tender.

'Poor darling,' he said, covering her hand with his. 'How vile. I wish I'd been there.'

'It would have been worse if you had,' said Charlotte, smiling at him weakly, and withdrawing her hand rather too hastily. 'I'd have cried all over you too.'

'And I should have taken you off for a most extravagant and wonderful lunch and dried your tears.'

'Well,' she said, smiling at him slightly shakily, 'you weren't.'

'Do you ever think of giving up? Going back to England and doing something else?'

'Never,' said Charlotte simply. 'Never for a single instant.'

'Well you're a brave girl. Why not?'

'Firstly,' she said simply, 'because I love it. And secondly because I'm not going to let them beat me.'

Later, much later, he began to talk about himself. Charlotte had no idea what the time was; everything had lost any sense of perspective, she seemed to be inhabiting some strange world with no conventional areas of time and space. She was no longer tired, but in an oddly calm, slightly distant state. They had moved to one of the couches; Dawson had brought in, at Jeremy's request, a large pot of coffee. Charlotte had looked at it, and asked if she could possibly have tea. 'How very English. Of course you can. Can't she, Dawson?'

'Of course, sir.' He reappeared five minutes later with a silver tray laid with cup, milk, sugar, hot water, and a huge variety of tea bags, Indian, China, fruit and herb of every possible description, and withdrew again with a slight bow.

Charlotte giggled. 'I'm sure if I'd asked for Horlicks, he'd have delivered it.'

'Of course he would. That's what he's there for.'

'Not to act as chaperon for hapless young girls?'

'I don't think you're hapless at all,' he said, looking at her very seriously. 'And no, not at all. He has a very efficient blind eye which he can turn when required.'

'I see.' She looked at him thoughtfully. 'How extremely spoilt you are. How does it feel, Mr Foster, to be the man who has everything?'

'I wouldn't know,' he said, 'I am nothing of the sort, you see.' And he set out to disabuse her of any notion that he did indeed have everything and was therefore happy. He had everything certainly, he said, that money could buy, but that was most assuredly not enough.

Charlotte, who had grown up on the fringes of great wealth, while not actually possessing it, was nevertheless intrigued by the stories: the private jets to take him to wherever he wanted on a whim, the island bought for a house party, and used only two days a year, the house in Jamaica built and never occupied, the fleet of servants in every house, the bodyguards, the helicopters, the yachts, the endless trail of parties, of beautiful women, of the quest for pleasure. He talked of it not boastfully, but casually, almost sadly.

'All I ever wanted,' he said, 'was love.'

'But you've been married to Isabella for eight years,' said Charlotte. 'That must mean something.'

'It means we suit one another very well,' he said. 'I don't make demands on her, nor she on me, except socially. Our secretaries put our diaries together, once a week, and the result of that liaison is a mass of parties, dinners, benefits, trips. But we are two lonely people. Or certainly one lonely person.'

'And what are you looking for?' said Charlotte interestedly.

'Oh,' he said, reaching out and stroking her cheek, 'I am looking most tirelessly for love.' There was a long silence; her head was spinning very slowly and gently.

'And if you found love,' she said, 'would things change? Would you and Isabella cease to suit one another?'

'I can't tell you that,' he said, picking up her hand and kissing it. 'I have never quite discovered it. I have come near, but not near enough.'

'Well,' said Charlotte, helping herself to some more tea in an attempt to become sober, 'speaking for myself, the order would have to be a little different. I would have no wish to start helping you to find love, and then be relegated to a sub-clause in a weekly meeting between two secretaries.'

Jeremy looked at her, and his eyes were very dark, very searching. 'I think I can promise you,' he said, 'that if we were to find love, you and I, then I should want to change things very quickly. Very quickly indeed.'

'Well,' said Charlotte, confused, almost frightened by the turn the conversation, their evening, was taking, telling herself he was a master at such pretty speeches, even while she enjoyed it, 'well Jeremy, I don't imagine it's going to happen.' She stood up rather purposefully. 'It's been lovely. Really really lovely. But it's – ' she looked at her watch – 'five o'clock. I have to be in the office by seven. Will you have your very discreet driver take me home?'

He looked at her and sighed. 'Dear me,' he said, 'the English schoolgirl again. So sensible.'

Charlotte felt stung, horribly hurt, thinking how this quality she projected hung about her, how often Gabe had taunted her about it, and her brother too. She flushed, and felt tears rising behind her eyes. Her head cleared suddenly. 'I'm sorry,' she said. 'Sorry to be so English, so sensible.' She turned away. 'I don't always mean to be.'

'Charlotte,' said Jeremy, and his voice was very soft, 'I'm sorry. I didn't mean to upset you. I like the Englishness, really I do. I think it's very – sweet.'

'Do you?' said Charlotte with a sigh. 'Most people don't. Most people think it's awful.'

'Well I don't. And I'd like to say thank you for listening to me. Being with me. It's been a wonderful – evening. Will you join me here again? Some time?'

'Well – perhaps,' she said, 'I'm not sure that it's entirely a good idea.'

'You're very sure of yourself, aren't you?' he said, standing up, looking down at her rather sadly. 'Very self-confident. I envy you.'

'Oh, Jeremy,' said Charlotte, smiling at him in a genuine disbelief, 'how can you say such a thing? You aren't exactly a poor shy blushing violet yourself. As we say in England,' she added.

'Well, now there you're wrong,' said Jeremy, and the dark sadness was behind his eyes again. 'Very wrong. I would give the world to be self-confident, to know what I really want to say and do. As you so clearly do. That's very difficult, you know, when you have a father like mine. Even when he's dead.'

'You must miss him,' said Charlotte suddenly.

'Yes,' he said, 'yes, I do. Very much. He might have been domineering and demanding, but he was the kindest person I ever knew. I feel – very tired, very weighed down without him. And it's such a special relationship, isn't it, with one's father?'

Charlotte stared at him, and felt an overwhelming sadness herself, not just at his loneliness, his clearly genuine grief, but at her own sad half-father, whom she loved so much, lost to her also for so much of her life these days; and she thought of her other father, and all the years they had spent without one another's company, and her eyes filled with tears again, and Jeremy stood up, and took her quite quietly and gently in his arms, and said, 'Charlotte, poor sweet Charlotte, don't cry, don't,' and

400

the sadness, combined with her exhaustion and with the strangeness and excitement of the situation she found herself in, and her earlier, disturbing exchange with Gabe, all suddenly blended, transformed into something intense and overwhelming, and before she could even begin to analyse it, she felt it, felt it in her body, warm, liquid, almost shocking, and Jeremy recognized it, felt it too, and he drew her more strongly against him, and said her name just once, again, very quietly and then he started to kiss her, tenderly, sweetly, and Charlotte, afraid suddenly, cautious, anxious, drew back. Whatever happened, however hurt, however angry he was, she must not, could not let this thing go any further. It was wilfully, stupidly dangerous, and she had to get away, quickly, at once, before any harm was done.

'There you go again,' he whispered, very quietly, his hands in her hair, 'the cool, self-contained little English girl,' and a shock of anger and of pain shot through Charlotte, in some strange way increasing her hunger, and in that moment she forgot everything, all sense, all caution, and as much to rid herself of that label, that awful, bossy, schoolgirly label, as to satisfy her aching need, she drew herself against him again, her own mouth searching, soft, not in the least self-contained.

And then without knowing quite how, she was lying on a bed, in the room beyond the studio, and Jeremy was very tenderly, very carefully, in between kissing her with increasing urgency, removing her clothes with a swift, clearly highly practised skill, and again without analysing how, she was naked, quite quite naked, and so was he, kneeling above her, smiling at her, and her body was crying out for him, longing to feel him, to have him there, there in her; she could feel her hunger for him growing, burgeoning, like some slowly opening flower, she was soft, warm, liquid for him, longing to be filled, she could no more have denied him and herself than leapt out of the great window into the night sky. She opened her arms, and he came into them, and lay above her, gently, carefully; she could feel his penis growing now, pressing against her, towards her, beginning to be in her, and she moved gently, thrusting at him, and he began to kiss her breasts, very lightly, carefully, slowly, teasing the nipples with his tongue, drawing back, looking at her, and then down again, kissing, warm, languorous, infinitely tender, and each time the hunger darted down, down through her body, trailing heat and something that was almost pain in its wake; and she opened to him, on and on, drawing him into her, insistently, urgently, and she could feel the great depths of her desire lighten into something nearer pleasure, a rising, a reaching to him and for him. He was kissing her mouth now, his own slow, gentle, and his hands were beneath her, holding, moulding her buttocks; she was quite quite lost to everything, everything but a fierce

401

concentration that was not just physical, but emotional as well, a longing, a desperation for release. She was sweating, thrusting at him frantically, in a swift, almost jerking rhythm, her body arched, her head thrown back, careless of everything but her own need; her entire physical existence concentrated into the approach of her climax, and she saw it as a brilliance before her, heard it as a thunder in her ears, and she cried out again, and again, and thrust frantically on and on, and it was there, there, granted to her, a sweet, fierce, nearly painful thing, tumbling, falling endlessly, spreading out and out in great circles of pleasure within her, and finally finally it was over, fading into quiescence, and she opened her eyes, and saw Jeremy above her, smiling at her, tender, but strangely triumphant; and with a pang that abruptly and hideously removed all the pleasure, at a single stroke, in a single moment, she realized exactly, precisely, what a dangerous thing she had done.

Chapter 33

Baby, early spring 1985

Baby was sweating slightly. The doctor seemed to be taking a phenomenally long time over his examination. He was peering into his eyes now, first one then the other, grunting and hmm-ing. Baby felt a strong desire to make a silly face at him.

'Yes well. Nothing too serious – hopefully. You're probably just tired. You work too hard. And we mustn't forget you did have that coronary – what? – two years ago. Look, I'll arrange for you to see a neurologist later this week, and he can check you over. Now when did you first notice this numbness? A couple of months ago, did you say?'

After he left the consulting rooms Baby wandered down Harley Street, feeling marginally better. The guy had to know what he was talking about. If it was something really serious that he suspected he would have had him into hospital that day. Doctors worked like that. The more time they took over doing things, the less serious the things were. And really he had no serious symptoms. He wouldn't have been able to leave seeing anyone this long if he'd been worse. It was several months now, and it certainly hadn't got any worse. Well it was maybe a little worse. Just a little numbness in his right hand sometimes, a difficulty in handling his keys. The coronary had made him a hypochondriac, that was his real problem. And he was working very hard, with Praeger's London launch coming up in April. Very hard. Life wasn't easy at the moment. He hailed a cab and went to his office in St James's.

Thinking about the launch reminded Baby about Angie, and the fight they had had the night before. Baby had complained that she wasn't giving him the support he needed, and he felt her work could go at least on the back burner. She had security now, she didn't need it, it wasn't so much to ask. Angie had said it was a great deal to ask, she loved her work, it was as important to her as his lousy bank, which (she would like to remind him) he had only inherited rather than created himself, and she would like to know what security she had. Mary Rose was flatly refusing to give Baby a divorce, and she was no nearer being Mrs Praeger than she had been ten years earlier. She had the twins to consider, and she was absolutely not going to put herself in a vulnerable position by becoming totally dependent on some man.

Baby had said that he was not some man, he was her husband elect, the father of her children, and as such he had some right to her support. Angie had told him if he wanted her support he could make some supportive gesture, like making over some Praeger shares to her. Then she might just possibly feel a little more secure.

It was not the first time she had made this suggestion, and Baby replied, not for the first time, that it was so far out of line as to be purest fantasy. Whereupon Angie told him to go fuck himself and went to bed in the guest room.

No wonder, he thought, he was feeling the strain.

His secretary, a pretty girl called Katy Prior, with awe-inspiring legs, was waiting for him with a large jug of fresh coffee – 'Making fresh coffee is your major job, I cannot drink that lousy instant stuff,' he'd said when he'd hired her – and some messages.

'Dr Curtis phoned. Could you make Friday for the appointment. And your wife called.'

'My wife? Would that be – ' Baby's voice trailed away awkwardly.

'It was a London call, Mr Praeger,' said Katy helpfully.

'OK. You'd better get her. She'll be at her office. You have the number, don't you, honey?'

'Yes, Mr Praeger. Oh, and a Mr Soames-Maxwell rang. He wants to talk to you.'

'Oh Jesus,' said Baby.

Angie was very chilly; she was going to be out that night. She hoped Baby had no objections. Baby said, almost equally chilly, that he had none, and told her he was going to New York at the weekend, for a main board meeting.

Then he rang Soames-Maxwell.

'Baby! Hi. Nice of you to call. I wondered if we could meet?'

'I don't think so,' said Baby wearily. 'What did you want to talk about?'

'Oh – I'm a little worried about Max. I didn't want to bother his – Alexander. Of course I may have to. But I wondered if we could talk first. I'm very happy to buy you a drink.'

'Thanks,' said Baby, 'but I can buy my own.'

'Well maybe I should call Alexander. Charlotte tells me he isn't too well . . .'

'When did you talk to Charlotte?'

'Oh, a few days ago. I try to stay in touch. Or I could talk to Georgina. She might – '

'No,' said Baby, suddenly seeing Georgina's white face and large, haunted eyes looking at him on the morning after the party as she and Charlotte told him what they had found out about Virginia. He had a duty to look after those children. Virginia's children. 'No, don't do that. I'll come and meet you. Where do you suggest?'

'The American Bar at the Savoy. Where else?'

Baby walked to the Savoy from the office. For the second time that day he felt he needed the fresh air and exercise. He dreaded these encounters with Soames-Maxwell. This was the third. It wasn't just that he intensely disliked the man, and disliked still further the corner he had them all in; he found the thought of him having a relationship with Virginia literally nauseating. He had fought it fiercely at first, despite all the corroborating evidence: had sat in the Savoy, where Soames-Maxwell always insisted they met, and told him and tried to believe it, that he felt there was nothing established, no proof, that he had no claims on them. And Soames-Maxwell had leant forward, a slightly sympathetic smile on his face, and said, 'Oh, but I think I do. Your brother-in-law, Lord Caterham, certainly is not Max's father. Max told me that. Your sister and I had a very – what shall we say – intense relationship. For many years, but particularly at the time when – well, Max would have been conceived. He looks like me. He is like me. The more I know him, the more I see it.'

'Well, I'm afraid – ' said Baby.

Soames-Maxwell smiled at him. 'I'm not afraid. In fact I'm delighted. But we can have some tests done if you like. If that would make you feel more – cooperative towards me.'

'What kind of tests?'

'Oh, blood tests, tissue typing. I believe that's very accurate.'

'Well,' Baby had said, 'we can discuss that another time perhaps.'

There was a silence. Then he said, because he was too curious not to, 'When – when did you last see her? My sister?' The words seemed to come out against his will.

'Oh – the summer she died. She flew down to Key West for a couple of days. We took a boat out, did some snorkelling. She was still extremely beautiful.'

'Was that your boat?'

'Oh, no. I sold her in what – seventy-five. My money was just sailing away in that boat, much as I loved her.'

405

'Was that when you went to Vegas? To conserve your assets?'

'No. No, I was hanging between Key West and Nassau for a long while. I sold my house on Cuba the year after the boat. Stayed with friends, mostly, you can do that for a long while, you know. Then they started moving off, dying off. Life was changing. But your sister was a constant. Fun, loyal, she was so good to me. And now – well, I have Max. It's very nice for me. Very nice indeed.'

'Yes,' said Baby. 'Yes it must be.'

'I know,' he said, with another dazzling, flashing smile, 'I know you think I'm going to try and milk the relationship. Milk Max.'

'Oh,' said Baby, looking at him with contempt. 'I cannot imagine what can have given you that idea.'

'Well – I kind of get that feeling. Clearly I was wrong. Anyway, I'm not going to.'

'I see.' Baby had watched him closely. He had no illusions that Soames-Maxwell was going to let them off the hook; he was mildly intrigued by the man's tactics. Did he really think they were all going to accept him, make him their friend?

'I just want a home. A nice home. At my age – I'm quite a little older than you – one doesn't really want to be living in cheapjack hotels in places like Las Vegas. Especially when you've known something so very much better.'

'No. I suppose not.'

'Do you think I could have another drink? I was right, they do mix them superbly here.'

'Yes, of course.' He called the barman over: Soames-Maxwell was drinking champagne cocktails, somewhat surprisingly. Baby would have expected bourbon or even beer.

'Now then, where was I? Oh yes, a home. A nice home. That's all I want. And of course a little spending money. For the upkeep.'

'I wonder if you could come to the point.'

'Of course. Now I naturally wouldn't expect to live at Hartest. Not at the moment, anyway.'

'What do you mean by that?'

'Well, maybe one day. When Max inherits. He could find a small wing for his old dad. Meanwhile, the house in Eaton Place would do me just fine. I'll just stay there, not be a nuisance, you don't have to worry.'

'Mr Soames-Maxwell, I do assure you there is no question of your living at the house in Eaton Place. It is a family house, it belongs to my brother-in-law.'

'Yes, but I understand nobody else uses it much. It seems a waste of a very nice house. It would do me perfectly. Near Les Ambassadeurs. I was a member there, you know. I'm so delighted Max has joined. We went there last week.'

'Indeed? Well that must have been very nice for you.'

'Yes, it was. I was very tempted to tell a few people there, old friends, you know, old colleagues at the tables, that Max was my son, but of course I didn't.'

'Of course not.'

'And as long as I'm comfortable, I never will. You have my word on that, Mr Praeger. Or may I call you Baby?'

'Call me what you like,' said Baby wearily. 'Mr Soames-Maxwell, I think you should understand a few things. First, what you are saying amounts to blackmail. Second, the Caterham family is not cash rich. Third, there is no question of your staying at Eaton Place. Or at Hartest. Do I make myself clear?'

'Yes you do. Now let me take those one by one. First I don't mean to blackmail you. But I think as an old friend of the family – well of your sister – I am entitled to a little consideration. Second, I am quite ready to believe they are not cash rich. But, I suspect, not quite on the poverty line. And I imagine some of you Praegers have a dollar or two to rub together.'

Baby stood up then. 'You will have to excuse me,' he said, 'I'm sorry. I have an urgent appointment with a lawyer.'

Baby had talked to Charles St Mullin together with Charlotte; despite the awkwardness of the situation, he liked him very much. He was straightforward and charming, almost a caricature of an English barrister. Baby found a relationship between him and Virginia easier to contemplate than one with Soames-Maxwell, but he tried to avoid the contemplation altogether.

'It's a horrible mess.' Charles St Mullin sat looking out over Lincoln's Inn. 'Very hard to see quite what we – you can do. This man has no claim on any family money whatsoever. But – '

'I know he has no claim. But morally, I suppose we do in a way,' said Charlotte.

He smiled at her. 'Charlotte, I'm very much afraid that morals don't come into it.'

'No. Sadly. But what I meant was that Max is obviously getting very involved with this bastard – sorry, unfortunate choice of word – and wants to do something for him, not unnaturally. And it could be argued that it would be very hard for Max to walk away from him and send him back to his den in Vegas.'

'Well, I think Mr Soames-Maxwell would probably have quite a lot to say if he did. To the press, for a start. I mean, that's the worry, isn't it?'

'Yes. Yes it is. Well, not just the press, simply people. It would be the most wonderful story. And it would just about break Daddy's heart.'

Baby was intrigued by her reference to Alexander as Daddy, and St Mullin's acceptance of it. They had obviously come a long way together, these two, in what was clearly a close, if odd, relationship.

'Yes it would,' Charles agreed. 'Well clearly we have to shut the man up. But it won't be easy.'

'Do you think we should let him stay at Eaton Place?' said Baby.

'Not really. The sooner he's out the better.'

'Yes, but how do we get him out?'

'Start by talking to Max, I suppose. He must see it's dangerous.'

'I don't think he does. But anyway, assuming we can persuade him to leave, what should we do?'

'Charlotte, my darling, I don't know. I really don't. Whatever we offer him, he will clearly ask for more. I am tempted to start by trying to frighten him off.'

'What, you personally?'

'Me and my good friend the Law. It's worth a try.'

'Well look,' said Baby, 'let me talk to Max first. Charlotte has to get back to New York, don't you, darling? Max gets back from one of his modelling trips on Saturday, apparently. I'll take him out to lunch and talk to him then. Thank you for your good counsel, Charles.'

'That's all right. My pleasure. I feel I have a strong duty to try and look after your interests.' He smiled and shook Baby's hand.

Charlotte gave him a kiss. 'I think your sense of duty may be severely strained quite soon.'

'I'll speak to you when I've seen Max,' said Baby.

'Fine. Meanwhile I'll see if I can't come up with anything else.'

'It'll need to satisfy Max too. That won't be easy.'

Baby had called Max the moment he was back in London from his trip. 'Max, it's Baby Praeger here.'

'Hi,' said Max. He sounded less than welcoming.

'You don't sound terribly pleased to hear from me.'

'Let's say I'm suspicious.'

'Really? Of what?'

'Of what you might be going to say,' said Max impatiently. 'If you're going to tell me to get Tommy off your backs, you can get off mine. I like him, he's my father, and I intend to look after him.'

'Max, he doesn't need looking after. He can look after himself very nicely.'

'If that's the case, how come he's been on the breadline in some hole in Vegas for years?'

'Max! He's not some tragic underprivileged old tramp. He was a very wealthy man. He got on the breadline, as you call it, by his own fecklessness. He's not a charity case.'

'No, I didn't say he was. But he needs help and I'm going to give it to him.'

'By offering him a permanent home at Eaton Place?'

'Well – yes. It's nice to have him there. It's fun. We're enjoying ourselves.'

'Max, it isn't yours to make available to him. It's your father's.'

'Alexander is not my father, Baby. Tommy is and I want to help him.'

Baby hung on to his temper with an effort.

'But Max, I understand that and I think it's really nice. But you can't instal him at Eaton Place.'

'Look, Baby,' said Max. 'I don't quite know why Alexander allowed our mother to behave as she did. I don't know what on earth was going on between them. But it seems pretty sick to me. And I find it hard to see why I should feel any particular loyalty to Alexander.'

'Max, how can you! He's been wonderful to you.'

'Well – he's been OK.' Max sounded weary. 'He didn't exactly have to work his fingers to the bone, did he? Just set us down in the heart of his little kingdom and watched us grow.'

'Max, that's not true.'

'I'm afraid it is. It's no use, Baby, you can't emotionally blackmail me. I'm going to help Tommy.'

Baby had put a proposition to Max: it was St Mullin's idea. 'Make it quite quite clear, and in writing, that the offer is to him, and him alone.' He said that since Max clearly required a London base of his own, not one to share with the Earl of Caterham (who had indicated he might be needing the London house himself rather more frequently in the future), and that since the Earl should not be worried by detail, Baby proposed to make available to Max a small house in London which Max could use rent-free 'for the foreseeable future, not exceeding a period of five years'. It would revert to Baby sooner, should Max find himself somewhere of his own to live. Very fortuitously, Angie had such a house available, in Pond Place, Chelsea.

To the enormous relief of the family (and to the slight puzzlement of Charles St Mullin) Max accepted this offer. When Soames-Maxwell phoned Baby to thank him (with rather more grace than Max had shown) Baby said coldly that the house was for Max, and Max alone.

'But there is no stipulation that he may not have house guests?' said Soames-Maxwell, and his voice was very amused.

'Unfortunately not,' said Baby and put the phone down.

Since then he had been summoned by Soames-Maxwell once more; Max had run up a gambling debt of £5,000 at Les Ambassadeurs, and neither of them could pay it. After checking carefully that it had indeed been Max's debt, Baby paid it. But he had come to dread any calls from Soames-Maxwell; and their inevitable consequence, a meeting in the Savoy Hotel.

Soames-Maxwell was already there when Baby came in; he stood up, and held out hs hand. Baby ignored it. He noticed that Soames-Maxwell was looking slimmer and rather better dressed than when he had first turned up at Hartest.

'Baby! Hi. You're looking tired.'

'I feel tired,' said Baby. 'I work very hard. Unlike some people,' he added and then regretted it, feeling it had sounded childish.

'Oh, we work hard, Max and I. He at his modelling, I at the housekeeping. Of course there is not a great deal to do in that tiny little house, it can be cleaned very quickly. Which is something in its favour. Although we are a little cramped.'

He smiled at Baby. 'What will you have?'

'I'll have a bourbon,' said Baby. 'What point are you trying to make?'

'Oh, that the house is a little too small for us.'

'Well, that is unfortunate,' said Baby, 'very unfortunate. Perhaps Max should try to earn a little more money, and then he could purchase something larger.'

'That's what I wanted to talk to you about. Max's money.'

'Oh yes?' Baby took a slug of bourbon. 'What about Max's money?'

'It isn't enough.'

'Enough for what?'

'His needs.'

'Oh for God's sake,' said Baby. 'My wife read an article only last week, about the fees these models can earn. Max was quoted as turning over a hundred thousand pounds a year. Of course it's enough.'

'Press articles are notoriously inaccurate,' said Soames-Maxwell, 'but he does earn, I have to say, a little over half that.'

'And you're telling me that isn't enough.'

'I'm afraid I am.'

'And what,' said Baby, with a very heavy sigh, knowing the answer, 'what has that to do with me?'

'Well, Max has debts to settle.'

'But what kind of debts, for God's sake? At what level are you living to need more than – what – fifty thousand a year? When that's spending money?'

'Well you see,' said Soames-Maxwell, 'it's what Max is spending it on. That's the problem.'

'I'm sorry,' said Baby, 'I don't understand.'

'It's the membership of Les Ambassadeurs,' said Soames-Maxwell, with a heavy sigh. 'And of course now I've had to join the Clermont as well.' He spoke as if joining the Clermont was on a par with the need to buy a season ticket, or a new pair of shoes.

'Mr Soames-Maxwell – '

'I wish you'd call me Tommy.'

'Mr Soames-Maxwell, I am simply not prepared to pay your gambling debts. I'm sorry. Max will have to cut his expenditure, or ask his – ask Alexander.'

'He already has. The answer was fairly predictable.'

'Well honestly, it isn't my problem. You have to solve it in your own way.'

'But of course it is your problem. Everything to do with Max is your problem. He's your sister's son, and Virginia was what you and your family made her.'

'Oh God.' Baby felt sick. 'You're very fond of telling us about your relationship with Max. Couldn't you take some responsibility for a change?'

'Baby – ' Soames-Maxwell leant forward and for the first time Baby saw a flash of genuine concern in his eyes. 'Baby, I know none of you would believe it, but I am very fond of Max. I have tried. Really I have.'

'Look,' said Baby, 'you send Max to me. I'll talk to him.'

'I don't think he'll come.'

'If you want the money,' said Baby, 'he'll have to come.'

Tommy Soames-Maxwell looked at him. There was a sliver of respect in his blue eyes. 'All right,' he said, 'I'll send him along.'

Baby left the Savoy feeling mildly panicky. Everything seemed to be closing in on him, in some claustrophobic nightmare. The interview with Soames-Maxwell had set the seal on it. He sat in a cab, on his way home, thinking about Virginia, wondering for the hundredth, the thousandth time, what had driven her to do what she had, and thinking too, thinking with a wrench of his heart of how useless their relationship must have seemed to her, that she had to deceive rather than confide in him.

Something had happened to her, in those early days, weeks of her marriage, that had changed her totally, and he, none of them, had understood, realized even; something that she had had to bear alone,

411

without any help from any of them. Remorse, many years too late, flooded Baby. There was nothing, nothing at all, he could do now. Except, perhaps, try to save Max from one of the worst of her mistakes.

Chapter 34

Angie, 1985

Angie was extremely annoyed. No, she wasn't annoyed. She was angry. Furiously, steamingly angry. With Baby, primarily, but to an extent herself. She had really blown it, she thought, glaring at the nanny as she bustled about the kitchen, sterilizing bottles and mixing formula on the Saturday morning that Baby had left for New York; why she had no idea. God, it would be a relief to get out of this house into something bigger. It had been just slightly over-sized for her on her own, and the occasional overnight visitor. For herself, Baby, two babies and a nanny it was grotesquely too small. Well, the new town house at least was very nice. Her temper improved just momentarily as she contemplated the great cream mansion in Belgrave Square, floor after floor of huge, lofty rooms, even now being painted, papered, plastered, carpeted, miles of silk and brocade hung at its high windows, pantechnicons of furniture delivered daily to its doors. All at the most incredible expense. Baby's expense. And the one thing she had always wanted, a country house, that was to be hers too; the last thing Baby had said to her as he flung out of the door the night before, was 'You might start looking at houses in the country, darling, for the weekend. I'm told Hampshire is very nice, give you something to do.' Give her something to do; as if she needed it. But it was at least something worth doing.

Unlike the other little tasks Baby seemed to have in mind for her: joining the wives' mafia, getting on the charity circuit, hostessing ladies' luncheons, partners' dinners, throwing cocktail parties, attending functions. When she had her company to run, to take care of, her own money to make. What did Baby think he was doing to her; who did he think he had married?

Married? There was a Freudian slip. Marriage seemed as far away as ever; she had imagined a delay, but that once the twins had been born, a most highly visible fait accompli, Baby would push through a divorce and they would be married. And here they were, two little boys eight months old, and she seemed set to remain Miss Burbank for the rest of her life. An unmarried mother, with no security and a great many disadvantages. And Baby was expecting her to give up her work, leave her company, her beloved company that she had built up herself from

413

nothing – well, almost nothing – to go uncared for, and devote her entire life to him. Him and his stupid bloody bank.

Angie poured herself a cup of black coffee; God, she was getting as dependent on caffeine as she was on alcohol. She was suddenly, sharply, reminded of Virginia and their first meeting, when she had sat pretending she liked coffee. She had come a long way since then.

She was part of the family now. Or nearly. And precious little good it seemed to be doing her. It added to her anger, thinking just how little.

Suddenly, on a whim, she picked up the phone and dialled the Hartest number. Baby wanted her to find a country house; who better than Alexander to help her find one – and maybe alleviate her loneliness at the same time? She waited, drumming her fingers on the table, while Fallon went to fetch him to the phone.

'Alexander? This is Angie here. Alexander, what are you doing this weekend. . . ?'

They pulled up in front of Hartest just before lunch. Alexander was waiting for them on the steps. He came towards them holding out his hands and smiling.

'Angie, how very nice. What a lovely idea. It was such a dull weekend before.'

'Alexander, it's very nice of you to be so welcoming. And to my family too. This is my nanny, Sandra Jenkins. Sandra, this is Lord Caterham. And these are my children, Alexander, this is Samuel Praeger, otherwise known as Spike, and this is Hugh Praeger, otherwise known as Hughdie. Both good American nicknames, you see.'

'They're very fine,' said Alexander, smiling benevolently, if vaguely, at the twins. 'And nanny is dying to play with them. Sandra, if you follow me I'll show you where the old nurseries are, and Nanny Barkworth will take care of you.'

A gratifyingly goggle-eyed Sandra took Spike up the steps, and Angie followed with Hughdie; Nanny appeared from the inner hall looking very disapproving. 'You'd better give him to me quickly,' she said to Angie, taking the baby, indicating clearly that she felt there was not a moment to be lost if Hughdie was to be saved from some appalling and imminent fate, 'and you come with me,' she added sternly to Sandra, over her shoulder. Sandra followed meekly, straightening her brown Princess Christian hat, which Spike had tried to pull off. 'Very silly, I always thought, having a brown hat,' said Nanny looking her up and down. 'You really couldn't expect it to stay on, not with a baby around.'

'No,' said Sandra. She was clearly far too overawed to argue with this particularly breathtaking example of Nanny's logic.

*

'Now then,' said Alexander, handing her a cup of coffee in the library, 'I took the liberty of ringing some agents in Marlborough and Bath and so on, as soon as I knew you were coming, for some particulars of houses. There's what sounds like an extremely pretty house in Gloucestershire, quite near Stroud. I'd recommend looking at that.'

'How big is it?' said Angie doubtfully. Pretty sounded a bit cottagey, not at all what she had in mind. If Baby was going to make her entertain clients in the country, he was going to provide a very nice background for her to do it in.

'Oh, not very big,' said Alexander, 'but charming. A classic, small eighteenth-century house.'

'Well we do want something quite big,' said Angie. 'There's the twins, and the nanny, and other staff as well, and we'll be entertaining quite a lot.'

'Oh, I think this would allow for that,' said Alexander, smiling at her slightly amusedly. 'It has eight bedrooms. And a stable block which you could convert if you wanted to, if you really felt cramped.'

'Oh I see,' said Angie. She felt silly suddenly. 'Well, yes, I could look at that.'

'Do. I think it would be worth it. And there's another one, about ten miles from here. How's your map-reading? Tomorrow I might come with you, if you would like that, but today I'm very busy.'

'My map-reading is excellent,' said Angie. 'And I'd like it very much if you came with me. Thank you.'

She was very happy driving around Wiltshire, looking at houses. She forgot her rage at Baby, her insecurity about her future; the countryside was just tipping over into early spring, the air filled with the oddly human cries of the lambs, the bright blue of the sky shot with drifting cloud, the sheets of Wiltshire landscape soft and rain-rinsed, mellowing in some indefinable way. The hedgerows were studded with snowdrops, and even some early budding primroses; and the birdsong was an almost tangible thing, endlessly rising and falling through the long afternoon. Angie was surprised at the pleasure it all gave her; she was not normally sensitive to such things, the country to her was the bits in between the towns. But Hartest always mellowed her, made her aware of her surroundings, and in her endeavours to appear to Alexander the sensitive, charming person he would like, she found herself (to her own surprise) genuinely enjoying what lay about her.

None of the houses was right; but she returned to Hartest at dusk relaxed and full of stories to tell him, and after paying a fairly perfunctory

415

visit to the nursery, where Sandra was bathing the twins under Nanny's deeply disapproving gaze, she went downstairs to the room where she had first slept over twenty years ago, and bathed and changed ready for dinner with Alexander.

She had chosen her dress with great care: it had taken her longer to settle on that than it had taken Sandra to complete the whole of the twins' packing. Something sexy, but not vulgar; sophisticated but not dull; Jasper Conran had cracked it for her, as so often he did, in a dark grey jersey dress, modestly high-necked, charmingly mid-calf, cut on the bias, swirling over her hips, clinging to her breasts. She wore it with black boots, and a very large Butler and Wilson baroque pearl choker. She spent a long time on her hair, putting it up, pulling it down, settling finally for something between the two, with tendrils of hair loose, as if they had slipped the black velvet ribbon that sleeked the rest of it back.

She wasn't quite sure why it mattered so much; she didn't fancy Alexander – well, she didn't think she did. She liked him very much; he had always been courteous towards her, courteous and kind, but there was something more than that, she decided, giving herself a last glance in the full-length swing mirror in her room, spraying herself with Rive Gauche, glossing over her lips yet again. Struggling to define it, she could only say that she wanted to be pleasing to him, make him enjoy her.

She was deeply, romantically intrigued by him, he had always seemed enigmatic to her, and she was inevitably far more so now, knowing of the new mystery about him, about Virginia, about the marriage, about his children's parentage, which Baby had told her about and then told her to try and forget.

'Try and forget,' she had said, staring at him, half amused, half shocked by the story, 'Baby, how could I forget such a thing?' and he had said she must, she must put it out of her mind now, at once, not let it enter any relationship or conversation she had with Alexander or indeed anyone else in the future, that it was a sacred, secret family trust. 'He will not, cannot talk about it; he's withdrawn from it entirely, Charlotte says, doesn't give any kind of credence to any of it.' And she had said of course she would never mention it, never allude to it, and she had meant it, known she would not indeed, for any kind of duplicity came easily to her, but it had given Alexander a strange, almost glamorous intrigue for her, made her regard him as someone of infinite curiosity. She smiled at herself and went out of the room; she was greatly looking forward to her evening.

*

It was a curiously happy one. He was relaxed, easily talkative; he had changed greatly, she realized, getting to know him again, from the dashing young man she had known when he and Virginia had been young and newly married, and he had met her at the station and shown her Hartest for the first time. Some of the changes saddened her, he was vague, forgetful, every so often seeming to withdraw into himself altogether. But he was gentler, less challenging than he had been, and in many ways easier to talk to; they sat and had champagne in the library before dinner and she told him about the houses, and what she had thought about them, and the one she was going to see tomorrow, in Gloucestershire, near Burford, and he had said he would certainly go with her, and be her chauffeur; and he asked her about Baby and the bank, and how Baby was adjusting to life in London, and she had told him (of course) that everything was wonderful, that Baby loved London, that they were very happy, that the house in Belgrave Square was beautiful, pausing only momentarily when he had asked her how Baby had adapted to fatherhood again, and saying, just a little sadly, that he was a wonderful father, but that she herself felt slightly insecure, anxious for her sons, that they were illegitimate, not Praegers, not safely in line for the inheritance of the bank and the fortune, that Fred III was just a little hostile towards her − 'But then who could blame him?' she had said, laughing, winding a tendril of hair around her finger, 'I am the scarlet woman, I came between Baby and his wife.'

And he said yes, indeed, that was true, but love was a powerful and almost uncontrollable thing, and that Baby had, he knew, been unhappy with Mary Rose for a long time, and that their children were after all grown up now, even Melissa, grown up enough to handle a divorce, and that it was good that Baby should have a second chance. They were in the dining room by then, eating the most delicious trout Angie had ever tasted, by candlelight; she smiled at him, and said she would feel rather better about everything if there was indeed a divorce that the children had to face, but that she greatly feared there never would be.

'Well,' he said, 'well, you will have to be patient, I'm afraid. I found it the most difficult thing of all to learn myself, but I managed in the end, and after that everything else seemed quite simple.'

It was a strange answer; Angie was slightly nonplussed. A silence fell; to ease it, she suddenly said, without meaning in any way to be challenging, 'Alexander, tell me about your childhood. I'd really like to know. Was it happy, here in this beautiful house?'

It was one of her talents, her most powerful attributes, to display, and indeed genuinely to feel, interest in people and their lives; and it was hard to resist her. Alexander looked at her thoughtfully, poured them both another glass of wine (velvety claret that he said went wonderfully well with fish) and started to tell her.

'My father was very cruel,' he said, 'the cruellest person I have ever known. He wasn't just cruel to me, he was cruel to my mother.'

'You mean he hit her?'

'Yes, sometimes. Mostly he just said horrible things to her. Told her she was ugly and stupid and – well, other things.'

Angie was proceeding carefully; she didn't press him on the other things.

'And you?'

'Oh, both things for me as well. He beat me. Quite savagely. With a riding whip.'

'Why? What for?'

'Oh – anything. If I didn't eat my lunch. If I wasn't well. If I used a wrong word or failed to know my tables. Every morning he tested me on my tables. I never could do maths.' He smiled at her slightly shakily. 'I don't know why I'm telling you all this.'

'I asked you to,' said Angie. She had been sitting very quiet, very still, her eyes fixed on Alexander. He was pale, and the hand holding his glass was very tense.

'Well – you invite confidences. And confidence.' He smiled at her quickly. 'He also used to beat me if I wet my bed, which I did quite often. He would come in in the night to check, or very early in the morning. Nanny used to try and get to me first; but she never quite knew when he was coming. And if the bed was wet, he beat me there and then, and then made me go back to it and sleep in it.'

'How horrible,' said Angie.

Alexander looked at her. 'I don't know why I'm telling you all this,' he said again, 'when we could be talking about you.'

'I'm not very interesting,' said Angie.

'On the contrary,' he said, 'I think you are very interesting indeed. You fascinate me.'

'How old were you when he stopped beating you?' she said, ignoring this.

'Nineteen.'

'Nineteen! Alexander, why did you stay?'

'I didn't have a choice, I felt. Of course he was quite mad. Had I been born into a poor family I would have been rescued, I expect, taken into care. But when such things go on in a house like this, there is a conspiracy of silence.'

'What did you try to do about it?'

'Not a lot. If I made a fuss, it was worse for my mother. She was very brave, very spirited, but in the end she gave in too. We both did. We just went along with it.' He was silent for a long time; Angie sat and looked at him, very still.

'It was a prison,' he said, 'a snare. There was no escape.'

'Couldn't you have told a – a doctor or something?'

'I did once. Told the GP. Silly old fool. He came up here and told my father that he thought he might need help. That he should see a psychiatrist. My father's reaction was very interesting. He took me along to a mental hospital, not far from here, where he had a friend who was a consultant. He told this man I wanted to do medicine, and made me watch them giving electro-convulsive treatment to some woman. It was ghastly in those days. You didn't have an anaesthetic. I – was very upset. I was sick. And my father said, quite casually, in the car going home, "You want to do that to me. Don't you?" I said I didn't, that he had misunderstood, and he kept on and on, shouting at me, saying I wanted to do it to him. When we got home, he beat me. Very savagely. We never tried again.'

'This is a terrible story,' said Angie. She felt genuinely shocked; her eyes had filled with tears.

'I'm sorry. Very sorry.' Alexander looked stricken. 'I should never have started. Do forgive me.'

'No,' she said, 'there's nothing to forgive. I asked you. I'm just so sorry. So he died – how? And when?'

'He had a heart attack and died, when I was at Oxford. I've never forgotten how I felt when I heard. Not even relief, not even happiness. Just a great peace. The funeral was probably the happiest day of my life, until my wedding.'

'And your mother? What did he do to her?'

'I told you. Beat her. Said horrible things to her. Worse.'

Angie looked at him. She saw pain and horror in his blue eyes, and she could imagine what the worse things had been. She had seen bad things herself, amongst her friends and their families, but nothing, she felt, could compare with the claustrophobic horror of this. She sat there, and then she leant forward and took his hand, very gently, and sat there, holding it. She felt very close to him, suddenly, almost as if they had been making love. Alexander looked at her, and tightened his grip on her hand. There were tears in his eyes now and he was obviously moved, shaken by telling her, by remembering.

'I'm sorry,' he said, 'so sorry. I shouldn't have said so much. It's not a pretty story, I'm afraid. Not dinner-party conversation at all.'

'This isn't a dinner party,' said Angie, 'and we're old friends. Aren't we?'

'I would like to think so,' he said, and raised her hand to his lips and kissed it; and then, with a visible effort, breaking out of the strange, intense mood that had been created by his story, 'Come along, let's go into the library and have some coffee, and discuss how we are to get to Burford tomorrow.'

'Alexander – '

'Yes?'

'Alexander, supposing you hadn't had any children. And this house had to pass from your family. To another branch of it. Or be sold. What would you feel about that?'

'I don't think,' he said simply, 'that I could bear it. I think I would rather burn it down.'

'I see,' said Angie.

In the morning he was very cheerful. Max had phoned, he was coming to stay for the night, arriving around teatime from Heathrow. He had been on a trip to Japan, Alexander said. He seemed excited, touchingly so, at the prospect of Max's visit.

'Well,' he said, 'we had better be on our way. Do you want to bring those children of yours?'

'God no,' said Angie, appalled.

The house near Burford was exquisite; a low-built L-shaped seventeenth-century manor house in golden Cotswold stone, called Watersfoot Priory. Behind the house was a walled garden, and beyond that a water garden; there were stables, a tennis court, 'Even room for a swimming pool,' said Angie ecstatically. 'This will do. I want to go and phone the agent and settle things now.'

'Won't Baby need to see it?'

'Baby likes what I like,' said Angie, sweetly firm.

They went to a pub for lunch and Angie asked them if they could provide some champagne; Alexander told her no pub would have such a thing, but they produced a bottle, a little warm, but good champagne nonetheless, and they drank it with the cheese sandwiches that were the pub's excuse for lunch, laughing at the incongruity.

Afterwards, they were both too drunk to drive; it was a glorious day, so they went for a walk. Unselfconsciously, Angie took Alexander's arm.

'Thank you for coming. It made it so much better. I wouldn't really have been that decisive on my own. And I think the agent thought you were my husband, so he didn't dish out quite so much horse manure.'

'I'm flattered if indeed he should think such a thing,' said Alexander, smiling down at her.

'Why?'

'Well, I must be almost old enough to be your father.'

'Oh, don't be ridiculous. An illegal father if you were. And in that case, so is Baby.'

'I suppose, yes. But he looks younger than me.'

'That really is ridiculous,' said Angie. 'Oh Alexander, it's been such a nice day. Such a nice weekend. Thank you. It's really cheered me up.'

'Well,' he said, 'I can tell you I've enjoyed myself more than I can remember for a very long time. A day of innocent pleasure. I have always liked the distinction between the two kinds of pleasures, innocent and wicked.'

'Yes,' said Angie, 'I remember you telling me that, long ago. Wicked pleasures sound more fun, I have to say.'

'Oh no,' he said, 'not at all. I prefer the innocent ones.'

A muddy Land-Rover shot past them, full of dogs and people in Barbours, shrieking with laughter. Angie looked after it thoughtfully.

'Oh dear, I hope I'm going to do all right here. Fit into country society.'

'I think country society will be lucky to have you,' said Alexander, smiling down at her, 'and if they don't take you immediately to their hearts, they will have me to reckon with.'

'You are so nice,' said Angie, reaching up to kiss his cheek. 'Just so nice.'

He bent and returned the kiss; for a moment, just a moment, she felt his mouth on hers, pausing on it, almost thoughtfully, then moving swiftly away. He looked down into her eyes, very seriously, very intently.

'This will not do,' he said, trying to sound lighthearted, 'this will not do at all.'

Max was at Hartest when they got back, sitting in the library, drinking whisky. He stood up when they walked in, and grinned slightly maliciously.

'Aunt Angela! What a surprise. And what have you two been up to, off all day together, and leaving those poor little babies unattended in the nurseries. That nanny of yours is a peach, Angie; do I detect the hand of Baby in her engagement?'

'Certainly not,' said Angie loftily. 'Baby didn't even meet her until the twins were born.'

'Well, you're very trusting. Or generous. Or something. How are you, Alexander?'

421

'I'm well, thank you, Max,' said Alexander. 'How was Japan?'

'Foreign. Didn't really like it, to tell you the truth. The only really good thing that happened was I got on some crazy game show.'

'Max! You didn't! I'm impressed,' said Angie.

'It isn't very difficult. If you can stand up and talk in Tokyo you get on a game show. It's a funny old place. You can't understand what's going on. The only word I learnt to recognize was *kaui*. Pronounced cow-ee. If you hear that at an interview, you know you've got the job.'

'Why were you doing interviews?' said Angie. 'Weren't you on a working trip?'

'Well I was, but I went for a couple of things while I was there. I'm a bit – well, strapped for cash. Can we have a word about that, Alexander, before I go?'

Alexander looked as if Max had hit him.

'Before you go? You've only just got here.'

'Yeah, I know, but I have to be in town by nine. Sorry, thought you realized that.'

'Well,' said Alexander, with a sigh. 'I'm a little disappointed. But it's nice to see you anyway. Shall we all have tea?'

'Yes, great. Can we have it in the kitchen with those babies?'

Angie laughed. 'Do you like babies?'

'Yes I do,' he said, quite seriously, 'I like them very much as a matter of fact.'

Sandra was visibly desperate when Angie went to find her in the nursery.

'Angie, I really don't think I can take much more. She's crazy, and she talks to me as if I was a child molester. She actually said this morning she thought it would be better if I took up something else. But then she went on to say that as the babies were half American, she supposed there was some excuse. Honestly, it's been terrible.' She looked sulky; Angie felt mildly remorseful.

'I'm sorry. You can have tomorrow off, if you like. To make up for today.'

'And yesterday. I'm not really supposed to do more than one weekend a month.'

'Sandra, you wanted to come down here,' said Angie firmly.

Serve her right. Teach her to be snobbish.

After tea, during which Nanny held forth at great length on the dangers of foreign food, no one was quite sure why, Alexander and Max disappeared and Angie and Sandra went upstairs to pack. As she carried her brown Hermes gladstone bag through the hall, Angie heard Alexander shouting; she paused, fiddling with the strap.

'It is outrageous,' he was saying, 'outrageous. This is the last debt of yours I will ever settle. Get out! Get out and back to London to that – that horrible life of yours.'

She ran to the front door and down the steps, and was putting her bag in the boot of the Mercedes when Max came running out. He looked very white and shaken.

'Max,' she said, 'Max, what is it? Can I help?'

'Oh shit,' he said, and brushed his arm across his eyes. 'Shit shit shit. No, Angie, but thanks.' He slammed the door of his car and roared off up the Great Drive.

Alexander hugged her when she left. He looked pale too, but far more composed than Max.

'It's been so nice, Angie. Come again. I look forward to having you as a neighbour. And give my regards to Baby.'

'I will.'

She drove in silence all the way home, thinking about Alexander and the mystery of him.

The phone rang by her bed just as she was going to sleep. It was Baby. How was she, how were the babies, was she missing him? Angie told him she and the babies were fine and ignored the third question.

'Darling, I won't be back until Tuesday.'

'Why the hell not?'

'Well, I have to see some people while I'm here. Seems silly not to. I'll be at Heathrow at midnight on Tuesday. Can you meet me?'

'I'm very busy on Tuesday,' said Angie, 'sorry, Baby.'

He sounded very subdued. 'OK, I'll get myself home. Lots of love, darling.'

'Goodnight, Baby.'

When she had put the phone down she suddenly felt very unhappy. What was happening to their relationship? Why was she so hostile to him suddenly? And why was Baby staying over in New York? All his clients, all his business, were in London now. He was always out these days, night after night. He always said she could be with him if she liked, but since she wouldn't come, he had to manage on his own. For God's sake, he couldn't be seeing someone, could he? Someone in New York? Angie thought suddenly and vividly of Caroline Whittiam, godmother to Spike, childhood friend of Baby's who had come over for the christening, and possessor of a pair of legs so long and perfect that other women made sure to wear long skirts if they knew she was to be at a dinner party, simply to avoid comparison. She had considerable suspicions about their relationship. Like most mistresses, Angie had never met any of Baby's other friends until she became his official partner. Could he be seeing Caroline while he was over there? What a horrible thought. No, that was impossible. Apart from anything else, he had scarcely enough sexual energy for her, let alone someone else. Shit. That didn't mean a lot either. He always used to tell her he would be practically impotent with Mary Rose, and then rush down to the Village and screw her over and over again. Angie lay in the darkness, sweating slightly. It was possible. Just. He was still, in spite of everything, a very attractive man. And an extremely rich one. It might also explain his reluctance to let her have any shares. No, that really was ridiculous. The whole thing was ridiculous. Baby adored her. He was helplessly dependent on her. Too dependent. It was a turn-off. Everything was fine. She was just being silly. Angie turned onto her side, and began to masturbate. She always did that, to calm herself. She had to do it quite a lot these days; Baby's performance left more and more to be desired. As her body exploded obediently into orgasm, it was not Baby's face that swam before her eyes, nor the arrogantly sexy one of his nephew, but the gentle, aristocratic features of Alexander, Earl of Caterham.

Chapter 35

Angie, 1985

Alexander became her friend. Right through that spring, when she was negotiating for, buying, refurbishing Watersfoot Priory, when Baby was increasingly detached from her and involved in launching Praegers – the inaugural party at Spencer House had been finally booked for early June, that being the first available date – she saw him almost weekly, sometimes merely lunching at Hartest with him, occasionally staying overnight there (still more occasionally with Baby, who had nodded briefly over Watersfoot and told her to go ahead). It was a strange friendship, she could see: he was a cultured, upper-class Englishman with a passion for country life and eighteenth-century architecture, she was a hustler from the East End of London, whose preferred reading, apart from her own balance sheets, was *Vogue, Vanity Fair* and the gossip columns, and who developed withdrawal symptoms twelve hours away from the shops. And yet, they had found a genuine interest in one another's company. He admired her, and she admired him; he was even, vague and slightly careworn as he was, in his own way very sexy. She couldn't quite analyse his sexiness, and it was clearly very different from Max's swaggering variety, and Baby's too, but it was there all right: a kind of grace, an easy self-awareness and an ability to appreciate, to acknowledge sensuality in others. And his life intrigued her; when Alexander talked of the house, the estate, and thus the broader aspects of his life, his horses, hunting, shooting, the ebb and flow of his year, she was, for some reason, not bored but intrigued. The intrigue was slightly detached, but it was genuine. And she liked to hear him talking about his children (trying to imagine a similar involvement in her own and entirely failing), his anxieties about Max, his pride and delight in Charlotte, his adoration for Georgina – 'She's your favourite, isn't she, I can tell' – 'Not exactly my favourite, but the one I get on the best with, have most in common with.' And by the same token, she found, she could talk to him about her own life, her sense of isolation from Baby and the bank, and indeed from Baby himself, and of being different from the other wives (while in no way wishing to be like them, to join them); her own business, her intense pride in what she had accomplished, the fascination of the property market and its ebb and flow within the country's prosperity, the absolute necessity to catch it at the right moment; and her past, the past before Virginia, she found she liked talking to him about that, the early days with Johnny and Dee, her modelling, her friendship with M. Wetherly. She censored it a little here and there, coloured it up occasionally, but basically she could talk endlessly and happily with him.

'Did you have fun with Virginia?' she asked Alexander one Sunday in late May, as they walked round the lake. She had gone to visit him after her weekly inspection of Watersfoot; she was discouraged by that as well, it was still a shell, and the swimming pool was certainly not going to be operational this summer.

Alexander looked slightly warily at her. 'What sort of fun?'

'Oh – I don't know. Did you do silly things, tell each other jokes, give each other ridiculous presents?'

'I – don't think so, no,' said Alexander. He looked rather sad and distant; Angie changed the subject. It had been a silly question anyway, anyone who had known Virginia could have seen that having fun was not one of her talents. Angie had liked Virginia, and she had been very sorry for her, but she had never been the sort of person Angie had aspired to be. Although knowing what she did about her now, sympathy seemed to have been a bit of a joke; envy would be a more reasonable emotion. All those lovers! Clever bitch. How the hell had she managed that? And why couldn't she have been a little more careful about the consequences? The whole thing was a riddle that intrigued Angie increasingly as she got to know Alexander better.

'How's Georgina?'

'She's fine. She'll be home in a month.' He looked happy. 'I miss her so. I understand she has plans to invite Kendrick and Melissa over to stay again. I presume that will be all right with you?'

'Perfectly,' said Angie, who very much wanted to establish more of a relationship with Baby's children; they seemed much more interesting and agreeable to her than her own. 'I had hoped of course that they would be able to stay at Watersfoot this summer, but that looks increasingly unlikely.'

'Well, you must come for a longer stay here in that case.' He smiled at her. 'With the children.'

'You like children, don't you?' said Angie carefully.

'Oh I do,' he said, 'very much. My children have been a source of immense pleasure to me. I like them at all ages. Even as tiny as Spike and Hughdie. I would actually have liked some more, a real old-fashioned Victorian family, but – '

426

'But what?' said Angie very quietly.

There was a long silence. Alexander looked particularly remote, particularly sad; then he said, equally quietly, 'Oh, well, you know, it was just not to be. Virginia was not – strong. It seemed selfish to insist on any more. And I – we – had Max by then, Hartest had its heir. That was the main thing.'

'Yes. Yes of course.' She looked at him. The veil of vagueness had dropped very heavily; no chance of any further confidences now. She tucked her arm into his and started walking just slightly more quickly.

'Poor Alexander. You must be lonely too.'

'Well.' He smiled at her. 'I am, in a way. But I do have the house to keep me company.'

'Yes. Yes, I suppose you do. I can't say mine is much use to me. I require something a little livelier.'

'Never mind, my dear. When this launch is over, I expect Baby will have more time for you. What a beautiful watch that is. You know you really shouldn't wear something like that on country walks, you might drop it in the mud, lose it.'

Angie looked down at her small wrist bearing the diamond and emerald watch from Tiffany, the first of the really good jewellery Baby had ever bought her, The First Fuck watch he had always called it, and she had worn it ever since.

'Oh,' she said, 'oh, it wouldn't – ' she hesitated – 'come off. It has a good clasp. Very good.'

She had nearly then, very nearly confided in Alexander about the watch, had nearly said it wouldn't matter. What on earth was she doing, telling him – or nearly telling him – such a thing? He thought she was squeaky clean, a really nice, morally upright person. What on earth would he think of her if he had known that the Tiffany watch was a fake, copied for her in Hong Kong one weekend, so that she could sell the original and use the money to finance a particularly desirable (and expensive) vacation in the company of a particularly desirable (and expensive) young man? While Baby had been on one of those endless family trips of his. It had pleased her so much, that manoeuvre, it had been so simple to execute and so foolproof really. Baby had no idea about jewellery, he would never have realized the watch was a fake. And it was a very good fake, nothing tacky, she had spent money on it. And yet sometimes, when Baby had been especially tender, especially loving, had talked about the watch and the occasion it had marked, she had felt uncomfortable, as near to guilty as she knew how.

She looked up at Alexander and hesitated for a moment, and then she said, 'Did you ever do something that you were proud and ashamed of at

427

the same time? Something so neat and clever you could hardly believe you'd done it?'

428

Chapter 36

Alexander, 1969–70

He could hardly believe he had done it. It had been so simple, so easy, and it had achieved so much, everything he had hoped for. And they did deserve it. All of them. He could scarcely believe the selfishness, the self-obsession of the way they had been behaving, using one another, upsetting one another, dragging one another down. It might have been all right, just might have been, if they hadn't involved him. Well not exactly him, but his territory. His house. The London house. Used by Baby and his mistress, without his permission, without his knowledge. Or so they had thought.

He kept hoping, for days after he heard Virginia talking to Baby, that she would mention it, ask him if it was all right, say, even, that she hoped it was all right. But – nothing. Nothing at all. He found it very shocking. Nothing could have persuaded him more of her total disregard for his feelings – and her absurd regard for her brother's – that she could deceive him quite so blatantly. He loved her so much, so very very much, and she knew he did – and yet she abused the love, and the trust, in this way.

He had listened to the telephone conversation between Baby and Virginia about Baby borrowing the house with a sense of growing distaste; he had picked up on it quite by accident, the phone had been ringing in the hall and he had answered it and the moment he heard the long-distance operator he had known who it was.

The two days he had known Baby and Angie were there, in the house, had made him almost ill. He had kept out of Virginia's way, saying there was a great deal to do on the farm (which was true). He hardly slept, those nights; he lay awake, beside Virginia, staring into the darkness, trying to calm himself. At three o'clock on the second night he got up, and went outside; it was a clear, starry night, with a soft, half-waned moon; he walked up the Great Drive a little way and looked back at Hartest, etched in all its perfection against the silver sky, and felt as always comforted by it, eased from his misery. There was a dim light up at the top of the house, on the nursery floor; he thought of little Max sleeping there sweetly, his heir, the heir to Hartest: no one would ever know, not even Virginia, how he had felt when he had finally held Max in his arms, looked down at the tiny crumpled little face and seen the succession finally safe. An odd tranquillity and a great triumph: he had been very supportive, very loving to Virginia over the girls, and over the other, tiny, sad little Alexander, but until this moment, until this strong, beautiful boy had been born, he had not known any true peace of mind.

And now Virginia had to drag her family, her crass, womanizing brother into this idyllic world he had created with her and it hurt, it hurt badly. It was an abuse of his love and his trust for her.

He could see he was not going to be able to forgive Virginia. He went and inspected the house in Eaton Place: there was some superficial damage, a stain on the bedroom carpet, a couple of the large wine goblets missing, presumably broken. It was at least clean and tidy. He had stood in the master bedroom and wondered if they had been using his bed: the thought made him physically sick.

He had to wait a year to sort things out. It was a long time, but he was used to being patient.

The affair between Baby and Angie seemed quite serious. He wasn't surprised. Baby would be attracted by cheapness. He was basically cheap himself. He found a letter to Baby that Virginia had written, lying on her desk, waiting to be posted; he steamed it open. Baby seemed to have set Angie up in an apartment in what Virginia referred to as 'The Village'. Greenwich presumably. 'Please please be careful,' Virginia had written, 'I know you're very fond of her, but there is so much at stake.'

Well, they were going to have to be very careful indeed, all of them, with him to deal with.

Virginia looked at him over breakfast one morning in early July. 'Alexander, darling,' she said, with that careful smile of hers that he had come to know meant asking a favour, telling him unwelcome news, 'do you terribly terribly mind if I go to New York for a few days later this month? Before we go on to this new house of Baby's on Sconset.'

'Good gracious,' he had said, forcing a smile, 'this is very sudden. Whatever has happened?'

'Oh – very exciting new client.'

'Who is this exciting new client?'

'I'm sure I mentioned him before. Very rich real-estate man. New house on Long Island. Quite near Beaches.'

'No,' he said, 'I don't think you did. What's his name?'

'Oh – Franklyn,' she said after a moment's hesitation. 'Ted Franklyn.'

'Well darling, I certainly don't want to come between you and your clients. You and success.'

'Wonderful,' she said. She was looking a little pale, he noticed suddenly, pale and heavy-eyed. It was a particular look that he had come to recognize.

'Are you feeling all right, Virginia?'

'What? Oh – yes.' She didn't look at him. 'Absolutely fine. Tired, but fine. I could do with a break. You too. I know you don't want to go to Sconset, but I do think it'll do you good.'

Alexander sighed. The last thing in the world he wanted was to go off on some bloody seaside holiday with Virginia and her family; but Baby and Mary Rose had bought this new place, and they had been invited; he had said, naturally, that his family could go if they wished, but he would stay in England. Georgina had first begged and pleaded with him to go, and then cried when he said he wouldn't, and he had heard himself giving in, agreeing to spend ten days there at the end, after which they would all come home; it still seemed to him an appalling waste of time but he could never bear to upset Georgina.

'Well – maybe. I certainly don't want to go. But yes, of course you must go to New York. Will you be staying with your parents?'

'No, I don't think so. No I won't. I can never work there. I'll be at the Pierre.'

'Fine. Well, it all seems to be settled. I can't quite see why you're asking me.'

'Don't be silly, Alexander. You know I wouldn't go if you really minded.'

'Do I?' he said. 'Do I know that?'

'Of course you do.'

'Well that's all right then. I presume you'll be back for the twentieth, though.'

'The what?'

'The twentieth, Virginia. The summer garden party. You know? The one you always enjoy so much.'

'Oh God, Alexander, I'm so sorry. So terribly sorry. It completely slipped my memory. And yes, I do love it. It's one of my favourites. But I had thought – '

'Yes, Virginia? What had you thought?'

'Well I had thought I could go straight on to Sconset. From New York. If it wasn't for the – the garden party. I mean that would be much more – much easier. And I am tired. As you said. But – '

He felt her falter, knew she was wondering if she could get away with it, with not being at the garden party.

'I hope no client is more important to you than your life here with me, Virginia,' he said, picking up his coffee cup, returning to *The Times*.

431

'No, Alexander, of course not. I'll be back. And then go again.' She sighed. He smiled at her encouragingly.

'Good. That's settled then.'

She called from New York five days later. Could he possibly manage without her, just this once, at the garden party? And then send the children on the plane with Nanny? She was terribly busy, and extremely tired, not feeling well at all, in fact her mother's doctor had said she should have complete rest for a few days. He had been most emphatic, as a matter of fact, that she should not rush backwards and forwards across the Atlantic. If Alexander didn't believe her, or wanted to check, the doctor was more than willing to talk to him. She just felt that it seemed madness to come back, just for one day; no one would miss her, after all, it was him and the children the tenants and everybody liked to see.

'*I* shall miss you, Virginia,' said Alexander. 'I shall miss you very much. And Nanny hates flying so much.'

'She doesn't, actually. She told me last time she really enjoyed it. She can stay at the house for a day or two, and then come back. She'll have a lovely long holiday after all, without us.'

'She doesn't like holidays.'

Virginia sounded exasperated. 'Well, if you're really so worried about Nanny you could come over earlier with the children.'

'Thank you, no.'

'Well, I'm sorry, Alexander. But I really can't help being ill.'

'In this particular instance,' he said, 'I think you probably can.'

He gave in of course, as he always did, when she trapped him like this; what kind of a husband would insist his exhausted, sick wife made an unnecessary trip across the Atlantic for a one-day function? But there was a blind blanket of fury in his heart, that she could have forgotten, was prepared to neglect, to forgo something so important to him, to Hartest, should put herself first. She was cheating now and cheating badly; he knew what she wanted, he knew she wanted to be with Baby, to talk to him, to share her troubles. And no doubt to share his. Perhaps make another offer of free accommodation for him and his little tart.

Alexander stared blankly out of the window. This was not how he had envisaged things at all.

He wanted to punish her. He wanted to punish all of them. He had no idea if the affair was still going on between Baby and Angie, but he had seen Baby using the phone in the village earlier in the day, and he could imagine why it had been. He sat and looked at them round the supper table, contrasting it with his garden party supper table, the first night on Sconset, and hated them. All of them. Not just Baby but Mary Rose for her blind complacency, and (although they were not physically present) Fred for his outrageous, overbearing arrogance and Betsey, for contributing to that arrogance, for persisting in her myth of a happy family. And Virginia of course. Certainly Virginia: for her terrible disloyalty. On many counts.

So – how? How to maximize his knowledge, to cause the most pain? And to ensure that any action he took could not be traced back to him.

Later, he went for a walk on his own. He needed to think.

The plan came to him two days later, as he sat reading on the deck, as they called it. Ridiculous name. Virginia had announced she was going in to New York. That in itself had angered him. He had a very shrewd idea why she had to go, but it still angered him. He had trekked all this way to be with her, to please her, and she promptly left him. She could surely have gone earlier. But at least it enabled him to carry out his plan. It was so simple he almost choked on the apple he was eating. He could do it easily. Tomorrow would be fine. He could do it in the afternoon. That would cause maximum havoc. And it would hurt all of them, neatly, beautifully. And they would never, ever dream of how it had happened.

He slept peacefully that night for the first time for weeks.

Next day, after breakfast, he went to his room, scribbled some notes on a piece of paper. He didn't need to memorize them, but he did need to get the accent absolutely right.

They were all in the garden.

'I have to go into the village,' he said, 'I want a newspaper. A New York newspaper. See you at lunch.' The children waved, and he left them, and pedalled slowly into the village of Sconset, rehearsing aloud as he went. He walked into the Chanticleer restaurant; they were all known there, the proprietor was friendly, waved him towards the telephone near the back of the restaurant, poured him a beer. It was very quiet; the only person around was a cleaner.

Alexander picked up the phone slowly; he was nervous now. He had written the number down; he sat looking at it for a while. It was a pity that Betsey, the only innocent person in this whole mess, had to be hurt along with the others, but she would probably benefit in the end. Make Fred a little less arrogant. And there really was no way he could spare her. She was absolutely essential to his plan. Of course there were still hazards. Betsey might be out. Virginia might answer the phone. No, that

433

was very unlikely. It was always Banks. It was one of his jobs. Yes, unless something very extraordinary had happened, Banks would answer the phone. And then he could ask for Betsey and then it would be straightforward. And if she wasn't there, wasn't going to be back, he would move onto Plan Two, and give the message to Banks. It wasn't as neat, but it would do. The message he had written sat looking at him from the card propped in front of him. Yes, it was perfect. He took one careful mouthful of the beer, and picked up the phone again.

'Mrs Praeger?' The accent was perfect, one of his best, thick oily Brooklyn. Poor Betsey, he thought, she would never hear a Brooklyn accent again without feeling upset.

'Yes, this is she.'

'Mrs Praeger, I'm sorry for disturbing you, but I'm very anxious to contact your husband.'

'Well he's not here.' Betsey's accent, her terminally anxious tone, came over more strongly on the phone. 'He's in his office. Why don't you call him there?'

'Well naturally I did, Mrs Praeger, but he's out and it is a little urgent.'

'Well I'm sure he won't be long,' said Betsey, 'did you speak to his secretary?'

'She was temporarily out of the office also.'

'Oh I see. Well – can I help in any way?'

'Well – I certainly would appreciate that. This is the Cholly Knicker-bocker column here. I wondered if you would care to comment on the story that your son has been seen a lot around town with an English girl? A Miss Burbank? Who used to work for your daughter? I believe she has an apartment in the Village, which your son visits from time to time. I'm sorry? Oh no, Mrs Praeger, there certainly isn't any mistake. I picked up the story from a very reliable source. I'm afraid I can't reveal it. But I can tell you it was someone close to Mr Fred Praeger. Mr Praeger Senior.'

So simple, so easy. He could scarcely believe he had done it.

Chapter 37

Charlotte, 1985

It was blowing up a little. The sky was as brilliant as ever, the sea as fiercely green-blue, but it was roughening. The raft rocked, gently at first, then more aggressively; Charlotte gripped the sides of it more firmly with her hands, afraid she would fall off. The water felt almost cold as it washed over her legs. She hadn't realized how hot she had been; she wondered briefly if she was burning. Another wave; another lift of the raft on the water; and suddenly, just for a moment, a drift of cloud over the sun darkened the day, and the sea turned almost grey. She was startled at the change, felt vaguely threatened; the curving shore looked suddenly far away.

'Turn over,' said Jeremy's voice, gentle, almost amused in her ear. 'Turn over onto your stomach.'

'I can't,' she said, laughing, 'I'll fall off.'

'No you won't. I've got you.'

'Yes you have,' she said, laughing still but more resignedly, and turned carefully, cautiously, afraid of slipping into the water. As always when she was making love to Jeremy, her mind was focused with a fierce, painful concentration; every other thing in the world was cancelled out. Had a hurricane been blowing, had they been in danger of their lives, she would still have thought only of her body, and its needs, and the gratification he could bring her.

She lay on her stomach, and felt him settling on top of her; felt his penis huge and warm in the crease of her buttocks. His hands were beneath her, holding her breasts; he was kissing her neck, tenderly, slowly. Her hunger increased, intensified; she pushed her back up, slightly, so that it was arched, so that he could have access to her. Another wave; she slipped, thrust up again, slipped again. Frustration and tension increased her desperation for him; she sighed fretfully, arched for the third time, thrusting at him, felt him enter her, slowly, steadily. Her vagina clenched triumphantly round him; he pushed, harder, she felt her entire body invaded, oddly stable suddenly, in their rocking, sea-washed bed.

She felt, faster than usual, her greed growing, the heady, irresistible climb towards her climax, pushed, urged on by the rhythm beneath her; she clasped the sides of the raft more firmly, riding the sea, riding her pleasure. She felt cast adrift from reality, from herself even, from everything on earth except the glorious sensation of him within her forcing her, pushing her, drawing her; his penis feeling, in the midst of her, so large, so strong, so powerful she could scarcely contain it. And then, as the raft rose again, as they rose with it, as she struggled to hold him, as he thrust again and again, and she felt his own climax, slow at first, then growing, throbbing, flowing inside her, her own came in a sweet almost heavy rush to meet him, and she rose halfway to her knees, crying out, clenching, clinging within herself to the delight and to him.

Afterwards, they went sailing; there was a strong sea running. Jeremy was a superb sailor, and all she had to do was let the jib in and out, and dive across the boat whenever he changed direction. It was quite enough that day. They went far out to sea; she sat on the side of the boat, leaning out, her feet crammed under the rope for safety, and looked up at the sails, pushing, straining against the wind as she had pushed and strained against him, and felt a great sense of tenderness and release. She looked at Jeremy, concentrating fiercely on the boat and its passage, as he so often concentrated on her, his brown body tense, lashed with spray, his strong hands, the hands that knew her and her body with all its idiosyncrasies so well, holding the ropes with the same strong, sure skill, and the journey through the water, cutting, soaring, relentlessly onwards seemed to echo the pleasure, at once smaller and larger, they had just shared on the raft, and he smiled at her suddenly, and read her thoughts and shouted above the wind, 'I love you!'

Charlotte didn't believe it, and she knew he didn't believe it either, but it was good to hear nonetheless.

They had been lovers for six months now, six heady, frightening months. At first she had been terrified, afraid of Isabella finding out, of her grandfather finding out, of anyone finding out; but Jeremy was a most skilful philanderer, greatly versed in the art of secrecy and concealment. He courted her (as much to amuse himself as to reassure her) by strange anonymous phone calls, by letters hand-delivered by constantly changing messengers in what came swiftly to be their own code; he arranged meetings in hired apartments, quirky, out-of-town hotels. He owned a tiny cottage on the furthermost tip of North Haven in the Hamptons, where he took her for a wonderful twenty-four hours, driving her out along the Expressway in a rather elderly Volkswagen Beetle which he had bought particularly for the occasion, and holding her hand and murmuring soothingly to her as they sat on the creaky ferry that took them across from Sag Harbor while she literally shook with terror that her grandfather or one of his friends from the Hamptons would recognize her; once there, they never left the cottage, but simply made love endlessly, and ate the meals painstakingly prepared by Dawson and packed in hamper and ice box, complete with champagne, wine and 'other substances for me, and for you if you want them', accompanied by hour-on-hour instructions from Dawson: 'Four p.m. uncork claret, five p.m. place half-baked bread in oven, six p.m. spread steaks with herb and garlic butter, light barbecue grill, seven p.m. toss salad, dress (ready-cooked) baby potatoes with chives and mayonnaise, remove ice cream, raspberry mousse and summer pudding from ice box, place in fridge to soften, take cheeses out of fridge' and so on right through to 'one a.m. latest, remove lobster meat from freezer to defrost overnight, also hash browns'; and then finally 'eight a.m. squeeze oranges, add to chilled champagne, place croissants in oven, hash browns in microwave, grind coffee beans'.

'Are you sure,' said Charlotte, smiling at Jeremy over her breakfast Bucks Fizz, and eating her way greedily through a large plate of hash browns, 'are you sure he hasn't also written down there "Seven a.m. awake mistress by kissing nipples, seven fifteen, turn attention to lower parts of body, seven thirty bring mistress to first orgasm of day"?'

'He might have done,' said Jeremy, smiling at her, 'but I wouldn't have needed to look at the instructions.'

'How long has Dawson worked for you?'

'Ten – no eleven years.'

'He's a wonder. I wish I could thank him for this weekend.'

'I'll thank him for you. And I hope you don't feel he should have all the credit.'

'Most of it,' said Charlotte. 'Can I have another croissant?'

She gradually became less frightened. Her main emotion, apart from an almost tangible sense of physical well-being, was guilt. From the moment she had been able to think straight after the first time she had gone to bed with him, up in his workroom, that strange, exhausting, difficult night, she had been shocked at what she had done, at tumbling into the trap, led by her own weakness and greed, of not only allowing him to make love to her, but allowing him to know how much she had needed and enjoyed him. She was under no illusions about either of them; they suited one another very well. He was a self-indulgent, spoilt, charming man, and he had wanted her and led her most skilfully into the trap whereby he had been able to have her. And go on having her. And she was using him, and she forced herself to recognize the fact, using him

437

to ease her loneliness, to soften her sense of rejection, to distract her from her helpless passion for Gabe, to amuse her, to make her laugh – and primarily, overwhelmingly, to give her physical pleasure. And there was no harm in any of it, she managed to persuade herself, unless Fred found out; and then there would be harm on a scale that made Charlotte tremble, and in her more sober moments, which were many, she cursed herself for having arrived in so vulnerable a position. If only, she thought, as she lay awake sometimes worrying about it all, if only she had not gone with him to the studio that night, had said she was too tired, that she must go home. Or if only she had not gone to bed with him, simply headed home straight after dinner; or if only the sex hadn't been very good, and she had been able to tell him that she would never see him again. But it had been good, very good, quite amazingly good in fact, and he had seen that and liked it and, given his considerable charm, and his exceptional position in her life, the thing had taken on a momentum all of its own, and she had (afraid of offending him, hurting him, making him think she had been using him) continued to see him 'once more, just once more' a great many times. And it was a trap, albeit a very, a frighteningly, pleasant one, and she felt herself becoming more and more ensnared, and more and more troubled by its eventual outcome.

Jeremy was a skilful lover, Charlotte was sexually hungry (a fact she had not fully recognized before), and the combination of the two factors was highly satisfactory. Charlotte was shattered, almost shocked by the sensations he could evoke in her. She was not very sexually experienced herself; she had a healthy appetite, first aroused by Beau Fraser, titillated by various young men at university, but never properly and wholly satisfied by anyone. Jeremy set out to teach her what her body could achieve in terms of pleasure; and its achievements were considerable. He was patient, tender, and resourceful in bed with her; he led and she followed, they discovered an almost immediate and surprising compatibility and the pathways they explored together were extremely pleasant. Charlotte was occasionally surprised by how pleasant they were. She had heard many rumours about Jeremy Foster and his depravities, and initially she had been nervous of what he might wish to do to her, ask of her; but as the weeks went by she decided the rumours were ill-founded and rooted in envy and suspicion – of his gilded life, his vast fortune, his charm, his looks, his legendary success with women. She had heard he was bisexual, that he was homosexual, that he ran orgies, that he did a lot of drugs. After several months, Charlotte had seen evidence only of the drugs.

She managed not to think about Isabella very much. She was very often away, she patently led her own life, and had very little time to spare for Jeremy, and Charlotte felt that gave her a right of sorts to have an affair with him. She had no intention of breaking up the marriage; the thought of being married to Jeremy was highly unappealing. And so most of the time, she tried not to worry, simply to enjoy herself. But the situation did not, she knew, entirely suit her. And it was so extremely fraught with danger.

Her affair with Jeremy had certainly not changed her attitude to Gabe. She still felt exactly the same about him: obsessed. It was wearing her down, that obsession; it was like a sickness, a constant pain, ever present, wearing, raw, even when she had forgotten about it herself. It made her tired, irritable, out of sorts when she allowed herself to dwell on it, or when he had treated her particularly badly. Most of the time she tried not to dwell on it, to ignore it; but sometimes when she was low, when she was particularly worried about Jeremy, when Freddy's hostility became especially apparent, when she was worried about Alexander, or missing England, she would feel it in a great hopeless wave of depression and wonder how much longer she could stand it. He continued to treat her badly: rude, arrogant, unappreciative for the most part, but one thing she knew had changed; he regarded her now as part of his strength, and an asset, and when things went well, when a good deal was pulled off, a new client won, some danger averted, he would grin at her and say, 'Well done team,' and take her out for a drink with the others, or even occasionally hug her in a brotherly sort of way. Charlotte never knew whether it was a good sign that he should hug her, or a bad one that he patently regarded her as one of the guys. In either case, it seemed worth it, to have some physical contact with him, however meagre. She was always afraid that Jeremy might guess how much she fantasized about Gabe (occasionally, to her own distress, even as they made love) but she was clearly a better actress than she realized, for he was so deceived by her protestations of hatred for Gabe that he teased her about being secretly in love with him.

More and more, Charlotte feared, she was turning into the kind of person she most disapproved of.

When Jeremy had first suggested three days' holiday in the Bahamas she had gone white with terror and told him he must be crazy. Then she had grown used to the idea, told herself it was probably safer to be with him there than in New York, realized she had not had a proper holiday for over two years and, ground down by his formidable persistence, weakly given in. The thought of it was so enchanting, so beguiling, three whole days in the sunshine, three whole nights of sex, three days and three nights of fun, that she actually found herself looking forward to it. She bought a lot of very expensive beachwear and evening clothes, told Gabe she was taking a very overdue vacation (and numb with terror told Fred and Betsey too), and booked a return flight to Nassau, sitting at JFK in a trembling panic that Fred would suddenly turn up, join her flight, be in some impossible way at Nassau airport when she got there to be met by Jeremy. But he was not; and Jeremy laughed at her white face and wild eyes and led her by the hand to his private jet that was sitting on the runway and flew her to Eleuthera airport, and then led her into his white Rolls which was waiting for them there, and drove her to the Cotton Bay Club, near Rock Sound, an enchanting hotel on a curve of beach, where he had booked them in as Mr and Mrs James Firth.

She got back to New York tanned, relaxed and pleased with life. They parted at Nassau very fondly, and Jeremy gave her a Rolex Oyster watch as he kissed her goodbye. 'To remind you of your time as a sea creature,' he said smiling. Charlotte gave him a hug, and said she didn't need a watch to remind her, but that it was a lovely idea anyway. She had always wanted an Oyster; she sat and stared at it all the way to New York.

She got home after midnight tired but very happy. She was no longer living with Fred and Betsey; her affair had driven her finally into a home of her own, a very nice studio apartment on the Upper West Side. It had one huge sitting room, a small bedroom, a walk-in closet which was almost as big as the bedroom, increasingly stacked with extremely expensive clothes (this aspect of her relationship with Jeremy intrigued her in a dispassionate way: she had never been interested in clothes before and now she thought of them a great deal), and a small bathroom and kitchen.

She had the walls painted white, hung full-length, natural-coloured slub silk curtains at all the windows, bought a few modern couches, coffee tables and chairs and a very large bed, and settled into single living with great relish. She entertained Jeremy there only occasionally (fearing a surprise visit from Fred, who had actually dropped in on her twice in the ten weeks she had spent there, quite enough to be nerve-racking) but Chrissie was a frequent visitor, and so were Melissa and Kendrick; she had even given a small supper party for her grandparents and Mary Rose, and all three of her cousins (although Freddy had cried off at the last minute pleading pressure of work), a markedly unrelaxed occasion, but one which she felt had established her as an independent person in the family's eyes.

There were two messages on her answering machine: one from Gabe, asking her to call him at the office, whatever time she got back, the other from Chrissie saying she had missed her. Charlotte made herself a jug of coffee, poured a cup and dialled Gabe's direct line.

He had been irritable about her holiday; asked her three times if it had been really necessary. He was obviously now going to extract his revenge.

'Gabe, hi. It's me. I'm back. What's wrong?'

'Nothing really.' He sounded strained, odd. 'Could you possibly come over? Or could I maybe come and see you? I'm sorry, but it's important.'

'Sure. Why don't you come here? I've done enough travelling for one night.'

'OK. Where are you?'

'Apartment Five, 793 Central Park West. OK? I just made a big jug of coffee.'

'Thanks.'

He sounded very unlike himself. Charlotte was puzzled. She put her holiday clothes away, changed into some jeans and a T-shirt. For good measure, she sprayed herself liberally with Y by Saint Laurent, and put a bottle of champagne in her tiny freezer. Well, you never knew.

Gabe arrived twenty minutes after his call. He buzzed. 'Hi, Charlotte, it's me.' Charlotte pressed the entryphone button; she felt sick already.

Sex was clearly the very last thing on Gabe's mind. He scarcely looked at her as he came in, shook his head distractedly as she offered him a drink, asked for a black coffee and didn't mention the fact she'd been away. Charlotte sighed, threw a regretful glance at the events of the last three days and the person she had shared them with, poured a second large coffee for herself also, and settled down at the other end of the sofa. There was clearly no question of them meeting in the middle.

'This Bloom deal,' said Gabe quietly, after draining his coffee mug, 'you haven't mentioned it to anyone, have you?'

'Of course not,' said Charlotte impatiently. 'You know I wouldn't. I hope,' she added slightly balefully. The Bloom deal was a hot issue, the big one that they had been working on for weeks. Bloom, a large paper and print conglomerate, was initially being chased by four predators; two had dropped out, leaving only a Praeger client, Tarquins, and one other firm, represented by Clarkson Wellington, another comparatively small bank, interested. It was a sensitive one, because the money being talked was so huge: out of proportion in relation to the value of the company: as in so many deals these hectic days. It was not unusual for banks to act as 'common carriers' for merger money and to lend money to any number of bidders in pursuit of the same prize. 'No one was remotely interested in

441

what they were getting, of course,' said Gabe, stretching out his long legs with a heavy sigh, 'simply the interest on the loan. We just dropped out of the bidding. I really don't think Blooms is worth that kind of money. It's been talked up too much. The price was getting silly. It just wasn't in Tarquins' interest. It would have backfired on us.'

'So?' said Charlotte. So far nothing was new, and her long day was catching up on her.

'Well, so we were flying out of a small private airfield in Washington. I went to the men's room. While I was there – '

'Yeah, yeah, someone turned the tap on and asked you what was happening,' said Charlotte. The leaking of information in the men's room, under cover of a running tap, was becoming something of a cliché in the merger and acquisition world.

'No, wrong. I got a call. In the washroom. It was from Beaufort.'

'Beaufort! Gabe, how did he know you were there?'

'Precisely. Got it in one.'

Beaufort was one of the leading arbitrageurs, in on every deal, examining it, analysing it, assessing it, taking a position on it, prime mover on the junk bond bandwagon, leeching upon the frenetic activity of the merger and acquisition business. He was also suspected – widely suspected – of insider dealing. No one had proof, and officially of course no one acknowledged it; but somebody, many somebodies, had to be doing it, the network was wide and complex and those somebodies were pulling it all together, organizing the astonishing accuracy of the dealings that were going on and the Midas-like pickings that they resulted in. The number of people involved with the somebodies could only be guessed at. It was entirely clandestine, run like some vast subterranean empire, with a coded language, its business conducted behind the closed doors of private houses and apartments, in cars parked on strange lots, on telephones with numbers known only to half a dozen people. And for the most part people didn't talk, didn't become citizens of the empire (although the prizes for those who did were shatteringly high, perhaps as much as 5 per cent of the profit of a transaction), but everyone knew it existed, while of course nobody knew at all. It was a gilt-edged conspiracy, suspected, feared, talked of, marvelled at, but for a long time unprovable, undetectable, the money earned disappearing into Swiss bank accounts, the conversations and transactions never recorded, never referred to. And in the empire Beaufort was one of the rulers: a rather quiet, plain man, with a shock of dark hair and painfully honest grey eyes, talking quietly in restaurants, in bars, at receptions. He had risen to power, like Boesky and Levine, on the back of the boom and the junk bond bonanza, playing with Wall Street and its satellite companies like so many amusing toys, confident, careful, watchful – and rich, earning vast fortunes as they did so.

'So – let's get this straight,' said Charlotte. 'He just phoned you. In this men's room?'

'Yup. We'd had a really tough meeting. Out at Bloom's place near Washington. But it was over and like I said we were at this private airfield. And Beaufort knew I was there. It was – weird.'

'And what did he say?'

'Well, he said we should keep talking, keep the price moving.'

'Because he has some stock already?'

'Obviously. So not only did he know about the deal in enough time to acquire stock, but he knew we were pulling out.'

'So – someone in the meeting was in touch with him.'

'Yes. Either one of us, or one of the Blooms people.'

'But – who was there from us?'

'Me. Fred. The lawyers. John Clark.' John Clark was the new junior associate, pale and thin, with a large adam's apple, lower down the pecking order even than Charlotte, too frightened to so much as breathe if Gabe turned his attention on him.

'Well there's your answer,' said Charlotte with a quick grin. 'He's obviously your spy.'

'Sure.' Gabe took a large gulp of coffee. 'This is nice coffee, Charlotte.'

Charlotte felt as if she had been awarded the Nobel Prize.

'Lawyers?' she said, determinedly keeping her attention on the matter in hand.

'Unlikely. It was Mason, who's been with the firm for about a thousand years, and Matt Jacobson who would be hung, drawn and quartered before he took so much as a paper clip away from Praegers.'

'Well, I was in Nassau,' said Charlotte, 'so it certainly wasn't me. I don't see that it matters greatly, Gabe. I mean, you said no, presumably.'

'Yeah, sure I said no. But I might not have done. That's the point. And they knew. That's the other point.'

'Why are you asking me anyway?' said Charlotte. 'You know it couldn't have been me.'

'I had to ask you,' said Gabe.

'Why?' she said, edgy now.

'Well because I thought you might have some ideas. And because I have to. In case of any reprisal. Have to show I did everything I should have done.' He scowled at her. She felt the old throb of simultaneous excitement and outrage at him. Bastard, keeping her out of bed at – what – two in the morning, quizzing her about a crime that he knew she would never commit. She scowled back. Then she said, 'I'm very tired, Gabe.

Now that you've completed your investigation, could you leave me, do you think?'

'Sure. Sorry.' He stood up. It was so unusual for him to apologize that Charlotte felt her jaw threatening to drop. 'It was just – disturbing.'

'I suppose,' she said slowly, 'the point was that Fred was there. Actually there. Could have heard about it. Or heard it.'

'Precisely. Lightning sharp as usual. God, Charlotte, I sometimes wonder if you have a brain at all, inside that pretty little head.'

Charlotte stood up and opened the door. 'Goodnight, Gabe,' she said. 'It's so nice to be back.'

'See you in the morning. Don't be late.' He looked at her for a moment or two, his eyes travelling over her, and then grinned. 'You look very well. The seaside obviously suits you.'

She found his remark and his careful consideration of her almost as exciting as all the sex she had had with Jeremy over the past three days.

In the morning Gabe was irritable, edgy. She got in at seven and found him already at his desk, his watch off, swearing into his Quotron.

'I have to go to Rome for a couple of days,' he said, 'big conference there. Your grandpa just told me. I could do without it.' He looked at her fiercely, as if it was her fault.

'Do any assistants get to go to this conference?'

'Yes they do. John Clark gets to go.'

'I see.' She felt stung, oddly rejected. All the shit she took from him, and then when he could have done something nice, he made a point of publicly not doing so.

She sighed; Gabe looked up at her and grinned.

'I didn't think two days alone with me would please you too much. That's second prize. You get first.'

'Which is one day alone with you?'

'No, two days without me. Handling this divestiture with Peacheys. OK?'

She stared at him. She could feel a flush rising under her tan: this was the first time in eighteen months he had suggested she might be able to do anything more difficult than bind papers together.

'Handle it? On my own?'

'For fuck's sake, Charlotte, you should be able to by now. It's extremely straightforward. Three buyers. Closing in two days. We're looking for at least six seventy-five, but you know that. Try and push them to seven. You can always go and ask Grandpa if you get into deep water.'

'Oh shut up,' she said, but she was smiling. 'Thanks, Gabe.'

She looked at her watch, on her newly browned wrist. 'Coffee and bagels?'

'Yeah, thanks.' He had followed her eyes, noticed the watch.

'Very nice. Memento of the vacation?'

'Of course not,' she said, blushing furiously, angry with herself for wearing it her first day back.

'He must be very rich,' he said and laughed.

'He is,' said Charlotte, trying to sound dignified.

Gabe went off after lunch; she said goodbye to him feeling already sick with nerves at the thought of her divestiture. She told herself it was stupid; just a little matter of accepting the highest bid for a small, healthy little company in Ohio. Couldn't be simpler. The bids would all be in in the morning; she just had to field them, and then accept the highest – or most suitable – and go ahead and send off the contract. Nothing to it.

She hardly slept.

The phone rang shortly after lunch, Gabe's personal line. The voice was quiet, slightly Southern in accent.

'Is Mr Hoffman there?'

'I'm sorry, he's not. He's out of town until Monday. This is his assistant speaking. May I help you?'

'I think not. Just tell him it was about the Bloom deal. We spoke two days ago. Goodbye.'

Shit, thought Charlotte, that must have been Beaufort. What was going on? Why did he think Gabe was worth pursuing? And how did he know that number? Only half a dozen people did. It didn't make sense. Well, maybe it did. Gabe was a star. A star, privy to many many deals. Worth tying up. She hoped to God he was actually not in the process of being tied up. This was all a little fishy. Then she remembered his anxiety, his patent distress, and shook herself. Gabe was many unpleasant things, but he was honest. If he was less honest, her own life might be more bearable, she thought, sighing. He might make an effort to be kind to her, patient, to pretend he found her at least not distasteful. 'Yes, and then you'd be even worse off, Charlotte Welles,' she said aloud, 'given food for hope. This thing will starve itself to death soon.' She scribbled a note to Gabe and put it on his desk: 'The phantom caller from the airfield called. Wants to talk some more. I think. On Tuesday?'

Next morning she travelled in early. It was so nice without Gabe, she thought, walking briskly up Pine Street at a quarter to seven. She felt so secure, so in charge, so confident. Not even the worry about Peacheys

445

was getting her down. One day, she thought, embarking on her favourite, well-worn fantasy, one day . . . She'd have him sitting in some satellite office, leaping up and down when she rang for him, waiting nervously to show her some figures, agreeing with her every utterance. Although she knew that was highly unlikely. Probably he'd be gone, she thought. He wouldn't stand for more than a week of her being in charge. Well, half in charge. She mustn't forget Freddy. Nice though that would be.

As she walked into her office, Freddy was coming out of it. He looked startled when he saw her.

'You're very early, Charlotte. Trying to cope without Gabe?'

'I am coping without Gabe, thank you. And what are you doing in my office?'

'Not actually yours, as I understand it. Or have things changed? I was just leaving a note for him, as a matter of fact. About a lunch on Tuesday. I got a message by mistake. How was your vacation? What did you do?'

'Great. Short but very sweet. I was sailing. You know how much I love sailing, Freddy.'

'Yes of course. I can't remember, did you say you were going alone?'

'I didn't say anything, Freddy. But as matter of fact, I didn't go alone. I went with a friend.'

'Oh I see. Nice watch, Charlotte. Present?'

'Oh – yes. Well, sort of.'

'Your friends are obviously well-heeled.'

'Some of them. Please excuse me, Freddy, I have work to do.'

He walked out of the office.

She spent a very nice weekend at Beaches with Betsey; Fred had flown to join Gabe in Rome. They shopped, walked on the shore, went to the movies and ate hamburgers like two truanting children.

When she got back, there was a message from Max. He was doing a job for *Seventeen* magazine and staying at the Hilton. Could he come over, maybe she'd like to cook a meal for him? If he didn't hear he'd be over at eight.

Oh God, thought Charlotte wearily, dialling his number. Why did life have to be so complicated? Max had gone out.

'This is great,' said Max, wandering into the kitchen where she was making them some coffee. 'I love it. That stove doesn't look exactly well worn.'

'Nobody in New York uses a kitchen for cooking anything except toast and coffee,' said Charlotte. 'The big apartments all have huge, gleaming stainless steel affairs, with ovens and hobs and microwaves and God knows what, and they never ever get used. New Yorkers would think you very strange if you cooked dinner for them. If you ask people over for dinner, you mean you're going to take them out. Then you get to the restaurant and work the room and throw a fit if you don't have the best table. It isn't very relaxing. Max, look, about supper this evening. It's a bit awkward. Tomorrow would be better.'

'Are you expecting someone? You are! Is it Jeremy, I wonder?'

Charlotte felt the floor rock beneath her. 'How on earth did you – '

'Darling, you look as if you're going to faint. I heard you on the phone to him at Christmas, that's all.'

'Max, you're disgusting, listening to people's phone calls.'

'Maybe, but you certainly learn a lot. Don't worry, I haven't said anything. Promise. Is he nice?'

'He's – very nice. Yes. But it isn't serious, if that's what you're thinking.'

'No, of course not. I mean I wasn't.' He grinned at her. 'It's all right, Charlotte, I'll leave in a minute. We can have dinner tomorrow. I don't want to come between you and true love.'

'It isn't love, I told you.'

'Even better.' He looked at her shrewdly. 'You're looking very – glossy. How much did that coat cost?' He nodded at the three-quarter-length fox jacket she had thrown on the couch when she came in.

'Oh,' she said, blushing, 'I can't remember.'

'Charlotte, don't be so jumpy. I don't care who you're going around with. Anyway, I want to talk about me.'

'Well that'll make a change.' But she smiled back at him.

'You look very good. Slimmer than I can ever remember. Love suits you.'

'I told you I'm not in love,' said Charlotte irritably.

'Oh, not with the sugar daddy. But with friend Gabe, I suspect. I'd put money on it, even.'

'Well, you'd lose your money. I can't stand him, I keep telling you.' She changed the subject. 'So what did you want to talk about, Max?'

'I've been thinking. What would you think about me going into the bank?'

'The bank? Max, you're crazy. You'd hate it.'

'I don't think so. I get a kind of a buzz, listening to you talking about it all; the games you guys play. I think I'd like it. And it certainly beats sucking in your cheeks and watching some pervert getting his rocks off over you through his zoom lens. I'm just so sick of that whole scene, Charlotte, I can't tell you. I just got ticked off like some naughty little boy

447

for having to cancel out on a job; I couldn't help it, I was ill. And the novelty has worn off in a big way. I have to do something. So I thought I might give it a try.'

'There's more to it than giving it a try,' said Charlotte primly. 'You either have to do it or you don't. But I suppose you might like it. There's a lot of boredom there as well, you know. And you get ticked off a great deal, I can tell you. Anyway, you'd have to ask Grandpa or Uncle Baby, it's nothing to do with me. Incidentally, how is Uncle Baby? Have you seen him lately?'

'Not very. I think he's OK. Why?'

'Oh – nothing. Well, I don't think he's very well. Did you notice how thin he'd got at Christmas? And he looks really drawn.'

'Haven't heard anything,' said Max. 'But I'll make some discreet inquiries if you like.'

'Please. I would. Poor Uncle Baby, I feel so sorry for him. And Angie's such a bitch and – '

'She's not so bad,' said Max easily. 'She's been very good to me.'

'I daresay,' said Charlotte tartly. 'She'd be good to anything with a cock to play with.'

'Charlotte! Dirty talk. Did you learn that sort of thing from Jeremy or Gabe?'

'Neither,' said Charlotte. 'But I tell you, Max, if you want to hear dirty talk, you should go to the trading floor. I heard words there I didn't even know what they meant. I could just tell they were filthy. They talk it all the time. It's amazing.'

'I like the sound of the trading floor,' said Max. 'Could I visit it tomorrow, do you think?'

'You *would* like it. That's an area of banking you'd feel thoroughly at home in. Yes, come in tomorrow. You can meet my friend Chrissie. She always says it's the biggest casino going.'

'Sounds fun. Yeah, I'd be interested. When should I come? I'm working till at least four.'

'That'd be OK,' said Charlotte. 'Roll up then.' She was feeling increasingly edgy, waiting distractedly for the door buzzer to go, longing for Max to leave, but managed to ask with a rather chilly politeness after Tommy. 'Talking of casinos,' she added rather tartly.

'He's OK,' said Max. 'Charlotte, I wish you'd give old Tommy a chance. He really isn't so bad.'

'I'm afraid I find it very difficult to believe that,' said Charlotte. 'He's sponging off you, Max. You and all of us. With a bit of blackmail thrown in. I think that's terrible.'

Max had learnt to live with his family's attitude towards Tommy, but it still upset him. 'Charlotte,' he said. 'Tommy doesn't mean any harm. He's a bit of an old roué, but he was kind and supportive to me, and he's really very grateful for the little house in Pond Place. And he doesn't spend nearly so much money at Les A these days. He's even got a job of sorts.'

'Really?' said Charlotte. 'What kind of a job?'

'Oh, it's acting as secretary for some charity. For some old ladies, whose husbands were in the air force or something. He really enjoys it, and it keeps him out of trouble.'

'I doubt that,' said Charlotte.

At that moment her buzzer went. Charlotte could feel herself blushing. She went over to the entryphone.

'Yes? Oh – oh, hallo. Well no – oh, well – ' She put her hand over the receiver and looked at Max. 'How long are you planning to stay?'

He grinned. He had never seen her so flustered.

'Oh – only long enough to meet him. Then I'm off. Have him up, darling, and then have him. I won't get in your way.' Charlotte glared at him, and then spoke into the phone again.

'Come on up. My young brother is here. But he's just leaving.'

Jeremy walked into the studio a few minutes later, carrying a bottle of champagne in one hand and an enormous bunch of red roses in the other. He was wearing an exquisitely cut suit, and had a large brownish sable coat slung across his shoulders. He smiled at Max, and held out his hand.

'Hi. I'm Jeremy Foster. You must be Max the Model.'

'Fraid so,' said Max. 'Not for much longer, I hope. Good to meet you. I'm really sorry I have to leave, but I'm due somewhere in a few minutes, Charlotte tells me.'

Jeremy laughed. 'Oh darling, for heaven's sake. This is family stuff. I've met Max before when he was about – what – twelve? Max, stay and have a drink with us, tell us what you're doing. We have plenty of time.'

'Thanks,' said Max. He was carefully ignoring Charlotte's frantic eye signals. 'That'd be great. Just a quick one, though. I met your wife once or twice. We even worked together. One nice lady.'

'Very nice,' said Jeremy easily, 'we've been together for a long, very nice time. We're really good friends.'

'Well that's nice,' said Max.

When he had gone, Jeremy took Charlotte in his arms and kissed her for a long time. 'I really love you,' he said. 'I love you to pieces.'

'It's me that's in pieces,' said Charlotte, 'and you don't love me.'

'Yes I do. And I want to give you a really stupendous present. To say

449

thank you for you. What would you like? A mink coat? A diamond ring? A box at the Opera? Just say the word.'

'What I'd like,' said Charlotte with a sigh, 'is a really nice long spell of peace and quiet, with nothing happening to me whatsoever.'

'I'll see if I can fix that,' said Jeremy.

What followed were the most terrible seven days of Charlotte's entire life.

The divestiture at least had gone all right. More than all right. Charlotte felt she had won her spurs. Or whatever you won in banking. A raise probably. Of the three initial contenders for Peacheys, she had been left with one: a series of nail-biting silences, interspersed by carefully timed phone calls, had persuaded her solo player that he was still one of a chorus, and that he was lucky to be in on the act at all. Charlotte closed the deal with the offer price twenty cents a share up.

Gabe walked in at midday. 'Hi. How's everything?'

'Fine,' said Charlotte. 'How was Rome?'

'OK. Rather foreign.' He was sorting through the messages on his desk. 'What's this about a lunch tomorrow? Message from Freddy.'

'Oh yes. He came in while you were away. Something about a mix-up with a date of his.'

'I don't know anything about a lunch,' said Gabe. 'What's he on about?'

'Well I don't know either,' said Charlotte irritably. 'Did you see the other message from me. From Beaufort?'

'Beaufort. Beaufort? For Christ's sake, Charlotte, how do you know it was him and what's he doing phoning me here?'

He looked white and shaken. Charlotte was surprised. 'Well, I think it was him. He said to tell you it was about the Bloom deal and that you'd spoken before.'

'Shit. Why's he hounding me? I just don't get this.'

She shrugged. 'I just wanted to let you know.'

'But the message isn't here.'

'It must be.'

'Charlotte, it isn't. What did it say?'

She thought a minute. 'It said something like "The phantom caller from the airfield rang. Wants to talk more." '

'And you wrote that down?'

'Yes I did. What's so terrible?'

'What's so terrible is it's indiscreet and cretinous.' His eyes were dark and angry.

'Oh Gabe, don't be ridiculous. Of course it isn't. It could mean anybody, anything. I was quite careful about it.'

'Oh, very careful!' His voice was heavy with sarcasm. 'Careful would have been not writing anything down, careful would have been just telling me, careful would probably even have been telling him I was away and you couldn't get in touch.'

'Oh for God's sake,' said Charlotte irritably. 'Don't be so over-sensitive. Nobody, but nobody could make anything of that message.'

'Many people could make a lot of it,' said Gabe briefly and walked out of the office.

Freddy came to talk to Charlotte and Gabe just before lunch. He gave his icy smile. 'I hear you just handled a deal without Gabe,' he said.

'Oh, well – not really,' said Charlotte. 'Just finished it off.'

'Grandpa's acting like you saw through the entire sale of Gulf Oil on your own,' said Freddy. He was trying to smile, but his eyes were very hard, his voice harsh.

'Well,' said Charlotte, slightly helplessly, 'you know Grandpa.'

'Yes I do, Charlotte,' said Freddy, and she was frightened by the hatred in his voice. 'I certainly do.' He was looking very pleased with himself.

'I wanted to let you know,' he said, addressing himself to both of them, 'before the official announcement, that is, that I'm off to Harvard Business School this September, as you know. And confirmed as a junior partner on the main board, as from now, but with effect from my rejoining the bank. I'm moving into the Heir's Room next week.'

'Great,' said Gabe. He stood up and shook Freddy's hand and clapped him on the shoulder, as if the news was a tremendous surprise and Freddy had won his partnership in the face of really tough competition. Charlotte, feeling sick partly at Gabe's display of sycophancy and partly at the fact that Freddy was clearly making his way much faster than she was up the Praeger ladder, forced a smile onto her own face.

'Brilliant, Freddy. Well done!'

'Yes. I am naturally very pleased.' He looked at her, his pale blue eyes rather watchful.

'I'm giving a dinner here. On Friday. In the main dining room, to celebrate. I'd like you both to come. It will be mainly family, which naturally includes you, Gabe, and a few major clients. Clement Dudley, Jeremy Foster, a couple of the International Paper people. Eight. Black tie. See you then.'

He left, making it very plain that there was no question of a refusal. Gabe met Charlotte's eye in open conspiracy for the first time she could ever remember.

'He clearly needs a pair of bigger boots,' he said simply.

They were working late on Thursday evening. To Charlotte's annoyance, she had had to cancel dinner with Jeremy. Gabe sensed her distraction, and was increasingly irritable with her.

And then his phone went. It was Fred III. Could he get on down to Fred's office right away.

Gabe, looking just slightly thoughtful, went. Summonses to Fred III could never be taken entirely lightly. Little more than two minutes later, Charlotte's phone went. It was her grandfather. 'Get on down here,' he said.

When she got to the office, the atmosphere was hideous. Gabe was white, his eyes like huge dark holes in his head. His fists were clenched, and he was staring at Charlotte as if he had never seen her before.

'Ah. Charlotte. I believe this is your writing?' Fred pushed a piece of paper at her; she didn't need to look at it.

'Yes. Yes it is.'

'Perhaps you'd like to explain what it means.'

'Well – it doesn't mean anything. I don't think. It was just a message. For Gabe.'

'From?'

'Well, I don't know.'

God, if only she knew what Gabe had said so far, how much she could say, whether she was making things better or worse.

'You don't know. It reads as if you know. "Your phantom caller," it says, "wants to talk some more." Clearly you knew he'd called before. Come along, Charlotte, I would like a slightly fuller explanation.'

Charlotte looked helplessly at Gabe. He hadn't moved; his eyes hadn't moved either.

'I – well – '

'Charlotte, do you know who this person was, or do you not? Please answer me.'

'Well – I'm not sure.'

'Charlotte, I hope you're not trying to do a cover-up job here. Out of loyalty.' Fred's voice was at its lightest, its most seductive.

'No. No, of course not. I mean there's nothing to – ' Her voice trailed away.

'Right then.' Her grandfather sat back more firmly in his chair. 'Let me put the question more simply. Was the phantom caller as you put it, was he Beaufort or one of that crowd?'

Charlotte thought fast. She decided total honesty was the only way out of this. Covering up was simply making everything look worse for Gabe. 'Yes. Yes I believe he was.'

'Why do you believe so?'

'Because – because Gabe had had a call two nights before. From – one of them.'

She didn't dare look at Gabe, but she heard him sit down suddenly. She knew then she had made a bad mistake. Clearly he had been denying any knowledge of what the message meant.

'Oh really. Do you know which one?'

'Beaufort,' said Charlotte. All was lost now, she might as well just give up, and tell everything. It made life simpler.

'And how do you know?'

'Gabe told me. He was very upset. And worried.'

Fred looked at Gabe. 'Is this true?'

'Yes it is.'

'Then why the hell didn't you say so?'

'I didn't think you'd believe me.'

'Fine. Why shouldn't I have believed you?'

'Because it was so – unbelievable,' said Gabe. 'I get a call in the men's room in the middle of the night, at an airfield where no one knew I was, from Beaufort, wanting to talk business. How the fuck would he have known I was there, if I hadn't told him?'

'Don't use that language in this office,' said Fred.

'Sorry.'

'I don't know. I have to tell you I do find it hard to believe.'

'Well there you are.' He looked at once sulky, angry and as if he was going to burst into tears.

'And then you tell Charlotte about it?'

'Yes.'

'When and where did this conversation take place?'

He was talking to Charlotte now.

'At – two in the morning. In my apartment.'

'Dear God,' said Fred, 'this gets worse. Is he often in your apartment at two in the morning?'

'Thankfully no,' said Charlotte coldly. Fred's eyes skimmed over her; for the first time he looked mildly amused.

'He came specially. To ask me if I'd talked to anyone. He was very worried. I know he'd never talked to Beaufort before.'

'So how do you suggest Beaufort knew where he was?'

'I haven't the faintest idea,' said Charlotte. 'We talked for ages about it.'

'Gabe? Any explanation?'

'None,' said Gabe wearily.

'Well, I don't get it,' said Fred heavily, 'and I'm not sure if I believe you. I'm going to make some inquiries. If I think you've even exchanged the time of day with these guys you are out of a job, and never mind if your grandfather was my godfather. OK?'

'OK,' said Gabe. He was looking more cheerful now suddenly; clearly hopeful again. 'Could I ask you something?'

'You could ask.'

'How did you get hold of that message?'

'Dick handed it to me just now. When I was coming back into the building. Someone had left it on his desk around an hour ago. He said he hadn't seen you, Gabe, all day, and he told me to give it to you. You know how he thinks he runs this place really.'

'Yes, I do,' said Gabe. 'Well – just a thought.'

'I'll see you both tomorrow,' said Fred. 'Goodnight.'

He didn't look at them; they were dismissed.

'Gabe, I'm so sorry. So very sorry,' said Charlotte, half running beside him as he stalked along the corridor. He turned to glare at her; he looked so angry she thought he was going to hit her. Then he pushed ahead so fast it was impossible for her to keep up. When she finally got into the office he was pouring, most unusually for him, a paper cup of bourbon. She looked at him warily. He bolted it down, poured another, looked at her over it. She sat down, her legs suddenly weak.

'You're a silly bitch,' he said, 'a stupid silly bitch.'

'I'm sorry,' she said again.

Gabe bolted the second cupful of bourbon. Then he said, and she never forgot it for as long as she lived, 'But you were great. Thanks. Have a drink.'

She went over to him with her own paper cup and looked at him very steadily as he half filled it.

'That's OK.'

His eyes met hers, and somewhere in their depths there was a new warmth, a friendliness, an acknowledgement that she was not entirely distasteful to him. Then he said almost casually, 'Fred made a call that night. Straight out of the Bloom meeting. He said he had to call home.'

'So?'

'So I don't know. It might be interesting to know who was there. At the house I mean.'

'Yes,' said Charlotte. 'Yes I suppose it might.'

Charlotte decided not to go home and change before Freddy's dinner; the Friday night traffic would be terrible and might make her late. She took her dress in with her: red crepe, slithery and draped, from Mme Grès in her new ready-to-wear American line. It was a dress she would never

454

have worn a year ago – a bold, extravagant dress which she knew didn't even suit her, she was too short and too baby-faced for it – but it was certainly a dress to go to the lions in. And she had a feeling they were ready for her.

'Charlotte, how nice!' Freddy was standing by the door of the dining room, greeting his guests. 'What a very grand dress. I do hope the occasion proves to be up to it.'

'Oh, of course it will, Freddy,' said Charlotte, smiling at him sweetly. 'It is already, surely. Here's a little congratulatory gift.'

She had spent a lot of much-resented time choosing a gift for Freddy and had finally settled on a gold moneyclip from Tiffanys. She resented giving it to him; she would have loved to have given it to Alexander or Charles, but clearly something was required. He took the exquisitely wrapped package and set it unopened on the small table beside him. 'How kind of you, Charlotte. Thank you so much.'

'My pleasure, Freddy.'

'Charlotte, dear, you look lovely and so sophisticated in that dress!' It was Betsey, smiling rosily above a mass of aubergine frills.

'Grandma, hallo. I'm so glad you're here. Where's Grandpa?'

'He's coming, dear. He's on the phone to Baby.'

'Ah. Er – how is Baby?'

'Fine, dear, I think.' Betsey sounded mildly puzzled. 'Why?'

'Oh – nothing.'

'Now here's Clement. Clement, dear, you've met my darling grand-daughter, haven't you?'

'Indeed I have.' Clement Dudley's stern face softened into what for him represented a smile: a just detectable softening at the edges of his mouth. 'I hear you are doing great things here, Charlotte. About to be promoted – or am I speaking out of turn?'

'You certainly are.' It was Fred; he had come into the room behind her. 'That's a very long way off. Especially at the moment.' But he winked at Charlotte as he spoke, and then eased Clement Dudley away from her. Charlotte stood, her heart thumping pleasurably fast. Promoted! To – what? VP? Must be. That was amazing. Fantastic. All the misery, the worry, the exhaustion of her week fell away; she felt warm, excited, pleasedly happy. She was doing all right: she must be. In spite of everything, her grandfather was pleased. She would shine at Praegers yet. She turned, smiling rapturously as she felt a light hand on her back, and found herself gazing into Jeremy's eyes.

'Oh! Jeremy. Hallo. How are you? Is Isabella here?'

'She is indeed. Over there, talking to Gabe.'

455

A pang of jealousy, irrational, violent, shot through Charlotte. Isabella was beautiful, charming, amusing, all the things she knew she was not; and Gabe was a sure-fire victim for such things. She looked across at the two of them, Isabella talking animatedly, Gabe laughing – he hardly ever laughed – his eyes taking in Isabella's six feet of dark beauty, and thought how she must seem to him, a short, dull, bossy English prefect. She sighed, and Jeremy laughed.

'Hey! What was that about?'

'Oh – nothing. I was just thinking – well, how lovely Isabella was, and how much I'd love to be tall and – and amusing.'

'Yes, and she is frigid, and interested only in herself,' said Jeremy. 'Believe me. Very very different from your lovely self.'

Charlotte took a deep breath. 'Jeremy – I – '

But Freddy had come over to them: Freddy with an oddly pleased look.

'Jeremy, how nice of you to come. You look very well.'

'Oh I am,' said Jeremy, 'extremely well. I just had a little holiday, you know, last week. Did some sailing, that sort of thing.'

'Oh really? Doesn't Isabella mind your going off without her?'

'No,' said Jeremy. 'She doesn't. She hates sailing. But how do you know, as a matter of interest, that she wasn't with me?'

'Oh, I saw her. At the MOMA opening. I was there with my mother. And my grandmother. We invited her back for supper, but she couldn't come. She was just a little put out that you weren't there. She was with that interior designer, what's his name, Dusty Winchester. So amusing. So effete. They were off to Elaine's. Oh, not just the two of them, I don't want to be putting ideas into your head. Quite a crowd were off. Although from what I know of Dusty, he's not exactly a threat to any marriage.'

Charlotte had just taken a sip of champagne; she swallowed it very fast and almost choked. Freddy had been with Betsey that night. At the house at East 80th Street. And Freddy – dear God, Freddy had been at Gabe's desk that morning, with that nonsense about the lunch date.

'Excuse me,' she said and moved across the room. Gabe was standing alone now, watching Isabella who had turned her lovely eyes on Fred.

Fred adored Isabella; he said she was the perfect woman. 'And the perfect wife,' he would add from time to time. 'Like mine. Only mine's better-looking of course.'

'Gabe,' Charlotte whispered, 'Gabe, come outside a second.'

'What? Oh, all right. Better not let Grandpa see us though. He'll think we're off to meet Beaufort.'

Outside in the corridor, she looked at him, half triumphant, half scared.

'Gabe, Freddy was at the house that night.'

'Fred! How do you know?'

'He just said so. He was at that – at some opening or other, with Betsey and Mary Rose. And then went back for supper. And Gabe, he was rooting through your desk that morning. It's him, it must be.'

'Holy shit,' said Gabe. 'Holy, holy shit.'

The evening was nearly over; she had got through it. Fred had made a short speech and Freddy a longer one. Everyone was chatting now; Fred III was leaning back in his chair laughing at something Isabella said to him. Charlotte felt almost faint with exhaustion and strain.

Freddy was watching her.

'Charlotte! Are you all right? You look a little pale.'

'Oh no. No, I'm fine. It's all right. Just a bit too much brandy.'

Everyone was staring; conversation had ceased altogether. Betsey looked concerned. 'Charlotte dear, are you OK?'

'I'm fine,' she said. 'Really.'

'You were looking so well,' said Freddy. 'Almost as well as you, Jeremy. Look at the pair of them, matching suntans. Or almost. You've been away too, haven't you, Charlotte? Last week, like Jeremy. Quite a coincidence.'

Charlotte froze; she could not have moved if she had been ordered at gun point. She forced herself to meet Freddy's eyes, his ice-cold blue eyes, staring at her in a kind of triumph, and realized suddenly, with clarity and absolute certainty, exactly what he was going to do. She was to be crucified, publicly, in front of her grandfather, Betsey, Isabella, Gabe, all the partners; everyone who mattered in her life. Knowing, knowing she was done for, that there was no escape of any kind, gave her courage; she smiled back at him, lifted her chin.

'Yes,' she said, 'wasn't it?'

She saw Fred look at her sharply, look at Jeremy; she met his gaze almost boldly.

'And where was it you went, Charlotte? The Bahamas, you said, I think?' said Freddy.

'I didn't actually say,' said Charlotte.

'Oh, I'm sorry. I thought you did. But weren't you sailing? With some very rich friend, I believe you said, who gave you that beautiful watch.'

'Yes, I was sailing. In the Bahamas,' said Charlotte. She was flushed now, looking down, but aware that Jeremy had drawn away from her, physically distanced himself as far as he could. There was a long silence.

'I think,' said Isabella, looking at Jeremy with some distaste, 'we should leave, if you will excuse us, Fred, Freddy. We have to go to Aspen in the morning, for a weekend's skiing. It's been such a lovely evening. Thank you so much.'

Fred stood up slowly. He was still looking at Charlotte as if she was something totally abhorrent to him; with an obvious effort he switched his eyes to Isabella. 'Of course. It's been great to have you with us. Thank you for coming. Jeremy, goodnight.' He shook Jeremy's hand briefly, avoided looking at him. They moved to the door. The whole party was breaking up. Charlotte sat utterly still, her head bowed, waiting. Only as Gabe passed her, on the other side of the table, did she look up, meet his eyes. He was looking at her with an expression she had never seen on his face before: she was too sick at heart to try to analyse it.

And finally they were all gone, and Betsey was banished, slightly puzzled and upset, to the car. Fred closed the door and leant against it.

'Is it true? Were you with Jeremy Foster? In the Bahamas?'

'Yes,' said Charlotte. 'Yes, I was.'

There was a long silence. Then:

'I'm so disappointed in you,' he said. 'So absolutely disappointed. You'll have to leave. You realize that. Go home. Maybe to the London office. I don't know. But you can't stay here. Not after this. You're a fool, Charlotte. An absolute fool.'

'I know,' she said. 'I know I am.'

Fred walked out and slammed the door.

Later, much later, lying in her bed, when she could cry no more, she drew comfort from just two things. One was that she had managed to retrieve the Tiffany moneyclip from the pile of presents for Freddy. The other was that she had analysed the expression on Gabe Hoffman's face. It had, without a shadow of doubt, been jealousy.

Chapter 38

Max, 1985

At four thirty p.m. they still hadn't done a single shot. The first model had arrived with spots and a headache, and couldn't fit into any of the skin-tight dresses; she said she was about to have her period and always blew up, it wasn't her fault. She was sent away, and they waited an hour while another girl was found. She had no spots, nor was she about to have her period, but she had no bust, and the dresses looked ridiculous on her. By this time the make-up artist who'd only been booked for two hours had left. Finally at almost four o'clock a very pretty, slightly debby girl arrived who fitted and suited the dresses perfectly; her name was Gemma Morton, she was seventeen, fresh from Benenden, and had only ever modelled twice before. It took a long time to get her hair right, and she made a mess of doing her own make-up and they had to send for another make-up artist, but finally she and Max were posed in front of a rather weary trio on the bandstand, in ever-more-absurd poses, and at six o'clock it was a wrap as the photographer, who fancied himself as a film cameraman, put it.

'Drink?' said Max to Gemma Morton.

'Yes, that would be very nice.'

She was dark, with a mane of long hair, big brown eyes and a just slightly chubby face. Her body on the other hand was not in the least chubby, she had long, slender, rangy legs and a very nice full bosom. Max decided he could really fancy her.

He took her to a pub in South Audley Street; he hoped she didn't have expensive tastes, he only had three pounds and he knew the cash machine wouldn't give him any more. She asked for a Campari soda. Max had half a pint of bitter. It left just enough over to buy her one more drink if she proved interesting.

'Have you been modelling long?' she said, pushing her hair back off her face and smiling at him rather ingenuously. 'It's fun, isn't it?'

Max, who had grown used to cool, world-weary models, found her rather engaging. 'Quite a while,' he said, 'long enough to be finding it less fun.'

'I really like it. I'm actually supposed to be still at school, doing my A levels, but I was really hating it, and I'm not actually very academic, so

459

Daddy said I could do this for a bit, and see how I got on. I'm probably going to do a History of Art course next year at the Courtauld. I want to work in a gallery.'

She smiled at him again.

'And what does Daddy do?' asked Max.

'He's a stockbroker,' said Gemma. 'It used to be a really boring job, but he's just started getting all these machines in, you know, ready for Big Bang. Have you heard about Big Bang?'

'Just about,' said Max.

He looked at her with new interest. Since Charlotte's fall from grace in New York, Fred III had made it very plain to Max that there was no chance of an opening in the bank for him. And Max was getting tired of modelling. Very tired indeed. Gemma's father was highly unlikely to be anything but a very large fish in the stockbroking pond; maybe he would be able to help him achieve his new ambition. He remembered a phrase from Gabe Hoffman, whom he had met after his morning with Chrissie Forsyte: 'When London goes upstairs,' he had said, 'it's going to be really wild.'

'Would you like another drink?' he said. 'I'm supposed to be on the wagon, watching my weight.'

Max had been genuinely enraptured by what he had seen on the trading floor at Praegers. He had sat next to Chrissie, silently captivated, staring past her across the vast room: a hundred white-faced people, a hundred black and green flickering screens, three hundred phones, all ringing, voices fighting with one another for a hearing. Huge clocks on every wall told the time in London, New York, Tokyo. He had no idea in which city he was, in which he was meant to be, he was in some indeterminate country with a new language, a new time scale, an entirely new culture, and he felt, given the minimum guidance, he could find his way around it with ease.

Chrissie smiled at him. 'Where was I? Oh yes. What we're doing is gambling, basically Did you ever gamble?'

Max nodded. 'Just occasionally.'

'That's all it is. Gambling. On a price. Of currency, on this desk; stock next door; commodities over there. Currency is the most exciting.'

A sudden hush fell on the room; Max looked up. The chief trader, a stout, swarthy man with an expression of ferocious intensity, had raised both his arms. There were great rings of sweat under them.

'Come on quick, give me dollars, give me yen.' Several people shouted at him; he listened to the tangled mass of information, for ten, maybe twenty seconds, turned, looked out of the window, spoke into his own phone.

'Some big order's come in,' said Chrissie. 'That's Chris Hill. They're all like that, but he's the most like it. He is just the greatest. You should watch him. If he'll let you. He works a twenty-hour day. Last year his wife spent one whole day with him. Christmas Day.'

Another girl came up to them. She smiled. 'How you doing, Chrissie?'

'Good,' said Chrissie, 'good. This market is just flying today.'

'I know,' said the girl. 'I know, I feel it.'

Max was so hyped up by then he could almost feel it himself. Suddenly he had seemed to have a nice, neat, and most pleasurable plan for his future. Fred III could give him a job either in New York or even London, and he could in due course get a fair-sized chunk of the bank for himself. Which would help to pay for the upkeep of Hartest, which was quite clearly prohibitive. Max had no idea of the details, but he did know the whole place hung on a knife edge.

And then Charlotte had had to blot her copy book in that idiotic, crass way and get sent home to London, in disgrace.

And as a result, there was the shadow of scandal and disgrace hanging over not just Charlotte, but the entire family, and as a further result there was no hope whatsoever (or so it seemed) for the Viscount Hadleigh to take up a position within the aegis of Praeger and Son, however much he might have taken it into his head that that was where he most wished to be, most wanted to do.

However (as it was often remarked around the photographic studios and more exclusive parties and night clubs and dinner tables of London), if Max Hadleigh fell down a sewer he would undoubtedly emerge clutching not just one, but a large handful of gold watches; and in the newly discovered arms of Miss Gemma Morton, model and debutante, he seemed set fair once again to do exactly that.

Chapter 39

Baby, 1985

Baby came through customs and looked for his driver; no use even thinking that Angie might be there. Parkinson held out his hands for Baby's bags, neat and expressionless in his grey uniform.

'Good evening, sir. Welcome back.'

'Thanks, Parkinson.'

'Good trip, sir?'

'Yes, on the whole.' Baby was tired; the news he had received in New York had not been guaranteed to make him feel any better. 'You have to take the rough with the smooth, don't you, Parkinson?'

'Yes, sir. The car is right outside, sir.'

Baby wondered if Parkinson would have said anything different if he had told him he had spent the entire five days in a gay brothel and encountered therein not only the President of the United States but the Queen of England, and decided he wouldn't.

It was early evening; in the spring dusk, even the landscape around the A4 looked quite pretty.

'Is Mrs Praeger at home, Parkinson?'

'No, sir. She asked me to give you this, sir.'

He handed him a letter; Baby felt slightly sick as he tore open the envelope. Angie's rather ugly, childish handwriting was at least easy to read.

'Dear Baby, Welcome back. I hope you've had a good time in the bosom of your family. It's been pretty exciting here, the twins are both well and Sandra has given in her notice. I have to be out this evening, with a client in deepest Essex. You should understand and sympathize with that one. May be late. Angie.'

Well, that was very affectionate. Made him feel glad he'd come back. What on earth was he supposed to have done? All those years, all that closeness, and now she was colder towards him half the time than Mary Rose had been. Baby folded the letter and put it in his pocket. He'd hoped to be able to talk to her this evening, tell her everything. Well, it could wait. It wasn't going to go away.

'Straight home, sir?'

'Er, no. No, let's go via the office. I'd like to pick up my messages, see what's been happening.'

'Very good, sir.'

They reached the Mall at seven o'clock, and promptly got stuck in a long line of taxis. Baby looked back at Buckingham Palace, and then towards Admiralty Arch and the awesomely classic beauty of Carlton Terrace. To his right, St James's Park, with its tangle of trees and birds and water, was sinking into the dusk. The sky was that deep dark turquoise seen only on clear spring evenings; the buildings were dark against it. Baby smiled, in spite of his gloom.

'This is a beautiful city of yours, Parkinson.'

'If you say so, sir,' said Parkinson, drawing up outside Praegers in St James's.

'I do, Parkinson. I do. Wait for me, will you? I won't be long.'

The building was in darkness; the night porter, just settled in with his sandwiches and his *Penthouse*, came to the door grumbling. When he saw it was Baby he switched on a polite obsequious smile and turned the *Penthouse* over on its face.

'Mr Praeger, sir. How are you, sir? Good to see you back, sir.'

'Very well, thank you, Willings. I'm just going up to my office. I'll be down in a while.'

'Very good, sir.'

Baby got into the lift, went up to the first floor. His office was in darkness, the desk horribly empty and un-busy-looking. He felt slightly sick looking at it, then told himself that of course it would be tidy, that he had been away, that Katy would have tidied it. But there were very few letters in the in-tray for him to see, just a few hopeful notes he had dictated, suggesting meetings, waiting for signature. He always hoped that when he went away things would by some magical process improve, gather momentum, but it had clearly been as dead as the week before he went. The days were increasingly quiet and empty, now that they had worked their way through so many major introductions. Baby sighed and went over to the window. Then he heard a sound from the neighbouring room and there, working away in her small pen, was Charlotte. She looked at him slightly sheepishly.

'Hallo, Baby. How are you?'

'I'm – OK,' he said slightly heavily. He was beginning to feel very tired. 'You're working late.'

'Well, I'm used to that, remember. This was early afternoon to Gabe. And I have things to do.'

'I'm pleased to hear it,' said Baby. He sighed.

Charlotte looked at him. 'Anything I can help with?'

463

'I'm afraid not, honeybunch. Don't worry. Are you – settling down all right?'

Charlotte had been in the London office for three weeks now; working for one of the assistant directors, ostensibly doing the same work she had done in New York, but in fact he knew she was finding it dull. Dull and slow. The whole operation was dull and slow. Like me, thought Baby, leaning against the door for a moment. He felt deathly weary. Charlotte looked at him.

'Uncle Baby, are you all right?'

'Yes, I'm fine. Just tired.' He looked at her and thought that she looked tired, too, tired and pale and subdued. He reflected on the wretched time she had been having; it might have been her own fault, some of it, she might have behaved extremely foolishly, but she was only twenty-three years old; and no doubt, in a lonely city, Jeremy Foster with his formidable charm and glamour had seemed fairly irresistible. Much of the blame for Charlotte's behaviour had to lie with him. But as usual, Jeremy would have got off scot free, while someone else paid the price. He had called Baby, full of expressed remorse, asked him to keep an eye on Charlotte for him. Baby had said shortly that he had no option, and rang off, making it plain that in this particular instance the client was not totally in the right. He smiled at Charlotte now, told her she looked as if she needed cheering up, and asked her if she would like to have a drink at the Ritz with him before he went home.

He sat silent over his drink, his mood sober. Charlotte, aware of it, said quietly, '*Are* you all right?'

'What? Oh, yes I'm fine.'

'You don't look fine,' she said firmly. 'You look awful.'

'Well – you know. Things aren't brilliant, are they? At the bank. You must see that for yourself. We just aren't getting many of the big ones. I'm pinning my hopes now on the opening. I can't quite understand where we're going wrong, people come and see us and seem impressed. Then they go cold on us. Gus says it's because we're American and new boys in town.' He sighed, then made a visible effort to smile at her. 'How is everyone treating you? Do you like Gus Booth?'

'Everyone's treating me fine. Thank you. Gus Booth seems very nice.'

'Well, he's certainly busting a gut for us. I was lucky to get him. He's out working on our behalf right now, talking to Tom Phillips from Boscombes. Big regional newspaper chain. I'm very hopeful about that one, as a matter of fact.'

'Good. Let's hope.'

464

He decided to broach the subject. 'Feeling any better about – things, darling?'

'Oh – ' she sighed, clearly wary of saying anything harsh about his friend, 'you know. One gets over these things, I'm told. I just can't believe I was that stupid.'

'Well – Jeremy is very clever,' said Baby, 'not to mention charming and persuasive. I don't think you should blame yourself too much.'

'Well I do,' she said, brisk suddenly. 'It was a ridiculous thing to do. Really ridiculous. It's quite right I should take the consequences.'

She sounded like her old self again, suddenly, very English, very well brought up. The combination of that with her new sophistication, her slimness, the expensive-looking black dress she was wearing, with the triple rope of pearls (he had noticed a great change in Charlotte's wardrobe since he had last spent much time with her) was very sexy. He could see why Jeremy had fancied her.

'How were you getting along with Freddy?' he said suddenly.

'Oh – fine. He's doing really well, isn't he?'

There was a note in her voice he couldn't quite analyse; jealousy probably. Well, it would do her good to lose her place in the sun for a while. Poor old Freddy had suffered long enough.

Conversation between them was very stilted; it saddened Baby. He finished his drink, asked her if she'd like another. 'No, thank you. I ought to be getting home.' She was staying in Eaton Place while she looked for a flat.

'Heavy date?'

'Yes. With a washing machine.'

'Ah.' He produced his credit card and asked for the bill; it came, and he picked up the pen, and for the first time in this particular situation, the horror happened. He couldn't grip it, couldn't sign his name. He fumbled, sweating, looked up at the waiter, smiling awkwardly, desperately.

'Sorry,' he said, 'cramp. So sorry.'

'Here,' said Charlotte, putting a ten-pound note quickly onto the tray. 'My treat. I owe you anyway.'

He looked down, when the waiter had gone, infinitely miserable. 'Sorry, darling.'

'Uncle Baby, you just have to talk about this. What is it? Does Angie know?'

'No,' he said with a heavy sigh, 'no, we're not communicating too well just at the moment. I don't talk to her about anything very much.'

'Well, tell me. It might help.'

Baby told her.

465

He walked into the house an hour later, after dropping her off; it was very quiet. Angie was always out, her evening in Essex, or wherever she was, had become the rule rather than the exception. He saw more of Mrs Wicks (who was installed in the new house, as at St John's Wood, in the basement flat) than he did of Angie; she would often pop up of an evening, as she put it, if he was alone, and cook him a little something. 'You must eat,' she would say severely, and if Baby protested would tell him he looked terrible, more terrible every day. 'Worse than Mr Wicks looked, before he died' was one of her favourite remarks. Even in his depression Baby found this so unlikely that it always cheered him up, and he would obediently eat the soup, or the toasted sandwich, or the Welsh rarebit that was her speciality and that she had introduced him to. She never ate with him, but sat and watched him with great attention, refilling his glass constantly the moment it was more than half empty, and giving him detailed accounts of what had happened in the various soap operas she watched. Baby would become rather drunk rather quickly, and get more than a little confused about which soap was which, so that on the rare occasions when he watched *Dallas* or *Dynasty*, or *Coronation Street*, he would expect J.R. to walk into the Rovers Return, or see Hilda Ogden going into shoulder-padded combat with Alexis. He knew Mrs Wicks was saddened and even embarrassed by Angie's behaviour, but they were both too loyal to her to say so, and found a solution in never mentioning her at all, which made their relationship all the more bizarre. Mrs Wicks also took a great interest in the bank's affairs; he once rather rashly admitted that he didn't have a great many clients, and she had insisted on giving him her savings, and the money Angie had put by for her (£10,000), to invest; she knew it wasn't a lot, she said, but every little helped. Baby told her gravely that indeed it did, and invested it himself in some gilts for her. He often told her, and meant it, that she was the nicest female he had ever known, barring his own mother.

Angie came in just after midnight. She was slightly flushed, and looked very pretty in a little sliver of a black dress. She ran up the stairs and into their room, came over to the bed where Baby was reading, bent to kiss him. Baby looked at her coolly.

'Hallo, Baby. Welcome home.'

'Thank you.'

'I'm sorry I couldn't be here to greet you in person.'

'I'm sorry too.'

'But you know, Baby, better than anyone, business is business.'

'Indeed. And how busy you are, aren't you, Angie?'

She looked at him, and he saw a careful look come into her green eyes. 'I'm sorry?'

'I said you seem to have been very busy. How was this evening?'

'Boring.'

'You don't look particularly bored. That's a very pretty dress to wear to – where was it?'

'Essex.'

'Ah yes. Did you just go to – Essex? Nowhere else?'

'No of course not.' She sounded impatient. 'I went out with the commuter traffic as a matter of fact, it was a nightmare, very stupid of me, left town at fiveish, and hit Romford at seven thirty.'

She came over to the bed, leant down to kiss him again. Baby turned his face away.

He went into the office early; Gus Booth was already there at his desk. He looked up and smiled. 'Baby! Welcome back.'

'Thanks, Gus.' Baby sat down rather heavily on the edge of his desk. He felt weary, and his bones seemed to ache. 'How was last night?'

'I'm sorry?'

'With Tom Phillips. Your dinner.'

'Oh – no go, I'm afraid.'

'Oh God.' Baby sighed. He felt sick suddenly; aware of how much he had been hoping for some good news. 'So – what went wrong?'

'Well – the usual, I'm afraid. Feels we're too much of a new boy. Don't have quite the weight. Maybe we can get in touch a little later. Keep the lines of communication open. Et cetera et cetera.'

It was a long day: a long week: a long month. They got a number of small, a couple of medium-size accounts; but it was not enough. Not enough to get them flying, up there with a chance, talked about, looked at, considered. They were failing, before they had begun. And because time was running out on them, every day made the failure more serious, the situation harder to turn around. It was not a serious failure, but it was most clearly not a success. And given the investment, the backing, the associations they had, it should have been. But the competition was intense. Not for nothing was a new bunch in the Square Mile known as the Thundering Herd, comprising most of the big American names – Chase, Security Pacific, Shearson Lehman, Goldman Sachs (together with the inevitable Japanese names – Nomura, Daiwa, Nikko). In the absurdly heady piratical climate of the run-up to Big Bang, where there were more dawn raids than dawns, companies endlessly under scrutiny and attack, bid for, bought, merged, restructured, relaunched, where it was said there was not a meeting room in London available even for breakfast, where planeloads of merchant bankers roared off every morning in pursuit of their prey, Praegers UK was a wallflower at the ball.

'We have to do something,' said their new PR consultant, Compton Manners, to Baby over lunch, a few weeks before the launch. 'We have to do something to get your credibility up. That's the problem. No credibility.'

'Well that's your problem,' said Baby, unusually irritable. 'I hired you to give me credibility, Compton. So far, you've hung onto it.'

'I know. I admit it. I'm very sorry. We've done all the right things. The reception, the breakfasts, playing on the Praeger name. But it isn't carrying the weight. What we need –' He stopped, stared at Baby. 'I just had an idea.'

'Well, we certainly need one or two of those,' said Baby. 'What is it?'

'Your brother-in-law. Lord Caterham. Would he help, do you think?'

Baby stared at him. 'In what way? What could Alexander do? He wouldn't know a client if it spat him in the eye.'

'He doesn't need to. He just needs to lend us his name.'

'How do you mean?'

'Well – allow me to plant a few stories about the family. Maybe what's known as a photo opportunity at the house, with the children. With Charlotte, primarily, as she works for you, but maybe the others too. So that Praegers is linked with this very English dynasty. I really think it would help, Baby. Could you ask him, do you think?'

'I'll ask him,' said Baby. 'I don't know how much good it would do, but I'll ask him. I'd ask God to sit in on a photo opportunity if I thought it would do any good. But I'm not hopeful. He's a cold fish, my brother-in-law, and he has an absolute obsession with that house of his. But you never know.'

'Well, we have to do something,' said Manners. 'Otherwise you'll just have to pack up and go back to the Big Apple.' He smiled and tried to make it clear he was joking.

'From where I'm sitting,' said Baby, 'that looks like kind of a nice idea. Give me a few days to think about it, Compton. I'll get back to you.'

He decided to ask Angie what she thought of the idea. She was so close to Alexander, maybe she could even broach the subject for him. He hadn't talked to her about anything for so long; maybe it would break the awful cold circle they had got themselves into. He called her at her office, and asked her if she was going to be home early that evening, that he wanted to talk to her; she sounded cool, distant, but said she'd try not to be too late. She was seeing clients, she told Baby briefly; he was too depressed, too heartsick to question her. He went home early himself with a heavy heart, picked at a plate of Welsh rarebit Mrs Wicked cooked for him, and was watching television in his den when he heard her car. In spite of everything, his heart always lifted when he knew he was going to see her; he went to the top of the stairs to greet her.

She walked in through the front door and stood staring up at him; she was very pale, and her make-up was smudged. She had been crying; she looked almost dazed. Baby stared at her, wondering what had happened.

Angie started to walk up the stairs towards him and she was crying again, now, great tears brimming over in her green eyes. Baby held out his arms, and she went into them, blindly, like a child. She stood there for a while, her face buried against him; then she stood back, studying him very intently, as if she had never seen him before. Finally she spoke.

'Why didn't you tell me?' she said.

Charlotte had told her; had phoned her and said she wanted to see her, told her there was something she simply had to know.

'Bossyboots,' said Baby, half irritated, half relieved. 'I'm sure she thinks she's still running the school council.'

'Well maybe. But I'm grateful. I don't know what might have happened to us if she hadn't.'

They were sitting up in bed, toasting their reunion – a spectacular one – in champagne, misery and fear temporarily held in abeyance. Baby tried to explain why he hadn't wanted to tell her. Why he hadn't wanted to tell anyone about it. It was because he felt somehow, he said, that while he didn't talk about it, didn't name it, didn't give it any recognition, it didn't really exist. The minute he said hey, look everyone, I have this terrible thing, and everyone started saying, hey, Baby Praeger has this terrible thing, he would be watched, worried over, sympathized with, stamped 'invalid'; until that happened, he could pretend, tell himself it was nothing, a few odd little symptoms, small unimportant blips in his personal mechanism. He had enough troubles at the moment, without adding sickness, terminal fatal sickness to them. If he ignored at least that one, maybe, just maybe it would go away. Or at least stay dormant, quiet. That was exactly how he visualized it, an obscene, sleeping beast; he did not want it disturbed.

'But you were doing such harm,' said Angie. 'To both of us. If I'd known I'd – '

'Yes. What would you have done?'

'Oh – you know. Been nicer.'

'Well – I'm sorry. It was my way of coping.'

'Pretty funny way,' said Angie. 'How many doctors have you seen, and how sure are they?'

Compton Manners phoned him the following afternoon.

'Hallo, Baby. Have you talked to your brother-in-law yet?'

'No,' said Baby. 'No, I haven't. I'm sorry.'

'Please give it a try, Baby. We could do something good there.'

'I'll ask,' said Baby.

'Alexander! Hi, it's Baby.'

'Hallo, Baby. How are you?'

'I'm fine. Asbo – Alsoblutely – ' Baby realized with a sudden sick horror that he was having trouble enunciating his words. It hadn't happened before, but he had been told that it might. It was one of the earlier symptoms. Something he should look out for, not be too alarmed by. Just a slight slurring occasionally – at first. Later you sounded permanently drunk, and then you couldn't speak at all. They had also said it shouldn't happen for a while yet. Not at the very early stage. So – was the stage not so early? Or was he galloping rather swiftly towards a later stage? Panic engulfed Baby, blind, hot panic. He felt sick, gripped the edge of his desk with his hand. His weak hand. It seemed reassuringly strong and normal. He swallowed hard, told himself not to be a neurotic fool. 'I'm fine,' he said firmly.

'You don't sound fine.' Alexander seemed concerned. 'What can I do for you?'

'I – wondered if I could come and see you. Want to ask you something. Over the weekend, maybe? We might come down to Watersfoot. Angie's dep – dep – ' Christ, it was going again – this was a nightmare – 'desperate,' he said finally, his voice very loud, 'desperate for me to spend some time there.' There, he'd got it out. It was OK. Just a silly slip. Nothing really.

'Of course,' said Alexander. 'I'll be delighted to see you. Sunday morning? Baby, are you sure you're all right?'

'Oh! Oh, yes of course. Fine. Honestly. Just a – a bit too much to drink. Heavy lunch. That's all. Tried to cut it down, but it keeps creeping up on me. You know what they say. Once a drunk always a drunk.'

'Oh yes,' said Alexander. 'I know what they say.'

Chapter 40

Alexander, 1973

'Once a drunk always a drunk.' The doctor had looked at Alexander very solemnly. 'I'm afraid your wife is a fairly bad case. Her drinking seems to be rooted in a disturbance, a neurosis, that I have been unable to get to the bottom of. She has worked very hard, we all have. And she's off it now. But you have to remember that she will always, always be at risk. Any strain and she becomes totally vulnerable.'

Alexander had nodded. 'Yes. Yes, I understand.'

'But – with care, and patience, and a strong wish of her own to succeed, she should be all right.'

'Good. Yes, that sounds good.'

'You must be watchful, Lord Caterham. Don't put temptation her way, don't leave her alone if she is upset or stressed, try to save her from any unnecessary trauma.'

'Yes of course. I love her very much. I want her to succeed.'

'I know you do. I've been very impressed by your patience and your forbearance with her. She's lucky to have you.'

'Well – I have tried. I intend to keep trying.'

'Good.'

It was true; he did want her to succeed. He had been frightened by the drinking, as well as upset by it, and sorry for her. And horribly, hideously grieved by the death of the baby. He often wondered why he was not more angry with her about that, about wilfully killing her child, which was what it had amounted to, but he was not; he had seen her own terrible grief and remorse, had known he was to a degree to blame himself, and anger was the one emotion he did not experience. But he had been afraid, and he had been revolted. It had been hideous to see the beautiful, cool woman he loved so much become ugly, stumbling, fumbling, dependent.

When she had started drinking, gaily, foolishly self-indulgent, it had irritated him, it had never amused him; but the irritation had never, as it logically might have done, turned to anger, it had turned to fear.

He watched her flirting, behaving outrageously at parties, and he had had the humiliation of half carrying her out as she giggled foolishly, waving to everyone in sight; and he had been terrified. And he had hated the hangovers, the white-faced headaches, the lying in bed, the vomiting (insisting she had eaten something that hadn't agreed with her), it had all revolted him.

He had tried so hard to stop her, tried reason, tried hostility, but she had ignored the former, and the latter had made her worse, had made her drink for comfort, for reassurance. It had been such a relief when she had told him she was pregnant; now, he thought, surely she would have to stop.

But it hadn't worked that way; she had been so fearful, so anxious that the third baby would be a boy, so emotionally vulnerable, she had drunk for comfort, increasingly as the months went by.

And then the baby had been born, and had died, tiny, white, sad little Alexander, with his stick-like limbs and his large clumsy joints, his tiny eyes, his restless, painful movements, leaving him with a sorrow so deep and dreadful that he had wondered how he would ever feel anything else. He had been angry then, he had raged, but not at Virginia; he had raged at Fate, at himself, at the doctors, anything, everything, but the sad, sick woman who had lain in her hospital bed and said she wished she was dead, she was so sorry and so ashamed.

And then after that it had got worse; she had drunk more, harder, to forget, she had refused help, had refused even to try, had told him that she needed it, that it was the only thing that didn't let her down. Alexander had never forgotten the agony of hearing her say that, of seeing her face when she said it, her bleak, hostile face. And still he had not given up, had gone on trying to help her; even when she had attacked him with her broken glass, and he had had to have stitches in his neck, he had still continued to be hopeful, loving, tender with her.

It had been terrible to witness her suffering in the clinic, dreadful to see, to feel her withdraw from him; but still he went on, visiting her every day, bringing her an endless supply of different soft drinks, the cigarettes she had started to smoke, plying her with chocolates, and gradually she came back to him – frail, frightened, and very dependent.

Her dependence pleased him; it made the problems, the unpleasantness less hard to endure. He liked the way she clung to him, even physically, asked his advice about everything, seemed unable to do anything without him at her side. The one thing that did grieve him, angered him even, was the way she refused to go home to Hartest.

She did in the end of course; after visiting her parents, and having a holiday with Baby, she said yes, she could go back. It had hurt too, the way she had been so afraid of it, not recognized the beautiful, healing atmosphere of the place, he had found that absolutely incomprehensible, and the way too she clung to him in the car, held his hand so tightly as she walked up the steps that his knuckles were red and tender afterwards. It had been a rejection of himself, a threat almost, he felt, to everything that most mattered to him, to them both; but she had conquered it, had settled again into her life and role as mistress of the place, and in time he had begun to forget.

And then Hartest was really threatened. Threatened financially. He had lost money on the stock market, more on his failed stud farm; but the really bad news had been that the place was infected with dry rot and subsidence. 'You need a new roof,' the man from the dry rot company had said, 'and a virtual rebuilding.' The initial estimate had been between four and five million. Alexander had almost nothing. The farm had never made a profit, in a good year it broke even; he had no money at all, no cash, everything he possessed was bound up in the house and the land.

Panic struck Alexander; blind, unreasoning panic. He had gone out and stood at the top of the Great Drive, looked down at the house, standing exquisitely golden and serene in the sunlight, and tried to visualize it crumbling, rotting, dying. Tears had sprung to his eyes. Somehow he had to get the money. He couldn't fail Hartest. He couldn't.

Virginia was in New York. She spent more and more time there. He hated it, but he let her go. It made her happy, and kept her safe. He called her, told her what had happened, listened impatient, shocked, but hardly surprised as she told him she had very little of her own personal fortune left, asked her (shrinking from talking to Fred, from revealing his incompetence) if she thought Baby would help. She said she wasn't sure if he would be able to do anything, but that she would ask him; she phoned next day to say such a large sum was outside Baby's discretion.

'Then I will have to talk to your father.'

'Well, Baby has offered to talk to him first. To pave the way. Would you like that?'

'Very kind,' said Alexander shortly. He found it increasingly difficult to be civil to Baby.

Fred had been intolerable; smug, playing cat and mouse, suggesting he should sell his Van Gogh, his Monet. Alexander sat quietly, willing himself to remain calm, pretending to consider the suggestions. When Fred said he should open Hartest to the public, set up a motor museum and a funfair, he felt physically sick; he closed his eyes briefly, feeling the room sway round him. Then he managed to smile, to look positive.

'What I really hoped for,' he said carefully, 'was a loan. On a strictly business basis, of course.'

And Fred had looked at him, his sharp eyes snapping with amusement, and said no, he would not even consider it, and then, as if eager to extract as much pleasure from the interview as possible, had added that he would give Alexander a very good price for the Monet.

He would probably have spared Virginia even then; had she not sided with her father over the house, and said opening to the public seemed to her a sensible thing to do, that Blenheim and Castle Howard had not been damaged by the experience, that at least the house would be safe. He had been so angry, then, he had wanted to hurt her so much; and it had been then, at that moment, that he had seen what he would have to do.

It had been quite complex, really, pulling all the elements together; but he had enjoyed it in a way.

Suggesting to his mother that he took Georgina up to stay with her, that had been a master stroke: 'Ma?' he had said, 'Ma, I think this nonsense has gone on long enough. I am terribly terribly sorry to have been loyal to Virginia, in keeping the children from you; it has been very difficult, but I can see I was wrong. If you will forgive me and allow me to at least bring Georgina up to see you, it would make me very happy. She is the most amazing child, mature far beyond her years, I know you will love her.'

And after an initial coldness, his mother had been so delighted, so eager to meet her grandchildren, that her pleasure alone eased any guilt he had been feeling. And then once they had been there, seeing how much she liked Georgina, how happy she was, it had been ridiculously easy to suggest that she should meet Charlotte and Max too. It would be very bleak for Virginia, alone at Hartest, without the children, with no Easter egg hunt to run, no lunch party, no one to talk to. But then it had been bleak for him, alone there too, even though he had had the children, for almost two months; she would see perhaps how hard it was for him to bear, and be sorry. And it had been a master stroke taking the children off on a camping trip, so they wouldn't even be at the castle if she wanted to speak to them.

It had been quite easy, finding out about her new prospective clients. They were all listed in her files. Virginia's efficiency was awe-inspiring.

And then they each received a call, from her doctor at the clinic, and

474

then from himself, saying she was really not very well just at the moment, not well enough to be taking on any more work, and that it would be a kindness simply not to give her the business; that had been easy too.

And a similar call to Catriona Dunbar, telling her that Virginia was simply not up to taking on the strain of the Riding for the Disabled Committee (which Virginia had told him she had decided to accept, that she was pleased to have been asked) and that the kindest thing she could do was pretend it was too late, that they had someone else on the committee now.

Probably that would be enough. Of course he couldn't be sure; but the situation was very promising. She would be alone, vulnerable, depressed. Nanny was away, and she would be too hurt at Catriona's rejection to spend any time with the Dunbars. He had made sure that the door to the cellar was unlocked. It might not work, but it probably would.

When they got back from Scotland, she had undoubtedly been drinking. She wasn't quite drunk, but she had been drinking. He could smell it on her breath. He was distant with her, cold.

Next day she was drinking again. And then the children went back to school, and she went to London and he left her forty-eight hours and then went to find her, and she was hopelessly drunk. And that night, as they sat having dinner, he told her that it was going to break his heart, but he thought he would have to open Hartest to the public after all. He followed her out to the kitchen; she was making herself a hot drink, she said. The hot drink smelled reassuringly of whisky. He drove back to Hartest that night.

Baby phoned him. He said he had called Virginia in London, as Alexander had suggested, and that she had sounded very drunk. Was she drinking again? Hadn't she just been to a clinic to dry out?

Alexander had said, yes, she was drinking, heavily, and he didn't know what to do. The doctor had said it was the strain, worry about Hartest. He was distracted and worried himself, unable to care for her adequately. And of course her clinic bills had been enormous, running into thousands.

Baby said he would pay the clinic bills and asked what Alexander was going to do about Hartest.

Alexander told him he simply didn't know.

★

He arranged for Virginia to go back into the clinic. He rang Baby and told him, thanked him for his help.

Fred rang. He said he couldn't have Virginia sick again, that it was disgusting and appallingly bad for the children and both family names, and that if the new roof was going to cure her, then there had better be a new roof.

When he saw how happy Virginia was at the news, he almost managed to persuade himself that he had been telling Baby the truth.

Chapter 41

Angie, 1985

'OK, I want the whole truth,' said Angie. 'No hedging, no sparing my feelings. Just tell me. Please.'

She was very pale; her eyes looked enormous. She was wearing jeans and a black sweater, and cowboy boots. Dr Curtis smiled at her.

'You look hardly old enough,' he said, 'to be Mr Praeger's wife. More like his daughter.'

'I'm not his wife,' said Angie briefly, 'and I do assure you I'm a lot older than his daughter. But I do love him and I live with him, I'm the mother of some of his children, and I need to know what I'm in for. I'm getting a little tired of all this evasion.'

Dr Curtis looked at her sharply. Her lip and her voice had quivered just momentarily.

'I'm sorry, Miss – '

'Burbank.'

'Burbank. I didn't mean to be evasive. You're obviously a brave girl. All right, then, I'll give you the whole truth. Mr Praeger has, as you know, motor neuron disease. A wasting away of the cell stations and the neurons, that is to say nerves from the brain, responsible for moving muscles. As they waste, the muscles waste. There is a consequent weakness throughout the limbs. As the disease progresses, the arms and legs become not only weak but stiff, and they often twitch. Walking becomes increasingly hard and it is very difficult for the patient to hold anything.' He paused. 'Is this really what you want to know?'

She nodded, her eyes fixed on his like a rabbit with a fox.

'I wouldn't say I want to. But I need to.'

'Very well. Later, there is a problem with the control of speech – it will be slurred initially, eventually becoming almost unintelligible. Eating is another problem, swallowing is difficult, and there is a danger of choking. Some patients – ' He paused.

'Yes? Some patients what?'

'Some patients tend to dribble, they cannot control the flow of saliva, you see.'

'Oh shit,' said Angie.

'Your – Mr Praeger's chest muscles will become weak, his breathing may be difficult, especially at night.'

'Treatment?' asked Angie very quietly.

'None, really. Physiotherapy can be helpful. Gentle swimming can help the muscles. Splints can be made to help the grip. Drugs can ease the muscular jerking.'

'And – what is the prognosis? I mean how long does he have?'

'It's hard to say. Three to five years. Maybe less. Few people live for more than five years after diagnosis.'

'I see,' said Angie. 'Well, thank you. It may seem a little hard for you to believe but I feel better now. Does Mr Praeger know all this?'

'I have given him a slightly – shall we say – sanitized version. I have certainly not buoyed him up with false hopes.'

'Good. None of it sounds too sanitized.' She smiled briefly. 'So Dr Curtis, what should I do? Should he be encouraged to give up work?'

'Absolutely not. If he enjoys it. But I have to say, in all honesty, I don't think he will be able to work for very long. He – '

'Yes?'

'He seems to be deteriorating quite fast. The right hand is considerably weaker than I would have expected at this stage.'

'Oh.' It was a small bleak sound.

'The worst thing, of course, is coming to terms with it. And living with it. Recognizing what has to happen. Accepting what help can be given. False hopes are definitely not helpful. He must confront it, and try to accept it.'

'He'll confront it all right,' said Angie, 'but I don't think he'll ever accept it.'

Angie felt very odd, frightened and yet oddly calm at the same time. She went for a walk in Regent's Park, looked at the trees with their fresh green leaves and thought inconsequentially that soon they would turn dusty and brown and start to die, and it seemed oddly and harshly appropriate. She thought of Baby, and what was going to happen to him, saw him frail and immobilized and helpless, his vigour gone, his capacity for extracting pleasure from every corner of his life gone, saw him frail and weak instead of vital and strong, and for perhaps the first time in her life she did not think for a moment of herself, of what it would mean to her, but wondered simply how he would bear it.

Chapter 42

Charlotte, 1985

'You cannot be serious!' McEnroe's petulant face stared up at the umpire, his racket hanging from an arm limp with disbelief.

Charlotte smiled indulgently at him; he reminded her of Gabe.

'Spoilt brat!' said a voice beside her. 'Needs a good thrashing if you ask me.'

'Maybe,' said Charlotte politely. The voice belonged to Brian Watson, MD of Watson and Shell, one of their most important new cliens. 'Mr Watson, your glass is empty, let me find you some more champagne.'

'Thank you, Charlotte. Very kind. Never normally drink at this hour, of course. Need m'nerves soothed, watching that young whipper-snapper. Should have been sent to a decent school.'

'Yes, I expect so,' said Charlotte carefully. She held out the glass to Baby who was on her other side, nursing the ice box with the champagne in it. 'Mr Watson's glass, Baby. Are you all right?'

'Yes, of course I am,' he said irritably. Irritability was one of the major symptoms manifested by his illness at the moment. Charlotte had never expected to feel sympathy with Angie, but she quite often did these days. Baby passed her the bottle of champagne with his left hand.

'Oh, marvellous!' Brian Watson was beaming, his hostility to McEnroe temporarily halted. 'Did you see that ace?'

'Yes,' said Charlotte, who hadn't, passing the glass back to him, 'and I saw that one,' she added as McEnroe took his third straight set and the Centre Court roared its usual slightly grudging approval. 'Shall we go in search of some strawberries, Mr Watson?'

She filled him a large bowlful, smothered it in cream, took it to him as he sat between Baby and Gus Booth in the hospitality tent, and then excused herself. 'I want to get an extra programme,' she said, 'I'll be back in a minute.'

God, this corporate entertaining was hard work; she'd always loved Wimbledon, but this didn't seem too much like fun at all. Well, if it was helping Baby keep the clients he'd got, it was worth it. The client list still wasn't looking terribly healthy, even after the launch at Spencer House. And they had a very important prospective client coming along a little later, Jerry Mills from Nicolsons, the electronics people. She rather liked Jerry Mills, he was large and brash and vulgar and fun, very different from the stuffy Brian Watson. And Mrs Watson, with her refinement, her tutting at McEnroe's behaviour, her ceaseless royal box watching. She had hardly seen a single game since the Princess of Wales had arrived.

'Charlotte!' said a voice. 'Hi. How are you?'

'Sarah! I'm fine. How lovely to see you.' Sarah Ponsonby had been at school with her, they had been prefects together in the sixth.

'I thought you'd gone to New York.'

'Oh – I came back. Long story.'

'But you're still working with Praegers?'

'Oh, yes of course. What are you doing?'

'I've joined you. Well, your world. I'm working for Routledge.'

'Routledge! Really? Is it fun?'

'Great fun. Of course I'm just a frightfully small cog in the wheel, but I have my sights set higher. Gus Booth is with you, isn't he? How do you like him? I've met Jemima a few times, you know she's a Routledge by birth, and she's an absolute hoot.'

'Oh, he's very nice,' said Charlotte, 'not exactly a hoot, but still. He's here, actually. Are you working, Sarah, or watching the tennis?'

'Working,' said Sarah with a sigh. 'With a special brief to take care of an important new client. Very lechy. Every time McEnroe swears, he pats my thigh. Oh, God, here he is.' She switched on a careful smile. 'Mr Phillips! I hope you're not deserting us.'

'Of course not. Just looking out for Mrs Phillips, that's all. She's late. Spot of bother with the babysitter.' He nodded at Charlotte and smiled. 'Enjoying the tennis?'

'Oh, I'm sorry,' said Sarah, 'Mr Phillips, this is an old school friend of mine, Lady Charlotte Welles. Charlotte, Tom Phillips. A very important person indeed.'

'How do you do,' said Charlotte, smiling, taking Tom Phillips' hand, feeling its moist, warm, over-effusive grasp. 'What do you do that you're so important, Mr Phillips?'

'Oh, run a little company,' he said, smiling back at her.

'Little company!' said Sarah. 'He runs Boscombes, Charlotte, you know, who own all those zillions of local papers.'

'Of course,' said Charlotte. The name did ring a bell.

It was not until the evening, back at Eaton Place, that Charlotte made the connection. She recalled, with great vividness, the evening at the Ritz. It had been the evening Baby had told her about his illness; when she had made the decision to tell Angie; and the evening he had been telling her his worries about Praegers' rather limited success. And what had he said? She heard his voice quite clearly in her head: he had said, 'Gus Booth is working for us right now. Talking to Tom Phillips, from Boscombes. I'm very hopeful about it.'

But Tom Phillips and Boscombes had failed to come up trumps, to deliver, to join Praegers, and Baby had been visibly upset when he told her.

And they had gone to Routledge instead; that in itself did not mean a great deal, nothing at all probably, except for a further memory, very recent, of Sarah's voice saying, 'Gus Booth is with you. Jemima's a Routledge by birth.'

At first Charlotte had been too unhappy, too homesick for New York and for Gabe and her life there to care what happened to Praegers UK, but after a few weeks and learning about, being forced to face the implications of, Baby's illness, she had become involved, concerned, determined for them to do well, to prove to Fred they could succeed. And it was therapy of a sort.

She wasn't sure what made her most unhappy: her banishment from New York, her humiliation at Jeremy's hands, or the removal of Gabe from her life. They were each, individually, misery enough: set together as components of a whole, they were a source of very severe pain. Jeremy had called her repeatedly and written to her; she had refused to talk to him, to return his calls, she tore his letters up.

Days without Gabe were dreadful and dead: empty not only of his presence and the constant turmoil he had created in her, but the excitement of working with him, the constant charging of adrenalin; and it was hard for her to separate that from the misery of losing the job she had loved so much, the sense that she was making some kind – quite some kind – of progress, that she was climbing, steadily and relentlessly, towards her ultimate, heady goal. Cast into what seemed like the sleepy backwater of the London office, her future uncertain, uncharted, she felt lost, confused – and unmotivated. The man she was working for, Peter Donaldson, was nice: not a mover and a shaker exactly, but highly competent, and extremely kind and considerate. The main problem was that the days moved at a pace that seemed not just slow, but virtually static; she had left a roller coaster and found herself on a treadmill.

Praegers had seemed set to do so well, they were a blue-chip bank, and what did it matter that they were – what was it Gus Booth had called them? – new boys in town? There were dozens of new boys in town and they were all doing really well. Why not Praegers?

*

She was having lunch with Charles St Mullin next day, and decided to talk to him about it. She talked to Charles about almost everything that happened to her; he had become her best friend. In her initial misery she had been tempted to resign from Praegers, and train for the Bar, follow in Charles's footsteps. She had even discussed a change of course with Charles; he had advised her not to make it. He said he felt she had banking in her blood and that she was going to succeed at it. And partly because she knew he was right, partly because she could still see the expression of intense pleasure on Freddy's face as he engineered her downfall in New York, she set aside the temptation to leave. She was going to stay at Praegers and she was going to win, and one day she would outflank Freddy, and Praegers would be at the very least half hers.

Meanwhile, Charles was enjoying having her in London again, he said; in fact he felt like writing both to Jeremy Foster and Freddy Praeger personally, to thank them for delivering her back to him.

They met every week, over long gossipy lunches, discussing the past, their respective presents, and to an extent their futures and how much of them might be shared.

'So I expect it's silly,' she said to him, after outlining her story about Routledge and Praegers, 'but I just think it's faintly fishy. Don't you?'

'I don't know enough about your world to know,' said Charles, 'I think you need to do a little more investigation into the background.'

The investigation proved easier than she had expected.

Charlotte wasn't sure what she thought about Gemma. She seemed sweet but slightly ridiculous, clearly besotted with Max, hanging on his arm and his every word. 'She's exactly what he doesn't need,' she had said crossly to Georgina, who was spending a weekend in London with her, 'making him think he's God, boosting his ego. If there's an ego in the world that doesn't need boosting it's Max's.'

'Oh, he's not that bad,' said Georgina, 'and maybe the love of a good woman is what he needs.'

Charlotte sighed. Georgina had always been inclined to be blind to Max's faults. 'He doesn't need anything, except perhaps getting away from that awful Tommy.'

'Well I don't know,' said Georgina. 'He came to Hartest the other weekend, with Gemma, Max I mean, and he was really nice to Daddy. You know how Daddy longs for him to be the devoted son. Well I really thought he was trying.'

'He's up to something,' said Charlotte briefly. 'How's Kendrick?'

Georgina's pale face flushed, and her eyes became soft and bright and larger than ever.

'He's fine. Not long now till the summer. He sends me lots of tapes,' she added with almost childlike pride.

'Tapes?' said Charlotte, amused. 'Who by?'

'Himself, stupid. Talking. He's no good at letter writing, he says, well he isn't, so I write to him and he sends me tapes back. It works really well.'

'Good,' said Charlotte slightly absently. 'Georgie, do you think you could try and talk Daddy into letting us do this photo session at Hartest? For the press? It just might help Baby.'

'I can't think how it could,' said Georgina, 'but anyway, I don't need to. He's agreed. Angie's asked him. I thought you knew.'

'No I didn't,' said Charlotte with a stab or irritation. 'Nobody told me.'

Compton Manners had managed to persuade the *Mail on Sunday* to run a feature on the two dynasties, as he called the Praegers and the Caterhams.

A photographer and a writer spent a long Sunday at Hartest, trailing the family round the house and the estate: they were photographed on the front steps, in the library, on the flying staircase, and at the top of the Great Drive (most of them on horseback) with the house standing below them like some exquisitely painted backdrop. Even the twins were photographed, in a boat on the lake, with their mother and father and their cousin Max.

Everyone was slightly surprised that Max had agreed so readily to come; he had arrived with Gemma in her Peugeot 205, 'Both of them stepped straight out of a commercial,' said Georgina; Gemma had been dazzled by the day, and stayed most discreetly out of all the pictures until Max hauled her into the one of the steps, and gave a rather reckless quote to the journalist about having found the right woman for him at last.

What was even more surprising was that Alexander had actually submitted to the camera twice. 'I'll hold your hand, it won't hurt,' Angie had said, laughing, 'come on, Alexander, just for me,' and he had stood between her and Baby at the foot of the flying staircase, looking very much the eccentric aristocrat, dressed in his shabby breeches and riding boots, shirt open at the neck, a rather vague smile on his face.

The pictures appeared in the centre spread of the paper the next weekend, captioned 'The Real Life Dynasty' and making much of the link between Praegers and the Caterhams; Compton Manners rang to congratulate Baby and asked him to thank Alexander. His satisfaction was greatly increased in the morning when there was an item about the

483

families in *The Times* City Diary, and on Tuesday, when the *Telegraph* mentioned the link in a story about what it called the Hidden Billions, the stately homes of Great Britain.

'It should help a lot,' he said. 'Watch.'

He was right; two of the three companies currently being courted by Praegers had signed by the end of the week.

But Jerry Mills signed with Routledge.

Max had had dinner with Gemma and her parents several times now; Dick Morton, charmed and impressed by Gemma's new, extremely aristocratic boyfriend, was equally delighted at Max's interest in the banking fraternity, and told him he could come and spend a couple of days in the office if it really appealed to him. 'I'm hiring a lot of people,' he said, 'a lot. These are exciting times.' The one black mark he felt chalked up against Max was his career. And his youth: 'But time will take care of that,' he said to his wife, 'and he seems very mature for nineteen.'

Mrs Morton, who was half in love with Max herself, agreed fervently.

'It's a gas,' said Max to Charlotte, over a drink one night. 'I really like it. Old man Morton has offered me a job as a trainee. They're huge, you know, Mortons. They're not being swallowed up by some investment bank. Clarkes have bought an interest, but basically they're setting up as corporate brokers. Market makers, the new buzz words. With a full service, corporate finance, security trading, underwriting, analysts, the lot. I think I can have a good time there. Only thing is, my income would be cut by about ninety per cent. But I think it'll be worth it. Alexander is giving me a bit of a sub. He's really pleased about it.'

'I'm sure he is,' said Charlotte, realizing suddenly why Max had been so amenable to taking part in the photo session, and had spent several weekends at Hartest with Gemma now. 'You're a clever little chap, aren't you, Max? Pleasing everybody, impressing Daddy with your new job, Gemma with Hartest, oh it's all very neat. What does Tommy Soames-Maxwell have to say about it?'

'Oh, he thinks it's fine,' said Max. 'As long as we can survive financially. He's been very supportive.'

'How nice of him,' said Charlotte sarcastically.

'Oh, don't be so miserable about it all,' said Max easily. 'You should be glad I'm thinking of going legit. And that I've got a nice steady girlfriend. Who isn't married.'

Charlotte felt herself flushing.

'Don't look so tragic, Charlotte. You want to forget all about Jeremy Foster, and set your cap for Gabe Hoffman instead. Now he *is* a good egg. I can't think why you don't snap him up.'

'I don't want to,' said Charlotte irritably, and then seeing Max looking at her particularly knowingly, decided to change the subject.

'Max, it's just occurred to me you can probably help me with something. Can I trust you?'

'No,' said Max. 'You know you can't.'

'Well, I have to. I need some information.'

'Charlotte! You're not asking me to breach the Chinese wall, I hope. See how I'm picking up the jargon already.'

'Amazing,' said Charlotte. 'No, it isn't that. But I want to find out about Gus Booth. I don't trust him. I don't know why. Baby thinks he's wonderful, but I don't. And I'm intrigued by something. Just see if you can pick anything up on the grapevine. See if your new friend Mr Morton has anything to say about Gus Booth. It'd be quite easy for you to mention him, they all know each other.'

'OK,' said Max. 'But if it puts Mr Morton off me, you'll have to persuade Baby to take me on.'

'No problem,' said Charlotte.

He rang her after his third week. 'I think I have a little information for you. Nothing secret, but possibly relevant. Which you may not have realized. Buy me dinner and I'll tell you.'

'I'll cook you dinner,' said Charlotte. 'I don't trust restaurants. Not when you're talking secrets.'

'The word is,' said Max, 'as you may know, apparently Gus Booth has just the hugest chip on his shoulder about not being allowed to work for Routledge. Well of course he can work for them, but can't ever get any higher. Because of not being a Routledge by blood. The word is that he only married the fair Jemima to try and get onto the board, and it's just no go.'

'Goodness,' said Charlotte, 'how intriguing. He doesn't seem like a man with a chip on his shoulder. Well, I must say he's much prettier than Jemima. And quite a bit younger. I often wondered about it. But I don't see what that's to do with us.'

'Well, I'll tell you. This is a man consumed by jealousy. And ambition. Even if it doesn't show. And a man to watch.'

'And. . . ?'

'God, you're not very quick, are you?' said Max irritably, pouring himself another glass of Alexander's 1982 Fleurie. 'This is nice. I'm not sure Alexander would be pleased we were drinking it.'

'*You* were drinking it,' said Charlotte primly.

'Bossyboots. Look, Charlotte, can't you see that a man in his position

485

is extremely well placed to trade? Information and so on. He could well still be trying to beat the blood ban. Is there anyone at Routledge you could do a bit of digging with?'

'Only Sarah Pousonby,' said Charlotte, 'and she wouldn't see any bad in Hitler if he smiled at her nicely. But maybe I can think of someone else. Thanks, Max. I'm sure you'll be running Mortons in no time at all.'

Charlotte began to watch Gus Booth as closely as she dared; his behaviour seemed beyond reproach. He came in early, left late, was unfailingly good-natured, charm itself. She was just beginning to think he had to be entirely above suspicion, when she went into his office late one night to pick up some files, and saw a message on his desk: 'Call J.M. 2.30' it said, followed by a phone number.

It was the work of a moment for her to ring. Jerry Mills's secretary said he was at lunch, and Charlotte rang off without leaving a message.

Mills was lost to them as a client. Everybody at Praegers had thought they'd landed him – at Wimbledon – until he went to Routledge. What possible reason had he for keeping in touch with Gus Booth?

She went to Baby, and told him what she suspected, what she thought, what she'd heard. Baby was appalled. Gus was a great guy, he'd slaved on their behalf. Pulled in a lot of business.

'Yes, and a lot of major clients have gone away again.'

'You really can't blame him for that. It's a very tough time.'

'Sure,' said Charlotte, 'but three of those people have gone to Routledge. Three. Gus Booth's father-in-law's bank. Baby, just think of that night when you took me for a drink at the Ritz. You said you really thought you might have got Boscombes. That Gus was having dinner with Tom Phillips. Then what happens? Tom Phillips says no. And a month later goes to Routledge.'

'Charlotte, we've talked to dozens of people. Dozens. They've gone all over the place. It's inevitable.' He was beginning to look angry. 'What good would it do Gus to have accounts going to Routledge from here? He doesn't benefit. He can never work there. It doesn't make sense. It's a fairy story. Now please stop interfering in matters you can't possibly know anything about. I have a very good relationship with Gus, he's loyal and supportive and I don't want any shadows cast over it by someone with no grasp of the situation, no understanding of what's involved.'

For the next two weeks she was very depressed. Baby was right, she had been acting like a Girl Guide. Or a prefect, she thought, cursing the old label that seemed so indissolubly fixed to her, certain that she was right about things, imposing her views on people, interfering in matters that were in no way her concern. And upsetting Baby, making everything worse when what he needed was an easy ride, a pleasant time. What did it matter – really – if Praegers wasn't setting London alight, she thought to herself moodily, walking home one evening as she often did to Eaton Place. Baby wouldn't be able to handle it all, even if they got every account they ever pitched for. It was probably much better that things should be quiet. And she had upset her relationship with Baby, which was the last thing she would have wished to do, when she was so fond of him, so concerned for him; he was cool towards her, no longer stopped by her desk for a chat. She really had made a total hash of everything, simply by (as usual) taking too much on herself, being sure she was right.

'You really are a disaster, Charlotte Welles,' she said aloud to herself, throwing a heap of carrier bags onto the hall floor. She had gone shopping to cheer herself up, Browns had had a sale, and she had bought two executive suits, and some very frivolous shoes by Maud Frizon to counteract their sobriety. She might just as well not have bothered; she was never going to be high-powered enough to wear them. She went out again and bought a large pizza for her supper; she might as well get fat again, and retire to the country.

Three days later she got into the office very early. As she walked in the front door, Gus Booth walked out. He ignored her totally. Charlotte went upstairs, into her office and then next door to Gus's. The incredible heap of papers on his desk was gone, the whole room was tidy and clear. She looked at it, startled. As she stood there, Baby came up behind her. He put his arm round her, gave her a hug.

'You're quite a girl,' he said, 'I owe you a big apology.'

He looked very pale, but he was smiling, albeit in a rather subdued manner.

'Crikey,' said Charlotte, lapsing as always into schoolgirl slang when she was particularly excited or upset. 'What happened?'

'Gus just – left. Come and have a coffee. I'll tell you all about it. I'm sorry I bawled you out, darling. Really.'

'Baby, I didn't actually recognize that as a bawling out. You should listen to your own father if you want to hear a bawling out.'

'I frequently have,' said Baby.

Gus Booth had been feeding clients to Routledge for months. Not all of them, naturally, but the ones he felt would be most prestigious. He would gain their confidence, then tell them in private that although Praegers was a great bank in New York, they just didn't have the clout, the experience in London. 'Take a look at my father-in-law's set-up,' he would say. 'He has a really great team there.'

And not unnaturally the clients would generally agree and take their business there. The ones that didn't were certainly not going to go to a bank where one of the senior executives was expressing doubt as to its capability. And the pack-of-cards syndrome was soon working very efficiently against Praegers.

'But why?' said Charlotte. 'I don't understand.'

'He thought if he sent them enough business, Routledge would bend the rules, make him a partner. Of course they won't. Ever. But he lives in hope. He's a fool. And what he has against me, in particular, is that I represent exactly what he can't have. Inherited privilege.'

'God,' said Charlotte, 'that's sick. How on earth did you find out?'

'Well, I just told Gus I'd had a very long chat with Tom Phillips. And with Jerry Mills. He was very quiet for a bit and then he asked me what I was going to do. I said I didn't know, and he just started talking.'

'Well,' said Charlotte, 'that was very clever. But suppose he'd called your bluff? Or asked them, even?'

'Well, that would have been fine,' said Baby, looking faintly surprised. 'I did have a long chat with them. Both of them.'

'But suppose I'd been wrong?' said Charlotte.

'Darling, the chat had nothing to do with you. Don't flatter yourself. I've been asked to serve on a charity committee. I wanted to know if either of them would like to join me.'

'Oh,' said Charlotte. 'So you weren't actually setting Gus a trap at all?'

'No, of course not,' said Baby. 'I never for a moment thought you were right. You obviously have much sharper antennae than I do. Fortunately. I owe you one, as they say. And I apologize again for being so – sceptical. Anyway, here's to a good run-up to Big Bang.' He raised his mug of coffee to her, and for a moment he looked young again, and handsome and carefree, the nightmare of his illness suddenly receded.

'To Big Bang,' said Charlotte.

She looked at her uncle thoughtfully. She wondered if he was quite as naive as he pretended. She supposed she would never know.

Chapter 43

Angie, 1985

So far, Angie thought, this wasn't working out too much like fiction. If they had been in a novel, and Baby had had an incurable disease, he would have spent his days maximizing on what life had still to offer him, and she would have been constantly at his side, sweetly serene, bringing comfort and cheer to him, easing his path, and helping others, notably his family, to do the same. The reality was that Baby was difficult, querulous, irritable, refused to do any of the things the doctor had advised, insisted on continuing to do everything, to work, to walk, to entertain, thereby exhausting himself (and becoming still more irritable), quite possibly, he had been advised, hastening the progress of his illness, and wouldn't allow her to tell anyone else in the family about it. It was as if, having told her, he wanted to transfer the entire burden onto her shoulders, and in some strange way, rid himself of it.

Her initial instinct had been to put her company in the hands of her very able deputy for however long was necessary; for the first time she could actually see her work as something self-indulgent and, to all practical purposes, unnecessary. But as the days went by, and Baby grew increasingly fretful and difficult, she changed her mind; her work, far from being self-indulgent, was a lifeline, an escape from the constant claustrophobic nightmare of what was happening to her. Instead of retiring, she shortened her working day, warned her staff she would be taking a considerable number of holidays in the near future, and put any plans for expansion on hold; and returned to the house and Baby every night refreshed and restored. And Baby, strangely restless, working with an energy and determination his staff had not seen before, was happy with the arrangement himself. Praegers was beginning to prosper now; three new major clients won during the summer, Gus Booth replaced by an Old Etonian, Tim Atkinson, acquired at some expense but proving himself infinitely worth it as he trawled what were still surprisingly well-stocked waters for clients, and the staff, motivated by the new and visible success, had turned what had been a collection of rather disparate people into a committed and even excited team.

'It's happening at last,' said Baby to Angie over dinner. 'Praegers has come alive. Just in time for me to do the opposite.' But for once he was smiling, good-natured.

Angie smiled back at him, and thought she would have given everything she had for him to be as well and as happy as he looked at that moment.

'I think we should go to New York,' she said to Baby, a few weeks after she had seen Dr Curtis. 'We must tell your parents, and I don't think it's news that can be relayed over the telephone. And we really have to tell the boys. And Melissa.'

Kendrick was coming over in the summer, for a vacation, to see Georgina and then taking her back with him. Surely, said Angie, he needed to be told before then? Georgina knew, she was bound to say something, it wasn't fair on her, to ask her to keep the secret. And if they were telling Kendrick, then they must tell Freddy.

'I don't see why,' said Baby mulishly.

'Oh Baby, don't be absurd. Quite apart from anything else, Freddy's future will be affected drastically.'

'Why?' he said again. He was clearly intent on making things as difficult as possible for her.

'Well because – because when you – if you – '

'Die?' said Baby, darkly, an aggressive light in his eyes.

'Yes, all right, die,' said Angie, struggling to be patient, 'or at least become ineffective, then Freddy will be taking over. Much earlier than he might have expected.'

'I wonder which of us will go first,' said Baby morosely. 'My father or me.'

Angie sighed, and tried to put her arms round him. He pushed her away gently.

In the end she did manage to persuade Baby to go with her to New York, to see Mary Rose and the children. 'And your parents, Baby, you must tell them.'

'Well,' he said heavily, 'well, we'll see.'

In fact they went to see Fred III together at Praegers; Angie sat in silence as Baby told him, and watched Fred become old and somehow shrunken before her eyes.

He sat looking at the two of them, in a silence so heavy that she could scarcely hold her head up, continue meeting his eyes.

'No hope then?' he said finally.

'No hope. I'm sorry,' said Baby, rather weakly. The apology came from the conditioning of a lifetime; Angie thought, with a flash of black humour, that Fred would probably even manage to bawl him out for this. But he didn't.

'Well,' he said. 'At least I – we know exactly where we are.'

'Yes. But it's not so terrible – yet, Dad.' Baby had forced a bright smile. 'I have years, I'm told. Years. The progress of the disease is very slow. We should be grateful for time to – to plan. To work out what will happen at the bank, to Freddy and – I suppose Charlotte.'

'Silly little thing,' said Fred irrelevantly. 'How is she?'

'She's fine. Doing well. She's a bright girl.'

'I've been telling you that for years,' said Fred irritably. He was clearly clinging to the subject of Charlotte, at having something different to focus on.

There was a silence.

'Max has been given a job at Mortons,' said Baby, in an attempt to keep the conversation on a less nightmarish level. If he had wanted to distract his father he could hardly have succeeded better.

Fred's brilliant eyes flashed, his face flushed. 'Mortons? A grandson of mine working for a British stockbroker? What on earth are you talking about?'

'Well,' said Baby patiently, 'he wanted to work for Praegers. If you remember. And you turned him down. He's genuinely keen.'

'Well, I was upset at the time,' said Fred, 'Charlotte had been fooling around. I didn't feel another Caterham was a good idea. But if the boy's really keen – well, I suppose it won't do him any harm. Mortons is a good firm. At least it'll get him away from that terrible life he's been leading.'

'Yes,' said Baby. 'I suppose it will.'

Fred sighed, returning before their eyes to the heavy, sad purpose of the conversation. 'Who on God's earth is going to tell Mary Rose?' he said.

'I already have,' said Angie.

Fred turned away from her, and looked down the street towards the waterfront. Then he swung round and jabbed savagely at his intercom.

'Peggy?'

'Yes, Mr Praeger.'

'Peggy, bring in a bottle of Krug, will you. And don't put any calls through. None whatsoever.'

'Mr Praeger, the Governor of the Bank of England is due to call at three thirty. If you remember.'

'I do remember. Tell him I'm out. And then have my car brought round to the front in – forty-five minutes, OK. And get my wife on the phone now, will you.'

'Yes, Mr Praeger.'

491

She came in with the Krug and three glasses. Fred III opened the bottle, poured it, handed first Baby and then Angie a glass.

'You're quite a kid, aren't you?' he said to her. 'Here's to courage.'

The interview with Mary Rose had actually had rather more of the elements of black comedy than tragedy. They had sat together in Peacock Alley at the Waldorf and Angie had ordered ice tea and Mary Rose had ordered orange pekoe, and Angie had told her that Baby was ill, and Mary Rose had implied in quite strong terms that if it was his heart then the blame was entirely down to Angie, for not supervising his diet properly. She had travelled some way down that particular road before Angie had managed to convey to her the details of the illness Baby was actually suffering from and that it was invariably fatal. Whereupon Mary Rose had glared at her and said, 'I don't know how you can come here in that ridiculous red coat and those terrible boots and tell me my husband is dying.'

She went on to upbraid Angie further on the shortcomings of English doctors, and their inability to diagnose and treat any disease more serious than the common cold; and then finally she stood up and said she had to get back to her office. 'I can't waste any more time on this sort of thing.' And then she had suddenly looked at Angie, and her face softened, and her eyes were no longer cold, and she said, 'I would like to tell you that I think it was very brave and good of you to come. I – I appreciate it.'

Angie sat staring after her, a most surprising haze of tears behind her eyes.

Baby told his children alone. He called them to the hotel, and Angie went out shopping; when she got back, he was alone, and very drunk.

'This is a shit of a thing,' was all he said.

The summer was actually fairly happy. Angie managed to persuade Baby to spend much of August at Watersfoot – 'Not because you're ill, Baby, no, because it's a time when quite a few people take just a few days off. And because we've spent around a million pounds on that house, and it might be nice to spend just a couple of weeks there.'

She sounded as exasperated as she felt; Baby grinned at her and took her hand.

'I'm sorry. Am I very awkward?'

'Very.'

'Will you take August off as well?'

'I will.'

'OK. Let's see if the kids can join us.'

The kids did. Or at least Kendrick and Melissa did. Freddy only came for a week and spent much of that in London. He was odd towards his father, almost cold: Baby surprisingly accepted it with cheerful grace. 'He doesn't know what to do, how to treat me. He's embarrassed.'

Angie thought there was another reason: that Freddy was feeling, however unwillingly, ambivalent about Baby's illness, knowing that he would get the bank sooner, and finding the prospect exciting, even in his undoubted grief.

'He's a cold little fish,' she said to Mrs Wicks. She found talking to her grandmother strangely helpful, in trying to survive some at least of the innumerable crosscurrents that were raging around her that summer. 'I can't stand him. And he's very very ambitious. But he knows it's wrong even to think about that. I think he's genuinely fond of Baby. And it's making him feel awkward. Or rather more awkward. Poor Charlotte, I don't envy her her business partner.'

'You're beginning to sound like someone quite different,' said Mrs Wicks, looking at her with a wry smile. 'This thing is going to be the making of you, Angela.'

'I don't think so,' said Angie with a heavy sigh. 'It's more likely to finish me off, I think.'

'Nonsense,' said Mrs Wicks. 'Tough stock, we Wicks.'

She needed to be of tough stock, Angie thought. Apart from the increasing problems of Baby's see-sawing morale, monitoring the progress of his illness (hideously fast it seemed to her), coping with the twins (and their new, fiercely protective nanny) she had to handle Kendrick and Melissa as well. And it wasn't easy.

She made an enormous effort to work on gaining Melissa's friendship, to break through Kendrick's slightly strained politeness. In the end she won Kendrick over by going on the offensive. She sat him down, literally, in the kitchen one night, after Baby had gone to bed, and Georgina for once was not with them (God, young love was wearing to witness), poured him a large glass of wine and said, 'Look, Kendrick, we have to talk.'

Kendrick looked at her nervously. 'Well I was just going to – '

'You weren't just going to anything,' said Angie firmly. 'And if you were it can wait. Kendrick, I know how you must feel about me, and I would probably feel the same, if I were you. The whole situation is hell. It isn't too much fun for me either, actually. But no doubt you think I've got myself into it and deserve anything I get.' She looked at Kendrick and grinned suddenly. 'Well, I have. And got more than I bargained for.'

Kendrick looked at her awkwardly and then at his feet.

'The thing is, we have to see it through together. After your father has – died – ' she forced the word out, knowing it was important she made him face it – 'you need never see me again. That's fine. I'd be sorry, because I like you, but that isn't very important either. But – well, for the next two or three years, or however long it takes, he's going to be a lot happier if we all seem to be getting along. I'm sure you feel it would be simpler if he was still with your mum, and of course it would, but life isn't like that. I'm with him now, and I really want to do my best for him. I – ' She paused. 'I love him, Kendrick. Very much. If we could be friends, or seem to be friends, it would make life a lot easier. What do you think?'

Kendrick was silent. Then he said, 'Well I – I don't know. Could I have another glass of wine?'

'Sure,' said Angie with a grin. 'Have the whole bottle. The whole cellar. I'm quite open about this, Kendrick. I'm out to buy your friendship.'

He smiled rather sheepishly back. 'Thanks. I'll make do with just the glass.' He drained it rather quickly; Angie refilled it.

'How's Georgina?' she said conversationally. 'She looked a bit tired, I thought.'

'Yeah, she is. She's been working very hard this vacation. And she has to take care of her father, you know, the burden very much falls on her.'

'He's not an invalid,' said Angie briskly. Typical of Georgina, to make a drama out of taking care of a perfectly fit man. Georgina had always irritated her. She should have *her* problems, she thought.

'No, but he is a little lonely,' said Kendrick earnestly. 'Georgina feels she has to be with him as much as she can. Charlotte and Max are in London all the time. It's a big worry for her.'

'Well, I see quite a lot of him,' said Angie briskly, not sure whether this was a good line to pursue or not, 'and he seems quite happy. He is vague, of course. But he always has been. Anyway,' she added, struggling not to appear unsympathetic, 'I'm sorry she's so tired. I hope you've had a good time together this summer, the two of you.'

'Oh we have,' said Kendrick. He had drained the third glass of wine by now. 'Um – the thing is, we – well, the thing is – Angie – '

God, will he ever get it out, thought Angie wearily. 'Yes, Kendrick?' she said.

'The thing is, we'd like to – to get engaged. But we feel that with Dad so ill and Alexander so – well, so lonely, it perhaps isn't the best time. What do you think?'

'I think,' said Angie carefully, 'it would be absolutely the best time. I know your father would be thrilled. And you can have a word with

Alexander yourself. Ask him formally for Georgina's hand. He'd like that. He's very old-fashioned. And if you want a good word put in for you, ask me. I get on very well with Alexander.'

'Thanks,' said Kendrick. 'Thanks very much. I really appreciate that.'

His pale face was flushed, his blue eyes still avoiding Angie's. Nevertheless, she felt acutely aware that she had won a considerable victory.

It was Max who helped her win Melissa over. Angie had grown close to Max over the past difficult weeks; he had been quite shocked and upset about Baby and asked her to supper with Tommy and him one evening.

'Oh, I couldn't,' said Angie, 'I can't leave Baby in the evening.'

'Why on earth not?' said Max. 'He'll survive. He actually looks perfectly healthy to me. Ask your gran to cook him supper. And you need a break, you look terrible.'

'Thanks,' said Angie. But she went.

She was rather touched by the two of them, and the trouble they took to cheer her up. They had booked a corner table in a small Italian restaurant where they clearly spent a great deal of time, and had a bottle of champagne waiting when she arrived.

'Of course we can't afford it,' said Tommy cheerfully when she remonstrated, 'but it's only the house one, and you're worth it.'

Tommy was full of funny stories, and Max told tales of his new life as a trainee at Mortons. They asked her about her business, and how she was managing to run it still while she had so much else to worry about; they told her they thought she was wonderful; they asked her if there was anything they could do to help. Angie told them not yet, but it was very nice to know they were there. They all got rather drunk and started swopping dirty jokes; Tommy then insisted on escorting her home by taxi, and when they pulled up just short of the house (just in case Baby was looking out of the window) he kissed her hand, and told her she was a brave lady. Angie went into the house feeling more cheerful than she had done for weeks.

She called Max in the middle of August, and said, 'You know you said you'd like to help. Here's your chance.'

She told him about Melissa; that she was rude, unhelpful, difficult with her father as well as to her, refused all offers of friendship, wouldn't even come to the family supper table unless she could find no way out, and then sat in silence, opting out of any conversation, and asked to be taken over to Hartest whenever Kendrick went with Georgina 'to see darling Uncle Alexander'.

495

'It's hurting Baby dreadfully. You know how he adores her. She's always had a thing about you, Kendrick says. Can you talk to her?'

'Sure,' said Max. 'Consider it done. I'll call her tomorrow, get her up to lunch or something. She'll like that. Silly little thing. How's Baby?'

'Getting worse rather fast,' said Angie, and was surprised to hear her voice tremble.

Melissa came back from her day in London with Max looking rather shamefaced, rushed into the kitchen and threw her arms round her father. 'It's lovely to be back,' she said, 'London is just gross. Can we all play Monopoly or something after supper? Angie, that is one great sweater. And something smells gorgeous. Would you like me to babysit for the twins tomorrow so you two can go to the movies or something?'

The fact that the nanny was there and scarcely allowed the twins' mother near them, never mind anyone else, and there was no cinema for at least twenty miles, appeared to have entirely escaped her; but it didn't matter.

Angie phoned Max to thank him two days later. 'She's still behaving like an angel. What did you do?'

'Oh,' said Max, 'applied a little emotional blackmail. It wasn't very difficult.'

It was weeks later that Tommy described to Angie, laughing, the precise nature of the emotional blackmail. 'He told Melissa he'd always thought she was a really nice person, the kind he liked being around, and from what he'd heard recently she was nothing of the sort, and that it made him really sad. Melissa apparently sat there with tears pouring down her cheeks, and promised to reform.'

'Well she did,' said Angie. 'It worked.'

Late that autumn, Baby started going to the bank only three days a week. His other hand was beginning to be affected, the slight slurring of his speech was an occasional embarrassment and if he was tired it got worse. He was increasingly irritable and bored, and sat around the house roaring at anyone who got in his way.

It was Max who cracked that particular problem too.

'I just might shoot myself one Monday soon,' Angie said to him cheerfully over the phone, when he rang to ask her how things were.

'Why specially Mondays?'

'Baby is just impossible on Mondays. He used to love them, getting back after the weekend, after the break; now he just sits and suffers, and makes sure I suffer too.'

'Tommy's at home on Mondays too,' said Max after a pause. 'Maybe he and Uncle Baby could get together. Tommy's got some ghastly new friend, a frightfully rich Arab called Al-Mahdu, who arrives with plastic bagfuls of money, and takes Tommy shopping with him. I'd much rather he was with Baby.'

'Yes – but exactly in what way?' said Angie doubtfully. 'I don't really want Baby sitting around waiting for casinos to open.'

'Well – no.' He hesitated for a moment. 'Leave it with me.'

Two Mondays later, Angie came in from her office at four, to find Baby looking radiantly cheerful.

'Tommy came to see me today. He's a nice guy really, you know. I know he's a bad lot, but I like him.'

'Really?'

'Yes. He's going to buy me some games.'

'What sort of games?' said Angie suspiciously.

'Computer games. There are the most amazing ones around, you know, real brain taxers. And then you can get backgammon, and a version of roulette – '

'Baby, you are not to play roulette with Tommy Soames-Maxwell. I forbid it.'

'Angie, I swear to you we won't play for money. Well, not big money. I think we can have a really good time. And – ' He hesitated. 'Those things are so easy to use, I can do it with my good hand. So don't go getting all schoolmissy about it.'

'I won't,' said Angie. She turned away, so he wouldn't see the easy, endless tears starting in her eyes.

And so it was that every Monday afternoon and sometimes on Thursdays too, Baby Praeger and Tommy Soames-Maxwell would sit in the drawing room in Belgrave Square playing backgammon and roulette and Dirty Scrabble for comparatively modest stakes and for hours on end.

'I really don't know what I'd do without you and Tommy,' said Angie to Max. They were having a drink after work one Monday; they quite often did, knowing their respective partners were very happily occupied with one another, knowing there was absolutely no hurry for either of them to get home. 'Or how I can thank you.'

She smiled at him and raised her glass, thinking how of all the family, apart from Alexander, she liked him best. He was such fun, so unfailingly good-natured, such good company. And he always looked so terrific; now that he had given up the modelling and no longer wore his hair slicked back in that awful trendy way, and just wore normal clothes, not those endless designer sweaters and ridiculous boots, he actually seemed twice as attractive. She looked at him now, lounging in his chair, wearing a beautifully cut dark grey suit and blue shirt, his fair hair just a little too long, the oddly dark shadow of his beard just beginning to show, his blue eyes snapping at her appreciatively, and she thought if she was – what – well, fifteen years younger she could fancy young Viscount Hadleigh rotten. As it was, of course, she simply regarded him in a rather maternal – or aunt-like – light.

'You could put in a good word with the family for old Tommy,' Max was saying slightly gloomily. 'They all loathe him.'

Angie thought privately, despite Tommy's kindness to Baby, that they loathed him with good reason; she saw him, as they all did, as a living time bomb, waiting with a deadly patience to go off. But she smiled at Max and said, 'I'm afraid the family don't regard me with exactly rose-tinted spectacles either. But I'll do what I can. Obviously.'

'Thanks,' said Max. He looked at her sharply suddenly and said, 'Don't you ever wonder about it all? Our motley collection of fathers and all that?'

'Not much,' said Angie briefly. 'The way I grew up, most people had a motley collection of fathers. I suppose it's a bit intriguing, why it should have happened, but actually, Max, I have more important things to worry about.'

'Sure.' He grinned at her. 'My big worry, between you me and the gateposts of the old stately home, is that Gemma might make something of it all.'

'Gemma?' said Angie. 'Why should she make anything of it?'

'Well,' said Max, looking slightly awkward, 'I think she likes who I am. And all that.'

'Yes, but she doesn't have to know, surely?' said Angie.

'Well not now,' said Max, looking more awkward still. 'But she might. If things got – well, more serious.'

'Oh,' said Angie, staring at him. 'Oh, I see.' There was a strange sensation somewhere in the area between her throat and her stomach; she asked the waiter to bring her another drink.

Going home in the cab she realized what the strange sensation had been. A strong and quite irrational sense of dislike for Gemma Morton.

In spite of his conversation with her, Kendrick had clearly not broached the question of an engagement with Alexander. Georgina had not mentioned it either; Kendrick had left at the end of the summer, and Angie saw Georgina, on her visits to Alexander, mooning about more theatrically than ever. She had once hinted to Alexander that he might

498

perhaps find Georgina just occasionally irritating, but he had been quite shocked.

'I enjoy her company more than anything in the world,' he said. 'With the possible exception of your own, of course. I can't think what I'd do without her. She is inordinately thoughtful and kind, and extremely mature for her age. No, she's a sweet child, Angie. My other two might well have something to learn from her.'

Kendrick and Melissa were coming over for Christmas; Freddy had begged pressure of work. Angie, knowing it would make Kendrick happier, proposed spending Christmas at Watersfoot; that way he would be able to spend a lot of time with Georgina. Baby complained, saying it was too much hassle, packing everything up; Angie told him she had never personally observed him packing so much as his own toothbrush, and ignored him.

They all went over to Hartest for Christmas Day; Alexander phoned Angie and said it would make his Christmas if they would come, that even Max would be there, that Nanny and Mrs Tallow were bored and lonely these days and had not nearly enough to do, and a family Christmas would keep them happy for months. He particularly requested that Mrs Wicks should come. Angie accepted gratefully, never having cooked a Christmas dinner in her life, even while reflecting aloud to Baby on the odd attitude of the upper classes towards their servants, and the fact that they seemed to be invited as much as cannon fodder for Nanny and Mrs Tallow as to give pleasure to Alexander.

'More like the cannons themselves, I would say, to consume the fodder,' said Baby. 'And there'll be plenty of that.'

Having given in to the suggestion that they should go to the country, he was in a benign mood. The progress of his illness had temporarily halted; he was no worse, and even managed to persuade himself from time to time that he was slightly better.

'He isn't,' the doctor had said to Angie, 'but it will do him no harm to think so.'

Mrs Wicks was very excited at the invitation, and had bought an entire new wardrobe for the holiday; Clifford had to spend the day with his elderly mother and she had not been looking forward to it.

'He didn't seem to mind my not being there at all,' she said to Angie crossly. 'Sometimes I think he prefers his mother to me.'

Angie told her she thought that was very unlikely.

She was very surprised that Max was joining them and said as much when he picked her up from her office on Monday en route to collect Tommy from the house in Belgrave Square; he looked at her, his blue eyes innocently blank, and said he couldn't imagine why. 'Christmas is the time to be with your family.'

'Yes, I know, but Tommy's your family too isn't he? Or so you're always telling us. What about him, all alone on Christmas Day?'

Max shot her a look of sharp dislike and said Tommy was spending the day with some old cronies at the Dorchester: 'He doesn't mind at all. And Gemma and her parents have a house in the Cotswolds and they've asked me there for Boxing Day.'

'Oh I see,' said Angie, 'still playing the perfect son and heir then, Max?'

Max stared at her and then put his foot down very hard on the accelerator of Charlotte's car. 'It really is nothing to do with you, Angie, if you don't mind my saying so,' was all he said. But the hostility she felt emanating from him was very strong. Perversely, she found it exciting.

They had a very good Christmas Day. Mrs Tallow cooked a superb lunch, they all played a lot of games, and exchanged a great many presents under the tree in the Rotunda, and then Nanny, to Angie's intense relief, pronounced the twins as overexcited and removed them forcibly to what she still called her Nurseries.

'Bossy old bag,' said Mrs Wicks under her breath to Angie, who told her to shut up and remember where she was; Mrs Wicks said that Nanny had gone to some pains to make her aware of where she was and that she had no right to be there. 'She actually started rambling on about people being born on the bottom end of the bed,' she said. 'I had to keep trying to tell myself she's a bit touched, just to stop myself from hitting her.'

Angie, realizing that Nanny had actually meant the wrong side of the blanket, and all too sure that she was not in the least touched, hastily agreed that she was. 'At least she's taken those children away. Let's be thankful, Gran. I'm going to have a sleep myself. Baby looks worn out as well.'

'Baby's fine,' said Mrs Wicks, smoothing her white and gold dress, and patting her red curls. 'We've had a very interesting talk about Florida. It sounds lovely. I thought I might take Clifford there after Christmas. Get him away from that mother of his. You should get Baby some Dubonnet, he seemed to prefer it to his wine. Earl Alexander looks very nice in that jumper, doesn't he?'

The jumper was one she had knitted herself from a pattern in *Woman's Own*, in a striking pattern of red holly leaves and reindeer heads on a green background; it was a measure of Alexander's regard for both Mrs

Wicks and possibly herself, Angie thought, that he had insisted on wearing it right through lunch.

'Very nice,' she said. She had given up trying to correct the endless variations Mrs Wicks made on Alexander's title.

'I'm going for a walk,' said Max. 'Anyone coming?'

He was standing by the fireplace in the library looking absurdly handsome and slightly dishevelled after acting as horses in a very good-natured way for the twins. Angie looked at him and felt a piercing thrust of sexual desire. She had tried without success that morning to celebrate Christmas with Baby in a way just slightly more carnal than opening parcels, and failed miserably.

'I will,' said Melissa.

Angie had been about to volunteer herself, and promptly shut her mouth again. She had no wish to tag along while Melissa flirted with Max. She at least had carte blanche to do so.

Kendrick asked at the end of the day if he could stay the night at Hartest. 'Georgina and I want to ride first thing, and it seems sensible.'

The excuse was so transparent that everybody laughed; they both looked awkward.

'Of course you can,' said Angie. 'I'll come over and fetch you both some time after lunch. You haven't forgotten we have to go and have drinks with our neighbours in the evening, have you? They specially asked for you, Georgina. They said they knew you when you were four and really wanted to see you again.'

'Fine,' said Georgina. She smiled at Angie, a sweet, rather careful smile. 'I think I might go and see Martin and Catriona in the morning. They're always on their own at Christmas. It can't be much fun.'

'We should have asked them,' said Alexander, looking stricken. 'I didn't think.'

Angie thought of the romantically tortured-looking Martin Dunbar and wished he *had* thought. 'Haven't they got any children?' she said.

'No,' said Alexander, looking particularly vague. 'I believe there was some problem.'

'What sort of problem?' said Melissa. She had been sitting half asleep, lolling against Max, her head resting on his shoulder, but the hope of a conversation that might be remotely sexual had woken her up. 'Is he – what's it called – impotent?'

'Melissa, please!' said Baby. He looked embarrassed. 'I do wish you'd learn to behave yourself and think before you speak. Please apologize.'

'I can't see what for,' said Melissa. She looked sulky. Angie sighed. So far Christmas had progressed fairly peacefully.

501

'For raising a subject that is most unsuitable, and for possibly offending most of the people present,' said Baby. 'Now say you're sorry.'

'Sorry,' mumbled Melissa.

'Anyway,' said Alexander, breaking into the silence, unusually tactful, 'as far as I understand Catriona was unable to have children. Very sad, as Martin particularly loves them so much. He often told me how much he would have liked a big family.'

'That is sad,' said Georgina, 'I didn't know that. And he'd have been the most wonderful father. He's so gentle, and so understanding.'

'Too much of that can be a bad thing,' said Mrs Wicks briskly, putting down one of her interminable glasses of Dubonnet. 'We've all been a bit too gentle and understanding with those twins today, Angela. We should take them home.'

The twins had found the piano in the library and were standing at it, banging their fat little fists on the keys; Angie looked at them, laughed, and said slightly reluctantly, 'You're right. Come on, Baby, pick up your sons and walk.'

Baby stood up and promptly sat down again. One of his legs seemed to have given way.

Driving over to see Alexander the next day, Angie felt extremely overwrought. The shock of seeing Baby's leg give way, the strain of being with Baby's children, her growing awareness of her attraction to Max, her own sexual hunger had all conspired to upset her badly. She had lain in the bath for an hour that morning, masturbating, trying to calm herself, but it hadn't really helped; the emptiness inside her seemed bigger, angrier than before.

Baby was in a furious temper, frightened by the incident with his leg, badly overhung, miserable at the prospect of several more days in the country with no access to medical advice. She had called Dr Curtis who had been good-natured at being disturbed over the holiday, and he had told her there was no need to worry particularly, that it was probably a freak thing, and that he would see Baby as soon as they were back in London. Baby told her to ask him if he would see him that day, if he travelled up, and to her intense relief Dr Curtis told her he wouldn't, which made Baby crosser than ever. She had left him inquiring of anyone who cared to listen what he was paying the fucking doctors for; as she thankfully shut the front door she heard Mrs Wicks telling him he should watch his language, there were children in the house. God, she thought, casting her mind longingly back to her life in St John's Wood before the twins had been born, how did anyone survive family life?

She drove much too fast over to Hartest; she always found speed a sexual release. It was slightly foggy and very icy, but she didn't care; she was so upset she felt a car crash would be almost welcome.

Alexander was alone, reading in the library when she arrived; Max and Charlotte had both gone over to visit Gemma and her parents, the Mortons. He got up to greet her and took her hand, bent to kiss her. In her overcharged state even that served to increase her physical misery. She wondered how Alexander had stood his enforced celibacy since Virginia died; or maybe he hadn't stood it at all, maybe he had had a girlfriend or two. If he had, it had been very discreetly managed. Or maybe he wasn't very strongly sexed, or maybe when you were older you didn't mind so much. Then she realized Alexander was very white and he looked shaken.

'What is it, Alexander, what's the matter?'

'Oh – I just had an upset with Georgina. She's gone off with Kendrick. For the day, she said. Then they just drove away. Didn't say so much as goodbye. I have to tell you, Angie, I'm very angry. With both of them.'

'Whatever about?' said Angie. She was so shocked she forgot the purpose of her visit to Hartest had been to collect them. 'The upset, I mean. You and Georgina are such good friends.'

'I know that. Oh, you don't want to hear. It's so annoying for you, too, when you've come all this way to collect them.' He tried to smile at her.

'It doesn't matter. I can wait. She's not –' an awful thought struck her – 'she's not pregnant, is she?'

'No,' he said grimly. 'Not this time.'

'What do you mean? Is she in the habit of being pregnant?'

'Well – she was expelled from her school for – for being in bed with some boy. And then it emerged, yes, that she was pregnant. She had to have an abortion. I wasn't very good with her, I'm afraid. Virginia had only just died.'

'I suppose,' said Angie slightly drily, 'that just might have had something to do with it. Her getting pregnant, I mean.'

'What? Oh, I don't think so,' he said quickly.

'So what's the matter today then?' she said, relieved that it couldn't be anything too serious. 'What's the fuss about?'

'Well – well yes, you do have to know. You're involved. Or at any rate Baby is. She and Kendrick want to get married. Of course it's absurd, out of the question. I told them so.'

'She and Kendrick. But that's great, Alexander. Why shouldn't they? I can't think of anything nicer, really.'

'It's quite impossible,' he said heavily. 'The whole thing has been an appalling shock.'

'But why a shock? You must have realized they were having a relationship? This is just a very nice logical development.'

'Of course I didn't realize they were having a relationship.'

'Then,' she said coolly, 'you're a fool. It's been going on for months and months.'

'I think,' he said, looking at her with great distaste, 'if you've known that you might have done the courtesy of informing me.'

'I think if you needed informing, you're a very blind man. What on earth did you think was going on? They're always together. Did you really not think they were sleeping together?'

'No,' he said, 'of course I didn't.'

'Well what *did* you think was going on?'

'I thought they were – well, just very good friends. They've grown up together, they're more like brother and sister. I could see they were fond of each other, of course. But I had no idea they – God, it's frightful. I would have stopped it had I realized.'

'Alexander, this is something out of the dark ages,' said Angie. She was beginning to feel slightly bewildered. 'Why should you have stopped it?'

'Because I don't like it,' he said shortly, and his face was very dark now, very heavy. 'I just don't like it.'

'Oh for heaven's sake. And anyway, you can't stop her, she's over eighteen. As a matter of fact I encouraged Kendrick to ask you if they could get engaged.'

'You?' he said and his face was heavy with distaste. 'You did that?'

'Yes I did. I thought it would be the correct and – and courteous thing to do.'

'You have nothing to do with any of this,' he said and his expression was so close to hatred she was quite shocked. 'Nothing. And of course I can stop it. Georgina is still heavily financially dependent on me.'

'Kendrick isn't exactly poverty stricken,' said Angie. 'And how dare you say I have nothing to do with this? I am very close to Kendrick. I just don't get it, Alexander, I don't see why you are so opposed to it.'

For the first time since she had known him he looked really angry. His whole body had tautened, his face had entirely lost its gentle, rather vague expression. He looked at her with an intense hostility in his dark blue eyes.

'You wouldn't get it, as you put it. Of course you wouldn't. It's far too involved and too subtle a problem for you. I told you I didn't want to discuss it with you. I knew there was no point in it. I think, Angie, you'd better go.'

Angie looked at him in genuine fascination. This was a man she had never seen before. She felt her own heart begin to thud rather pleasurably.

504

'I have no intention of going,' she said calmly. 'I'm sorry you're so upset, but I feel, apart from anything else, I have to defend Kendrick's interest. He's my – well, almost – my stepson, and he's extremely nice. Georgina would be very fortunate. Can you just give me one good reason why they shouldn't get married?'

'I have to say I find your attitude totally puzzling,' said Alexander. 'Apart from anything else, Angie, they're cousins. Cousins can't marry.'

'Oh balls,' said Angie. 'Of course they can marry. It's permitted in the Church of England. The vicar called the banns for some cousins only this morning. You're talking crap, Alexander, high-handed, intolerant crap. I'm surprised at you.'

'Please don't talk to me like that,' he said, and his voice was very icy.

'I think it's about time somebody did talk to you like that,' said Angie coolly. 'I thought you were a nice, liberal, loving father, and I find you're just a plain old dyed-in-the-wool tyrant after all. A hidebound, prejudiced, overbearing tyrant. I'll tell you what I think, Lord Caterham – ' some instinct was warning her now, to hold back, telling her she was on dangerous, deadly ground, but she was too angry, too excited to stop – 'I think you're just jealous, jealous your favourite daughter is in love with someone else, jealous she's close to someone, is having a sex life, jealous she wants to leave you . . .'

Alexander stood quite still, looking at her; he was ashen, his eyes blazing. He took a step towards her suddenly, and Angie felt an abrupt chill, not of fear exactly, but of dread.

'How dare you,' he said, very quietly, 'how dare you, how dare you say such things. Take them back, take them back at once.'

'I dare because they're true.'

'They are not true.'

'Of course they are true. Look at yourself, Alexander, look at the situation, go on, force yourself, just for once take it head on.' She was dimly conscious of talking of other things now, of pushing the frontiers of what she dared to make him confront. 'Stop running away, please, Alexander. Please.'

'You bitch,' he said quietly, and she felt a great rush of emotion reaching out from him towards her, and then quite suddenly he took her in his arms and kissed her furiously, hard, on the mouth. It was a very sensuous practised kiss; she felt his lips, hot, oddly yielding, his tongue seeking hers out, one of his hands tangling in her hair, then moving gently, agonizingly tender, on her neck. A snake of fire shot through Angie; she clung to him, whispering, almost gasping his name, her body straining frantically, desperately at his, feeling the great white heat of her desire obliterating everything except what she wanted, what she had to have.

505

'Please,' she said, 'please, Alexander, now, please.'

And he suddenly looked down at her, seemed to realize properly who she was, what he was doing, and his face was quite different again, dead, distant, and he put her away from him and said, 'No, no, Angie, we can't, we can't,' and 'Yes,' she said, 'we can, come on, let's go somewhere now, please, I have to have you, I do, I do.' She was flushed, there were tears in her eyes, her fists clenched, and he turned from her and almost ran into the house, and she followed him, through the Rotunda, down the corridor, into the gun room; she heard the door slam, and she pulled it open and went in after him.

He was standing by the window, his back to her. 'No,' he said, 'no, please leave me alone.'

'I can't,' she said, 'not now, I can't,' and she went towards him, turned him round, put her arms up round his neck, pulled his face down towards her, her eyes huge, dark with hunger.

'I want you,' she said. 'Please, Alexander, please, I want you so much, I'm so lonely, so unhappy, it won't hurt Baby, he'll never never know.'

And he looked down at her, and said, 'No, Angie, no, I'm sorry, I'm terribly terribly sorry,' and she looked back at him, half puzzled, half afraid, and said, 'Why, Alexander, what is it, I don't understand?' and he said, finally, his face infinitely wretched, 'I have to tell you now, at last. I'm impotent.'

Chapter 44

Virginia, 1960

She looked at him, half puzzled, half afraid; and he said, his face infinitely wretched, 'I have to tell you now, at last. I'm impotent.'

The room shook, shuddered around Virginia; she stared at him, and then shrank back onto the pillows, her body withdrawing from him as swiftly, as fearfully as her mind.

'I – I don't understand.'

'I'm impotent,' he said again.

She sat up, reached for her glass of champagne. She drained it, feeling the alcohol hit her bloodstream, reassuring, comforting. The room steadied, the nightmare receded briefly. She held out her glass. 'May I have some more?'

'Of course.' He filled it for her, then his own. He pulled on his robe; she never saw him naked again.

'I'm sorry,' he said again. 'So very very sorry.'

Virginia shivered. Her body, which had been so warm, so hungry a few moments earlier, felt chill and oddly withered.

'You're cold,' he said, 'here, put your robe on.'

'Thank you.' She put it round her shoulders, pulled the covers of the bed up. Her teeth were chattering slightly.

'Oh darling. Darling – ' He moved towards her; she pulled away.

'Don't. Don't touch me.'

'I'm sorry.'

There was a long silence. Then she said, 'Would you open the shutters please?'

'Of course.'

The warm, golden air filled the room; Virginia looked towards the window at the blue sky, the wheeling gulls. She closed her eyes, opened them again, as if willing the nightmare to recede. It didn't. Alexander was sitting looking at her, his face concerned, gentle. She felt a panic threatening to overtake her, and fought it back. She met his eyes with great difficulty and said, 'I think you had better explain.'

'I'll try.' He shifted on the bed, reached for a strawberry, held out the dish to her. She shook her head, feeling sick that he could even think she might be able to swallow, to eat.

'I don't quite know how to begin,' he said. 'It's so difficult.'

'I would say,' she said, 'that it isn't very easy for me.'

'No. No of course not.'

'Perhaps I should ask some questions.'

'Very well.'

'How long have you – have you known you were – '

'Impotent? Oh, for a few years. Always, I suppose, in a way. At least, ever since I could have been expected to function normally.'

'So – you've tried to have relationships?'

'Oh yes. God, I've tried. Many times. But – well, I always failed. Always. Or at least where there was any affection, any regard.'

'But Alexander, you – '

'Yes?'

'You have seemed to – want me. You've kissed me, held me, just now, you were – oh God.' She threw her head back, fighting down the tears.

'Of course I want you. I think you are the most beautiful, desirable woman I have ever known. I want you terribly. And I love you. It's so very important that you understand that, Virginia. I love you very much.'

'Oh for God's sake,' she said, and for the first time there was anger in her voice. 'How can you talk of loving me? How could you do this to anyone you loved?'

'I'll try to explain. Somehow. But first you must try and believe that I do, I do love you. You are exactly the woman I want to spend my life with. You're warm and tender, and clever and vulnerable. I fell in love with you immediately, that first day, over lunch. I wanted, from that day on, to marry you, to make you my wife.'

'But – '

'Virginia, you mustn't fall into the trap of confusing impotence with a lack of desire. I feel great desire. My body feels it, even displays it – at times. But – ' He looked at her, and there were tears in his eyes; then he bent his head. 'I looked at you, lying there, and I wanted you almost beyond endurance. I loved holding you, loving you. But I knew – well, I'm sorry. I can only keep saying that.'

'Have you tried to get help?'

'Oh, Virginia. Of course I have. I've seen doctors, psychiatrists, analysts, sex therapists. I've had electrotherapy, drug therapy, psychotherapy. Ever since I realized, the first time I tried to make love to a girl, I have tried to be cured.'

'How old were you then?'

'Sixteen.' He looked at her, smiled shakily. 'Very young. She was a village girl, of course – '

'Oh of course.' She sounded bitter. 'That's the aristocratic way, isn't it? In England? Christ. A village girl.'

He met her gaze steadily. 'Maybe. But I liked her, I was very fond of her, and I had known her for years, her mother worked for us. We played together as children. I had found the homosexual activity at school disgusting, terribly upsetting. But I did feel sexual desire. I keep coming back to that, Virginia, to wanting you to understand. And I wanted to – experience it.'

'But?'

'Well – I found it impossible. I failed. Failed totally.'

'And –'

'Well, I tried again. With another girl. It was the same. I began to worry. But I thought it was inexperience, not knowing quite what I was doing. Oh Christ.' He looked away from her.

'So when did you try to get help? Did you talk to your – no, I suppose not, not your parents, your father –'

'My father! Dear Christ, Virginia, had it not been for my father, I would be making love to you now. Or so they have told me, the shrinks. Or many of them. He – oh God, I don't want, I can't talk about that, not now –'

His eyes looking at her had tears in them again. She put her hand on his. For the first time she felt pity. 'It's all right. Another time.'

'Perhaps.' There was another silence. 'So – I started on this long, terrible path. I saw our GP. He was bluff, foolishly optimistic, told me to relax, that it would be all right. Then he sent me to a specialist. He gave me some bloody silly exercises to do before I attempted to make love. The shame, the absurdity of it made me worse. I tried again, with a girl at Oxford. But I was beginning to be very afraid, that word would get round. So I would dodge the issue, draw back. Literally.' He laughed briefly, savagely. It was an ugly sound. Virginia pulled the covers further up around her.

'Well, I don't think I need to go on. I've done the rounds, that's all I can say. Tried everything. They say it's hopeless.'

'And have you never, ever –' She kept failing to say what she wanted to; the words were too ugly, too frightening.

'Oh, like all impotent men, or most, I've achieved something with a few prostitutes. A doctor suggested that, and it worked. I was astonished, elated even. But with someone I care about at all, it's no use. I'm a classic case, they tell me. Absolutely classic. If I dislike, despise someone, I can make love to them. You might,' he said, with a slight smile, 'you might take some comfort from that.'

★

Virginia lay and looked again out of the window. So many emotions were raging in her, she was incapable of feeling any of them clearly. Disgust, fear, anger, shock; they all merged into a kind of wild panic, in which she trod, almost submerged, battling to maintain some kind of sanity.

She was silent for a long time; then she said, 'But Alexander, I can understand that you are – impotent. That you are capable of feeling love, desire even. What I can't understand is how you could do what you have done to me. Tricked me. Trapped me. When you say you love me.'

'Well,' he said, and there was a great softness and tenderness in his eyes, and an odd humour as well, 'well you see, I wanted a wife. Very badly. For many reasons. And I fell in love with you. And I chose you.'

'But that's – that's horrible.'

'Why? I have much to offer. As you know. You wanted it. Quite badly, I suspect.'

'Alexander, this is absurd. Whatever I wanted, had I known about this, about you, I would never, ever have married you.'

'No,' he said with a sigh, 'no, I realize that. Although I do flatter myself that you wanted me along with the rest. You were in love with me, weren't you, Virginia? It wasn't just the house, the title, and all that?'

'Alexander, of course it wasn't. Of course I fell in love with you. It wasn't the house and the title at all.'

'Ah, now here you are beginning to depart from the truth a little. And I begin to feel just slightly less guilty. Of course you wanted the title, the status – and of course you will want the house.'

'Alexander, I don't intend ever to see the house. I'm going home.'

'Well, we shall see.'

'There is nothing to see,' she said, and her face was shocked at his words. 'Of course I am going.'

'So,' he said, 'so I was wrong. You didn't – you don't love me.'

'Alexander, I can't love you. Not now.'

'Why not? Nothing has changed.'

'Well of course it's changed,' she cried out in an agony of frustration. 'You've tricked me. You are not who – what – I thought you were.'

'Nonsense. I am precisely what you thought I was. In all respects but one. One which I suggest we can overcome. Together.'

'You mean – ' her eyes were hopeful, eager even – 'you mean, you think I can help you to – to be better?'

'No, I fear you cannot do that. I know you cannot. I have to tell you that in all informed opinion – from several countries, including your own – you are doomed to failure. And because I find the failure so very painful, heartbreaking, I would prefer it that you did not attempt to go that particular route.'

'Then I don't know what you mean. And I can't consider staying. I want to go home. I want to go home now.' Suddenly her icy calm cracked; tears rose in her throat, choked her, welled into her eyes. She began to cry and then to sob hysterically. She lay back, beating the bed with her fists, lashing out at Alexander as he tried to get near her, to comfort her. He looked at her first with pity and infinite regret and then, as her hysteria increased, almost with fear.

'Please,' he said, 'please don't.'

'Get away!' screamed Virginia. 'Get away. Get out of my sight. You're disgusting. I loathe you. It's terrible what you've done, terrible.'

'Don't,' he said, 'don't say that. It's not so terrible.'

She was so shocked, she stopped crying.

'Of course it's terrible. How can you say that?'

'Because it's true. Listen to me. Please listen.'

She sat silent again, great tears rolling silently down her face.

'Look,' he said, 'I do love you. I really do love you. I loved you straight away, and then I loved you more. And more. I loved your gentleness, your vulnerability, your great honesty. I loved your beauty and your charm. I thought you were a perfect perfect wife for me. And I wanted you. I wanted you so much. And I knew we could be happy together.'

'Alexander, this is – '

'Please bear with me. Virginia, I do have a lot to offer. Be honest. Forget the sex thing.'

'But – '

'Forget it,' he said, and his eyes were pleading, and oddly sad. 'I know you wanted the rest, Virginia. I know you did. I know you were dazzled by the thought of being a countess, the mistress of Hartest. Be honest, isn't it true?'

'Well – '

'Isn't it?'

'I – I suppose so.'

'You were. I know you began actually to want that as much as you wanted me. I found that hurtful initially, but – well, it helped me make my decision. It was success for you. You've been so put down by your father, in the shadow of your brother, always slightly mocked in the family, discounted however gently by the circle your parents move in, and I came along with this great glittering prize and all your family, all your friends, the press, everyone, was suddenly admiring, impressed, in awe of you. Virginia Praeger, her family's second best, was to be the Countess of Caterham, mistress of one of the most beautiful houses in England, mother of the future earl. It was a dazzling prospect, wasn't it, Virginia? Admit it?'

511

'Yes,' she said, and for the first time there was a coolness in her eyes. 'Yes it was. But – '

'And there were days, lots of days, more and more of them recently, when you weren't quite quite sure about me. I saw you looking at me, consideringly, sometimes, and I knew what you were thinking, and I knew you were stifling it. But I never ever felt for a single moment that I was not quite sure about you. I loved you on that very first day and I never felt so much as a flicker of doubt.'

'You have a very strange way of showing it,' she said. She felt calmer again. 'May I have some more champagne?'

'The bottle's empty. Shall we have some more?'

'Yes. Call room service.' Looking back she was to see her alcohol dependence began at that moment.

'Shall I get some more strawberries?'

'No, I hate strawberries. Get some raspberries.' Suddenly for some reason she felt light-headed, almost happy. She knew it wouldn't last, that the horror would return, but just for that moment, she felt good: indulged, greedy, powerful.

'Very well.'

He ordered; then returned to the bed.

'Are you still cold?'

'No. No, I'm not.'

'It's a beautiful day.'

'Yes.' She got out of bed, walked over to the window. The water of the Canale di San Marco stretched below and beyond her, an incredible shimmering blue; on either side of her stood the golden buildings of Venice, etched into the sky, echoed in the water below them. She tried to feel wretched, harmed – and failed; the beauty drove away the darkness. Alexander looked at her. 'Do you like it? Do you like Venice?'

'It's a little hard to say,' she said, and moved onto the balcony. The sun was warm; she heard the sounds of Venice, the endless cacophony of voices, the shouts of the gondoliers, the cries of the gulls, the sound of the water itself, mellowing, softening everything, soothing her despair. Alexander came out behind her. He held a glass of champagne in his hand, gave it to her.

'Here. Promise me – '

'Alexander, don't be ridiculous. I can't promise you anything. Of course I can't.'

'You can. You can promise me just to come and see St Mark's with me. Please.'

'I – '

'Yes, we will go later. You have to see it. Then you can leave. If that is really what you want.'

'Yes, Alexander, it is. It is what I want. Well, not what I want, but what I have to do. You have to see that.'

'Perhaps.'

'Not perhaps. You must.'

'Well. Here, take your raspberries.'

'Thank you.' She sat down, stretched her long legs out onto the ledge of the balcony. The sun felt hot, comforting on her face. She drank her champagne, picked the raspberries out of the basket. Suddenly she turned to him. 'Alexander?'

'Yes.'

'Alexander, what did you think – plan for us? I really would be intrigued to know.'

'Oh,' he said, 'a working arrangement.'

'I'm sorry,' she said, 'but I cannot imagine how such a thing could be.'

'Well,' he said, 'clearly I need an heir. I must have an heir. If I don't, Hartest and the title will go.'

'Well, somewhere there must be a taker for it,' she said. 'Some deserving distant relative. Living perhaps in a humble croft. A village person, maybe.' Her face was contemptuous.

'Virginia, you know how I feel about Hartest. I could not even consider letting it go to someone else other than my son. Other than someone who had been reared in it, fashioned by it. Someone who had been taught to love it, to value it, by me. I would rather demolish it stone by stone.'

'You really mean that, don't you?' she said, looking at him curiously.

'Of course I do. I really mean it. Hartest is what I love most in the world. I would do anything in the world to save it for myself and my children. Anything.'

'Why does it matter so much to you?' she said. 'Do you know?'

'Yes,' he said, 'I think I know. I love it because of its beauty, its history, its grace, of course, I feel it is part of me, it is somehow in the fabric of myself. But more even than those things is that it has saved me. Kept me sane. I would leave my father after some ghastly scene, be forced to listen to my parents fighting, quarrelling, or worse – '

'Worse? What?'

'I don't want to talk about that,' he said quickly, 'just try to understand. Whatever ugliness, whatever pain I had endured, I would walk into the house, or simply stand outside and look at it, and feel healed, comforted. It was like some calm, beautiful womb I could retreat into, where I was

safe and at peace. It is all the world to me, Virginia. Does that answer
your question?'

'I suppose it does.' Her voice was very distant and cool.

'Drink your champagne. Let me refill your glass.'

'I'm getting drunk,' she said and giggled suddenly.

'It doesn't matter.'

'I suppose not. So you need an heir. I suppose I am to go and get one for
you.'

'Yes.'

The simplicity of his answer, the calm assurance with which he said it,
stunned her; she turned towards him, stared at him, her eyes wide with
horror.

'Alexander, you can't – '

'Yes I can. I have thought about this very carefully. Very carefully
indeed. You shall have whatever you want. Whatever. You have only to
ask. I – want you to be happy. You may have lovers, as many as you like.
Of course you must be very discreet. But I won't – '

Virginia suddenly started to laugh, half-hysterical, wild laughter.

'Don't,' he said, 'please don't. I can't bear it.'

'*You* can't bear it. Alexander, do try to imagine how I'm feeling. This is
like being trapped in some nightmare. Some dreadful sick nightmare.
You can't bear it!'

The scorn, the disgust in her voice was harsh, heavy. He stood up,
looked down at her, and his face was white.

'I think I should go out for a while,' he said, 'we can talk more later.'

'Alexander, there's nothing to talk about. Please understand that.'

'No. No, maybe not.'

'Not maybe. There isn't.'

'Very well. But I would still like to go out. Promise me – '

'Yes?'

'Promise me you won't go while I'm not here. Please. I would want to
say goodbye.'

'Very well,' she said with a sigh. 'I won't go.'

When he came back she was asleep, back in the great bed; the shutters
were still open, and the room was filled with the late afternoon light,
darker, more intensely gold. Her dark hair was splayed across the pillow,
her face was peaceful, like a child's. He bent and kissed her, and she woke,
smiling up at him, reaching her arms to him; then he watched reality
come back to her, hostility to her eyes, hardness to her face.

'Hallo,' he said. 'It's getting late.'

'I feel terrible,' she said, 'I have a terrible headache.'

514

'It's the champagne,' he said, 'and that endless flight. I'm so sorry.'

'No,' she said. 'Alexander, no it isn't. It's what's happened, what's happening. Please try to accept that.'

'All right.'

'I'm going to have a bath. Could you get some tea? Some china tea?'

'Of course.'

'I've checked on flights. There's one tonight to London. I'd like to get it.'

'So you won't,' he said, 'you won't come and see St Mark's?'

'I don't think so, no. I'm sorry to have broken my promise. But I have to get away.'

'I understand.'

'I'm sorry, Alexander.'

He ordered a water taxi for her, watched her pack her overnight bag. The rest was still in her suitcases and trunks. She felt foolish, oddly ill at ease.

'Alexander,' she said, 'could you – would you – mind waiting for me downstairs?'

'Of course not.'

He went out. She suddenly felt terribly alone and frightened. More than anything in the world she wanted to talk to someone familiar and close. Her mother. Yes, she would call her mother. It was early morning in New York, she would be pleased to hear from her. She wouldn't tell her everything, just that she was coming home. She asked the operator to get the number for her. Banks answered.

'Hallo, Banks. This is Miss – Lady Caterham.'

'Lady Caterham! How good to hear from you. That was a beautiful wedding, if I might say so. The staff all enjoyed it so much.'

'Thank you, Banks. Could I speak with my mother, please?'

'Of course. Just wait a moment, Your Ladyship.' She could hear him savouring the last two words.

For the first time Virginia came against the reality of what she was going to have to do. What she was going to have to say. The number of people, the hundreds, the thousands, who would be intrigued, fascinated, whatever she said, whatever story she told, who would gossip, exchange theories, laugh, sneer possibly. It was going to be very painful, very ugly. Well, it was too bad. It had to be done. She had no choice.

Betsey's voice came onto the phone, breathless, happy.

'Darling, how lovely of you to call. I was just beginning to wonder about you. How are you, my darling? Oh, that was such a beautiful beautiful wedding. I was so proud, so very proud. And your father – oh Virginia, I have never seen him so moved. Never. Not even when Baby –

515

when you were both born. The last thing he said, when we got into bed last night, was, "I was so proud of her today. So proud of my little girl." ' Betsey's voice wavered. 'Oh darling, I'm sorry, getting emotional at you on your honeymoon. It's just that – well, how are you, darling? And how is Venice? Are you enjoying it, have you been to St Mark's yet?'

'No.' Virginia's voice seemed out of sync with her brain, it was unwilling to form words. She cleared her throat. 'No not yet. Mother – '

'I suppose you're tired. You must be terribly tired, actually. Is the hotel nice?'

'Yes, it's beautiful.'

'I'm so envious. I have always wanted to go to Venice. Your father never would take me. Well, I mustn't run on too much, Alexander doesn't want you spending too much time on the phone to your mother, I'm sure. Just so long as you're all right.'

'Yes,' said Virginia slowly. 'Yes, I'm fine. Thank you.'

'Good. Well send Alexander our love. And write me the minute you get to Hartest House, I don't expect anything while you're in Venice. Goodbye, darling. I'll send your love to your father. He was having the photographs rushed round to the bank this morning, he said he couldn't wait to start reliving the day. He said – oh maybe I shouldn't tell you this, yes of course I should, whyever not, he said it was ten times more beautiful a wedding than Baby and Mary Rose's and you were a hundred times a more beautiful and charming bride. I tell you, darling, you really have made him very proud. And me. And when Banks came in just then and said, "Her Ladyship is on the phone," well I just had to pinch myself.'

'You're such a terrible terrible snob, Mother,' said Virginia, and in spite of herself she smiled into the phone. 'Look, I'll call you again. Soon.'

'Darling, don't bother. Unless you want to. 'You'll be very – ' she paused delicately – 'very busy. There's such a lot to see in Venice.'

'Yes. Yes there is. Goodbye, Mother.'

She put the phone down and looked out of the window. Venice was blurred with tears.

'Baby? It's Virginia.'

'My sister the Countess. To what do I owe this honour, Your Ladyship? My goodness, Mary Rose is regretting marrying little old me. When she might have been a ladyship too. No consoling her last night, I can tell you.'

'Oh Baby, don't.'

'Sorry. Crass New World behaviour. I suppose over there titles are two a penny. Anyway, you're in two of the papers this morning, the *Times* and the *News*. And a big piece in Cholly Knickerbocker's column.

You know how we Americans do still love a bit of real blue blood. And *Woman's Wear Daily* are running a story too, they've been on to Mother apparently, asking if they can use pictures of you in your dress and your going away, she's so excited, she rang Mary Rose to tell her. Big mistake, that. Big. Heavy frost it brought on. I tell you, Virgy, you really are a star here. I just hope England is going to appreciate you as much.'

'Well – oh, Baby, it is nice to talk to you.'

'On your honeymoon! Virgy, don't tell me you're homesick. Isn't the gilded Earl keeping you happy?'

There was the faintest touch of contempt in his voice. Against all logic Virginia felt defensive about Alexander.

'Yes, of course – it's just – '

'Darling, I have to go. I'm sorry. Big meeting. Huge. Call me any time. Give my love to Venice. And make sure you go to the Guggenheim, it's gorgeous, and I am not a culture man, as you know, and of course you have to go to Harry's Bar. I want you to see it as your personal responsibility to keep the Yank flag flying in Europe. Although you're half English now, I suppose.'

'Don't be silly, Baby, of course I'm not.'

'Well, bye, darling. Thanks for calling. Lots of love.'

'Lots of love, Baby.'

She sat icy-still on the bed. She was still there, twenty minutes later, when Alexander came in.

'Virginia, the taxi's here. Would you like me to come with you to the airport?'

Virginia looked up at him. Her face was very pale, her golden eyes coolly blank. Then she smiled, a distant, tight little smile.

'Alexander, I think I may not leave tonight. I'm terribly tired. And hungry. Perhaps we could go out to dinner, I thought Harry's Bar would be fun, and then in the morning I might after all like to see St Mark's.'

Chapter 45

Georgina, 1985–6

It had been her fault, the whole ghastly thing. Her fault for hurting and upsetting her father so much that it had brought about a breakdown. How could she have done it, how could she, when she loved him so much, far more than Charlotte and Max did, when she and she alone had stayed loyal to him, refusing to consider seeking out some dubious, alternative father – Georgina couldn't even contemplate the word 'real', Alexander, tender, supportive, endlessly loving, was her real father – how could it have been her who had caused him such terrible, destructive pain?

She had sat by him, holding his hand, watching him helpless as he wept, great racking sobs, while they waited for the doctor to come, wishing she was a thousand miles away, that it was she who was enduring this pain, wishing she was dead. 'I did this,' she said, staring helplessly up at Angie, who was looking as stricken, as frightened as she was; and Angie had said, 'No, no, don't be silly, Georgina, of course you didn't,' trying to calm her. But it didn't help, didn't make her feel any better, she just kept hearing her own voice telling Alexander he was mad, that she should have realized it a long time ago, and seeing herself running down the steps after Kendrick, jumping into his car and telling him to drive away, not looking back.

Thank God, thank God she had felt so bad, so guilty; otherwise she might have stayed away for hours, all day even; they had driven to a pub and Kendrick had been upset too: 'Anyone would think I was some kind of a monster,' he said, staring moodily into his beer, 'a pervert, what does he have against me, what did I ever do to him?' And she had tried to comfort him, to calm him, to tell him that it had just been a shock, that her father would come round; and Kendrick had looked at her very strangely and said, 'But he's not even your father, not really, so why – ' and she had said, feeling he had hit her, 'Don't say that, Kendrick, please. I should never have told you, he is my father to me, I don't even want to *start* going down that road.'

And then she had begun to worry again, about Alexander, and she had told Kendrick she thought they should go back and he had said there was no way he was going to confront Alexander again, and she had finally said she wanted to go back anyway, and he had dropped her at the bottom of the steps and she had run in and heard the ghastly wailing coming from the gun room, and Angie had come out looking ashen and said, 'Oh, Georgina, thank God you're here, your father's had some kind of breakdown, I'm going to call the doctor, stay here with him, and I'll find Nanny.'

And she had gone in, and he was sitting there, his head in his hands, crying, sobbing, and she tried to put her arms round him, and he pushed her away and said, 'No, no, don't, don't touch me.'

And then Nanny had come in, with Angie, looking stern and concerned, but very calm and composed.

'He's been doing too much,' she had said severely, 'he's overtired, I knew this would happen,' and then she had sat down beside him and put her old arms round him and started patting and stroking him, and saying, 'There there, Alexander, it's all right, it's perfectly all right,' and gradually he had quietened and had clung to Nanny, whimpering and sobbing.

'He's not quite himself,' Nanny said, speaking to them over his head, as if they might have assumed that this was the way he often behaved, and Angie had nodded and said no, she could see that; and then Dr Rogers had come in, and tried to talk to him, and Alexander had pushed him away, shouting that he didn't want any bloody doctors near him; and finally Dr Rogers had given him a shot and suggested they helped him up to bed.

Later when he was sleeping peacefully, Dr Rogers had said, 'I would say, without knowing very much more, that he's had a complete mental breakdown. I'll call in a colleague in the morning. Was anyone with him when it happened?'

'I was,' said Angie. 'I'd been talking to him. He was upset. He'd had a – an argument with Georgina. Isn't that right, Georgina?'

'Yes,' said Georgina, feeling panic rising up in her chest, 'yes I'm afraid so. I – I – ' The room swam suddenly, and she had to sit down.

Angie put her arm round her.

'It's all right, Georgina. And then he started talking about Virginia – about Lady Caterham. And gradually he became more and more upset and then suddenly he was crying and then . . .' Her face was shocked, strained. 'I – I didn't know what to do. I'm sorry.'

'You did fine,' said Dr Rogers, 'but all that does confirm my diagnosis. Anyway, I'll ask Dr Simkins to come over in the morning.'

He stood up, closed his bag, walked out towards the stairs. Georgina followed him, so frightened she could hardly speak.

'Dr Rogers, I have to talk to you. It's all my fault. All of it.'

Dr Rogers turned and looked at her very benignly. 'I doubt that, Georgina,' he said, 'I really do. You mustn't blame yourself.'

'No, but you don't understand, we had a row, I said the most terrible thing to him. I told him – told him – ' Her voice trailed away. Dr Rogers smiled at her.

'Georgina, whatever you told him, it couldn't have done this to him. This is a severe breakdown. The unkindest words – and I'm sure they weren't that unkind – from a much-loved daughter could not possibly have caused it. Your father has had a lot of strain over the past few years. It hasn't been easy for him. I would say you've been a source of great comfort to him. The others have gone, haven't they? Left home.'

'Yes,' said Georgina. 'It might have been better if I'd gone too.' She wiped away her tears on the back of her arm. Dr Rogers smiled at her and gave her his handkerchief.

'Nonsense. I'm sure it was a very good thing you were here. And that you're going to be here in the next few weeks, to help him through this. Try not to worry. He'll be all right in a little while. You just help Nanny take care of him. Wonderful old girl, she is. You're lucky to have her. Goodbye, Georgina. Keep the handkerchief. I'll see myself out.' He turned and went down the stairs.

'Goodbye,' said Georgina, her voice little more than a whisper. She went back into the bedroom.

'Should I stay?' Angie was saying. 'I feel faintly responsible, but I really ought to get back to Baby.'

'It would be better if you didn't stay,' said Nanny sternly. 'He needs complete peace and quiet.' Her look and tone implied that Angie would be bringing in a large and noisy party complete with rock band at any moment.

'Well, that's fine then,' said Angie meekly. 'I'll get along home. Nanny, would you call me tomorrow when this Dr Simkins has been? Tell me what he says. Or should I be there?'

'No, that won't be necessary,' said Nanny, 'Georgina and I will take care of him. Won't we, Georgina?'

'Yes,' said Georgina very quietly. She set aside any hopes of seeing Kendrick before he left next day. She felt that if she had to devote the rest of her life to looking after her father it would not be penance enough.

Dr Simkins pronounced Alexander to be suffering from a severe breakdown and acute depression, probably suppressed for years since Virginia's death; he said he should be admitted to a private psychiatric nursing home for a few weeks until he began to improve. Since then Alexander had seen two other psychiatrists and shown some signs of the promised improvement; he had been moved home at the suggestion of the second, with a full-time nurse, and was at least more relaxed. In the nursing home he had been possessed by an appalling restlessness, and had paced his room all day and most of the night, sitting intermittently in his chair and staring blankly in front of him. Georgina had gone with Nanny to see him twice, and so had Charlotte and Max, but he had hardly seemed to recognize any of them, sitting silent while they tried to talk to him, make him smile, even show any emotion at all.

'Let him go home to that house of his he loves so much,' the new psychiatrist had said, 'and see if that doesn't do him some good.'

Nanny and Georgina had gone together with Tallow to fetch him, and the doctor had been right, it had worked straight away; as the car had swung round the corner out of the woods and into the Great Drive, Alexander's mouth had softened into a smile, and his blue eyes had filled with tears.

'How lovely,' he had said. 'Home.'

He was still not well, he was vague, still quietly distant much of the time, physically frail, and heavily dosed with antidepressant; but gradually, they watched him growing stronger, and by the time the spring came, and the daffodils were beginning to daub the meadows of the park with great banks of gold, he was beginning to talk, to smile, to be himself again.

She hadn't seen Kendrick since. Nanny and Angie had both urged her to go and see him off at Heathrow, but she refused. 'I can't leave Daddy. And Kendrick will understand.'

Kendrick did understand – at first. He told her on the phone he loved her, that of course she must stay with her dad, that he felt guilty too, just a little. But he was angry when she told him she had dropped out of college, and angrier and very hurt when she refused to go to New York for his twenty-first birthday in February: 'It's important, Georgina, it's only a small family celebration, but I really want you to be there.' Georgina had refused, saying she couldn't leave, that her father was still very ill, that her own birthday would certainly go, unremarked, at her own request.

'The doctor specifically said I should stay here, be with him, that it was important in helping him get better. I don't want to fail him, Kendrick.'

'You're taking this much too seriously,' said Kendrick, clearly irritated. 'He's getting better, you said so, and he won't miss you for two days, for God's sake. And whenever are we going to tell people, make the announcement?'

Georgina said that wasn't the point and she didn't know when they could make the announcement. Kendrick put the phone down. He called back to apologize, but things between them were strained.

She was walking in the woods one windy March day when she met Martin Dunbar. She had the dogs with her; they had been very subdued ever since Alexander had been taken ill, hanging about at the bottom of the stairs when he had been in bed, and haunting him now from the moment he appeared in the morning until he went back after supper. Even walks seemed to hold little pleasure for them; she had had trouble getting them out.

'Georgina!' said Martin. 'How lovely to see you. It's been such a long time. How's your father? I popped in last week, when you were out shopping, and he certainly seemed a little better.'

'Oh, he is better,' said Georgina. 'Definitely. Getting home to Hartest has made all the difference. He's talking quite a lot these days, and this morning at breakfast he even laughed, over Bernard Levin's column in *The Times*.'

'Well, that *is* good news. It must have been very worrying for you. And you must miss college. When are you going back?'

'Oh – I don't know. Not yet. Not till he's quite well.'

'What a good daughter you are,' he said, and his eyes were sad even as he smiled at her. 'Alexander is lucky to have you.'

Oh God, she thought, if only, if only he knew.

Kendrick didn't come for Easter; he was studying very hard for his finals. He begged her to go over, but she said she couldn't. 'Daddy's so much better, I don't want to upset things now. We go for quite a long walk every day, he says it does more for him than all the drugs. I'm sorry, Kendrick.'

'That's all right,' he said. His voice was rather distant; he seemed a long way away suddenly.

'Georgina? This is Angie. How's Alexander? I'm sorry I haven't been over lately. Things have been a bit – difficult.'

'Of course. He's better. Definitely. How are you?'

'I'm feeling pretty good, Georgina, thank you. I've rung to ask you to a wedding.'

'That'd be fun,' said Georgina cautiously. 'Whose?'

'Mine.' Angie's voice sounded triumphant, almost wobbly.

'Yours? But I thought – '

'Yes, we all thought. But Mary Rose has decided to give Baby a divorce. Just like that. So it means we can get married.'

'Oh Angie, that's wonderful news. I'm pleased.' Slightly to her own surprise, Georgina discovered she really was. 'When?'

'In just over a month. They're rushing it through. Last Saturday in April. Kendrick will be over of course, and Melissa and Freddy, and Fred the Third and Mrs Praeger – you know I've never even met her – everyone really. So keep it free, won't you, and find a really splendid hat.'

'I will.'

Georgina thought how odd it was that someone who had been as good as married to Baby for what was after all a long time should never have met his mother.

'When did you hear?'

'Oh, only about two hours ago,' said Angie. 'I haven't hit the ground yet. I expect Kendrick will be ringing you, but I wanted to tell you myself first.'

She's really excited, thought Georgina, smiling into the phone. She really does love him.

Kendrick phoned her later that night, and talked to her about it; he was clearly feeling a little confused, pleased he said for his father, but sad for his mother, impressed by the huge gesture she had made.

'I think she still loves Dad, and she just can't face the guilt of denying him what he so wants, now that he's – well, now he's ill.'

'Well, I think that's really nice,' said Georgina carefully, anxious not to upset Kendrick. 'How do the others feel?'

'Well, Melissa is of course in a great spin, planning her bridesmaid's dress, and her hairstyle, and wondering if Max might be best man, and Freddy is – well, a little quiet.'

'But he will come?' said Georgina anxiously. 'Uncle Baby would break his heart if he didn't.'

'Oh yes he'll come,' said Kendrick.

'And Grandpa and Grandma?'

'Yes of course. Grandma is terribly excited, almost as much as Melissa.'

'Well,' said Georgina, laughing, 'she never seems all that much older than Melissa to me.'

'And then there's us,' said Kendrick. 'We can talk to Dad now, can't we? Make it official. Specially as your dad seems to be getting better.'

'Yes,' said Georgina, 'yes, I suppose we can.'

Baby and Angie were married on a breezy gold and blue spring day, a registry office wedding in Oxford and then a blessing in the village church. It was a poignant occasion; nobody there able to quite forget that the only thing that had made it possible, for all its defiant happiness, its triumph, its courage, was the fact that Baby was dying.

The entire family and a few close friends were there, Fred III looking stern as Freddy pushed Baby up the aisle in a wheelchair dressed for the occasion in white ribbons. Betsey, her eyes very bright, clutched Fred's hand, dared by his fierce old face to cry. Melissa, as bridesmaid, looked ravishing in a dress from Mexicana, all endless layers of white lace and frills, with white roses tangled in her golden hair; it was remarked upon by most of the family that her attention seemed fixed more firmly on Max than on the bride and groom; as Max had not brought Gemma, saying the occasion was strictly family, she had him and her fantasies about him to herself. The twins, who were being restrained with great difficulty at the back of the church by their nanny, were dressed as page boys, in white sailor suits, and Mrs Wicks almost stole the whole show by appearing in a full-length white silk dress with a very floaty skirt, slashed up one side to the knee, revealing an extremely shapely leg, as Max remarked to Georgina in a hoarse stage whisper, designed to be heard by the legs' owner. She wore what could only be described as a coronet in her red curls, and over the white dress a silver fox jacket. She had refused to allow Clifford to come, as she said he would be an intruder; Baby proposed the theory later to Angie that she wanted a free hand with Alexander. Georgina caught sight of Nanny's face as Mrs Wicks arrived; her lips were folded in so tightly they were invisible, her eyes brilliant with disapproval.

Alexander, to everyone's surprise and pleasure, had insisted on coming; he said he felt much stronger, and he would not have missed it for the world. He was looking pale and particularly vague, and he clung rather tightly to Georgina's hand throughout the service, but he sang all the hymns very vigorously and smiled most benevolently on the bride as she came down the aisle.

The bride was wearing an utterly simple, low-waisted, ankle-length white crepe dress by Jean Muir, skimming over her body, demurely high at the front and slashed almost to her cleavage at the back (covered for the church service by a long matching jacket). She carried a great bouquet of white roses and freesia, and in her hair, as if to acknowledge the considerable effrontery of her virginal attire, she wore a coronet of blood-red roses. She looked very pretty and extraordinarily young, and when the vicar said, 'I now pronounce you man and wife,' she leant down and kissed Baby in his wheelchair and flung her arms round his neck.

'Theatrical nonsense,' Georgina heard Nanny hiss in Mrs Tallow's ear, but when she looked round, she saw that she was smiling.

Tommy Soames-Maxwell had slipped into the back of the church at the very last minute and then slipped out again, almost unnoticed by most of the guests, and driven swiftly away again; he had asked Angie if he might come, saying he would not miss it for anything if she would have him there, but he had no wish to embarrass or upset Alexander or anyone else in the family. Even Charlotte was mollified by this behaviour and told Georgina afterwards at the reception at the house that perhaps she had misjudged him just a little and he was not after all entirely bad. Georgina, who had a sneaking liking for the supposedly wicked Tommy, and knew from Max how kind he had been to Baby, said cautiously that she didn't think he was entirely bad either.

Fred III got up at the reception and asked everyone to raise their glasses to the bride and groom, on what was a wonderfully happy day; he said from where he was looking, Baby was an outstandingly fortunate man, and nobody was to be fooled by the wheelchair or any other damnfool nonsense into thinking otherwise. It was a charming and graceful little speech, entirely diffusing any awkwardness from the situation; nevertheless Georgina, looking at Baby and Angie through eyes blurred with tears, found it impossible not to wonder how long the marriage would be allowed to last, and how much that thought had shadowed the day for them.

Kendrick drove her away after the reception; he said he had no idea where he was going, but he wanted to get her away from everyone. It was still quite early, before seven, and dusk was only just beginning to settle on the Cotswold hills. Baby had been exhausted, although very happy, and it was tacitly agreed that everyone should quietly disappear. Georgina had been worried about Alexander and said she should drive him home, but he had insisted on going back with Nanny and the Tallows. He was very tired, he said, and certainly he had behaved slightly strangely at the reception; after shaking Baby's hand and telling him he was a lucky chap, and kissing Angie in a rather desultory manner, he had disappeared for the rest of the afternoon and was found by Charlotte playing with the twins in the nursery. He said he was sorry, but he hadn't felt like talking.

'Well now,' said Kendrick, pulling the car to a halt in a gateway on a particularly pretty lane. 'What do you want to do?'

'Oh, I don't know,' said Georgina, deliberately misunderstanding him. 'Go for a walk maybe. I had much too much champagne. I'll tell you what I'd really like to do,' she added, smiling at him, thinking how infinitely sexy he looked, in his striped trousers and black waistcoat, his morning coat discarded, his white shirt open at the neck. 'I'd like to go to bed with you. Well, there doesn't have to be a bed. Right now, if we can find somewhere.'

Kendrick lifted his hand, and pushed it into her hair; his eyes seemed to bore into hers, wide, dark with love. 'We'll find somewhere,' he said and leant forward and started to kiss her, very slowly, very lazily. Georgina returned the kiss, gently at first then with increasing intensity; she felt desire growing, burgeoning in her like some strong living being. Tamed, restrained by the past months, by grief, by guilt, by loneliness, it had finally broken free, was demanding release; she pulled away from him, her face solemn, intent.

'I mean it,' she said, 'I can't wait,' and smiling, he opened his door, walked round and took her hand, pulled her out, and with his eyes still fixed on her face, led her into the woods. She stumbled a little, in the high heels she had worn for the wedding, tripping over small roots, curling fronds of bracken; impatiently, she pulled them off, walked in her stockings, smiling up at Kendrick, a confident, reckless smile. They were deeper into the wood now, and the dusk was growing thicker, almost misty. 'Here,' he said, smiling, 'here is a bed for us,' and just below them a small hollow lay, filled with new bracken and great sheets of bluebells.

She ran into it ahead of him, smiling too, and sank onto the ground, holding out her arms to him; the last thing she remembered saying as the sweet all-consuming hunger took possession of her was 'We shall crush the bluebells,' and he said, 'Fuck the bluebells,' and then all she knew was his body on hers, warm, heavy, hungry too, his hands everywhere, on her breasts, her stomach, her thighs, her buttocks, and then her own body arched up to him, welcoming him into her, and as he entered her, she felt a sweet rich triumph, a sense of absolute pleasure and joy, and even while she moved, gave to him, while her whole being ebbed and flowed, rose and fell, she was able to think, to know, to feel quite clearly that this was not how it had been before, and might never ever be again.

When it was over, when finally they were quiet, lying there on their brackeny bed, smiling at one another, awed, almost frightened by the depths, the heights, they had travelled and accomplished, Kendrick pulled his jacket over her, folded his shirt under her head, and said, 'I love you, Georgina. I want you to be my wife.'

And Georgina looked up at him, courageous suddenly, joyful, strong, and said, 'I want it, Kendrick. I want it too.'

They went back to Watersfoot, and crept in the back door, aware that no one seeing them could fail to know what they had been doing. Angie and

Baby were up in their room; nobody else seemed to be there. Kendrick disappeared and came down with towels, jeans, jumpers, 'And two pairs of rather male briefs, I'm sorry,' and they went into the shower together, next to the utility room, and stood in the thudding water, and made love again, thoughtless, careless suddenly of who might find them there, and then they got dressed, Kendrick made them both mugs of tea and she sat in the den just looking at him and loving him, and not doing anything at all except thinking of pleasures past and the great happiness hopefully to come.

In the morning, Baby was unwell; they had been going to talk to him, to tell him their news and their plans, but Angie said he had a chest infection, that the doctor had said he must be kept quiet. She looked extremely tired, almost dazed; Georgina said that she should go back to Hartest and see Alexander, and asked Kendrick to come with her. Kendrick said he would stay; that maybe his father would like to see him later. Angie seemed grateful.

Later in the day, Baby was worse; a specialist was called, he was given more drugs, there was talk of hospital. Kendrick's voice on the phone was heavy; Georgina was frightened, angry almost, that the happiness that had been granted to Baby should have been so short-lived, so tantalizingly tenuous.

But next morning he seemed better; by the afternoon he was sitting up and shouting at everyone, and desperate for some time together, Georgina and Kendrick fled to London, leaving everyone in the country, and spent a wonderful twenty-four hours in Eaton Place, scarcely leaving the bedroom before Kendrick had to go back to New York to take his final examinations.

Less than a month later he came back, and the nightmare began.

He phoned Georgina from Heathrow; she was in the kitchen with Mrs Fallon, helping her make pastry. Alexander was in London; she often thought afterwards how her entire life might have worked out differently if he had been at the house.

'Heathrow! But Kendrick, you're in New York.'

'No, Georgina, I'm not in New York. I'm at Heathrow. I just told you. Separation from me has obviously affected your brain. Is there any chance you could come and meet me?'

'Of course, of course there is, I'll come straight away, but I'll still be nearly two hours, I should think. Oh, Kendrick, how lovely, how lovely. I'll be with you as soon as I can. In the arrivals area. Love you.'

'Love you too.'

Georgina's white Golf GTI tore up the M4 at a steady 110 without thought for speed limits, the police, or her own safety. Due entirely to the good offices of her guardian angel who was clearly working overtime on her behalf, she reached Heathrow in under ninety minutes.

Kendrick was waiting for her, lounging against a pillar in the arrivals hall; he was wearing a camel greatcoat and a slouch hat. 'You look like Dick Tracy,' said Georgina, kissing him.

'You don't look a bit like Breathless Mahoney,' said Kendrick, kissing her back, 'but I never did like blondes anyway.'

'That lets me off one big worry.'

'Can we go straight to bed when we get home?'

'Absolutely straight.'

'Thank God for that.'

'How's your dad?' asked Kendrick. He was looking very solemn, lying in the old-fashioned white iron bath in Georgina's bathroom. She had had it moved down from the nursery bathroom, when Nanny had had it modernized and put in what she called a sweety in avocado green.

'He's OK,' said Georgina cautiously. 'He's in London for a few days.'

'Better? He must be, if he's in London.'

'Yes. Better. But not well. Not really. The psychiatrist says we have to be very careful. Not cross him, not let him get tired. He's funny, his mind seems to have slowed down. It's hard to explain, things take a long time to get through. But once they do, he's fine.'

'Good.'

'Uncle Baby isn't any worse,' she said, 'I saw him last week. He was in good spirits. He and Tommy had found a whole batch of new games. I don't know what they'd do without each other, I really don't. You mustn't let on, specially not to Charlotte, but I quite like Tommy.' She was aware that she was running on, that she was nervous, anxious to postpone the moment when he began to try and discuss their future.

'Yes,' he said, 'I quite like him too. What I've seen of him.'

'Does your father know you're here?'

'No. Not yet.'

'Aren't you going to tell him?'

'Well,' said Kendrick, 'it depends.'

'Oh what?'

'I'll tell you. How are you finding it here, nursing Alexander?'

'Depressing. Boring. But you know I have to do it,' she added warily. 'For the time being.'

'The time being is dragging on a bit, isn't it?'

'Maybe a bit. Kendrick, what is this? And why exactly are you here?'

'I'm here to carry you off. To my enchanted castle. Aka my new loft conversion on the Upper West Side.'

'Is it gorgeous?'

'It's gorgeous. Huge rooms, huger windows, all light and white, overlooks the park.'

'It sounds perfect.'

'No it's not quite perfect,' said Kendrick.

'What's wrong with it?'

'You're not there.'

'Oh.'

'Georgina, darling, I do truly admire your devotion to your father, or rather to Alexander, and we will come to that in a minute – don't look like that Georgina, please – '

'Kendrick, you know very well that as far as I'm concerned Alexander is my father. I love him, he's been perfect to me all my life, and I simply have no interest in finding anyone else. And I don't care if he's Mr Wonderful, like Charles St Mullin, or if he's Mr Nightmare, like Tommy. As far as I'm concerned, it's Daddy, and he is Mr Perfect, and that's that. I wish I'd never ever told you about it.'

'Fine,' said Kendrick. His face made it very clear it wasn't.

'Well anyway, what were you going to say?'

'I was going to say that I thought it was my turn.'

'What do you mean?'

'Georgina, I love you, I've asked you to marry me, you've said you would, and I've waited what seems like a long time.'

'But Kendrick, what about Uncle Baby – ?'

'I've been doing a lot of thinking and I'm quite sure we should give him the pleasure of seeing it happen. And I want you living with me in New York. I'm going to be working there now and you're not working here, and it seems crazy. I was thinking about it last night and how crazy it seemed, and I just got on the plane and came to tell you. That's why I'm here. I think we should get married very simply and very soon, over here, and then move to New York. I know Dad's ill, and everything, but he certainly wouldn't want us hanging around here waiting for him to – well, that's what I think.'

This was a very long speech for Kendrick; Georgina sat listening to him, staring at him as he lay in the bath, her expression very distant. 'I see,' was all she said.

'Well, that's not a very passionate response. I thought you'd be racing off packing, buying a bridal gown, all that sort of thing.'

'No you didn't.' The flat voice matched her expression.

'What do you mean?'

'You didn't think that at all. You knew I'd argue, that I wouldn't be able to come.'

'Georgina, what do you mean, you wouldn't be able to come? Of course I didn't know that. I wouldn't be here if that was the case.'

'Because you know I have to look after Daddy. I have to.'

'Georgina, listen. Your father, unlike mine, is actually perfectly fit and well. He may live for another twenty years. Probably will. Are you going to stay here with him all that time?'

'No of course not. But he's had a breakdown, Kendrick, and it was at least partly my fault, and he's in a very vulnerable state. There's nobody else here, except Nanny and Mrs Tallow, to look after him. And besides the psychiatrist said we mustn't – force him. Make him face things he doesn't want to face. I can't leave him, I can't.'

'For how long can't you leave him?'

'Well – until he's better.'

'And how long do you think that might be?'

'Well – I don't know. Maybe a few more months.'

'But it's already gone on for months. It could become years. Am I to stay there all alone in New York indefinitely waiting for you? Because it doesn't seem a very happy prospect, Georgina. I just might not be able to do it.'

'What do you mean?'

'I mean I might have to rethink. I might feel you didn't love me enough to marry me. I might feel that coming second to your father was not very satisfactory. You must surely see that, Georgina.'

Georgina faced him. She felt very frightened, but she was not going to give in, not going to be intimidated.

'I'm sorry, Kendrick, but that's what I have to do. I can't fail him. Not now. He needs me.'

'I need you.'

'He needs me more.'

'Well in that case,' said Kendrick, 'I think I may as well get straight back to New York. It's very sad, but I don't see any alternative. Pass me that bathrobe, would you, Georgina, and maybe you'd be good enough to check on flights out tonight.'

Georgina passed him the robe. She watched him in silence as he wrapped it round him, reached for his clothes; his face was a fearsome blank.

'You're not serious, are you?' she said.

'Oh yes,' he said. 'Absolutely serious.' He looked at her with something close to dislike in his eyes. 'I love you so much, Georgina, so terribly much, I can't remember a time now when I didn't love you. But love needs nourishing, tending. It can't grow on without any encouragement at all. My love for you is being starved to death. Unless you do something about it it's going to die. For the last time, Georgina, are you going to come with me? We could be so happy.'

'No,' she said, 'no I can't. Not yet.'

'Then,' he said, 'I think we had better forget all about it, don't you?'

She drove him all the way back to Heathrow. Stony-faced, silent, unreproachful.

'Goodbye,' she said when they got there.

He looked at her, raised his hand, touched her cheek.

'Goodbye, Georgina,' was all he said.

And then the long journey back, without him, and for the first time since she could remember, no tape to listen to with his voice on. As she turned into the Great Drive, in the darkness, Georgina finally began to feel the pain, began to cry; by the time she was at the house she was sobbing, loud, desperate, racked sobs. She flung herself through one of the side doors, ran up the stairs into her room, slammed the door. For what seemed like hours she lay on her bed, crying, thinking of Kendrick, of the long time they had loved one another, of how much she loved him, dazed by the speed with which it had ended.

Half the night she cried. She heard three strike on the stable clock and then four before she was aware of time at all; and she was lying exhausted on her bed, unable briefly to cry any more, when the door opened slowly.

'Georgina?' said a voice. It was Nanny.

'Oh Nanny, I'm sorry. Did I wake you?' said Georgina, sniffing loudly, groping for a tissue.

'Hard to do that. I hadn't been to sleep,' said Nanny. 'What is it this time, Georgina?' She sounded cross; Georgina gave her a watery smile.

'It's Kendrick, Nanny.'

'What about him? Has he gone?'

'He's gone back to New York.'

'Well that was a short visit. Doesn't he like it here any more?'

'Not today he didn't. Well he didn't like me.'

'He should make his mind up. I thought he wanted to marry you.'

'Not any more, Nanny. Not any more.'

'So what's gone wrong?'

'I've gone wrong, Nanny. Or rather I haven't gone right, his way.'

'You're talking in riddles,' said Nanny, as if her own conversation was always perfectly straightforward. 'What are you going on about, Georgina? You always did have trouble expressing yourself.'

'Oh Nanny, don't scold me. I can't stand it. The thing is, Kendrick wants us to get married and then for me to go back to New York straight away, and I told him I couldn't.'

'Why?'

Georgina stared at her.

'Well because of Daddy, of course.'

'Oh,' said Nanny. 'Oh, I see.'

'I can't leave him, Nanny, I can't. Not even if it means losing Kendrick.' She had started crying again, staring up at the ceiling, her face swollen and ugly. 'He needs me. He needs me so much. And I love him, you know, I really really do. And I just don't think he could manage without me. Not now. I can't leave him, Nanny, I really can't.'

Chapter 46

Virginia, 1960

'I can't leave him, Nanny, I can't. He needs me so much. And I love him, you know I really do.'

Nanny looked at Virginia. It was the latest in a long series of conversations. The first seemed a long time ago now, but it wasn't really, only a few weeks. Virginia had been sitting in the small chair in the window in her bedroom; Nanny had been listening to her crying for hours, and unable to bear it any longer had come in.

'Is everything all right, Your Ladyship?'

Virgina looked at her and in spite of everything she managed to smile: a watery, lopsided smile.

'Not absolutely, Nanny. Not absolutely. Oh, I'm sorry, I didn't mean to worry you.'

She had been at Hartest nearly three months; a pale, rather subdued bride, struggling to make the adjustment to her new life, solitary much of the time, riding alone through the grounds, meeting her official commitments, making herself familiar with the house, its history, its demands. Alexander was still painfully proud of her, showing her off; only a month after they had reached England, he had insisted they gave a big party, to introduce her to all his friends and their neighbours in Wiltshire, supper for two hundred and fifty, in a marquee on the back terrace, with dancing afterwards. A great success, it was agreed, and it had been reported in the local press and even a couple of the London papers.

'It was too much for you, that party,' said Nanny, 'I told Alexander, His Lordship, that it was too much, too many people.'

'Well that was kind, Nanny, but of course it wasn't too much; I should be able to cope with a few people coming round.' She giggled weakly. 'You must think I'm hopeless. Really hopeless. Alexander should have married some stalwart Englishwoman with nerves of steel and an iron constitution.'

'No,' said Nanny simply. 'I think you're wonderful.'

Virginia looked at her, startled. 'That's really very sweet, Nanny. I don't see anything very wonderful in what I'm doing.'

'You're making Alexander – Lord Caterham happy,' said Nanny. She sounded stern.

'Well – he's making me happy,' said Virginia determinedly, and then burst into tears again. 'Oh Nanny, you'll have to excuse me. I'll be all right soon. Just tired, I suppose.'

'Yes, I suppose,' said Nanny. 'Well I will leave you. If that's what you want. Would you like anything? A cup of tea?'

'I'd love a glass of wine,' said Virginia. 'It's a funny time for it, I know, but that's what I'd really like. Do you think you could ask Harold to bring a bottle into the library? I'll be down in a minute for lunch.'

'Yes, if that's what you want,' said Nanny. She implied that it couldn't possibly be what Virginia wanted. She started to leave the room, then turned in the doorway.

'I do know,' she said, looking a little flustered, 'I do know how difficult everything must be for you. I just thought I should say that. I've known Alexander ever since he was a tiny little boy.'

Virginia stared at her. A very faint hope that there was someone she might be able to share the nightmare with began to uncurl somewhere deep within her.

'Well, Nanny, maybe you could be my friend. Maybe I could talk to you sometimes? I miss my mother particularly. She is such fun, Nanny, you'd really like her.'

'Indeed?' said Nanny, in tones that implied very clearly that she wouldn't.

'I did think,' said Virginia wistfully, 'that Alexander's mother might have made some gesture for my birthday. Sent a card or something. But she seems determined to be hostile.'

'She's very nice really,' said Nanny. 'It's unlike her to be unkind. She was always very kind to Alexander.'

Virginia looked at her, surprised. 'Well she's his mother, Nanny. She would be kind.'

'It wasn't always easy,' said Nanny. 'Lord Caterham, Alexander's father, didn't believe in kindness. He had to be stood up to.'

'He sounds a very difficult man,' said Virginia.

'He was dreadful,' said Nanny, and walked away. Virginia looked after her in surprise. It wasn't Nanny's style to criticize her superiors.

'Alexander, I know it's painful for you,' she said after supper a few days later, 'but I really would like to hear more about your father.'

'Virginia, I do assure you that you wouldn't like it.'

'All right, I need to hear more.'

'That is open to debate also, I would say.' He looked at her, almost fearfully, and then managed to smile. 'Why don't we talk about something pleasant? Like your father?'

'Alexander, please don't keep running away from things. I'm here, I'm trying to do my best; but you have to give a little.'

'I really cannot see,' he said, 'what good telling you about my father would do.'

'It might help me. It might give me an idea.'

'An idea of what, Virginia?' He looked very cold, icily angry. Virginia faced him steadily.

'Of how I might be able to help you. Of what we might be able to do.'

'Virginia,' he said, and the suppressed rage and misery in his voice made her shiver slightly, 'I have told you. There is nothing we, as you put it, might be able to do. And your amateur, phoney American psychiatry least of all. Now can we please change the subject?'

'No.' She stood up, her own rage giving her courage. 'No we can't. I have a right to know, Alexander, I really do. Tell me about it. Otherwise I'm leaving. Right now.'

He looked at her and visibly weakened, his anger gone. At that stage in their relationship when they both thought it possible, even feasible, that she might leave, she could seriously frighten him with the threat. Later it was empty, invalid; they both knew she would never go.

'Well – I told you. He beat me. Often. I – well, it gave him some kind of sexual thrill. Afterwards he would – oh God, do we have to do this?'

'We have to do this.' Virginia took his hand, held it, faced him steadily. 'Please go on.'

'Well – he would abuse me.'

'You mean sexually?'

'I mean sexually.'

'Oh God.'

'Well I can tell you. He seemed fairly far away,' said Alexander, with an attempt at humour.

'And – your mother. Did she know?'

'Yes of course she knew.' He looked surprised. 'He liked to threaten her with it. Threaten both of us.'

'Alexander, this is awful. Dreadful. Why didn't she leave him, take you with her?'

'She did. Twice. But then he found us, both times. Used terrible emotional blackmail. And she didn't have any money, and her own parents were dead, and then of course, you feel so foolish, so wretchedly foolish, being seen to be a victim, ashamed almost . . .'

'Yes,' said Virginia quietly. 'Yes, you do.'

'And I think in her own odd way, she was fond of him. Certainly she felt guilty about him. When he was in a good mood he had great charm, he was funny and immensely generous. He would suddenly rush her off to Paris, or Monte Carlo for the weekend, shower her with presents. Then they'd come back and she would make him angry, or I would, and the whole ghastly cycle began again.'

'I remember reading a paper on this,' said Virginia slowly, 'on women as willing victims. Addicted to violence, to pain.'

Alexander looked suddenly cold again, withdrawn into himself, his mood of confidence lost.

'I do loathe that American psycho-babble,' he said. 'Please don't use it on me, it really offends me.'

'I'm sorry,' said Virginia. 'Alexander, did you tell the doctors all this?'

'Oh, I did. Well one of them. A woman. An analyst. She was very clever, very skilful.'

'And –'

'Oh I don't know. It didn't do me any good.'

He sighed, and looked at her. 'Look, I'm finding this very painful. Could we change the subject, please?'

'Alexander, no, not yet. Did he – do anything else?'

'Isn't that enough? Not to me, no. But I would hear them sometimes.'

'Hear them what?'

'Oh, he would shout at her, hit her. And then –'

'And then make love to her?'

'Yes.' The answer slid out of him, clearly taking him by surprise. 'Yes. I knew that was what was happening. I learnt to know – the sounds. At first I thought it was pain, the cries of pain I'd heard earlier, I hammered on the door once, I was a brave little boy you see, telling him to leave her alone. She came to answer it, dressed in her robe; she looked strange to me, wild, but not unhappy. She told me to go to Nanny. Nanny was always there.'

He looked at Virginia and there were tears in his blue eyes; he tried to smile at her. 'It's casebook stuff, I'm afraid. They all say so, the doctors.'

'Alexander, when did you first try to get help?'

'I've told you. I was eighteen, went to the GP.'

'On your own?'

'Yes, of course.' He looked surprised.

'You never talked to your mother about it?'

'Of course not. How could I?'

'I don't know. Maybe not.' She thought of her own inability to communicate with her parents.

'Did anyone know? Apart from you?'

'Well,' he said, 'as much as she was able to understand it, I think Nanny knew. I broke down one day, in front of her. She said could she help. I said no one could help. She pointed out she'd known me from the moment I was born, that it had been a very close relationship. She has a great sense of humour really, you know.'

'I know,' said Virginia. 'I love her.'

'Well, I said I had a problem. A physical problem. That I was seeing some doctors. And she said, and I'll never forget it, she said, "Does that mean you won't be able to get married, Alexander?" And I said, "It might, Nanny, but let's hope not." We never mentioned it again.'

'I see,' said Virginia.

She went into Swindon to the public library, spent hours reading up impotence. Growing braver, she went to London, and made an appointment to see a specialist in psycho-sexual medicine. She gave a false name, told him about her husband who was impotent. She asked him if there was any hope. The specialist said it was always difficult, such cases, but it was possible. He would naturally have to see her husband, and treatment was long and often traumatic. He asked her to make an appointment for them to come together.

Virginia screwed up her courage (aided by several glasses of wine at dinner) and told Alexander about the specialist. She asked him if he would go and see him. He said he wouldn't, that he would never see any doctor again, that he was sick to death of seeing people, that she had no right to go round blabbing about their marriage all over London, that he had told her that nothing could be done. Then he stood up, hurled his glass of wine at her and ran out of the room and up the stairs. Virginia followed him; the door of his bedroom was locked.

'Alexander, please please let me in!'

'No.'

'Alexander, I shall scream if you don't.'

He opened the door. There were tears streaming down his face; he looked stricken, ashamed, almost afraid. 'I'm sorry,' he said, and held out his arms. 'I'm sorry about everything. So desperately sorry. Maybe you should go. Maybe you should go home to America.'

Virginia faced him steadily. 'I won't go,' she said, 'because I do seem, in spite of everything, to be very fond of you. And I want to help you. But you've got to promise me to see this doctor. You've got to.'

'All right,' he said. She closed the door behind her, and went into his arms.

'I love you, Virginia,' he said, 'I love you so much. I don't know what I would do without you now. I really don't.'

He started to kiss her. Virginia, overwrought, sexually starved, her loneliness and misery rising up in a great wave, returned his kiss, her body pressed frantically, desperately against him. She stroked his hair, caressed his neck, moved her hands slowly down his body. She still, in those days, hoped for miracles.

'Alexander.'

'Yes darling.'

'Alexander, when I was in New York I saw a most marvellous man. Well I didn't exactly like him, he wasn't marvellous in that way, but he was breathtakingly clever.'

'Really, darling? In which field? Interior design? Banking?'

Virginia took a deep breath. 'Psychiatry,' she said.

Alexander's face froze. His eyes shot ice at her. 'Please don't go on,' he said.

'Alexander, I promise I will never ever talk to anyone else about this for as long as I live, but – '

'Indeed, Virginia? I think I would utter a heartfelt amen to that. How dare you go talking to some quack about me and my problems? How dare you?'

'Our problems, Alexander. Ours. Please listen.'

'Virginia, I'm going out now. When I get back, can we recommence today, in a more pleasant way.'

Virginia got up. She stood in the doorway, barring it with her hands. 'Alexander, listen to me, God dammit. Listen.'

'I will not listen.'

'You will or so help me I'll kill you.'

'Indeed? By what means?'

'Alexander, please. Please.'

'No. Get out of my way.'

He pushed her gently. A black mist rose in front of Virginia's eyes, a black, swirling hot mist. She raised her hand physically as if to push it away; Alexander caught the wrist.

'Just stop it,' he said, and his face was contorted with rage. 'Just stop it. Leave me alone.'

'Oh yes,' she said, and her voice rose higher and higher into a scream, 'yes I'll leave you alone. I'll leave you, to rot here, rot away, without love, without me, without children to inherit this lousy beautiful prison you're so in love with. I'll leave you and you can just try and seduce some other poor wretched woman into thinking you're normal and she might want to marry you. I'll leave you right away, Alexander, in fact I'm going to pack now, at once. And you needn't worry, I won't tell anyone your lousy rotten secret; I would be ashamed, do you hear me, ashamed.'

'Be quiet,' he said, 'shut up, shut up, the servants will hear you.'

Virginia looked at him and suddenly she laughed, out loud, an ugly, harsh laugh.

'I'm so sorry, Alexander,' she said, 'how thoughtless of me. That would never do, would it? Not the servants.'

She was in her room, dragging things out of her drawers, when he came in. He was pale and looked very shaken; he sat down on her bed.

'Virginia,' he said, 'please try to understand. Please listen to me.'

'I've listened to you too much, Alexander. I don't want to hear any more. I'm going.'

'Listen. Please. Just once more. Then you can go. I'll drive you to the airport myself.'

'There's no need. I have a car.'

'I know you do. Listen. Please. Oh Christ . . .'

His voice was so strained, so desperate, Virginia stopped and looked at him. Then she sat down on the bed, her arms full of clothes, and said, 'All right. I'm listening.'

'I don't think you can possibly understand how terrible for me this is.'

'For you! My God!'

'Virginia, please. You said you'd listen. The awful dreadful humiliation. Knowing that I have to live with it for ever. Wanting you so much, loving you so much, knowing – well. The pain is unimaginable to you, I do assure you.'

She was silent.

'At first I was willing to try. Willing to undergo the treatments, the analysis, telling the story over and over again. It was like poking at a gangrenous wound. I told myself it would be worth it, but it wasn't. It never was. It never began to be worth it. Don't you see? And every time, the hope and then the despair. I can't get onto that spiral again, Virginia, I can't. I'm too afraid.'

'Not even for me?'

'Not even for you.'

She looked at him very steadily. 'Then I do have to go.'

'Very well. Of course.'

He went downstairs. Virginia continued to pack. When she had finished she called the airport, made a reservation; it would be easy to go home now, to face everyone, she had frequently thought this over the past months, she could just say that she and Alexander were miserable together and had decided to part. No humiliation, no horror; it would be fine. She was about to ring for Fallon when she looked out of the window. Alexander was sitting on the wall of the back terrace, facing the house. His shoulders were stooped, his arms were wrapped around his body as if trying to shield himself from some pain. As she looked, she realized he was crying, quite quietly, great tears rolling down his face and dropping onto his arms. Every so often he would raise his hand and wipe them away. He looked oddly colourless, all the life in him washed away.

Suddenly she saw him vividly, as he had been that first day, in the restaurant in New York, so smiling, so golden, so handsome, rising to greet her, holding out his hand, and she felt again her heart lurch and the lurch in her body simultaneously. She remembered how fast and how violently she had fallen in love with him; and she remembered too the growing doubts about him and her life with him, and how she had stifled them, wanting so much, longing, to be his wife, to be a success, to have admiration, respect, recognition as a person, to be, in fact, the Countess of Caterham.

And as she looked and as she remembered, her heart began to ache for him, not just with pity, but with love; she did love him, she realized, she loved him very much, perhaps more now than she had when they were first married. It was an odd, strange love, and it was not going to bring her great happiness; but love it was, and it was mingled with guilt, and the knowledge that she was not without fault, and she knew that she could not leave him, it would be too savagely, horribly cruel and she would never forgive herself.

She went slowly downstairs and walked out onto the terrace.

'I suppose,' he said, 'you've come to say goodbye.'

'No, I haven't actually,' she said, 'I've come to see if we could ride together after lunch. I'm just a little frightened of my new mare still, and I need your help with her.'

Later, of course, the reaction had set in. She had stopped feeling noble and tender and had felt angry and wretched instead. Alexander had gone to see the estate manager, and she wandered up to the nurseries, Alexander's old nurseries, and walked round, touching things, the crib, the high chair, the rocking horse, crying quietly. And Nanny had come in, from her room opposite, and had taken her hand and said, 'Madam, please forgive me, but I couldn't help overhearing some of your – conversation this morning, saying you were leaving. I thought perhaps I should tell you that I had – well, suspected there was something wrong. With Alexander that is. He did – tell me once. Not exactly of course. But I can understand why you're going. No one could blame you. I shall miss you, madam.'

And finally confronted by someone who would not judge, would not exclaim or be horrified, someone who loved Alexander and who she knew was coming to love her, Virginia said, 'No, Nanny, I'm not going. I'm staying. Not just for a while, as I had planned, but for good. But I will need your help and your support.'

And then she had begun to talk and to try to explain why she was staying, and what she was going to have to do, and Nanny sat in complete silence, listening to her, just holding her hand, and when she had finished, she said, as if Virginia had been discussing the arrangements for the weekend, 'I would suggest you change the drawing room curtains, Your Ladyship. Blue is such a cold colour, and especially with the stone fireplace.'

Chapter 47

Max, 1986

It was Thursday; one of Tommy's days for visiting Baby. Max decided to go and pick him up on the way home. Poor old Baby. It was ghastly the way he'd deteriorated so fast. He sat in his wheelchair, his legs limp and useless, his arms in splints. On bad days he sometimes had trouble supporting his head, and his speech was becoming increasingly impaired. The worst thing, as Tommy had remarked to Max, was that inside this frail shambles of a shell was a mind that was robust and impatient, condemned to a helpless loneliness. 'I don't know how he stands it.'

'I'd shoot myself,' said Max.

'You couldn't,' said Tommy sadly, 'you couldn't do anything as constructive as that.'

Angie answered the door herself; she looked tired and depressed.

'Hallo, Max. Come in. Drink?'

'That'd be nice. Can I see Baby?'

'Of course. Tommy's done a great job, as usual. I don't know what Baby would do without him.'

Mrs Wicks appeared in the hall.

'Oh, hallo, Sir Max,' she said, 'how are you? Angela, those twins need a good spanking, they're roaring round up there in your bedroom, squirting perfume at each other.'

'Oh, I don't care,' said Angie with a sigh. 'Go and give them one, Gran, if it'll make you feel better. Where's Debbie?'

'She's gone out. It's her night off.'

'Silly bitch,' said Angie irrelevantly.

'She may well be a silly bitch,' said Mrs Wicks, 'in fact I'd agree with you there, but she is entitled to her night off. She works hard.'

'Well so do I and now I'll have to bath the little buggers and put them to bed. Oh shit.'

She sat down on the bottom of the stairs and put her head in her hands; Max sat down beside her and put his arm round her.

'Look,' he said, 'Tommy and I are going out to dinner. With Gemma. Why don't you come too? I'm sure Mrs Wicks would babysit, wouldn't you, Mrs Wicks?' He turned the smile that had launched a thousand looks on Mrs Wicks.

'Course I would,' she said, batting her heavily mascaraed eyelashes at him. 'And then Baby and I can watch *Dynasty* together. You go, Angela, it'll do you good.'

Angie hesitated, then grinned at Max.

'You talked me into it,' she said.

They went to the Caprice. They couldn't really afford it, and it was clearly going to empty the bank account, but Tommy said Angie was worth it, and Max agreed. Angie's mood lifted swiftly; they had drunk a bottle of champagne before they left the house and she was flirting alternately with Max and Tommy, telling funny stories and dirty jokes, and darting across the room whenever anyone she knew came in to greet them extravagantly and ostentatiously.

Gemma grew increasingly sulky and increasingly silent; she was interestingly jealous of Angie; Max looked at her cross little face and, half amused, half irritated by it, perversely turned an increased battery of attention on Angie. Then halfway through the meal he felt remorseful and put his hand over Gemma's.

'You OK?' he said.

'I'm fine,' said Gemma. 'Just a little bored. That's all.'

'Oh darling, don't be silly. Join in the conversation a bit more.'

'I'm finding it a bit hard to get a word in edgeways, actually,' she said. 'And I can't see what's so interesting about selling flats to Arabs.'

'You're not listening,' said Max, 'what was interesting was that the Sheikh of whatever turned up with a hundred thousand pounds for Angie in a plastic bag from Anne Summer's sex shop. Why don't you try and change the subject if you're so bored?'

'Well, when I do say anything nobody seems very interested,' said Gemma.

'Nonsense,' said Max, 'we're all interested. Aren't we?'

'Aren't we what?' said Tommy, turning reluctantly back from a rather bawdy exchange with Angie about the size of his feet.

'Interested in Gemma,' said Max. 'She's feeling left out.'

'I'm not,' said Gemma irritably. 'Don't be silly, Max.'

'Gemma, darling little Gemma, of course we're interested in you,' said Tommy. There was a slightly nasty look in his blue eyes. 'Tell us all about your latest modelling job, darling, or perhaps the last two or three, and we'll all sit and listen with bated breath.'

Gemma tumbled straight into the trap. 'Well, it was for *Vogue*,' she said, 'and it was Jasper's latest collection, and he was there, and

543

Bailey was shooting, and Jasper said I was the only girl who could actually – '

Max, trying to concentrate, and ignore Tommy's wicked eyes fixed intently on Gemma's face, found himself disproportionately distracted by the sight of Tommy's hand creeping up Angie's slender thigh.

After dinner she said it was her turn and she would take them all to Tramp.

'I'd like to, and it'd be fun, please let me. Otherwise I'll get depressed again.'

'We'll come,' said Max and Tommy in unison. Gemma said she was tired and she might go home, but Max told her he would be very upset if she did that, and that he was looking forward to taking her back to her flat already.

It was a vintage night at Tramp. Jackie Collins was in town, and holding court; the Michael Caines and the Roger Moores were boogying happily on the floor; Viscount Linley and Susannah Constantine arrived with a large, and largely recognizable, party.

'I feel outclassed,' said Angie. 'Comfort me, Max.'

'You could never be outclassed,' said Max, 'but I'm certainly happy to try and comfort you. Come on and dance with me.'

She was wearing a slither of black crepe, short, cut low; her blonde hair was carefully wild. She looked terrific, Max thought; he told her so.

'Oh Max, don't. I'm old enough to be your mother.'

'No you're not,' he said, 'don't sell yourself short.'

He had undone his tie, his dress shirt was unbuttoned halfway to his waist. 'You look like one of your own photographs,' said Angie, slipping into his arms.

'You feel gorgeous,' said Max, and meant it. She was in terrific shape. She must be – what must she be, he wondered, taking in the smell of her, the warmth of her, finding her sweetly, pleasingly disturbing – thirty-fivish. A good age. A sexy, sensuous age.

He smiled down at her, into her green eyes.

'What were you thinking?' she said, amused.

'I was thinking you looked terrific.'

'Oh Max. Maybe for my age – '

'No, not for anything. Just terrific. How old are you, anyway?'

'I'm – ' she hesitated, then said with a slightly grim smile, 'I'm thirty-seven.'

'You look terrific,' he said again. 'Really good. I think you're gorgeous.'

He pulled her against him, slowly, thoughtfully, savouring the moment; he had wondered for a long time, he realized, how it would feel to be physically close to her. She felt very small, very fragile, moving against him; that in itself was arousing. And very warm. Her perfume was strong, heady; she smiled up at him, a careless, slightly reckless smile. 'This is nice,' she said. The DJ had put on an old 10cc number, 'I'm Not in Love'. 'My favourite,' she said; he could feel her moving against him, fluid, compliant; he began to move his hands over her, carefully, tenderly, caressing her back, her neck, and then moved downwards towards her buttocks. They were hard, high, small; Max felt desire, dangerous, hot, licking somewhere deep inside him, felt his body shifting within itself; this was good, this was very very good. She looked up at him, and her eyes met his, half amused, searching, brilliant. 'Angie,' he said, 'Angie, I – ' and then the record finished, the spell broke, the tempo changed, and she sighed suddenly, and said, mocking him, and he hated it, half hated her, 'Now Max, come on, this won't do, we mustn't upset Gemma any further,' and took his hand and led him back to the table, and he felt chilled and put down, and foolish at the same time, foolish and very young, for allowing himself to be carried away by a slow dance and – what was it, Tommy was always quoting that old guy Noël Coward – oh, yes, cheap music.

He drank two glasses of champagne very quickly, and tried to avoid her amused, thoughtful eyes.

A woman with the Collins entourage came over to them, held out her hands to Tommy, kissed him on the lips.

She was glossy, sexy, year-round tanned; Tommy put his arm about her, turned to Angie and Max.

'Sammy, meet Angie Praeger. And Max Hadleigh. Oh and Gemma Morton. This is a good friend of mine, Sammy Brown. What are you doing in town, Sammy?'

'Oh – a little shopping. Having fun,' said Sammy. 'A few stolen days from LA.'

'If I had the chance to be in LA,' said Angie, smiling at Sammy, 'I certainly wouldn't be here.'

'You know LA?' said Sammy.

'A little. I love it.'

'You should get Tommy to bring you over. Take a trip.'

'Oh – I'm a working girl, I'm afraid,' said Angie.

'Really?' Sammy looked bored. 'Are you Praeger as in Praeger the bank? Family?'

'Yes, I am.' Angie's voice was cautious; Max and Tommy stayed silent, following her lead.

'So do you know Chuck Drew from the New York office?' said Sammy.

'I've – met him,' said Angie.

'His wife is a great friend of mine. She is thrilled at the thought of moving to London.'

'Oh really?' said Angie. 'Well, I'm pleased for her.'

'Sammy, come and have a drink with us, darling,' said Tommy.

'Maybe later,' she said, kissing him rather lingeringly on the mouth. 'Don't go without giving me your number anyway.'

She went off to rejoin her party; Angie stared after her, looking puzzled.

'Now why on earth,' she said, 'should Chuck Drew be moving to London? Is Fred the Third up to something, do you think?'

'God knows,' said Max. 'Don't worry about it.'

'I have to worry about it,' said Angie, 'I'm afraid.'

The next day Angie called Max, ostensibly to thank him for the evening.

'I meant to ring earlier, but Baby was bad. He's better now.'

'That's OK,' said Max. 'And you don't need to thank me. It was fun.'

'I'm afraid Gemma didn't think so.'

'Oh – she was all right. Really.'

'I hope so.'

'Max, how do you think I can find out about Chuck Drew and why he might be coming to London?'

'Not sure. I'll ask Charlotte if she's heard anything.'

'Could you? I'm worried. It doesn't make sense. Thanks.'

Charlotte hadn't heard about Chuck Drew. She was upset. 'Maybe it's a mistake.'

'Maybe.'

'I think I might call Gabe. He'd know.'

'You do that,' said Max. 'Good excuse to make contact.'

'Oh, piss off,' said Charlotte irritably.

She rang Max a few days later.

'Gabe hadn't heard a word, but he's going to do some digging. He did say Freddy was being extremely pro-active, following up every possible lead. Apparently he's pulled out of Harvard after only a year, and he's building up a nice little empire there. Established in the Heir's Room even.'

She sounded upset. Max was sympathetic.

'Never mind. You'll get back soon, I'm sure. Grandpa seemed pretty sweet on you at the wedding.'

'Did you think so? I'm afraid I didn't notice anything of the kind. I think it'll be a long time before I get anywhere near Praegers New York again.'

'It's a terrible thing, sex,' said Max solemnly.

'What's sex got to do with it? Oh, Max, that was mean. God, I could kill Freddy. And Jeremy Foster.'

'Let me know if you need help. With either of them. It would be a pleasure.'

'Well,' said Max, 'we survived.'

'Only just,' said Jake Joseph. 'I need a drink.'

Jake was his mentor and officially his boss at Mortons. He was a dealer: short, heavily built, funny and deceptively relaxed, with a mind like a jet-driven razor. Dealing was in his blood. His great-grandfather had worked Stag Alley, the name given to Capel Court at the back of the Stock Exchange, where the spivs of the Victorian era had got news of a new issue of railway stock and dashed down the alley to cash in on it. His grandfather and father had been jobbers on the Exchange; with the coming of Big Bang, Jake was one of the market makers, the brave new world's jobbers, who would buy and sell on their own accounts for their own profits. 'I tell you,' he said to Max, on his first day at Mortons, 'this business is going to make Monte Carlo look like a car park.'

Jake often quoted Dick Morton's claim that he could walk onto the Stock Exchange floor and say immediately if the market was going up or down. 'I can sniff it.' It was the sort of remark that set Max's pulses racing.

After a few months at Mortons, Max was beginning to be able to sniff it too.

And today, 27 October, there was a great deal to be sniffed in the air.

They went out of Mortons and down to the Fenchurch Colony wine bar. The scene there more closely resembled something from a St Trinian's film than the sober world of the City of London. A heaving mass of bodies filled the small space, fighting to get at the bar; empties stood outside in the street, in the gutter, all over the floor, more reminiscent of beer cans than champagne bottles. The champagne was not being poured into glasses, it was in some cases being sprayed in the air, drunk from the bottle, carried off to waiting cars; the first day of the brave new world was being celebrated in a way that was to become legendary. Not to mention extremely distasteful to the Old Guard.

Big Bang itself had actually begun with something of a whimper. Ten days earlier, on the Saturday, there had been a full-scale rehearsal: everybody in, an imaginary script handed out to every firm in the City and the new technology – SEAQ, the Stock Exchange Automated Quotation – switched on; the most memorable event of the day was a breakdown of the entire system.

On the day itself, the jobbers – 'From this day forward we are market makers,' said Jake solemnly – sat at their screens, tapping more than slightly nervously, entering bids and offers on share prices into the system, and trying to adjust to knowing what every other market maker was doing, and also trying very hard to believe it was for real. It began quietly; they were nervous. Max watched Jake, always so cocky, so 101 per cent sure of what he was doing, staring at his screen, almost unblinking, sweat beading on his forehead, tapping numbers tentatively into it, swearing, shouting into his phone, cursing the salesmen, the analysts, the clients, the information he was receiving, Max, himself. It was hot, very hot in the room; the screens alone generated a lot of heat. The noise was intense, the atmosphere claustrophobic; everybody was, as Jake said, shit scared. Twice the system broke down; three times Jake took his phones off the hook and said he couldn't stand it any longer. And then suddenly, at about three o'clock, he looked at Max and his dark eyes were brilliant with excitement. 'I've got it,' he said, as if he had just learnt to ride a bicycle. 'It's OK. It's good. We're going to be all right.'

Max picked up on the excitement; it was frenetic, heady, all-consuming. He kept remembering things people had said – Chrissie Forsyte: 'The trading floor is the centre of the universe.' Jake Joseph: 'It's going to make Monte Carlo look like a car park.' And his Uncle Baby remarking that the trading floor gave him a hard-on, and he knew suddenly and sharply, with a sense of sheer pleasure, what they all meant. At the end of the day, after he had left Jake, light-headed with adrenalin as well as champagne, he took Gemma out to dinner and then to bed, and made love to her with an almost frantic enthusiasm.

He could never again quite break the association of sex and money forged in his mind that day.

Chapter 48

Angie, 1986

'I just found out exactly where my heart is situated,' said Baby. 'I felt it break.'

Angie looked at him, as he sat in the car beside her, being driven home from St James's, and felt her own heart hurting almost beyond endurance, her own eyes blur with tears. They had gone, at Baby's request, to the bank for Big Bang, to see the trading floor in operation for the first time; she had stood by his chair, with Charlotte, watching the increasingly frenetic activity, listening to the shouting, wondering if she would be able to make sense of it in a thousand years, and after an hour or so, when Bill Webb, the chief trader, came over to them and said, 'How does it match up with New York, Mr Praeger?' and Baby had answered that it matched up pretty well, that he was proud of them all, and had had only a little difficulty getting the words out, he had turned to her and said, 'Let's go home.'

'I shan't go in again,' he said, when she had got him settled in the drawing room, his teacup with its straw in his good hand. 'I'm an embarrassment, the clients don't like it, the other guys hate it, especially when my speech is bad, and I'd just rather not be there.'

She couldn't think of anything to say; no words of comfort came, no protestations that he was wrong; she just took his hand and kissed it, and tried to smile at him, and finally managed to tell him that she loved him.

'I'm pretty pleased about that,' said Baby, and fell asleep.

He slept a lot these days; she was glad that he did. The muscle twitching that plagued him didn't seem to prevent sleep; he was very tired a lot of the time. She supposed it was the drugs.

She went out of the drawing room quietly and down to the kitchen, and made herself a pot of tea, strong enough to stand a teaspoon in. Bugger champagne: when the chips were really down, she thought, you returned to your roots. She felt very weary suddenly, weary and heartsore. Watching Baby deteriorate had been like the worst possible nightmare: a living death that was neither swift nor merciful. He was so brave now: patient and calm, the bad temper of the early days quite gone. She kept telling herself maybe she should stop going to work, stop doing anything, but it was her lifeline, it got her through the dreadful days, enabled her to come back to him smiling, with stories to tell, thoughts to share. And besides, the doctor had said he could live for a year yet or even two. Whenever she thought of that, of him being condemned to this for two more years, Angie felt physically sick, and more than sick, violently angry. It was so unfair, so wrong; what had Baby done to deserve it? He had been a kind, good man, a loving father, a loyal son; for what wrongdoing had this piece of vengeance been wrought?

Fucking me, I suppose, she thought; fucking me, leaving his wife. Well, Mary Rose had been spared this, this misery, this pain: justice of a sort perhaps.

To distract herself from her pain, she rang Tommy. He sounded pleased.

'Darling, how nice to hear your voice. I'm all alone here. Max has spent all day personally supervising Big Bang, and now he's carrying through his own version of it with Gemma. How are you? You wouldn't like dinner, would you?'

'I'm fine,' said Angie, determinedly crushing the chill that always accompanied news of Max and Gemma, 'and I'd love dinner, actually, Tommy. But I can't.' She sighed and shifted in her seat, trying to ignore the ever-present ache of frustration in her body; she had no doubt that had Baby been in good health, she would have had little hesitation in launching into a dazzling joyful affair with Tommy.

'Ah well. I wasn't terribly hopeful. How's Baby?'

'Oh – you know. Pretty bloody awful. Tommy, I need your help. Are you still in touch with your friend Sammy?'

'Sometimes, darling, yes. Why?'

'I need some information. That's why.'

'Angie! You're not asking me to spy?'

'I'm asking you to spy.'

'And what would you give me in return for this – information?'

'Tommy, I've already given you a great deal. Don't be greedy.'

'Well, but darling, I get so tired of living in a cramped little cottage in a noisy London mews.'

'It's a whole lot better than a bedsit in Vegas.'

'Well, I know, and I do appreciate it. But we've outgrown it a little.'

'Tommy, I'm sorry to hear that,' said Angie briskly. 'You're going to have to shrink back into it a little. At least until you've paid off your debts. Primarily to me.'

'Oh well.' He sighed theatrically. 'Well, maybe I could stack this information you want against my credit account. How would that be?'

'I suppose it would be OK.'

'What do you want to know then, darling?'

'I want to know why she thinks Chuck Drew is coming to London. When. Who knows about it at Praegers. That sort of thing. If she's really best friends with Janette Drew she'll know. Women always tell their best friends everything, especially things their husbands tell them not to talk about.'

'All right, darling. Are you sure you don't want dinner?'

'Quite sure. But thanks anyway.'

It was a week before he came back to her. Sammy had been most forthcoming after Tommy had promised her a snort of the best-quality cocaine he kept for special occasions.

'Of course that's expensive, darling. I shall have to bill you.'

'Of course. Come on, Tommy, get to the point.'

'Well it seems that Chuck's move to London is Freddy's idea. And that it has the backing of most of the senior partners.'

'Does Fred the Third know this?'

'Apparently not.'

'Chuck hates Baby,' said Angie slowly. 'And he hates Fred the Third as well. Ever since – well ever since. But surely Freddy would know. Bit intriguing, wouldn't you say?'

'I would. There's something else, apparently.'

'What?'

'Is there someone called Chris Hill?'

'Yes. He's the chief trader. In New York.'

'Well, apparently he's been negotiating to move to Gresse.'

'Gresse! I don't believe it. Chris Hill lives and breathes Praegers. He's been there all his life. He's a senior partner. Why should he move to some bank twice the size, where he won't mean anything to anyone?'

'I don't know,' said Tommy. 'You asked me to find out what I could. I have. Now how are you going to thank me?'

'How would you like me to? Apart from buying Buckingham Palace for you?'

'Hartest would do. No, take me to some very flashy restaurant for lunch. I feel like showing off.'

'OK. You're on. How's your autobiography going?'

'Fascinating. I'm halfway through chapter one.'

'My goodness.'

They went to the Ritz for lunch. He was waiting for her at the table as he always was: he had been raised as a gentleman, he said, and he didn't keep ladies waiting. Angie looked at him and sighed. He really was a very attractive man. Now that he had lost some weight, was living more healthily, he looked wonderful. He was tall, almost as tall as Baby, with dark dark blue eyes, and very long, girlishly curly eyelashes. He had passed those on to Max. His face was thinner too, almost gaunt; his nose was aquiline, his cheekbones chiselled, his mouth curving and sensuous. He was Max, grown up, grown older, but not old; Max with a lifetime of experience, Max with a little wisdom, a touch of common sense. But not a lot.

Tommy smiled at her, kissed her on the cheek.

'Why the sigh?'

'Oh – nothing.'

His eyes moved over her appreciatively, lingering on her mouth. 'You look good, darling. Very good. In fact I can hardly keep my hands off you.'

Angie smiled, thinking how much more welcome that kind of information was than that she looked tired or thin, or that she was being wonderful.

'Let's have some champagne,' she said, 'you've done me good already.'

But halfway into the lunch her mind started to wander; she was still much beset with the puzzle about Chuck Drew and Chris Hill.

'You're not listening,' Tommy said plaintively. 'I was telling you all about my days with the dying dynasties of Palm Beach . . .'

'Dying dynasties! Tommy, honestly. What nonsense you – ' Then she suddenly clutched his arm, and went quite pale. 'That's it! Tommy, that's it.'

'I beg your pardon?'

'That's it. Of course! Praegers! It's a dying dynasty. Isn't it? Fred the Third is eighty-three this year. Baby is – well Baby is dying. Freddy's only – what, twenty-five or something. Charlotte is even less experienced. It's all very very fragile. It's my guess those partners are up to something. Think they can get hold of the thing.'

'But darling, I thought Praegers was family owned.'

'It is. I haven't got any of their bloody shares, even. And don't think I haven't tried. No, but Tommy, just think. What if something happened to Fred the Third now, before Baby died? Never mind if it's been left to Charlotte and Freddy. The clients would be nervous. They'd all threaten to move. There'd be a vote of no confidence, wouldn't there? Suppose Fred didn't even die, suppose he had a stroke or something. Of course. Drew and the others could swoop in, and then maybe – I don't quite see how Chris Hill moving to Gresse fits in, but I'm sure there's an answer. God, what a plan. It's really clever.'

'I can't think old Praeger wouldn't have thought of this,' said Tommy. 'He's not a fool, surely?'

'No, but he's very arrogant. And he thinks he can run the thing for ever. I must talk to Charlotte quickly.'

Charlotte listened to everything Angie had to say very carefully. Then she said, 'Maybe we should go to New York and see Grandpa and talk to him. Together. Don't you think?'

'Maybe we should,' said Angie.

But they didn't go.

Baby grew suddenly worse. Angie, watching him all through the next Sunday, noticed a new weakness, an increased difficulty with breathing. She called the doctor; he came at once, examined Baby, and then walked into the drawing room looking grave.

'I'm afraid he is very ill now. He has a chest infection, quite slight in fact, but because the muscles are so weak, it's causing the breathing problem. I can treat that of course, with antibiotics. But it's his heart that is really letting him down. It was weakened by the coronary years ago and now it's failing. I'm sorry, Mrs Praeger. Very sorry.'

It was the flowers from Mary Rose that finally made Angie cry. Until then, until she read the card, she remained icily brave, smiling graciously at all the callers, receiving phone calls, making arrangements. She insisted on the funeral being in the country, in the same church where she and Baby had gone to have their marriage blessed, only six months earlier. She said she knew it created logistical problems, but that Baby would have liked it.

She invited quite a lot of people to the funeral, friends, colleagues, family. She said she knew Baby would have liked that too, and the party she held afterwards, for over fifty people, with a buffet lunch, and a pianist who played all the music Baby loved best, the great early jazz numbers, Cole Porter, Rodgers and Hart. She said Baby's life had been one long party, and she saw no reason to let him down just because this was one he couldn't personally attend. She told everyone they were not to wear black, and they were not to expect an ordinary funeral; and indeed hardly anyone did, but when she made her entrance in the little church dressed in a brilliant red, rather short dress, with only the black ribbon holding back her hair to add a note of sobriety, there was a moment of almost tangible shock. Spike and Hughdie, who were still too small to perceive death as anything more than a rather temporary affair, stood on either side of her, dressed in pale grey linen coats, looking self-important, turning round constantly to beam at everyone in the congregation. She stood otherwise alone in the front pew; Freddy, Kendrick, Melissa and

Fred III stood behind her, together with the nanny, poised to rush the twins out if necessary.

Betsey had not come; she had been ill with angina, and the doctor had said that the strain of the journey and its dreadful purpose would kill her. She had argued fiercely and then suddenly capitulated and submitted to the shot of Valium he gave her with almost visible relief. Fred stood in the church, impassive, his back very straight, his head erect. He was now burying his second child and the pain was almost unendurable; but Fred had a courage and a toughness that seemed increasingly invincible. Only when Melissa slipped her hand into his, as the choir and the vicar came into the church, did his eyes fill briefly with tears. Then he shook his head impatiently, like an old war horse, cleared his throat and sang 'Lord of All Hopefulness' louder than anyone else in the church; although at the last line, 'your peace in our hearts, Lord, at the end of the day', his voice faltered, and he fished his handkerchief from his pocket and blew his nose rather loudly.

The service was very short, very simple; some prayers, a brief address, on Baby's courage and the example he had set; and one choirboy sang, most beautifully, 'I Know that My Redeemer Liveth'. Angie stood dry-eyed throughout, occasionally smiling down tenderly at one or other of the twins. But when Freddy read, as the lesson, St Paul's Letter to the Corinthians, his own voice shaking slightly as he finished on 'the greatest of these is love', she sat down abruptly and took both of them onto her lap, and little Spike looked up into her face and smiled with an expression of such trust and tenderness that everyone observed it through a blur of tears.

Later, when everyone had gone, Angie walked the quarter mile through the fields to the little church. It was a surprisingly bright evening, the end of a short winter day; the sun, sharply etched in orange, was slithering towards the dark hills. She walked over to Baby's grave, trying to believe and failing utterly that he was finally gone, had left her alone, that she was now to live in a world that did not contain his smile, his voice, his silly jokes, his love for her. She stood there, looking down at the freshly dug earth, seeing him again, as she had last left him, trying to smile, his courage and his gaiety infectious, intact, against all the horror, the misery, of what he had had to endure. She thought of him as he had been, when she had first known him, that evening when he had met her at the airport, smiling at her, telling her that Virginia had told him to meet her, saying, 'Now that I've seen you I can tell you I wouldn't have missed it for the world,' his eyes, laughing, appreciative, moving over her, arousing her, disturbing her even as he stood there, long before he touched her even, and she thought of him on their wedding day, in his wheelchair, looking at her with infinite love and pleasure as she hurled her arms round his neck in the church, and kissed him. She thought, too, of the months she had wasted, distanced from him, before she had known he was ill, and wondered how she could not have known, not have realized, when she had loved him so much; and tried to set the thought aside, knowing what useless, hopeless grief that would release. And then she moved forward slowly, looking at the flowers, reading the cards, trying to absorb what they said, what they really meant.

There were hundreds of them, great bouquets from his colleagues, a tiny bunch of white roses from Melissa – 'Darling Daddy, with my very best love,' a mass of lilies from Betsey and Fred – 'Baby. With pride and love. Mother and Dad,' her own red roses, exactly like the ones she had worn in her hair at the wedding – 'Baby. Thank you for everything. Angie. With my love.'

Dozens more, from the boys, from Charlotte and Georgina and Max, from her grandmother, from Nanny, Mr and Mrs Fallon, the staff in London and at Watersfoot, on and on they went, endless rows of them, all beginning already to curl, to wither in the frost. And then at the end of one of the rows, a simple bunch of cream roses, with a small card written in black in a perfect italic hand; she bent down to read it.

'Baby,' it said, 'With love, for happy memories. Mary Rose.'

And Angie stood there, and thought of Mary Rose, her happy memories so far in the past now, three thousand miles away, for she had refused to come; utterly alone, with no one in the world to comfort her, grieving for the young strong man, grown sick and old, who had married her and given her three children, and for a while had loved her and then had turned away; bereft she was, and half forgotten, those children far from her side, and Angie's heart quite suddenly fractured into grief and pain and she stood there in the almost darkness, sobbing quietly but with a dreadful, absorbing intensity, and she did not stop and she did not move until the red sun had begun to vanish and a sliver of new moon was rising tentatively in its place.

Chapter 49

Georgina, 1986–7

She had written Kendrick a note, sent it to Watersfoot so that it was waiting for him when he got there.

'Dear Kendrick,' it said, 'I'm so very sorry about your father. I know how much you loved him. Maybe we can talk after the funeral. Send my love to Angie. Georgina.'

The first time she saw Kendrick was as he left the church; he helped to carry the coffin out, but not even the grief on his face concealed the lash of emotion in his eyes as he looked at her, explored her face. She was wearing one of her voluminous long dark dresses, and she was very pale. She met his gaze steadily, her expression quite unchanged; she did not smile, nor did her face soften in any way. She was standing with Alexander and Charlotte and Max; she felt oddly detached from them, strangely vulnerable.

She watched him, imagining, enduring with him, the dreadful wrenching grief of saying finally goodbye to his father, of seeing his coffin go into the earth; and at the gathering at the house he avoided her, afraid, she knew, to so much as say hallo lest all the repressed emotion should find voice. But afterwards, when all the guests had gone, and Angie had walked down to the church alone, and Charlotte was marshalling her party to leave for Hartest, he came up to her and said, 'Please stay.'

She nodded, spoke to Charlotte, kissed her father and went back into the empty drawing room at Watersfoot; Kendrick walked in behind her and closed the door.

'Well,' he said, strained, awkward with emotion, 'well, how are you?'

'I'm fine,' she said. 'How are you?'

'Oh, good. Yes.' He nodded. There was a silence.

'I'm so sorry about your father,' she said, 'so sorry.'

'Yes, well. It's certainly better for him.'

'Yes. Yes, I suppose it is.'

'I've missed you,' he said suddenly.

'I've missed you too.'

'I'm – well I'm sorry things turned out how they did.'

He sounded very final; Georgina, who had been half expecting a gesture, a word that might mean he was retracting all that he had said, looked at him warily.

'Yes. I'm sorry too.'

'I just felt – well – '

'I think I know how you felt, Kendrick. You made it very plain.'

'It was important to me.'

'What was important to you?' She could feel all the wrong emotions rising in her, hostile, awkward emotions, a re-creation of her stubbornness on the dreadful night in May.

'That I – that we – well, came first to one another.'

'No matter what?'

'Yes, no matter what. It's the only way to function, Georgina. The only way I could see our lives developing together.'

'Well,' she said, crushing determinedly the very large painful lump rising in her throat, 'then it's just as well we're not going to live our lives together, isn't it? As we would never agree on that? On something so crucial.'

'Yes, I suppose so,' he said quietly. 'You don't feel any different then?'

Georgina looked at him. The past five months shimmered before her eyes, with their odd mix of misery and happiness, the loneliness, the courage she had found and the fear of what might lie ahead. She looked at Kendrick, whom she had loved so much, and she longed more than anything in the world to tell him what had really happened, what she truly felt. She walked over to the window, looked out at the darkness, thinking, trying to form the right words. It was a long silence; Kendrick broke it.

'Oh never mind,' he said, 'I'm sorry I even raised it. We're better apart. Much better.'

'Kendrick – '

'No,' he said, 'no, don't. I didn't actually think there was any more to say. I really didn't. I'm sorry if I've embarrassed you. You have your life here, and I have mine in New York. I'm building up a clientele for my painting,' he added with almost childlike pride. 'I guess it was just a childish romance we had. Just as well we found out before it was too late. I must go and see Grandpa, he looked terrible.' He held out his hand. 'Goodbye, Georgina.'

With an immense effort she met his eyes calmly, almost coolly. She took his hand, and said, 'Goodbye, Kendrick.'

'It obviously suits you,' he said, smiling at her slightly strangely, 'being without me. You've actually put on a little weight.'

It had been very soon that she had realized: almost immediately after they

557

had finally parted. She had woken up one morning, feeling extremely sick; sat up with a jolt, remembering the precise nature of the sensation with horrific clarity. She shot into her bathroom and threw up violently.

'Oh God,' she said wearily, sitting back on her heels, wiping her streaming eyes. 'Oh, dear God.'

She decided to keep the baby. She had actually decided it that morning, that first morning, as she sat on her bathroom floor. It was all she had left of Kendrick and she wanted it. It would be perfectly simple to bring it up at Hartest. Nanny would help. For the first time since Kendrick had walked away from her, through the doors of the airport, she felt a dart of happiness. At last, at long last, she was actually going to have a baby. No more remorse, no more grief. But a baby. A baby of her own. She didn't care what her father had to say. She was doing enough for him. He would probably be pleased, once he'd got used to the idea. She wandered round the grounds, stroking her perfectly flat stomach, feeling sick, smiling foolishly.

Nanny guessed quite quickly. She came into Georgina's room one morning, when she was lying down, recovering from a particularly violent bout of nausea, looking disapproving.

'You've done it again, haven't you?' she said.

'Yes I have, Nanny. Now don't scold me, I have enough to cope with. I'm pregnant and I'm having it, and that's that.'

'I suppose it's Kendrick's.'

'Yes of course it's Kendrick's. Really, Nanny!'

'Well, it's obviously doing you good.'

'I don't feel too good,' said Georgina, closing her eyes briefly.

'You look happier,' said Nanny.

'So you don't disapprove too much?'

Nanny looked at her. 'We've still got the crib,' was all she said.

After the funeral, when she could see she was to be alone with the baby, that there would be no marriage, no husband around to help her, and when she could see also that the bump in her stomach was growing so large it could not much longer fail to be noticed, she decided she must tell Alexander. He had a right to know; and if she was to live at Hartest, have the baby there, then clearly, however notional such an idea might be, she had to ask his permission.

He seemed well these days, but distracted much of the time; he was working on the estate full time again, brimming with plans for the spring: for earlier lambing, for breeding a new strain of deer, for starting a commercial dairy. Nevertheless she was worried about him; he spent a lot of time in the gun room these days and often she found him poring over the account books late at night. She had summoned the courage (knowing that such questions always made him angry) to ask him if he had financial problems, but he assured her, surprisingly calmly, that he hadn't, that it was simply that the financial implications of his new ideas were complex and made heavy demands on his time. He had been to London a couple of times ('Business, darling,' he would say vaguely if she asked him); what really concerned her was that he had been to New York more than once. When Georgina had expressed surprise and interest in those trips, had tried to ask him about them, why he was going, the dreadful familiar blankness came back into his eyes and she could feel him withdrawing from her; he refused to tell her, saying that it was entirely his concern, and afraid of distressing him further she changed the subject quickly. She spoke to Charlotte about it, who agreed it was strange: 'But it's no use trying to make him tell, you know what he's like.'

'I know,' said Georgina with a sigh, 'but it's so odd and he's so strange about it, it frightens me.'

'Oh, you shouldn't be that worried about it,' said Charlotte briskly. 'He looks very well. Leave him, Georgina. Don't push it, for God's sake.'

'I'm not pushing it,' said Georgina irritably. She found the way Charlotte and to a lesser degree Max tried to tell her how to handle Alexander, when their own involvement with him was so extremely limited, very trying. She had done so very much more than her fair share of caring for him through his illness, she felt the least they could do was acknowledge the fact, and treat her views and concerns with respect. But on the rare occasions when she had tried to express this point of view, Charlotte would deliver a pompous little lecture about how of course she was not alone, they were always there, she had only to ask, and Max would tease her and call her Miss Nightingale, so she gave up.

And she had to admit that Alexander did seem well, and on the whole relaxed. He was particularly delighted by Max's more frequent visits to Hartest (usually with Gemma), and Max's apparently increased warmth towards him; he would talk about them both when they had gone as if they had done something remarkable and even difficult, rather than simply driving down from London for lunch; Georgina found this especially irritating; she tried to tell herself she was being childish, that Max was a treat, something served up in great style every once in a way, while she was there every day, part of the furniture, nursery fare and of little interest – but it still stung her.

Alexander had been talking to her about his new dairy on one of their walks one dark day a week later.

'So I thought we could convert some of the old stables into a dairy,' he was saying, 'and start production in, say, April. There's such a big demand for yogurt and so on these days, ice cream maybe even, and we could call it the Caterham Dairy or something like that, so that it had a bit of character. What do you think?'

'I think it's a wonderful idea,' said Georgina. 'Really I do. Have you talked to Martin about it?'

'Of course. He's very keen. As a matter of fact he's coming to lunch today. Why don't you join us?'

'I'd like that.' She smiled at him. 'You know how much I love Martin.'

'Yes, he's a real charmer.' He looked at her, and said, 'Darling, I do think you ought to think about getting back to college now. I so appreciate how much you've done for me, but I'm fine now, and I hate to see you stuck down here wasting your life.'

'I'm not stuck, Daddy, and I don't see it as wasting my life.' Georgina took a deep breath and looked at him. 'Daddy, there's something I have to tell you. Something you need to know.'

'What's that, darling? You're not going to give up architecture, are you? It would be such a pity.'

'Well – I don't know. Maybe I'll get back to it one day. No – the thing is – well, Daddy, you see, I'm – I'm going to have a baby.'

He looked at her, and his face was more than expressionless, it was absolutely blank, white, as if someone had drawn it, drawn the features and then not put in any emotion whatsoever. His eyes particularly were lifeless: almost unseeing. Then finally he said, 'What do you mean?'

'I mean what I say,' said Georgina, puzzled. 'I'm going to have a baby. I'm pregnant.'

'Well it's ridiculous,' he said briskly, appearing to come slowly back to life. 'Of course you can't have a baby. You must – have it seen to. Like the last time. You'd better go and see that woman – what's she called? Page? Something like that.'

'Paget,' said Georgina. 'Lydia Paget. I have seen her. She's been looking after me. She's going to deliver the baby, I hope.'

'Georgina, you're talking nonsense. Nobody is going to deliver your baby. You're not married and you're much too young. Why hasn't this Paget woman talked to me about it? I have to say I think it's outrageous.'

'Daddy, *you're* talking nonsense,' said Georgina. This wasn't going quite as she had hoped. 'I'm twenty-two. I can do what I like.'

'And who is the father of this baby?' said Alexander. He was beginning to look angry now, a flush rising in his pale face. 'And exactly how pregnant are you?'

'I'm six months pregnant,' said Georgina, meeting his eyes, surprised and impressed at her own calm. 'And –' some swift, deep instinct warned her not to say, not to tell Alexander more than she absolutely had to – 'I would rather not say who the father is.'

'Oh really? And perhaps you can tell me why he hasn't married you, whoever he is, why he isn't here supporting you?'

'Because,' said Georgina carefully, 'we don't want to get married. We're not suited to one another, it wouldn't have been a good idea.'

'Well, I suppose I have to be grateful for that at least. So you're going to raise an illegitimate child instead, without a father, simply because suddenly you find you'd made a mistake. I presume he knows about the baby, whoever he is?'

'No,' said Georgina, alarmed, 'no he doesn't. I – thought it best not to tell him. It would be better, I thought, to be on my own.'

'Well, it sounds like a piece of extremely muddled thinking to me, Georgina, I have to say. And how do you think you're going to support this child? Where are you going to bring it up?'

'Well – ' She stared at him, beginning to be frightened now. 'Well here, I thought. I mean it is my home, and Nanny would – '

That had been a mistake. Alexander's voice rose.

'Nanny! I hope Nanny doesn't know about this, and has remained silent also? Because if she does, if she has – '

'No,' said Georgina hastily. 'She has absolutely no idea. I just thought – well, she's here and the nurseries and – well, I thought you might agree – '

'Georgina, I do not agree. Not to any absurd ideas you might have about bringing up your baby at Hartest. I cannot imagine how you could ever have thought of such a thing. You can pursue this insane plan if you must; I can see that it's a little late to do anything else now. But you will not do it here, and you'll get no help from me. I don't want you or your baby at Hartest. Do you understand? I want none of it. None.'

'Yes,' said Georgina, 'yes, I understand. Don't worry, Daddy, I'll remove myself, and the baby. Straight away. I'm surprised it's what you want, but I'll go.'

'It is what I want,' he said. 'I'm appalled at you, Georgina, appalled, that you could behave in such a stupid, amoral way and that you could be so incredibly insensitive as to think I would welcome you and your child here. You are no daughter of mine.'

'No,' she said, looking at him very levelly, 'no, I know I'm not. I never really believed it before. But I do now.'

She couldn't remember afterwards exactly what happened; she must have gone back to the house, packed, loaded up her car, gone to see Nanny, explained to her, and then driven to London, and moved into Eaton

Place: because at seven o'clock that night, that was where she found herself, sitting in the drawing room, still numb, very calm, and listening to Nanny's voice on the phone asking her if she was all right.

'I'm fine, Nanny, really. Now promise me, promise you won't tell anyone, or say anything to Daddy. He'll just blame you. I'm only going to be here a few days, and then I'll find a flat or something.'

'He's so childish,' said Nanny crossly, as if Alexander had thrown a fit of pique over some trifle, rather than told his favourite child to leave his house. 'But he will get over it, Georgina, he really will. You mustn't fret. He'll have you back, when he's got over the shock.'

'He won't,' said Georgina, 'and I don't want to be had back.' She heard her voice wobble.

'Now listen,' said Nanny, 'when are you going to see that doctor again? I don't like the thought of you up there in London, with no medical help at hand.' She made London sound like some remote Hebridean island.

'I'll see her tomorrow, Nanny, I promise. I'm fine. Honestly. Don't worry.'

She told Max first, the next day, after seeing Lydia Paget and getting herself booked into Queen Charlotte's to have the baby.

'I just don't get it, Georgina. I think you ought to tell Kendrick.'

'Well I may one day,' said Georgina, 'but I don't want to yet. And you're not to tell him, and if you do I'll – well, I can think of all sorts of things I'd do to you.'

She was grinning, but she could tell she'd struck home; Max scowled at her.

'Are you going to stay here?'

'No,' said Georgina. 'I most certainly am not. I don't want to, and I don't think Daddy would let me even if I did. I'm moving as soon as I can find somewhere.'

'Let's ask Angie,' said Max. 'She'll have lots of nice little nests for you, I'm sure.'

Charlotte was very cross too: that Georgina had not told her, that she had not told Kendrick, that she had let things go so far.

'He has a right to know, Georgina,' she said firmly. 'It's positively immoral not telling him. Perhaps I'd better go over and see him.'

'Of course you mustn't!' said Georgina, alarmed. 'I don't know why everybody thinks I can't handle my own life. I've made a decision not to tell Kendrick and I'm not going to. And you're not to. Anyway, I thought Grandpa would set about you with a computer terminal if he so much as set eyes on you in New York.'

'Yes, I'm afraid he might,' said Charlotte with a sigh. 'He's shown no sign whatsoever of forgiving me. Even so, Georgie, you ought to tell Kendrick. I really do think so.'

Angie, greatly to Georgina's surprise, disagreed with them all.

'It'll just cause a lot of hassle, if you tell Kendrick,' she said briskly. 'He'll come over and start mooning about, and think he's got to offer to marry you, and Mary Rose is quite likely to get involved, and who needs it? You'll be much better off on your own, if you ask me. Much less complicated. Don't let them bully you.'

She had found Georgina a very nice little flat in Chiswick, which she said Georgina could have for nothing for the time being at least; Georgina argued, and said she must give her something for it, that she had some money from investments, but Angie told her to shut up, that she needed every penny she'd got, and that she could pay her back one day.

'Bloody Alexander. What a pig,' she said. She had gone round to the flat to see if everything was in order, the day Georgina moved in.

Georgina looked at Angie, who seemed very upset and drawn, and altogether wretched. Well, it was hardly surprising; it was only a month since Baby had died.

Georgina slipped into an oddly peaceful routine, and soon felt as if she had been living in Chiswick for ever. She took great care of herself, feeling that however irresponsible it might be to become an unmarried mother, and one moreover with no gainful employment at her fingertips, she owed it to her baby to see that they were both as healthy as possible. She ate all the right things; she rested every afternoon; she saw Lydia Paget regularly for her check-ups and she went to antenatal classes at Queen Charlotte's every week, and lay on the floor with a lot of other pregnant ladies, learning to relax and to do special breathing exercises.

She had expected to feel bored and lonely, but she was neither; a curious tranquillity had taken her over. Everyone told her it was hormonal. She read a great deal, she walked for at least an hour a day and she redecorated the flat entirely, taking special delight in the nursery, which she painted white with huge golden sunflowers climbing up the wall, and a trompe l'oeil on one wall of a window looking out onto a child's picture-book scene of blue skies, white cotton-wool clouds and rolling eiderdown hills, studded with sheep and horses.

Charlotte and Tommy were her most frequent visitors: Charlotte to check on her and cluck over her and to put in at least ten minutes every time trying to persuade her to tell Kendrick, and Tommy just to chat (and also she suspected to check on her). So far the two of them had avoided arriving at the same time; it seemed bound to happen sooner or later.

Charlotte was worried and distracted about the office. Freddy had been on a couple of flying visits with Chris Hill, 'checking things out'. Bill Webb, the chief trader, had already threatened to leave, and so had Charlotte's immediate boss, Peter Donaldson.

'And I get to do the square root of nothing most of the time,' said Charlotte disconsolately. 'When I think of how fast I was getting on in New York – well – '

'Any chance of getting back to New York soon?' asked Georgina.

Charlotte shook her head and sighed. 'Absolutely none. Grandpa is still hardly speaking to me. I'm so sick of it, Georgie, I can't tell you. I keep talking to Charles about going into Law. I'm sure I'd be happier.'

'And what does Charles say?' said Georgina.

'Well, he says I have to remember what I'll be giving up, and how much I loved it in New York. And I suppose he's right. Anyway, I'm hanging on for now. I don't have much alternative.'

When she had gone, Georgina sat and thought about Charles. She hadn't met him, but he sounded incredibly nice. She wished she had a Charles: someone who cared about her, who she could talk about her future to, someone to advise her, someone who was hers. The nearest she had to such a person at the moment was Tommy, and he hardly came into the same category. Not that she wasn't very fond of him, she was. She had told Max so, and he had laughed in a rather smug way and said he'd told them all Tommy was a good egg and now they were all coming round to the idea.

'Charlotte isn't,' said Georgina.

'Charlotte gets more like a head girl every day,' said Max.

She missed Alexander a lot; that was her only real sadness. She loved him, very much, and they had been extremely close; the suddenness with which he had thrown her out of his life had literally shocked her. She also felt an appalling sense of injustice, and anger, that after all she had done, given up for him, he had not supported her when she needed him. At first she had expected to hear from him, had thought he would phone or write and say he was sorry, ask her to come home; but he didn't. Nanny phoned quite often to see if she was all right, and told her Alexander was still going round like a bear with a sore head, but that he never mentioned her. It hurt, Georgina found, exploring this piece of knowledge rather as if it was a sensitive tooth; it hurt badly.

And as the child within her grew, larger, stronger, more vigorous, so did her interest in, her speculation about, her feeling of need for her other, shadowy father.

Her other regular visitor was Mrs Wicks, who dropped in at least twice a week with a box of eclairs; she had heard about the baby from Angie, and she had always liked Georgina, so had taken it upon herself to play Mum, as she put it. The first time she came she asked Georgina if there was anything she fancied and Georgina had said promptly, 'A chocolate eclair,' and now they shared several over a cup of good strong tea each visit. Mrs Wicks was also knitting for the baby, and showering upon Georgina a vast number of bootees, bonnets and matinée jackets all in rather strong colours. She said she never could understand why babies had to be dressed in washed-out pinks and blues and had been particularly delighted when she had found some skeins of bright, rainbow-coloured wool at the Kilburn Market on her way to Clifford's flat. Nanny, who had been to visit Georgina a few times, had found the drawerful of luridly coloured clothes; when she heard their source her lips had been drawn in so tightly they could not be seen at all, and she had said she hoped Georgina wouldn't actually be dressing the baby in them, as you couldn't be too careful these days. She was very jealous of Mrs Wicks's regular access to Georgina, and told her not to take any notice of any advice Mrs Wicks might give her about the baby: 'She's an old woman, Georgina, she wouldn't know what was what at all any more.'

One afternoon towards the middle of December she was wandering round the Marble Arch branch of Marks and Spencers looking rather hopelessly for Christmas presents (and wondering whatever she might do for Christmas: clearly not go home, even if Alexander did ask her, which seemed increasingly unlikely, and the one on offer, to spend it with Tommy and Angie, didn't feel quite right) when she bumped into Catriona Dunbar right by the thermal underwear. Bump was the word; her stomach met Catriona before anything else did. In just the last two weeks she seemed to have grown dramatically. ('Carrying it right to the front,' Mrs Wicks had said confidently, 'got to be a girl.' Georgina had been slightly puzzled by this as all babies seemed to her to be carried in the front, but she knew better than to argue with Mrs Wicks.)

'Georgina!' said Catriona, rallying swiftly from what must have been a considerable shock. 'How nice. How are you? Your father said you'd gone back to university.'

'Oh – oh, yes I have,' said Georgina, not wishing to make Alexander appear a liar with all the attendant complications of such a scenario. 'I'm just up here for some shopping. How are you? And Martin?'

'Oh absolutely fine. Jolly busy, of course. Marvellous idea of your father's about the dairy, isn't it?'

'Marvellous,' said Georgina.

There was a silence. Then Catriona said, 'Well – I must be getting on. It's so crowded, isn't it, and I've hardly started. We'll see you at Christmas, of course. You'll come and have a drink or something, won't you?'

'Oh – yes, of course,' said Georgina. 'Thank you. Bye, Catriona.'

The next day her phone rang. It was Martin Dunbar. Georgina almost dropped it, she was so amazed. He sounded hesitant, and was clearly very embarrassed.

'Georgina. How are you?'

'I'm absolutely fine, Martin, thank you.'

'Good. Because my wife said – well – look, Georgina, please don't think I'm interfering, but does your father know about – well, the baby? I mean you're not – not – well, in any kind of jam, are you?'

Georgina felt a rush of tenderness towards him: that he should have the courage and the concern to ring her and broach the subject of what he clearly thought must be a secret to be kept from her father. She smiled into the phone.

'Martin, that's so sweet of you. I'm so touched. No, I'm not in a jam, I'm living in a very nice flat and I'm being well looked after by everyone. And yes, Daddy does know. Honestly. He's a bit upset about it, because I'm not married or anything, you know.'

Martin sounded relieved. 'Well, I was just – well, worried.'

'You're so nice to worry.' She felt close to tears at his kindness. 'Thank you. Um – how did you know where I was?'

'Oh, well, I asked Nanny,' he said, and sounded rather proud of himself at this piece of duplicity. 'I thought she was bound to know, even if your father didn't.'

The room swam in front of Georgina's eyes. To think of Martin, so painfully, desperately shy, seeking out Nanny, and asking her where he could find her, seemed almost unbelievable. For some reason she thought quite illogically of Lady Macbeth, and her command to her husband: 'Now screw your courage to the sticking point.' Martin must have had to do that, right to the sticking point; he must be genuinely and extremely fond of her.

'Look,' he was saying, 'if you do need anything, money or anything, I mean, you will let me know, won't you? Promise me. I'd hate you not to be properly taken care of.'

'Oh Martin,' said Georgina, 'I just don't know what to say. But yes, I promise I will. Let you know, I mean.'

'Good,' he said, and then after a pause, 'Well, I'd better go. When – when is the baby due, by the way?'

'Oh – the end of February,' she said, 'or thereabouts.'

'Well you'll let me know, won't you?'

'Of course I will. But maybe I'll see you before then. I hope so.'

'I hope so too. Will you be coming home for Christmas?'

'I'm – not sure,' she said.

Two days later, a letter arrived for her, the envelope addressed in Nanny's writing, from Alexander.

'Dear Georgina,' it said, 'I hope that you are well. I would not wish you to spend Christmas alone in London, and therefore I want you to know that you will be welcome at Hartest for the holiday. Your affectionate Father.'

She read it several times, half pleased that he was holding out an olive branch, however puny, half shocked at the letter's chill tone (despite the dutiful 'affectionate'). He was obviously still extremely angry, could not bring himself to apologize for his behaviour, or even to say he missed her. She could not help contrasting it with Martin's gentle, determined kindness. She set it aside, not sure what to do about it, and found that she felt rather sick.

Georgina was not home for Christmas, and nor was she with Angie and Tommy, or with Mrs Wicks and Clifford, which had also been on offer. She was in hospital. The day before Christmas Eve she had suddenly developed a dull ache in the bottom of her back, which had developed into quite severe cramps; Lydia Paget had promptly had her admitted to Queen Charlotte's.

'It's probably not necessary, but we can't be too careful. The head's engaged, and it's early for that. Don't look at me like that, Georgina, I'm sure you'll be fine. Bed rest for a week usually solves all these little problems.'

She lay, frightened and depressed, in the antenatal ward on Christmas Eve; it was largely empty except for a large black lady who was moaning gently in the next bed: everyone who was considered fit had been sent home.

Charlotte, who had rushed in to see her as soon as she heard, was sitting on one side of her bed, Lydia Paget on the other.

'Look,' said Lydia, 'there really isn't anything to worry about, I'm sure. The cramps have stopped, haven't they, Georgina, and the foetal

567

heartbeat is very strong. And the baby's lashing about. Look at him.' They all looked and laughed; Georgina's large stomach, under the hospital sheet, was heaving up and down. 'Now I know it's horrid being here for Christmas, but it's a great deal better than risking losing the baby. Look at it that way.'

The day after Boxing Day she had just been told she could get up for an hour when the ward doors opened and a tall, stooping figure wearing wellington boots and a Barbour walked towards her bed. He held out a rather tatty bunch of flowers and smiled at her.

'Martin!' she said, so amazed she could feel her jaw actually drop. 'How lovely to see you. What on earth are you doing here?'

'Well believe it or not I've come to visit you,' he said, looking rather helplessly round him.

'But I don't understand. Why aren't you at home? It's Christmas.'

'Oh, I'm not a great one for Christmas,' he said, 'I get very tired of it very quickly. And Catriona had to go and visit her mother in Bournemouth, she's not at all well, and I thought – well I thought I'd come and see you.'

'Well, that is just the nicest present I've had all Christmas,' said Georgina. If Santa himself had walked in, she thought, complete with Rudolf, she could hardly have been more amazed. 'Come and sit down.'

'Thank you.' He sat on the bed rather gingerly. 'Are you all right? Charlotte told me you were in hospital and I was worried about you.' He looked worried, she thought; the lines on this thin face were even deeper than usual.

'Honestly, Martin, I'm fine. It was all a silly false alarm. The baby has settled down again, and I'm allowed up this afternoon. Home in two or three days.'

'You must take care of yourself,' he said. 'Is there anyone to look after you when you do get home? Couldn't you go back to Hartest?'

'Well, Charlotte tells me Nanny's threatened to come up and stay with me,' said Georgina, ignoring the second question, 'and Angie has offered to have me, and Mrs Wicks, her grandmother you know, she says she could nurse me for a day or two, so I shall probably be killed by kindness.'

'Oh,' he said. 'Well, that's good. You look very well,' he added, 'it suits you.'

'Thank you,' said Georgina, patting her stomach. 'It certainly is very odd to be fat.'

'Um – what are you going to do when you've had the baby?' said Martin. 'I mean, where will you live? And is there anyone who can – well, look after you then?'

I shall look after myself,' said Georgina firmly. 'I plan to get a job. And I shall live in my flat. In Chiswick. It's very nice, you know. I'm not in some kind of attic.'

'Well that's good,' said Martin. 'I just wondered. I mean it's a lot for you to cope with.'

'Oh, not really,' said Georgina. 'Other people manage.'

'Yes, but other people usually have husbands,' said Martin. He sounded surprisingly firm. 'I really wonder if you've thought this through, Georgina.'

Georgina felt a stab of irritation suddenly. She'd been so pleased to see him, and now he was beginning to sound like all the others. Fussing away. Well, in a way it was quite nice, she supposed. Almost fatherly. This was more the sort of thing she'd expected from Alexander. She smiled at him.

'I know. And it really is so nice of you to worry. But I'm sure I'll be all right. Angie has suggested she takes me on as a trainee in her property company. I'd like that.'

'But you can't give up your architecture,' he said, looking quite shocked. 'You're so good at it, or so your father has always said, and you love it.'

'Well – I'm quite good at it. I can live without it.' There was another silence. Martin looked at his feet. The doors of the ward opened again, and Angie came in.

'Hallo, Martin!' she said, smiling at him. 'How lovely to see you again. What on earth are you doing here?'

'He's playing fairy godfather,' said Georgina. 'Very sweetly came to visit me. He was worried about me.'

'How nice of you,' said Angie, sparkling at Martin. She always moved into another gear when there was a new man around. 'What a good friend. Braving a maternity ward when you're not even related to any of the mothers. I call that courage.'

Martin seemed even more embarrassed; he blushed and smiled at her awkwardly and looked back at his extremely large feet.

'And did you have a good Christmas?' said Angie. 'And how's your wife?'

'Yes, very nice. Catriona is well, thank you. We were at Hartest on Boxing Day. Alexander was in good form.'

'Was he?' said Angie briskly. 'How nice.' Her expression made it clear she didn't want to hear anything about Alexander's good form. 'Doesn't Georgina look good? It suits her, don't you think? When I was pregnant with the twins I looked like some kind of a circus freak. Hideous.'

'I'm sure you looked very nice,' said Martin politely. 'Well, I think I

569

should be getting along now. I'm glad you're all right, Georgina. You won't forget what I said, will you? About – about help and everything?'

'No,' said Georgina, 'I won't. And thank you so much for coming and for being so kind. Bye, Martin.'

She reached up to kiss him; he returned the kiss briefly and then hurried off, struggling into his shabby Barbour as he went.

'He's so sweet,' said Angie absently, looking after him.

'Isn't he? I simply can't get over him coming,' said Georgina. 'It must have cost him an almost superhuman effort. Why on earth do you think he did it?'

'I suppose he was worried about you,' said Angie.

'Yes but – Angie, he never leaves Wiltshire. Never. I think the last time was for his wedding.'

'Well – maybe he fancies you.'

'Oh, now that is silly,' said Georgina. 'Martin – fancying anyone!'

'Excuse me!' said Angie. 'I had a very nice time with him at your father's party. Very nice. He was quite drunk and he came outside with me and – '

'And what?' said Georgina, laughing.

'Well and nothing. He just talked a lot. But I think he's very sexy. In that mournful romantic kind of way. I suppose it's the Russian blood.'

'What Russian blood?' said Georgina, staring at her. 'I didn't know Martin had Russian blood.'

'Didn't you? Oh, yes. Apparently his grandmother was Russian,' said Angie. 'His second name is Russian even. It's – now let me see. Yuri? No that's not right. Jurgen? No – Oh, I know, Yegor. Yes that's it.'

'Oh,' said Georgina. 'Well, you've got more out of him than any of us ever did, Angie. Yegor! What a name.'

'It's the Russian version of George, apparently,' said Angie, picking out the best grapes from a bunch by Georgina's bed. 'I reckon he was in love with your mum. He was telling me how beautiful she was.'

'Martin? Oh don't be silly. He's absolutely under Catriona's thumb. Never goes anywhere or does anything without her.'

'Doesn't mean he couldn't fancy someone else,' said Angie. 'Powerful stuff, sex.'

'Oh Angie, you're obsessed with sex,' said Georgina, laughing. 'Now I want to know what Clifford gave your gran for Christmas.'

As the time for the birth drew nearer she felt her spirit darken. She felt less brave, less optimistic; loneliness stalked her, and she longed, astonished at herself, for her mother who had died what seemed so long ago, when she herself had been no more than a child. She thought of her constantly, wondering if Virginia had felt what she was feeling: the physical weariness and discomfort, the fear of the ordeal of birth, the trepidation at the prospect of being totally responsible for another human being.

Ten days before the baby was due, Charlotte arrived in Chiswick to find Georgina lying on the sofa, trying to get comfortable.

'I wish I knew who my father was,' Georgina said suddenly. 'Where he was. I wish I could see him. You're so lucky, you and Max.'

'Georgie, I'm amazed,' said Charlotte. 'You always said you didn't want to know, that Daddy was your father, that – '

'Yes I know, I know,' said Georgina irritably, 'but being pregnant has made me feel different. I really feel as if I need to know. I miss Mummy too,' she added.

'I expect it's just because you and Alexander have quarrelled,' said Charlotte briskly.

'No, it isn't, I started wanting to know, thinking about him, before I'd ever told Daddy. It's obviously a strong primeval urge.'

'Well, maybe you should start even now and try to find him.'

'Oh, Charlotte, how can I? What clues do I have? Just that he's called George and he's probably very tall. I mean – well I mean! No, I just have to live without him. Make up with Daddy, and manage with him.'

'Have you heard from Daddy again?'

'Oh, once or twice. He's phoned. I know he's sorry. He hasn't said so, he's as cold as ever, but I can tell. I don't actually want to make up with him just now. I haven't got the strength.' She sighed. 'I expect when the baby's born I'll feel better about him.'

'Yes. Are you – scared, Georgie?'

'Yes. I am a bit,' said Georgina. 'I mean, I know there are all sorts of things you can have now, and it's not like it used to be, and Lydia will be there, but I look at this great bump and – well, it's quite a lot to get out, isn't it?'

She smiled slightly shakily at Charlotte.

'Oh, you'll be fine,' said Charlotte. 'Oh, by the way, Georgie, I met Martin last weekend, when I went down. He asked after you so sweetly, and made me promise to tell him the minute anything was happening. He said something really quite odd, actually. He said, "I wish she was having it down here, so I was near her." He really does adore you, doesn't he? It's sweet. I suppose as he hasn't got any children of his own, he might see you as a kind of substitute. A surrogate daughter.'

'Yes, I suppose he might,' said Georgina. She stared at Charlotte, feeling rather strange suddenly. Fragments of thoughts, of conversations, kept running through her head, linking and then drawing apart again. What was it, where did they lead? She sat up a bit and said to

Charlotte, 'I'd love a cup of hot tea. With sugar in. I've got a bit of a tummyache. And could you fill me a hot-water bottle?'

'Of course,' said Charlotte, 'and then I'll see you to bed before I go. When are you going to move in with me?' Georgina had promised to spend the last few days of her pregnancy with Charlotte, so that when she did go into labour Charlotte could deal with the practicalities, like phoning Lydia Paget and getting the ambulance.

'Oh – at the weekend, probably. Yes, I think I'll have a bath, and then go to bed.'

'I'll stay till you're out of it. Make sure you don't slip,' said Charlotte with a grin.

She drifted off to sleep even before Charlotte had left, still trying to work out what it was precisely that was drifting round her brain. She was dreaming now; she was running towards someone, someone very tall, walking away from her, with his back to her. 'George,' she was calling, 'George.' But he wouldn't turn round, and he was walking even faster now; Georgina ran harder herself; she was panting, and she had a horrible stitch that kept coming and going.

'Please!' she shouted. 'Please. Wait.'

And then she fell over and the stitch was worse, like a knife in her side. 'Ouch,' she yelled. 'Ouch, it hurts!'

She woke herself up with her yells. She was lying on her side, as she had fallen in her dream, and the stitch was still bad.

Georgina realized she was in labour.

'Come on then, love.' The ambulance man was kind and reassuring. Like a father. Shit, here was another one. They really did hurt. Maybe she was further on than she'd thought. God. It was lasting a bit of a time, this one. Oh, there, going again. That was better. Yes, he was so nice, the man. 'All right? How often are they coming?' he said. He and his colleague had lifted her into a kind of chair which was actually a stretcher, to carry her out of the flat.

'Um – well, about every ten minutes. I think,' said Georgina.

'Oh well, we've got plenty of time. You all right?' he said again.

'Oh – oh yes, thank you. Bit scared,' she said.

'Oh, you mustn't be scared, my love,' he said, patting her hand. 'Nothing to be scared of these days. You can have a nice epidural, not feel a thing. Who's your doctor?'

'Mrs Paget.'

'She's lovely, isn't she, Dick? Like a mum to her mums, I always say.' Dick nodded. 'Come on, sweetheart, in we go.'

Georgina smiled at them both; they were putting her in the ambulance now. 'And you're like fathers. Really.'

Something suddenly began to clarify in her rather confused brain. What was it? Something to do with fathers. And – oh, God, another tug. She clutched Dick's arm, closed her eyes, tried to breathe how she had been told. Gradually it faded. 'It hurts a bit,' she said, opening her eyes, trying to smile.

'You'll be all right,' said Dick, smiling back.

They had got to the admission room now. She had had another pain. It was really quite fierce. A nurse, kind but brisk, was pulling back the blanket. 'Can you get onto the bed by yourself? When this contraction is over.'

'Yes of course.' She spoke with difficulty, slithered off the stretcher onto the bed. It was hard; it suited the pain. It was more of a wrench now than a tug. She didn't like it very much.

'Now then. Let's have a little look. I'm going to examine you. I'll listen to the baby's heart first, and then do an internal. I'll be as gentle as I can.'

It wasn't gentle enough; the probing hand inside her, meeting the wrench, was awful. Georgina yelled.

'Sorry,' she said, embarrassed. 'I didn't mean to do that.'

'Don't worry. Try to relax.'

The wrench had receded; she tried to concentrate on something else. Now what had it been, that she had been thinking of then, the thought she kept trying to finish? Daughters: yes, that was it. And fathers. Something kept surfacing. Something someone else had said. And something she'd thought. What, what? Oh, yes, dear Martin, so kind, so concerned.

And Charlotte had said . . . yes, that was it, that because he didn't have any children of his own, maybe he thought of her as a sort of daughter. That was a nice thought. Very nice. But there was something else, something – oh God. Another one.

She screwed her face up, bracing herself. It was nasty. Really quite nasty. The nurse spoke to her firmly. 'You're doing it all wrong. You must relax. Not tense yourself. Didn't you go to classes?'

'Yes,' said Georgina, 'but it was easy then.' She smiled at the nurse. The nurse smiled back.

'Well, you've come quite a way, you'll be pleased to hear. So it's not too surprising the contractions are getting stronger. You're two fingers dilated already. Well done.'

'Isn't that – sort of halfway?'

'Well – yes and no. It's certainly progress. Now then, before we get you up to the labour ward, get you settled there, there's a couple of things

573

we have to do. I'll try and make it as pleasant as I can. Catch you between contractions . . .'

It seemed a long time before she was what the nurse called settled in the labour ward. She didn't feel very settled. She felt as if she was riding on a rough sea, rocking up and down, on peaks and troughs of pain. The wrenches were moving down a bit now, reaching from the depths of her stomach into her vagina, somehow, pushing at it. It was horrible.

'Is Lydia Paget coming?' she asked. 'I do want her here.'

The midwife, who was very large and very black, was kind. 'I know you do. We're trying to find her. Now just try, very hard, my dear, to relax, do your breathing. You've got a way to go yet.'

'Can't I have an epidural?' asked Georgina. She was beginning to feel frightened.

'Of course, but really I'd rather wait until Mrs Paget is here. She is in charge of you, you know. Just try and hang on, my dear. She won't be long, I'm sure.'

Another pain and then another. Come on, Georgina, do your breathing, concentrate, Angie had said it really worked. Bloody Angie. It *would* have done for her. Now she was something to do with this peculiar, complicated thought she was having. About Martin and fathers and everything. What was it? Shit, this was awful. Awful.

'Please,' she said through gritted teeth. 'It's quite bad. It's very bad. Couldn't you – '

'Well look,' said the midwife. 'I'll examine you again. See how you're getting on. Then maybe see about an epidural then.'

'Have you contacted Lydia?'

'Yes, I told you.' She spoke slightly wearily. 'She's on her way in. About half an hour. Maybe a little longer. She's been delivering another baby. Turn on your side, my dear. That's right.'

Half an hour. Maybe longer. God, she couldn't stand another half hour of this. She couldn't stand another half minute. It was terrible. One pain on top of another, endlessly tearing at her, wrenching through her. Where was all the wonderful pain relief she had been promised, where was the epidural, where was Lydia, for God's sake?

'Relax, my dear, relax, I have to examine you.'

Right. Relax. Come on, concentrate. Breathing definitely didn't work. Let's think again, try and solve this riddle instead. Martin. Fathers. Yes, that was it, she'd thought he was like a father that day he came to see her in the hospital. She remembered now. Fussing and bossing. Just like a father. So sweet of him to come, though, so kind. Now then, what did that have to do with Angie –

'Oh God,' she yelled at the midwife, 'stop it, stop it, it's horrible, it hurts so much.'

'Please, my dear, try and relax. Let me just – '

'I can't relax. I can't. Don't tell me to, it's fucking impossible.' She was crying now, and angry, hostile to the midwife, turning her head fretfully from side to side. She was beginning to shiver. 'I'm cold.'

The midwife had finished examining her; she was smiling.

'You're doing so well. You really are. And so quick. You're lucky.'

'Lucky! Quick!' She looked at the clock. Incredibly it was only half past three. This seemed to have been going on for ever.

'You're in transition, my dear. Any time now you'll be able to push. Almost ready.'

'But – the epidural – I want an epidural.'

'It's too late for that,' said the midwife, patting her hand. 'Much too late for an epidural. Your baby will be here in a very little while. I'm going to fix you up some gas and air, just to lift you over the contractions. We're going to beat Mrs Paget to it.' She fiddled about, beaming at Georgina as proudly as if it was her own baby being born. She handed Georgina the mask: 'Now when the pain begins next time, put this over your face and breathe deeply. It will help you a lot.'

Georgina tried it; it was horrible. The room swam, receded, rushed back at her, but the pain stayed right there, splitting her in two . . . A young doctor had come in, joined the midwife.

'Everything all right?' He was smiling, a knowing irritating smile.

'No it's not all right, it's bloody awful,' said Georgina. She had a long respite from pain, relaxed on the bed. 'Where's Lydia? I wish she was here, I want her here.'

'She's on her way,' said the doctor. 'But I think your baby will be here first. Now, let me have a look.'

Oh God, not again, thought Georgina, surrendering herself to the double agony. She pushed the mask away.

'Don't. I hate it.'

She yelled out as he and the pain joined forces in her body, then hauled herself back into a semblance of control.

Think, Georgina, concentrate, don't let it get the better of you.

'Right, you're fully dilated. On the next contraction, push. Push as hard as you can. OK?' He smiled at her.

The midwife took her hand, mopped her forehead. 'You're doing so well,' she said.

The contraction began. She was afraid of it at first, shrank from it, then felt it change, different from the others, strong, urgent, taking her over. She pushed, hard, frantically; the pain mounted, stronger and wilder.

'I can't,' she said, 'I can't. It's too bad.'

'Yes you can. Now rest. Wait for the next one. Just wait.'

She waited. God, it was worse waiting than enduring the pain. Distract yourself, Georgina, distract yourself. Come on. Back to Martin, to Angie, work it out, what was it?

'Push. Come on, push.'

She pushed. It was easier. She began to feel strong. She lay back in between the contractions, in a strange half world, alone, except for her baby fighting to be out of her, just the two of them, her baby and the pain; it was going to be all right, she was going to make it. Another pain, another push; another rest. Back to the thoughts. Martin. Angie. Angie's voice. 'I think he was in love with your mum.'

Martin. Daughters. Fathers. More pain; she could feel the baby's head now in her vagina, pressing, urging at it. The young doctor was smiling at her, excited. She liked him suddenly, she smiled back. 'I can see the head now,' he said. 'Next contraction he'll be here.'

Rest. He'll be here. He'd be here. A son. Maybe a daughter. Martin. In love with your mum. Something else. Christ, here it came again, what was it, what was it, push, Georgina, push, yes, that was it, that was it, she had it, she'd remembered, it was his name, Martin's name, his second name, the Russian name, what was it? Yegor. Yegor, he was called. Push, Georgina, push. Here he comes. Yegor, it's a Russian version of George. Martin, fathers, daughters, love, George, push just once more, push, George – yes, yes, that was it, George, George: Georgie.

And as she pushed her son out into the world, smiling, crying out in triumph, Georgina knew, realized finally and without any doubt at all, who her father really was.

Chapter 50

Virginia, 1964

All she had wanted was to show him the baby. He had phoned, said he wanted to come that very day, the day she was born, but she had said, no, he couldn't. It was too risky, it would look odd. He would have to wait. They would both have to wait.

It was four days before he finally came in. Four endless, happy, impatient days. Shy, agonizingly shy, hardly able to look at her, holding a big bunch of bright pink peonies.

'I wish they were roses,' he said. 'But Catriona's aren't out yet. Anyway, she might have noticed if I'd picked them. How are you?'

'I'm fine,' she said. 'Look. Isn't she lovely? Georgina. Such a lovely, grand, pretty name.'

He smiled at her, awkwardly. 'She's absolutely beautiful,' he said, gazing down at the small, sleeping baby, an expression of immense tenderness and awe on his face. 'So beautiful. I'm so happy.' And then: 'How – how was it?' he said, and blushed.

'It was fine. I wouldn't have believed how fine it could be. So quick, so easy. I actually enjoyed it. When she was born, I heard myself saying, "We did it, Georgie, we did it." I was so proud, you see. No drugs, nothing.'

'Oh, that's good,' he said slightly awkward, and then, 'You're very brave.'

'Not at all. Honestly.'

'I'm sorry she's not a boy.'

'I'm not. We can do it again, have another. Look, isn't she heaven? She's so long already! She's going to be so tall.'

Georgina's tallness, her thinness, her tendency to stoop as early as five, was something of a worry. It seemed to Virginia someone might, one day, notice it, remark on it. Well, Baby was very tall. Not thin, of course, but tall. And Fred III was thin. Although very upright, very erect. But that would do. Genetically that would do.

She was so happy, so terribly happy. Everything seemed to be going right suddenly. It was so good to have him there, within reach, within contact. She could see him, did see him, almost every day. God, she loved him. She found it hard to believe how much she loved him. He was her first thought every morning and her last thought every night. She would look at him sometimes, as he sat in the gun room with Alexander, when she went in to offer them coffee (she wondered if Alexander had ever noticed she only offered him coffee when Martin was there, the rest of the time she left it to Mrs Tallow to remember to see to it) and feel quite faint, she loved him so much, all of him, his gaunt face – like, what had she told him he looked like, oh yes, a gentle hawk – his long neck, his untidy straight brown hair, his stooping back, his long long legs, permanently clad in their shabby brown cords, his hands, large, slender, beautiful hands, clever skilful hands that made her cry out with pleasure, over and over again. God, she loved him. And it was so happy, so wonderfully wonderfully happy, their love affair, so uncomplicated, so completely devoid of pain.

She thought every day of the first time things had happened: when he had told her he thought she was beautiful (so stunned she had been, so amazed, pregnant with Charlotte at the time, as amazed that he could think her so with her grotesquely swollen body as that he should say it at all); when he had told her he loved her; his smile when she had asked him to make love to her, in the boathouse down at the lake that dark, dark night, joyful, bashful, confident all at once, the expression of awe in his eyes when she told him she was pregnant, that she knew it was his; picking the memories over like sparkling, shiny jewels on a thread. They got her through the bad times, those memories, when she felt she couldn't stand living with Alexander in the awful claustrophobia of her secret, for another day; when she actually quarrelled with Martin, quarrelled over Alexander and the ghastly farce of their marriage, when he wouldn't, couldn't understand how it worked, how she could stand it. The terrible time, when their other baby died, the poor, sick little Alexander, born too soon, born ill and fated to die, through her own fault, her own wilful wicked fault, her drinking, the awful, dreadful compulsive drinking that she could not, could not possibly, live without any more, not even when she had Martin, had Georgina, was going to have another baby. That had been the one time he had not been there for her; she had been in London of course, far from Hartest, from him; but she had longed for a phone call, a letter, a visit even. It was not such a very long journey, she had said to him; but he had said (when finally he did ring her, tentative, apologetic, sad) he had been too afraid, too fearful, not just of Alexander, but of her and of what perhaps he, as well as Alexander, was doing to her. But the memories, the happy memories, and her love for him, his love for her, got her through at all. Somehow.

He had been so hurt about Tommy, so horribly hurt. She wondered, very often, how she could have done it to him, how she could have done it at all; gone off and had an affair and slept with another man, a man she had hardly met, become pregnant by him – well of course, she hadn't expected to become pregnant, it should have been impossible, the way her dates had been, she just hadn't thought for a moment. She was not, of course, a very skilled user of birth control. But she had been so desperate for some fun, some laughter. However much she loved Martin, he wasn't exactly fun. She had always hoped that he never knew how she kept going back to Tommy, an addict to a drug; she went to enormous lengths to deceive him, to cover up, more like a wife cuckolding her husband, she thought, amused, than a mistress cuckolding her lover. At any event, she didn't think he ever did know, he thought that Tommy was a once in a lifetime, a piece of madness that had overtaken her, still recovering as she was from the death of the baby.

All those years they remained close and loved each other; sometimes able to see more of one another, sometimes less. Catriona, dear, hearty, blind Catriona had never had the faintest idea; nor Alexander either. She felt, they both felt, terrible, deceiving him, when Martin was his employee, and was supposed to be, indeed was, his friend; but the alternative was telling him and there seemed little virtue in that. The third alternative, of renouncing one another, they did not even consider.

It was ironic, really, she thought, that Georgina should have been Alexander's favourite child, as she was very much her own. She grew up quite unaware of the inordinate love of three parents: Virgina always made sure that Martin could be around on birthdays, at Christmas, that Georgina spent time with him. It gave her great pleasure, as Georgina grew older, that she liked Martin so much; and it amused her in a slightly anxious way to see them together, so extremely similar, both of them so tall, so thin, with their permanently anxious expressions, their rounded shoulders, their tendency to stoop. Her two gentle hawks: they smoothed the often rough edges of her life.

It had been her idea, the nickname; he had told her about his Russian ancestry, about his ridiculous middle name. 'I like it,' she said, 'it's lovely. I shall call you Yegor, I think.'
'Please don't,' he said, 'I hate it,' and Georgie had grown from that, it was as Georgie she thought of him, it was Georgie she loved; and it

irritated her, angered her almost to hear Georgina called Georgie, it intruded in some illogical way on the relationship, cheapened it, threatened it even. And at the same time it amused her that none of them ever knew why it made her so cross, why they had to avoid it.

All her married life she loved him; they grew, like a conventional couple, closer together as time went by, sharing simple pleasures in a way lovers can seldom do, picnics, walks, rides, even Christmas – and watching their child grow up. It always amused her to hear people say affairs were so unsettling, sources more of misery and distress than contentment. For her, her Georgie, and her love affair with him were the great joys of her life; and she died calling out his name.

Chapter 51

Charlotte, Spring 1987

Gabe's voice broke into Charlotte's sleep.

She dreamed about him so often, still, that there was no real surprise in the fact; it was only when she pushed herself with great difficulty towards proper consciousness – she always had trouble waking up – that she realized that she was actually holding the phone, and he was actually speaking to her, his voice strangely muffled but unmistakable, deep, throaty, slightly impatient – oh God, it was a sexy voice – saying her name over and asking if she was there.

She sat up abruptly, realizing the voice was so muffled largely because there were several folds of sheet in between her ear and the receiver, pushing her hair back, feeling her heart pound so hard that she was sure if she hadn't been in bed she would have fainted.

'Gabe,' she said, 'what on earth is it?' She looked at her clock: six a.m. 'It must be – what, one in the morning there.'

'I'm working,' he said, and she could feel his irritation reaching her across three thousand miles, 'we're busy here.' The implication that she could clearly not have anything more important on her mind than getting to the shops was very clear. 'Look, Charlotte, there's something I really think you should know. Dad told me not to get involved, but – well, did you know your grandfather is ill?'

'What?' she said, feeling a strange blank space where her stomach should have been. 'Of course I didn't know. What sort of ill? Why haven't I been told?'

'I thought you couldn't,' he said slowly. 'That's why I decided to call you. I just thought it was odd.'

'Gabe, please stop talking in riddles. Just tell me what's happened. Has he had a heart attack or something? Why hasn't Grandma been on the phone? I don't understand.'

'I'm not sure. No, he hasn't had a heart attack. More of a minor stroke, I think. It was – what, three, maybe four days ago. It isn't too terribly serious. But he's at home, and there are some odd things going on.'

'Gabe, what sort of things?'

'Well they certainly seem odder now I know you didn't know. Well, for a start, had you heard anything about Chuck Drew coming to London?'

'I had, actually,' said Charlotte slowly, 'but it was months ago. I was going to talk to Grandpa then, but then Uncle Baby died, and Peter Donaldson was put in charge, and I just thought it was a stupid rumour. I'm sure Peter doesn't know anything about it.'

'Well, check. Also – apparently Chris Hill is moving to Gresse.'

'Shit, Gabe. That was part of the same rumour. Why on earth should he do that? Now of all times?' Her mind was racing around feverishly, twisting and turning. 'If he's on the level, then he must know Grandpa needs him. And – '

'Yeah, if he's not, then he could turn the situation at Praegers to his advantage very neatly. I don't know. Anyway, I thought you ought to know. That's all.'

'I think I'd better come over,' said Charlotte. 'See Grandpa, see Freddy maybe. How's Freddy being?'

'Oh – pretty much the same, only more so.'

'And he hasn't said anything to you about it all? Or your father?'

'Nope. Nothing. Goes around looking important. That's about all.'

'Yes,' she said, 'yes, I'd better come. Anyway, I want to see Grandpa. And Grandma.'

'Well,' he said, 'let me know when you get here. It'd be nice to see you anyway.'

For the second time in five minutes Charlotte thought she might faint.

She wanted to ring Betsey straight away, but it was clearly out of the question for several hours. She got up, showered, dressed (noting to her intense misery that the waistline of the new Margaret Howell suit she had bought only a month ago was already tight, God, she must get back on a really good diet), packed a bag, booked herself onto a flight out of Heathrow late that afternoon, and went into the office.

She went in to see Peter Donaldson as soon as she arrived. She liked him more and more, and felt ashamed now of her dismissal of him as dull in her first wretched weeks in London. He had always been kind to her; he was supportive and generous, swift to give credit where it was due.

'Peter, I'd like to take a few days' holiday, if that's OK. My grandfather isn't terribly well, and I had a call this morning. I'm sorry, I know it's a bad time, but – '

Donaldson looked alarmed. 'I hadn't heard anything. I'm so sorry. Should I be doing anything?'

Well, that confirmed there was something strange going on. In the normal course of events, he would clearly have been notified that Fred III was not well, that changes might be taking place, that there was talk of Chuck Drew coming to London.

'No no,' she said hastily. 'Apparently he's very anxious no one should fuss. He's very sensitive about his health, you know.'

'Well, I expect he is,' said Donaldson. 'If I was eighty-four and running a bank I'd be more than sensitive.' He smiled at her, but she could detect the anxiety in his voice. His appointment had been slightly unexpected, and initially seen as temporary, when Baby had died. He had done a superb job, but he had never been confirmed as chairman, London. It was a sensitive point.

'Oh well, let's hope it's nothing, as usual,' said Charlotte. 'Anyway, I'll be back next Monday, I promise. And I'm not going till this afternoon.'

'Fine. But brief Billy Smith, won't you, on everything that might go through?'

'Of course.' Billy Smith was her assistant: bright, keen, ambitious. She knew she was lucky to have him.

She went back to her office, and asked her secretary for a coffee.

'Biscuits, Charlotte?'

'Oh God, no,' said Charlotte, suddenly fiercely aware of her waist band digging into her as she sat down, 'I'm on a diet, Liz. As from today.'

'Fine,' said Liz. She had, in the last six months, seen Charlotte on five different diets.

At lunchtime she called East 80th Street. Her grandmother came to the phone, sounding frail and something else – what was it? Cool. Yes, definitely cool.

'Charlotte! How nice to hear from you.'

'How is Grandpa?'

'Well – ' The voice hesitated. 'Well, he's coming along, I think. Yes, definitely coming along.'

'Is he in bed?'

'Yes dear, of course he's in bed. Have you been very busy, Charlotte, or something? I have to tell you he was a little hurt, not to have heard from you.'

'Grandma, I – I didn't know. Until this morning.'

'Oh Charlotte dear, don't be silly. I asked Freddy to call you straight away and he told me he had. When I didn't hear from you I checked with him.'

'Freddy – ' Charlotte stopped. She felt very cold suddenly, and very angry. How could Freddy have been so cruel, so ruthless? It was one thing playing power games in the office, but to try to manipulate her through the feelings of two old people was quite another.

'Grandma, I'm truly sorry. I – hadn't understood. I'm coming over tonight. Could Hudson meet me?'

'Well – ' Betsey sounded slightly warmer. 'Well, I expect so, dear. What time is your flight?'

'Gets into JFK at seven. Local time. If he's not there, I'll take a cab. Don't worry. Could I speak to – no, on second thoughts, just give Grandpa my best love, and tell him I'm coming. Bye, Grandma.'

She called Freddy's number. He was out all day, said his secretary, was there any message?

'Yes,' said Charlotte briskly, 'just tell him I called, and that it was thoughtful of him not to worry me about my grandfather's illness, but I would really rather have known.'

'Oh, right – er – fine.' The secretary sounded slightly awkward. She was obviously in on the conspiracy. Well, Charlotte thought, visualizing her sharply, over-crimped, over-glossed, with *Dynasty*-sized shoulder pads, she'd never liked her. If she got this thing sorted, she'd take great pleasure in telling her a few facts of life.

She called Gabe next. 'I'm coming over tonight. I'm going straight to the house. Maybe we could talk in the morning.'

'Sure,' he said. 'Give me a call.'

He sounded his old self, abrupt, detached. She sighed, and stopped even thinking about the biscuits she had turned down. The best thing Gabe had ever done for her was wreck her appetite.

Before she left, she called Georgina.

'Hi, Georgie. How's George? God, I wish you hadn't given your baby the same name as yourself.'

'Displaying his usual good healthy appetite,' said Georgina. 'I feel like that milking machine in the cowshed.'

'Do you mind being a milking machine?'

'I like it.'

'I'm going to New York for a few days. Grandpa isn't very well. Nothing serious, I don't think. I'll call you when I get back. How's Daddy?'

'Daddy's fine.'

Georgina was back at Hartest, with her baby. She seemed different: tranquil, happy, relaxed. She said vaguely, if anyone remarked upon it, that it must have been motherhood that had done it to her. To the amazement of everybody but Angie, who said he was displaying classic parental guilt, Alexander had arrived at Queen Charlotte's with a

584

bouquet of flowers so big he could scarcely be seen behind it, and tears in his eyes, and begged Georgina to forgive him, and to come home. She had said she wouldn't, and that she liked London and living on her own; after four nights of getting little more than two hours' unbroken sleep, and George developing both a cold and a nappy rash, she packed up her Golf and went gratefully home to Hartest and to Nanny. It was something of a relief to the rest of the family. They all loved her, but it was generally agreed that she was hardly capable of looking after herself, let alone herself and a baby.

Her grandmother greeted Charlotte in the first-floor drawing room at East 80th Street with arms outstretched. She looked older, Charlotte thought with a pang, much older. Charlotte had been over to see her soon after Baby had died, and she hadn't looked so bad then; she had still been in shock, perhaps. She was somehow collapsed-looking, not just shorter, as old people always become, and thinner, but without substance.

'Charlotte! It's lovely to see you. Come and sit down, darling. How was the flight?'

'Fine,' said Charlotte. 'How are you, Grandma?'

'I'm OK, dear. A little tired of course. You look tired too, Charlotte. I expect you've been working too hard.'

'Just a bit,' said Charlotte. 'But it's good to be busy. The London office is such a success now, Grandma, Uncle Baby did such a good job setting it up. He'd be so happy to see it now.'

'I'm sure he did,' said Betsey, her face suddenly alight at being able to talk about Baby. 'He was such a brilliant man. Such a success at everything he turned his hand to. I remember when he was just a little boy and he had his first bicycle, he was riding round the yard on it in just about five minutes. Your mother had so much more trouble, poor darling. And then – ' Her voice drifted on.

Charlotte listened, sipping her orange juice, longing for something stronger. After five minutes or so, she said, 'Can I see Grandpa?'

'He's asleep, darling. He sleeps a lot. And it's important for his recovery, Dr Robertson says. He's been so good, has Geoff, coming in every day.'

'I'm sure,' said Charlotte. 'Do you think he'll wake later, and I can see him? Or should I just go to bed soon? I'm terribly tired, it's two in the morning, my time.'

'You go to bed, darling. He was so pleased you were coming, although he pretended to be cross, of course. That you hadn't been before.'

'Yes, I'm so sorry,' said Charlotte. 'It was just a terrible mix-up in the office. I was out for about three days, and I never got the message. You should have phoned.'

'Well, dear, I would, but Freddy was so insistent you knew. I know how busy you are – '

'Not for you and Grandpa,' said Charlotte, kissing her. 'Now I think I might go to bed, if you don't mind. And stop waving those potato chips at me, Grandma, the temptation is making me feel quite faint.'

She was allowed in to see Fred after breakfast. He looked a lot better than she had expected, sitting up in bed, freshly shaved, his brilliant blue eyes sharp behind his glasses, spruce in his Brooks Brothers striped pyjamas, the bed littered with the *Journal*, the *Times*, and the latest copies of *Fortune* and the *Institutional Investor*. He glared at her, then held out his hand and pulled her down to kiss her.

'Took your time coming, didn't you?' he said. He spoke crossly, but there was genuine hurt behind his eyes.

'I'm sorry, Grandpa, I really didn't know. Nobody's fault, I was out of the office for a few days. Anyway, I'm here now. How are you?'

'I'm absolutely fine,' he said irritably. 'Damn chap Robertson won't let me out of bed for another day. It was nothing, nothing at all, just a dizzy spell. Probably had too much to drink at lunchtime. I want to get back to the bank, and he won't let me. Not for another week, he says.'

'That doesn't sound too long,' said Charlotte carefully, 'and I'm sure it's in good hands. I presume Pete is looking after things?'

'Well, after a fashion. Boy doesn't really know what he's doing,' said Fred irritably. Charlotte thought of the white-haired distinguished-looking Pete Hoffman, with his thirty-five years of banking history, and wondered how he would feel at being called a boy. Probably like it, she thought.

'Well, how's the London office? Donaldson still making out all right? I've been worrying about him, keep meaning to come over, sort it out.'

'Absolutely fine, really. He's a very good man, Grandpa. I mean, obviously you know how well we're doing.'

'Well? No I certainly wouldn't call it well. All right, was the best news Chris Hill could give me. Should be getting better results in this boom, Charlotte. Obviously Donaldson hasn't got the fibre. Pity. He'll have to be replaced. Just as soon as I'm up to it. Hill's got some good people he's put forward. Suggested Chuck Drew amongst others. He's very sound these days.'

'Grandpa – ' Charlotte's mind was whirling. 'Grandpa, I don't know what – ' She stopped. There was no point trying to tell him the picture Chris Hill had presented was wrong: not until she had a clearer idea what was going on. He would simply start bawling her out again and telling her she didn't know what she was talking about.

'Grandpa, what?' said Fred. He looked flushed suddenly, and frailer than she had realized. She backtracked hastily.

'Oh – nothing. It's lovely to see you. Grandma seems well.'

'Yes. She's getting old, of course,' said Fred, slightly dismissively, as if he was a young man in his prime. 'Worries about things. Now how long are you going to stay? Want some coffee, Charlotte, and what about a croissant?'

'I'd love some coffee,' said Charlotte, looking longingly at the croissant. 'Thank you.'

'And how are you making out? Doing anything much yourself yet? You should be. Clever girl like you. Damn fool you were, messing everything up here,' he added.

'I'm doing plenty,' said Charlotte. 'Loads of divestitures. Deal with lots of the clients myself. I'm loving it, Grandpa, really I am.'

'I hope that idiot isn't giving you too much to do,' said Fred. 'You can't run before you can walk. Probably time we got you back over here. How's that brother of yours?'

'He's fine,' said Charlotte, not even attempting to analyse how she felt at the prospect of coming back to New York, but experiencing a rush of pleasure that it was so clearly a possibility, 'he's doing really well, at Mortons. He's on the money desk. Making a fortune. He's just bought a Porsche.'

'A Porsche? I thought he was hard up,' said Fred. He looked rather cross. 'Or did your father buy it for him? I imagine not, the way things – ' He stopped suddenly.

'Way what things, Grandpa?' said Charlotte. 'What were you going to say?'

'Oh,' he said quickly, 'I don't approve of fathers buying toys for their grown-up sons.'

Charlotte let it pass. But she was faintly intrigued.

'Yes, well all the traders have Porsches,' she said. 'They leave a trail of them everywhere. Porsches and empty champagne bottles. They're like a lot of very overexcited little boys. At an endless party.' She realized she sounded rather prefectish and tried to lighten her tone. 'But it's all good fun. And very good for business.'

'I don't know that I like the idea of my grandson making a fortune for Mortons,' said Fred slightly petulantly, 'it doesn't feel right at all. If he's any good at what he does, he should be working for Praegers. I might tell him so.'

'I don't know that he'd want to change,' said Charlotte carefully; she

587

knew that Max's prime ambition these days was to move over and work for Praegers. 'He loves Mortons. And like I said they're paying him a lot of money.'

'Money isn't everything,' said Fred as if he had spent his entire life working for a pittance himself. 'What about family loyalty, eh? Doesn't that count for anything?'

'Well, but Grandfather, you said he couldn't have a job at Praegers,' said Charlotte. 'He asked you. It's not his fault.'

'Well, he was still doing that bloody silly modelling then,' said Fred crossly. 'He's proved himself now. Is he still going out with Old Daddy Morton's daughter?'

'Yes,' said Charlotte, struggling not to sound disapproving. She didn't like Gemma, she thought she was self-centred and empty-headed. 'Yes, they spend a lot of time together. How did you know anyway?'

'Your father told me,' said Fred.

'Daddy! When on earth did you see Daddy?' said Charlotte, amazed. Alexander and Fred's dislike of one another was legendary. There was something going on here, clearly; Fred's earlier remark was more significant than he was going to admit.

'Oh – last time he was over here,' said Fred briefly. 'Didn't you know about that?'

'Well, I knew he came. I thought it was – well, I didn't really know what it was,' said Charlotte lamely. 'You know Daddy. You can't get him to talk about anything if he doesn't want to.'

'Quite right too,' said Fred. 'And it's no business of yours that he came.' He looked a little uneasy. 'Now then, who's this coming upstairs? Oh God. Geoff, not again. I told you not to come back until I was ready for a game of golf.'

Charlotte caught Geoff Robertson on the stairs as he was leaving.

'How is he?' she said.

He smiled at her rather distantly. 'He's OK.'

'Not in any danger?'

'No. As long as he's sensible.'

'So will he be able to go back to the bank?'

He looked at her as if she was extremely stupid.

'No of course not,' he said. 'Well, only in the most minimal capacity. He had a heart attack, you know. It wasn't a very major one, but at his age, any one at all is serious. It's a miracle he's recovered to the extent he has.'

'Oh,' said Charlotte. 'Oh, I see.' She felt very helpless suddenly.

Geoff Robertson looked at her. 'They're a very good loyal bunch of men at that bank,' he said suddenly. 'Almost every day I get a call from one or other of them. Mr Drew, and Mr Hill. And young Freddy of course. Asking me how he is. Very concerned, they all are.'

'Oh yes,' said Charlotte. 'They are all very concerned. It's true.'

Gabe suggested they had a drink after work.

'Harry's Bar,' he said, 'six. I may be late,' he added, 'and I almost certainly won't be able to stay long.'

'Oh, fine,' said Charlotte.

She had drunk two large spritzers and was already feeling slightly light-headed when he finally came in at a quarter to seven. It was two years since she had seen him, and she realized, with the sweet pang of pleasure that began in her head and moved by a circuitous route through every possible area of her body, that she should abandon any thought that she might have had of falling out of love with him, or even of growing immune to the intense assault he launched on her senses by the simple fact of entering the same room as herself. He looked exactly the same; quite how she might have expected him to have changed she could not imagine, but against all logic she had. The same towering body, huge shoulders, long long legs that he never seemed quite able to find a satisfactory resting place for; the same wild dark hair, brooding brown eyes, rather full mouth; the perfect teeth, the reluctant smile, the crushing handshake (Charlotte, submitting her hand to the handshake, found herself shrinking from it even despite the considerable pleasure of being in at least some physical contact with him), and then, as he sat down opposite her, winding his legs carefully round the chair legs, the voice, the deep, dark, almost gravelly voice, God, she had missed that voice, oh God, she'd missed it: 'Hi,' it said, the much-missed voice, the much-loved voice, 'you've put on weight.'

Charlotte felt sick: with disappointment, with anger, with shame. She stared at him, and could think of nothing, nothing to say that wasn't foolish, self-denigrating, crass. She felt a blush rising in her neck, right up to her forehead; tears of sheer misery rose up behind her eyes. She looked down, looked away; then forced herself to meet his gaze. He was grinning at her now, his eyes dancing with evil mischief at her; he reached out and picked up her glass.

'Let me get you another. White wine?'

'Yes please,' said Charlotte.

While he was gone, she blew her nose, composed herself as best she could; when he returned she was smiling at him coolly.

'Well,' she said, 'only three quarters of an hour late. Not worthy of an apology, obviously. Don't worry, Gabe, I don't have too terribly much to do this evening.'

'He looked genuinely puzzled.

'I said I might be late,' he said. 'How's Grandpa?'

'Not very well,' said Charlotte. She was very nervous; she realized her hand was shaking. She took a swig at her glass, almost gulping it down; then realized with horror it was half empty.

'You've obviously been drinking halves of bitter,' he said, noticing. 'How's England?'

'Wonderful,' said Charlotte. 'It's marvellous to be back home.'

She looked at him and smiled radiantly; he smiled slightly uncertainly back. There was an expression at the back of the dark eyes that she couldn't begin to read.

'And the London office? Everything OK for you? I'm sorry it's not doing better.'

'Gabe,' said Charlotte with an effort at dignity, 'I just don't know why you have to say things like that. Knock everything that isn't Praegers New York. The London office is doing just fine, we're making loads of money, and I'm personally – '

'Hey,' said Gabe, 'get down off that extremely high horse, will you? I'm not knocking anything. I'm just playing back information. I genuinely thought you were having a tough time over there.'

Charlotte stared at him. 'Why?'

'Well, that's what the word is. All over our building. London isn't making out. May have to close. Send over reinforcements, et cetera, et cetera.'

'Well it's a filthy lie,' said Charlotte. 'I just don't understand it.'

'I think I could begin to,' said Gabe. 'Cheers. It's nice to see you. Even if you have rounded out a little.' He grinned at her. She scowled back at him.

'You certainly know how to make someone's evening,' she said. 'Thanks.'

'Oh for God's sake,' he said. 'You haven't got any less touchy, have you?'

'Gabe, I'm not known as touchy in any other company,' said Charlotte with an effort at sounding lighthearted. 'I do assure you it's entirely a change that you wreak in me.'

'Well I'm extremely sorry,' he said, and clearly didn't mean it. 'It just slipped out. I didn't mean to offend you.'

'Perhaps we'd better change the subject,' said Charlotte.

'Perhaps we had.'

There was a silence. Then she said, 'Freddy is definitely up to something. He told Grandma he'd told me about Grandpa.'

'Did he? Little squirt.'

'And there's something else,' she said, 'Geoff Robertson, that's the family doctor, says he gets called almost every day by Chris Hill or Chuck Drew or Freddy, about how Grandpa is.'

'How sweet,' said Gabe.

'That's what I thought.'

'Chris Hill is definitely negotiating with Gresse,' he said. 'Definitely.'

'How do you know?'

'I have a girlfriend who works there.'

'Oh,' said Charlotte. She felt sick again, and drank the rest of her spritzer very quickly.

'Apparently he's about to sign.'

'I just can't make it out. Why should he move now?'

'God knows. But they've got some incredible package for him, and their chief trader's talking to Lehman.'

Charlotte sighed. 'Well, maybe he's on the level. Maybe he's a good guy.'

'If he was a good guy, he'd stay on.'

'That's true. What does your dad think?'

'He doesn't think anything. Keeps his nose clean, my dad does. Always has. Retirement only a few years off, you see.'

'That's not a very nice thing to say about your father.'

'Charlotte darling, we're not all loyal little family sycophants like you.'

Charlotte stood up. Her eyes were blazing. At that moment she could happily have killed him.

'How dare you,' she said, and her voice was shaking, and for once she didn't care. 'How dare you. I am not a sycophant, and I might say, Gabe Hoffman, I have never noticed you turning down the opportunity to work at Praegers, to take the King's shilling, and follow in your father's footsteps. If you disapprove so much of nepotism, why aren't you working at Lehmans or First Boston? It isn't just natural brilliance that's got you where you are, in fact, I'd say natural brilliance was probably the least crucial ingredient in the extremely nice little brew you've concocted for yourself at Praegers. I'm going home, Gabe. I don't know why you ever bothered to arrange this evening. You obviously don't want to see me. Please let me know if you hear anything else about my grandfather. Or perhaps if you do you'd better pass it on to somebody quite different. Nothing to do with my family. I'd hate you to feel you'd furthered the Praeger nepotistic cause any further.'

She turned and half ran out of the door, and up the steps into Hanover Square. She wasn't quite sure why she was so distressed: she supposed she had simply forgotten how vile he was, how deeply he could hurt her. She had hoped, without realizing she had hoped it, that he had in some way come to reciprocate the way she felt, had actually wanted to see her, was concerned for her as well as for her family and the bank. Hurt pride was added to the usual pain. She started walking very fast in the direction of Wall Street and Broadway. She would get a cab home quickly and sit and talk to Betsey and Fred. That would make her feel better, soothe her battered ego. They loved her.

She cut into New Street and then suddenly realized that it was quite deserted, very dark and that she was being followed. A tall youth in a donkey jacket and a woollen hat was uncomfortably hard on her heels. Oh for God's sake, Charlotte, she thought, you've just got reinfected with New York paranoia. In England this would just have meant there was someone walking very close behind you.

Nevertheless she speeded up her pace; the youth did likewise. She felt fear now, start in her belly, clutch at her guts; sweat broke out in her armpits. She walked still faster, stumbled, almost fell; he was virtually behind her.

She righted herself, pulled her coat round her: 'Hey,' said a voice, 'hey lady, what's the hurry?'

She ignored him, walked on; he was beside her now, tall, threatening. He looked down at her, and his eyes were very glittery, evil in the lamplight.

'I said what's the hurry.' He put out his hand, took her arm.

She shook it, trying to get free. 'Leave me alone.'

'Ah!' he said, in a phoney British accent. 'You're English. How is the dear old mother country?'

'It's fine,' said Charlotte. She was still hurrying along. Maybe if she could keep him talking, she could get up into the comparative safety of Broadway.

'Good.' Suddenly, with a speed and force which shocked her, he pushed her into a doorway. She tried to scream; he put his hand over her mouth. It smelt. She twisted her head, backwards and forwards.

'Please let me go,' she mumbled against the hand. 'I have some money. Please let me go.'

He moved his hand from her mouth, put it round her throat, pinning her to the wall. He reached with the other hand for her bag, pulled out the wallet, stuck it in his pocket.

'Can I go?' said Charlotte. 'Please. I won't say anything.'

'Hey,' he said, 'you're a real upper-crust little lady, aren't you? I always fancied a bit of class. I'm in no hurry. No hurry at all.' He still had her pinned to the wall of the doorway by her throat; he pushed his face into hers. His breath was foul; his lips slobbery. She screamed briefly, and then his hand was on her mouth, silencing her. His hand was groping at her jacket now, seeking out her breast; panic engulfed Charlotte.

'Please don't,' she said, 'please.'

'Oh, but I want to please,' he said, and stood back from her grinning. Charlotte summoned all her strength, raised her leg and kneed him in the crotch.

'You bitch,' he said, but it didn't do what she had hoped, make him loosen his grip, he pressed harder on her throat, started moving his hand into her coat again.

She felt herself shrinking, shrinking, high up within herself, unable to think, unable even to fear, just revulsion, revulsion and nausea; and then, just as she knew there was no hope, no escape, he was pulled off her, and somebody, somebody large, strong, furiously, viciously strong, had him on the ground, and was belting him, punching him, and saying 'You filthy, filthy fucker' over and over again. It was Gabe's voice: Charlotte stood there, staring at him, watching him punch the youth, turn him over, pull his hands together behind his back, drag her wallet out of his pocket.

He turned his head and looked up at her, briefly, and she could read nothing in his face, nothing at all, except a terrible, tender concern.

'Are you OK?' he said.

She nodded helplessly.

'He didn't. . . ?'

'No. No he didn't do anything. Really.'

Gabe picked the man's head up almost casually and then knocked it down onto the street again.

'You silly bitch,' he said almost conversationally. 'You silly silly bitch. Walking around in these streets as if you were in some goddamned English village. It's time you wised up.'

'Gabe,' said Charlotte, scarcely able to believe she was hearing this attack, when she had been so frightened, so near to being raped, 'Gabe, how dare you – '

'Oh, shut up,' he said, and stood up. The man was whimpering now and half conscious; Gabe threw him into the doorway.

'Come on,' he said, taking Charlotte's arm. 'Let's get you home. This joker isn't going anywhere.'

'Shouldn't we call the police?' said Charlotte.

'Yeah. We'll go to the office. Are you really OK?'

'Yes I'm fine. But won't he run away?'

'Well, he doesn't look too well up to running. If he does, he does. I can't leave you here, and I can't take him with us. Come on, let's get to the office. All right?' She nodded, speechless. Her legs felt very weak suddenly. Gabe put his arm round her waist, helped her along; she kept stumbling.

They reached the bank; the night porter let them in.

'I'm just going up to my office,' said Gabe briefly.

'Right-oh, Mr Hoffman. Still a lot of people up there.'

'Gabe,' said Charlotte, 'let's go to my – my other office. It'll be quiet there. I don't want a fuss.'

'Won't it be locked?' he said.

'I have a key.'

They went in, turned on the lamp. Charlotte sat down rather feebly in one of the low leather chairs by the fire. It had been waiting for her, this room: her equivalent of the Heir's Room, a rather grand, beautifully furnished, clearly important office. Fred had shown it to her on her first morning before whisking her down to her grey pen. 'You can move in when you've earned it,' he had said. She had never so much as taken a call in it, but she had stood in it from time to time, wondering if she would ever be able to claim it.

Gabe called the police.

'Yeah,' he said, 'I'll come and meet you. Corner of Beaver and Broad. Five minutes.'

'I'll be back,' he said to Charlotte. 'Don't go away.'

She managed a half smile. 'I won't.'

He was back in fifteen minutes, closed the door behind him. He had a bottle of brandy with him.

'OK. They carted him off. No problem. I thought you might need this. Got any glasses in here?'

'Yes, I think so. In that cupboard there.' She pointed to a cupboard by the fireplace; it had several glasses in it, of varying sizes.

He poured a large glass and handed it to her. Charlotte gulped at it; it was soothing, warming, welcome. Gabe looked around him, at the panelled walls, the flower-filled grate, the large desk, the Indian carpet.

'Nice little place you've got here,' he said.

'Oh Gabe, don't,' said Charlotte wearily, 'I can't help it and anyway, you know I never used it.'

'You will though, won't you?' he said and there was a wary expression in his eyes.

'Yes, I suppose so. I hope so. Oh – let's not talk about it. I feel awful.'

Gabe gave her some more brandy, then stood by the fireplace looking down at her. 'Like I said, you're a silly bitch,' he said suddenly, 'that was asking for it, you know. Fucking asking for it.'

Something exploded in Charlotte: something vast and sad and horrific in its strength. She stood up and turned on Gabe, started to pummel at him with her fists, sobbing at the same time.

'Shut up, shut up, shut up,' she screamed through her sobs. 'You're harsh and cruel and vile. How can you talk to me like that when I – when I –'

'When you were mugged,' he said, and he was shouting too, 'yeah, and when you could have been raped or killed, and all for nothing, the price of a bit of stupidity. You women never learn. Never.'

He grabbed her fists and tried to hold them still; Charlotte pulled them away.

'I hate you,' she said, 'I hate you so much.'

She turned away from him, dashing her hand angrily across her eyes.

'Don't,' he said, and his voice was different, quieter suddenly, almost gentle. 'Don't say that. I don't like it.'

'Oh you don't? Why not? Does it not suit your great arrogant fucking ego?'

'No,' he said, quieter still. 'I don't like it because I love you.'

A shock went through Charlotte, a physical, shuddering shock. She felt it in her head, and she felt it deep within her body, and she felt it in her heart. She turned round slowly and stared at him; his face was white, his eyes very dark. He looked at her deeply, heavily seriously, almost sombre; he raised his hands towards her, then dropped them again.

'Gabe,' she said, aware even as she spoke that it was a cliché, an absurd cliché, 'Gabe, did you say what I thought you said?'

'I don't know,' he said. 'What I said was I love you.' He scowled at her. 'Unfortunately.'

'Why unfortunately?'

'Why unfortunately: because you're so difficult, and spoilt and self-centred and arrogant and bossy and moody and –'

'*I'm* difficult and arrogant!' said Charlotte. 'Gabe Hoffman, you should take a look at yourself. I have never known anyone more difficult and arrogant than you – oh for God's sake, what am I saying, what am I doing?' She went over to the door, locked it, and stood with her back to it, looking at him. He had taken his jacket off, and his shirt was crumpled; his face seemed more lined than usual, his hair more wild. He was still scowling, but his eyes had softened.

'I don't know quite what to say,' he said.

'Nor do I,' said Charlotte.

Gabe stepped forward, stood looking down at her. He was close enough now for her to touch him; she put out her hand tentatively, lacked the final courage and dropped it again.

'Dear God,' he said and picked up the hand, turned it over and kissed the palm. Very slowly, very languorously. Charlotte closed her eyes briefly, felt the hot molten sensation of desire invade her. Gabe took her face in his hands, and kissed her, on the mouth. His lips were very heavy, very strong, his tongue slowly exploring her mouth; Charlotte kissed him back, gently, almost nervously at first, then with a growing, surging urgency. She was still dazed, shocked, she still dared hardly move.

Gabe put his arms round her, pulling her against him. He was kissing her harder now, saying her name, over and over again; his hands began to move down her, caressing her back, lingering on her waist, pausing, then moving again, down to her buttocks. She pushed against him, grinding her hips, gently but urgently; she felt as if her desire was a live thing in her, reaching out, searching for him; she felt him respond, and pulled her mouth away from his, smiling up into his eyes.

'Thank God for my carpet,' was all she said, and lay down on it, holding out her arms.

He began to unbutton her shirt; she sat up impatiently, tearing it off, and her bra too, lay down again, her eyes fixed on his. She could feel her nipples hard, erect, and at the same instant, as his mouth went to work on them, his tongue teasing them, playing with them, a heat, a liquid heat reaching down from them into the deep, aching depths of her. He pulled away again, started removing his own clothes; he was naked now, and as she stared up at him, at his heavy muscular body, the dark hairs covering his chest, his arms, the flat hard stomach and the jutting penis, standing out from a great mass of pubic hair, she moaned, moaned with longing and pleasure and disbelief at what was happening to her.

He knelt again and pulled her skirt down, off, and then her panties; he kissed her breasts again, then her mouth, her shoulders, her neck, frantic as if he could not have enough of her. And then he bent further, kissed her stomach, her thighs and then tenderly, very slowly moved again, lay above her, and she could feel him there, there, oddly gently, urging at her, sweet and slow. 'I love you Charlotte,' he said again, and she thrust at him, suddenly, swiftly, crying out, and he was in her, invading her, filling her, with a huge, strong, wild pleasure. She could feel herself beginning to climb now, already reaching, grasping for release; her body, moving with his, sweetly rhythmic, slowly at first, then faster, faster, advancing, retreating, rising, falling. She wrapped her legs round him, round his waist, feeling him deeper still; a shot of pleasure so bright, so violent she was almost afraid of it.

He was still suddenly: then pushed, pushed, reaching into her, seeking out her climax, drawing it from her; she felt the final climb, the great

596

triumphant soaring into pleasure and she arched her back and cried out again and again, feeling him respond, now following her, now leading her and then at last he groaned and spasmed and slowly he was still.

'Good God,' he said after some little time. 'Dear God, how very unbritish you are.'

'No I'm not,' she said, and even in her pleasure heard indignation in her voice. 'I'm not unbritish at all.'

'Charlotte,' said Gabe, 'do stop arguing.'

They lay there for a while; then she began to feel cold, shivered. Gabe reached out and got his jacket, laid it over her; kissed her tenderly, held her closer.

'That was kind of nice,' he said.

'Yes it was. And kind of unexpected. Totally unexpected, I would say.'

'I cannot believe,' he said, 'that you didn't know.'

'Didn't know what?'

'That I – well, loved you. Fancied you. Wanted you.'

'Gabe, of course I didn't know. I'm not clairvoyant. How could I have known?'

He grinned. 'I thought women did know these things.'

'Well – sometimes. If the man is charming, polite, complimentary. If he's rude, boorish, aggressive, it's a little harder.'

'Was I rude and boorish?'

'Yes you were.'

'Yes, I guess I was.'

'Why were you rude and boorish, Gabe?'

'Well, because you were so fucking arrogant and touchy and difficult. It was like getting close to a piranha. I felt if I did, I'd be dead. I thought you disliked me. I thought you – well, it doesn't matter.'

'Well, it doesn't matter now,' said Charlotte. 'It doesn't matter at all.'

Later, she started to get dressed; bashful suddenly, concerned about her rounded stomach, her full breasts. 'I'm fat,' she said. 'I look awful.'

'Don't be silly,' he said, reaching out, outlining the curves with his hand, 'I like you that way. It's how I remember you, when you were sixteen, when I first set eyes on you, at your grandfather's party, ripe and plump, with a bloom on you, like some gorgeous peach. I thought you were beautiful. When I said in the bar you'd put on weight, it was meant to be a compliment.'

'Well,' said Charlotte tartly, 'it didn't come over that way. And I wouldn't recommend you saying it to any of your other girls. They won't see it like that either.'

597

'I don't have any other girls,' he said.

'Yes you do. Don't lie.'

'Yes, I do. I won't lie.'

She finished dressing, pulled on her jacket even, chilled suddenly at his words. She fumbled in her bag for a tissue, avoiding his eyes.

'Hey,' he said, 'what did I say?'

'Oh – nothing.'

'Yes I did. What was it? The other girls? That was it, wasn't it? God, you're touchy, Charlotte. Touchy and difficult. I don't know if I can handle this, I really don't.' But he was smiling. 'I'll tell you something,' he said suddenly. 'When I found out about you and Jeremy Foster, I could have killed him. And then probably you. I never really felt jealousy before then.'

'I didn't love him,' said Charlotte. 'I really truly didn't.' She looked at Gabe very solemnly. But her heart was singing.

'Shit,' he said, 'where's my watch?' They started to look for it.

'Why did you take it off?' said Charlotte, laughing.

'I always take my watch off,' he said, 'when I'm doing anything important. You know I do.'

'Yes,' she said, 'yes I suppose I do. Here it is, look, under the chair.'

He put it on, smiling at her. 'Come along,' he said, suddenly brisk, 'I think I should get you a cab. Send you home.'

She stared at him. 'There's no hurry, Gabe. Honestly.'

'Charlotte, I'm sorry, baby, but there is. The night is young. I have work to do. Several hours of it.'

'Oh for God's sake,' said Charlotte. 'I just don't believe it.'

'Charlotte my darling,' he said, 'you'd better believe it.'

Charlotte hardly slept that night. The combined effect of her attack, Gabe's declaration of love and some extremely intense lovemaking had left her almost sick with tension. She felt literally shocked, assaulted by a series of emotional memories: fear, outrage, relief, anger, wonder, pleasure, and above all a wild happiness. It was impossible to rest.

She finally got up at six, showered, put on a track suit and went for a walk in Central Park. She supposed Gabe would have told her it was dangerous, but there seemed to be even more joggers than muggers.

He called her after breakfast. 'You OK?'

'I'm fine. Thank you.'

'Good. I have a lot on today. If you're free tomorrow that'd be good.'

'I'm free.'

'I'll call you in the morning,' he said and rang off.

Charlotte put the phone down, trying not to feel aggrieved. A love affair with Gabe was clearly not going to do a great deal to massage her ego.

She had lunch with Fred. He was irritable, drinking red wine. Betsey kept telling him not to, which only served to make him drink more. After a while, tired of being contradicted, even when she said it was two o'clock and it quite plainly was, Betsey retreated to her room for a rest; Charlotte frowned at her grandfather.

'You shouldn't be so horrid to her. She's only trying to look after you.'

'I know,' he said, 'and I don't like it.'

'You're a bad-tempered old man,' said Charlotte companionably.

'I know it. Charlotte –'

'Yes?'

'Oh – nothing.'

'Try me.'

'It's business. Bank business.'

'Good. I like business. I like bank business even more.'

'Chris Hill came to see me this morning,' he said.

'Oh yes?' Charlotte felt her heart pounding a little harder.

'The fool wants to move. To Gresse. They've made him an offer he says he can't refuse.'

'Well – he's only human. And he has – what – four daughters? Expensive.'

'Yes, yes, I know. But I've offered to top anything they can offer.'

'So?'

'So there's one thing they're offering that I can't.'

'What's that?' asked Charlotte.

'Shares.'

'But Chris has shares in Praegers, surely?'

'Yes he does, but only a very few. Gresse are offering him a large number. And thereby a substantial share in the profits. He says he can't resist that. Having part of the company, having control.'

'Well – you can't offer him shares,' said Charlotte. 'Praegers is Praegers.'

'Well – yes, it is.' Fred's old face was sad suddenly, hurt, the lines etched very deep. 'But with Baby gone, I have to have totally committed partners. Freddy – and you – are very young. Inexperienced. You'll need support. Guidance. And I certainly need Chris Hill. At this point, more than at any time I can remember. He's a brilliant man. He holds that trading floor together.'

'So what are you saying?' said Charlotte, afraid almost to hear the answer, knowing what it was going to be.

'Oh,' he said with a sigh, 'I don't quite know. But I can't afford to lose Chris Hill. That much I do know.'

'Grandpa.'

'What?'

'Grandpa, I'm sorry if this makes you cross. But I just think you should take a hard look at what's going on. I mean – '

Fred glared at her. 'If you're going to start interfering,' he said, 'you can go home. I don't want to listen. And I don't want to listen because you don't know what you're talking about.'

Charlotte sighed. It was hopeless. 'Well – all right,' she said. 'But I hope you won't regret it.'

'Well I won't.' He sighed, and looked at her, his face softer suddenly.

'I'd like to have you back here, I think,' he said, 'with me. The time has come.'

Charlotte hardly slept that night. Not because of Gabe, or even because she was clearly about to be restored to New York, but because of the sudden awful realization of where Freddy and Chris Hill, and Chuck Drew and God knew who else, were going and how they were going to get there.

'It's Machiavellian,' she said to Gabe next day. They were walking in the park, in the afternoon; it was already nearly dusk. He had promised to be round after breakfast and finally arrived well after lunch. 'I had to do some work,' he said as if that was entirely satisfactory explanation enough. Charlotte didn't actually care. She was too strung up to care about anything.

'Chris Hill has Grandpa over a barrel. He'll get some shares, obviously. I don't know how much – seven, ten per cent maybe. Then no doubt the others will move in. Use it as a lever.'

'He won't give any to Chuck,' said Gabe. 'He doesn't seem to have too high an opinion of him. Won't care if he leaves, I should imagine. I can see why. He's a pretty dull guy.'

'He's not always been dull,' said Charlotte and told him what Baby had told Angie about Chuck's insider trading, years before.

'Good God. So why is he still there?'

'Grandpa forgave him. Apparently. It was a very long time ago.'

'More to it than that,' said Gabe. 'Has to be. Your grandpa never forgave anybody anything. Not if they'd threatened the bank.'

'Well – I don't know. I have a feeling Angie does, but – anyway, maybe Chuck's just going to ask to move into London and oversee it. I daresay Grandpa would agree to that. All these stories about what a disaster it is.'

'Well, my dad will stay loyal,' said Gabe. 'No doubt about that.'

'Well, no doubt. But if Chris has lots of shares and he doesn't, might he not feel a little miffed? I would.'

'Possibly. Tell you what, I think Bart Kegan is in on this thing. He's very close with Freddy, always buttering him up.'

Bart Kegan was the youngest of the senior partners: good-looking, charming, oily. He was famous for having enough suits to wear a different one every day for at least a month. 'I loathe Bart,' said Charlotte.

'Do you?' said Gabe. 'I'm surprised. Most women adore him.'

'I'm not most women.'

'No, that's true.' For the first time that day he took her hand, kissed it, smiled at her, kissed her mouth.

'You got some free time now?'

'I have,' she said briskly. 'Don't tell me you have.'

'A little. Shall we go back to my place? I'll cook you dinner.'

'That'd be nice. Gabe – we ought to try and do something about all this. Would your dad help, do you think?'

Gabe hesitated. Then he shook his head. 'Not a chance. He's phobic about politics. That's why he likes Praegers. He says because it's family there aren't any.'

'There weren't,' said Charlotte gloomily. 'Well – maybe I'll have to be brave. Talk to Grandpa.'

But she didn't get a chance. When she got back much later that night, Fred was in hospital. He'd had a second heart attack. And before he had it he'd made seven and a half per cent of Praeger shares over to Chris Hill.

'You do realize,' said Gabe when she told him, 'that they can get rid of you now?'

Chapter 52

Max, Spring 1987

Max put his hand up to his face. A red mark stood out on his cheek, where it had been struck.

'That hurt,' he said.

'Good,' said Gemma, 'it was meant to.'

'You bitch,' said Max. 'You little bitch.' But he was smiling.

'Don't smile.'

'Gemma, darling, I shall smile if I want to.'

'And don't call me darling.'

'Why not? If I love you.'

'You don't love me. You treat me really badly.' Gemma's exquisite little face was flushed, her eyes bright with unshed tears. She pushed her mane of dark brown hair back from her forehead, and then stood facing Max, her hands on her narrow hips.

'You look as if you're going to whip me,' he said.

'I'd like to.'

'Hey,' he said, 'that'd be fun.'

'Oh Max,' said Gemma irritably, 'please don't start fooling around. I'm so angry and so hurt.'

'I don't see why. I've taken you out every night this week, next weekend we're going to stay with your friends in Norfolk, I just organized a dinner party single-handed to celebrate your birthday, I keep giving you the most fantastic fucks, what more can I do?'

'Max, I want you to come away with me and Mummy and Daddy to Paris this weekend. It's my birthday treat.'

'Gemma, I'm sorry but I can't. I've been promising Tommy for months I'll take him to Hartest. I can't let him down now.'

'But why does it have to be this weekend? When it is my actual birthday on Sunday?'

'Because Alexander is away, and he and Tommy don't get on.'

'So you and Tommy are going to spend the weekend alone, in that house?'

'Yes, we are.'

'Well, am I allowed to come?'

'No you're not.'

Gemma looked at him, her eyes very watchful. 'Sometimes, Max, I think the rumours about you and Tommy might just possibly be true.'

Max walked over to her and grabbed her arm. He felt very frightened suddenly, more than he would have believed possible.

'What rumours?' he said and he could hear his voice shake slightly.

'You know perfectly well what rumours. That you and he are lovers. I think it seems quite feasible, really.'

Max stared at her. He felt weak with relief, and intensely amused. He began to laugh.

'Oh,' he said, 'that. Well, my darling, I would have thought you would be the first to know that couldn't be true.'

'God, Max, I hate you.'

'No you don't. You adore me.'

'I don't.'

'Well, we won't argue about it. Come on, we're late.'

'I'm not coming.'

'Oh yes you are,' he said, laughing, drawing her into his arms, kissing the top of her head tenderly, 'and when we get back, you can come a great many times more.'

She did; but long after she had gone to sleep, Max lay beside her, staring into the darkness, living and reliving the moment when she had talked about the rumours about him and Tommy, and wondering just how long he could keep the secret safe within the family.

He wasn't even sure quite why he was so frightened. At worst it could only be an ugly rumour; Alexander would deny it, obviously. Families like theirs had always attracted scandalous gossip; everyone liked hearing it, but no one really believed it. It would be different of course if there were other claimants to the house and the title, but there weren't. No cousins, no uncles; really it was absurd to be so neurotic about it. It was in everyone's interest to confirm him as the next Earl of Caterham. Including Tommy's. It wasn't going to do Tommy any good at all to have Max declared as a bastard son, with no right to Hartest. All Tommy wanted was a comfortable lifestyle. Well, maybe a little better than comfortable. Nevertheless Max was frightened, and he supposed it was because of the ugliness of the story. He had loved his mother very much and been proud of her; he might have rejected her since, might have labelled her a tart and Alexander a feeble cuckold, but Max was a snob, and he liked his situation in life, the beautiful house, the proud title. It was coming to mean to him far more than he would ever have imagined; it was reassurance, security, status, all the things that learning about his history, about Tommy even, had robbed him of. That day in Ireland, when Charlotte had told him about Virginia, she had effectively orphaned him; he had lost a father and rejected a mother. All that was left to him after that was the fiction: and it was a reassuring, important fiction. It gave him a past, gave him a background. He had grown very fond of Tommy, but Tommy was not the person he wished to be. And he despised Alexander, as a person; but only Alexander could give him his place in the sun.

He knew that when he had been modelling, fooling around, getting expelled from Eton, taking drugs, he had put himself at risk; he had not been the heir Alexander wanted. At sixteen, eighteen it hadn't seemed important; now it mattered increasingly to him. The old family joke about Georgina being the favourite, the one who loved Hartest, the future Earl of Caterham, occasionally seemed just slightly sinister. He was, against every possible odds, a touch anxious about the small George.

He had not really ever thought Alexander would do it, leave the house to anyone but him; but it had been enough of a possibility from time to time to rock his complacency, disturb his self-important ego. And once George had been born, he began to think harder about his relationship with Gemma. The more respectable, the more stable he appeared, the better. He would be twenty-one this year; he was seriously considering becoming engaged to her. She was the kind of girl he could imagine being his wife, being the Countess of Caterham: beautiful, well educated, raised in the right traditions. Her father might be a businessman, but he was a country gentleman as well: charming, hospitable, civilized. And Alexander liked Gemma, approved of her. That was important. God, it made him angry, having to worry about Alexander's approval. When it was something he so basically despised.

Max sighed and turned over, flung his arm around Gemma. She pushed it off again, frowning slightly in her sleep. She was a selfish little cow. Of course he adored her. And when she was in a good mood, she was fun. And a great lay. There really was no reason against asking her to marry him. No reason at all.

Max determinedly shut the one reason, the one absurd, insane reason not to marry Gemma out of his head, turned his thoughts to the next day at Mortons and what it might bring, and finally went to sleep.

He was sitting scowling at the screen some time in the middle of the next afternoon. He had just gone short on a deal, sold 5,000 shares he hadn't yet bought and the fucking things were going up, not down. Shit shit shit; he stared at the screen, banging his desk in frustration. He really should have learnt his lesson at Christmas; he had sold 10,000 Australian shares that were dropping like so many stones before lunch on Christmas Eve, confident he could make a huge profit buying them back that afternoon, and then when he'd got back, two bottles of champagne down, you couldn't get a line to Australia for a million pounds. Everyone was phoning their gran, their mum, their auntie to say Happy Christmas. The Stock Exchange closed before he got through. In the end he gave up and when he went back after the holiday, the shares had gone right up. He had cost Mortons quite a lot of money that holiday; Jake Joseph had laughed and said it was the sign of a good trader that he could cut his losses and just concentrate on the next trade. 'You'll have to make it up again over the next few weeks though, my son. Otherwise Daddy-o will not be pleased.'

Max had made it up again in ten days. He was very good at his job.

'Max! Call on one!'

'OK.' He picked up the phone, still staring at the screen. 'Max Hadleigh.'

'Hi, Max Hadleigh. It's Charlotte Welles here.'

'Charlotte, where are you? I can't talk to you now, I'm in the middle of a trade.'

'I'm in New York, and stop showing off.'

'Still? I thought you were coming back yesterday.'

'I was. But Grandpa's had another heart attack. Oh, only minor, I've seen him since, but he's in hospital. Grandma's distraught. I have to stay. And there are some nasty things going on. Really nasty.'

'What sort of nasty? Charlotte, I told you I can't talk now. I – shit, hang on a minute.'

The shares had suddenly dropped. He watched them for a minute or two, saw them go down another point, then went back to the phone.

'Ring me tonight, will you? Or later? Or can I call you?'

'Yes,' she said, 'call me. As soon as you can. I'm at East 80th Street.'

The shares had dropped some more. Max hesitated, then made a decision. They might drop further, but he couldn't be sure. He called the broker offering them and clinched the deal, then sat back, savouring the familiar heady sensation that was half physical, half mental. It was true, Jake was right, this game was sometimes better than sex.

He picked up the phone again.

When he had finished listening to Charlotte it was lunchtime; he told Jake he was going for a beer and went for a walk. The City was busy, the streets jammed, people rushing about looking important. He walked slowly, thinking; down Fenchurch Street, along Lombard Street, past the Cornhill, and along to Threadneedle Street and the Bank of England.

Nobody who lived their lives in the Square Mile could help but be physically affected by the place, the strange contrast of the wild pace of day-to-day business, and the shadowy, narrow streets, the tall formal buildings, the sense of history, of time gone, measured not just in years but money, greed, profit, loss, success, failure. He stopped opposite the back of the old Stock Exchange and went into Throgmortons, down the faded grandeur of the stairs into the bar, and ordered a beer. It was full of market makers and journalists, shouting, telling dirty jokes, boasting about the morning's trades and stories; Max stood pretending to read the *Financial Times* and hoped no one would recognize him. They didn't. He didn't usually drink at lunchtime, but he felt confused, disoriented, not himself. He decided he was hungry and went into the Long Room, further down still, and sat at one of the absurdly long rows of tables, like some subterranean city itself, ordered steak and kidney pie, and tried to work out how he felt about what Charlotte had told him. He certainly wasn't sure how he felt about Fred III's offer. It was what he had wanted so much a year ago; now he was settled, doing well, had friends, Dick Morton thought well of him. Did he really want to move? He'd have to start all over again, Miss Bossyboots would be queening it over him, he'd have to endure the suspicion, resentment, all over again. Was it worth it?

Then he thought of the possible ultimate prize, of being a partner at Praegers, part of the family, and decided maybe it was. The sky really would be the limit there. Fred hadn't promised that, Charlotte had said, but she had also said she knew he had meant it. He had made inquiries about Max, had heard he was good. 'It certainly isn't because you're family and he thinks he ought to, rather the reverse. But he does hate to think of you at Mortons, doing well, making money. Anyway, he says he'll top whatever they pay you. You'd be in London, of course. At first anyway. I wish you would, Max. It would help. Strengthen my position.'

Well he certainly wasn't going to say yes Grandpa, thank you Grandpa, I can't wait Grandpa. He'd think about it.

That stuff about Freddy was really intriguing. Scary in a way. If Charlotte had got it right, she could lose her place in the sun. And on the board. All the more reason for him to go in with her, join forces. It was all very cloak and dagger: more like fiction than fact. But it made sense. Freddy had always hated Charlotte, she had said he was insanely jealous of her, and with Baby no longer there the bank was vulnerable. He could see that. And if Fred was going to snuff it – God. What a nightmare.

Charlotte had sounded extremely cheerful, for someone under duress. She said Gabe Hoffman had been very helpful, and then gone a bit girly.

Maybe they'd finally got it together. He'd always thought they should. He'd thought Hoffman a good egg. A lot better than that ghastly Foster. How could Charlotte have got mixed up with someone like that, Max wondered, pushing his pie crust round his plate. What a naive creature she must be. Well, she still seemed like a head girl to him with that brisk bossy voice of hers; not sexy to his way of thinking, but obviously to some. Maybe schoolgirls were one of Jeremy Foster's things. Anyway, that was hardly the point. Charlotte had said she would be back in a week or so, and she hoped he'd have made up his mind by then. She said Freddy was threatening to come to the London office with this Drew person, and she'd like to have Max there.

There was of course the problem of Gemma. She wasn't going to like the idea of him leaving Mortons. She enjoyed the fact that he worked for her father; it gave her further control over him. Sometimes Max felt that their whole relationship was just another adornment to Gemma, something to deck herself out in, to show off. She loved everything about being his girlfriend, about being half of a trendy, quasi showbiz and yet archetypically smart, socially acceptable couple. She liked the way they had an entree not just to the chic world of fashion, the creative haute monde, moving in the same circles as Jerry Hall, Yasmin Le Bon, the Geldofs, the David Baileys, rock and pop stars, fashion editors and writers, but also to the rock-solid, blue-chip world of the English aristocracy. She found herself written up in features, sought after for quotes about herself and Max in magazines like *The Face* and *Arena*, and *You* and *ES*, as well as starring with him in the society pages of *Tatler* and *Harpers*, at parties and balls and point-to-points. It all suited and excited her; there seemed no limit to where they might not go, find themselves, and she was charmed by it.

Gemma was first upset, then furious when Max broke the news. Tears welled up in her great brown eyes, and then when she had stopped being tearful, she turned on him.

'How could you? After all Daddy's done for you. Really, Max!'

'Gemma darling, he hasn't been paying me for nothing. Yes, he gave me a start. It's been great. But I've done well there. I haven't been a liability. Rather the reverse. Made him some money, even. And now I want – well I think I want – to make out on my own.'

'On your own! Oh sure. In your grandfather's bank. With your sister holding your hand. I think it's pathetic. I really do.'

'OK,' he said easily, 'I'm pathetic.'

He suddenly fancied her rather fiercely. He often did when she was

607

being particularly stormy. 'Look, darling, I'll think about it, OK? Now can I take you home, please, and pleasure you for a bit.'

'No,' said Gemma crossly. 'You can't. Not unless you promise – oh Max, stop it. Don't.'

He had his hand up her skirt; smoothing over her thighs, her slender, silky, glorious thighs. He moved a little further, feeling for the edge of her stockings, Gemma always wore stockings and very frilly suspender belts. She was that sort of girl. Max forget about the bank, forgot about everything. He had to get her home.

'Come on, darling. Let's go.'

'But – oh, well, maybe. We can talk about it in the car.'

She gave him a sulky smile. Max found it rather hard to walk out of the restaurant, his erection was so strong.

'Shit,' he said, as they drove along, 'I just remembered. I don't have my door key. Tommy has it. I'll have to pick it up on the way. He's at Angie's.'

'Oh Max, no. Can't we go to my place?'

'No,' he said, 'I have to go home. Early start tomorrow. It won't take a minute.'

They had stopped at some traffic lights; his hands were in her panties, fingering tenderly at her pubic hair. She was deliciously wet. 'God, you're gorgeous,' he said.

'Oh – well, all right,' said Gemma. She was very responsive to flattery.

'Max!' said Angie, giggling gently, as she opened the door. 'How lovely.' She was very drunk and very obviously stoned. 'Come along in. We're drinking tequila. And having just a tiny smoke.'

'I won't come in,' said Max, grinning at her. 'What happened to the bridge game?'

'Oh, it finished. Please do come in. I have a present for Gemma for her birthday. And I'd like it anyway.' She was looking gorgeous: tousled and flushed, her green eyes very large and bright, moving over his face, up and down his body. 'Please, Max!' She leant forward and kissed him briefly; she smelt heady, hot, exciting. Max hesitated. 'Well – '

'Oh darling, please. Come on.' She called over his shoulder down the steps at Gemma sitting in the car. 'Gemma, come along in. Have a quick drink. I have a birthday present for you.'

'I really don't think we can, thank you,' said Gemma slightly frostily. 'We have to get home.'

Max suddenly felt irritated. Unfriendly little bitch. Here was Angie being generous and thoughtful and Gemma couldn't have the courtesy to say thank you.

'We'll come in,' he said. 'Gemma, come on. Just ten minutes.'

'I really think we should get back.'

'Oh, don't be dreary,' said Max irritably. 'I know what's on your mind, but it'll be even better after some of Tommy's hash, it's the most fantastic stuff. He absolutely refuses to tell me where he gets it.'

'Come on in then,' said Angie rather loudly, 'only don't make a noise and wake the nanny.'

'Angie, my darling, the nanny's out,' said Tommy patiently. He had appeared behind her in the doorway. 'You said goodbye to her yourself. Told her not to come back, in fact.'

'I didn't!'

'You did.'

'Oh well. Come on, you two.'

Max waited for Gemma and then walked into the house and up the stairs to the drawing room. Angie was giggling on the sofa.

'What did she say, the nanny, when I told her not to come back?'

'She just laughed,' said Tommy. 'I could really fancy that girl. Fantastic tits.'

'Oh, that's what Baby used to say,' said Angie, and burst into tears.

Tommy promptly started cuddling her; Max poured her another tequila and sat down and cuddled the other side; Gemma stood looking at once sulky and embarrassed.

Angie stopped as suddenly as she had started, pushed them both away and smiled radiantly round.

'Let's play strip snap,' she said.

'What on earth is strip snap?' said Tommy.

'Like snap, only instead of giving up your cards, that is, as well as giving them up, you take something off.'

'I like it,' said Max. He felt a new sexual excitement now, more sensuous, less predictable than the one he had felt in the restaurant. 'Tommy, are you going to make me one of those reefers of yours, or do I have to do it myself? Gemma, do you want one, darling?'

'I – I think really we should go,' said Gemma. 'I'm tired.'

'Nonsense. This will revitalize you. You'll be telling me you have a headache yet.'

'I do,' said Gemma, 'actually.'

'I have some wonderful pills,' said Angie, jumping up.

'No really, don't bother,' said Gemma. 'I don't like taking pills. Mummy and I see a homeopath. That's so much better for you.'

'Oh God,' said Max, turning away from her. 'Come on, folks, let's get on with this game.'

'I won't play if you don't mind,' said Gemma awkwardly. 'I'll just read or something.'

'Oh, don't be such a pain in the arse,' said Max. 'Of course you must play.'

'Max, I don't want to.'

'Well, Gemma, I want you to.'

She looked startled at the coldness in his voice; Angie and Tommy exchanged glances.

'I'll deal,' said Tommy quickly. 'Let Gemma do what she likes, Max. It's her birthday.'

Half an hour and two more tequilas later, Angie was down to a black lace teddy, Max was wearing his boxer shorts – 'Lovely silk, darling,' said Angie, stroking them appreciatively – and Tommy was almost fully dressed. Gemma was rather determinedly playing solitaire.

'I'm hungry,' said Angie, standing up. 'I'm going to fix us all a sandwich. Anyone want anything else?'

'I don't even want a sandwich,' said Max, his eyes moving over her rather intently, 'I want another tequila. Quickly. And then maybe another game. Angie, do you still have the old roulette wheel?'

'Oh my goodness,' said Angie, moving over to him, stroking his hair gently, 'what a keen little gamesman you are. Like father like son, eh Tommy? I bet you know where the old roulette wheel is.'

'Absolutely,' said Tommy.

And then they all realized, with a swiftness that froze them into sobriety, what they had said; and they all looked at Gemma, their eyes full of horror, like three naughty children.

'Of course he's not my father.' Max was sitting in the small drawing room in Pond Place, looking rather sick. He had left with Gemma rather hurriedly, leaving Tommy to help Angie tidy up, as he put it. 'Does he look like my father?'

'Yes he does.'

'Well so does Alexander. I mean Dad.'

'Not as much as Tommy does.'

'Oh for God's sake. Now you really are scraping the barrel. It's pathetic. Honestly, Gemma, I don't know how you can read so much into a bit of drunken mickey taking. You're more of a child than I thought.'

'Max, I really am not that stupid. And it all makes perfect sense. Suddenly.'

'Oh balls. What does?'

'Your devotion to Tommy. Your funny relationship.'

'Oh Gemma, you're crazy. It's you who's talking nonsense now. It's too absurd. Do you honestly think that some American guy could be my father? I'm Alexander Caterham's son and heir. You ask him. He'll tell you.'

'I might,' said Gemma. 'I just might.'

'Well go ahead,' said Max lightly. 'I'm sure he'll be delighted to reassure you.'

'Well who is Tommy then? What's the bond between you?'

'He was an old friend of my mother's. Who was American, as you may care to remember. He was down on his luck and we get on well, and – well, that was it really.'

'But why do you live with him? In this – ' she looked about her – 'this funny little house?'

'Why shouldn't I live here? It's a very desirable neighbourhood.' He spoke lightly, trying to diffuse the tension.

'Oh, come off it, Max. Why don't you live at the house in Eaton Place? That really is a desirable neighbourhood.'

'My father likes to use it when he comes to London. He doesn't want us camping all over it. He always made that clear.'

'So why do you live with Tommy then? Why not on your own? Or with someone your own age? A friend?'

'Gemma, Tommy is a friend. He just happens to be a lot older than me. I really like him, he's fun, he helps with the rent. I don't know, it works.'

'Well, I think it's funny. I'm not convinced.'

'Gemma, if you start gossiping about this ridiculous idea of yours about me and Tommy I swear to God I'll break your neck.'

'Oh for God's sake,' said Gemma. She sounded very tired suddenly. 'All right, Max. Come on, take me home, will you? I'm tired. It's been a horrible evening.

Max looked at her.

His mind was racing, running over possibilities, dangers, safety nets. There was one thing he could do. It might not convince her. But it would certainly shut her up.

'Gemma,' he said, 'will you marry me?'

Chapter 53

Georgina, 1987

She just hadn't known how to tell him. Every time she thought of a way of doing it, she saw his thin, anguished face suffused with colour and embarrassment, and rejected it again. The first few days after the baby was born, it had obsessed her, almost as much as the baby himself. She would lie there in her high bed, holding the baby, or feeding him, or simply gazing at him awed as he lay there, still in the preferred foetal position, her son, in all his perfection, the tiny hands clasping one another, the small legs curled up, the thatch of dark hair, the unfocusing blue eyes, concentrating fiercely, with the whole of his minuscule being, on the various things that made up his life: sleeping, crying, feeding. And between experiencing sensations of such love, such tenderness, and a protectiveness so fierce she would not have been able even to imagine it before, she thought of Martin, who was so important a part of the baby's existence, and knew he had to know that she knew, must be allowed to see the baby, hold him, love him, be a part of his life, as he had now in some strange almost retrospective way become part of hers. And she could simply not see how.

It kept her awake, wondering about it: as much as the cries of the other babies, the greedy demands of her own. She was not even sure if he knew that she knew. She had never hinted that there was anything remotely irregular in her relationship with Alexander: rather the reverse. Her devotion to him over his illness had implied tremendously strong filial bonds. So how could she do it? Could she say, 'Martin, I know I'm your daughter and I'd really like to talk about it?'

Or 'Martin, this is your grandson.' Or 'Martin, shall I start calling you Daddy?'

No. Not really.

The whole thing was immensely difficult. And delicate.

And then she had the idea of calling the baby George. It was a nice name anyway. It suited him: he looked like a George. Martin would be sure to comment on it. And then she could say – well, she wasn't sure what she'd say, but she felt the conversation would take care of itself after that.

The relief was so intense she finally fell deeply and sweetly asleep and had to be shaken awake by an irritable staff nurse saying if she wanted to do the night feeds she must wake up and do them, otherwise they'd give the baby a bottle.

She told Charlotte first. Not about Martin, but that the baby's name was George. She wanted to try out her reaction. It had been typically bossy. 'Georgina, you can't give your baby the same name as yourself. You just can't.'

'Yes I can. It's a nice name.'

'But it will be so confusing. You'll be sure to call him Georgie and – '

'No I won't,' she had said, very firmly. 'That's the one thing I won't call him. He's called George.'

'Well I think it's very silly,' said Charlotte.

Georgina looked at her awkwardly. 'There is another reason,' she said.

'What other reason?'

'Charlotte, I – I know who it is.'

'Who who is? Georgie, do stop talking in riddles.'

'Who Georgie is. Who – oh Charlotte, do stop being dense.' And she sat up in bed and pushed her hair back irritably, her eyes fixed on her sister.

'I'm sorry, Georgina, I don't – ' and then Charlotte had stared at her, awed, almost afraid to say anything, anything at all. And finally she said, 'You mean, you know who your – your father is?' She spoke in a whisper, looking anxiously over her shoulder at the next bed; as it was occupied by an Indian girl surrounded permanently by an enormous number of relatives, it seemed unlikely they would be overheard.

'Yes. Yes I do.' Georgina smiled at her, feeling as she had once when she had rushed in from school and up the stairs to tell her mother she had won the art prize. 'I do. And it's – Charlotte, you're not going to believe this, but – promise me you won't argue, because I do know – '

'Georgie, for God's sake, tell me. I shall hit you in a minute.'

'It's Martin.'

'Martin! Martin Dunbar! Oh Georgina, that's nonsense. Of course it isn't. It can't be. Martin, but he's so – '

'So what?'

'Well he's so – shy.'

'So am I. And he's tall, and terribly thin, and he stoops.'

'So do lots of people.'

'I know, I know. There's more. Listen.'

She told her. About Martin's kindness and concern, his monumentally courageous act of visiting her in hospital, the way his attitude towards her had become so paternalistic.

'Yes but darling – '

And then the more important things, the name, Angie's conviction he had been in love with their mother.

'Don't look like that, Charlotte. I know. OK? I just know. Can you tell him, please, that I've had the baby. Tell him it's a boy, but not what the name is.'

She decided not to tell Max. It was too much like hard work. She just let him tell her that calling the baby George was a bloody silly idea and left it at that.

She had a very shrewd idea that Nanny had at least had her suspicions. She had nodded slightly grimly when Georgina told her the baby's name and said, 'Very suitable.' On the other hand, it could just have been Nanny.

She wondered if Angie might put two and two together and make one of her very neat fours. She was so sharp and shrewd. But if she did she didn't show it. She just nodded and said, 'It's a sweet name,' and asked Georgina if she'd like to borrow her nanny for a few days, or come and stay with her. Georgina often felt bad these days about not liking Angie more.

She had been so pleased when Alexander had appeared in the ward, she burst into tears. He had come and put down his huge bouquet of flowers and taken her in his arms and kissed her and told her he loved her and he was sorry he had been so stupid and that she was a clever girl and he loved her and begged her to go home to live at Hartest with the baby. She had said she loved him too, but that she wanted to stay in London; she would go down every weekend, she said. She had wondered if there might be some reaction about the baby's name from him; but there wasn't. He had simply said he thought it was charming that she liked her own name so much she wanted to perpetuate it.

When she had finally – well, hardly finally after only three days – capitulated and gone home, Alexander had been visibly moved. She had sat in the library, by the fire, feeding the baby, and he had sat opposite, watching her, his eyes soft with tenderness, and perhaps a slight sadness. 'I only wish your mother could have seen this,' he said. He hardly ever mentioned Virginia; Georgina was surprised.

Nanny had received them both with immense relief, and had George tucked up firmly in the crib, his disposable nappy replaced by a good strong terry towelling one, his Babygro by a Viyella nightie before Georgina could turn round.

'I'm very pleased you're here,' Nanny said, 'I was worried about him up in London with that woman.'

She made it sound as if George had been conducting a wild and unsuitable love affair; it was a while before Georgina realized she had been referring to Mrs Wicks.

Martin hadn't visited her in hospital. She had been, against all the odds, surprised and, she had to admit, disappointed. She kept telling herself that one visit to London in a decade was probably as much as he could reasonably be expected to make and certainly to a maternity hospital; nevertheless it hurt. Then the day before she was due to come out, a big bouquet of flowers arrived, from him and Catriona, and a card from Martin, saying, 'Dear Georgina, We are both so pleased. I very much look forward to seeing you when you come down to Hartest. Do be in touch.' From Martin, under the circumstances, that was quite a big gesture.

She had finally seen him when she had been back at Hartest for about three days. She was sitting in the nursery, winding George, when she heard a car on the drive; she looked out and saw it was his Land-Rover.

Georgina felt slightly sick and faint, rather as if he had been her lover. She gave George a final pat on the back, wrapped him in his shawl and walked rather slowly down the stairs. When she got to the bottom Martin was nowhere to be seen. Feeling silly, she went through to the front hall, and heard him talking to her father in the corridor. She followed their voices.

'Hallo,' she said. 'Hallo, Martin.'

'Georgina, darling, can't stop now,' said Alexander, 'crisis in the dairy. Two of the cows are sick. Martin came to alert me. Martin, hang on a minute, I'll just call Bill Withers, see if he can get up here.'

He disappeared into the gun room; Georgina looked slightly awkwardly at Martin.

'Hallo,' she said.

'Hallo, Georgina. How are you?'

'Oh – feeling much better. A bit tired, you know, but all right. Look, this is my son and heir. Isn't he beautiful?'

Martin looked at the baby and there was a very odd mix of expressions on his face: tenderness, happiness and something close to awe, but most of all, an intense and burning interest, a searching of the small features, an almost fervent study of everything about him. It was that more than anything else which told Georgina she was right.

Finally he turned to her and said, 'And what are you going to call him?'

'Well,' she said, her heart thumping almost painfully, 'I'm going to call him – '

And then Alexander had reappeared, flustered, impatient. 'Come on,' he said, 'Withers is meeting us there.'

And Martin was gone.

It was a week later that she met him again; she had (greatly daring, for Nanny disapproved, saying it wasn't natural) bought a sling, so that she could walk about with the baby strapped to her; she was wandering down the path towards the stables, and he was hurrying up it, towards the house.

'Hallo,' he said, 'you're looking better.'

'Thank Nanny. She won't let me near him half the time. So I get lots of sleep.'

'Can I walk with you a little?' he said, looking slightly awkward.

'Of course. I thought you seemed in a hurry.'

'Oh – not really. I was actually thinking I might see you. At the house. I had an hour to spare.'

'Oh.' She smiled at him, confused, feeling herself blush. This was crazy; she was acting (again) as if he was a lover. 'Yes,' she said, 'come with us. We're on our way to the stables. Or maybe the lake.'

'The lake's a longer walk,' he said. 'Let's do that. If you feel up to it.'

'Of course.'

'You were going to tell me the baby's name,' he said, 'the other day.'

'Yes,' she said, 'so I was.' There was a pause: come on, Georgina, get it out. 'He's called George,' she said and met his eyes very steadily.

'Ah,' he said, and then, his expression quite unfathomable: 'After you?'

'Well – partly. It's a nice name. And it's – ' her courage failed her – 'oh, I don't know. Do you like it?'

Martin Dunbar stopped walking. He turned and faced her, and he looked immensely sad and oddly amused at the same time. 'I like it very much. Very much indeed.' There was a long long silence. Georgina stood staring at him, her heart thudding. Finally Martin said, quite casually as if remarking on the weather, 'Nobody else really knew this, but your mother used to call me Georgie.'

'Yes,' said Georgina. 'Yes, I sort of guessed that. It's why I gave him the name. Actually.'

Martin didn't say anything; but he looked at her, sharply, searchingly, and then he smiled at her, a radiant, all-consuming smile, and put his arm very gently round her shoulders.

'I'm very proud of you,' was all he said.

★

They walked for nearly an hour, talking, talking. It was very easy. He didn't ask her any of the crass questions, how long she had known, or how she had guessed, and she didn't ask him how any of it had happened. He just talked to her about Virginia and how much he had loved her, what a special person she had been, how good a friend; he said that of course Alexander and Catriona had never known, never suspected how close they had been, and it was far far better that they never should. He said that watching Georgina grow up had been a great joy to him; he said she had always been his favourite.

She told him that it was lovely for her that he was so near, especially now that she had George, and she was so pleased she had come home to Hartest. She said she hoped they would see more of each other in the future, and she said how silly it was that you could live next door to someone and not see them for weeks on end. She asked him if he thought Catriona would mind if she brought George to the house sometimes, and he said that Catriona would be delighted. It was so sad for her, that she had been unable to have children, he felt terrible for her; of course she had always rather assumed it was his fault. They had never, he said, with an embarrassed smile, gone in for any of those awful tests: just agreed to live with it.

'I'm so please you came back to Hartest too,' he said, 'it's lovely for all of us. I was so afraid I was going to lose you.'

Over the next few weeks they grew closer. They walked together, they sat and chatted sometimes in the house while Martin was waiting to see Alexander or when he had left him; she took George down to the house to visit both him and Catriona. Once or twice, greatly daring, she met him in Marlborough and he took her to lunch in a pub. 'It's a great treat for me to be able to spoil you,' he said. He absolutely accepted and supported her decision to have George, and moreover not to tell Kendrick about him. 'If the relationship wasn't working, then it's far better to be on your own.'

She wondered at first how he equated that philosophy with the condition of his own marriage, but she came to see that against all the odds, that was a relationship that did work, in its own way, that was perfectly happy.

She discovered that he liked, cared about many of the same things as she did: music, paintings, beautiful houses: 'Even though ours is so ugly. I had a little trouble coming to terms with that when we first moved in; but Catriona liked it and I've grown accustomed to its face.'

He told her things she had never known about her mother and which it was good for her to hear: about how fiercely loving she was towards them all, how loyal to Alexander ('She never would hear a word, not a word of criticism about him'), how courageous. He defended her when Georgina said she was always going away, leaving them all: saying her work was important to her, that she had a great talent, that it gave her the strength to go on fighting her alcoholism, her sense of failure, her feeling that her father was always disappointed in her.

He told her charming anecdotes about her mother, illustrating her charm, her talent for the small, thoughtful gesture ('Catriona once confided in her that she loved Scottish dancing, and every year on her birthday your mother would give a small party and after supper we would all dance, you were always away at school'), her beauty ('People just used to stare at her, Georgina, people who didn't know her well, she really was lovely').

She never asked quite how and why it had all happened, and she never told him about Charles St Mullin and Tommy or discussed Charlotte and Max in any way. Partly because she was too shy, too fastidious to do so, and partly because neither of them saw a need to transgress the shadowy but strong boundaries they had set up. Within those boundaries she felt safe, reassured, happy, they contained everything she felt she needed to know, and they neither damaged nor threatened Alexander in any way. She could see that it was odd of her to be able to accept them, accept the boundaries, that most people would have been obsessed with curiosity, but she was grateful that she was able to do it. Beyond them was danger: and she had no wish to court it.

And the best thing of all, perhaps, was that Alexander had absolutely no idea that she had found her other father, solved her own mystery – or how extremely happy it had made her.

Chapter 54

Max, April 1987

The sun was streaming in through the chapel windows. Gemma's veil swept almost the length of the aisle. Her dress by Anouska Hempel was in cream silk, hung with a thousand drop pearls. She carried only a white prayer book, with a trailing garland of lily of the valley; her eyes were cast modestly downwards.

'You'll have to liven up a bit, darling, you look like a fucking nun.' Nige Nelson was scowling at the polaroid he had just taken. 'And those shoes are all wrong. Too high. Got any others?'

The fashion editor, who was young and terrified of Nige, rummaged through the heap of plastic bags. 'These?' she said. 'But they're still high.'

'Useless. Why don't you girls ever learn? Gemma, have you got any, darling?'

'No,' said Gemma loftily. She sounded cross. 'Max, there wouldn't be any in the house, would there?'

'I shouldn't think so. Not really Georgina's thing, white satin high heels.'

'What about your mother's things? There are lots of her clothes still there, aren't there? I saw them the other day.'

Max felt a bolt of rage. God, she was insensitive. 'I'm sorry, Gemma, but I'm not about to go rifling through my mother's clothes, just to provide accessories for some lousy fashion shoot.'

'Oh shit, let's just go with it,' said Nige wearily. 'It's getting late, the light's going. Come on, Gemma, nice smile at your bridegroom, darling.'

Gemma gazed adoringly into the eyes of the Moss Bros clothes horse beside her.

'Too virginal,' said Nige. 'Come on, darling, work at it a bit. Now where's the fucking crimper gone? Outside having a joint, I suppose. Oh there you are. Can we have a bit more hair? And the eye shadow's too bright. Tone it down, will you? Quickly, for Christ's sake. Otherwise I'll have to use artificial light, and my turd of an assistant's forgotten a cable.'

Max was beginning to seriously regret offering the chapel at Hartest to *Brides Magazine* for the day.

★

He drove Gemma back to London in a sulky silence. She was animated, overexcited. 'That went well, didn't it? It was so lovely, standing there, thinking of our wedding. I think when I marry I might get my dress from Anouska, what do you think?'

'I really don't know,' said Max.

'Nige is a pig, but he's a brilliant photographer. I'm sure they'll be really great. Your father might like to have some, don't you think?'

'I don't think, no,' said Max. 'I think he'd hate it.'

'Why?'

'Oh, forget it. If you don't know, there's no point my trying to explain.'

'You're in a nice mood,' said Gemma. 'What's the matter?'

'The matter,' said Max, 'is that I found I didn't actually like having the chapel filled up with a load of creeps and perverts, and – '

'Oh, for God's sake,' said Gemma, 'you gave your permission. And they're not creeps and perverts. They're good fun. Which is more than I can say you were today.'

'Well I'm extremely sorry. I hadn't realized my role was anything other than janitor.'

'I'm going to go to sleep,' said Gemma, curling up in the corner of her seat. 'There's no point talking to you. But let's hurry. That party starts in an hour. We'll miss the whole thing if we're not careful.'

'Good,' said Max.

Max had been with Praegers just over three weeks now; he had a salary that was roughly half as big again, a very generous bonus package and a 1 per cent share in the bank, which Fred had made an extremely vague commitment to increase at some unspecified time in the future. Nevertheless he wasn't altogether happy; he missed Jake and the other lads at Mortons, and he missed something else as well, something indefinable. Gabe Hoffman, over on a short trip, told him what he thought it probably was as they talked briefly one night, waiting for Charlotte to finish work: 'You have to know you're on a solid base. Old Fred is a megalomaniac tyrant, but he knows how to run a company. I guess Gemma's dad is the same. Praeger UK is a bit of a leaky vessel, I'd say, and now you've got a dodgy crew moving in. It'll probably get fixed up in time, though. Don't worry.'

Max tried not to worry. The dodgy crew had arrived: Chuck Drew in late March, with a couple of associates, and in April Freddy joined them.

'Grandpa wants me to get a good footing with the clients this end,' he said to Max loftily. 'It's only a year's posting, but it will ensure everybody knows me personally. I think it's an excellent idea.'

Max nodded.

'Oh, and by the way,' said Freddy, looking at him, his blue eyes icy with dislike, 'you do understand, don't you, that you are to remain on the trading side? There is absolutely no question of your taking up a true executive position. No client contact, except at the most rudimentary level. Grandfather explained that to you, I'm sure.'

'No,' said Max, 'not that I recall.'

'Ah. Well he certainly stressed that to me,' said Freddy.

'Well in that case I'll certainly try to remember,' said Max.

The atmosphere in Praegers UK was not merely less happy than it had been; it was uneasy. Peter Donaldson was still nominally heading it up, but Chuck Drew was doing a good job of demoralizing him, and denuding him of status and responsibility, countermanding his instructions, negating his decisions, muscling in on his meetings, undermining his relationship with his staff. Charlotte, who liked Donaldson, was upset and said as much to Freddy. Freddy turned eyes on her that were dark with dislike and told her not to interfere in matters that did not concern her.

'But it does concern me. He's my boss.'

'Then I suggest you concentrate on working for him,' said Freddy. He was almost as angry at Charlotte's prospective move to New York as he had been about Max's arrival in the London office.

'He feels threatened,' said Max. 'He thought he'd got rid of you.'

'According to Gabe, he still could,' said Charlotte. 'He and Chris Hill and Chuck have a majority shareholding now. Well not now, but when – if Grandpa goes.'

'He'll never go,' said Max easily. 'He's immortal.'

Chuck Drew was a masterly tactician. He was an exceptionally good-looking man, tall, slim, with brown hair and blue eyes, superbly dressed and very charming; he was a generous host, both in the finest restaurants in London, and at his home in Sloane Street, a fine tennis player, a good raconteur. It was extremely difficult to see him as a villain; even Charlotte found herself laughing at his jokes, enjoying his overt appreciation of her work. It was only when he had been in the St James's offices for two months that she realized that what she was doing became less responsible and interesting every day, that her client contact had been dramatically reduced, and that somehow whenever a mistake had been made, her department seemed to have made it. And then Chuck would put his arm round her, tell her she was usually such a clever girl, that everyone made mistakes, that he even made them himself at times, and that of course no one was going to hold it against her.

He was evil; but he was hard to hate.

There were some very unpleasant sharp practices going on at Praegers as well. It hadn't taken Max long to discover them. Jake had given him a crash course in what to look out for in his first week at Mortons.

'There's piggy-backing. Big favourite. You meet someone at a party who says I'm thinking of putting half a million into ready-mixed concrete. Can you give me a ring tomorrow. So you go in with the lark, buy half a million worth yourself, see the price go up, and then sell them to your client. You make your profit and your commission. And watch for the rings. Five guys from one of the big institutions. Agree on a stock over lunch, ring five different market makers and order fifty thousand from each one. Zoom goes the price. Easy peasy. Any client in the know can have lots of fun and games. And then there's the contract-note dodge. Very neat. Very neat indeed. You're a bit short of money, so you make up a client. Buy and sell shares for him. Get lots of lovely commission.'

Within a month of Drew's arrival at Praegers, Max had either observed for himself, or heard of, both contract-note dodges and piggy-backing. It was only on a small scale, but it was certainly going on. He told Charlotte, who told Donaldson; Donaldson said short of telling Fred III, there was nothing he could do. 'Those are Chuck Drew's men, and he'll neither believe it nor care.' He sighed. 'I don't care too much myself, Charlotte, to be honest. I think I'm about to be sent on holiday.'

'Oh, that'll be nice,' said Charlotte, misunderstanding. Donaldson smiled grimly.

'You don't understand. It's the old joke about the holiday, you know? "He has two holidays a year and they're both six months." '

'Oh God,' said Charlotte. 'This is a seriously bad mess. What do we do, Max?'

'I don't know,' said Max. 'Sit it out, I guess. I wish I'd stayed at Mortons.'

'I don't,' said Charlotte. 'I need all the help I can get.'

'There's not much I can do,' said Max.

'No, but at least you're here.'

'Yes, and you're going back to New York.'

'Not yet. Grandpa keeps putting it off. I don't know what he's playing at.'

Fred III, against his doctor's advice, was back at work almost every day – playing at lots of things, and hugely enjoying them. He had adopted in the New York office the practice Bobby Lehman had instigated at Lehman Brothers, when he was choosing a successor: he put all the top executives in a committee and rotated their functions every month. It was a most effective way of confusing and demoralizing all the partners.

'Well, at least Chuck Drew isn't in that league,' said Charlotte to Max.

'No, but he's doing a lot of damage here. I wonder – ' He looked at Charlotte. 'I just wonder if that isn't part of a game.'

Charlotte shook her head. 'I don't think so. Grandad must have decided he trusts him. And of course he's completely blind about Freddy. I must talk to Angie some more about Chuck. She knows something more than she's said.'

Charlotte seemed to be part of another game: one day Fred would say he wanted her over in New York in a matter of weeks; another he would talk vaguely about the autumn.

'It's so frustrating,' she wailed to Max. 'I don't know what I'm supposed to be doing.'

'I expect it's quite frustrating for poor old Gabe as well,' said Max.

'Oh do shut up,' said Charlotte.

There were other disreputable things going on. Chuck Drew had imported several Arab clients: everyone was instructed to respect their still Croesan wealth and to do everything they asked. This was fine as long as it extended only to meeting them with ever more lush limos at the airports, using the bank's cars to take the wives shopping, escorting them to polo games, keeping bank clerks behind sometimes for two hours checking and changing up to fifty thousand pounds' worth of dollars which they were handed in grubby plastic bags five minutes before closing time, and meeting their immense gambling debts – sometimes for weeks at a time until they settled. It was not unknown for a single client to run up debts of a million a week at the casinos. But when Peter Donaldson was asked to organize whores to accompany the men to the polo matches, he said enough was enough and finally resigned. Fred III was told by Chuck Drew that he had resigned on health grounds; Donaldson, who knew when he was beaten, didn't argue. Charlotte cried the day he left, and said she couldn't believe how quickly things had gone downhill, and she and Max and all the other traders took him out and got him extremely drunk.

And then there was something much more sinister going on. At first it manifested itself in a few isolated incidents, and it never affected Max. But once or twice John Fisher, one of the salesmen he had become friendly with, came back from a meeting with Chuck looking concerned.

'What's up?' asked Max. 'Had your bonus cut?'

'No,' said Fisher. 'No. It's nothing. Honestly.'

Max shrugged. 'OK. Don't tell me.'

After this had happened a second time, he took Fisher out and got him drunk. Fisher told him he had been put under pressure by Chuck to push shares in certain companies in which he personally had no faith.

'And in which I guess our friend has an interest,' said Max. 'Well don't do it.'

'No. Well, but – that's easy to say. He'll check on it. Oh – I don't know. It happens all the time, I'm sure.'

He sounded miserable. Max grinned at him.

'Course it does. Don't worry. It's all in the game, as my friend Jake would say.'

But he knew it would not have happened at Mortons; and it should not have happened at Praegers.

'The Chinese wall is developing chinks,' he said to Charlotte. 'Watch it. We may have something tangible to hit Drew with soon.'

One of Chuck Drew's imports was an analyst called Vernon Bligh. Max disliked Vernon at first sight; he was very tall and thin and he wore a signet ring with a crest on it and an Old Etonian tie. 'There's a jeweller in Ealing knocking out those crests,' said Max to John Fisher, 'all the boys are ordering them. Jake told me about him. And I can tell you the nearest Bligh ever got to Eton was a day trip to Slough.'

He spent a happy lunchtime quizzing and tripping up Bligh about his house, his year, the games he'd played, the prep school he'd come from.

'Game set and match,' he said cheerfully to Fisher as they got back to the office. 'Did you see his face when I said I remembered seeing him one Fourth of July? The relief. The fakes always fall for that one.'

'I didn't get it,' said Fisher nervously. 'What's so great about the fourth of July?'

'Because it's the Fourth of June at Eton,' said Max patiently. 'Fourth of July is American Independence Day.'

Bligh undoubtedly had Chuck Drew's ear. And was in his pocket. Analysts need to be honest, above reproach; if they are not they're dangerous. They look at companies, assess their value, and then advise the salesmen on the viability or otherwise of a forthcoming issue. Vernon Bligh advised the salesmen however Chuck Drew told him. Several of the clients found their stock heavily promoted and sold, and rewarded Chuck handsomely. If the companies did not then perform quite up to scratch that was felt to be the shareholders' problem. But in the early days that summer, when share prices continued to soar to unprecedented heights, there was no problem anyway. A company needed to be almost totally incompetent for its shares to lose value; money was always available for shoring up. On paper the new Praegers UK was doing well: a considerably increased client list, and an immensely active trading floor. Fred III, Gabe reported from New York, never stopped singing Chuck Drew's praises.

Georgina called Max at the bank. She sounded upset.

'I don't know what to do, Max. Everyone says I have to tell Kendrick about George and I just don't want to.'

'Who's everyone?' Max had most of his mind still on the screen. There was something going on: a lot of shares were climbing. Big bid coming in, maybe.

'Well – Charlotte mostly. And Nanny. It's because Aunt Mary Rose is coming over.'

'What on earth for?'

'Oh – some book research. She's been in touch with Daddy.'

'I can't see what difference that makes. Even if she finds out. George doesn't have to be Kendrick's baby.'

'No, but I expect he can still count.' Georgina sounded gloomy. 'And Daddy says he's bound to let it out. I mean that George exists.'

'I wouldn't have thought that necessarily followed,' said Max. Shit, this thing was big: another three points.

'Why not, Max? Max, are you listening?'

'Yes. Yes I'm listening.' God, he wished she'd let him get back to the screen; it was like trying not to come. 'What I mean is, I don't see why Alexander can't be asked to keep his mouth shut. He's quite good at keeping secrets, I would have thought.' He knew it sounded harsh; he didn't care.

'Oh Max, don't. Poor Daddy, he tries so hard. Well anyway, I thought I might go and stay with Granny Caterham for a few days. She has asked me. I'd be safe up there. What do you think? At least I wouldn't actually bump into Mary Rose.'

'Good idea,' said Max. 'Very good idea.'

'Good.' She sounded pleased. 'Well if you think so, I will.'

'All right, Georgina. That's settled then.' It was very sweet the way she asked him for advice: as if he was both older and wiser than she was. He was very much aware he was neither.

'Max! Call on three!'

'Max! Will you take a look at this screen! It's going crazy.'

'Max! Have we missed something, or have we missed something?'

'I've got to go,' he said to Georgina. 'Have fun in Scotland.'

625

It was an oyster that did it; an oyster was the catalyst that brought them all so close, so dangerously, powerfully close. Max was sitting at his desk the day Mary Rose was due to fly in to London, trying to calculate how much commission he had made in the past month and considering putting down some money on a new flat, when the phone rang.

'Max? This is your father.'

Max hesitated briefly, thinking, imagining Tommy; then realized it was Alexander. Alexander sounding frail and distant.

'Max, I'm not well. I've eaten an oyster. Ignored the old dictum, I'm afraid. No R in June.'

'No. Alexander, I'm sorry. You sound dreadful.'

'I feel dreadful. It's all most – most unattractive, I'm afraid. I can't ever remember being so ill. Horribly ill.'

'Yes, well they're nasty things, oysters.'

'Indeed they are. Now listen, Max. Mary Rose is arriving this evening. At Heathrow. I had promised to meet her.'

'You had?' Max was astonished. Even given that Mary Rose had arranged to see Alexander, it seemed surprising he was actually coming to London to meet her.

'Yes. It seemed only courteous. After all, she has no friends in London now. Anyway, I quite clearly can't.'

'No-o.' Max's attention was still half on his commission.

'Max? Max, are you there?'

'Yes, I'm here.'

'Max, I'd like you to meet her. Take her out to dinner this evening, see her into her hotel.'

'Alexander, I can't do that. I'm going to the theatre.'

'Well, maybe Charlotte could – oh God, Max, I have to go. Meet her, would you please, and look after her. We can talk again in the morning.'

'Yes, all right,' said Max, alarmed at the pain in Alexander's voice. 'Don't worry. Have you had the doctor?'

'Yes, I have. Goodbye, Max.'

The phone slammed down. Max looked at it, and sighed. He and Gemma had been going to the theatre. He had got tickets for *Phantom*. She was going to be absolutely furious . . .

He buzzed Charlotte's phone to ask her if she could help, but she was having dinner with old friends. 'And I'm not letting them down, Max, it's been arranged for a long time.'

'No, all right, all right,' said Max crossly. 'It's not my problem either.'

'I'll look after her,' said Tommy. 'Don't worry about it. You can tell her you have theatre tickets, and you'll be back as soon as possible. She'll understand. We can all have a nightcap together then.'

'Tommy, I can't help feeling this is dangerous.'

'Max! Do you really think I'm going to spill the beans? You know how discreet I am. I'll be an old family friend, and charm itself. I promise. Besides, I'm curious to meet your aunt.'

'Well – I suppose it might – oh, but Alexander will be furious. I can't think why he's so bothered about her, he never liked her.'

'Max, by the time I've finished with the lady, she won't tell Alexander. Don't worry. I'll take her to the Rue St Jacques, I think. I imagine I have carte blanche on expenses for the occasion? Yes, I thought so. You can come and meet us there at – what – eleven?'

'Oh – all right. Yes. That'd be great. Tommy, you're ace.'

'Don't talk about aces, Max. I did have a poker school planned for tonight.'

Max walked into the restaurant just in time to see Tommy raise his brandy glass to Mary Rose, and her smile at him, reach out and cover his hand with her own.

'Tommy,' she was saying, 'you are absolutely the very first, indeed, the only person to understand how I feel about that. I'm amazed that someone outside the family could be so sensitive to the situation.'

'Goodness,' he said, smiling at them both, 'I seem to have arrived at a delicate moment. Shall I go away again?'

'Of course not,' said Tommy, gazing up at him, his very blue eyes innocently wide. 'We're delighted to see you.' Max noticed that he had not moved his hand. 'Come and sit down. Is Gemma not with you?'

'No,' said Max, 'she had a headache.'

This was a slight understatement for the screaming tantrum Gemma had thrown when she heard he was not after all going to take her out for an expensive dinner *à deux*, but it was adequate for the occasion. He bent and kissed his aunt. 'How are you, Aunt Mary Rose?'

'I'm well thank you, Max. Your friend Mr Soames-Maxwell has been looking after me so nicely.'

'I'm delighted,' said Max, pulling up a chair. 'I'm only sorry I couldn't be with you myself.'

'Poor Gemma,' said Tommy, finally and slowly withdrawing his hand. 'Would you like some Armagnac, Max?'

'How kind,' said Max, smiling at him through faintly gritted teeth.

'I was just telling your aunt,' went on Tommy, picking a very large Romeo y Julieta from the box the waiter had offered him, 'how well you were doing at Praegers, and that I thought it might be just a little hard for her to see the bank filling up with Caterhams. That she must feel her own family has been perhaps a little sidestepped. After what must have been a great deal of hard work, raising them and so on.'

'Well, we're half Praeger,' said Max, smiling easily at Mary Rose, after flashing an intensely dangerous glare at Tommy. 'Don't forget that. And of course Freddy is very important at Praegers now.'

'Of course,' said Mary Rose coolly. 'But just the same, it was always understood, at least until Charlotte stepped in – ' she made it sound as if Charlotte had taken over Praegers entirely of her own volition – 'that the bank would be one hundred per cent Freddy's, in due course.'

'Well, yes, but that was a long time ago,' said Max. 'Blood on the tracks, eh, Tommy?'

'I beg your pardon?'

'Old expression of Tommy's. So have you two been having a good evening? I'm so sorry neither Alexander nor I could meet you.'

'To be perfectly frank with you,' said Mary Rose, with a glance at Tommy under her lashes which Max realized was meant to be flirtatious, 'I'm quite glad you didn't. Oh, no offence, of course, Max, but Mr Soames-Maxwell and I have had the most charming evening. He was telling me how he came across you in Las Vegas, and how you and the rest of the family have been so good to him.'

'Oh really?' said Max, smiling slightly nervously. It would be useful to know quite what Tommy had been saying. 'Er – did he explain the family connection?'

'Oh yes of course,' said Tommy, 'that my grandmother and Betsey were classmates. Back in the distant past.'

'Oh. Oh yes, of course.'

'And then Mr Soames-Maxwell – '

'Tommy, please!' said Tommy, smiling into her eyes.

'Yes of course, Tommy. Tommy has been regaling me with wonderful stories about staying with the Kennedys at Hyannis Port, and how he knew Hemingway, and all kinds of interesting people, in fact I was telling him that if he has any problem with a publisher for the book he's writing I should most certainly be interested.'

'That does sound fascinating,' said Max. 'I'm delighted.'

'Well,' said Tommy, 'I can only say that I too have had a most wonderful evening. It's so rare that one finds a sympathetic listener.'

Mary Rose smiled at him; she was flushed with a mixture of wine, flattery and pleasure, and looked nearer to pretty than Max had ever seen her. He suddenly remembered his father's anger when he had insulted Mary Rose, and how Alexander had defended her, and the other occasions when he had proclaimed her attractive (and even sexy). He himself had obviously never found the key to her.

Tommy was talking again. 'But now I really feel, as you are in Max's excellent hands, I should take myself home. It's getting late, and I have an early start tomorrow. Max can take you to your hotel. Could you get me a taxi?' he said to the waiter, who was hovering with the bill. 'And I think Viscount Hadleigh will be settling that.'

'Can't we drop you off in the car?' asked Mary Rose. 'It's outside now, I can see it, and I always rather like a drive round London at night. So pretty.'

'Oh, it's terribly out of your way,' said Max hastily. 'No, we'll get you a taxi, Tommy.' He was studying the enormous bill: a bottle of vintage champagne, a bottle of a vintage white burgundy, caviar, a *mille-feuille* of salmon and the Armagnac, the cigar – Tommy had certainly gone to town.

'Nonsense,' said Mary Rose firmly, 'I know exactly where Pond Place is, Tommy has been telling me about it – well, I certainly know where the Meridiana is – it will take ten minutes at this time of night. It's the least we can do, Max, after Tommy has been so extremely kind.'

'Fine,' said Max, and so it was that five minutes later they were bowling down through Soho and on to South Kensington and he was thinking how extremely unwise he had been after all to have taken Tommy up on his offer.

'Oh how charming!' said Mary Rose. 'A mews house. I've never been inside one, you know, New York is not rich in mews, and they always look so impossibly small one can't believe there's room in there for people to live.'

'Well of course, they were built for horses,' said Tommy, 'but they seem to convert well. Although it is extremely small. Extremely,' he added with a meaningful look at Max.

'Horses! Yes, of course. Do you know I had never quite realized that. Oh, it does look delightful, could I possibly see inside?'

She was flirting with Tommy again, ignoring Max, the full battery of her charms turned on him.

'Aunt Mary Rose, you must be awfully tired,' said Max. 'Another day, perhaps.'

'I am not tired,' said Mary Rose, with a sudden return to her waspish self, 'not in the least. You appear to think I am in my dotage, Max, or approaching it. Tommy, you and I are the same generation, are we not, and we are not in the least tired.'

'Indeed not,' said Tommy. 'After an evening like this, I feel absolutely refreshed.'

Max kicked him. He did seem to be getting carried away.

He was never sure afterwards if Tommy invited Mary Rose in to punish him for the kick, or just to add some additional spice to his adventure; whatever the reason, he did it.

'How very delightful,' said Mary Rose, 'just for a moment, then.'

And they were sitting in the tiny sitting room, under the stairs, drinking the excellent coffee that Tommy always made, Max putting on a great show of not being sure where everything was, with murder in his heart, when a taxi pulled up outside, there was a thunderous knocking at the door, and Georgina stood there, with George sleeping soundly in a moses basket at her feet.

Chapter 55

Georgina, July 1987

She had been too shocked, too surprised to lie. It had been as simple as that. Had she been expecting to see Mary Rose it would have been different, but she had not, and neither had she expected to have to answer the question. The question that had haunted her ever since she had said goodbye to Kendrick at Baby's funeral, nearly a year ago. Most people didn't ask it, or not aloud, anyway, they waited politely, expressing interest in, admiration of the baby, hoping to be told; and when they were not, they gave up, moved on, and she could continue in her own safe silence.

But Mary Rose was not most people; and when she had said, 'Well, Georgina, and who, might I ask, is the father of this child?' she had answered (fearing that Mary Rose actually knew or certainly had suspected), 'It's Kendrick,' and then all had been lost, hopelessly lost, and the carefully constructed edifice of the life she had been making for herself and George crumbled away as if it had almost never been.

If only, if only she hadn't gone to the mews; if only she had gone to Eaton Place. But she had been afraid that Mary Rose might be there. If only she had stayed in Scotland another day. But George had had a cold, and seemed to be developing a cough, and Scotland was cold and damp, and she had been worried about him, and wanted to get back to Nanny more than she had wanted to avoid Mary Rose. If only she had caught an earlier train, and not missed her connection to Swindon. But her grandmother had insisted the later one was better, more reliable and had a proper refreshment car. And so it went on and on, if only, if only, but, but. And the end result had been that when she found herself confronted by George's grandmother there had been no way out of it that she could see but to tell the truth.

'Well,' Mary Rose said, 'I shall call Kendrick at once. I have no doubt he will want to come to England immediately. I fear it will be most distressing for him. Your behaviour is worse than immoral and high-handed. It is extremely cruel.'

Georgina supposed it was. She had not seen it in that way at the time, she had been too busy seeing herself as a victim; but looked at from Mary

Rose's, from Kendrick's viewpoint, it was true. She had been cruel and arrogant: she had robbed him of his child. It was an awful, awful thing she had done. She lay awake until the dawn, listening to George snuffling and sneezing against her breast, and then she called Charlotte and told her what had happened and borrowed her car and drove home to Hartest to wait for Kendrick.

He rang her that afternoon; he sounded subdued and very detached. He was coming to England next day, he said; perhaps someone could meet him at Heathrow. Georgina said someone would. She lacked the courage to go herself; in the event Mary Rose, who had moved down to Hartest, still in a state of violent rage, drove to the airport and fetched Kendrick. Georgina found that alarming: the thought of her pouring outrage and venom into his ear the entire journey.

She waited for him sitting on the front steps, holding George; it was a brilliant summer day. The sun had gilded the parkland, the lake was a sheet of glass-like blue; there was a shimmer of heat on the Great Drive. The house and all about it was wrapped in an intense, golden stillness; Georgina sat, savouring it, wishing she could shut the gates of Hartest, keep herself and George safe from the rest of the world.

When she saw the car, coming through the lodge gates, she stood up, oddly calm; she went into the house and up the stairs, and gave George to Nanny.

Then she went down again, and sat on the South Terrace. It was very hot; she could feel the sweat trickling down between her heavy breasts. The horses in the paddock were switching their tails and shaking their heads against the relentless flies; beyond them, the woods looked cool and dim and inviting. She was just wondering wildly if she could run away into them and hide, when she heard footsteps behind her in the dining room, and turning, she saw Kendrick framed in the doorway.

'Hallo, Georgina,' he said.

'Hallo, Kendrick. How are you?'

'Tired. Hot. Thank you. Where's the baby?' He made it very clear he did not wish to engage in small talk.

'He's – with Nanny. I thought it would be – ' she smiled rather uncertainly at him – 'too corny if I had him in my arms. I can take you up, or you can go on your own, now or later if you'd rather.'

'Suddenly I have a say in things,' said Kendrick shortly. 'Yeah, I'd like to see him. Now, if that's allowed.'

'Of course. Shall I come?'

He shrugged. 'As you wish.'

He had put on some weight, she thought, he looked older, somehow, different. More self-assured, more of a man. Well, he was twenty-three. They were both twenty-three. Not children. Grown-ups. Parents.

He followed her up the stairs. He was silent. He looked very grim. Georgina realized suddenly that he was experiencing the fear of every parent, awaiting the first sight of a child. For Kendrick, George was about to be born.

They reached the nursery landing, and stood outside the door; Georgina's heart was beating very hard. Nanny's voice came out.

'Come along, George, let Nanny wash your tummy.'

Georgina looked at Kendrick and saw his face change, and saw quite clearly in that moment what had happened, what small miracle had been worked. That sentence had brought George alive to him. He was not just a baby, a thing, something that had been kept from him, something he should have known about. He was a person, a real person, who had a tummy and enough willpower to be doing something to stop Nanny washing it. Very slowly Georgina reached past him and pushed open the door, and they looked in.

Nanny was kneeling on the floor, on the battered old cork bathmat, bending over the bath; in the bath, with his back to them, was their son. It was a chubby slightly rounded little back that he had and the bottom on which he sat was very small, with two large dimples, one on each buttock. His hair was dark, and curled sweetly and damply on his small, tender neck; his head was bent over something in the water, something on which his whole being was focused. Nanny looked up and nodded at them, and then returned her attention to the baby; Kendrick moved into the room, and George heard him and turned round. He looked up at him, his small face intrigued at this new entry into his world; a thoughtful small face, wide-browed, snub-nosed, with large blue eyes and a neat, solemn little mouth. It was a yellow plastic duck he was trying to get hold of; Kendrick looked at it, and his expression softened, changed again. Georgina, watching him, felt her eyes fill with tears. She had been holding that duck, as she sat on the bath, talking to him, the night he had left her. The night George had been conceived.

The baby looked up at his father and studied him, and Kendrick smiled at him, nervously, awkwardly; George waited a moment, and then his face slipped, slowly and almost carefully, as if he had to concentrate on it, into a smile of its own, a toothless, delighted grin, a look of infinite merriment. And Kendrick stood there, and looked at the baby, and Georgina, seeing her child in a strange way for the first time, thought as she had done when he had been born, understood what people meant when they talked about their love for their children, how all-consuming

633

it was, how protective, how powerful, making the careless thoughtful, the weak strong, the cowardly brave, the selfish selfless, and she could see that Kendrick felt it too.

Later he said, 'I just don't know how you could do it, Georgina. I just don't know.'

'Well,' she said, 'well, there didn't seem much choice. At the time.'

'Oh really,' he said, 'no choice. No decision. Your baby, yours to do what you thought best with. Is that right?'

'Well – yes. No. Oh, Kendrick, I don't know. I tried to tell you. At – at the funeral. I – I couldn't.'

'And you never tried again. You never even tried. You decided to rob me of fatherhood, of the closest most crucial relationship I could ever have. All by yourself, you made that decision.'

'Yes,' she said, 'yes I had to, really.'

'And did your family have anything to say about it? Charlotte, Max, Angie, your father – I suppose you all decided I need have nothing to do with it, that it was a Caterham baby? It's outrageous, Georgina. I can hardly believe it of you.'

'Kendrick, it wasn't like that. And anyway, they all said I should tell you. But you – well, at the funeral, you seemed not to want to have anything to do with me any more. I thought, if I told you, it would seem like emotional blackmail – '

'Oh for God's sake. Don't you think it was more important than that? There's a new creature in this world, has been for what, half a year, half mine, part of me, and I've been allowed to know nothing of him.' He looked at her coldly, angrily. 'If I ever wanted convincing that I should never marry you, you've done it for me now. I could never live with someone who could be so arrogant, so devious.'

'Oh Kendrick,' said Georgina, pain eating at her almost unbearably, 'I can't listen to this any more. I did my best, as I saw it. I'm sorry.'

'My mother thinks we should get married,' he said.

'You don't look as if you altogether agree with her.'

'Georgina, I – I'm trying to be very honest here, so don't start crying – '

'I'll try not to. I don't cry nearly so much these days.'

'Good. Look – '

'Kendrick, you don't have to say anything if you don't want to. You've hardly arrived. There's plenty of time.'

'I do. I do have to say things. Quite a lot of things. It's important.'

'Oh.' Georgina felt sick and rather frightened. She had not expected any such discussion to take place; certainly not so soon. She was not prepared for it in any way; Kendrick had been returned to her life, a stranger, a sombre, distant stranger, and she was confused and disturbed by the changes as much as by his presence.

'You see, I did love you. Very very much. And I did want to marry you. But – well, Georgina, whatever your reasons, you cut me off from you, and things have happened, and time has passed, and – well I don't know that we could be together again now. Really I don't. What do you think?'

'I don't know what to think,' said Georgina quietly. 'Is there – have you got – got someone else?' She was surprised at the courage required to ask the question.

Kendrick didn't look at her. There was a long silence. God, she thought, oh God, he has, he's in love with someone else, he wants to marry her; and she was stunned, physically hurt by how much she minded.

'Well,' he said at last, 'I don't quite know how to answer that question.'

'Kendrick,' said Georgina, with a stab of irritation, a rush of spirit, 'either you have or you haven't. It's not something you can be not sure about.'

'Well, what I mean is, yes, I do have someone.'

'Oh,' she said, very quietly. 'Oh, I see.'

'Someone I'm very fond of. But – well, certainly not that I had thought of marrying. Or hadn't got around to thinking of marrying.'

'Oh,' she said again.

'This is a ridiculous conversation,' he said, smiling at her suddenly. 'We're discussing marriage as if it was a contract, as if you were a client or something.'

'Marriage is a contract,' said Georgina slightly crossly.

'Georgina, you're just being awkward now,' said Kendrick. 'Yes of course it's a contract, but you know that's not what I meant. The point is that we certainly shouldn't get married because we feel we should, or because my mother feels we should, or because we have a baby.'

'No,' said Georgina.

'We have to talk a lot more,' he said, 'a lot. I need to get my head together. And I'd like to get to know my son a little more. Is he around this morning? Could we take him for a walk or something?'

'Yes,' said Georgina, jumping up, relieved that the difficult conversation was temporarily at least at an end. 'Let's. Nanny won't like it, because he's supposed to be in his pram now, but he's not Nanny's baby, is he?'

'Goodness me,' said Kendrick. 'That really is heresy. Come on, then, let's go and borrow our baby.'

They spent a lot of time together over the next few days, talking, walking, sitting, playing with George. Georgina, having spent the best part of a year telling herself she didn't need Kendrick, didn't want him in her life any more, fell steadily deeper in love with him every day. It was confusing, it was dangerous, she was haunted by the thought of the other someone (of whom he had never spoken since), but it was irresistible. She had loved him for too long, too much, had known him too well, she realized, to find herself regarding him dispassionately, as a happy memory. He had been the first, the great love of her life, he had fathered her child, he had been for a long time the man she had planned, had wanted to marry; and he was not now to be slotted easily and neatly into her life as a memory, as part of her past, as a friend, however dear. It was interesting, she thought, lying awake restless through the whole of one hot night, how much she found herself wanting him physically again. At first, she had seen him only in emotional terms; she had in any case been dead to desire for a long time, but now each day the longing for him was fiercer, deeper, hungrier. She started remembering with extraordinary vividness what it had been like in bed with him, his tenderness, his intensity, the way he had understood her, known what she wanted, given it to her gently, fiercely, infinitely lovingly. The memories made her fretful, wretched; she was physically uncomfortable with desire for him, she could scarcely sit still in his presence any more.

She had no idea how he felt about her emotionally; he was sweet, gentle, tender, affectionate, but she did not know if he still felt love for her. But physically she feared he felt nothing; his behaviour towards her was one of a loving brother. He never touched her, except perhaps to usher her through a door, never kissed her except once to say goodnight. He sat and watched her sometimes, feeding George, and it was with a most dispassionate, albeit pleased look on his face; as if she was someone he had never felt anything for, as if she was some remote, distant relative or friend. Georgina remembered the way they had been so physically obsessed with one another that they could scarcely bear to sit on opposite sides of the table, to be separated by a chair's distance; now she might as well have been the chair itself, she told Charlotte fretfully, for all the notice Kendrick took of her.

Mary Rose on the other hand was very pressing about their marriage. She sat them down after lunch on the Sunday and told them there should be no doubt about their future.

'Of course you should marry. You're both free. The child needs two parents. Whatever Georgina has done – ' she made it sound as if she had gone rushing off with some dissolute stranger, Georgina thought, rather than bearing Kendrick's child alone, with some degree of courage – 'whatever she has done, the child is not to blame. You had planned to marry once, as I understand it, I cannot imagine why I wasn't told, but one learns to endure these slights from one's children, you planned to marry once, so clearly the prospect is not entirely distasteful still. You're both free. You must marry and give – George – ' she seemed to have trouble with the name – 'a stable background.'

'But Mother,' said Kendrick, 'we've both changed. Neither of us is sure that we want that.'

Oh God, thought Georgina. Oh Kendrick. One of us hasn't changed. One of us is sure. One of us is quite sure. She looked at him and smiled determinedly brightly.

'Kendrick,' said Mary Rose severely, 'life is not easy. Nobody could know that more than I do. I have had a great many disappointments and hardships in my life. But one has to try and do the right thing.'

'But Mother,' said Kendrick, 'it might not be the right thing.'

'Oh of course it's the right thing,' said Mary Rose impatiently. 'The two of you have a child, and the child needs a father and a mother. How many more times do I have to point that out to you? He is your joint responsibility and you have to face up to it. And I have to tell you that I think you should live here, Kendrick. Bring the child up here.'

Georgina stared at her. Even she had not considered that, not in her wildest dreams.

'Mother, you're being ridiculous,' said Kendrick. 'I don't want to live here. My home, my work is in New York.'

'Oh nonsense,' said Mary Rose, 'you're an artist, you can work anywhere. You've always liked Hartest, liked England. You and Georgina could live here, bring the child up here. I have to tell you, Kendrick, I think you have a certain right to it.'

'Mother, what on earth do you mean? A right to it?'

'Kendrick, Georgina's sister is to have a large share of Praegers. And now Max is working for the bank as well, and no doubt trying to inveigle himself into the share structure. I might say that would happen over my dead body, but that is neither here nor there. At any event, I would see a certain justice in your having a share of Hartest.'

Alexander had come into the library, and was listening carefully to what she was saying. He came forward and put his hand on Georgina's shoulder.

'Mary Rose, I have to protest at that,' he said, quite lightly. 'Hartest of course goes to Max. He is my son and heir, he is the future Earl of Caterham. Kendrick has no claim on it whatsoever. Hartest is not a company, to be divided up.'

'Of course it isn't,' said Kendrick hastily. He was still very wary of Alexander. 'Mother, it's madness what you're saying. Madness.'

'I'm afraid I don't see it quite that way,' said Mary Rose. 'I see it as common sense, but we can talk about it some more at another time. But Alexander, would you not agree that Kendrick and Georgina should marry? For the sake of the child if nothing else?'

'I don't know,' said Alexander. 'I have always thought there is only one reason for marriage, and that is love.'

He smiled at them, his vague, rather sweet smile, and went out of the library again. Georgina got up quickly. 'I have to go and feed George,' she said, 'excuse me.'

She sat in the nursery, looking down on George's small dark head, thinking about Mary Rose's words and how perfect it would be if Kendrick could be persuaded to do what she said.

'So that's it,' said Charlotte when Georgina told her later. 'She's always been crazed with jealousy about me. She sees this as a chance to get even. How extraordinary. Well of course she just doesn't understand, does she? She's American. Of course Max must have Hartest. It's his. You can't start dividing it up into flats, or something.'

'I don't see why not,' said Georgina, 'I don't see why we couldn't all live here.'

'Georgie, you're mad,' said Charlotte, 'and I don't think Max would like it, one little bit.'

'I think you're forgetting something,' said Georgina and there was a strange expression in her tawny eyes. 'Max is actually not Daddy's heir. Well, he's his heir, of course, but he's not his son.'

'Georgie, have you gone out of your head?'

'No. I'm just talking facts,' said Georgina coolly. 'I'm sick of you all pushing me around and telling me I'm mad and I don't know what I'm doing. As a matter of fact, I don't see why Kendrick shouldn't be entitled to some of Hartest, if we were married. And I'll tell you something else, if Aunt Mary Rose knew about Max, she would really go to town, and I don't know that I'd entirely blame her.'

She was very upset. She had ignored Charlotte's shocked face, her suddenly wary eyes, refused to continue with the conversation and had gone running out of the house down the front steps and towards the stable yard. She had just taken the small winding path that led towards the lake when she heard her name being called; Kendrick was running after her.

'Georgina. Georgina, are you all right?'

'No,' she said, 'no, not really.' She was crying; she brushed the tears angrily away.

'What is it?' said Kendrick. 'Tell me.'

'I'm surprised I need to tell you,' said Georgina. 'Everybody discussing us, telling us what to do, telling us we ought to get married, that we shouldn't get married, that you ought to live here, that we'd be perfectly happy if we just put our minds to it – '

'And do you think we would?' said Kendrick. He was looking very serious.

'Oh, I don't know,' she said, too upset, too angry to be anything but direct, 'but it's not up to them, it's up to us. Isn't it?'

She was crying harder now, her voice harsh, almost ugly with anger.

'Yes it is,' said Kendrick, 'it's entirely up to us.' He put his hand out and touched her face. 'You've been very brave,' he said, 'very brave. I think you're wonderful.'

Georgina stared at him. 'I thought you thought I was arrogant. Cruel. Wicked.'

He smiled. 'I do. But I think you're wonderful as well. Come on, let's go to the lake.'

'They'll think you're proposing to me,' she said, smiling through her tears.

'Well, they can think what they like. I just want to make you feel better. Come on.'

He took her hand, and they walked along together in silence for a while. Georgina felt soothed, calmed; her physical longing for him also strangely eased by the minimal contact.

'Well, what do you think?' he said, after a while.

She was startled. 'About what?'

'Oh, not our getting married. About my mother's proposal we should live here and I should be a sort of joint heir to Hartest.'

She looked at him carefully. 'Well – I don't know.'

'I kind of fancy it,' he said, and then winked at her. 'It's all right. Well I do, of course, you know how much I love it. It's nonsense, and we both know it's nonsense. But just think what she'd do,' he added casually. 'If she knew. About Max. And oh God, if Freddy knew.'

'Yes,' said Georgina. 'Just think.'

It was a good thing, she decided, that he was such an extremely nice person. Otherwise he might, he just might, put the knowledge to good use.

She went up to bed early; she was terribly tired. Then at about one in the morning, she heard George crying; she dragged herself wearily out of bed.

639

He was fractious; he seemed to be getting another cold. She tried feeding him, but it didn't seem to settle him; he wasn't really very hungry. He was very wet; she changed him, put him in a clean nightdress, and then found the sheet of his cot was wet as well. The airing cupboard was empty; damn. Then she remembered there was a whole row of sheets airing down in the scullery; she put one of George's shawls round her shoulders, picked up the baby, and went downstairs.

She was back on the first-floor landing, thinking how heavy George was getting, that it was no joke carrying him up and down three flights of stairs, when she heard a door open; it was Kendrick's. He looked worried.

'Everything OK?' he said. 'Is George OK?' He had become very protective of the baby.

'George is fine,' said Georgina. 'But he was wet and I had to go right down to the scullery and get a sheet. I'm just going to put him back to bed.'

'I'll come with you. If I may.'

'Of course you may,' said Georgina. 'You can carry him, he's really heavy.'

They went back upstairs and she made up the cot and put George back in it; he smiled sweetly up at them, and fell asleep again almost at once. They hung over the cot, one each side, smiling indulgently down at him.

'He's a very nice baby,' said Kendrick. 'You did well there, Georgina.'

'*We* did well,' said Georgina, smiling at him, and then became aware that the shawl had fallen off, that her nightdress was open, that her breasts were very much on display and that Kendrick was staring at them, as if he had never seen them before. She did not move, and neither did he; then very slowly and gently he reached out and touched one of them, caressing it, moving his fingers until they surrounded the nipple, massaging it very very gently.

'Be careful,' she said and in spite of herself, her emotion, her intense joy, she laughed, 'you'll get a great spray of milk over you if you're not careful.'

'I like that,' he said, 'I like it so much, that you're feeding him, feeding the baby. I love watching you do it. It makes me feel – oh, I don't know – peaceful.'

He moved forward, and took her hand, and bent and kissed her very gently on the lips.

'What a strange, silly relationship this is,' he said quietly, drawing back. 'Here we are, once lovers, now parents of a very nice baby, and we never touch one another.'

Georgina didn't speak; she didn't dare. She stood there, staring up at him.

'They've certainly changed, your breasts,' he said, 'they were so small, so tiny. You used to complain about them, do you remember?'

'Of course I do. But they've worked well, you see, they do their job.'

'Indeed they do,' he said, and lifted his hand and outlined one of them again, his hand holding it, his thumb smoothing it; Georgina could stand it no longer. She moaned gently.

Kendrick looked at her, alarmed, took his hand away. 'Did I hurt you? Are they sore?'

She shook her head, still afraid to speak, and took his hand and lifted it to her mouth and kissed it and then put it back on her breast. She felt consumed by him; she could feel her entire body given up to desiring him. Kendrick looked at her, startled, wondering, then bent his head and kissed her again; harder this time, more questioningly, his tongue in her mouth, and his hand, still moving, stroking, fondling her breast and then, slowly, wonderfully, moving very tenderly and gently, down her body towards her stomach.

'To think,' he said, very quietly, 'you housed our baby there.' And suddenly he went down on his knees in front of her, and started to kiss her stomach; his hands were on her buttocks, holding them, working at them. Georgina felt literally faint with longing, with great strong thrusts of hunger for him; she looked down and put her hands on his head, willing herself, struggling to keep still. Kendrick's tongue was working at her now, she could feel it, in her pubic hair, seeking out her clitoris; she stood there, trying to be silent, throbbing, pushing deep within herself. She threw her head back, biting her lip, her hands wild in his hair; she felt a climax growing, quickly, sharply, easily, so easily. His tongue was working harder now, he was breathing hard, his hands pushing her against him; she could feel his fingers in her anus, the whole of her body was fused and confused, entirely focused on the growing, growing, wild, strange sensation he was creating in her. She felt herself beginning to tremble; her legs felt weak, her body hot, hot and frantic. Kendrick pulled away from her, smiled up at her, his hands moving up her again, reaching for her breasts, holding them, smoothing them, and then quickly returned to her, with his tongue, teasing, thrusting, pushing, and she cried out, cried out with a pleasure so fierce, so drawn out, so central to the whole of her being, that it was like pain.

She sank to the floor, then; he was kneeling and, clumsy with greed and desire still, she slithered onto him, fast, urgently, savouring the joy, the great leaping pleasure remembered of his penis in her, sat there astride him, moving slowly, gently, still alight with pleasure from her climax, and he moved with her, pushing, thrusting, up, up, and she began to climb again and felt him rising too, heard his breathing become heavier, faster, felt his hands holding her, urging her to him, and then it happened, and he climaxed too, on and on, throbbing, breaking in her, and she caught it and came with him again, more gently, more tenderly this time, echoing his own, and then at last it was over, and they stayed there very quietly on the nursery floor, for a long time, while their son slept, just smiling at one another and unable to find anything at all to say.

She slept late and deeply; she had many strange dreams, heavy, almost sombre dreams, labyrinthine in their depth. In the last one, as she surfaced towards morning, she was fighting, fighting to get to the light, it was so dark, so dark and she had been alone in the darkness and Kendrick was out there, in the light; something was happening, there was a shouting in her ears getting louder as she came to the surface, and then she heard someone screaming, screaming her name, and she awoke and shot out of bed, and to the window; it was Nanny, and she was next door, leaning out of the window herself, and below her, she could see the pram, George's pram, on its side, just below the terrace, and running into the house, with the baby in his arms, white-faced, shouting her name also, was Alexander.

The baby was fine: he had an egg on his head, where he had fallen out of the pram, but Dr Rogers had checked him over and sent him into Swindon to have him X-rayed, and there was nothing wrong, no concussion, nothing at all. In fact George had celebrated the day by cutting a tooth; as Georgina had fed him his apple sauce for tea, she had felt something hard under the spoon and there it had been, a tiny white jagged edge. It had made them all feel better, that tooth; restored the day to normality. When George had finally gone to sleep and Georgina and Kendrick were sitting, weak with reaction, in the library, Alexander had come in and shut the door, and offered them both a brandy, and she had finally managed to ask him to tell her again, in proper detail (for it had all been so confused before), what had actually happened, what he had seen.

He had been walking up from the stables, he said; one of the dogs was snuffling round on the terrace. 'He found some interesting smell under the pram; maybe George had had a rusk or something, I don't know. Anyway, he must have nudged it; and I saw it very slowly, at first, begin to move. The terrace is level, of course; but towards that end it does slope a bit, and then of course there are the steps. It was a nightmare, all in such slow motion, as these things always are. I ran and ran, but I couldn't get there in time; just saw it turn and start to tumble down the steps. It was a miracle, a miracle, it wasn't worse.'

'Oh God,' said Georgina, 'and I was asleep, how could I have slept so late – ' She looked at Kendrick, confused, reminded forcibly of the night, of how she could indeed have slept so late and so deeply – 'I suppose Nanny must have put him out there. That's when babies sleep, of course, in their prams, after the ten o'clock feed. Oh God.'

'Yes,' said Alexander, 'yes, I'm afraid it was Nanny.'

'Daddy, what do you mean, you're afraid?'

'Georgina, she – oh, dear, this is so difficult to say, to face, but she is getting very old, I'm afraid.'

'So?' Georgina stared at him.

'Darling, when I got to the pram, I'm afraid – very much afraid – the brake was off. Nanny had failed to make it safe. She really is not to be trusted any more.'

Chapter 56

Alexander, July 1987

It had been unlucky, that. So unlucky. If he had been a little longer reaching the pram, perhaps, a little slower – but no, the baby had been thrown out, thrown out onto the soft earth. He should have left him strapped in, perhaps. That might have been better.

Well, he had tried. And he had failed.

It had been such a clever plan. The biscuit under the pram, the dog, deprived of its breakfast, hungry, the brake off, the pram positioned so carefully, pointing towards the steps. Nanny, safely up in the nursery, Georgina asleep – asleep after her disgusting behaviour the night before, did she really think she had not been heard, those cries, those awful, raw cries; talking on the landing to Kendrick, waking him up, and then – then.

He had been very upset, very disturbed by the conversation with Mary Rose. The thought of that boy, living at Hartest, with Georgina, with the child: what did they all think Hartest was, some kind of hotel, to be broken up and shared out? He had been working for so long, all these years, struggling to keep it, keep it safe, keep it whole, keep it his, keep it for Max, and now that cretin calmly proposing it should be divided up, equating it in some crazed way to the bank. It was obscene, disgusting. It made him feel physically sick.

So much the worse that he had failed; if the child had been no more, then there would have been no question of a marriage. She could not possibly consider it. But could he, should he try again? Not for a long time, a long long time. And then it might be too late.

Chapter 57

Max, August–September, 1987

Max looked into the policeman's face. It was the worst sort: young, pale, supercilious, a suggestion of spotty.

'Good morning, sir. Would you care to tell me how fast you thought you were driving just then, sir?'

'Oh – ' said Max carefully. 'Oh, I'm afraid a little too fast, Officer. I'm sorry.'

'How much too fast, sir, would you say?'

'Well – maybe twenty mph too fast?'

'I think a little more than that, sir. We recorded it at between ninety-four and ninety-eight. Over quite a long distance, sir.'

'Good Lord,' said Max.

'Yes, sir. Could I see your licence, sir?'

Well, that had done it, he thought, released finally and driving at a very sober sixty-nine on towards London. He'd get a huge fine. Certainly have to spend an inordinate amount of money on a solicitor. Maybe he should get rid of the Porsche. The police did look out for them. Bloody silly idea really, staying at Hartest overnight, and then trying to beat the rush into town. God knows why he'd done it. Well, God might know, but he didn't. He just wasn't thinking too straight at the moment. And he knew why that was. He was worried. Properly, seriously, sleep-disturbingly worried. About rather too many things.

There was Praegers. That was the least of his worries, he supposed. On a scale of one to ten, it only rated about a five. But it was difficult there, uncomfortable, the atmosphere increasingly unpleasant. It didn't greatly affect the trading floor, but it was horrible for Charlotte. Her nice boss gone, her job increasingly difficult, and that little tick Freddy breathing down her neck as well. But none of that was a gut-eating, mind-warping worry. Not like the business about Georgina and Kendrick and this insane nonsense about Kendrick living at Hartest. Of course it was nothing more than a demonic gleam in that crazed woman's eye; and Kendrick was still farting about in that dreamy, half-arsed way of his, saying he wasn't sure if he did want to marry Georgina or not. God, if he'd been Georgina, he'd have kicked him hard where it hurt. There she was, poor kid, dying of love and misery in front of their eyes, coping with the baby all on her own, and Kendrick didn't even have the decency to come to some kind of a decision about the whole thing. She kept on defending him too; she'd tried to explain to Max only last night, tears in those great eyes of hers. Max often wondered if Georgina had ever passed more than twenty-four hours without crying.

'It's so hard for him, Max. He can't decide what's right, you see. He can't make up his mind if he loves me or – or her. And whether it would be dishonest to marry me, in that case. He's such an honourable person, you see, that's the trouble.'

Max took a very clear-sighted view of Kendrick's honour; and from where he was sitting it took a pretty flexible form. He seemed to have the very best of both worlds, a girlfriend in New York (who was also standing patiently by, waiting for him to make up his mind: what did the guy have going for him, for fuck's sake?) and another one in England, who was bringing up his baby, uncomplainingly asking for no more than a kind word whenever he condescended to come over and visit her. Max would have been very tempted to help Kendrick towards a decision with a few well-chosen words, had he not promised Georgina faithfully to keep out of it, and had he also not been afraid that pushing Kendrick in one direction might be counterproductive and propel him very fast in the other. And in the direction of Hartest, and his taking up residence there. Of course in fact that would never, could never happen; it was out of the question, anybody could see that, Kendrick kept on insisting that his home was in New York, that he would not dream of settling in England, and Max was quite sure that even if he changed his mind, even if (to please Georgina, who was more English than the Union Jack) he agreed to live in England, then they would not, they most definitely would not be living at Hartest with their baby. Hartest was not a commune, for Christ's sake; it was a house, a family house, part of the estate, to be preserved against all costs, and it was his, as the future Earl of Caterham, to do as he liked with. There was no way a whole flotsam and jetsam of assorted relatives and their children were going to move in on it, and that was the end of the matter. He would not allow it, and in the short term Alexander would never allow it. Except that – and this was where the worry took on an edge, a painful, stomach-knotting edge – Alexander did adore Georgina, and he adored the baby these days, and he kept on and on about how wonderful it was to have a grandchild, and to feel immortal, and to see the continuation of the Caterham line. Every time he said that Max felt as if he was going to puke. Stupid, sentimental claptrap; the old fool was going gaga. It was a strange kind of immortality; if his wife hadn't whored around, there would have been no continuation of any line. Thank Christ, thank Christ, Kendrick didn't know about all that. Georgina might be naive and unworldly, but at least she hadn't been so stupid as to tell Kendrick. He'd asked her a few weeks ago, after they'd had a bit of a barney about the whole thing, and he had said what a crazy, totally unthinkable idea it was, that she should live at Hartest with Kendrick.

'I don't see what difference it would make to you, Max, you always said you didn't care about Hartest, and you hardly ever come here.'

Max said that was quite untrue, that he cared very much about Hartest, and he came there a great deal these days, and Georgina said she didn't call lunch once a month a great deal and as far as she could see it was just showing it off to Gemma and making sure she knew what a great prize she was getting.

That had upset Max; they hardly ever argued, he and Georgina. But he had been scared, and he had felt he had to ask her, and she had looked at him, her face very set and rather stern, and said that no, of course Kendrick didn't know, it was family business and should be kept amongst themselves.

Nevertheless, it was a worry; and it wouldn't quite go away.

Max's other source of anxiety was Gemma. This was actually more of a gnawing unhappiness than a worry. He had known she was spoilt, vain, self-centred; he could match her on those qualities with ease. What he had not properly realized was that beneath the slightly vapid charm of her personality was no real warmth, no kindness, no generosity. On a good day, he felt quite fond of her; on a bad one he actually disliked her.

'Max? Good morning, my son.' It was Jake, calling from Mortons. 'Good weekend? How is the young lady?'

'I don't know,' said Max shortly. 'I haven't seen her since Friday. She and Mummy went to Paris for the weekend, shopping.'

'Lucky Mummy. There's something going on in the futures market, by the way. Which is not why I called. Meet me for lunch? Or after work? I have a rather interesting little story for you.'

'Oh really? Better make it after work. I'll come up there.'

'OK. Champagne bar Corney and Barrow?'

'You're on.'

John Fisher came down to his desk looking ghostly pale. 'What's up?' said Max. 'Hangover?'

Fisher smiled at him with an obvious effort, nodded his head. 'Yup. Sure.'

It was clear he wasn't telling the truth. 'Shall we have lunch?' said Max.
'No. No I can't,' said Fisher. 'Not today. Big issue on. Sorry.'
'Please yourself,' said Max. 'What's the issue?'
'Oh – electricals,' said Fisher.

Max idly flipped through the company reports, looking for news of an electrical issue. There was none. He stopped worrying about it. The dollar was up, the mark was down, the pound was flying, and someone had tossed him for the first trade of the day. His worries receded; he had more important things to think about.

Jake was sitting in the corner of the champagne bar looking smug, a bottle of house champagne in front of him, three quarters empty.
'You're late.'
'Sorry. Got embroiled with the dollar. Good day?'
'Yeah.' Jake poured him a glass of champagne; Max drained it, and poured them both another.
'I'll get another bottle.' He went to the bar and ordered house champagne; a Japanese next to him was paying for a bottle of Cristal Rose at £100.
He smiled at Max. 'Good times!' he said.
'Yeah,' said Max, 'very good. Long may they last.'
The Japanese nodded enthusiastically, and Max grinned back. One of the most agreeable things about working in the City was the sense of heady optimism in everybody. It certainly beat the neurotic anxieties of the modelling business.
'Now then,' he said to Jake, settling down again in the comparative peace of their corner, 'what's this story?'
Jake looked even more smug.
'There's a couple of very interesting little real-estate companies started up.'
'Oh really?' Max felt bored; if this was just about a tip, he wasn't interested.
'Yeah. Shops and garages mainly. Outer London. And beyond, if my information is correct.'
'So?'
'Well, so they're using cash. To buy sites, to build, to fit out.'
'So?'
'According to my informant, it's Arab money.'
Max guessed Jake's informant was one of his brothers. He had three: all in Special Branch. Jake said their job required much of the same qualities as his.
'Oh Jake, for God's sake. We all know about the Arabs and their cash.

It pours into Praegers every day. And who's your informant anyway? You read too many of those thrillers.'

'Friend of the family. As you might say. Anyway, this money isn't coming into Praegers. Or indeed any bank. It's straight into the bricks and mortar.'

'What, in petro dollars?'

'No, you fool, someone's changing it for them. But it's not seeing the inside of any bank account.'

'Uh-huh. You mean it's dirty money?'

'Could be. Very dirty. Or so my informant assumes.'

'Who's your informant, Jake?'

Jake tapped his nose. 'Never inform on an informer. Let us say he's in the employ of the government.'

'You mean he's a cop?'

'I didn't say that. Did I?'

'No you didn't say that, Jake. Well, it's all very exciting, but what's it got to do with me? Why are you telling me anyway?'

'I'm telling you because I think you might recognize a tie-up here. And given the situation at Praegers, you might find it useful. Now as I understand it the money's coming into the country in Swiss francs. Then being changed here again for sterling.'

'Shit,' said Max.

'Precisely. What was that new account you announced on a few months ago? That electronics company?'

'Shit,' said Max again. Then he said, 'Oh for God's sake, Jake. There are zillions of Swiss companies.

'I'd look at the board,' said Jake. 'I did. Lot of funny names on that board. Not all of them Swiss. Arab, quite a few of them. Including a Mr Al-Fabah. Now isn't he a client of yours? Or rather of your Mr Drew's? If I had to put my money on anything right now, I'd say Mr Al-Fabah was having some money laundered for him very nicely, washed and starched and ironed, and then bringing it in here and using it for buying his shops.'

'Well someone's got to be changing the francs,' said Max.

'Indeed they have. Look into it, my son. I would. And if you get anything that might interest me and my friend, let me know, there's a good lad.'

After that they dropped the subject. They were pleasantly drunk; they went downstairs to the restaurant; there was a party of traders sitting extremely noisily over a bottle of 1939 Armagnac which had cost them £145.

'They're betting on the number of drops left in it,' said the manager rather wearily. 'I wish they'd just hurry up and finish it.'

649

Jake knew one of the traders; he and Max were invited to join in the game.

It ended at eleven; Max had lost £100, Jake had won £500. He said they should go to a club; they went to several. At five, it didn't seem worth going home. Max and Jake went back to Mortons, crashed out on the floor for a couple of hours and then staggered down to the restaurant for breakfast.

'I'll have to get a shirt,' said Max. 'This one stinks.'

'I've got a couple in my desk,' said Jake. 'Keep 'em there for emergencies. Let me have it back.'

'I'll do better than that,' said Max. 'I'll get you a new one.'

'That's my boy,' said Jake.

Max got to Praegers at eight. It was already buzzing. Shireen, Chuck's very sexy new secretary, was whisking along the corridor, her arms full of files; Max reached out and patted her inviting little bottom. She turned round and frowned at him and dropped the files.

'That was your fault,' she said, trying to sound cross.

'I'm sorry. Let me help you pick them up.'

He carried them along the corridor for her, put them on her desk. 'There you are, darling. Any time you need me, just say the word. In fact, why don't I buy you a drink tonight, just to show you how sorry I am?'

Shireen hesitated. Max knew what she was thinking: that he was not Chuck's favourite person and that he was engaged to the girl who adorned the cover of her *Cosmopolitan* that month. But vanity and greed won.

'That'd be nice. But I mustn't be long, I have to meet my girlfriend.'

'Tell her to join us.'

One thing led to another that evening. Shireen found herself plied with champagne, told she was a clever girl and ought to consider training as a dealer, and then taken out to supper at Langans. She did refuse to go back to Praegers with him, to pick up the shirts he had bought for himself and Jake that day; a week ago her friend had gone back to the bank she worked for late at night with one of the traders, she said, and they had finished up having sex on the floor.

'Doesn't sound too bad,' said Max, grinning at her.

'Well it was, actually,' said Shireen, 'the night porter watched them on the security video.'

Max finally drove her home to Bromley in his Porsche and fell exhaustedly into bed at two, not before eliciting from her the information that Chuck was away the following week for two days in Zurich, visiting the new electronics company. Max remarked casually that he thought he had been there last week as well and Shireen said yes, he was always going over, it was such an important new client, and Chuck was just about the most conscientious, as well as the kindest, most generous boss she had ever known. Every time he went to Zurich, she said, he brought her some really nice present back. Max said he had thought the electronics company was in Geneva, and Shireen said it was, but Chuck often visited a contact in Zurich at the same time.

It all seemed to be fitting together very neatly.

He told Jake, but he didn't tell anyone else. Charlotte had enough to worry about.

Jake told him it was certainly interesting, but his friend would need something a little more tangible. 'Like knowing there was a numbered bank account. He must be doing something with the money. The commission on laundering is at least twenty per cent.'

'I'll keep working on Shireen,' said Max.

John Fisher was looking more terrible every day. He wouldn't tell Max what the matter was, but one day in early September he said he couldn't stand it any longer and resigned. That afternoon Chuck Drew sent for him, and he came out of the office looking even worse and said he had agreed to stay on, and that Chuck had given him a raise.

'Are they blackmailing you or are they blackmailing you?' said Max.

'Don't be ridiculous,' said Fisher. He had lost a lot of weight.

It had seemed such a good idea, the party. It was Max's idea, born out of a row he had been having with Gemma. He said it was time they had a party. Gemma said they'd had a party and Max said he didn't call the middle-aged bash put on by her father a party and he wanted a proper one. It was he said (casting his mind about slightly wildly) to celebrate his twenty-first birthday; Gemma said that wasn't until December and it was bad luck to do it early, and Max told her he would celebrate his birthday whenever he fucking well liked. Gemma told him she was sick of his filthy language, and Max took her home; next day he apologized, but the party still seemed a good idea. He wanted a real party, an epic party, he said, he wanted everyone there. He told Gemma it could be to celebrate their engagement again if she liked, that was fine by him, just so long as it happened. Appeased by the thought of yet another public confirmation of her future as the Countess of Caterham, Gemma agreed.

Angie offered them her house. 'I'd love it. I could do with a party.'

Gemma threw a tantrum at the prospect of the party being at Angie's. 'It will turn into her party, and that awful old woman will be there, and anyway people will think it's odd.'

'If you mean Angie's gran, I do assure you she'll be at the party wherever it is,' said Max, 'and if anyone thinks it's odd, I don't want them there.'

Charlotte however told him he couldn't have his twenty-first and engagement party at Angie's. 'Gemma's right. Have it at Eaton Place.'

'I don't think Alexander would like that,' said Max. 'And anyway I'd be worried to death about things getting damaged.'

'I think he'd like it very much,' said Charlotte, 'and I really think most of your guests are past the stage of throwing up in the drawing room.'

'Want to bet?' said Max gloomily.

But Charlotte was right; Alexander was delighted, and said he would send out the invitations in his name.

The whole thing got out of hand very quickly. By the time Max and Gemma had drawn up a list of friends, it was already looking like a hundred people; then Alexander said, given the nature of the party, there must be some family. Max said OK, as long as that included Melissa – which led to Georgina saying of course it did, and so must it include Kendrick – which meant inevitably that Freddy must be sent an invitation. 'And Mary Rose,' said Tommy firmly. 'She must come, if her children are there. I shall look after her. We can dance together, how wonderful.'

Fred and Betsey were sent an invitation but turned it down, both pleading ill health; Catriona and Martin Dunbar were also invited at Alexander's insistence. Max complained vociferously about them, saying that if Catriona was coming, he might as well have the rest of the stables, and that Martin was enough to put a damper on the Rio Carnival and if they came he'd cancel the whole thing. Georgina told Max he was rude and insensitive and that the Dunbars were a great deal nicer than most of his horrible friends and rushed out of the room in tears; in the event they refused also, but Max had often wondered since why Georgina had been so upset about it all. She was a very odd girl at times. He supposed it was Kendrick's bloody dithering that was making her so stressed. Max resolved to have a word with Kendrick at the party.

The guest list grew to 150, then to 200. The house was not big enough. There would have to be a marquee. 'That'll be great,' said Angie happily, 'we can have a disco out there, and dancing.'

The date set was 10 September. 'Everyone will be back from

holiday,' said Max, 'and people like Melissa won't have gone
yet.'

The entire financial community of London appeared to be comin
a very large slice of the Sloane population as well. Charlotte looked
slight trepidation on the mix of the Jake Josephs, and Max's colleague
the trading desk, and Gemma's girlfriends, almost all of whom seemed
work in art galleries or were applying for jobs as chalet girls. Max told he
not to be so old-fashioned: 'Those girls need waking up a bit, they'll all have a ball.'

The Mortons had accepted, but had said (to Max's relief) they could not stay very long; they had a house-party of Japanese financiers in the country that weekend.

Much of the modelling fraternity was coming, including the American girls able to work their bookings to be in London for the weekend, almost every photographer Max had ever worked with, and a considerable smattering of designers and journalists; the whole thing was being seen as the launch of the autumn party season, and anybody who had not received an invitation and could possibly imagine themselves to have a right to one was making hasty plans to be out of the city that night, lest their social disgrace should be witnessed.

Two days before the party, John Fisher came to Max looking deeply embarrassed and said he couldn't after all come to the party. 'I'm sorry, Max. Family problems. Got to go home.'

'Oh for fuck's sake,' said Max. 'I don't mind you not coming, well I do, of course, but I do mind you lying to me. Tell me what's going on, John; I might even be able to help.'

Fisher looked more desperate than ever; then he said almost inaudibly, 'I don't know what to do.'

'I know what you're to do,' said Max. 'You're to come and have a drink with me tonight and tell me what's going on. You're going to end up in a bin at this rate.'

It took two bottles of beaujolais to get John Fisher talking; Vernon Bligh had been putting huge pressure on him to push certain issues, when he'd refused a couple of heavies had arrived at his flat, offering to break his legs, and when he'd actually given in his notice, Chuck Drew had sent for him and said they had enough on him to report him to the Securities and Investment Board. He suggested to Fisher that he would be wiser to stay, and then clapped him on the back and gave him a raise, telling him his future in Praegers UK was looking very rosy.

'Oh for God's sake,' said Max. 'Why on earth didn't you say anything before? We can take you to old man Praeger, and get this whole thing wrapped up. He won't listen to anything Charlotte and I say; but this'll do it for us. Swear you'll come. Next week. Then you'll be off the hook.'

'Yeah, but I've still been breaking the law,' said Fisher desperately.

'Don't worry about it,' said Max. 'Have any of the other salesmen been going through this?'

Fisher didn't know; he said it was not something you talked about in the men's room; Max said he was sure they had and that they'd sort the whole thing out the following week. He poured Fisher, looking more cheerful than he had seen him for weeks, into a taxi, went home and called Charlotte. Charlotte was just going to the airport to meet Gabe but said she'd call him and discuss it later. She didn't actually ring and came in next morning looking slightly sheepish and very sleek, with dark rings under her eyes; Max grinned at her and said she obviously had more important things on her mind than a little insider trading, and the whole thing had better wait until after the party.

That evening Alexander phoned from Hartest; he said he was desperately sorry, but he was feeling extremely unwell. He had gone to bed with a bad headache and Nanny had taken his temperature and it was over 104. It didn't look as if he would be able to come to the party. Max grinned at the thought of Nanny standing sternly over Alexander and taking his temperature and, suppressing a considerable sense of relief, said it was a great shame, but he was sure they could manage. Georgina, who had already moved into Eaton Place with George, was worried that she should go down and take care of Alexander, but Max told her she had done enough for the old bugger and that he'd be fine in the care of Nanny.

'Yes, but – ' said Georgina.

'Georgina, now what?' said Max wearily.

'Well, Nanny is a bit unreliable these days,' said Georgina. 'I never told you, but she left the pram brakes off some time in the summer and George nearly had a horrible accident. That's why I couldn't leave him there for the party.'

'How odd,' said Max. 'She seems totally *compos mentis* to me still. Anyway, I don't think you can compare Alexander to a six-month baby. I'm sure Nanny won't poison his milk or push his bed out of the window. Relax, there's a good girl. You can call in the morning and see how he is.'

Georgina rang in the morning and got Mrs Tallow, who said that Lord Caterham was still in bed, that it was the influenza apparently, but she was sure there was nothing to worry about, and that she would look after him. Georgina said could she speak to Nanny and Mrs Tallow said Nanny had gone to stay with her sister for a few days, while George was away.

Georgina told Max she did think Nanny could have stayed to look after Alexander, when he was ill, and Max, trying not to sound as irritated as he felt, told her that if Nanny was going doolally, it was better that she went away. Georgina sighed and started packing up George's things. He was going to spend the night at Angie's house, with the twins and Angie's nanny.

Georgina and Angie both arrived at seven o'clock, saying they thought Max might need some help. Georgina was wearing one of her white flowing Victorian robes, with her hair drawn back in a plait, and white roses twisted into it. She looked very arresting and about fifteen. Angie looked a little more than fifteen, but just as arresting, in a scarlet sequin and lace strapless catsuit – 'It's from Jacques Azagury and even I thought it was a little expensive' – her blonde hair a wild cloud round her face. Max looked at her and decided he would have to avoid dancing with her at all costs. Gemma would go completely apeshit.

'Come in,' he said, 'it's chaos.'

It was; four of the waiters and the doorman had not arrived, a large garland of flowers had just fallen down, Brian Prufrock, the caterer, was having a tantrum because one of the waiters who *had* arrived had said that maybe the seafood vol-au-vents should be served alongside the smoked salmon spinwheels, rather than separately, the disc jockey had fused all the lights, there was no sign of Gemma, who had promised to be there by six at the latest, the marquee seemed terribly cold, and the Mortons had phoned to say could they come slightly early, to have a quick drink 'and then we'll just slip away and leave you in peace'.

'You go and get changed,' said Angie, 'I certainly don't want to have to chat up the Mortons. Georgina, you go and shut the waiters up and tell that old tart Prufrock he can serve the vol-au-vents on his arse if he wants to, and I'll get some heaters brought round for the marquee.'

Max stood in the shower, wondering yet again why he had ever thought the party was a good idea.

Things got a bit better after that. The waiters all arrived, so did the doorman, the DJ came back, bringing his pianist friend, and then two heavies appeared bearing enormous industrial heaters.

Charlotte materialized on the doorstep, glossy but unfamiliar, her dark hair drawn back in a chignon, her golden eyes heavily made up, catlike; she looked very slim, very chic, thanks to a week of nothing but citrus fruit, and was wearing a white silk jersey body and wraparound skirt from Dona Karan. He heard Tommy's voice behind him, slightly shaky:

'Jesus,' he said. 'Jesus, you look like your mother.'

655

'Tommy,' said Charlotte, handing him her jacket, 'Tommy, I've told you before, I don't find that particular line of chat very attractive.'

'I'm not trying to be attractive, darling, I'm being truthful,' said Tommy. He smiled, but his eyes were oddly sad. 'You also look absolutely gorgeous. Come along in, and I'll try and keep my hands off you.'

'I'll help you,' said Charlotte.

'Where's Gabe?' said Max.

'Working,' said Charlotte. 'Sometimes I wonder if he thinks the bank is more important than me, and sometimes I know he does.'

'Good man,' said Max.

The party suddenly took off on a roller coaster at about nine o'clock. Cars rolled along Eaton Place in a never-ending procession; people came into the house, into the hall, took glasses of champagne, shrieked at Max, at Gemma, at one another, at the Mortons who had somehow become part of the receiving line in Alexander's absence, kissed, exclaimed at the flowers, at Gemma's dress, and moved into the great golden massing warmth of the party beyond them.

Gemma, who was looking very pretty in a midnight-blue taffeta ballgown from Anouska Hempel, had arrived just after eight, extremely upset about her hair, which Leonard had curled and which she had wanted straight. 'Well, go and hang it under the shower,' Angie said briskly. Gemma glared at her and proceeded to ignore her from then on. She managed to stay at Max's side, smiling, kissing and shrieking, until the arrival of Opal. Gemma had heard all kinds of rumours about Max and Opal, the six-foot daughter of an African chieftain; looking at her, she felt suddenly they must have been true. Opal was wearing red crushed velvet shorts, and an absolutely see-through white chiffon blouse which revealed her magnificent black breasts. She nodded coolly to Gemma, and then put her arms round Max's neck, and kissed him on the lips.

'Max, darling. It's so lovely to see you. Life hasn't been one bit the same without our trips. And I haven't really enjoyed a session since that one I was in the bath, remember, and you were the butler. For that horrible bubbly stuff.'

Max returned her kiss, moving his hands slowly and appreciatively up and down her back, resting them briefly but lovingly on her bottom. 'I obviously did something right. Opal, this is Gemma Morton – '

'Max's fiancée,' said Gemma quickly, holding out her hand. 'How do you do.'

Opal took her hand for the briefest moment and dropped it again as if it had burnt her. 'Max, we must talk later.'

'My my,' said Angie, who had been passing through the hall during this confrontation, looking after Opal's languid figure weaving a swathe through the crowd, 'I don't think she and Gemma are going to get along too well.'

'Tough,' said Max. He looked at her, and suddenly he didn't care about Gemma, didn't care about anything.

'You look incredible,' he said, and bent to kiss her briefly, putting his hand tenderly on her small firm backside.

Angie looked at him and smiled briefly.

'Max, if you want to fondle my arse that's fine by me, but it's an exclusive arrangement. It has a jealous streak, does my arse. It doesn't like sharing favours with other people's. Like six-foot models.'

'I find that very hard to believe,' he said, and although his expression was amused, there was a touch of pain in his eyes. 'Ricci! Lovely to see you. I'm so glad you could come. Angie, this is Ricci Burns, hairdresser to the rich and lovely. Ricci, my aunt.'

'I wish all the aunts were like you,' said Ricci Burns.

Mrs Wicks had brought Clifford, to whom she was now engaged. She was in a maroon taffeta ballgown, embroidered in green sequins; her hair had been freshly permed and stood out from her head in an orange halo, and entwined in the halo were a great many small pink roses. It was the first time Max had met Clifford; he shook his hand heartily.

'You're Mrs Wicks' fiancé. You're a lucky man,' he said.

'In what respect precisely?' said Clifford. He was looking round him rather disapprovingly, a glass of orange juice in his hand.

Max thought maybe Mrs Wicks had been right in her fears that the party would be too much for him.

Kendrick had arrived on his own at about nine o'clock, looking rather wild-eyed. He had drunk two glasses of champagne very quickly, before going to find Georgina. Her great eyes lit up as she saw him, and she flushed with pleasure. Silly little thing, thought Max; why can't she see through him?

Freddy, Mary Rose and the Drews arrived together, about ten minutes after Kendrick. Freddy smiled coldly at Max and shook his hand rather limply; Chuck Drew on the other hand pumped his arm energetically several times. 'It's great of you to ask us,' he said, with his college-boy grin. 'Really great. This is my wife, Janette.'

Janette was a hard-edged American Wives League girl: blonde, lacquered, glamorous, fascinated. If he had decided to give her a rundown on the state of his bowels, Max thought, she would have stood there, an intrigued expression on her face.

'It's just wonderful to meet you,' she said. 'We're enjoying it so much. You must tell me who did the flowers, they are just incredible.'

Max told her it was the same girl who had done Fergie's wedding and wandered off while she was saying, 'Oh my goodness, that is just so exciting, Chuck did you hear – '

Mary Rose was talking animatedly to the Mortons, who were still there.

'Isn't this a lovely house?' she was saying, 'although nothing can possibly compare to to Hartest, can it?'

Lucinda Morton slightly coolly said they had not yet visited Hartest, although of course she knew it.

'Oh really!' said Mary Rose. 'Of course my children virtually grew up there. They think of it as one of their family homes.'

They were all going in to supper when Melissa arrived with her new boyfriend, Jonty Hirsch. She was wearing a black jersey dress from Giorgio di Sant Angelo which clung so lovingly to every crevice of her raunchy little body that even the mound of her crotch stood out, and she had only to bend over one of the black mirrored plates of canapés to reveal her taut high breasts in all their glory, including the nipples. She kissed Max and then took Jonty's arm again rather too possessively. She looked pale and slightly tearful, and had what looked like a bruise on her forehead. Jonty had slicked-back dark curly hair, and his skin looked as if it had not been outside for weeks; he was very thin. He was wearing black leathers, and his boots had high heels. He was smoking a Gauloise cigarette.

'Melissa darling, are you all right?' said Max, looking at her drawn face. 'Whatever happened to your head?'

'Oh, I walked into a door,' said Melissa, smiling brightly. 'Max, this is Jonty Hirsch. Jonty, my cousin Max Hadleigh.'

'Hi,' said Max, holding out his hand.

Jonty did not reply, nor did he take the hand; he blew a mouthful of smoke at Max, nodded tersely at him and looked at the throng beyond.

'This is a bit of a crush,' he said to Melissa, 'let's just see who's here and then split.'

'Oh don't be silly, Jonty,' said Melissa, 'it's a fabulous party.' She sounded nervous, and hurried after Jonty who had stalked off.

'Well *he's* a little charmer,' said Angie.

Gabe had still not arrived; Charlotte was looking furious.

'He said he'd be half an hour at the longest. It's not fair. It's just not fair.'

She was almost in tears.

Georgina was actually in tears. Max found her in the kitchen, picking at some discarded canapés.

'What's the matter?'

'Oh – nothing. Really.'

'Is it Kendrick?'

'Well – yes. No. Oh Max, you're not to say anything to him. He's very upset.'

'Max, is this your sister? The one you're always talking about?' It was Jake Joseph. 'Would you let me get you supper, and make a lonely young man perfectly happy?'

'Oh – really, no I don't think I could – I mean Kendrick's going to – ' Georgina's voice tailed off.

'In that case I may have to shoot myself,' said Jake. 'Could you at least show me to a suitable room?'

Somewhat amazed, Max watched Georgina smile rather weakly and go off with Jake; by the time they reached the supper line, she had visibly cheered up and the next time he glanced in their direction, she was actually laughing.

Funny old thing, sex, he thought.

Tommy had taken Mary Rose away from the Mortons, and was standing in the supper line with her.

'There's nothing like a family party, is there?' he was saying as Max went past.

The Mortons were sitting with the Drews and Freddy, who signalled to Charlotte as she went past.

'You seem to be on your own, I thought Hoffman was over here. Do come and join us.'

'You're so kind,' said Charlotte. 'Maybe a little later.'

The pianist had just finished playing 'Yellow Submarine' as written by Mozart (requested by Jake Joseph) and 'Rock Around the Clock' as written by Mantovani (requested by Mrs Wicks); he was very clever.

Freddy stood up, held up his hand. 'I would like to hear,' he said, as silence fell, smiling slightly, his eyes on Charlotte's face, ' "You're the Tops", as performed by Bach. As a fugue, perhaps.'

Polite laughter from most people; to anyone who had known Virginia, had known Charlotte, had known Fred, it was an ugly in-joke. The pianist smiled. 'Sure,' he said. 'That's easy.'

He began to play. Max saw Charlotte drain her glass, pour another, look over at the door for Gabe for the hundredth time that evening. He saw Mary Rose look suddenly sad; saw her look almost angrily at Freddy. And he saw Georgina stand up, and half run out of the marquee, and Kendrick follow her.

Georgina left; simply left. She had rushed down the steps, Kendrick said, when Max caught up with him in the hall, and got into a taxi.

'I don't know what to do. Where do you think she's gone?' He looked wild-eyed.

'To Angie's house, I should think,' said Max. 'George is there.'

'Oh. Of course.' Kendrick looked at him, relief in his eyes. 'Yes, I'll call her there in a minute.'

'You do that,' said Max. 'But first you might care to tell your brother he's an unpleasant bastard.'

'I'm – sorry,' said Kendrick, 'I agree. It wasn't kind.'

'It wasn't. Oh, and Kendrick – '

'Yes?' Kendrick looked at him coldly.

'Stop messing Georgina about, would you? It's time she knew where she was.'

'I'm sorry?'

'You heard. Stop playing silly buggers with her. It's not fair.'

'I don't quite see what it's got to do with you,' said Kendrick.

'Oh really? Well I think that's rather insensitive of you. She's my sister. I care about her. OK?'

'Look Max,' said Kendrick, and there was a flush on his face now, 'I resent your tone. I care about her too. Very much.'

'Well from where I'm sitting, it doesn't look like that,' said Max. 'It looks like you don't care about her at all. If you can't make your bloody mind up, then why don't you bugger off back to New York for good?'

'Well that would suit you nicely, wouldn't it?' said Kendrick.

'I'm sorry?' said Max.

'Get me out of your hair. Remove any possible threat to having your inheritance muscled in on.'

'Kendrick, are you quite mad? I really don't follow you at all.' Max could feel himself flushing now, feel fear as well as anger rising in him.

'Don't you? Have you really not been told of the suggestion that I should live at Hartest, if Georgina and I were married? I can't believe that. Georgina very much likes the idea.'

'I have,' said Max, 'I dismissed it for the nonsense it clearly is.'

'I don't see it quite that way,' said Kendrick. 'Georgina adores England. She adores Hartest. I'm an artist. I can work anywhere. If I do marry Georgina, it could be the best thing, for all of us. Particularly our son.'

'Oh for God's sake,' said Max. 'Don't give me that. Of course you can't live at Hartest. It's not some kind of holiday house. It's Alex – it's my father's house. It will be mine. It goes with the title.'

'Oh really?' said Kendrick, and the expression on his face was careful, almost cunning. 'And it's really yours, is it? No doubt about it?'

'Of course it's mine,' said Max. He could feel himself beginning to sweat.

'Well,' said Kendrick, 'I think there might be some kind of doubt about that. Or certainly there could be. If – certain facts came to light. Now I don't give a toss about any of it, Max. Don't worry, I'm not about to start spreading nasty rumours. But if I do decide to marry Georgina, I have to tell you I think it might be very nice to live at Hartest.'

'Then I sincerely hope you don't,' said Max. He felt sick, and very cold, but he stayed calm. 'Now you'd better call Angie's house and make sure Georgina's there. As you care about her so much.'

He waited while Kendrick made the call; Georgina was there.

'She wants me to go over and see her,' said Kendrick.

'Fine,' said Max. 'Don't hurry back.'

He went to find Charlotte. He had to talk to someone. She was sitting looking slightly aloof on the stairs with Tommy; he had managed to make her laugh.

'Tommy, could I borrow Charlotte for a bit? I need to talk to her.'

'Sure. As long as you return her.'

'I will.'

'Bloody Gabe!' said Charlotte as they walked away. 'I could kill him. Look at the time, it's nearly midnight. I really don't – '

'Shut up, Charlotte,' said Max.

'I'm sorry?'

'I said shut up. We have a big problem. I just have to talk to you about it. I'm sorry.'

He told her. She listened, finally distracted from her rage over Gabe.

'You know,' she said, 'I don't know how we thought this wouldn't all come out sooner. It's only because we've been so brainwashed by Daddy. To ignore it, to pretend it isn't there. In a way I'd be relieved.'

'Well I wouldn't. Charlotte, how did he know?'

'Oh, I expect Georgina told him. In fact I'm sure she did.'

'But she told me she hadn't.'

'Did she?' said Charlotte, and for the first time that evening she smiled. 'Good old Georgina, I didn't think she had it in her to be devious. And I saw her chatting away in the supper queue with your funny friend Jake. It must be motherhood, toughening her up.'

'Oh for God's sake, Charlotte. The point is, he knows. And he's poised to take advantage of it.'

'Well, I don't know how much he can take advantage of it. And he's a nice person anyway, I always thought. The only thing is – dear God, suppose he tells Freddy?'

'Exactly. Or Mary Rose. Or maybe he has.'

She shook her head. 'No. No, we'd know if he had. That's for sure. Do you think he really plans to move into Hartest?'

'God knows. He seems keener on that than marrying Georgina, if you ask me.'

'Well. Maybe it's not such a bad idea.'

'Charlotte, it's a bloody awful idea. I'm not having it.'

'Dear me!' said Charlotte, looking at him, half amused. 'Quite the little feudal lord all of a sudden. I thought you despised Daddy and the title and the whole damn thing.'

'Not the whole damn thing,' said Max, looking suddenly morose. 'Just – Alexander.'

'Look, Max,' said Charlotte, 'this isn't getting us anywhere. You have a party to run and I have a – '

She stopped; Gabe had just walked in the door. He looked at her and said, 'Hi. Sorry I'm late. Big run on the dollar.'

'How fascinating. You must find someone to talk to about it,' said Charlotte, deceptively sweet. 'I'm leaving. Goodnight, Gabe. Night Max, lovely party.'

'What on earth's the matter with her?' said Gabe. Max looked at him; he was obviously completely baffled.

'Gemma, for fuck's sake will you come on down and have supper,' said Max.

'No,' said Gemma, 'I won't.' She was sitting on the edge of the nursery bath. 'Not unless you promise not to go on touching up every female that comes near you. It's disgusting, first that model creature, then Angie, and then I saw you stroking that other girl, the plain one with the straight hair.'

'What plain one? I never stroke plain girls. Oh, you mean Jennifer? She's not plain. We go back a long way, Jennifer and me. I looked after her on her first trip.'

'How nice for her,' said Gemma. 'Well, I'm not coming down. OK?'

662

'Fine. You stay up here and play with yourself. Nobody else is going to.'

He went down to the marquee and over to Freddy's table. Freddy was sitting looking superciliously across at the dance floor, watching Chuck and Janette Drew doing a demo-style waltz.

'You little squirt,' said Max.

'I beg your pardon?'

'You heard. You're a cruel, vicious little squirt. How dare you do that? Upset my family. It was unforgivable.'

'I think you're over-sensitive,' said Freddy. 'I personally saw it as a trip down memory lane.'

'Oh, go fuck yourself,' said Max.

By midnight the entire party had moved into dance mode. The marquee was packed; the financial element and the media merged happily together in a hot, grinding mass. Jake Joseph was draped over one of the chalet girls, his hands firmly grasping her buttocks. One of his policeman brothers was doing an extremely energetic pelvic thrust with an Art Gallery, eyes closed, head on one side. Mrs Wicks was jiving with Tommy, while Clifford stood morosely on the edge of the floor. Two gay photographers were dancing in a spectacular fashion together in the centre of the floor, and two model girls were smooching on the edge of it. Three young dealers were spraying each other with bottles of champagne. Opal was dancing a solo, her arms waving wildly above her head, her face contorted in an orgasmic grimace.

'Nice friends you've got, Max,' said Angie.

'They are, very nice.'

'It's going well, isn't it? Is Melissa all right, do you think?'

'I think so. Don't greatly fancy her bloke.'

'No, he's vile. Where's Georgina?'

'Gone back to your place. With Kendrick.'

'Good on them,' said Angie.

'It's not quite how you think,' said Max soberly. 'Look at Mary Rose. She's having such a good time talking to Daddy-o Morton. She's practically persuaded him to open an art gallery.'

'They're not still here, are they?' said Angie incredulously.

'Yes they are.'

'And where's their daughter?'

'Sulking. Over there, look.'

'You'd better go and dance with her.'

★

What seemed like very much later, he found himself dancing with Angie. Gemma was in the clutches (and seemed happy to be there) of a male Art Gallery.

'You dance like a black guy,' Angie said to Max as the music changed to a slower beat and he took her in his arms.

'What does that mean?'

'It means you have rhythm. Fantastic rhythm.'

'Well,' he said lightly, 'you know what else they say about black guys. Do you think I could match up to them in that way too?'

'I doubt it,' said Angie. Her green eyes sparkled up at him; she looked smug.

'Do you have a lot of experience of that, Mrs Praeger?'

'Enough.'

'Ah.'

Max held her more tightly; he could feel his erection growing through his trousers. She responded, squirming her body against him.

'Sorry,' he said, smiling down at her. 'Can't help it. It's that – outfit.'

'I like it.'

'The outfit?'

'No, the effect it has on you.'

'Good.'

The music changed; slower still, Dylan's voice cut through the room, raw with sex. 'Lay Lady Lay . . .'

Max pulled Angie closer. 'Angie – '

'Yes, Max.'

Suddenly Max couldn't stand it any longer. He had had just enough to drink; he felt smoothly, recklessly in control. He couldn't even see Gemma; it was almost too easy. He had wanted Angie for so long now, he couldn't even remember a time when he hadn't. She looked up at him, and met his eyes; she smiled a slow, confident smile. Max smiled back. 'You look very arrogant,' she said.

'I feel arrogant,' he said. 'Come on. This thing has gone on long enough.'

He knew she would know what he meant.

Upstairs, in one of the spare bedrooms, she lay on the bed. Max pushed the door behind him, and walked towards her. His face was very intent, very serious.

'I've never said this before,' he said, 'to anyone. I think you ought to let me mean it. I love you.'

'Oh,' said Angie. She sounded surprised. 'Oh Max, of course you don't. Maybe you think you do.'

'No. I do. Can I please take that ridiculous garment off you?'

'It's a lovely garment.'

'It's lovely, but it's ridiculous. You'll look better without it.'

'Max, it cost nearly a thousand pounds!'

He laughed, suddenly and oddly very happy. 'Only you could say that. At this point. Maybe that's why I think I love you. Well, let me take a bit of it off. Maybe five hundred pounds' worth.'

'Oh, all right! Undo the zip. That must have cost about a hundred.'

She sat up, turned her back to him. He came up behind her, pushed her hair away, kissed the back of her neck. It was very warm, it smelt, it felt, of desire: of perfume, tinged with sweat. He moved his lips slowly down her backbone; he put his arms over her shoulders, slipped them inside the top of her sequined bodice, seeking out her nipples, caressing them, stroking them with small, delicate movements. Angie moaned very softly.

'You're so lovely,' he said, 'so lovely.'

He began to undo the bodice, slipping his hands under her breasts, moving them down her body, feeling her flat stomach, her thick tangle of hair, her moist, sweet sex.

'You're so warm,' he said, 'all of you, so warm.'

Angie turned round suddenly, her face raw with desire. She put her arms round him, lay back, pulling him onto her. Her hands went inside his trousers, exploring his buttocks, moving tentatively, gently. Max was kissing her now, hard, harder, his tongue working in her mouth; he felt liquidly hot, wildly sweetly out of control.

She sat up suddenly, smiling; her catsuit was half off now, she was naked to the waist, her hair wild and tumbling around her. She reached out, began to unbutton Max's shirt, her hands slipping down inside his trousers.

'Oh God,' he said, and he bent down and began to kiss her breasts, tenderly, carefully, as if they were very delicate and might break.

'I love you,' he said again.

And then the door opened and Gemma came in.

He found her, crying, in the kitchen, just standing there, sobbing amidst the dirty plates and empty bottles, the great skirt of her ballgown trailing in the spilt wine, tears running down her face, like a small child.

'Gemma – please – don't – ' There seemed little to say. He fell silent again.

'Just get out, will you,' said Gemma, quite politely.

'Gemma, I can't. You know I can't. I want to help.'

'That's very rich,' she said. She stared at him, her large brown eyes still

665

brimming with tears, her face blotched and oddly ugly. 'You want to help. The only way you could help is by going away and never coming back. Excuse me please, Max. I want to go back to the party.'

He watched her go; as she passed the end of the corridor, he saw Jonty Hirsch speak to her. Hirsch was holding a bottle of bourbon; he said something, offered it to Gemma. She took a swig from the bottle, smiled at him. He said something else to her; she hesitated, walked back into the kitchen, got two glasses out of the cupboard.

'Gemma,' said Max. 'Gemma, be careful of that guy. He's drunk and he's been snorting coke for the past hour.'

'Max,' said Gemma, looking at him with such dislike it made him quail, feel weak and withered, 'Max, just leave me alone, will you? You've made it very plain you have other interests. You stick to yours and let me find my own.'

'Have it your own way,' said Max. But he stayed, watching them both. He saw Jonty pour a large tumblerful of bourbon and drain it. And then another.

He saw him fill the tumbler again, and hold it out to her. He saw Gemma hesitate, then take it and drink it, very quickly. He watched Hirsch staring at Gemma, his eyes wandering down her body, lingering on her breasts. He moved quietly down the corridor towards them; they ignored him, seemed unaware he was there. He heard Jonty say, 'So who are you, exactly?'

'I'm Gemma Morton. I'm engaged to Max. Melissa's cousin.'

'You shouldn't mess with him,' said Jonty. 'He's a wanker.'

And then he leant forward and kissed Gemma hard on the mouth.

'Jonty!' Melissa had appeared in the corridor. 'Jonty, come on. Let's go.'

'Oh, spare me!' said Jonty. 'I wanted to go, you didn't want to go. Now I want to stay. Nice girl here –' he indicated Gemma – 'shame about the rest.'

'Jonty!' She put her hand on his arm; Jonty raised it as if to hit her. Melissa stared at him; her eyes were frightened but she stood her ground.

'Leave her alone,' said Max. There was a touch of extreme menace in his voice.

'Go fuck yourself,' said Jonty. He caught Melissa's wrist in his hand and twisted it round. She winced.

Max suddenly and very swiftly went into action; so fast nobody quite saw how he did it. Jonty was on the floor.

He stared at Max for a moment, then stood up; his hand went into his pocket and then he shot it out again; he moved slowly, menacingly towards Max.

'Look out,' said someone, 'he's got a knife.'

Melissa had moved suddenly, between them; she put up her arm. There was a flash of steel, and a spurt of blood; and then suddenly Jonty was pinioned, his arm twisted up behind him, his face distorted in pain, the knife on the floor. Tommy Soames-Maxwell, with the skill born of a hundred bar-room brawls, had him helpless; he raised one leg and kneed Jonty violently in the buttocks. Jonty yelled out.

'Good,' said Tommy, almost conversationally. 'Hurt you, did it? I'll do it again in a minute. I always enjoy teaching manners to people like you. Max, call the police.'

'I already did,' said Angie. She had appeared from nowhere, was bent over Melissa, frantically bandaging her wrist round and round with table napkins. They turned relentlessly red.

'He must have got an artery,' said Max. 'Shit, is there a doctor in the house?' He felt terrible. Everything was happening extremely slowly.

'Call an ambulance,' said Angie. 'Fast.' Melissa was very pale now, almost green.

'Look,' said Tommy, 'tie a tourniquet round her arm. Max, take this chap over, would you, I'll do it. Give me some more napkins, Angie. Rip them up. OK, Melissa, now try and sit up a little more and put your head down between your knees, and let me just tie this round, it'll have to be tight, may hurt a bit, but it'll stop the bleeding. There. That should do it.'

He smiled at her, sat down beside her, put his arm round her shoulders. She lifted her head, and smiled at him weakly. 'You should choose your friends more carefully, darling,' he said. 'Come on, stay with your head down.'

'I feel sick,' said Melissa suddenly, and threw up all over the floor. Then she began to cry.

'Where's her mother?' said Tommy.

'She's left,' said Max, adding a silent thank God.

'No she hasn't,' said Mary Rose and walked into the hall. Max looked at her: she was very calm, very composed. She was always good in a crisis, he thought. It had been the same when Baby had his heart attack; he had never forgotten that. 'I was trying to get a cab.'

The police and ambulance arrived at almost the same moment; Melissa was sitting with her head against Tommy's shirt, still looking very green.

The police were hustling Jonty out. Angie met Mary Rose's eyes rather shamefacedly. 'There's been a bit of a problem,' she said.

'So I see,' said Mary Rose, icy cold. She sat down on the other side of Melissa, and looked at Tommy. 'What happened?'

'She got mixed up in a fight,' said Tommy, 'I think she'll be OK. Here's the ambulance men.'

They looked at Melissa, at her wrist wrapped in the bloodstained napkins, and tut-tutted a bit.

'Looks like you need a stitch or two, love,' said one. 'Come on, we'll fetch the stretcher. Who did this tourniquet?'

'I did,' said Tommy modestly.

'Nice job,' said the other one.

'I'll go with you in the ambulance, Melissa,' said Mary Rose. She was white with shock herself.

'I want Tommy to come,' said Melissa. She was very distressed.

'Better if neither of you came,' said the ambulance man. 'Follow in a car. We may need to give her a whiff of something. That must hurt a lot. Has she had anything to drink?'

'Er – almost certainly,' said Max.

'God!' said the ambulance man, in tones that spoke volumes.

'We'll both follow you then, darling,' said Tommy to Melissa. 'Go on, poppet, we'll be with you all the way. Max, can I take your car?'

'Sure,' said Max. 'You've got a key, haven't you?'

'Yes, sure,' said Tommy, 'I'll go get my jacket . . .'

Melissa was put onto the stretcher and carried out; Mary Rose stood staring after her; then she followed Angie and Max and Gemma through to the front door, waiting at the bottom of the stairs for Tommy.

'I really don't know,' said Angie, conversationally, and to no one in particular, 'what this family would do without Tommy.' She was very white herself. 'He just saved Melissa's life, Max, I hope you realize, and probably yours as well.'

Mary Rose turned and looked at them both; they were standing side by side with Gemma just behind them. She was very still, and her eyes were thoughtful, careful.

'Just who exactly is he?' she asked. 'I really am not stupid, you know. I can see there's some mystery about him. I think I have some right to know.'

Max and Angie stood silent and utterly still. Gemma looked at them, the pair of them, from one to the other, and Max saw in her eyes, read in her face, that she had seen her chance now, her chance to avenge herself for the moment when she had come in and seen him and Angie, Angie naked to the waist, with his head bent over her, kissing her breasts. He looked at her, at the hatred and the humiliation in her, and he watched her and he waited, waited for the words, the dreadful, destructive, savage words, knowing they would come, and that there was nothing any more that he could do about them, nothing at all. And after the endless silence, Gemma smiled suddenly and waited, clearly, plainly, savouring the moment, before she spoke.

668

'Tommy Soames–Maxwell is Max's father,' she said. 'Isn't that right, Max?'

Chapter 58

Charlotte, September–October, 1987

Betsey would probably be all right, the doctor had said. Probably. If they took great care of her. It had been very nasty, but she was strong: for her age. Complete rest, no worries, and she'd probably be all right.

'So I'm taking her to Beaches,' said Fred. 'She loves it there. It's her house. Not mine. And we're just going to sit there, and look at the ocean, and I'm going to see her get well again.'

'Fine,' said Max. 'I'm sure you will. Give her our best love. When she's a little better, we'll come over and see her.'

He put down the phone and looked at Charlotte.

'There really is nothing we can do. This is not the moment to go rushing over there with shock horror stories. It's not fair on him and it's not fair on Grandma. It's a wonder she's alive at all, poor old thing. Breaking two ankles at her age. And knocking herself out at the same time. Apparently she was unconscious for almost twenty-four hours. They thought she would never come round.'

'No,' said Charlotte. 'No, there's nothing we can do.' She felt rather sick. The enormity of the mess they were all in hit her suddenly. 'So what do we do now?'

'God knows. Carry on, I suppose. Nothing much else to do.' He sighed and looked moodily out of the window. 'It was the one bright light on the horizon, going over there and shopping Chuck. Shit. What a mess. It's just not fair.'

Charlotte looked at him. It always infuriated her when Max perceived his misfortunes as being unfair, and down to the machinations of some malevolent Fate.

'Max, it's all your own fault,' she said, 'you got yourself into it, the whole thing, with Gemma and Tommy and everything. You must see that. It would serve you right if Gemma talked to the entire British press about it all.'

Max stared at her. There was a silence. Then he said, 'You really are still the head girl at heart aren't you, Charlotte? So endlessly po-faced and bossy and sure you're right . . . Don't you ever have any doubts about yourself and your own behaviour? I reckon Gabe's had a lucky escape.' He stood up and walked towards the door. 'I'm going to see

670

Angie. At least she doesn't sit in judgement on everybody all the time.'

Charlotte felt tears sting behind her eyes; she bit her lip and looked down at her hands, examining them as if she had never seen them before. She thought, inconsequentially, that they looked rather like schoolgirl's hands still, with their short unpainted nails, their lack of jewellery. Bloody Max. He was so childish, so amoral still, so totally irresponsible. His party, his own engagement party and he'd been up in one of the bedrooms with Angie. She was trouble. God, she was trouble. They just about deserved one another, those two.

Her phone rang. It was Georgina. Her voice sounded small, tearful. 'Charlotte? It's me. Can I come over?'

'Of course you can. Maybe we should go down to Hartest. See Daddy. It's only Saturday morning. Even if it does feel like the middle of next week.'

'What about Gabe?'

'Gabe's gone,' said Charlotte briefly. 'Back to New York. It's just not going to work, Georgie. Let's talk about something else. Where's Kendrick?'

'He's gone too. We don't seem to do too well at this love business, do we?'

There was a lot to talk about. Georgina was upset too; very upset. Kendrick had finally told her at the party that he had made his decision: he couldn't marry her. His girlfriend in New York, Gail, had put the pressure on him and it had made him see that she was the right girl for him. She was what he needed; she was going to get behind him and see he was successful.

'He's right,' said Georgina with a sigh. 'I can see it's right. Kendrick's so gentle and everything. If this – Gail – is strong and powerful, that's what he needs. It hurts, I feel awful, but I can see it. I'll get over it in time. I suppose. At least I've got George.'

When they reached the house Alexander was much better. In fact he seemed perfectly all right.

'Just a twenty-four-hour thing, obviously,' he said vaguely. 'I'm so sorry I missed the party. How did it go?'

'Oh, it was fine,' said Charlotte.

She drove back to London on Sunday after lunch; Georgina had seemed surprisingly calm. She hadn't told Alexander about Kendrick; she said she couldn't face it yet.

'He'll be upset for me, I know he will. And then I'll get upset again. I'll tell him in a day or two.'

671

'What about Max and Gemma?'

'Oh God no. That really will upset him. You know how fond of Gemma he is.'

'Well,' said Charlotte with a slightly grim smile, 'he's very fond of Angie too.'

'Charlotte, don't be silly. Max isn't going to marry Angie.'

'I wouldn't put anything past Max,' said Charlotte.

'Well,' said Freddy the next morning, walking into her office. 'I hear there's some doubt about Max's inheritance? How exciting, Charlotte.'

'You hear wrong,' she said coolly. 'There is absolutely no doubt about Max's inheritance.'

'Oh really? I didn't know that bastards could inherit titles.'

'Max is not a bastard,' said Charlotte, 'and he will inherit the title.'

'I think you might be wrong there,' said Freddy. 'I have a lawyer friend. I plan to consult him.'

'Fine,' said Charlotte. 'You do that, Freddy. Just what do you have in mind anyway? Claiming Hartest and the title for yourself?'

'No,' said Freddy. 'I wouldn't want that great heap of trouble, thank you. But it seems to me that Kendrick's son might have more of a claim to it. I could be wrong.'

'You are wrong,' said Charlotte. 'And Freddy, you might keep your filthy innuendoes to yourself. There are laws against slander, you know.'

'It's not slander if it's true,' said Charles St Mullin, 'as of course you know. The only person who might confirm it of course is your friend Tommy Soames-Maxwell.'

'No friend of mine,' said Charlotte with a shudder. 'Although I have to admit he's been very good about this. Charles, what about this inheritance business? Can Max inherit Hartest? And the title?'

'If your father wants him to, he can certainly inherit Hartest. It's entirely down to him. He can leave anything or nothing to Max. I have no doubt that he's taken care of it. Now on the title, that varies with individual cases. Some, most indeed, specify that the eldest son inherits. Others that the oldest child, be it male or female. Your father could perfectly well have discovered that an illegitimate son was able to inherit the title. Or that the ducks on the lake could have it. The real point it seems to me is that Max is registered and acknowledged as Alexander's son. By Alexander himself. I know of no legal precedent for this precise situation, but it would take a huge lawsuit to dislodge him.'

She was wretched at work. Freddy and Chuck had seen to it that she was

672

stripped of all responsibility; she was working for one of Chuck's henchmen and virtually reduced to doing grunt work. The days were long and painful: 'But there's nothing I can do about it,' she said to Max, 'just stick it out and wait until we can get Grandpa to see what's going on.'

'If he lives that long,' said Max. He sounded grim.

Georgina phoned at the end of the week. She was upset and worried. George wasn't well. He kept getting tummy upsets. The doctor had checked him carefully, and couldn't find anything wrong. 'But he's miserable and he's losing weight. I don't know what to do.'

'What does Nanny think?'

'She says he's teething.'

'He's probably teething then,' said Charlotte. 'Don't worry. Did you tell Daddy about Kendrick yet?'

'No, not yet. I can't face the fuss, Charlotte. I just can't.'

'I should leave it then.'

'I think I will.'

She phoned two days later. George was better.

'There you are,' said Charlotte. 'Nanny was right.'

Betsey was slowly recovering. She was very frail, Fred said, but every day she ate a little more, slept a little less.

'I hope you're looking after her well,' said Charlotte severely.

'Of course I am. I haven't left her since it happened.'

'Shall I come and see her?'

'I think she'd like that.'

'I'm going to visit Grandma,' she said to Max. 'Just for a day or two. I'm hardly crucial here in the office.'

'Fine. Are you going to talk to Grandpa?'

'I don't think so. He sounds as if he couldn't take it. But I just might.'

'Are you going to see Gabe?'

'I don't know,' said Charlotte, 'that's entirely up to Gabe.'

'Is it?' said Max.

She booked a flight to New York for the following Monday. When she told Freddy where she was going and why, he looked at her with his coldest, most fishlike stare and said, 'I hope you don't have any plans to talk to my grandfather about the bank and your situation in it.'

'He's my grandfather too,' said Charlotte, 'and I shall talk to him about whatever I like.'

'I wouldn't if I were you,' said Freddy. 'I have a letter here, that I've drafted to Nigel Dempster and Ross Benson. Would you like to read it?'

He handed it to her. It read: 'Dear Sir, There could be a story for you in the background of my cousin, Maximilian, Viscount Hadleigh. There is a suggestion that his true father is Mr Tommy Soames-Maxwell of Pond Place, Chelsea. I shall be delighted to help you as far as I am able, with further information if you care to contact me.'

'You shit,' said Charlotte. 'You little shit.'

'Don't worry,' said Freddy. 'I have no intention of sending it. Unless I hear you've been talking to Grandpa about anything that you don't like at the bank. OK?'

Charlotte smiled at him very sweetly. 'Freddy!' she said. 'Are you trying to tell me that there's something irregular going on that Grandpa wouldn't be happy with?'

She had the satisfaction of seeing Freddy's pale skin turn a very unattractive shade of purplish pink.

She phoned Georgina just before she left. 'I hadn't thought, I'm sorry. You could come with me. Do you want to?'

'Oh – no,' said Georgina. 'I don't think so. I might see Kendrick. And anyway, George isn't well again. I'm taking him to a specialist on Thursday.'

'Oh Georgie, I'm so sorry. Try not to worry.'

'I'm trying,' said Georgina.

When she got to Kennedy, she scanned the line at the barrier looking for Hudson. He wasn't there. Charlotte sighed; she was tired. She had turned away and started fighting her way through the crowd out towards the cab rank, when she heard her name.

'Hallo, Charlotte.'

It was Gabe.

He drove her quite fast into the city in his Mercedes two-seater. Charlotte didn't speak; nor did he, except to tell her he had heard she was coming from his father and had told Hudson not to come. Fred and Betsey were not expecting her until the morning, he said. He didn't touch her. He looked very fierce.

When they got to Gramercy Park, he put the Mercedes in a parking lot and said, 'I'd like you to come up to my apartment.'

'What for?' said Charlotte. She knew it was a very silly thing to say, but she was fighting not to sound bossy.

'So that I can go to bed with you, you silly bitch,' said Gabe.

'Oh,' said Charlotte. 'Oh, all right.' That time it was easier.

Having sex with Gabe was quite unlike having sex with anyone else she had ever known. She told him so, as they lay some time later, slightly apart, holding hands, occasionally kissing.

'Not that I have an enormous amount of experience,' she said hastily.

'How is it unlike?' he said. He sounded rather pleased with himself. 'Oh – I don't know. It's so – so single-minded.'

She had often thought this; his expression as he turned to her (after removing his watch) was exactly as it was when he swooped into his Quotron: ferociously, almost angrily intent, his eyes dark and burning, seeking, searching, knowing what he wanted, what he was doing.

'Well, you wouldn't want me to be thinking of something else, would you? Like work?' He laughed suddenly. He didn't often laugh; it was one of the things she perversely liked about him, it added to his intensity. She smiled at him.

'No of course not. Gabe . . .'

'Yes, Charlotte.'

'Gabe, I'm sorry if I – well, if I – '

'Oh for God's sake,' he said, and he sounded very amused. 'Now what are you trying to say?'

'If I'm a bit – well, bossy sometimes. I'll try and be more – amenable in future.'

'Charlotte,' said Gabe, 'if there's one thing I can't stand it's amenable females. Why do you think I fell in love with you? Because you're so bloody stroppy, that's why.'

'Oh,' said Charlotte meekly.

Fred III looked very old and very frail suddenly. She supposed it was the fear of losing Betsey. Betsey actually looked better than he did, she had some colour in her cheeks, and the combative gleam in her eye whenever the nurse came in to check her pulse, her blood pressure, her ankles and the bruises and swellings on her head, where she had hit it when she had fallen, indicted to Charlotte a greater sense of well-being than her appearance initially indicated.

She spent her days in the sun room, reading, talking to Fred, doing her tapestry. She was delighted to see Charlotte; she told her she was looking very well, but a little thin.

'We'll feed you up while you're here, darling.'

'How's the bank?' asked Fred, over lunch. 'Everything going all right? Getting on with Drew OK, are you? I'll have you back in New York this autumn.'

'You've been saying that ever since the spring,' said Charlotte.
Fred glared at her and poured himself a bourbon.

After lunch Betsey sent Fred off for a nap. 'My accident has taken it out of him, dear,' she said, 'and I must confess I'm finding him a little trying. He will fuss. I think really it would be better if he went to the bank, at least a couple of days a week. But he won't hear of it.'

While the nurse was putting Betsey to bed, after supper, Fred poured himself and Charlotte a glass of Armagnac and lit a cigar.

'She's very frail,' he said. 'I worry about her. I miss the bank, of course, and I'd like to be there, maybe just a couple of days a week. But I wouldn't leave her. Not at the moment. She likes to have me here.'

By the end of her stay with them, Charlotte was able to engineer a compromise whereby at the beginning of October, Fred would go back to the bank two days a week.

'I have to get this thing settled,' he said moodily. 'I really do. I'm not going to live for ever. And the bank's vulnerable. I must establish a good modus operandi, for taking care of it until such time as you and Freddy are able to take it over.'

'Is – Chris Hill firmly settled again?' asked Charlotte. 'No more flirtations with anyone else?'

'Nope,' said Fred, looking very pleased with himself. 'Good man. But it's a lopsided arrangement, him having those shares, and I know that. You didn't think I hadn't thought it through, did you?'

'No, of course not,' said Charlotte.

'Freddy and you getting on all right?' he said after a pause, his face obscured by cigar smoke, as it always was when the answer to a question was important to him.

'Yes,' she said. 'Yes, fine.'

'Good. I'm glad he's having that experience over there. Good for him. Anyway, I shall be back in Pine Street in a week or so, and then once I've got it straight, your grandmother and I are going on a world cruise. She's dreamed of one all her life, and I don't want her to miss out on it. I've got the tickets as a matter of fact. Kind of a second honeymoon, I thought. We sail on October fifteenth.'

'It sounds gorgeous,' said Charlotte politely.

'Yes, I think it will be. I can't stand holidays of course, but as I say, I think I owe it to your grandmother. She's done a bit for me in her time.'

'She certainly has,' said Charlotte.

★

676

Gabe came out on the Sunday, for lunch. Charlotte had confided in Betsey that she was in love and Betsey, always excited by romance, insisted she asked him over. Charlotte had been nervous about the effect on her grandfather of knowing she was having a relationship with someone at Praegers, but he was rather touchingly pleased that it was Gabe.

'Your grandfather was one of the first partners in the bank,' he said to Gabe, 'I'd like to see that tradition continue. I've relied on your father's support a great deal over the years. He's a very clever banker. I shall miss him.'

Neither Charlotte nor Gabe betrayed by so much as a flickering eyelid that they considered it hard to imagine that Pete Hoffman would not outlast Fred III at the bank.

After lunch, Charlotte and Gabe walked along the shore.

'Quite the little blue-eyed girl, aren't you?' he said. He sounded sombre.

'Oh for God's sake, Gabe,' said Charlotte. 'For the thousandth time, I can't help it.'

'No, but I can,' said Gabe.

'What do you mean?'

'I can help being there.'

'Gabe, what are you talking about?' said Charlotte.

Gabe turned to look at her. 'I don't know that I could stand working at Praegers,' he said, 'when you're running it. You and Freddy. It would be – hard.'

'I don't see why,' said Charlotte.

'Then you're very stupid,' said Gabe, and he sounded genuinely angry. 'How can I work for a bank, even as a partner, when my – when you are its chairman? It would be intolerable. I couldn't stand it.'

He stopped, threw some stones into the rolling ocean. Charlotte looked at him. His face was dark, intent on its task. She smiled suddenly, thinking of the other times she had seen that look. She took his hand, started dragging him up towards the dunes.

'Come on. Up here.'

He followed, still half angry; Charlotte turned as she reached the dunes, put her arms up, around him, pulled his face down to hers.

'I love you,' she said. 'It won't matter.'

'It will matter,' said Gabe, 'but I love you too.'

He started to kiss her, his mouth hungry, greedy; very slowly, but determinedly, he pushed her down onto the sand.

'There are people coming,' said Charlotte, pointing down the endless shoreline. 'Look.' Three, or was it four, tiny figures were moving slowly but relentlessly towards them.

'We must beat them to it then,' said Gabe. He was lying in the sand now, cradling her beside him in the crook of his arm; his other hand was working at the zip of her jeans. He had it down; Charlotte raised her hips, eased herself out of them. The sand felt soft and very cool beneath her bare buttocks.

Gabe had undone his fly; his penis was large, erect. Charlotte wriggled down, took it in her mouth, started working at it, licking, teasing, tugging. She felt her own excitement mounting, rising; her breathing quickened. Gabe's hands were in her hair, holding her head; she heard him moaning.

'Oh, I love you,' said Gabe suddenly, and pulled her up, turned her over, pushed, thrust into her. She rose up to him, felt with incredible speed and urgency her climax growing, growing, leaping; she flung her arms out, her head back, clutching the grass on the dunes. Above her a gull soared, high, swift, swooping, like her own pleasure; she followed it with her eyes, with her body, pulling, reaching, circling Gabe; and then it came, a great burst of light, bright wrenching pleasure, and the gull and she cried out together, in a strange lonely triumph, and Gabe held her to him, close, tight, and she felt him following her; and as they lay, their pleasure eased and softened, she heard voices and laughter, and she looked into his eyes, his dark, probing eyes, and said, 'We only just made it.' And laughed aloud with happiness and triumph.

'That was a first for me,' he said, kissing her gently.

'What do you mean?'

'I had to keep my watch on,' he said.

Later they swam, diving endlessly beneath the great gentle rollers; and then lay, their skin salty and cool in the autumn sun.

'What a day,' said Gabe. 'What a good day,' and he smiled at her, and took her hand and kissed her fingers and said, 'Charlotte . . .' and she said, 'Yes Gabe?' and he said, 'I really have to go now, I have work to do,' and instead of being angry or even upset, she laughed, laughed aloud, because she knew him so well, and what she knew was what she loved.

'What a very nice young man,' Betsey said, over supper. 'Are you going to marry him, Charlotte?'

'I don't know,' said Charlotte, carefully vague, and then she added, 'he's married already really.'

'Oh darling, no!' said Betsey, looking shocked.

'To Praegers,' said Charlotte, and laughed, and Betsey laughed too and said she had learnt long ago to see Praegers not as a wife, but a mistress.

'And the wife, if she is clever, always has the last laugh.'

'Then I must try to be clever,' said Charlotte, smiling at her.

It was bad in the office, Gabe had said. Chris Hill, secure, arrogant in his position, was throwing his weight about, waiting impatiently for Fred to finally go, for Freddy to come back, for power. The surging soaring stock market, the apparently ceaseless boom, the rise day on day of the Dow Jones, all added to his image of a man who could not lose. His following, the degree of confidence felt in him at Praegers, was immense. Pete Hoffman, on the other hand, angered, hurt by the tip of balance in the boardroom, demoralized by the lack of recognition from Fred, was waiting simply these days for retirement, too tired, too damaged to fight.

'But he would, wouldn't he?' said Charlotte. 'He would fight, if he had the power and the shares and the clout, he would fight with us, with me.'

'I don't know,' said Gabe, 'I really don't.'

She tried very gently talking to Fred, suggesting Pete was offered shares as well, to retore the balance of power. Fred, a little less gently, told her she did not entirely know what she was talking about, that he had it under control, that he was working things out. And every day he hesitated, every day he grew older and frailer, every day the danger increased.

The night before she left for England, she was talking to her grandfather after dinner. Betsey was peacefully asleep; every day she grew stronger.

Fred lit a cigar.

'How do you see things out there in the markets?' he said. 'How does your friend Gabe see them?'

Charlotte was flattered by his interest. 'I think he sees it as a peak,' she said.

'Oh really? And does he see a trough following it?'

'Oh – not a trough. But he says it can't go on rising for ever. The Dow Jones is pushing three thousand, isn't it? That's awfully high.'

'Mmm.' Fred looked at her, drawing on his cigar. 'And London?'

'Well, it's just as dizzy. The FT is at – '

'Yes yes, I know what it's at,' said Fred impatiently. 'And I know Chuck thinks it's built on rock. But have you picked up any feeling that it might not last in Britain much longer? From anywhere else?'

'No,' said Charlotte. 'Everyone I know thinks it'll go on for ever. The Tories getting back in was crucial; steadied everything down again. And you know how the City feels about Lawson, they love him. He's the Messiah as far as they're concerned.'

'Well I don't know.' The cigar had gone out; Fred spent a while lighting it again. 'There are some small but vital signs out there. I had dinner with Trump the other week. He's selling quite a bit. Much more significantly, Goldsmith is getting out of everything. Selling his stock, his houses, the lot. Well, he's a little eccentric these days, of course. Obsessed with this AIDS business. I don't know. I just have a feeling – ' He puffed out the smoke, his face suddenly obscured. Charlotte sat listening, a sudden sense of chill in her body. 'I just have a feeling there might be a dip ahead. I think it's all overheating. And people have got too damn greedy.'

'Do I have to worry?' said Charlotte lightly, giving him a kiss. 'Should I be selling my shares?'

'Oh no, darling. You don't have to worry. You're quite safe. And so is Praegers.'

It was 22 September.

On her return she went down to Hartest. Georgina was distraught. George was no better. He would recover for a bit, and then become ill again. He didn't look well. Even Charlotte could see that. He was very thin, and fretful, and his skin was dry and rough-looking.

'It's the dehydration,' said Georgina miserably. 'Poor little boy.'

Dr Rogers had said if he wasn't better in a few days, he would admit him to hospital as an in-patient.

Alexander seemed equally distraught. 'He's been so good,' said Georgina, 'he pushes him around in his pram for hours, trying to get him off to sleep, and the other night when I was up with him he heard me and came and sat with me for hours.'

'Well, he's very fond of George,' said Charlotte, 'and he is his grandchild after all.'

Alexander wasn't looking very well himself. He was very thin, and pale, and he had shadows under his eyes. He had been upset about Gemma and Max, he told Charlotte: 'That was no way to behave. She was a sweet little thing. I'm ashamed of Max, Charlotte, I really am.'

'Well,' said Charlotte, 'I know all that, but if he didn't in the end want to take things further, then it was best to break it off. And at least everyone who said he was going to marry her for her money has been proved wrong. That would have been really bad.'

'I didn't know there was any question of that,' said Alexander. His voice was sharp suddenly. 'And why should he need to worry about money anyway?'

'Well, I suppose Hartest is a big expense,' said Charlotte carefully, 'and – '

'What on earth do you mean?' said Alexander. His eyes were very hard suddenly. 'Hartest pays its way. It always has done. I resent very much the implication that Max might need some kind of a handout to keep it going.'

'Oh Daddy, don't be silly,' said Charlotte. 'Of course he doesn't need it. I didn't mean that. But Gemma was – is – jolly rich, you know. Anyway, Daddy, I think it's probably for the best. Max is very young, much too young to get married.'

'She was doing him good,' said Alexander fretfully. 'He'd steadied down a lot. I had so hoped – well, there's nothing I can do about it.'

'Nothing,' said Charlotte. She kissed him. He looked at her and said suddenly, 'Did your grandfather say anything about me while you were there?'

'No,' said Charlotte, surprised, 'no he didn't. Except to ask after you, of course. Why, was there some reason he should have?'

'Oh no,' said Alexander quickly. 'No reason at all.'

It was 27 September.

Chapter 59

Georgina, September–October 1987

Georgina had never been frightened before, she realized. She had never had this kind of awful, black nightmare filling her. Everything else receded in the face of it, of what was happening to George; to the endless pitiful sound of him vomiting, to his cries of pain, his wailing, his increasingly thin little body.

Some days he was fine; that was the strange thing. He would eat, smile, keep the food down. She was still breast feeding him, of course; he only had a modest amount of solid food: scrambled eggs, a little soup, apple sauce, yogurt. And that was all home-grown and cooked; it wasn't as if she was relying on some terrible mass-produced stuff.

There had been all that awful publicity recently, about baby food – any food – being contaminated by the animal rights people; she wouldn't have risked it anyway, even if she had been living in a high-rise flat in a London street, rather than safely at Hartest, with their own cows and chickens and vegetables. She cooked, increasingly carefully, kept soup, vegetable puree in the freezer; refusing to allow Nanny or Mrs Fallon to help her. Well, she had to be as careful as it was possible to be. And anyway, it certainly wasn't his food. He had had allergy tests, of course: and horrible things called barium meals and barium enemas, his poor little body probed and abused by doctors trying to solve the puzzle. Everything was negative.

'I'm so afraid it's something like – well something really dreadful,' she told Martin on one of her increasingly rare walks with him, 'some disease. Something inherent.'

'You mean like lukaemia?' he said, putting his arm round her.

'Well – yes,' said Georgina. 'Yes, I suppose so.'

'Have they suggested it might be?'

'No. No, they haven't. But they are going to do some extra blood tests. I know that's what they think.'

She stared at him; his face was blurred through her tears. 'I love him so much, Martin. I didn't know what love was, before. You can't imagine.'

'Oh,' he said and he smiled at her very gently, 'oh Georgina, I think I can.'

★

For several days after that George seemed better. He hadn't been sick for days; he had been sleeping; he had been guzzling greedily at her breasts. She felt much better. Maybe it was over. Maybe it was just one of those extraordinary, inexplicable things that would never be solved.

She slept with him beside her; he didn't wake at all in the night; in the morning he was almost rosy. She bathed him, smiling with pleasure at him, even while she grieved over his little legs, so round and dimpled a few weeks ago, now strangely straight.

'You're going to be well now, aren't you?' she said. 'You're going to be all right for Mummy.'

George smiled radiantly at her.

She went downstairs; the kitchen was empty. George was obviously hungry; she decided to give him some Farex with his apple sauce. He loved that.

There was a jar of apple sauce in the fridge, carefully covered; she had made it yesterday. She got it out, mixed it with the Farex and a little Hartest yogurt.

'Here,' she said, 'here, darling, lovely lovely, your favourite.'

George smiled at her, savoured the food, smacking his small lips. She smiled, happy. This was the fourth day. He was obviously getting much much better.

Suddenly George was sick. Violently, horribly sick. Several times. He was obviously in pain; his legs were drawn up and he was screaming.

Georgina called the doctor; then she changed her mind and put him in the car and drove at top speed to the hospital.

She rushed into Casualty; the woman was supercilious. 'Name? Date of birth? Religion?'

'Oh for God's sake,' said Georgina, 'what does it matter what religion I am? My baby's really ill. Please please let me see someone, please, quickly.'

'You can see someone as soon as there's someone to see,' said the woman. 'It's a very busy morning. Now if you'd like to sit there and wait.' She waved imperiously in the direction of the row of chairs. They were almost all occupied. Trembling, Georgina sat down. The woman next to her had burnt her hand; she was trying not to cry, holding onto her husband. The man opposite was drunk; he was dribbling and he smelt awful. He kept cackling at her and once or twice he came over and tried to tickle George. She pulled the baby away from him, and he swore and sat down again.

After a while, George was sick again. She mopped him up with a handful of Kleenex. He smelt awful. He cried endlessly, his little fists clenching and unclenching with pain. Panic rose in her, cold clutching panic.

She stood up again, went over to the desk. 'Please,' she said, 'please let me see someone. I'm so worried.'

'A lot of people are worried,' said the woman piously, 'you have to wait, I'm afraid. Doctor shouldn't be much longer now. Your baby doesn't look too bad to me.'

George vomited again, and then appeared to lose consciousness.

Frantically Georgina tried to find his pulse; she couldn't. His little white face lolled back over her arm. He was breathing, but she couldn't believe it was for much longer.

'Poor little thing,' said the drunk. He came over and tried to chuck George under the chin.

'Leave him alone,' Georgina almost screamed. 'Just leave him.'

Everyone stared; she didn't care. She got up suddenly, and walked very determinedly down the corridor looking at the curtained cubicles.

'I don't know where you think you're going,' said the woman, running after her, 'but you won't get attention that way.'

'I'm not getting it just sitting there,' said Georgina. She thought she had never hated anyone before as she hated that woman. She looked at her almost detachedly. 'You are a very stupid woman,' she said, hardly able to believe her own voice. 'Now just leave me alone.'

She pulled aside one of the curtains at random; an Indian doctor was bandaging a little boy's hand. He looked at her with a mild interest, but none of the outrage the woman was displaying.

'Please look at my baby,' she said. 'Please. I'm afraid he's going to die.'

'He certainly doesn't look very well,' he said. 'I hope you brought him straight in. Delay can be fatal, you know.'

Georgina opened her mouth and screamed.

George didn't die. They kept him in for observation; he was not sick again that day, but he was very unhappy, he had bad diarrhoea and his pulse was weak. Georgina breast fed him, and rocked him, and felt afraid, and alone, and wished only that she could be ill, could suffer, could be in pain, and that George could be well, smiling, strong again.

That evening, when she had lost all track of time, Alexander suddenly appeared in the ward; he was carrying a big bag.

'Clean clothes for him,' he said. 'How is he?'

'He's very bad,' said Georgina, and burst into tears.

'He doesn't look too terrible,' said Alexander, 'and he's at least asleep.'

'I know. But he's so weak. And dehydrated. And his pulse is weak. They nearly had to put him on a drip.' She was trying not to cry.

Alexander sat down opposite her, looking at the baby. Then he suddenly said, 'Kendrick should be here. With you. Helping you.'

'Oh Daddy,' said Georgina with a sigh, too weary, too heartsore to consider the effect of her words, 'Daddy, it's all over between Kendrick and me. All over. We're not going to get married or anything. I'm sorry. I should have told you before.'

It was very strange, she said to Charlotte, but it was from that night that she dated George's real recovery. He was allowed home next day and he wasn't sick, and stopped crying with pain, and he put on weight and thrived.

'I kept expecting a relapse and it never came. It was wonderful. It was as if – well as if telling Daddy about Kendrick, getting that off my chest, had something to do with it.'

'Well, it can't have done,' said Charlotte, 'it can't possibly.'

'No, I suppose not. Unless there was some strange anxiety in me communicating itself to George. What do you think?'

'I don't think that sounds very likely,' said Charlotte, 'but anyway, it doesn't matter. George is well again. That's the really important thing.'

'Yes,' said Georgina, 'of course that's the really important thing.'

Chapter 60

Max, October 1987

'God, you look gorgeous. I might have to ask you to marry me.' Max's voice was low, throbbing with intensity.

'Oh Max, honestly.' Shireen looked up at him in the lift, from beneath her long spiky eyelashes. 'Don't be silly.'

'I'm not being silly. That dress is a peach. An absolute peach.' He put his mouth to her ear, looked cautiously about him at the other impassive faces. 'I have a huge erection just looking at you.'

'Oh Max,' said Shireen again. 'Do be quiet. Anyway, it's not a dress, it's a suit.' She looked down complacently at the black jacket and skirt. 'I got it from Next. They call it the City Look.'

'Nice pearls too,' said Max. 'Very executive.'

'Do you like them? They were a birthday present from Chuck. He brought them from Hong Kong for me.'

'Good old Chuck,' said Max. 'God, I envy that man. Fancy a drink after work, Shireen?' He put his mouth to her ear again. 'I might have some news for you, from my friend at Mortons.'

'Ooh – yes.' Shireen looked excited. 'Yes, all right, Max. Usual place?'

'Usual place.'

The usual place was the Fenchurch Colony wine bar; Shireen had now met Max there four times, as he progressed her entry into the world of the dealer.

The entry was fictitious, of course; he had asked Jake about it, for form's sake, and Jake had said very solemnly, tapping his nose the while, that he would certainly see what he could do. He had even met Shireen with Max once, and talked to her at some length about a trader's life and how she would enjoy it and what prospects for her there might be in it; in exchange for this information and (as Shireen thought) promotion of her cause, and several glasses of champagne a time, Shireen chattered artlessly about what was going on in the office in general and between Chuck and Freddy in particular. It was a double double of course; they knew it wasn't entirely artless and she knew they knew, but as long as that was how it appeared, then no one could get heavy with anyone.

'My goodness,' she said that night, settling into her chair, tugging her micro-skirt down over a millimetre or so of thigh, 'my goodness, what a day I've had.'

'Oh really?' said Max, filling her glass.

'Yes, really. There's this big deal going through, you know Bretts, the flash jewellery people – '

'Yeah yeah,' said Max, 'one of Freddy's faves.'

'Yes, that's right. I do like that Barry Brett, he's really lovely to me. He promised me one of their gold chains with the pearls in, you know, at trade, next time he comes in. I hope he won't forget. Well anyway, they've acquired a big stake in Langleys, you know, that posh jeweller. It was a dawn raid,' she added with a complacent expression.

'My goodness, Shireen, you have all the jargon these days, don't you?' said Max.

'Well,' she said, 'you know, you pick up a lot just listening. Well anyway, Bretts' shares have roared away, of course, but so have all the rest – '

'Of course,' said Max.

'And now they want to make a bid for Langleys, but there's some other company after them, some American company, and so the shares have gone even higher, and Bretts haven't got enough cash to bang in an offer of their own.'

She sat back looking very pleased with herself.

'So?' said Max. 'My goodness you're a clever girl, remembering all this,' he added hastily. 'I don't know how you do it.'

'So, well I don't know,' said Shireen slightly lamely, 'but I do know that Chuck really wants Bretts to get it, and he and Freddy have been on the phone all day, trying to help them.'

'Mmm!' said Max thoughtfully. 'How much money is Brett looking for?'

'Max,' said Shireen suddenly, 'Max, are we here to talk about my career or Chuck's deals?'

'Oh God, Shireen, I'm sorry. Your career of course. Now look, I've talked to my friend, Jake, you know? And he says there's nothing at Mortons just this minute. There was that slight hiccup at the end of the summer, remember, and they're just a bit cagey. But everything's looking fine now, and Jake says he thinks they will be looking for people at Citicorps any minute and he's going to put in a word for you there.'

'Oh,' said Shireen. She sounded disappointed. 'I thought it was going to be a bit more, you know, solid than that.'

'It's quite solid,' said Max. 'Don't knock it. If Jake Joseph's recommending you, you'll get the job. No messing. Now then, talking

687

of solids, shall we go and eat? I shall fall over if I have any more of this stuff.'

'Yes, that'd be nice,' said Shireen. 'Can we go to Langans again?'

'Of course,' said Max.

He smiled at her, his most come-and-get-it smile, the one that had sold so many thousands of shirts and pairs of jeans and Ts and even boxer shorts what seemed like a very short time ago. God, life had been simple then. How on earth had he got into this kind of mess?

'Three hundred and fifty million pounds,' said Shireen, through a mouthful of smoked salmon. 'I just remembered, that's what it was.'

'What what was?' said Max. He had just been wondering if he had the nerve to go back to Angie's house at – what would it be – one, and try to get into her bed. Probably not. She was strict about that sort of thing.

'What Brett needed. To bid for Langleys.'

'That's a lot of money.'

'Yeah well,' she said, pressing her legs artlessly against his under the table, 'you can get money easily these days, can't you? Even that much?'

'Oh you can,' said Max.

It was 5 October.

'Have you ever bought anything from Bretts?' said Max to Angie. They were lying in her large bed, after some outstandingly good sex; Angie turned to him, her green eyes very amused.

'Of course not. Load of tat. Why?'

'Oh – just wondered. My little friend Shireen was talking about them.'

'They're quite a successful little chain,' said Angie. 'High-street stuff.'

'Yes, well, they're putting in a bid for Langleys.'

'Oh really? Bit up-market.'

'Yes, I know. Bit expensive too. Three hundred and fifty million, I'm told.'

'Small beer these days,' said Angie.

It was 7 October.

He was in love with Angie. There was just no debating it. He loved her. He loved everything about her. He loved her angelically hard little face, with its great green eyes, and he loved her ingenious, greedy, slender body, he loved her sense of fun and he loved her tough, clear-sighted pragmatic mind and he loved her dubious moral sense, at once so devious and so honest; he loved all those things. He only wished there was some chance that she might love him.

Max knew that if he lived to be a hundred, he would never forget the night of the party. The heady, reckless flight to the bedroom; Gemma's pain; the fight; Gemma's revelation; Melissa gone to hospital; Jonty gone, Tommy gone, the guests gone, everyone gone; the police finally gone, statements taken, detailed, painstaking statements; Gemma driven home, silent, weeping, to her parents, left with them, with helpless apologies; and finally, just him and Angie alone in the house, shaken, sobered, exhausted – and yet strangely, oddly exhilarated.

She had turned to him and said quite simply, 'So now what do we do?' and he had looked at her, very serious, and said, 'Shall we go upstairs then?' and she had looked back just as serious, and her eyes had been most unusually direct, candid, and she had said simply, 'Yes.' He had taken her hand and led her upstairs; they had gone into the bedroom where they had been before, and she had stood there, her eyes fixed on his, and moved forward and begun to kiss him, sweet, honeyed, questing kisses, her body pressed harder and harder against his, her arms wrapped more and more tightly round him. She had stood back suddenly, and grinned and said, 'Time for the hundred-pound unzip, Max,' and he had undone it, right to the bottom, and she had slithered out of the catsuit, dropped it on the floor and stood there, quite, completely, amazingly naked. Max had thought about Angie, imagined her naked for so long, it was hardly a surprise at all; and yet the greatest shock he could have imagined. Desire roared through him, stunning him, shaking him; so thin she was, so perfect, flat-stomached, slender-thighed, but with those ripe, rich brown breasts, quite full, with large dark nipples standing out, and a great thick bush of quite reddish pubic hair.

He moved forward; he felt very strong suddenly. He took the breasts in his hands, bent his head, began to kiss them, his tongue working on the nipples. He felt them harder still; he moved his hands down, tenderly, down her back, down to her buttocks, so firm, so strong. Max had always averred you could judge a woman's sensuality by her buttocks; if they were hard and taut, her appetites were strong. Angie's were very hard, very taut.

'Get your clothes off, you bastard,' said Angie suddenly. 'I can't stand this very much longer.' And while he was tearing off his shirt, his trousers, his pants, she moved and lay on the bed, her arms flung above her head, her legs slightly splayed, staring at him.

'Oh God,' she said, 'oh God,' and that was all, and then he was on her, holding her, afraid of failing her, of not doing right by her, and yet so desperate, so hungry for her that he could scarcely contain his body and what it needed, had to do.

'Stop,' she said suddenly, 'wait.' And she turned him over, and looked at him, smiling down, staring almost consideringly at his penis, and then slowly, very slowly, she knelt astride him and lowered herself tenderly onto him, very slow, very very cautious; she was lusciously, wonderfully wet, and neatly tight; he felt her enclose him, felt the glorious sweet warmth; 'Be still,' she said, 'be still,' and he thought how strange the words were, to come from her, so formal, so firm, and of course he couldn't, he couldn't be still, and almost at once he began to thrust, up into her taut, tender welcome, feeling the waves, the great surging, pushing, overwhelming waves breaking out of him, out, out into the freedom, the release of her, of Angie, of Angie his love.

Later, hours and hours later, he said, 'Angie, I meant it, what I said earlier. I love you. I know I do.' And 'Oh,' she said, 'oh Max, don't talk such nonsense, don't say such things, how can you love me, me of all people?' and she smiled, but there was a pain behind the smile.

'I do love you,' he said, 'of all people, of course I love you. I love you more than anything. I've loved you since I was sixteen years old, and I first saw you, that lunchtime at the Ritz. Do you remember?'

'Oh, I remember,' said Angie, smiling at him, her green eyes soft suddenly. 'Baby and I had just gone public, it was such fun to be out together, not hiding in endless bedrooms, and he said, "Look, that's my nephew over there with that extremely beautiful girl." '

'And what did you think? What did you say? Or don't you remember?'

'I remember what I said,' said Angie, 'although I probably shouldn't tell you, I said, "He's fairly extremely beautiful himself," and I remember what I thought, I thought what a spoilt, arrogant little brat you must be. And I was right.'

'That isn't fair,' said Max. 'That really isn't fair.' He felt genuine hurt suddenly.

'Of course it's fair,' said Angie briskly. She pulled the sheet up over her suddenly. 'I'm cold.' Max sighed. The mood of closeness, of love, felt shattered.

'So I don't mean anything to you?' he said. 'You're just fooling around. Is that right? I'm this week's man.'

'Max,' said Angie, 'Max, don't. Don't spoil things. This is so new. Of course you mean something to me. Of course you do. But I don't know how much yet. Max, I'm still hurting. From Baby. Give me a chance.'

'I'm sorry,' he said, and he meant it. 'I forgot. I'm a fool. And I'm really sorry.'

'It's all right,' said Angie. 'And you're not a fool.'

Since then they had been together a lot. If Max had had his way he would have been with her all the time. But he didn't.

Angie said she needed space, time, her independence. She had her company, which she had neglected, she had her twins, whom she had neglected rather more, and she simply couldn't commit herself totally to a relationship at the moment. Max found it hard. He had always had what he wanted; had achieved it with comparative ease. He had never, he realized, had to wait, wait for anything. It was very uncomfortable.

He saw her two or three times a week; and that was good. Very good. They had fun. Angie told him she hadn't had so much fun since Baby had been young. Max liked that.

He stopped worrying, without understanding quite why, about Freddy and Mary Rose, about Hartest and Alexander. Any emotional energy left over from his job was expended on Angie. They ate out a great deal, went dancing, saw shows, watched videos over Indian take-aways. They also had a lot of very good sex. Angie's inventiveness, appetite, and sheer pleasure in bed (and in the car, and in the park, and in the shower and in the drawing room, and once, rather memorably, in a box at the theatre) slightly awed Max. He had always thought of himself as a bit of a stud. He discovered that compared with Angie he was a novice. And every time, afterwards, however wild and close and fused they had been, she seemed to withdraw from him, to retreat into herself, to go away from him again, to become a single and quite separate person.

One day, he promised, one day, he would make her stay.

One night, soon after his dinner with Shireen, he took Angie to the Ritz. 'For old times' sake,' he said.

It was packed; all the restaurants in London seemed permanently packed, even in the week, even on a Monday. This was a Monday. Monday, 12 October.

They had a good dinner; over a second glass of Armagnac (during which Angie made a rather interesting suggestion as to what she might do to Max with the Armagnac she had at home), Max looked across the room and saw Freddy passing the doorway, en route to the gents', with another man. He looked young and very flashy; he thought it was Brian Brett.

'Excuse me,' he said to Angie. 'Nature calls.'

He followed Freddy in, just in time to see him turn into the row of urinals. Max shot into one of the cubicles and bolted the door. Shortly afterwards, he heard Freddy's voice.

'Right, Brian. Back to the ladies.'

'Yes indeed. A lovely lady, Mrs Drew.'

'Isn't she? Chuck's a lucky man.'

'Indeed. Now Freddy, while we're alone, I have to tell you I could be a little strapped for cash on this. I calculate I'll need something in the order of – well let's say sixty on top of the usual loans. Is there anything – well, that you could suggest?'

'Oh good Lord yes,' said Freddy. 'No problem at all. We can underwrite that sort of figure. Don't worry about it, Brian.'

'Great. Well, we shall all benefit from the proceeds, no doubt.'

'No doubt.'

'Sixty,' said Max. 'Sixty what, do you suppose? Sixty thousand? Sixty hundred thousand?'

'Nah,' said Angie. 'Million.'

'Yeah. I guess. That's a lot of money,' said Max, 'for a bank this size to underwrite. And I bet it's not the only one. Freddy's so bloody greedy. It's the thought of the commission.'

'Not a lot of money these days,' said Angie. It was 12 October.

'Shireen,' said Max, 'do you hear a lot of talk of mezzanine finance these days?'

'Oh yeah,' said Shireen, 'all the time. Freddy's very keen on it.'

It was 13 October.

Max talked to Charlotte. 'I think Freddy's overextending the bank's credit. I really do. We should tell Grandpa. Fast.'

'We can't,' said Charlotte. 'He's off on his cruise. On his second honeymoon, as he put it.'

'When?'

'Um – tomorrow.'

'I think we should try.'

'OK.'

Charlotte phoned Fred III. Max sat by the phone listening.

'Grandpa? Charlotte. Listen, I need to talk to you. What? I know you're going tomorrow, I wanted to say have a great trip and – look, I'm sorry, I know you're busy but it's important. Listen Grandpa, there's something you have to know. It's about Freddy. He's – Grandpa, please. Please listen. He's – well he's overextending. He's lending a lot of Praegers' own money. Well I don't know exactly, but it's pretty serious. Well, I just do know. I can't tell you quite – what? Oh, Grandpa, please please don't do that. Please. It won't – '

She looked at Max, her face troubled. 'He cut me off. He's talking to Chuck. Now we've had it.'

It was 14 October.

Chuck bawled them out. Quite pleasantly, but very firmly. He finished by pointing out that at such time as Fred III retired, Charlotte's share of the bank no longer meant quite what it had done and she had to learn to do what she was told. 'I can't fire you,' he said, 'but I can make your life pretty uncomfortable. I would keep a clean profile if I were you.'

It was 15 October. There was a rumour on the radio of jitters on the New York Stock Exchange. Nobody took a great deal of notice.

Max was sitting at his desk at lunchtime when the *Daily Mail* called. Would Max like to comment on the story which had reached them that the Earl of Caterham was not in fact his father?

Max told them there was no story, that he had absolutely nothing to say, and that they should speak to their own lawyers about the laws of libel.

He put the phone down, feeling very sick, and went to see Charlotte.

'The cat,' he said, trying to sound amused, 'seems about to leap out of the bag.'

'What cat? Max, what are you talking about?'

'I think Freddy's talked to Nigel Dempster.'

'What?'

'Well, he did warn us,' said Max.

'I'll talk to Charles.'

Charles told them they would be best advised to keep quiet. 'Say nothing. Keep saying nothing. Tell Alexander and Tommy to say nothing. You can't actually sue, when the story's true, and it might damage the girls as well. Ride out the storm.'

They remembered his words rather vividly over the next twenty-four hours.

Max and Angie and Charlotte shared a curry that evening and tried to persuade themselves that Nigel Dempster had better things to write about than them. Charlotte tried to ring Gabe, but he was out.

'Does he know?' asked Max idly.

'No,' said Charlotte briefly.

They watched the news and the weather forecast, more from inertia than anything else; they were told that it was going to be a slightly windy night. Charlotte left early, and went home to bed. Angie and Max also went to bed, and fell asleep talking, without having made love.

'I would never have believed this possible,' said Max sleepily into Angie's hair. 'You must be losing your grip.'

693

'Nothing wrong with my grip,' said Angie, sleepier still. 'It's just that there's nothing to grip on to.'

Max woke up to hear an incredible noise: a screaming in the air, and a tearing noise outside the window. He got up and looked out of the windows and wondered if he was still dreaming – or watching an old B movie. The plane trees all around the square were bent almost flat, straining at their roots; an enormous sheet of what looked like metal was literally flying through the air. It was a huge street sign; it crashed into a tree and fell, awkwardly. Dark shapes were hurling along the ground like great black rats; they were, he realized, dustbins. Clouds of dust, tangled with sheets of newspaper and polythene, swirled along the street, caught in the branches of the broken trees. It was completely deserted; he looked at his watch. It was two in the morning. He ran to the back of the house, looked over at the gardens; a great tree had fallen, crashed from a garden two houses along, crushing the fences. The roof of the conservatory extension, Angie's pride and joy, was smashed in by another fallen tree; half the shrubs had been torn up and were either twisted and caught up in the trees' branches, or vanished altogether.

'Angie,' shouted Max, running back into the bedroom. 'Angie, get up. It's a nightmare out there. It's the end of the world. Get up.'

Angie shot out of bed.

'What is it? Are the boys OK?'

'Don't know,' said Max. 'I'll check.'

Up on the fourth floor, the little boys slept sweetly, impervious to the drama; the nanny was staring out of the window, transfixed.

'The lights have gone,' she said. 'I just tried. Angie, do we have candles?'

'Sure. I'll get them. I'll just buzz down and see if Gran's all right.'

'Mrs Wicks isn't there,' said the nanny, 'she was with her – her friend.'

'Oh God,' said Angie, 'I hope she's OK. What is this, what's going on?'

'I told you, it's the end of the world,' said Max.

In the morning they could see that it was not the end of the world. But it was the beginning of the end of a great many smaller ones.

The television was not working, but the radio was full of it, of stories of the greatest hurricane to have hit England for over 100 years, great destructive gusts running at up to 120 miles an hour, causing almost inestimable damage, of great forests torn up, of tons of shingle being thrown from Brighton beach smashing windows and doors, of horse boxes and caravans, lifted like so many toys and tossed around in the air, of roads and railway lines blocked by fallen trees, of people dead. It

694

was a disaster such as the gentle climate of Britain had scarcely ever produced.

Their telephone was out of order; Max walked down a Piccadilly strangely deserted in the blustery sunshine, and used the public phones in the Ritz. He called Hartest; Georgina sounded cheerful. They had lost several trees down the Great Drive, the boathouse had been literally tossed into the air, a couple of the stone statues had been lost from the terrace, and half the stable roof had gone, but they were comparatively sheltered, they were lucky. Martin and Catriona had several windows smashed, and had lost a lot of their roof. Alexander had been up all night, fretting, pacing the house, worrying about the slates, the domed roof on the Rotunda, the tall downstairs windows, but everything was all right and he was calm now, busy with Martin and the circular saw, clearing the drive.

Charlotte had not even heard the storm.

Mrs Wicks and Clifford had been asleep – 'In separate rooms, I hope,' said Angie, 'they're not married yet' – but Clifford had woken to hear the window of his back basement smashing as a metal dustbin was blown against it. He had greatly enjoyed coping with the emergency and activating his generator. It had put him in mind of the Blitz, he said, when he had been an air-raid warden.

Max had coffee in the Ritz dining room, and then decided to go to Praegers. It was still strangely deserted; the trains and tubes were not running, there were hardly any cars. Hundreds of suburban roads had been blocked by the falling trees; people were literally trapped at home.

He suddenly remembered, with a sense of dread, about the Dempster column. He bought a paper and opened it with shaking hands. There was nothing. He felt initial relief and then intense anxiety again. There was tomorrow and tomorrow and tomorrow . . .

Max walked down to St James's and along to the Praeger building. There was nobody there. He used his pass key and went in; the lift wasn't working so he walked up the stairs to the fourth floor. It was eerie. No lights, no sound. It was cold.

He went into the trading room; the screens were all dead.

'Shit,' said Max aloud.

He walked along the corridor and down the stairs slowly to the first floor. The executive floor where Chuck and Freddy had their offices. Maybe he could put the desolation to good use.

Chuck's door was locked; well, it would have been. Shireen would have the key, but Shireen wasn't there. Trapped by fallen trees out in Bromley, no doubt, where she lived. Max hoped she was all right. He was actually rather fond of Shireen.

He tried Freddy's office. That was not locked. He pushed the door carefully, slowly. This was great. He could go through Freddy's files and – 'Good morning, Max.' It was Freddy. He smiled his chilled smile at Max. 'Not many of us in. Can I help in any way?'

'No thanks,' said Max, furious at himself for being caught, at Freddy for being there. 'Your flat was obviously OK.'

'Fine. Just a little damage in the square gardens. And you?'

'Oh – not too bad.' He didn't want to get involved in discussion of damage to houses; didn't want Freddy to know where he had spent the night.

'And Hartest?' said Freddy. 'Any damage there? Have you spoken to your – to Lord Caterham?'

Max looked at him very coldly. 'No,' he said, 'he was out, moving trees. But I spoke to my sister, and she was fine. How kind of you to be concerned, Freddy.'

He went back to the Ritz and tried Mortons. No reply. He decided to go into the City. There were a few buses running; he got one as far as Chancery Lane and then walked. Most people were friendly, eager to talk, drawn out of their usual reticence by the drama; but as he walked down Fleet Street, he saw people, quite ordinary respectable-looking people, helping themselves to shoes, jumpers, shirts from broken shop windows. It was a sobering sight: the English, looting. He reached Mortons at about eleven; there was nobody there, so he walked on to Coates Cafe. Coates Cafe had a small clutch of people there, dealers mostly, enjoying an extremely leisurely breakfast. They'd been there for hours, they told him; then they were going to try the screens again. Jake wasn't there.

By midday a handful of the dealers were working; things, they said, were sluggish. Max shared a liquid lunch with a couple of friends, and then at around three decided to go home to Pond Place. The quiet, the emptiness was beginning to get on his nerves. It made him uneasy. As he passed St Paul's a cab came past, and he got in it. The cab had its radio on. In the first few hours of trading, said the newscaster, the Dow Jones Industrial Average had crashed by over 100 points. It's biggest ever one-day fall, the bland, emotionless voice said. And so it was that the news began to drift into London. The real news. The real news of the real disaster.

It was 16 October.

The weekend was quiet. The phone lines were restored. Angie called a builder friend on Saturday morning, and had him send over some men to fix the conservatory roof. She and Max and the boys got in the car and drove around in a great convoy with what seemed like half the population of London, looking at the damage in the parks. It was a sad and ugly sight. On the Sunday Charlotte said she was going down to Hartest. Max went with her. That was sad too. At least a hundred trees had been torn up in the parkland, and lay where they had fallen, like great moribund dinosaurs. Alexander was very upset. He loved his trees; he paced up and down the drive, looking wretched. He grieved over the boathouse too; it had been put up by his grandfather, he said, it had been part of the fabric of his life. Max grew impatient with him; he felt sorrier for the Dunbars, who were virtually homeless. Georgina had suggested they move into Hartest, while their roof was fixed, but Catriona had refused to consider it. Georgina said she wasn't sure if it was shyness, or simply a feeling that she ought to be at home. Either way, Alexander said he was glad they hadn't accepted the invitation.

And then it was Monday. Monday, 19 October. Still nothing in the *Mail* Diary. Max went in early. He felt keyed up, edgy, not sure why. When the screens first went on, he blinked, thought it must be an error. They were a mass of red. Just endless red. Vernon Bligh rushed over to the trading desk, his smirking expression gone, panic engrained suddenly on his sharp features. 'The market's one twenty down,' he said and his voice was hollow with shock. It was normally five, at the most ten.

Max felt himself begin to sweat; he got on the phone and called Jake, who was calm, almost amused. 'Told you,' he said, 'told you it was too much. Only thing is to sell. Sell fast. And pray for a dead-cat bounce, and then sell short.'

The dead-cat bounce is an old and very sick joke in the banking fraternity. It is said that if a dead cat hits the floor of a securities house, it will bounce. Between hit (when prices are at their lowest) and bounce there is money to be made.

Max sold. He did not sell alone. The market went down and down, into a black hole of despair. The cat lay comatose all day.

Every share went down by 25 per cent. Several by 50 per cent. And the really wild high fliers by 70 per cent. The dealers sat at their screens and tried to hold back the red sea. But they failed. It was panic, on a screaming, nightmarish, despairing scale, sharply intensified by the fact that for many of the dealers, personal fortunes were melting away as well. By mid-morning they sat at their desks, head in hands, faces wiped blank by despair, most of them refusing to answer their telephones. Or just staring at their screens in disbelief, watching the dollars pouring off the New York market.

By that evening at least one eighth had been wiped off London share prices.

Max and Tommy went out that night to eat at the Pizza Express in the Fulham Road. It was full of people, all talking quite cheerfully about the crash. Had everyone heard, everyone was saying, three, four billion pounds wiped off the stock market. Nobody seemed to take it very seriously; it was just another chapter, a bit of excitement, in the fairy story of Easy Money. As they drove back along the Fulham Road there was a report on the radio: Wall Street had fallen 500 points. 'Jesus,' said Max, 'it can't have done. Five hundred. Not five hundred.'

It had.

The crash followed the sun, rolling round the world from East to West. In the morning Tokyo went down, then Hong Kong. After London, New York again. By Tuesday night the London Stock Exchange had lost a fifth of its value. Some of the richest financiers in the world were wiped out; Australian markets suffered hideous damage, as a result of the Hong Kong suspension of trading. Rupert Murdoch lost $700 million in one day. Robert Holmes à Court was ruined. Everyone talked in superlatives. John Phelan, chairman of the New York Stock Exchange, talked about financial meltdown. Jimmy Goldsmith forecast the end of the world.

There were various theories advanced as to its cause: that the stock market had simply overheated; that it was part of the inevitable rise and fall pattern of the stock market, and after the phenomenal rise there must be a correspondingly phenomenal fall; that it was initially at any rate a result of programme trading, the process whereby if a stock moved to minus 2 per cent, the signals went out on the screens to sell; that trades were made much more quickly than they had been pre Big Bang and the panic chain was set in motion faster; that there was no control, as there would have been pre Big Bang, from the jobbers who could have called at least a temporary halt, stopped the panic selling. Whatever the reason, the market fell and fell, on a great unstoppable roller coaster.

The dead cat did bounce briefly; on the middle of Tuesday in New York, evening in London. There was talk of suspending trading on the New York Stock Exchange, which was at that point in touch with the White House. It wasn't suspended and the market rose by 200 points; but as the insurers moved in, selling furiously on the futures market to protect their investors, it fell again, lower still.

By the Wednesday, what had been a shocking excitement, a near fantasy, had become hard reality. Hundreds of thousands of people were ruined. And Max saw Freddy Praeger, sitting at his desk in St James's, ashen, shaking, chain smoking, refusing to go home, and realized the full extent of what he had done to Praegers.

That weekend, Tommy received a call from the *Daily Mail*. So did Max. Max rang Hartest; Nanny answered the phone.

'Nanny, you may get a call from the press,' he said.

'We have already,' said Nanny.

'Oh God. What did you say?'

'I told them your father was away. And that if they had nothing better to do than ring us up, they should start looking for different jobs.'

'Nanny, you're wonderful.'

On the Monday Freddy and Chuck took off for New York.

And the story was in the diary:

Max the Mystery Man

Persistent rumours surround the background of Maximilian, Viscount Hadleigh to the effect that Lord Caterham is not in fact his true father. Viscount Hadleigh, who works as a dealer in his American grand-father's bank, Praegers, has been too busy in the aftermath of the crash to comment on the story, and Lord Caterham was unavailable at the family's Wiltshire seat yesterday.

Lord Hadleigh, a colourful character, who has worked as a photographic model for several years, and who was until recently engaged to Gemma Morton, debutante daughter of Richard, the stockbroker king, now spends much of his leisure time with Mrs Angela Praeger, the widow of his uncle 'Baby' Praeger. Mrs Praeger, who runs her own property company, has been close to the family for many years.

Mr Tommy Soames-Maxwell, a close friend of the family, who shares a house with Viscount Hadleigh, was also unavailable for comment over the weekend.

Max rang Angie. 'The shit's hit the fan,' he said.

'I know. I suppose it could be worse.'

'It could. It could be on the front page.'

'Just keep saying nothing,' said Charles. 'It's the only thing that will work.'

Jake Joseph called. 'What's all this, my son? I always said you were a little bastard. Seems I was right.'

'It's a load of shit,' said Max. 'Just a complete fabrication.'

'Of course it is,' said Jake. 'I hope this doesn't mean your gorgeous sister was born on the wrong side of the blanket as well.'

'Oh go to hell,' said Max irritably.

Tommy rang to say he was really enjoying it and couldn't he just make up one story to tell them?

Max said if he did, he was a dead man. Dead by starvation.

Several other people called. Max decided to use Nanny's line. It seemed to work.

Max took Shireen to lunch at the Ritz.

'It's exciting you being in the papers,' she said, looking at him interestedly. 'How did that story start?'

'I can't imagine,' said Max, 'but you know what they say. Never believe anything you read in the papers.'

'Yes,' said Shireen, gazing at him, her eyes interestingly bland, 'and you know what else they say. There's no smoke without fire.'

Max looked at her thoughtfully. 'If you promise not to say anything to anybody, I'll tell you how it started.'

'Oh Max, of course I promise.'

'It's an old old story that's gone around for years. It's because some half-witted servant we had went around saying that I was adopted. It resurfaces from time to time.'

'But why?'

'I told you. She was half-witted. And my father had fired her. I suppose it was her idea of revenge. She just went on putting it about. That's all. But you really must not talk to anyone about that.'

'Oh Max, you know I won't.'

Max gave her some more champagne, patted her hand and turned the conversation to Praegers. There seemed a strong possibility that Praegers London was going belly up.

'Bretts went right down the pan, apparently. And that was just one of Freddy's little games,' said Max to Charlotte. 'He's off to do a whitewash job. See what they can haul out of the ashes. While Fred's away.'

'Well they can't do much,' said Charlotte. 'Fred's not stupid.'

'They can buy some time. Praegers New York hasn't done too badly. I just talked to your friend Gabe. They have huge reserves, and they weren't seriously exposed. It's my guess Chuck is going to try and transfer some money from New York to London, to cover the losses.'

'He can't do that, surely. Not without Grandpa knowing.'

'He probably could. Chris Hill would have access to the funds. He could certainly authorize a transfer. But Grandpa would pretty soon know about it. I suppose they can at least buy some time.'

'Not a lot, I hope,' said Charlotte.

When Max was getting ready to leave that night, the girl in reception phoned up to him.

'There's a couple of reporters down here,' she said. 'What shall I do with them?'

'Just ignore them,' said Max.

He went along to see Shireen.

'The press is downstairs,' he said, 'don't start talking to them, will you? You'll have your picture all over the papers in no time.'

'Max, of course I won't.'

Max rang Nanny and told her to unplug the telephones.

The following day, both the *Mail* and *Mirror* had a picture of Shireen on one of their inside pages, and a story about what the *Mail* described as Below Stairs Talk, and the *Mirror* described as the Servant Girl's Revenge.

Charles was cautiously optimistic; he said if this was what the papers were reduced to, they clearly hadn't got anything more tangible to say.

Nanny was indignant, and said Max could have warned her, but that she and Mrs Tallow had both dealt with the reporters very firmly, and told them the girl in question had left twenty years earlier.

'I told you not to talk to them,' said Max.

'I wanted to talk to them,' said Nanny. 'Mrs Tallow and I are enjoying it.'

'Oh,' said Max humbly. 'Well, don't say anything more, will you, Nanny? And keep it from Alexander.'

'Don't worry about it,' said Nanny.

Shireen was defiantly apologetic.

'They promised they wouldn't use it, they said they just wanted some background.'

'Just the same, I told you not to talk to them. Honestly, Shireen.'

'Sorry, Max.'

Max grinned at her. 'Never mind. You can repay me one day.'

The strange thing was, he found, now that the thing he had been dreading for so long, the doubt over his parentage, had been publicly cast, that people were talking about it, discussing it, gossiping about it, debating it, he simply didn't care. It seemed infinitely foolish somehow, unbelievable, as unlikely to him as it sounded, as it looked, there in the paper, in black and white.

He was almost – not enjoying it, but just possibly savouring it. He embellished and embroidered the story of the sacked servant, and when nobody seemed to be interested in it any more, he was almost put out.

'I think,' he said to Charlotte, 'we may have laid the ghost.'

'I think you're speaking a little soon,' she said.

Freddy and Chuck came back after three days. They looked tired, but considerably more cheerful. There was something else about them; something Charlotte and Max didn't like.

'They look as if they've got something on us,' said Charlotte. 'I'm worried.'

They had come in at midday; they went for a long lunch at the Ritz, and then continued drinking for some time in the boardroom. At six o'clock Chuck wandered into the trading room.

'Come and join us in the boardroom,' he said, 'have a drink.'

'Sorry. Got a prior engagement,' said Max cheerfully.

'This is more important,' said Chuck, with one of his plastic smiles. 'I think you'll agree when you hear.'

Max went down to the boardroom with a sense of vague anxiety but no more. He could not believe Chuck and Freddy could have pulled off anything very dramatic. Charlotte was there, looking equally cheerful.

Chuck had his back to them as they went in; he turned to face them.

'Sit down,' he said. 'This business in the papers must have been awkward for you.'

'Not really,' said Max. 'It seems to have died a death now. I wonder how they got the story in the first place.'

'I can't imagine,' said Chuck. 'Drink?'

'No,' said Max. 'Thank you.'

Chuck shrugged. 'You could need it,' he said. 'Charlotte?'

'No thank you,' said Charlotte. 'Er – is everything all right?'

Chuck turned innocent eyes on her, gave her his most charming smile.

'Absolutely fine. Why shouldn't it be?'

702

'Oh – we thought there were problems. After the crash.'

'Well naturally we have problems. Everyone does. But nothing that can't be contained. No cause for serious concern.'

Charlotte's eyes met Max's. They've done a transfer, said her look. Chris Hill's played ball with them.

'Good,' she said. 'I'm so pleased.'

'Now,' said Chuck, 'are you sure you don't want a drink?'

'Yes, I'm quite sure,' said Charlotte puzzled.

Chuck shrugged. 'OK. You're going to take this neat then? No watering down? No Valium?'

'Chuck,' said Max. 'Take what neat? Get to the point.'

'OK. It's about your house, Max. Or rather your – your father's house.'

Max felt a thud of alarm. What on earth did Hartest have to do with all this?

'Yes?'

'He's very fond of it. Isn't he?'

'Of course he is,' said Max irritably. 'It's a beautiful house and it's the family seat.'

'Er – yes. That means it actually belongs to the family and all that?'

'Yes of course.'

Chuck shook his head, regret oozing out of his brown eyes. 'Sorry. It doesn't.'

'I beg your pardon?' Max was too shocked, too caught off guard to respond in a way that was at all clever.

'I said it doesn't.' Chuck smiled at him, sat down on one of the arms of the great carver chair that stood at the head of the table. 'I'm sorry, but you're wrong. While I was over there, I did quite a lot of investigation into the bank's affairs. Very complex, some of them. Your grandfather has some very interesting assets. The ranch, for instance, in Venezuela, worth billions now. A fortune in Swiss francs. And then, this English property.'

'What?' said Max. He felt very sick suddenly. Freddy was standing by the window looking at him, smiling his dreadful chill smile.

'Hartest House,' said Chuck ' – is that its correct name? – belongs to Praegers. Of course it's small beer, as you say over here. But every little is going to help at the moment. Unless of course you can let me have – let me see, what was it? – oh yes, six million pounds right away, I shall have to put it on the market. I'm calling in the loan.'

Alexander sat, his head in his hands, at the table in the gun room.

'It was years ago,' he said, 'years and years. Your mother was still alive.

Fred let me have the money; there was dry rot, right through the structure, and the house needed a new roof. It was a formal arrangement; I wouldn't have agreed to anything else.'

'Nor would Grandpa,' said Max grimly.

'Possibly not. Anyway, things have been difficult lately. The estate hasn't entirely been paying its way. I got – behind with the repayments.'

'How far behind?' Charlotte's voice was oddly harsh.

'Oh – I haven't paid for – well, for about three years.'

'Three years! Daddy, that's a long time.'

'Yes, I know. I'm sorry. Darling, don't look at me like that.'

'I'm sorry. I wish we'd known, that's all.'

'Yes, well. I didn't want to worry you. I went to see Fred, last year. He was – quite good about it. Really. Told me to sort it out as and when.'

'That doesn't sound quite like Grandpa,' said Charlotte. 'And – ?'

'Well – I had planned to. Of course. At such time as I got straight.'

'And things are looking pretty crooked still?'

'Yes. I'm afraid so.'

'Was there anything in writing then? Last year I mean. From Grandpa?'

'Er – no. Not exactly. At the time he wasn't too well.'

'Shit,' said Max.

'Daddy,' said Charlotte, feeling rather cold, 'Daddy, do you have a copy of the mortgage document? That I can show my lawyer friend?'

Alexander's face had taken on its helplessly distant look. Charlotte felt her heart begin to sink.

'No. Yes. Oh, I don't know. Does it matter?'

'Yes, Daddy. Yes, I think it does. But I'm sure it can be sorted. I mean there's no way Grandpa is going to allow them to call in that loan. It's ridiculous. We're family.'

'Grandpa's away,' said Max, 'on his second honeymoon. Remember?'

'Max, don't be absurd. This is 1987. People are contactable, even on the high seas.'

'I suppose so.' Max sounded gloomy.

They started going through his files. They were a nightmare, as disorderly as Virginia's had been orderly. Vets' bills were mixed up with instructions to his bank, accounts from his stockbroker with letters to the children's schools. Finally, after a long weekend of searching, they found the relevant document. Charlotte took it to Charles St Mullin.

'Have you read it?' he said.

'Yes I have. I'm just hoping I've misunderstood.'

'I'm afraid you haven't.'

The agreement Fred III had entered into with Alexander was not quite a

704

standard mortgage. It stipulated that in the event of Alexander defaulting on the payments, the house became the property of the bank. 'In other words, Chuck Drew was justified in making his threat. Making up the arrears would not be sufficient. But you do have twenty-eight days,' said Charles. 'That's how long it would take them to get a possession order. All is not completely lost.'

'Grandfather is an old bastard,' said Charlotte. 'I can't believe he would have done this.'

She was very upset.

They sent Fred a fax on the liner currently off the coast of Fiji – at least he was unlikely to have seen the English papers there, thought Charlotte – asking him to call them on the subject of the mortgage on Hartest. After twenty-four hours, when there was no reply, Charlotte sent a second one, marked urgent.

An hour later, Betsey called. The line was surprisingly good.

'Grandma, how lovely to hear from you. Are you having a good time?'

'Wonderful, darling. I feel seventeen again.'

'Oh, that's great. And Grandpa?'

'Grandpa is having the time of his life. He's organized a poker school, and he's also absolutely determined to win the quoits championship.'

'Well that's great too. Er – Grandma, is it possible to speak to Grandpa?'

'No, dear, I'm sorry.' Betsey sounded embarrassed. 'He was – a little annoyed at your letter. He had left the strictest instructions that he was only to be contacted in a real emergency. He's spent hours, you know, talking to them all about the crash, and he says enough is enough, and he wants to be allowed to have the rest of his holiday in peace.'

'But Grandma, this is a real emergency. We could lose Hartest.'

'Oh darling, surely not.'

'Grandma, we could. Please please tell him. It's very involved, and I'll explain if you like, but we could.'

'Well – maybe you'd better talk to him. I'll try and get him to call you.'

They waited for a call from Fred; none came.

After another twenty-four hours, Charlotte looked at Max. 'What do we do? We can't force him to talk to us.'

'Send another fax?'

'We could try. Spell it out.'

Charlotte and Max spent hours on the letter (to be signed by Charlotte), struggling to sound urgent without being peremptory, concerned but not hysterical, reproachful (towards Freddy and Chuck) but not recriminatory. They finished by saying they knew Fred would

705

not want his grandchildren to lose Hartest through what was clearly an administrative hiccup.

'I hope that'll be all right,' Charlotte said nervously to Max as they sent the fax.

'Of course it will be,' he said.

It wasn't all right. Fred sent her a furious fax back accusing Charlotte of paranoia, Alexander of gross inefficiency – 'I told him to get the thing sorted when he came over' – and the lot of them of whining hypocrisy. 'If you're so concerned about saving your house, I suggest you do what should have been done years ago and make it pay its way. Turn it over to the public. I've told Chris Hill and the board to deal with it in my absence. I'm sure they won't see you on the streets. Please allow me to finish my holiday in peace.'

'Oh God,' said Charlotte.
'Shit,' said Max.
Georgina burst into tears.

'What I can't understand,' said Charlotte, 'is why Grandpa is being so Machiavellian. What's it to him, for God's sake? Why does he want to see Hartest go down the pan?'

'I think,' said Angie slowly, 'that he just doesn't like Alexander. I think he suspects Virginia wasn't happy with him, and I also think the whole thing about Hartest, you know, Alexander refusing to turn it over to the public when he can't actually afford to run it, and insisting it stays a family house, just enrages him. Baby told me he was furious with Alexander when he asked him for the money for the roof and the rebuilding. He told him he ought to give it up then. Alexander refused, point blank, and there was a big scene. Why Grandpa gave in in the end was something of a mystery.'

'I wish I'd known,' said Max, punching the air furiously with his fist. 'I wish I'd known the bloody place was mortgaged. I never dreamt, never for a moment.'

'Well, nobody did,' said Angie. 'Even Baby thought Fred had just given Alexander the money. Because of Virginia. Apparently the worry had driven her to drinking again.'

'Evil old bastard,' said Max.

Chuck Drew told Max he had a buyer for Hartest. 'A cash buyer. My client, Mr Al-Fabah. He's looking for an English property. He's wanted one for some time, and considers Hartest would be perfect. In fact, I was going to phone your father and arrange for Mr Al-Fabah to see it this weekend. He has some very interesting plans for it.'

Max thought about Hartest. He thought about it, standing there in its small, sheltered kingdom, in the heart of the parkland. He thought of all the times he had stood at the top of the Great Drive, looking down at it, and taken it totally for granted, seeing it simply as home, somewhere to live, to be looked after, to take his friends to show off, and he felt sharply ashamed. He thought, as if he was actually seeing it for the first time, of the way it stood, as if carved out of the sky behind it, gracious, welcoming, perfectly proportioned, the curving steps, the tall windows, the pillars studding the front, the great dome of the Rotunda pushing up into the sky; he saw the parkland filled with the grazing deer, the black and white swans on the lake, the Hart a ribbon of blue winding into the woods. He thought of how, as you pushed open the great front door and went into the house, it was quiet and cool and calm; he thought of the flying staircase, soaring up from the Rotunda, and suddenly, sharply, he saw his mother coming down it, smiling at him; he thought of running up the staircase and along the corridor and up again to the nurseries and to Nanny when he came home from school; he thought of being in the gun room with Alexander, his favourite room then, small, dark, wood-panelled, smelling of leather and wood and the dogs, being there on his twelfth birthday when Alexander had given him his first gun. He thought of the parties at Hartest, huge dinner parties, garden parties, dances, shooting lunches, meets, the house providing a perfect backdrop, an endlessly gracious setting for English country life and its gentle, unchanging rhythm. And he thought of Al-Fabah in all his infinite vulgarity, his black-crow-like wives, his Chanel-clad call girls, his stretch limos, his bodyguards, his gold rings, his gleaming little dark eyes, he thought of him, getting his hands on it, moving in on it, and he felt physically sick. And for the first time he saw Hartest as Alexander did, something infinitely precious, infinitely dear to him, something to be preserved at all costs, from all comers.

'We have to stop it,' he said to Charlotte. 'There must be something we can do. Someone who can help.'

Chapter 61

Charlotte, November 1987

Everyone thought, of course, that she'd approached him. Nobody would ever, had ever believed, that she'd bumped into him as she left the Pine Street offices, after a fruitless appeal to Chris Hill for a stay of execution. Even when it was all over, they wouldn't believe her. And why should they? It was such an extremely unlikely story. But it was true.

'Charlotte!' he had said. 'Charlotte, how lovely to see you. And why are you crying? What's the matter?'

And she had looked up at him, and instead of scowling at him, spitting in his face, as she had always vowed she would do if she ever saw him again, she had been so pleased to see him, to see someone civilized and friendly and unthreatening, that she had smiled at him, and said, 'Oh Jeremy, it's lovely to see you too.'

Al-Fabah wanted Hartest. He wanted it very badly. He had been to see it twice now, arriving in his limo, with Chuck Drew and a different girl each time, his bodyguards with them in a second car, waiting outside, staring up at the house, wandering round the grounds, shouting at one another, laughing, throwing stones in the lake.

Charlotte had no faith in the success of the trip to New York, but she felt it had to be made. 'We certainly won't persuade Chris Hill if we don't ask him.'

Chris Hill was asked and was not persuaded.

'I'm sorry, Charlotte,' he said, looking at her as if she was a distasteful small insect, 'but I can't delay things any longer. Praegers London, as you know, took a considerable pasting in the crash, and it would be wrong of me not to take any measures which will help to restore its fortunes.'

He had called London; Chuck Drew had told him that Mr Al-Fabah had the money, and wanted to expedite matters. He was tired of living in hotels; he wanted a house.

'The workmen would like to start in a week or so, Charlotte,' he said. 'I hope you'll be able to be cooperative.'

Charlotte walked out of his office and slammed the door.

And then she went down to the street. And then she met Jeremy Foster.

'Come along, my darling,' he had said, 'let me see if I can't cheer you up. How about tea?'

Charlotte found herself nodding rather weakly (the weakness contributed to by certain rather sharp physical recollections).

He took her to the Palm Court at the Plaza and bought her a wonderful cream tea, which she had amazed herself by wolfing down, and was amazed still more by the fact that not only did she stop crying, but she started talking to him, and giggling and generally feeling a great deal better. She had forgotten how he could always do that to her: charm her, amuse her into a state of careless, almost reckless happiness. And then somehow it had been much later, almost six o'clock, and they had moved into the Oak Bar and had a bottle of champagne and she had started telling him about Hartest and the Arabs and how she couldn't bear it, couldn't bear any of it, and if only, if only Fred had been around, none of it need happen, or at least probably need not happen; and Jeremy had said how much did she need, to get her out of the mess, to save Hartest, at least until Fred came home, and she had said six million and he had said dollars or pounds and she had said pounds, and he had told her it was hers, for at least the foreseeable future, for old times' sake, and because he had been so sorry, so terribly terribly sorry about what had happened and he had missed her and at least this way he would be sure of seeing her occasionally, as he thought he might insist on a stage payment of ten pounds a day or maybe a week, to be delivered personally by her, probably to the studio; and she had said no, no, she couldn't possibly take that sort of money from him, and he had said nonsense, of course she must, it was nothing to him, nothing at all, or certainly very little, he had made a very serious amount of money only weeks before, having (entirely thanks to some advice from her grandfather) sold a great deal of stock at the top of the market and stashed the money away safely in all kinds of extremely safe and secure places. And then he had added (having seen her face, reading the expression on it) that of course she need have no worries about him and his motives, there were no strings attached whatsoever, except that they might be friends once more and have the occasional cream tea. He was a totally reformed character, he said, his marriage was in a very healthy condition, there was a new little Foster on the way, and he had heard besides that she was very much involved with a charming young man at Praegers, and he was hoping for an invitation to the wedding.

'You can regard the whole thing as a business deal if you wish,' he said, 'we will have the lawyers draw up any number of documents, and when Hartest is safely and unarguably yours again, then you can think about how you would like to repay me.'

And finally, Charlotte had given in, unable to resist the glorious prospect of Hartest being safely and unarguably hers, or rather Alexander's, and in no danger of any kind from Mr Al-Fabah, or Chuck Drew or Freddy Praeger or even her grandfather.

And then, slightly the worse for rather more than half the bottle of champagne, weak, foolish with relief and happiness, she had been leaving the hotel with him, actually coming out of the door, and Jeremy had had his arm round her, and she had been laughing up at him and kissing him first on one cheek and then on another, and she had looked down to the bottom of the steps and there looking up at her was Gabe Hoffman.

It had been the most terrible row. The worst Charlotte could ever remember. Gabe had told her she was a slut and a whore, and that as far as he was concerned their relationship was over; she had told him he was crazed with jealousy, and arrogant beyond all belief; if he thought she would even consider continuing in a relationship where trust played no part whatsoever he must be in serious need of psychiatric treatment.

It went on for hours, the pair of them caught in an endless vituperative vortex; finally Charlotte, exhausted, despairing, too angry to feel pain, left, just walked out.

Charlotte was in her small office at the bank one afternoon, trying not to think about life either with or without Gabe, trying to believe the endless frustration and boredom of her working life would one day come to an end, when the phone rang on her desk. It was a call from New York and it was Fred III.

'Charlotte. Get over here fast, would you? And bring Max with you.' He spoke as if he was on the other side of London, rather than the Atlantic. 'I'd like to know what the hell is going on.'

'Grandpa! I thought you were still on your cruise.'

'Oh, I got tired of that. Dreadful people. All old. Couldn't stand them any longer. And your grandmother was worried about you and that house of yours. Quite unnecessarily, I hear.'

'Yes,' said Charlotte, 'yes, it's fine.'

'I didn't like what I heard about that. And I've been hearing other things, Charlotte. Things I don't like at all. I really need an explanation.'

Charlotte told him he would get one.

She and Max booked themselves onto a flight next day. They talked to John Fisher first.

'Are you with us? If we need you?'

John Fisher went first red, then white. Then he said he was.

710

'We'll ring you,' said Charlotte.

Fred was in his old office; he looked tanned and well. He was chewing on a new cigar.

'Sit down,' he said, gesturing at the chairs opposite the desk, as if they had just walked in from another part of the building, rather than travelled three thousand miles. 'Do you want coffee?'

'Yes please,' said Charlotte. 'How's Grandma?'

'She's perfectly well. Never better.'

'Good,' said Max. Fred glared at him.

They waited, while the coffee was ordered, brought in, poured.

'OK,' said Fred. 'Let's start with the house. Is it true Jeremy Foster gave you the money to clear the loan? That you went whining to him?'

'No,' said Charlotte.

'Oh?'

'I didn't go whining to him, and he didn't give me the money. It's a business arrangement and – '

'Oh really? And how do you propose to pay back such a sum? For God's sake, Charlotte, have you no sense of any kind? First you compromise yourself and the bank's good name, by becoming the mistress of a major client – '

'Grandpa, that's not – '

'Be quiet. You had an affair with Jeremy Foster. It was an appalling thing to do. Appalling. And now, just as people might be beginning to forget about it, you re-establish the relationship.'

'Grandpa, I didn't.'

'Oh really? I heard, from a fairly reliable source, that you were seen coming out of the Plaza Hotel with him. Behaving in a fairly indiscreet way.'

'Yes but – '

'And the next thing I hear is that you hand over his draft for six million pounds. It is almost beyond belief, Charlotte. I've told Chuck Drew to repay the money into Foster's bank account. I will not have it.'

'What? You did what?'

'You heard me. The money is going back.'

'But it can't. It's nothing to do with you. Grandpa, that is so unfair.'

'I think it's perfectly fair and it has a great deal to do with me. I will not have the reputation of the bank compromised. I find it almost incomprehensible that you should feel it is perfectly acceptable to take money on such a vast scale from a major client. I have to tell you that any faith I might have had in you has been severely shaken.'

Max was very white. He stared at Fred in silence for a while and then

711

said, 'Grandpa, let's talk about some other trust that might be shaken. Let's talk about your grandson for a start. Do you know what he's been doing to Praegers? Putting it on the line, that's what. Underwriting money that he has no right to, in order to promote deals and clients in which he has a vested interest? Do you know how much Praegers lost in the crash? Personally, unnecessarily, not through client companies losing money. Around one hundred million.'

'Oh for God's sake,' said Fred. 'I've looked at the portfolio. You're talking nonsense.'

'You mean the hundred million's gone back. Well, you might take a look at what's been going on here then,' said Max. 'I have a very shrewd suspicion some large transfers have been made.'

'I will,' said Fred, and he put out a finger and stabbed on the intercom. 'Get Chris Hill in here, will you? You'd better know what you're talking about,' he said to Max, 'or you could be up on some very nasty charges indeed. And don't think the fact you're my grandson will help you, because it won't.'

Chris Hill came in looking very calm, very in control.

Yes, he said, he had made certain transfers to London. They had been well within his discretion, and had merely been designed to protect London in the uneasy days after the crash. Freddy had been perhaps slightly reckless, but he had only been acting from an excess of enthusiasm. He did not believe Fred III would find anything seriously untoward in the management of any of the accounts.

'You will,' said Charlotte, when Chris Hill had gone. 'You'll find plenty. Salesmen have been victimized. We have actual evidence. From one of those salesmen.'

'Oh really? A friend of yours no doubt?'

'Yes, a friend,' said Max, 'but an employee of Praegers long before we even knew him. I'll get him on the phone for you, right now. He'll tell you.'

Fred looked, for the first time, uncertain. Then he said, 'Maybe later.'

'Grandpa,' said Charlotte, 'a lot of bad things have been going on. Honestly. Sharp practices, things you'd never tolerate. Buying up huge blocks of shares, to push the price up, before the clients bought them, insider trading. Even, we think –' She stopped, too afraid suddenly to go on.

'Even what?'

'Oh – more of the same.'

'And what have you been doing all this time? I have heard very little evidence of your making much impression on things.'

'Grandpa, I haven't been allowed to do anything. I'm back on grunt work.' She looked at him and tried to smile. 'Honestly. It's been – difficult.'

'Ah,' said Fred. 'So now we come to it.'

'I'm sorry?'

'You've been feeling sorry for yourself. Jealous. Resentful. A very good hotbed for nurturing dangerous fantasies. Good God, Charlotte, I'm shocked at you. It's pathetic. Time you grew up a little.'

'Grandpa, they are not fantasies. Please talk to John Fisher. Please.'

'Oh, John Fisher. Is that your victimized salesman?'

'Yes it is.'

Fred hesitated. Then he said, 'No, I really don't think it's necessary. It's all very clear to me. I think you'd both better get out. Go back to London. I don't know quite what I'm going to do about you. About your futures. But I certainly need time to think. And you'd better tell that father of yours to get out of Hartest. It's back on the market.'

'Grandpa, you can't do that. You can't. It's his home.' Angry at herself, Charlotte felt tears at the back of her eyes.

'Indeed? I seem to remember a fairly substantial little shack in London. I don't see him quite on the streets. Now if you would be good enough to excuse me, I have a great deal to do.'

'What do you think they did?' said Charlotte. 'How do you think they put the money back?'

They were sitting in a taxi, driving back to Kennedy. Charlotte was stunned, numb with shock. She knew she should have been angry, outraged, but she couldn't feel anything. Not even a confrontation with Gabe Hoffman in the corridor when he had stared at her stony-faced and then turned on his heel had pierced her feelings. Max, white-faced beside her, had not said a word since they left Pine Street.

'God knows. God knows. I could try finding out from Shireen. But what good would it do? He's blind. He's crazy.'

'He's dangerous,' said Charlotte, 'the whole situation is dangerous.'

'Who for? Not us. I fancy our time as employees of Praegers is over. At least we won't have to worry any more.'

'What about Hartest? We have to worry about that.'

'I'm not at all sure he can make us pay the money back.'

'That is, if they've cleared the cheque,' said Charlotte.

'Shit,' said Max.

★

Chuck Drew had not cleared the cheque. He told them, smiling his most charming and regretful smile, that he had been so busy, he had failed to present it until the day before. And now Fred had specifically requested that he withdrew it.

'I would hate to jeopardize our relationship with our most important client,' he said, 'and your grandfather feels very strongly about it. Our relationship with Mr Al-Fabah has also been a little strained, so if he feels that a purchase of Hartest House may now after all be possible, then we shall be oiling a great many wheels all at the same time.'

'We've got to do something,' said Max. 'We've got to. Before we all sign on with the Social Security. I'm going to talk to Shireen. She's our last hope.'

He called Charlotte at home two nights later, sounding excited. 'Got him,' he said, 'I think.'

'How? Why?' said Charlotte.

'Apparently the money was put back by way of recalled loans and interest payments, things like that.'

'So?'

'So they were from the Swiss company.'

'God. How did you find out?'

He hesitated. 'Don't tell Angie. I had to promise to take Shireen to Paris for the weekend. With her mum.'

'Oh Max. Honestly.'

'It's all very well,' said Charlotte later, 'but how do we get Grandpa to believe that?'

'We have to get my little bird to sing. He'll believe her.'

'Why should he?'

'Simply because she doesn't really understand what she's saying.'

'And how will you get her to do it in the first place?'

'Oh, I've got an idea,' said Max.

Charlotte sat and listened while he got on the phone to Jake Joseph. And while he told Jake that if he could get Shireen a job as a dealer, as an assistant, as anything, even if it was only going to last for a week, he would do anything, anything in the world for him he liked.

'She's not stupid,' he kept saying, 'she's very quick. She might even be good at it. Shit, Jake, my whole life depends on it. I'll be your friend for life. I'll invest all my money in Mortons. I'll get you membership of Les A. I'll take you to Paris with Shireen and her mum. Please. For old times' sake. Go on, you bastard, you know you can do it.'

Finally, after nearly half an hour, Max grinned into the phone.

'You're a hero. Yes, you are. And yes, I'll arrange a dinner with her. I'll arrange a dozen. Yeah. Thanks, Jake. You're a true friend.'

He put down the phone and smiled at her, exhaustedly triumphant. 'Right. Jake's going to offer her a job as a trainee dealer. On his desk. He says he'll probably get fired, and I said that was fine, he could come to Praegers.'

'Max, you're in no position to offer people jobs at Praegers.'

'I *will* be able to,' said Max, 'after this.'

'And who does your friend, Mr Joseph – who I have to say I found rather nice – want to have dinner with?'

'Georgina,' said Max.

'Georgina! Surely not!'

'Yeah. He says she's the sexiest girl he's ever met. He says he only has to think about her and he gets an erection.'

'Oh,' said Charlotte. She suddenly felt rather bleak.

When Max told Shireen he had fixed for her to have a job at Mortons, and that he'd like her to go and see his grandfather with him in New York, by way of showing her gratitude, she looked at him rather shrewdly beneath her spiky black eyelashes and said she didn't see why she should, and that if he wanted her to start betraying Chuck's confidence she wasn't going to.

Max told her that if she didn't, the job at Mortons would probably not materialize, and Shireen said that was blackmail. Max said it was nothing of the sort, it was a trade, and he hoped she wasn't about to miss out on her very first one. Shireen said she'd think about it.

'She'll come,' said Max to Charlotte.

The three of them went to New York next day. Fred III refused to see them at Pine Street, and told them to get straight back to London, but when he got home to East 80th Street that night, they were all sitting in the upstairs living room, with Betsey. Betsey had her most formidable expression on, and told him that if he didn't listen to what Max and Charlotte and their perfectly darling friend had to tell him, she was moving out.

Fred roared at her that she had no business interfering in what she didn't know about, and Betsey said she knew about people, and when push came to shove, she'd put her faith in Max and Charlotte rather than Chuck Drew and Freddy.

'All you have to do,' she said, 'is listen to them.'

'Wrong,' said Max. 'All you have to do is ask Shireen a few questions. But I'll tell you what the questions are.'

'I really don't know quite what all this is about, Mr Praeger,' said Shireen, standing up, holding out her hand, tugging her skirt down over her small bottom with the other, 'but it's certainly very nice to meet you.'

Fred looked at her, and it was perfectly obvious that he believed her. He sat down, lit a cigar, and said to Max, 'OK. Tell me the first question. I'll take it from there.'

'Ask Shireen,' said Max, 'where the money came from that Chuck put back in the bank after the crash.'

Fred asked Shireen; and Shireen told him.

Chapter 62

Angie, November 1987

It was absolute madness of course. Absolute bloody madness. Angie lay in bed, staring into the darkness and contemplating her madness. She could not in her wildest dreams have imagined anything crazier, more counter to any of the cool logic that usually governed her actions.

Max had asked her to marry him and she had not said no. She hadn't said yes either, but she certainly wanted to.

It was ridiculous. She couldn't imagine what she was doing. OK, so she loved him. She really did. She'd been fighting it for a long time, that love. She'd managed to convince herself for a while that it had just been sex; she'd wanted him, and there had been no more to it than that. But then she had had him, over and over again, and it had been really very good indeed, and it had gone on getting better moreover, and she had had to admit to herself that there was more to it. She loved him. Spoilt, arrogant, difficult, demanding as he was, she loved him. She thought about him all the time. She wanted to be with him all the time. She had fought that too; she had told him right from the beginning, made it very clear after that first night, the night of the party, that there was no way he was going to move in with her, no way he was going to spend more than a couple of evenings a week with her, and then, for God's sake, that hadn't been enough for her either. She worked so hard at the other evenings, seeing other men, entertaining her clients, playing with her sons (whose company she was actually beginning quite to like, now that they were something just slightly more than wailing, whining parasites). And they had been all right, the other evenings, but she had found herself thinking, at the end of every one, that it would be nice when tomorrow, or the day after tomorrow or the day after that, she would be seeing Max again.

The weekends were so much better when he was around as well. Weekends in London, or even at Watersfoot, weren't up to much otherwise. Friends tended to be with their families. Men tended to be with their wives. Divorced men were tied up with their children. And the men who were available were somehow not quite right. And they needed to be right, for a weekend. Or even a whole day. They didn't like the country. Or they didn't like London. Or they didn't like her children.

Max liked London and the country, and he seemed to like her children. So weekends with him were fun.

Max was fun. Fun as Baby had once been. Uninhibited and imaginative and fun. They just had a good time together. With the boys, or without the boys. He thought nothing of putting the boys in the car and driving to Alton Towers and spending the day on the rides. Or driving round Windsor Safari Park three times, and making faces at the monkeys with equal enthusiasm each time. Or sitting watching the same cartoon videos over and over again, on a diet of Big Macs and strawberry milk shakes. On the other hand, neither did he think anything much of bribing the nanny (with the loan of his Porsche) to work a whole weekend and taking Angie to Paris. Or Milan. Or spending twenty-four hours in bed, watching blue movies and drinking too much champagne and occasionally doing the odd drug, and seeing how many times they could both come. He enjoyed both kinds of pleasures equally. Some of them innocent, a few of them wicked. She remembered Alexander talking about that, the two different kinds of pleasures, all those years ago. He had been more of a pleasure-seeker himself in those days.

Well, Max was certainly young enough to be a pleasure-seeker. He was still only twenty-one. God. Twenty-one. What was she doing? She was thirty-nine, and she was having a wild and a very serious affair with a boy who was indisputably young enough to be her son. But then that was the whole point: it wasn't just an affair. She could have coped with an affair, it would have been fine, very suitable, very fashionable even. She loved walking into restaurants and clubs with Max, loved people talking about them, staring at them, loved informing fellow guests at parties how old she was and how old he was. No problems, no ties, just fun. Fun and sex. Great.

Only she had to go and get involved. Had to realize how much she missed him when he wasn't with her. Had to face that she was jealous of him if he was with someone else. Had to say that she looked forward to seeing him with an intensity that startled her; had to recognize that when he walked into the house, into the room, into someone else's room, joined her at a party, and smiled at her, that lazy, sexy smile, she felt her heart lurch with a mixture of pleasure and desire.

OK. Well that was all right. She loved him. She could admit that. She loved him. She'd been in love before. Well, hadn't she? OK, not very often. With her first boyfriend. Well, she'd been very young then. With Baby. For years and years. And – who else? The photographer? No. That banker guy? God, no. She was not given to falling in love. She didn't actually like it very much. It removed her from control. Probably the nearest she'd ever been to loving any man, apart from Baby and the first boyfriend, had been Alexander. Dear old Alexander, she'd been so fond of him. Well, she'd blown that one. To say things had never been the same was an understatement. He was so clearly embarrassed by her now, avoided her, hated being in the same room as she was. She wondered if he had ever thought she might talk. Tell his ghastly shameful secret. She never had. She never would. Not to anyone, not to Max, not to Tommy, not to anyone. It was best left, buried, safe, with Virginia.

Poor Virginia. Poor woman. God, why had she stayed with him?

She sometimes wondered if it might not be better if the children knew. Rather than regarding their mother as some kind of a whore. But then – how would they regard their father? If they knew? Some kind of a nut case? Or worse? No, it was better to leave things as they were. Not that she had any choice in the matter. And besides they seemed to have survived it. They were all a bit damaged, of course – but then who wasn't? Everyone had something they had to learn to live with. And this lot had certainly had plenty of compensation.

God, they were spoilt. She had very nearly lost her temper with them when they had all been moaning about their problems. They quite literally believed they had a right to all of it: money, beautiful houses, powerful jobs. It was pathetic really. She was beginning to sort Max out a bit; but the others, the girls, they were a lost cause. Georgina particularly: so she was an unmarried mother. Big deal. Everyone was always saying how marvellous she was, coping all on her own. She had a vast house, staff, a loving supportive family. Angie could have told them all a few things about coping on your own. Maybe this relationship with Max's sharp little friend Jake would develop. Jake was besotted with Georgina. He had set her on a pedestal, and stood below it worshipping her. It didn't seem to be doing him a great deal of good. Georgina remained graciously, gently distant from him. Angie was quite sure he hadn't been to bed with her yet. She must tell Max to tell Jake to knock her off the pedestal. Drag her off somewhere and screw her rigid. He was exactly what Georgina needed. Funny, down to earth, sexy: far better for her than dreamy old Kendrick. Who had actually seen some sense himself and chosen his tough New York girlfriend, to steer him through life. What Alexander would make of Jake as a partner for his beloved, his favourite child, she couldn't imagine. But he needed shaking up a bit too. He was the worst culprit when it came to living in a dream world.

Charlotte did it as well. She had grown up with that bloody silver spoon in her mouth, or two of them, really: the Caterham inheritance and the Praeger one. OK, so she worked hard, and at least had some grasp of commercial realities. But she had been outraged when she had thought she was going to lose it all. And now of course she hadn't had to.

719

Everything was looking pretty good for her. Restored to her throne: back in New York: the old King's favourite. Forty per cent share of the bank hers in the fullness of time. But she seemed to have lost Gabe.

He had promptly resigned from Praegers, when he'd heard about Charlotte. He said he couldn't even think of staying, with her in a more senior position. He was setting up a hot shop, and no doubt it would do extremely well. He had an awesome reputation, Max said. Thirty-two years old and a star. A serious star. Charlotte was a silly bitch if she let him go.

There'd been talk of Max going to New York. There still was. For now he was to stay in London. Fred, with a great deal of smoke-blowing, had asked him how he felt about the bank and his role in it. Max had told him he loved dealing and hadn't thought about anything as serious as a role. Ultimately, his role was that of the Earl of Caterham, but it seemed a pretty long way off. But he'd told Angie that she was wrong about Hartest. Thinking he was going to lose it had been pretty seriously scary. It was his, safely his – Fred had written off the loan, and he was going to have it. Greedy little sod, Angie said; but she smiled tolerantly as she said it.

Freddy had been seriously disgraced: not fired, but cast out into the wilderness of the trading floor. Told he must earn his place in the sun again – and it was going to be a long haul. That had been Fred's solution, and it had been a clever one. But he'd be forgiven. The old buzzard was a great one for family. He was already saying Freddy had just been led astray, that he was young, impressionable, ambitious. Meanwhile, Pete Hoffman had been made chairman. He was certainly one of the good guys. Chris Hill and Chuck Drew fired. That had been good.

She looked at her clock. It was nearly six. She must have been awake for hours. She was sleeping very badly these days. Very badly. It was adding to her tiredness, her entirely unaccustomed lack of stamina. Oh, God, thought Angie wearily, switching on her light, picking up the latest copy of *Tatler*, what on earth was she going to do?

Over breakfast she called Tommy. She had to talk to someone; she couldn't stand it any longer. Tommy was the most pragmatic person in the world; he made her look like a romantic.

'Tommy? I need help.'

'Darling! What an irresistible thought. I'll come right round.'

He arrived, looking concerned, with a rather small bunch of roses.

'I couldn't afford any more,' he said. 'If you want a bigger bouquet, you'll have to give me the money.'

'No, really, Tommy,' said Angie. 'You're much too kind. But I couldn't think of it.'

She made him some coffee. 'Aren't you having any?' he said.

'No. I'm off coffee. I'll just have some tea.'

'Whatever's the matter with you?' said Tommy. 'You normally take it intravenously.'

Angie told him.

Max arrived at the house that night looking wary. He was carrying a much bigger bunch of roses. Angie looked at him suspiciously.

'What's this about?'

'I'm very sorry,' he said, 'but the pigeon has come home to roost.'

'Meaning?'

'Promise you won't be too angry. It's just that I've been thinking about it all day, and I can see I've got to bite the bullet, and tell you.'

Angie's heart thumped very painfully and very hard. It seemed to have shifted to somewhere up in her throat. She sat down suddenly. He was leaving her. He'd found someone young and fallen in love with her. Well, at least it would resolve matters. She wouldn't spend any more nights racked with indecision.

'Well,' she said, 'come on, Max, don't faff about. What is it? What do you want to tell me?'

Max looked at his feet and then up at her again. 'I – I have to take Shireen to Paris. She's cashing in her promissory note. Her and her mum. This weekend. I'm very sorry. But it was the deal I made with her, when she – '

Angie threw her head back and laughed, for a long time. She couldn't ever remember feeling more lighthearted and -headed.

'Oh Max, for God's sake,' she said, 'I know. I remember. And of course I don't mind. It's the least you can do. How's she getting on at Mortons?'

'Well,' said Max. He looked rather smug. 'She's a natural, Jake says. She's coping with the whole thing.'

'Good. I'd have hated to see her go down the pan.'

'Yup. Me too. So you really don't mind?'

'Of course not. How is Jake, and has he ravished Georgina yet?'

'He's fine and he hasn't.'

'Ask him down to Hartest for the weekend, and lock them in the stables or something. That should do it.'

'Mmm.' He sounded doubtful. 'Do you really think it's a good idea? Those two?'

'Yes I do. I think it's great. The chemistry's there.'

721

'OK, I'll give it a go. It's a good idea. Will you come too?'

'No. Your dad wouldn't like it.'

'Angie – there's something I've always wanted to know. Always wondered.'

'What?' said Angie cautiously.

'Well – did you ever – that is, with Alexander – I mean – '

'Max!' The absurdity of the notion made her laugh aloud again. 'Max, honestly. If only you knew!'

'Knew what?'

'Oh – how much he'd hate it,' she said hastily. 'Listen, Max, I have to talk to you. Sit quietly and listen.'

He sat down, looking at her. His dark blue eyes were concerned, almost afraid. Angie's heart contracted with love. Shit. Bloody love. Nothing but trouble.

'What is it?' he said. 'Is something wrong?'

'Yes. No. Well, it might be.'

'Angie, you're talking in riddles.'

'I know. I'm sorry. But I talked to Tommy and he said I had to tell you. Straight away.'

'Tell me what?' He had gone rather pale.

'It's – well, it's rather delicate.'

'What is? For God's sake, Angie, this isn't like you.'

'I know. OK.' She hesitated, took a deep breath. His reaction to this would actually settle matters. Once and for all. Tell her what she ought to do. 'Max, the thing is, I'm pregnant. With – with your baby.'

There was a long silence. Max stared at her. He went whiter still. He looked away suddenly, stood up, walked over to the window, looked out.

Angie felt first pain, than panic running through her, stabbing at her.

'OK,' she said, 'that's it. I knew I shouldn't have told you. Sorry, Max. Forget it. Big mistake. Big.'

'Angie,' said Max, and he turned round slowly, and his face was still expressionless, but his voice was shaky, oddly deep. 'Angie, it's the most ridiculous thing I ever heard. Honestly. Ridiculous. God knows what everyone will say.'

'Well,' she said, and she laughed suddenly, 'I expected all kinds of reactions, but not this one. So what are you saying, Max? What exactly are you saying?'

'I'm saying this settles it, you silly cow. Once and for all. We can get married. And it had better be quick. I don't want any more little bastards cluttering up the Caterham line.'

Chapter 63

Alexander, November 1987

It was so horrible, he felt sick. All the time. Max, marrying that little slut. Telling him calmly that it was going to happen. Sitting there, on the sofa in the library, holding her hand, the pair of them smiling at him.

Her, Angie, his wife's little East End charity case, coming to live here as Countess of Caterham. It was disgusting. What on earth was Max thinking about? She was old enough to be his mother. Apart from anything else, she wouldn't be able to provide him with an heir. They obviously hadn't considered that one. And she was so totally wrong. Wrong for Max, wrong for Hartest. Quite sweet, in her way; he'd been fond of her once. But common, vulgar, ignorant. No taste. You had only to look at that house she lived in in London, with its ankle-deep carpets and those dreadful fancy curtains, to see what she'd do to Hartest. It would be as bad as the Arabs. Worse, possibly. God, this was a nightmare. No sooner had he got rid of one spectre, of that dreadful boy Kendrick coming to live here, than he found himself confronted by another.

Unpleasantness. Scandal. There had been enough of that lately. It had half amused, half angered him that they thought he had seen none of the stories in the press. They seemed to regard him as some kind of half-wit. It had been worrying, that: not as worrying as Fred III's threat to sue the press. Ringing him up like that, across the Atlantic, asking him what he thought they should do about it. Everyone knew the way to handle the press was keep quiet. Well, he'd dealt with Fred all right. And made sure Hartest was finally safe at the same time. They all thought he was so stupid. So vague and stupid. It was probably just as well, otherwise it would be much more difficult for him. But sometimes he thought that he would love to tell them. He would tell them. One day.

But not yet. He had to sort out this marriage of Max's first. Why on earth couldn't Max have stayed with Gemma? Sweet, suitable child. He really had been happy about that. She had loved Hartest, loved Max; she looked right, she was right.

Stupid, crass boy; it was absurd.

It had to be stopped.

Chapter 64

Angie, Christmas 1987

'Let's have Christmas here,' said Angie. 'At Watersfoot. I'd like that. It'd be fun.'

'OK,' said Max. He was lying, with his head on her still concave stomach, looking extremely contented. 'Just think, Angie, he's in there. My son. It's amazing.'

'It might be your daughter. And anyway it's not just yours. It's mine as well.'

'Nah. It's a boy. I know it. And if it's a girl you can have another.'

'Max, I'm a little old for raising vast dynasties. I still can't quite believe I let this happen. I hate being pregnant. I hate babies. I told you, this is the last one.'

'Well, we'll see. You don't think we ought to have it at Hartest? Christmas I mean?'

'No,' said Angie sharply, 'I don't. Alexander hasn't really got used to the idea yet. About us. I don't feel – comfortable with him.'

Max shrugged. 'OK. We'll stay here. That's fine. I don't mind. But you're wrong about Alexander. He's really happy about it. He told me. Tears in the eyes. Poor old sod. I'm afraid he really is a bit gaga these days. Not quite all there.'

'Yes,' said Angie, 'I think you could be right. But he's very sweet. He wouldn't hurt a fly.'

'No, of course he wouldn't,' said Max. He sounded slightly shocked.

They were getting married on New Year's Day. In the registry office at Marlborough, family only. Angie was still in a state of shock. It was not only from the realization that she was pregnant, although that had been disturbing enough. 'You're a clear case of the last-minute syndrome, Mrs Praeger,' her doctor had said to her. 'The old wives would have us believe it's a last-ditch stand on Mother Nature's part. Medical science can't verify or explain it, but certainly a great many babies are born in their mothers' fortieth year. And those very low-dose pills do have a failure rate. Miss one, and you're vulnerable, miss two, and you're certainly at risk.'

She had of course; she had missed two. The night of the party and the next night, with all the dramas and tensions, the excitement of at last, at long last being in bed with Max. Even so, it was unlike her; the rigid efficiency that normally ruled her life would have seen to such things. 'I'm obviously getting soft,' she said to Max, 'I have to get a grip on myself.'

And then the almost frantic eagerness with which Max had greeted the news; she had expected him to be at best cautiously pleased, not ecstatically happy and determined to marry her. She had counselled caution, said they must wait, get used to the idea still, that Max must be absolutely certain of his motives. Max had told her she was a silly bitch and that he was absolutely certain; after two weeks of exuberant daily declarations of love and determination, she gave in, because she wanted to more than anything else in the world, and said she would marry him, soon after Christmas. She was feeling lousy at the moment anyway; and they had to tell the others. They hadn't told them about the baby; one shock at a time, they felt. Let them get used to the idea of the marriage first.

Alexander had been sweet: vague, but happy, had kissed her tenderly and said it was wonderful that at last she was really going to be part of the family. Georgina had been quite sweet too; a little more guarded, but she had made a nice little speech about how lovely it was to see Max so happy, and she thought Angie deserved to be happy too. Charlotte had clearly been appalled. She had forced a smile, said how lovely and congratulated them both, but then after a strained ten minutes had hurried off, pleading an urgent call to New York. She had looked actually upset; Angie was torn between feeling hurt and wanting to shake her by the hand and tell her she'd every right to feel upset, she would do as well, it was an extraordinary liaison for Max to make. But she was too happy to care.

Three days before Christmas she was sitting at Watersfoot, wrapping up presents and waiting for Max to arrive from London, when the phone rang. It was Alexander.

'Angie, my dear. I know this is asking a lot, but I wondered if you would come over this afternoon. Or perhaps early this evening, around six. For a drink. I'd so love to see you.'

'Alexander, I'd love to come, but I am rather busy. Christmas, you know.'

'Oh.' He sounded disappointed – worse, deeply upset. 'Well. Never mind. It's just that I – well, I've been worrying about a few things, Angie. Silly I expect, but I would like to discuss them with you. But never mind. Of course you're busy. Especially at Christmas. Living alone has made me selfish.' His voice sounded shaky, almost tearful.

'Alexander, I – ' she said.

'Oh, don't worry about me,' he said, 'I'm sorry, my dear. Of course it's much too far for you to come. I just thought – well, never mind.'

'Alexander, of course I'll come,' she said, 'I'd like to see you too. I can bring your Christmas present. Is Georgina there?'

'Yes. Yes, she should be. She's going to have supper with the Dunbars a little later, but I know she'll be pleased to see you.'

'Good. Well look, I'll be with you in about – two hours? I'll just finish here, and make sure the twins are OK. They're at a party. And then I'll be on my way.'

'Thank you so much, Angie. I do appreciate it. I shall look forward to seeing you, my dear.'

She arrived at Hartest at about six thirty. The traffic cutting across Marlborough had been terrible. As she turned off the road across the downs, and into the twisting winding lane that led to Hartest, she noticed that her petrol was very low. Damn. She should have filled up before. Oh well. Too late to do anything about it now.

Alexander was waiting for her on the steps; he looked tired, but his face was soft and welcoming as she ran up the steps. She handed him his present, and kissed him. 'Happy Christmas, Alexander.'

'And to you. What a beautiful parcel. Come in, my dear. Would you like a drink, or some tea?'

'Tea I think, Alexander. I've got to drive back.'

'Fine. Mr and Mrs Fallon are out, I'm in charge. Come down to the kitchen, I'll make it for you.'

Angie followed him down to the great kitchen. Suddenly, inconsequentially, she remembered vividly the first time she had seen it, when Virginia had been radiant with happiness over the newly born Georgina, and Alexander had been young and dashing, and Charlotte had been a little girl in red wellingtons; it seemed a long time ago.

'Is Nanny here?' she said.

'Nanny's gone to see her unfortunate sister in Swindon. For the whole Christmas period.'

'So you really are all on your own?'

'Oh yes. Well, Georgina will be here, of course, and George. As I told you, they're at the Dunbars' this evening. And Charlotte is arriving tomorrow. Sugar?'

'Yes please,' said Angie.

Alexander didn't have tea. He poured himself a large whisky.

'Well,' he said, 'let's go up to the library.'

He sat down in one of the large shabby leather chairs on one side of the fire; Angie sat in the other.

There was a silence.

'Alexander,' she said, 'Alexander, I – '

He interrupted her. 'You must think me very foolish,' he said, 'to be worried about you and Max. But I can't help it. Max is – '

'Very young,' said Angie.

'Well, yes. And impressionable. Of course I'm delighted he's going to settle down. And of course I'm delighted that it's with someone we all know and like so much. But – '

'I know what you're going to say,' said Angie, 'I'm old enough to be his mother.'

'Indeed.' He smiled at her rather awkwardly.

'You're not the first person to express that point of view.'

'I'm sure not. I just worry, you see, that – well, in a few years – '

'Of course. I'd worry too. If he was my son. I am worried. But we've talked about that. And decided to take it head on. When and if it happens.'

'I see. Well – that's reassuring in itself. That you've considered it.' He poured himself another whisky. 'And then of course there's the matter of children. I'm not sure – oh dear, this is very delicate – '

'Alexander, it isn't so delicate. You think I'm too old to have children. To provide an heir for Hartest. Is that it?'

He looked at her awkwardly. 'Well – yes. I suppose it is.'

'Well . . .' She hesitated, still not sure as to whether she should tell him. 'Well, amazingly I'm not. We haven't – told anyone else yet. But – well, I'm pregnant. Now. With the heir to Hartest. Slightly surprisingly, I have to say. But of course I'm not that old. I'm still actually in my thirties. By the skin of my teeth. I hope you'll be pleased.' She had been looking into the fire; she turned to face him again, caught him off guard. His expression was extraordinary: just for a moment she saw in it intense surprise, shock in fact, almost – what was it? Horror? No, that was too strong. But certainly a very violent emotion. It was – yes, it was fear. How odd. She felt fear in herself: just for a moment. Then it was gone, so swiftly she thought she must have imagined it, and he smiled, warmly, put out his hands towards her. 'Angie, my dear, that is truly lovely news. Many congratulations. Well, it certainly removes one of my greatest worries. I think this definitely calls for some champagne. Driving or not. You must have some. We must have some. You can have a little supper with me afterwards, a sandwich or something. You'll be fine. Or – ' he looked at her anxiously again – 'are you not allowed to have champagne?'

'Oh, I think so.' She didn't actually want any, but she was so pleased at his reaction, so touched at the effort he was making that she knew she must have some. 'I'd love it.'

'Stay there, my dear. I'll fetch it. I won't be long.'

He came back with the tray, smiling; popped the cork, poured her a glass.

'Aren't you having any, Alexander?'

'Oh – well, you know. I've been drinking whisky. It won't quite go. But a little, yes, of course. We must drink to the baby's health.'

He poured himself a glass; a rather small glass, she noticed, raised it to her.

'To the heir! To my grandson!'

'The heir,' said Angie. She felt slightly silly. She drained her glass rather quickly, held it out for more. She noticed he hadn't touched his, after the first sip.

'How are you feeling? And when is – is the baby due?'

'Oh – in June,' she said quickly. 'And of course we'll be married in a week. So he'll be very legal. Very legitimate.'

'Of course.' He smiled again. 'I note you expect a boy?'

'Yes, well, you know, I think it's more the power of positive thinking. Being determined, you know? That it will be.'

'And how do you feel?'

'Oh – fine. Better than with the twins, actually.'

'Good.'

She realized the room was spinning slightly. She'd obviously drunk too much too quickly. Shit. She somehow wasn't enjoying this very much. It was uncomfortable. She wished Georgina had been there. Or even Mrs Tallow.

She smiled slightly nervously at Alexander.

'I feel a bit dizzy. Too much champagne. Could I take you up on that sandwich?'

'Of course. I'll fetch it for you. You stay there, and rest. I'm so sorry, my dear.' He looked concerned. 'I'll bring you some coffee as well, if you like.'

'That'd be nice. Thank you.'

She sat for a while, leafing through a copy of *The Field*, trying to tell herself she didn't feel as drunk as she actually did. She felt sick as well now, and she had a bad headache. And the room, unless she concentrated really hard, rocked a bit. If only, if only she hadn't had the champagne. It had been really, seriously stupid. Although she'd always been perfectly all right before, on champagne, when she'd been pregnant with the twins. Well, she was older now. Maybe she should be more careful. She wondered if she'd be all right to drive home. Maybe she should ring Max and get him to fetch her. She looked at her watch: already nearly eight. He'd probably be home any minute. She went over to the phone and dialled Watersfoot; the nanny answered.

Max wasn't home; but yes, she'd tell him when he came in to phone Angie at Hartest. Angie sat back and decided to try and relax for an hour or two. Then if she felt better, she'd go.

Alexander came in with a tray of sandwiches, a bottle of Perrier and a pot of coffee.

'Right,' he said, 'this should sort you out. Smoked salmon. Is that all right? It was all I could find in the fridge.'

'Lovely,' said Angie. 'Just what I want.'

She wolfed down three of the sandwiches, and drank two glasses of Perrier; the room steadied a little. She felt less sick.

'You look better,' said Alexander, smiling at her. 'You obviously need feeding up.'

'Eating for two,' said Angie, smiling back.

There was a silence. Then he said, 'Angie, there was something else. I –'

Angie took a deep breath. This was it. And she was feeling uninhibited enough to meet it head on, cope with it. She leant forward, put her hand on Alexander's knee.

'Alexander, don't. Don't even say it. I know it must have been awful for you, that terrible day, it's haunted me ever since. I'm so terribly sorry. But I have never ever told anyone and I never will. Really. I swear it.'

Alexander looked at her and an expression of great bewilderment spread over his face.

'I'm sorry?'

A fresh wave of dizziness hit her; but she ignored it. She had to get this out of the way, aired, so that it would recede again, safely, into the background of all their lives.

'Alexander, I'm talking about the morning when you told me you were – about your – about the impotence.'

There. She'd done it. She'd said it.

'I'm sorry?' said Alexander again.

'Alexander, don't, you don't have to pretend. Really you don't. You told me and I respected it, and I just wanted to reassure you that as far as I'm concerned it never happened. I never knew. I'll never tell Max, never tell anybody. Don't worry about it, please.'

Alexander nodded. His eyes had their vague look. He was obviously thrown by her broaching it. But at least it had been done.

'Yes,' he said, 'yes. Good. Thank you.'

'Do you want to talk about it? At all?'

'No,' he said. 'Oh no. No I don't think so.' There was a long silence. And then he looked at her, and his face was quite different suddenly. It was not vague at all, it was sharp and very intense.

'So you knew?' he said. 'You did know?'

'Alexander, of course I knew. You told me.'

There was a very long silence. Then he said, and his voice sounded very strange, almost rehearsed, 'Yes. Yes of course I did. I remember now. Yes of course.'

Another long silence: then he said, 'Perhaps I do want to talk about it. Perhaps it would be a good idea. I never have, you know. Not since – since Virginia.' There were tears in his eyes now, she saw; he was looking out at the parkland, bright with the frosty moonlight. Angie sat motionless, silent; waiting.

'I could always – perform with prostitutes,' he said. 'With people I didn't care about. I'm a classic case, it seems. Freud describes it as the need for a debased sexual object. What he refers to as the affectionate current and the sensual current are adrift. Oh, I could lecture on the subject for many hours, you know.' He smiled at her, slightly shamefaced. 'I had a lot of treatment. Horrible, some of it. It never did any good.'

'Never?'

'Never. That was why I came to love Hartest so obsessively, of course. It became the focus for all my frustration, all my love. If I couldn't have a wife, children, I could have Hartest.'

'I see,' said Angie. The room seemed to be rocking again slightly.

'But I wanted a wife. I wanted children. Had to have children. And then I met Virginia. And I just loved her. I took one look at her and loved her. It was cataclysmic. I would have done anything for her. Anything. Died if necessary. I worshipped her, Angie, I really did. You have to believe that.'

'I believe it,' said Angie quietly. His voice had become monotonous, but absolutely compelling.

'She was everything, everything I wanted, needed, that Hartest needed. She was beautiful, cultured, charming, amusing – and she was good, Angie. She was terribly good. Kind. Concerned. And she loved me too. I know she did.'

'She must have done,' said Angie, staring at him.

'So I did it. I did the unforgivable thing, and married her.'

'Knowing?'

'Knowing. Oh, I went back to the therapists, the psychiatrists, everyone, hoping, praying. But – well, yes, knowing. I can't quite tell you what I thought might happen. I still don't know. I turn my mind from it.'

'Alexander, why didn't she guess? How could she be so naive, so stupid? I just don't understand.'

'She was very young,' he said simply. 'She was a virgin. It was a long time ago. She had led a very sexually sheltered life. It's hard for someone like you to understand – '

'It certainly is,' said Angie tartly.

'I can only tell you the truth. What happened.'

'Which was – what?'

Alexander took another drink.

'I – managed to deceive her. I told her I didn't want to sleep with her until we were married. I was quite ardent. In my own way. The desire is still there, you see, this is what nobody understands.'

'I see.'

'I have to say in my defence,' he said, and his expression was suddenly lighter, 'that she was very anxious to become the Countess of Caterham. She liked the idea very much. She was so much in the shadow of Baby, you know. She needed to be important herself.'

'I see. Well, I can understand that. It was a big shadow, Baby's.'

'So – well, we were married. I don't want to talk too much about it all. But she was very loyal. She stayed with me. Had our children. I do think she must have loved me.'

'Alexander, when you say she had your children, what exactly went on there? Did you just send her out to find some – some fathers?'

'Yes.' The simplicity, the directness of his answer shocked Angie; she felt slightly sick suddenly. In the depths of the house a phone was ringing.

'I'll get that,' he said, 'excuse me.'

He came back smiling. 'That was my mother. Calling to say – Happy Christmas.'

The mention of Christmas brought Angie back to normality. She looked at her watch. Nearly half past nine. She felt chilled suddenly, chilled and threatened, without knowing why. Why wasn't Max back, why hadn't he phoned?

Alexander was talking again. He had once again refilled his glass. She forced herself to concentrate, to listen attentively to what he was saying.

'Virginia was an alcoholic, you know.'

'Yes,' said Angie quietly, 'I do know.'

'I drove her to it, I expect,' he said. There were tears in his eyes again.

Angie looked at him. There seemed very little she could say.

731

'And nobody, Angie, nobody in the world knows about – about me. Except for yourself. And Nanny.'

'Nanny!'

'Yes. She always knew. She knew about the marriage, everything. In her own, rather simplistic way. But she would never tell. Never. She loves me, and besides, she promised me and she promised Virginia. Who she also loved very much.' He looked at Angie again, almost defiantly. 'She really did love me, you know, Virginia.'

'I believe you,' said Angie.

He sighed and looked at her. 'It would be terrible if anyone knew, Angie. Terrible. I had a few worries, when there were all these stories in the paper. Fred Praeger threatened to sue, you know. But I – well, I eventually managed to persuade him not to.'

'We all thought – oh nothing,' said Angie, staring at him.

'I know. You thought I didn't know. Of course I knew. I'm not a fool.' His eyes were different, suddenly: watchful, cunning.

'Alexander, of course you're not a fool. Um – how did you persuade Fred?'

'Oh,' he said, 'I just said that certain things might come out about Virginia. Which I might be driven to revealing. If I was really being hounded. I said I'd feel better if Hartest was safe again.'

'Oh,' said Angie. She felt sick again. God, he was evil. She wished he'd stop telling her things. She forced herself to smile at him. 'Well, anyway, Alexander, I'm not going to tell. I promise. I never told anyone. Not even Baby.'

'Really?' He sounded distant, almost detached.

'Really. And I never ever will.'

There was another very long silence. Alexander just sat, staring at her. Angie felt panic mounting in her. She felt trapped, nightmarishly trapped. She had to get away. She had to. She realized suddenly that she was sober, quite able to drive.

'Alexander, I must go. It's very late. Could I phone?'

'Yes. Of course. I wonder though if you could do me a great kindness first?'

'Of course.'

'Well – I promised to collect Georgina from the Dunbars. Her car is off the road. Some trouble with the electrics. It's only a couple of miles down the road. Only I'm afraid I've drunk rather a lot, I don't think I'm safe to drive.'

'Yes, of course I will,' said Angie, relieved at the thought of getting away from the house. 'The only thing is, I'm very short of petrol. I've only got just enough to get home. Could I take your car to fetch Georgina?'

'Yes, please do,' he said, and he seemed almost relieved at her words. 'That's a very good idea. It's out in the front. The old Bentley. You'll enjoy driving that. And I'll ring Watersfoot and tell them you're just leaving.'

'Angie, hallo. Do come in. What a nice surprise.' Catriona Dunbar opened the door; Angie smiled at her, thinking how extremely plain she was, and how much a flattering hairstyle and a little make-up would help. Why didn't these women do something about themselves?

'I've come to collect Georgina. And George. I hope it's not too early, but I've got to go, and Alexander's had a few too many drinks this evening.'

'How very kind. She's in here, talking to Martin.'

Angie followed her into the drawing room; it had that look she had come to know rather well and be constantly amazed by, endemic to the country houses of upper-middle-class England, a kind of cultivated shabbiness.

'Hallo, Angie,' said Georgina. 'Are you all right? You're very pale.'

'Yes, I'm fine. Just a bit tired. Come on, Georgina, we must go.'

'Martin,' said Catriona, 'aren't you going to offer Angie a drink?'

'No, honestly,' said Angie. 'I have to get back to Watersfoot, and it's a long drive.'

Georgina put George into the back of the Bentley and got in beside Angie.

'It's nice to see you,' she said politely, 'but – why are you here?'

'Your father rang me, asked me over. He – wanted to talk.'

'He didn't tell me he was going to ask you.'

'Well – he was in a bit of a funny mood. I think he's better now.'

'Good. Angie, can I ask you something?'

'Of course.'

'It's just that you seem to be able to talk to Daddy. And – well, if I wanted to leave Hartest, and – and go and live in London for a bit, with George, do you think he'd be all right?'

'Would this be anything to do with Jake Joseph?'

'Well – it might.'

'I think your father would be absolutely fine,' said Angie. 'He's not nearly as fragile as he makes out, you know.'

'Angie – thank you very much. And I think it's really nice about you and Max. Honestly.'

'I'm glad somebody does,' said Angie.

Alexander was standing on the steps when they got back. He was smiling. Georgina ran into the house with George, after kissing her briefly.

'See you over Christmas.'

'Thank you, Angie, so much,' said Alexander. 'I've phoned Watersfoot, spoken to the nanny. I said you were on your way.'

'No Max yet?'

'Apparently not.'

'Oh well.' The bastard. Still out drinking. Just the kind of husband she needed. 'Thank you, Alexander. It's been a – a nice evening. Call me any time you want to talk.'

'I will.' He returned the kiss, looked at her rather intently for a moment; then he suddenly took her in his arms, held her very close to him.

'Now I want you to drive very carefully, Angie. You look tired.'

Chapter 65

Alexander, 1980

'I want you to drive very carefully, Virginia. You look tired.'

She did look terribly tired. Far too tired to drive all the way to Hartest and to deal with distraught children when she got there. He had really needed her to stay. To talk everything through, to decide what they were going to say and do. He hadn't been quite sure what might happen after that, but he had thought there might have been several alternatives. In the event, however, he had had no choice. He had had to act rather quickly.

It was just as well, really. There was no room for fear, for indecision. Quickly, carefully, it had had to be done. While she was getting a few things from her luggage, to take down with her. The only danger had been that she might look down into the street. While he had the bonnet up. But he had only been checking the oil, he would have told her, and a loose lead he had noticed, when he had been looking at it the other day.

'Don't worry if that warning light comes on,' he said to her, 'it's a fault in the wiring. I've booked it in for a service, on Friday. Terribly overdue. You really should take more care of your cars, Virginia.'

'Yes, Alexander,' she had said wearily.

He told her that he would be down the following day. To give the children his love, to tell them whatever she thought best. He gave her a kiss, held her closely for what seemed a long time; he was afraid that he might give himself away, weaken. She looked up at him, half surprised. Then he forced himself to smile, to let her go. It was the only thing to do. It really was.

He watched the Golf move slowly off down the street, waving to her, smiling. But its lights were blurred by his tears.

He went into the house to wait.

The only real danger was that the brakes would fail too soon.

Chapter 66

Angie, December 1987

Angie put her foot down the minute she had turned in the forecourt and was in the Great Drive. She felt oddly wretched, slightly sick again. Alexander was clearly more disturbed than she had thought. He certainly seemed to have some trouble confronting reality. The whole encounter had been difficult, frightening even. She didn't quite know what she should do.

Talk to someone. To Max perhaps. To Charlotte. Charlotte was so sane and sensible. But what should she tell them? That their father was – what? Mad? But he wasn't. He was very confused, very intense – but not actually mad. Certainly he was harmless. But it did seem to her he needed help.

Angie shivered suddenly and turned up the heating in the BMW, switched on the radio. She felt herself to have been in the heart of some horror, and she wanted to escape, to get away. Well, she was going home. Home to Watersfoot, to the children; home to Max. The weather had deteriorated. It was icy, and it was slightly foggy too. She decided to call, to tell him again that she was on her way. It would make her feel safer, less beleaguered. She stopped the car, just at the top of the Great Drive, as it turned away into the woods, and picked up the phone; shit, it seemed dead. She shook it, stabbed at the buttons; nothing happened. Oh, God. Now if she ran out of petrol, she was really in trouble. She debated going back to the house and rejected it. It really wasn't worth it.

She moved off again, glanced at the gauge: it was pretty far down. Baby had often told her to carry a spare can. She had always told Baby there were always men around with spare cans. Not tonight there wasn't. Now there was a warning light on; flickering, settling into intensity. What was that? The fuel warning system, presumably. She really ought to take a little more interest in her cars.

Well, she should be OK. She had driven a long way in her time, with fuel gauges jammed on empty. Not so much these days, but when she had been young, and hadn't had any money. She was always driving around on a wing and a prayer then. She'd only run out once, and that had been on the Pacific Coast Highway, and she'd been wearing cut-off denims, and she'd had plenty of gas in the tank in no time. This was different, though. This was Wiltshire, and it was foggy and she wasn't wearing cut-offs. She was – Christ, this car was going fast. Sixty-five. She hadn't meant to put her foot down quite so hard. And a very windy downhill bit of road ahead. 'Concentrate, Mrs Praeger,' she said aloud. 'Think what you're doing.'

Chapter 67

Alexander, December 1987

It was seeing her stop that did it; that broke the spell. Until then, it had been exactly the same, the sadness of the parting, the kiss, the admonition to drive carefully, and the tail lights blurring with his tears. And the knowledge that it had been necessary. Discovering she knew, that had made it doubly so. He really had had no idea. Obviously it had been that dreadful day, when he'd had the breakdown. She must have been there. He couldn't remember, but it was the only explanation.

Of course she'd sworn not to tell. Well of course she would have done. He certainly didn't believe her. He couldn't. Couldn't risk it. Especially after talking to her like that. It had been foolish, in a way, allowing himself to talk. But wonderful: such a release. No, he couldn't possibly have done anything else. There had been no choice, just as there had not with Virginia. It was very very sad, because in a way he was fond of Angie. He always had to get fond of them. That was the trouble. That was the whole terrible, humiliating trouble. She was engaging. In spite of everything he found her engaging. That dreadful vulgar parcel she'd brought; very sweet, really.

He'd done much the same thing to the car as he had to Virginia's. Not quite so undetectable, but still very clever. What he'd done to the Golf had been masterly. Injecting the brake fluid hose with water. So that when it heated, it had turned to gas. And then all the efforts of the brakes had gone into compressing the gas. Doubly effective as the car started going really fast on the motorway. Poor Virginia. She hadn't had a chance.

It had been more difficult with the BMW. Pretty, flashy car that, like its owner. But he'd known what to do. He'd studied it, planned it very carefully for days, weeks. Practised with Georgina's. Attached a flexible blade round each of the brake pipes from the chassis. And then every time the car turned a corner, it cut into the pipe and the fluid began to leak. There were so many corners, as you drove away from Hartest. It would be a miracle if she survived.

But then, seeing her stop, he suddenly remembered. His jacket: it was in the car. He'd gone out wearing it, and then it had been getting in the way, making it harder to work quickly; he'd taken it off and thrown it in the back. He would have remembered it, retrieved it, if it hadn't all taken longer than he'd expected; one of the blades had been awkward, wouldn't fit tightly enough, had threatened to snap, he'd had to get another. And seeing the lights of the Bentley coming back down the drive, he'd just slammed the door and run to the steps. He hadn't panicked, of course; he never did. He stayed very very calm. He'd just been slightly rushed. That was all.

But he thought he probably should get the jacket. There was just a chance that someone might examine the car, ask questions, inquire as to why the jacket was there. Especially as it had a couple of small screwdrivers in the pocket.

Well, he could catch her up. Easily. The Bentley could outpace that car in the lanes easily; it held the road better, and besides he knew every twist and turn, which she would not.

He could just tell her he'd been checking her petrol gauge: that he'd been worried about it, and thrown the jacket in then. She had been quite worried about getting home; she wouldn't stop to question him, to think. And after that – well. It wouldn't matter. She'd be gone. Safely gone. Away from Max. Away from Hartest.

Alexander hesitated for just another moment. Then he ran down the steps and got into the Bentley.

Spring 1988

ANGIE

She'd lost the baby. Through the long hours of that night, as she sat in Casualty with Tommy, and waited, while Max had been caught up in the dreadful grisly sadness of Alexander's death and its practical consequences, she became slowly and relentlessly aware of a strong pulling ache in her back; then the sharp cramps began, then the bleeding. They tried to stop it, but it was hopeless; late the following afternoon, she miscarried.

She had cried, cried for hours, from shock as much as grief; Max had wept too, had stood at the foot of the bed looking at her, his face suddenly, sharply older, not touching her, just telling her he loved her, that it would make no difference, that there could be other babies.

They had both known it wasn't true.

She and Tommy had talked for hours the night Alexander died. He had stayed with the car, while she and Max had gone to Marlborough, to the police. While they were at the hospital, he told her he had found certain evidence that her brakes had been tampered with, and that he had removed it. 'And did you realize Alexander's jacket was in your car?'

'In my car? No, of course not.'

'He must have left it there. Possibly why he was chasing you. I put it back in the Bentley.'

They agreed it was quite unnecessary that anybody should hear about it, that it would serve no useful purpose. Alexander had been terribly drunk, and his car had crashed, and that was the verdict that would no doubt be brought in. They talked for a long time; Angie, who had had the sensation of being still in a nightmare, had felt herself slowly awakening to calm and a degree of normality.

'The guy was a psychopath,' Tommy said casually, as he listened to her, as he heard the dreadful sad story of the marriage, as they untangled together the elaborate mesh of his plan to kill Angie, 'and like all psychopaths, terribly clever. Every detail taken care of. You sent to collect Georgina, her car probably quite healthy in the garage. Mr and Mrs Tallow, Nanny, all away. We called, you know, and he told us you'd left.'

'When?'

'Oh – ninish.'

'God. He told me that was his mother. I couldn't think why you hadn't phoned.'

'Well anyway, we came to meet you. It was so foggy. Thinking you'd be nearly home. Then we phoned again, from the car, thinking we'd missed you, and Georgina said you were just talking to Alexander outside. It got a little worrying, after that. So we drove on. Your car phone wasn't working.'

'I know. He must have – fixed that too.'

Angie shuddered. She felt threatened still, deeply shocked. She was holding Tommy's hand, as if it was a lifeline, her link with reality. Then she said, 'But he wasn't really a psychopath. Surely. He seemed nice, Tommy, a lot of the time, gentle and – and sad. I loved him, in a way, I really did.'

'About as gentle and sad as a black mamba,' said Tommy, 'and most psychopaths are nice a lot of the time. What characterizes them is a complete lack of any sense of guilt.'

'Tommy, just why did he want to kill me? What had I done? Was it because I knew about – about him?'

'Possibly. There might have been some quite different reason. Maybe he didn't like the idea of your marrying Max.'

'But he seemed so – pleased.'

'Darling, you're so naive. They're very cunning, these guys. Terribly clever.'

'Tommy – do you think he killed Virginia too? All those years ago?'

'He might have done,' said Tommy. 'Quite possibly.'

'Oh God. And then – '

She told him about Alexander's conversation with Fred, about Virginia. 'You're right. He was clever. Horribly clever. And there was that strange business of Georgina's baby too, being so ill. Could that have been him?'

'Could have been. Although again, God knows why.'

Angie shuddered again.

'I was lucky, wasn't I?'

'Very lucky.'

Tommy looked at her. 'I really don't think any good could come of anyone else knowing about all this, do you? We should keep very quiet about it, don't you think?'

'Well of course we should,' said Angie. 'Very very quiet.' She sighed heavily.

'Are you OK?' said Tommy.

'Yes, I'm OK. Tough stuff, we Wicks, you know.'

And then the pain had begun.

She had refused to marry Max on New Year's Day. She had told him it was because it seemed wrong, with Alexander so recently killed, but that was not the reason. She knew it wasn't, and she felt he knew too.

She had gone home to her house, after the miscarriage, and he had come home to her. He had been gentle, tender, sad. He told her he loved her; she told him she loved him. ·

The thought kept coming to her, unbidden, in those first days, how terrible it would have been if Alexander had indeed been his father; if he had perhaps carried some of those dangerous, deadly genes.

Angie was a strong person, but for weeks after the crash she had nightmares, and waking nightmares too, when she heard Alexander's voice again and again, telling her quietly and tenderly to drive carefully, that she looked tired: knowing that he was sending her wilfully to her death.

The terrible irony was that Max seemed to be developing the same almost obsessive love for Hartest; from treating it carelessly, casually, he seemed genuinely to have started to care about it, insisting they spent every weekend there, talking for long hours to Martin and to Georgina about it; it had been the cause of one of their first real rows. She had been complaining about having to go there one weekend, and Max had told her she was making a fuss about nothing, and she had said *not* nothing, it was cold and it needed decorating and he had said perhaps she would like to tell him what needed doing to it, and she had made some proposals, to carpet the rooms, to put in some en suite bathrooms, to double glaze at least some of the windows, and he had gone crazy. And she had completely lost her temper and told him he was an arrogant, offensive brat obsessed with his mausoleum, and he had told her the mausoleum, as she put it, was one of the most beautiful houses in England and he loved it very much. They made up that night in bed; but it had been a startling episode.

After a few weeks they began to quarrel more, she and Max; he was pressing her to marry him, she was still refusing. He accused her of not

742

loving him; she told him she needed time. The only place they were truly happy was in bed.

Then one night, he was very late back. He came in after midnight, drunk; and more significant than drunk, evasive.

Angie knew what that meant. That he had been with someone else. And although it had hurt, horribly badly, she had been relieved. He was going to grow away from her, grow out of love with her; and that was the only thing that could possibly happen, to save the pair of them.

She took a huge decision that night; she told him she thought he should leave, return to Pond Place, or move into Eaton Place. She made more fuss than she felt like making, just to expedite the thing. She said she wasn't prepared to have him in her house, if he was going to fool around with other people.

It was a brave thing to do; she knew if she had been overtly noble, told him she wanted him to feel free, he would have stayed with her longer from a sense of guilt.

It didn't work straight away, of course; he was remorseful, said he was sorry, that he would never leave her. But a few weeks later, he was late home again, and she threw him out.

She was extremely unhappy, for a long time. Well, a long time for her. Several weeks.

Then Tommy, dear Tommy, asked her out to dinner one night, and one thing led to another, and she began to feel very much better very quickly.

GEORGINA
She missed him so much. So terribly much. Of all of them, she had loved Alexander the most and he had loved her the most in return; she knew that. And she missed him and she mourned him dreadfully. It seemed to her almost impossible that she would never see him again, watch his slightly stooping back as he wandered about the house and grounds he loved so much, see his face as he looked at her fondly across the dinner table every evening, hear his voice as he talked to her, always courteous, considerate, as if she was some visiting acquaintance, instead of his daughter.

He had been buried in the little graveyard by the chapel, beside Virginia and the baby Alexander; his headstone read simply: 'Alexander. Earl of Caterham. Beloved husband of Virginia, father to Maximilian, Charlotte and Georgina.' He would have liked that. It would have pleased him. It said everything.

She had stayed alone at Hartest for a while, with Nanny and George, trying to come to terms with it, trying to think what to do. George missed him too; Alexander had been so sweet to him always, played with him, taken him for walks round the park.

She had been relieved when Max and Angie postponed their marriage (although sad for them, of course, about the baby); having to celebrate, trying to pretend she was pleased about it, would have been very hard on top of coping with her grief.

Then as the weeks went by, and they were clearly less happy together, quarrelling a lot, she began to hope they might not marry at all. She didn't feel guilty for hoping it; anyone could see it had been the craziest plan. She liked Angie better these days, but she still didn't exactly get on with her, and she was certainly not the wife for Max.

Martin had been wonderful; very gentle, very understanding. He might, she thought, have minded how upset, how unhappy she was, felt some jealousy, or at least some awkwardness. But he didn't, he let her talk endlessly, let her wonder how and why it had all happened.

'I shouldn't have let him go,' she had said over and over again, 'I knew how much he'd been drinking, I should have stopped him. But I didn't. And anyway, why did he go? Why should he have gone?'

Martin told her she must not blame herself; that in any case she couldn't have stopped him. He must have thought Angie had forgotten something, or wanted to tell her something. She had hardly been out of sight, Georgina said, when he had left. Obviously he thought he could catch her up easily.

And then when Angie had skidded, and he'd swerved to avoid her; Angie must have been driving too fast, to hit the stile like that. Georgina found it very hard not to feel some sense of blame towards Angie. But it had been foggy, foggy and icy; and Angie said Alexander had been flashing at her and hooting, it had distracted her. That was what had caused her to skid; she had lost concentration. Over and over again Angie had said she didn't really know why Alexander had come after her; but that they had been discussing Christmas, and she had suggested various things. Maybe he had remembered something, wanted to tell her something. Or give her a message for Max. It was very unlike Alexander, Georgina thought, and it seemed a terrible thing to die over, a social engagement. But she was obviously destined never to know. She had to accept it. There was absolutely no doubt that Angie had been very upset indeed; and that she and Alexander had parted on the warmest possible terms. The last thing she had heard Alexander say, as he stood watching

Angie's car going up the drive, was, 'She's very sweet really. Very sweet indeed.'

MAX

It had been very difficult. All of it.

He'd felt terrible about Alexander's death. Guilty and genuinely grieved. And then Angie losing the baby, that had been awful. His baby. Their baby. It had been a very long time since Max had wept, but he had wept then, at the thought of his son not being born, not growing up, not learning to love him. A death as well, of a sort.

And then Angie had been impossible. OK, he'd been ready to make allowances at first. Of course she was wretched, physically frail, shocked from the night Alexander had died. It had been a ghastly experience for her. Although he still felt there was something odd about it all, something she wasn't telling him. Why on earth had Alexander been chasing after her – so fast he had crashed? Why had Angie been driving so fast? First she'd said the brakes seemed to have failed, later she'd just said she skidded. It just didn't make sense. Any of it. He supposed he would never know. He asked Angie if they'd had some row, and Alexander had maybe wanted to try and make it up, but she said no. He had to admit he had had his fleeting suspicions for a while, about what on earth Angie had been doing there that evening in the first place; but she had been so amused by that (once she had recovered), so adamant that she had no idea why Alexander had been chasing after her, that he had finally set the matter aside, as an unsolved, unsolvable mystery. For all of them. Alexander was gone; and Max had felt a strong, strange sense of loss and misery over his going; but he managed to persuade himself there was nothing to be gained by raking over and over the thing, trying to find a solution.

Alexander had obviously been very confused: look at the business with the phone calls, saying Angie had left when she hadn't. But he really couldn't believe (having thought about it endlessly) that there was any more to it than that. Angie had had a horrible time; but she had survived, thank God. She might have died as well.

Tommy had been great: good old Tommy. Seen to a lot of the admin, the next day, notified the authorities, got Angie's car towed away and seen to, looked after her, God, he'd been right about Tommy and they'd all been wrong. Against some opposition from Charlotte he'd suggested Tommy moved into Eaton Place. Nobody used it, and if they did, there was still plenty of room. Tommy had been very pleased although he said he would still have preferred Hartest. He was a country gentleman at

745

heart, he said. Max told him to forget his heart and be grateful he could pretend to be a gentleman.

After Angie threw him out he'd gone back to Pond Place, while he thought what to do. He didn't want to live in Eaton Place with Tommy; he'd never liked it and he wanted to be on his own. For a while.

He was very unhappy. Even though he could actually see that it was for the best, that maybe the marriage wouldn't have worked, he still loved her. He loved her very much. The thought of life without her was empty and chill and pointless. OK, so he had been out with a couple of girls; actually got into bed with one of them. It hadn't meant anything; certainly hadn't meant he didn't love Angie, was ready to leave her, to get over her. He was surprised she'd reacted so strongly. Maybe she hadn't loved him as much as he'd loved her. The thought hurt him; it made his heart ache.

Work was good, though: a great comfort. Max loved Praegers. He loved it more and more. He got as much pleasure, still, from doing a good deal, as he had on the very first day. And it was more difficult these days; the easy ride was over. Of course everyone knew you couldn't stay a dealer all your life; probably not after you were thirty. Younger than that. Maybe. But then there were all the other things, the things Charlotte was so besotted with, the mergers, the takeovers, the manipulation of people and money; it was irresistible. One huge casino. Who was it had said that? Oh, yes, that nice girlfriend of Charlotte's, Chrissie Forsyte. Pretty girl. Great legs. He might look her up next time he went to New York. Now that he wasn't going to be a married man.

And Fred had told him he could have a share in Praegers, maybe take over London, in the fullness of time. And he wanted that. He wanted it like he wanted sex. It was physical. It made his balls ache. And it also meant that he would have some money. Real money. To pour into Hartest.

He didn't mind how much it cost; anything now to keep it for the family, to save it from the National Trust and the day trippers and the tickets at the gate. In that at least, he felt exactly like Alexander: proprietary, fiercely protective. It was his memorial to Alexander, that, keeping it safe. He was happy to see it swallow up a great deal of money; although he was extremely grateful that Fred, by way of a very large conciliatory gesture, that he did not entirely understand, had waived the mortgage repayment altogether. That had been before Alexander had died, even. Angie said he should just be grateful and not pursue things any further, and he'd agreed. Fred had in any case issued dire warnings that any future financial demands must be met from the estate's own resources.

Poor old Fred. He'd looked very old, very frail when he and Charlotte had gone over to New York to see him. A lot of the bluster had gone out of him.

Anyway, Hartest was his now. Beyond any kind of doubt, it was his. He had read the words of Alexander's will: 'I bequeath Hartest House with contents and all its lands, estates and titles, to my heir, Maximilian Frederick Alexander Welles, Viscount Hadleigh' – clever, carefully chosen words – and had laughed aloud with pleasure.

But the fact remained, he was miserable. Very miserable. He'd rung Angie only the night before, suggested they had dinner: no strings, he'd said, he just missed her. And she'd made some feeble excuse about being very tired, going to bed early. He had a feeling she was seeing someone. Already. He didn't know how she could.

Max woke up early these days; he supposed it was a sign of age. He got up, went for a run, came back, and was standing in the shower when the phone rang. Shit. Seven in the morning. Who would ring him at seven?

'Max Caterham,' he said into the phone. He hadn't quite got used to that, to not being Max Hadleigh.

'Max?' said a voice. An American voice. 'Max, this is Opal. I just hit London. I was so sorry to hear about your dad. Listen, are you free for lunch today? I know you're a married man, or nearly, but it'd be good to see you.'

Max thought about Opal. He thought about her incredible legs, her full breasts, that amazing neck of hers, her small neat head with its tightly cropped hair; he thought about her wonderful raucous laugh, and her capacious appetites. He suddenly felt much better.

'I'm not married, Opal,' he said, 'not even nearly. Let's have lunch. I'll book a table at the Caprice for one.'

'Great,' said Opal, 'but I'm sorry about the marriage.'

'Oh,' said Max, 'it's OK.'

And he realized it was true.

CHARLOTTE

Everyone else was all right, thought Charlotte irritably. Max had been very upset for a bit, about Angie, but he was fine now, having a wild old time, as far as she could make out, in London.

Georgina had said that Angie had been very upset for a while about the whole thing; Charlotte slightly doubted that. Well, she might have been upset at the prospect of not becoming Lady Caterham, of being mistress of Hartest, but anything more than that seemed unlikely. Angie's feelings ran about as deep, in Charlotte's view, as a puddle in a drought. She was an opportunist and a very skilful one, and the only person she was capable of being in love with was herself. And Max had not been able to recognize the fact. Nor had Baby, of course. Both of them falling for the old ploy, the pregnancy. God, how did the woman get away with it? Anyway, Georgina had also said that Angie was seeing Tommy Soames-Maxwell. Now that was a match made in heaven. Or rather hell. Max had had a very lucky escape. And was no doubt beginning to appreciate it.

Alexander's death still puzzled her. As she knew it puzzled Georgina. What had he been doing, chasing after Angie in the freezing fog, when they had just spent several hours together? It was totally inexplicable. She had questioned Angie closely, as Georgina and Max had done, but Angie had stuck to her story. She had no idea; she could only suppose that he had suddenly remembered something – or maybe he had not been following her at all. She had seemed genuinely upset, genuinely baffled; but Charlotte was still not satisfied. She was quite sure that Angie knew something. Not necessarily incriminating, but something. In fact she had pursued her line of questioning for so long and so intensely that in the end Angie had actually burst into tears and Max had told her to leave Angie alone. She had given in then, followed the family line; but it continued to trouble her. She couldn't accept that she would never know. Her mind did not work like that.

It was Nanny who finally made her feel better about it. 'Stop fretting, Charlotte,' she said, 'you're like a dog without a bone.'

'With a bone, Nanny,' said Charlotte automatically.

'No, without,' said Nanny. 'There's no bone there to chew.' And then she added, 'Your mother died, after all. Much better that way.'

Charlotte knew what Nanny meant; not that it was better both her parents were dead, but that it was better to leave things quietly alone.

She gave Nanny a kiss and told her she would try to take her advice.

Charles St Mullin said that he thought she should take positive steps to alleviate her loneliness in New York and hold out if not an olive branch at least a leaf to Gabe Hoffman. Charlotte said she would die first, and Charles kissed her and said that would rather defeat the object.

She was at least having a good time at Praegers. A vice president now, and a highly effective one. She had her own team of eleven people, which she ran with efficiency and skill, if not tact. Pete Hoffman thought the world of her. So did Fred III, who seemed stronger again suddenly and

748

came in at least twice a week, for rather long afternoons while he interfered in the workings of every department and wasted a great deal of time and then went home and told Betsey that he really didn't know what would happen if he ever had to retire.

Freddy was making the best of a fairly bad job, with a surprisingly good grace; he had simply, for the time being at least, accepted that he was lucky to have been retained at all and was working very hard. Everyone told him that sooner or later he would be restored to at worst junior partner level, that Fred was already talking about his being led astray and overambitious, but he certainly wasn't behaving as if he believed them. He was racing against time, and his grandfather's retirement; the strain was visible.

Mary Rose, whom she saw occasionally, never mentioned the matter of the rumours about Max again. Charlotte had a shrewd suspicion that Freddy had told her to keep her mouth shut for his sake. Mary Rose had in any case mellowed; she had published one of the year's best-selling art books, a work on wall paintings in France, and was happy with her publisher boyfriend.

But Charlotte was miserable. Lonely and miserable. She felt, at twenty-six, a failure socially. Well not exactly socially, she would then tell herself; she had hundreds of friends, she was always out, partying, clubbing, attending openings, presiding over charities. She had several extremely enthusiastic admirers. She was actually a great success socially. So – what was she? A personal failure. Yes, that's what she was. She had messed up the one great relationship of her life; and by running another, highly irregular, one she had endangered her entire future.

She saw Gabe occasionally; at functions, benefits, in restaurants. He would nod at her coolly, had even said good evening to her once. He was running a very successful financial hot shop; he had several blue-chip accounts, everyone was talking about him.

'But he's not happy,' Pete Hoffman said to her, one afternoon, when he caught her reading about Gabe in *Fortune* magazine. 'He misses you. There still isn't anyone else, you know.'

'Well that's a shame,' said Charlotte, smiling sweetly at him, 'but I'm sure he'll find someone in time.'

One day in late April, when the days were beginning to lengthen, she was sitting in her office reading, catching up on her journals, when an item in one of the smaller publications caught her eye. Gabe Hoffman, it said, was reported to be courting Michael Browning, of BuyNow, for his new in-house publication account. Talks were quite advanced, and Browning had told the reporter that he was sure he and Mr Hoffman could do business.

Charlotte read this several times, and each time the red spots before her eyes grew bigger, and the pounding of her heart grew more stifling. Gabe Hoffman! Stealing Michael Browning from her, from Praegers. That was her own account, that publication division. Pete Hoffman had given it to her to take care of. It was a new field for Browning. And Gabe was just muscling in, thinking he could take it. How dare he. How dare he! The bastard. You just didn't do that sort of thing. You didn't. Everyone knew Praegers had a very special relationship with Browning. She was surprised at Michael Browning herself, as a matter of fact. God, it was a dirty world, these days. Dirtier than ever since the crash.

She sat there for a while, getting angrier and angrier and then in the end she couldn't stand it any longer. She called Hoffmans and asked to be put through to Gabe.

'Good afternoon,' said a honeyed secretarial voice. 'Mr Hoffman's office.'

'Give me Mr Hoffman please,' snapped Charlotte.

'May I ask who's calling?'

'Yes, you may. It's Charlotte Welles.'

'One moment please.' There was a long silence; then the honeyed voice came back.

'I'm afraid Mr Hoffman is busy right now. May I have him call you?'

'No,' said Charlotte. 'No you may not.'

She slammed the phone down. She was shaking.

She thought quickly, furiously. Gabe was only across in the World Trade. She would go over there. She'd force him to see her. If she was there in the office, he'd have to. She would make a scene until he did.

She stood up, dragged on her jacket, picked up her bag and set off; ran down the stairs, up Pine Street, turned right into Broadway and then crossed towards the great forecourt of the World Trade. She looked up at it. He thought he was safe in there, insignificant little bastard. Well he wasn't. He wasn't.

She went in. Hoffmans was on the sixty-fourth floor. She bluffed her way up there and then came against the stony wall of reception. The girl was terribly sorry, she said (having called Gabe's office), but he couldn't see anyone. He was terribly busy.

'Give me that phone,' said Charlotte, snatching it from her hand. 'Hallo. Is this Mr Hoffman's secretary? Listen to me. This is Charlotte Welles. Would you be so good as to tell Mr Hoffman that if he won't see me I shall take all my clothes off in reception and start screaming. Yes, that's correct. Thank you.'

She put the phone down, smiled sweetly at the girl behind the desk and waited. After about thirty seconds another girl came out. She looked nervous.

'Miss Welles?'

'Not quite correct,' said Charlotte. 'But basically yes, that's me.'

'I'm afraid Mr Hoffman – '

Charlotte unbuttoned her jacket, and took it off. Then she kicked off her shoes. She eyed the girl and started on the buttons of her shirt.

'One moment please,' said the girl hastily. She picked up the phone.

'Gabe? I really think you should see this lady. She seems a little upset. Yes. Fine. Yes. I'll do that.'

'Come this way,' she said to Charlotte.

She led her down a corridor. Hoffmans was small, there were only perhaps half a dozen offices, all set around the bull pen.

The secretary led Charlotte to the last door in the corridor and opened it.

'Gabe. Here you are,' she said nervously and promptly vanished, clearly terrified of getting caught in the crossfire.

Gabe looked up. His face was contorted with rage.

'How dare you!' he said. 'Force your way in here, create a scene, threaten my staff. It's outrageous. Please leave immediately. Or I shall have you thrown out.'

'You dare to talk of being outrageous!' said Charlotte. 'You! You're stealing my clients. How dare you do that. That really is outrageous. Outrageous and unethical.'

'Of course it's not unethical,' said Gabe. 'It's the way the Street works. We all have a right to each other's clients. Grow up, Charlotte, for God's sake.'

'Oh balls,' said Charlotte. 'Don't give me that, Gabe. Not in cases like this we don't. I just don't understand you. Michael Browning has such a special relationship with us, and your father – '

'Who?'

'Michael Browning.'

'Charlotte, I have to tell you I don't know what you're talking about,' said Gabe. He seemed to be telling the truth. Charlotte stared at him. Then she thrust the cutting at him.

'Really? Well, look. There you are. Discussing – what does it say – advanced talks with him.'

'Charlotte,' said Gabe, and there was a suspicion of laughter behind his dark eyes now, 'Charlotte, have you never heard of a journalist getting things wrong?'

'Oh Gabe, don't give me that.'

'Charlotte, of course I'm not after Browning. This is a new account, my father's account. I do have some integrity. For God's sake, the stupid fucking reporter got the two Hoffmans mixed up. Are you really so dense? Call him if you don't believe me.'

'Oh,' said Charlotte. She felt a bit sick suddenly. 'Oh well. You could hardly blame me for believing it. For being angry.'

'I would disagree with that,' said Gabe, 'and I think you owe me an apology. Actually.'

'Oh you do? For what?'

'For not checking the story. For making a ridiculous scene. For embarrassing me.'

'If you think – ' Charlotte began.

'No, I don't think. I know. I know you're too stubborn and too arrogant and too stupid ever to apologize. I found that out long ago. But I had forgotten quite how stubborn and arrogant and stupid you could be.'

Charlotte stared at him. He had got up from his desk now, moved round, and opened the door behind her. His expression was unreadable.

'I had also forgotten quite the effect your arrogance and stupidity had on me. How it could actually at times be almost counterproductive.'

'I don't know what you mean,' said Charlotte.

'Come with me,' said Gabe. 'I think I need to explain a few things to you.'

He took her by the arm and ushered her, none too gently, back down the corridor. There was a large door at the end, labelled Conference Room. He pushed it open. It was in darkness; the April evening light filtered very pale now through the long windows. Gabe pushed her inside, followed her, slammed the door.

She turned to face him, stormy, still so angry she could hardly breathe.

'Charlotte,' he said, 'since you're never going to be any less arrogant or stupid or stubborn without my help, and since those qualities are going to seriously damage your prospect of success in the future, I feel I have a certain duty to try and do something about it. Now then. Listen to me, you silly bitch. I shall attempt to steal accounts from you until I choose to stop and I hope very much you will do the same to me. The day you stop and the day I stop, we'll probably lose interest in one another altogether.'

'I don't know what you're talking about,' said Charlotte, rather feebly. 'And I don't have the slightest interest in you in any case.'

'Of course you do,' he said irritably. 'And while we're on the subject of your interests, would you be good enough to tell me if you're still seeing your friend Mr Foster?'

'Oh for God's sake,' said Charlotte. 'I never was seeing Mr Foster, as you put it. Well, not since – not since. You're obsessed.'

'Maybe I am,' he said quietly, 'but I find it very hard not to be.' He had stopped talking and was looking down at his shirt cuff, fiddling furiously with his wrist.

'I'm going,' said Charlotte, trying rather belatedly to sound controlled and businesslike, 'I have a great deal to do.'

She turned towards the door.

'Don't go, Charlotte,' said Gabe. 'Please.'

'I'm afraid I have to,' said Charlotte. 'Gabe, this door is locked.'

'I know it is,' said Gabe, 'I locked it.'

'Then please unlock it,' said Charlotte. 'And what on earth are you doing, Gabe, fiddling with your cuff like that?'

And then she looked at him, and realized he was smiling at her in a very particular way, and very much against her will, found herself smiling back at him.

And then she looked at the table and realized what he had been doing, fiddling with his cuff.

He had been taking his watch off.